the

yada yada
Prayer Group

&

the

yada yada
Prayer Group
GETS DOWN

neta jackson

THOMAS NELSON
Since 1798

NASHVILLE   DALLAS   MEXICO CITY   RIO DE JANEIRO   BEIJING

Published in Nashville, Tennessee, by Thomas Nelson. Thomas Nelson is a trademark of Thomas Nelson, Inc.

Published in association with the literary agency of Alive Communications, Inc., 7680 Goddard Street, Suite 200, Colorado Springs, CO 80920

Thomas Nelson, Inc. titles may be purchased in bulk for educational, business, fund-raising, or sales promotional use. For information, please e-mail SpecialMarkets@ThomasNelson.com.

Scripture quotations are taken from the following:

The CEV © 1991 by the American Bible Society. Used by permission.
The Holy Bible, NIV. © 1973, 1978, 1984, International Bible Society. Used by permission of Zondervan Bible Publishers.
The NKJV, © 1979, 1980, 1982, 1990 by Thomas Nelson, Inc., Publishers.
The Holy Bible, NLT, © 1996. Used by permission of Tyndale House Publishers, Inc., Wheaton, Illinois. All rights reserved.
The King James Version of the Bible.

"If Not for Grace," written by Clint Brown. Copyright © 2000 Tribe Music Group (administered by PYPO Publishing) BMI.

This novel is a work of fiction. Any references to real events, businesses, organizations, and locales are intended only to give the fiction a sense of reality and authenticity. Any resemblance to actual persons, living or dead, is entirely coincidental.

ISBN-13: 978-1-59554-474-2 (SE)

Printed in the United States of America

07 08 09 10 11 QW 7 6 5 4 3 2 1

the

yadayada

Prayer Group

To my sisters in the women's Bible study

of Reba Place Church

—you know who you are!—

who loved me anyway and stretched my faith.

And to Dave

—best friend, husband, writing partner—

who had the vision for this book in the first place

and believed in me in the process.

Prologue

CHICAGO'S NORTH SIDE—1990

A soft mist clouded the windshield of the Toyota wagon, playing catch-me-if-you-can with the intermittent wipers. Apartment buildings and three-storied six-flats crowded the wet narrow street like great brick cliffs. The woman behind the wheel of the Toyota drove cautiously through the Rogers Park neighborhood of north Chicago, looking for Morse Avenue.

At least it wasn't the typical macho Chicago thunderstorm: blowing in on big winds, shaking the trees, darkening the skies. *Boom! Crash! Flash!* Sheets and sheets of rain . . . and then just as quickly rolling away, leaving puddles and sunshine. A midwestern girl at heart, she usually enjoyed a good storm.

But not today. She hated driving in a heavy rain, especially on unfamiliar city streets with her kids in the car.

Mist . . . swipe . . . mist . . . the gentle rain softened even the rough edges of this Chicago neighborhood as she peered past the wipers looking for street signs—

A dark blur rose up suddenly in front of the car through the thin film of mist. Startled, she stomped on the brake. *Swipe.* The clear windshield showed a dark bedraggled shape—man? woman?—banging a fist on her hood. Heart pounding in her chest, the driver fumbled for the door locks. *Oh God, Oh God, what's happening?*—

"Mom-meee!" A frightened wail from the car seat behind her stifled the woman's first instinct to pound on the horn.

"Shh. Shh. It's okay." She forced her voice to be calm for the children's sake. "Someone walked in front of the car, but I didn't hit him. Shh. It's okay." But she gripped the steering wheel to stop her hands from shaking.

With one final bang on the hood, the figure shoved its fists into the pockets of a frayed army jacket and shuffled toward the driver's-side window. The driver steeled herself, heart still racing. Now she was going to get yelled at. Or mugged.

But the person hunched down, tapped gently at the window, and whined, "Change, lady? Got any change?"

Anger and relief shredded her anxiety. Just a panhandler. A woman at that, surprisingly small and bony beneath the bulky army jacket and layers of scarves. But the nerve! Stopping her car like that!

The driver rolled down her window a mere crack.

"Mom! Don't!" commanded her five-year-old man-child in the backseat.

"It's okay. Give Blanky to your little sister." She peered at the woman now standing just inches from her face. Dark-skinned, bug-eyed, the army jacket damp and limp, buttoned askew . . . the mist clung to the woman's uncombed nappy hair like shimmering glass beads.

"Got any change?" the panhandler repeated.

The driver channeled her voice into assertive disapproval. "You shouldn't jump in front of my car! I could have hit you."

"Need food for my baby. And diapers," said the woman stubbornly. She peered though the crack in the window into the backseat. Her voice changed. "You got kids?"

The driver was tempted to roll up the window and move on. Her family had made it a rule not to give money to panhandlers. Even a suburban mom from Downers Grove knew a dollar was more likely to find its way to the corner liquor store than be spent for bread and diapers.

But she hesitated, thinking of her two preschoolers in the backseat. What if the woman really *did* have kids who needed food and diapers?

Still she hesitated. Then an idea popped into her head. "Uh . . . I was just headed for Uptown Community Church on Morse Avenue." *To pick up my husband,* she could have added. Uptown had invited men from several suburban churches to volunteer once a month in an "urban outreach" to homeless men and drug addicts. "If you stop in there, I'm sure somebody will help you."

The woman, damp and glistening, shook her head. "Been there b'fore. Don't wanna wear out my welcome. Just a little change, lady? A dollar will do."

If you do it unto the least of these, you do it unto Me.

The driver sighed. Life would sometimes be a lot simpler if years of Sunday school lessons didn't follow her around like Jiminy Cricket sitting on her shoulder. What would her husband do? After all, he came to this "outreach" today because he wanted to help people like this woman.

On impulse, she leaned over and pulled up the lock on the passenger side of the car. "Get in," she said to the woman standing in the mist. "I'll take you to a grocery store."

"Mom!"

The panhandler scurried around and got in the car. She didn't put on the seat belt, and the driver tightened her mouth. She couldn't be this woman's keeper about *everything*. She turned and glared at her five-year-old before he opened his mouth again.

Now what? She had no idea where a grocery store was in this neighborhood! She'd passed the Rogers Park Fruit Market a few blocks back, but it probably didn't carry stuff like diapers. What she needed was a Jewel or Dominick's.

Or maybe her son was right—this was crazy, picking up this woman!

Then she saw it: Morse Avenue. She could ask at the church where to find a grocery store. Turning onto the busier street, full of small stores with security grids on the windows, she watched the door numbers slide by. There. She slowed beside the old two-story brick storefront that housed Uptown Community Church and turned off the ignition. The wipers died.

The woman in the passenger seat narrowed her eyes. "Thought we was goin' t' the store."

"We are," the driver chirped brightly, hopping out of the car. "I just have to let my husband know that I'll be a little late. Be right back." She opened the back door. "Come on, kids." Another encouraging look at the woman in the front seat. "I'll only take a minute."

With her daughter's legs wrapped tightly around her waist and the boy plodding along in sulky silence, the mother pulled hopefully on the handle of the glass door. *Oh, please open.* Relieved when it swung outward, she hustled up the narrow stairs to the second floor that had been remodeled into a large open meeting room. She stood uncertainly at the top of the stairs, looking for her husband among the small groups of volunteers scattered around the room who were talking, some praying. There he was. She caught his eye, and he acknowledged her with a smile. *Could I see you a moment?* she mouthed as she motioned at him.

The kids hugged their daddy as she explained the situation. But instead of being pleased, his voice rose. "You picked up a panhandler? In the car? Of all the—"

A tall thin man with wispy gray hair and wearing a Mr. Rogers sweater suddenly appeared beside them, smiling warmly. Her husband shook his head, still incredulous. "Uh, Pastor, this is my wife . . . honey, you tell him."

Feeling foolish now, she described the woman who had stopped her in the street and her intention to get the woman some groceries. "She said she's been here before. But I've got the kids . . . do you think it's okay?"

Uptown's pastor nodded, his large Adam's apple bobbing. "I know the lady. Last time she was here, I tried to get her into a detox program, but she didn't follow through. Probably not too anxious to see me again." His warm hazel eyes hinted at the compassion he no doubt handed out as freely as meals and good advice. "She can be a nuisance but is probably harmless. Sure, get her a bag of groceries . . . but as a general rule? Don't pick up panhandlers."

Relieved, she got directions to the nearest supermarket and ruffled her son's hair. "Okay, kids. We'll just help this lady out then come back and pick up Daddy." She picked up her daughter and reached out for her son. The boy pulled away from his mother's hand but allowed himself to be guided back down the stairs and out the door.

"Now be nice," she muttered under her breath as they approached the Toyota. "We're supposed to help people, even when it's inconvenient." Right.

"Hey, Mom, look!" Her son pointed an accusing finger at the car.

The woman was gone.

1

I didn't really want to go to the "women's conference" the first weekend of May. Spending two hundred bucks to stay in a *hotel* for two nights only forty-five minutes from home? Totally out of our budget, even if it did include "two continental breakfasts, Saturday night banquet, and all conference materials."

Now if it had been just Denny and me, that'd be different. A romantic getaway, a second honeymoon . . . no teenagers tying up the phone, no dog poop to clean up in the yard, no third grade lesson plans, no driving around and around the block trying to find a parking place. Just Denny and me sleeping late, ordering croissants, fruit plates, and hot coffee for breakfast, letting someone else make the bed (hallelujah!), swimming in the pool . . . now *that* would be worth two hundred bucks, no question.

I'm not generally a conference-type person. I don't like big crowds. We've lived in the Chicago area for almost twenty years now, and I still haven't seen Venetian Nights at the lakefront, even though Denny takes Josh and Amanda almost every year. Wall-to-wall people . . . and standing in line for those pukey Port-a-Potties? Ugh.

Give me a small moms group or a women's Bible study any day—like Moms in Touch, which met at our church in Downers Grove all those years the kids were growing up. We had some retreats, too, but I knew most of the folks from church, and they were held at a camp and retreat center out in the country where you could wear jeans to all the sessions and walk in the woods during free time.

But listening to the cars on I-90 roaring past the hotel's mani-cured lawn? Laughing like a sound track at jokes told by high-powered speakers in tailored suits and matching heels? Having to take "after five attire" for a banquet on Saturday night? (Why would a bunch of women *do* that with no men around to admire how gorgeous we look?)

Uh-uh. Was not looking forward to it.

Still, Avis Johnson, my boss—she's the principal at the Chicago public school where I teach third grade this year—asked if I'd like to go with her, and that counts for something. Maybe everything. I've admired Avis ever since I first met her at Uptown Community Church but never thought we'd be pals or anything. Not just because she's African American and I'm white, either. She's so calm and poised—a classy lady. Her skin is a smooth, rich, milk-chocolate color, and she gets her hair done every week at a salon. Couldn't believe it when I found out she was fifty and a *grand-mother*. (I should be so lucky to look like that when Josh and Amanda have kids.) I feel like a country bumpkin when I'm around her. My nondescript dark brown hair never could hold a "style," so I just wear it at shoulder level with bangs and hope for the best.

Not only that, but when we moved from suburban Downers Grove into the city last summer, I applied to teach in one of the public schools in the Rogers Park neighborhood of Chicago, where we live now, and ended up at Mary McLeod Bethune Elementary, where Avis Johnson just happened to be the *principal*. Weird calling her "Avis" on Sunday and "Ms. Johnson" on Monday.

Avis is one of Uptown Community's worship leaders and has tried to wean its motley congregation of former Presbyterians, Baptists, "Evee-Frees," Methodists, Brethren, and No-Churchers from the hymnbook and "order of service" to actually participating in *worship*. I love the way she quotes Scripture, too, not only from the New Testament, but also from those mysterious Minor Prophets, and Job, and the Pentateuch. I mean, I know a lot of Scripture, but for some reason I have a hard time remembering those pesky references, even though I've been in Sunday school since singing "Climb, Climb Up Sunshine Mountain" in the toddler class.

People at Uptown want to be "relevant" in an urban setting, which means cultivating a diverse congregation, but most of us, including yours truly, aren't too comfortable shouting in church and start to fidget when the service goes past twelve o'clock—both of which seem par for Sunday morning in black churches. Don't know why Avis stays at Uptown sometimes. Pastor Clark, bless him, has a vision, but for most of us transplants, our good intentions come with all the presumptions we brought from suburbia. But she says God called her to Uptown, and Pastor Clark preaches the Word. She'll stay until God tells her to go.

Denny and me—we've only been at the church since last summer. That's when Honorable Husband decided it was time white folks—meaning us, as it turned out—moved back into the city rather than doing good deeds from our safe little enclaves in the suburbs. Denny had been volunteering with Uptown's "outreach" program for over ten years, ever since the kids were little, driving into the city about once a month from Downers Grove. It was so hard for me to leave the church and people we've known most of our married life. But Denny said we couldn't hide forever in our comfort zone. So . . . we packed up the dog, the teenagers, and the Plymouth Voyager, exchanged our big yard for a postage stamp, and shoehorned ourselves into a two-flat—Chicago's version of a duplex—on Chicago's north side.

But frankly? I don't really know what we're doing here. Uptown Community Church has a few black members and one old Chinese lady who comes from time to time . . . but we're still mostly white in one of the most diverse neighborhoods in the U.S.—Rogers Park, Chicago. Josh says at his high school cafeteria, the black kids sit with the black kids, Latino kids sit with Latinos, nerds sit with nerds, whites with whites, Asians with Asians.

Not exactly a melting pot. And the churches aren't much better. Maybe worse.

In Des Moines, Iowa, where my family lives, I grew up on missionary stories from around the world—the drumbeats of Africa . . . the rickshaws of China . . . the forests of Ecuador. Somehow it was so easy to imagine myself one day sitting on a stool in the African veld, surrounded by eager black faces, telling Bible stories with flannel-graph figures. Once, when I told Denny about my fantasy, he snorted and said we better learn how to relate across cultures in our own city before winging across the ocean to "save the natives."

He's right, of course. But it's not so easy. Most of the people I've met in the neighborhood are friendly—friendly, but not friends. Not the kick-back, laugh-with-your-girlfriends, be-crazy, cry-when-you're-sad, talk-on-the-phone-five-times-a-week kind of friends I had in Downers Grove. And the black couple who lived upstairs? (DINKS, Josh called them: Double-Income-No-Kids.) They barely give us the time of day unless something goes wrong with the furnace.

So when Avis asked if I'd like to go to this women's conference sponsored by a coalition of Chicago area churches, I said yes. I felt flattered that she thought I'd fit in, since I generally felt like sport socks with high heels. I determined to go. At worst I'd waste a weekend (and two hundred bucks). At best, I might make a friend—or at least get to know Avis better.

THE LOBBY OF THE EMBASSY SUITES HOTEL in Chicago's northwest suburbs was packed with women. An intense hum rose and fell, like a tree full of cicadas. "Girl! I didn't know *you* were coming!" . . . "Where's Shirlese? I'm supposed to be roomin' with her." . . . "*Look* at you! That outfit is *fine!*" . . . "Pool? Not after spending forty-five dollars at the salon this morning, honey. Who you kiddin'?"

Avis and I wiggled our Mutt and Jeff selves through the throng of perfumed bodies and presented our reservations at the desk.

"Jodi Baxter? And . . . Avis Johnson. You're in Suite 206." The clerk handed over two plastic key cards. "If you're here for the Chicago Women's Conference"—she added with a knowing smile—"you can pick up your registration packet at that table right over there."

Avis let me forge a path back through the cicada convention to a long table with boxes of packets marked A–D, E–H, all the way to W–Z. As we were handed our packets emblazoned with CWC in curlicue calligraphy, I noticed a bright gold sticker in the right-hand corner of mine with the number 26 written in black marker. I glanced at the packet being given to the woman standing next to me at the A–D box who gave her name as "Adams, Paulette"—but her gold sticker had the number 12.

"What's this?" I asked the plump girl behind the registration table, pointing to the number.

"Oh, that." Miss Helpful smiled sweetly. "They'll explain the numbers at the first session. Don't worry about it . . . Can I help you?" She turned to the next person in line.

Humph. I didn't want to wait till the first session. I was nervous enough surrounded by women who seemed as comfortable in a crowd of strangers as if it were Thanksgiving at Grandma's. I didn't want any "surprises." Avis waved her packet at me over the heads of five women crowding up to the table between us and nodded toward the elevators. We met just as the door to Elevator Two pinged open, and we wheeled our suitcases inside.

"What number did you get?"

"Number?"

"On your packet, right-hand corner, gold sticker."

"Oh." Avis turned over the packet she was clutching in one hand, along with her plastic key card, purse strap, and travel-pack of tissues. "Twenty-six. What's it for?"

I smiled big and relaxed. "I don't know. They'll tell us the first session." Whatever it was, I was with Avis.

As it turned out, we didn't need our key cards. The door to Suite 206 stood ajar. Avis and I looked at each other and stole inside like the Three Bears coming home after their walk in the woods. The sitting room part of the suite was empty. However, through the French doors leading into the bedroom, we could see "Goldilocks" sitting on the king-size bed painting her toenails while WGCI gospel music blared from the bedside radio.

The stranger looked up. "Oh, hi!" She waved the tiny polish brush in our direction. "Don't mind me. Make yourselves at home."

We stood and stared. The woman was average height, dark-skinned, and lean, with a crown of little black braids sporting a rainbow of beads falling down all around her head. Thirties, maybe forties; it was hard to tell. Her smile revealed a row of perfect teeth, but a scar down the side of her face belied an easy life.

7

Avis was braver than I was and said what I was thinking. "Uh, are we in the right room? We didn't know we had another room-mate."

The woman cocked her head. "Oh! They didn't tell you at regis-tration? Suite 206, right?" She capped the nail polish and bounced off the bed. "Florida Hickman—call me Flo." She stuck out her hand. "Avis and Jodi, right? That's what they tol' me downstairs. Anyway, I was going to room with this sister, see, but she had to cancel, and I didn't want to pay for a whole suite all by myself. Had to sell the kids just to get here as it is." She laughed heartily. Then her smile faded and she cocked her head. "You don't mind, do you? I mean . . . I don't need this whole king-size football field to myself. Unless . . ." Her forehead wrinkled. "You want me to sleep on the fold-out couch?"

My good-girl training rushed to my mouth before I knew what I was saying. "Oh, no, no, that's okay. We don't mind." *Do we, Avis?* I was afraid to look in Avis's direction. We had pretty much agreed driving out that since it was a suite, we could each have a "room" to ourselves. Avis was definitely not the stay-up-late, sleepover type.

"Oh. Well, sure," Avis said. "It's just that no one told us." I didn't know Avis all that well, but that wasn't enthusiasm in her voice. "I'll sleep on the fold-out," she added, wheeling her suit-case over to the luggage stand.

I noticed that she didn't say "we." I stood uncertainly. But our new friend had generously offered the other side of the mammoth bed, so I dragged my suitcase into the bedroom and plopped it on the floor on the other side of Florida's nail salon.

Well, this was going to be interesting. I had thought it would be quite an adventure to get to know Avis as my roommate for the weekend. As members of the same church, this was a chance to get beyond the niceties of Sunday morning and brush our teeth in the same sink. But I hadn't counted on a third party. God knows I wanted to broaden my horizons, but this was moving a little faster than I felt ready for.

As I hung up the dress I hoped would pass for "after five" in the narrow closet, I suddenly had a thought. "Florida, what number is on your registration packet?"

Florida finished her big toe and looked at it critically. "Number? . . . Oh, you mean that gold sticker thing on the front?" She looked over the side of the bed where she'd dumped her things. "Um . . . twenty-six. Why?"

2

As I walked between Avis and Florida toward the ballroom where the Friday night session was going to be held—feeling rather like the white stuff in an Oreo cookie—I could hear keyboard, drums, and bass guitar already pelting out some contemporary praise song I wasn't familiar with. As loud as the instruments were, however, I could hear a woman shouting, "Glory! Glory!" amid similar repetitions from other powerful female voices.

I cringed. Were we late? The schedule said the first session was at seven o'clock, and my watch said only six-fifty. No way did I want to walk in after the thing had started and have people stare at me. On the other hand, maybe it was a good excuse to just slip into the back and observe from afar.

But I guess we weren't late because there were still quite a few people milling around, finding seats, and greeting each other with enthusiastic hugs. I needn't have worried about people staring at me because no one seemed to care a spit. In fact, several women squealed when they saw Florida, as if they could hardly believe their eyes that she was here, but she didn't introduce me to any of her friends.

Meantime, I gave up any hope of sitting in the back because Avis was moving steadily toward the front, where people were already walking back and forth in the space between the front row and the platform, waving one arm and praying out loud over the music. *Oh, please God,* I groaned, *not the front row.* No telling what was going to happen during the meeting, and I didn't want to be a target for some well-meaning prophecy or someone who decided I needed to be slain in the Spirit.

Fortunately Avis turned into the fifth row back—still too close to the front to my way of thinking—and went all the way to the end of the row next to an aisle. Same as she does at Uptown Community, because she likes to move about during worship. I sighed. *Relax, Jodi. Don't be so nervous.* After all, I knew Avis—not very well, but still—and trusted her to be rock solid when it came to the Christian gospel. Whatever was going to happen at this conference, Avis thought it was going to be good and had invited me to experience it too. Like I said before, that counted for something.

There was no actual "beginning" to the first session. But right about seven o'clock the worship band swung into another thumping contemporary song and a lady with mocha-cream skin and a red suit came onto the stage with a hand-held mike and revved us up like a cheerleader at a football game. "Come on! Come on! Let's hear you praise the Lord!" We all stood, and everybody was moving to the music in one way or another—stepping, clapping, waving hands. Five hundred female voices tackled that song like a powder-puff football team: "Cel-e-brate . . . Je-sus . . . Celebrate!"

I clapped and sang along with everyone else and started to enjoy myself. This was good. If only Amanda and Josh could see me. Denny too. My family thinks I'm too stiff. The kids love to go to Cornerstone in the summer—the music festival out in the cornfields of Illinois sponsored by an aging group of Jesus People—and they come home pumped. We tried it as a family when Josh was in middle school, camping on the grounds, choosing from various sessions by the likes of Tony Campolo, Ron Sider, and John Perkins, and listening to all the Christian bands. I tried not to walk around with my mouth open staring at the kids with green spiked hair and dog collars sporting Jesus T-shirts. "I Broke the Rules—I Prayed in School" . . . "He Blew My Mind When He Saved My Soul" . . . "He Who Dies with the Most Toys—Still Dies." But by the time we got home, my ears were ringing and I wanted a T-shirt that said, "I Survived Cornerstone!"

We'd been singing in the ballroom about twenty minutes when I realized we were only into the second song. At forty minutes I wondered if we were ever going to get to sit down. Didn't these women ever get tired? But Avis and Florida were still going strong at sixty minutes.

Finally the speaker for the evening was introduced: Evangelist Olivia Mitchell, from right here in Chicago, though I hadn't heard of her before. She was about my age—in her forties—and very attractive. Not just her looks, which were fine enough. But she moved and talked like she was comfortable in her own skin.

Whew! She laid it on thick, coming off the platform, speaking directly to this woman or that one, about needing to be "women of purpose" and "living into our destiny."

I scrunched down in my seat, hiding behind the women in front of me. Destiny? Who had time to think about destiny! Trying to keep up with a classroom of thirty third-graders, half of whom could barely speak English, much less read it, two teens with raging hormones, a happy-go-lucky husband who was more generous than thrifty, and a full schedule of church meetings at Uptown Community, I felt lucky to wake up each morning knowing what day it was.

But listening to her challenge us to "be the woman God created you to be" started me thinking. Who *did* God create me to be? Did God have a particular purpose for Jodi Baxter? If so, I couldn't put words around it. I grew up in a solid Christian home—well, after my dad got "saved" when I was still in preschool. We not only went to church on Sunday, prayer meeting on Wednesday, and Pioneer Girls Club on Saturday morning (Boys Brigade for my brothers), but we had family devotions every night after supper, which I didn't mind if they were short, but we always prayed "from the youngest to the oldest," and my dad tended toward long-winded prayers. Every Sunday morning we had to say a Bible verse from memory at breakfast, and John 3:16 wasn't allowed as a fallback. I knew the Ten Commandments and the nine "Blesseds" of the Sermon on the Mount, and even though we were "no longer under the law but under grace," I definitely knew what was expected of a good Christian girl from Des Moines.

But who was that little girl, really? Baby of the family (a fact I shamelessly milked to my advantage whenever possible) . . . nuts about teddy bears (I'd collected one hundred stuffed bears by the time I went to college, a feat that impressed no one) . . . a scaredy-cat about bugs and big dogs (giving my two big brothers plenty of fuel for driving me crazy) . . . dreamy and romantic (of *course* I would get married to a dark-haired, handsome man and live happily ever after) . . . told everyone I was going to be a missionary to Africa when I grew up (which I never put together with big bugs and scary animals).

What did that safe, protected, idealistic little girl have to do with—

The voice of the lady in the red suit broke into my thoughts. "—the number in the little gold dot on your registration packet," she was saying. *Aha!* I thought. *The mystery is about to be revealed.* I felt around under my padded chair for my registration packet, even though I knew my number by heart: twenty-six. "This is the number of the prayer group you have been assigned to for the weekend," she went on, waving a packet. "Each group will have ten to twelve women. Roommates will be together in the same group; otherwise we have mixed up people from different churches and different parts of the city. After all, ladies, a major purpose for this Chicago Women's Conference is to break down the walls and link hands with our sisters . . ."

The red suit with the hand-held mike went on giving instructions, but my mind was already leaping ahead. A small group— now that might be more my speed than a huge crowd. On the

other hand, I backpedaled; a small group was a pretty intimate setting for a group of strangers. I craned my neck and looked around
the ballroom. Pretty diverse all right—if 80 percent black and 20
percent "other" counted as diverse. If this conference was supposed
to draw together women from a broad spectrum of Chicago-area
churches, where were all the white churches from Elmhurst and
Downers Grove and Wilmette?

The worship band and singers struck up a thunderous chorus
of "Awesome God" as the rest of us began to file out of the ballroom to our "prayer groups," presumably, though I'd missed where
we were supposed to go. But Avis and Florida were "twenty-
sixers," too, so all I had to do was follow along—

"Mmm. Getting on toward my bedtime," Avis's voice murmured behind me. "Maybe I'll just go back up to our room."

I turned, opening my mouth in protest. But before I could say
anything, Florida jumped in. "Now I *know* these touchy-feely
groups aren't my thang." A touch of street slang slipped in, making
me realize I didn't know cucumbers about this woman. "Though it
ain't my bedtime, that's for sure." She laughed, her beaded braids
shaking around her head. "But I sure could do with a cup of coffee
and a—"

"Whoa, whoa! Just a minute." I was surprised to hear my own
voice throw a block on the deserters. I looked at Avis, who was stifling a yawn. "You got me into this, girlfriend." (Whoops. The
moment the handle slipped out of my mouth, I was sure I'd gone
too far using the familiar tag I'd heard all around me that night.
But I rushed on.) "The prayer groups sound like a major part of

the weekend, so I'd like to go." (Yikes! Was that true?) "But I don't want to go alone." (*That* part was certainly true.) "Come on. Let's go together. It's for prayer, after all." Now I was getting shameless. The Avis I knew on Sunday had a big thing about prayer. But just in case, I looked at both women and added hopefully, "Please?"

Florida crinkled her eyes at me and her mouth broke in an open grin. "Girl, you are so funny! You beggin' me to come to this prayer group thang?" She wagged her head, setting the little beads to dancing again. "Okay, okay, I'll come. Just give me a moment to get some coffee and a cig. Meet you in ten minutes in . . ." She looked at something she'd scribbled on her packet. " . . . Room 7."

I watched her bounce through the crowd and disappear toward the general direction of the coffee shop. "Think she'll show up?" I asked Avis, who now looked resigned. I took that as a good sign and steered us toward the bank of meeting rooms that circled the ballroom. "Maybe that's why God put Flo in our suite," I blabbered on, "so we could be in this prayer group thing together. She could use some deliverance from those cigarettes, for one thing." Obligation and guilt—I was good at laying it on thick.

"Ten o'clock," Avis announced as we fought our way through a river of women in the hallway, hunting for their meeting rooms. "I'll stay till ten o'clock. Then I turn into a pumpkin."

I smiled to myself as we sidled into Room 7. The clock on the wall said 9:05. Ten o'clock was fine with me. I couldn't imagine praying longer than an hour with a bunch of strangers anyway.

Four circles of chairs filled the four corners of the hotel meeting room, with a large printed number hanging on the back of one chair in each circle. Avis and I headed for number twenty-six, where several women of differing ages, sizes, and colors were already beginning to fill the twelve chairs.

Twelve chairs. Twelve women.

I had no idea.

3

vis and I sat down on two of the folding chairs beside each other. I tried to save a seat for Florida, but a large black woman with close-cropped reddish hair and big gold earrings handed me my tote bag that I'd put on the seat and sat down with a *whumph*. I shrugged and tried a smile. "Hi. My name is Jodi."

"Adele." The woman gave a short nod.

O . . . kay. That was a ragged start. Almost all the seats were filled now, with just a couple vacant. Well, if Florida showed, she'd have to fend for herself.

For a few minutes, everyone just sat silently or talked to the person next to them—their friend or roomie, I presumed. But by now the clock said 9:15. If someone didn't get this thing rolling soon, we wouldn't have any time for prayer or whatever it was we were supposed to do.

I took a big breath. "Well, I'm not sure what we're supposed to do, but I don't know most of you so maybe we could just go around the circle and introduce ourselves."

"We've got nametags," said Adele, voice flat.

She might just as well have sat on me. I felt my face go hot.

Just then Florida slipped into the vacant chair on the other side of the circle. She looked around curiously, taking in the awkward silence. "Y'all didn't wait for me, did you? What are we doin'?"

"Uh . . . introducing ourselves, I think," said the woman next to her. Hispanic-looking. Slightly plump, but pleasant face, her dark wavy hair pulled back into a ponytail at the nape of her neck. She grinned at Florida. "Why don't you start?"

I could have kissed the lady. The ball had been dribbled to the other side of the circle, giving my face time to return to its normal pasty hue.

"Who, me?" Florida shrugged. "Oh well, why not. My name is Florida Hickman. I'm five years saved and five years sober, thank the *Lord*. Got three kids. Two are living with me right now; the oldest one is ADD, otherwise they doin' good. My husband works full time"—she gave a little laugh—"lookin' for work."

"Uh-huh. Kick the loser out," muttered Adele.

I nearly fell off my chair. The nerve! I imagined myself Walter Mitty-like telling the woman to shut up. But no one else must have heard her, and Flo just carried on. "But thank God, I got my GED, passed the civil service exam last year, and got a job at the Chicago post office that puts food on the table. So I can't complain. I'm blessed!" She smiled sweetly at the Hispanic lady. "Now you."

I wanted to snort. Florida let drop more in sixty seconds than

I would in a month of Sundays, given the same situation. What kind of precedent did *that* set?

"*Si.* No problem." The woman next to Flo gestured with every sentence. "I am Delores Enriques from Iglesia del Espirito Santo, and I work as a pediatric nurse at Cook County Hospital." I couldn't speak Spanish, but I was pretty sure she said "Church of the Holy Spirit." Delores's eyes rolled up, as though searching her brain for more information. "Um, my husband, Ricardo, drives truck, and we have five kids, from five to fourteen." She shrugged. "Guess that's it—oh!" She turned to the slim young black woman on her other side. "This is Edesa, from my church. She babysits for my kids, and she's good—but don't nobody steal her!" Delores gave the young woman a squeeze.

Well, it was rolling now. Edesa seemed shy, with a trace of an accent. Jamaican? Haitian? Didn't Haitians speak French? Why would she end up at a Spanish-speaking church? Edesa didn't say much, just that she was a student at some community college, but I didn't catch which one.

I hadn't really noticed the woman next to Edesa. But when she spoke, her voice was soft, cultured, almost European—which startled me because she was black. Not black-black, like some Africans I'd met, but rich brown, like Starbucks coffee beans. And she wore a scarf in an African print tied smartly around her head and wore a matching tunic in orange and black. How could I *not* have noticed her?

"I am Nonyameko Sisulu-Smith. Just Nony is all right," she added, seeing that several of us didn't quite get it. "My homeland

21

is South Africa, but I came to the States to go to the University of Chicago, where I met my husband, and so here we are. I love the Lord, and that's why I'm at this conference." She gave a little shrug as if to say *that's all.* I wanted to say "More! More!" But she had already turned to the tall Asian girl next to her. "This is Hoshi Takahashi. She is a student in my husband's history class at Northwestern University—he's a professor there." Nony's smile now was wide and genuine. "Hoshi just became a Christian!"

The young woman nodded and smiled and nodded. "Yes! My name is Hoshi. I am student from Japan. Like Nony say, she tells me about Jesus and I am new Christian." She beamed. "Glad to be here. Glad to know all of you. Glad to practice my English!"

Okay, I was impressed. Prayer Group Twenty-Six was practically a mini–United Nations.

Silence reigned. I leaned forward slightly to see if there was someone hiding between Hoshi and Adele. Nope. It was Adele's turn.

The big woman sighed. "Adele Skuggs, just like it *says* here on my name tag. 'Adele's Hair and Nails' on Clark Street in Rogers Park, if any of y'all want a makeover." Her voice seemed to take on a smile at the mention of her beauty shop, and I glanced at her. She had a small gap between her two front teeth I hadn't noticed before. I quickly looked back at my lap. "Oh, yeah," Adele added, "I've been a member of the Paul and Silas Apostlic Church on Kedzie since I was in the children's choir. Me and Chanda over there." She nodded at another woman we hadn't got to yet. She folded her arms. She was done.

My turn. I suddenly felt about as interesting as an economics textbook. But I couldn't invent an exciting persona on the spot—besides, Avis was sitting next to me—so I stuck to the truth. "My name is Jodi Baxter. I'm married, have two teenagers, and I teach third grade at Bethune Elementary in Rogers Park." I skipped the born-in-Iowa-recently-moved-from-the-suburbs part. I was sure everybody would automatically think *Hick Chick.* "I'm a member of Uptown Community Church in Rogers Park, and Avis Johnson, who is the principal of the school where I teach, invited me to this conference . . . so, here I am!"

"What kind of church is Up-town Com-mun-ity?"

I was startled by Adele's question. No one else had gotten questions. And the way she pronounced every syllable of the church name made it seem like a challenge.

"Uh, it's nondenominational. Just . . . Christian. You know." It sounded lame.

The big shoulders next to me shrugged. "Just asking. All sorts of *unitys* and *communitys* out there. Just 'cause you put the name *church* on somethin' don't mean anything these days."

I didn't trust myself to speak. What *was* this woman's problem?

Avis came to the rescue. "I think it's my turn. My name is Avis Johnson, and as Jodi said, we both attend Uptown Community Church in Rogers Park. I grew up Church of God in Christ but began attending Uptown a couple years ago because I like the emphasis on bringing people to Jesus, not bringing them to a denomination. Like this conference. We're about Jesus, right? Unless you tell me different, I assume that's why we're all here."

Thank you, Avis, I breathed inwardly. I kept my eyes riveted on my friend's face, not daring to look at Adele on the other side of me.

"And I'm glad to have us introduce ourselves," Avis continued, "but I think the whole idea is to spend some time praying. So maybe we can move along and share some prayer needs. Or pray for the conference itself. Speakers . . . praise team . . . women who need healing in their lives."

With that admonition, the remaining women in the group quickly introduced themselves:

Chanda George, Adele's friend, had a Jamaican accent that was a little hard to understand. I wondered why she and Adele weren't sitting together. Maybe they just attended the same church so they got put in the same prayer group.

Leslie Stuart ("Just call me Stu," she said) was in her mid-thirties, long and shapely, with big eyes and long blonde hair with dark roots. Didn't say what church she came from, just that she was a real estate broker in Oak Park, Chicago's first suburb to the west. "I think we should pray for the peace of Jerusalem," she announced.

The peace of Jerusalem? Seemed a little off the mark at the moment, though the Middle East was a hotbed in the news. But the middle-aged white lady on the other side of her immediately said, "Amen! As Jerusalem goes, so goes the world. And as long as we're praying for peace, pray that I don't knock off my husband. I won't go into details. Details, shmetails. If you're married and human, you know what I mean." She rolled her eyes and sighed.

Chuckles around the group broke the crust of awkwardness and seemed to let in a breath of fresh air.

"Oh. My name is Ruth . . . Ruth Garfield. I'm new to this Christian thing, too. Popular in my family, I'm not. And if I knock off my husband, they'll definitely blame it on being a lapsed Jew."

The chuckles burst into outright laughter. "You are a cool lady!" Florida said, wagging her forefinger at Ruth. "Maybe we could knock off our husbands together." She simpered at the rest of the group. "Just kidding. Just kidding."

"*Sure* you are, honey," muttered Adele next to me.

There was still one person to go. Another white girl—woman, rather. At first glance she looked young, her short hair bleached blonde on the tips and combed in the spiky look popular in those big Calvin Klein ads on the sides of buses. She wore denim overalls, which, I had to admit, looked youthful and cool but out of place among the carefully dressed women in pantsuits and business dresses, and Nony in her exotic African garb. But as she pursed her lips, as though considering what to say, I realized her eyes betrayed hardships beyond her years.

She shrugged. "I'm just . . . Yolanda. They call me Yo-Yo. Don't know why I'm here. I'm not really into this Jesus thing you talk about. But you guys are all right. I'm cool with that." She shrugged again. "I'm with her"—she jerked a thumb in Ruth's direction.

"A cook she is, at the Bagel Bakery in my neighborhood." Ruth winked. "She makes pastry to die for."

That's interesting, I thought. "Where'd you learn to cook, Yolan—uh, Yo-Yo? Professionally, I mean."

Yo-Yo's lips tightened, and for a brief second her eyes took on a wary look, like a cat in a corner. Then the shrug again. "Lincoln

Correctional Center." She let it hang in the air. "Prison," she added.

Lincoln? The new Illinois women's prison? I could have slapped my mouth. I'd only meant it as a friendly question.

Yo-Yo glanced around the quiet circle. "What'd I do—punch everybody's bozo button?"

"Don't you worry about it, honey," Adele spoke up. "We all got skeletons in our closet of one kind or another . . . *all* of us."

I didn't dare glance at Adele. Did she mean that for me?

Yo-Yo leaned forward, elbows on her knees, worn athletic shoes planted widely on the floor. "I'm not ashamed of it. Not like I axed anybody or anything. Served eighteen months for forgery. Had my reasons. But I did the crime, served my time. It's behind me now." She sat back, casually hooking one arm over the back of the chair. "Ruth, here, put in a good word for me at the bakery, helped me get a job. Ain't easy to get work after you've done time."

Gosh. I felt like I'd opened Pandora's box. Obviously there was a lot more history to Ruth and Yo-Yo's relationship than met the eye. And what did Yo-Yo mean, "had my reasons"?

"I'm sure it hasn't been easy." Avis's voice broke into my thoughts. "I'd like to pray for Yo-Yo, if that's all right with the rest of you—and you, Yo-Yo?"

Once more Yo-Yo shrugged. "Hey, if it makes you feel good. Just . . . you know. Don't get all hyper."

Avis stood up, moved to the outside of the circle behind Yo-Yo, and began to pray. "Thank You, Lord. Thank You, Jesus," she began.

That was smooth. Avis had a kind of authority—not bossy, just firm, confident—that gathered up the loose ends and knotted them so they wouldn't fray any further. At least we were finally praying—which was the point, after all.

"Others of you, feel free to pray," Avis invited a few moments later. To my surprise, Florida knelt down in front of Yo-Yo, laid a hand on her denim knee, and began to pray in a loud voice, praising God for new beginnings. I wasn't sure how Yo-Yo reacted to being the focus of attention, because my own eyes misted up, and I had to fumble around in my pockets for a tissue.

After a while, Avis moved behind Ruth, laid a hand on her shoulder, and began to pray for the marriages in the group that were on rocky ground. Ruth and Florida had been pretty blunt about theirs . . . didn't know about any of the others. At least my marriage was solid, thank God.

At one point I glanced at the clock: 10:47 . . . and Avis was still going strong.

4

It was almost 11:30 by the time Avis and I got back to our room. Florida said she'd be up in fifteen minutes—probably stepped out for another cigarette. Told us she'd be real quiet when she came back. I hoped so. I was *tired*.

"You didn't leave at ten," I teased as Avis pulled out the sofa bed in the "sitting room" part of the suite. I found two puffy pillows on a shelf in the closet and tossed them in her direction.

"I *knew* it would go late," she grumbled, unzipping her suitcase and pulling out a black-and-gold caftan. Man, it looked comfy—and a whole sight more elegant than Denny's Chicago Bulls T-shirt that I usually wore.

"Sorry you stayed?"

"Hmm. No." Avis carefully wrapped her head with a black scarf—to preserve her hairdo, I presumed—and knotted it on her forehead. "Once we got to praying. It was the idea of sitting around talking with a bunch of strangers that put me off."

I studied her curiously. That was the part I liked, once we escaped the cast of thousands—well, hundreds—in the main session. "Oh. Sorry if I got us off track by asking everybody to introduce themselves." I wasn't *really* sorry; somebody had to get us rolling. But the introductions had gone rather long.

"You surprised me, jumping right in like that. But I think people were glad you did," she said. *(Except Adele,* I thought, but kept that to myself.) "We can spend more time praying the next time we get together," Avis went on, picking up her toilet kit and disappearing into the bathroom. "What time did we agree to?" she called back.

I raised my voice. "Nony suggested 7:00 A.M. Before breakfast. Think anyone will show after going so late tonight?" I was personally hoping we'd all oversleep. At this moment seven o'clock sounded like the crack of dawn. But the water was running in the sink now, and there was no answer.

By the time I used the bathroom and came out, Avis was in bed and the lights were out in the sitting room. I left the bathroom light on and the door open a crack for Florida and crawled between the sheets of the humongous king-size bed on the side next to the window. My body was tired, but my mind still felt all wound up. The main session had been pretty good, even if it was loud. Prayer Group Twenty-Six was going to be interesting. I liked knowing a few more people at this conference by name. Maybe I wouldn't feel so out of place.

The door to the suite clicked open, and two seconds later Florida slipped into the bathroom and shut the door. When she came out, I lay still, hoping she'd think I was asleep. I was too tired to do any more talking. But opening my eyelashes a crack, I noted she had her beaded braids wrapped in a scarf like Avis's. Must be an African-American thing. But her big Chicago Bulls T-shirt? I grinned inwardly. Just like me.

SOMETIME DURING THE MIDDLE OF THE NIGHT, I awoke and went to the bathroom. By the time I came back into the bedroom, my eyes had adjusted to the darkness, and I stopped short. Florida wasn't in the bed. Her side was rumpled, and I was pretty sure I remembered when she'd crawled in. Remembered I'd been glad it was a king, which left lots of room for two people not used to sleeping in the same bed.

But where had Florida gone? Surely she didn't have to have a cigarette in the middle of the night! Curious, I opened the French doors between the bedroom and sitting room and peeked in. Only one lump in the sofa bed. I tiptoed in, shuffling old-lady slow so I wouldn't bang into something. There was another lump on the floor between the sofa bed and the window. The air conditioner—hardly needed in early May—was humming steadily. Florida? Why was she sleeping on the *floor?*

I crawled back into the king-size bed feeling confused. Sure, it felt awkward to sleep in the same bed with a virtual stranger. When it turned out we had three in our room, I would have preferred sharing the bed with Avis. Or sleeping by myself on the sofa

31

bed, lucky Avis. But I hadn't thought about how Florida might feel. Was it just too weird sleeping with a white girl? Nah, I told myself. Couldn't be that. Florida seemed cool with that. No chip on her shoulder—not like that Adele. But a sense of rejection settled over me like the kid who got no Valentines.

Suddenly I missed Denny terribly. Missed reaching out and resting my hand on his arm, feeling the rising and falling of his steady breathing as he lay on his side. Missed snuggling against his bare back and fitting my body into the curve of his legs. Missed the comfort and safety that his mere presence fed into my spirit. Missed knowing that I *belonged.*

I even missed the kids. Missed getting up in the middle of the night to go to the bathroom and peeking into their rooms to be sure everyone was okay. That was when I fell into my deepest sleep, knowing we were all under one roof, safe and sound and together.

Did they miss me? Was anyone losing any sleep at the Baxter house because Mom . . . Jodi . . . wasn't under that roof? Did the house feel incomplete without me?

I sighed. Probably not. Teenagers were too self-centered to even notice Mom was gone. And Denny . . . he would miss me, sure. But once he fell asleep? He wouldn't notice I was gone till morning.

Lying there awake, taking up a miniscule slice of space on the king-size bed, I felt terribly alone . . . and lonely. It wouldn't feel so bad if the conference was over tomorrow—make that today, since it was obviously past midnight already. But I'd paid for two nights. *Two long nights!*

From here, Sunday felt like an invisible speck on the distant horizon.

I WOKE UP TO THE SOUND OF THE SHOWER. Rolling out of bed, I pulled back the "blackout" hotel curtains and was nearly blinded as a wash of sunlight poured into the room. Blue sky . . . sunshine . . . what a great day to go for an early morning walk. Denny and I often walked to Lake Michigan on weekend mornings, only a few blocks from our house. "The lake," as everyone calls it, is Chicago's playground, lapping at the sandy beaches and rocky breakwaters that define miles of parks along the shore, filled with joggers and bikers, in-line skaters and dog-walkers, picnickers and bench sitters, volleyball players and windsurfers, kids and old folks and family reunions. The lake is what made city living bearable for me and a million or so other small-town transplants.

But the steady hum of cars and eighteen-wheelers on I-90 reminded me that on this particular Saturday I was a prisoner in a fancy hotel with undoubtedly *no* place to go walking except the parking lot.

What time was it anyway?

The door to the bathroom opened as I squinted at my watch—six-twenty—and Avis emerged in her caftan with a plastic bonnet over her night scarf. I hadn't seen a plastic bonnet since high school days, when my mother wore one in the shower to protect her monthly permanent. Avis looked at Florida's empty side of the bed, jerked a thumb in the direction of the sitting room, and whispered, "What gives with that?"

I shrugged . . . just as Florida wandered through the French doors in her big T-shirt. She stopped, seeing us both just standing on either side of the king-size bed. "It's not time to get up yet, is it?" She yawned. "Bathroom free?"

"Sure," I said automatically. But I'd been up long enough now that the urge to pee was growing stronger. "On second thought, just let me go and it's yours." I dashed into the bathroom. From the relative anonymity behind the almost-closed bathroom door—like a pink-tiled confessional—I called out, "I was worried about you when I found you missing in the middle of the night. What happened?"

Florida laughed from the other side of the door. "You snore, girl! Had to find me another bed if I was going to get any sleep."

I was so startled I stopped peeing in midstream. "Oh, gosh, Flo. I'm sorry!" I didn't know I snored. Denny never complained. I emerged a moment later feeling both embarrassed and contrite. "It's terrible to pay all this money for a hotel room and end up on the floor. I'll trade tonight, okay?"

"Hey, don't you worry about me. I'm a light sleeper—*anything* wakes me up." Florida disappeared into the bathroom. "Besides," she called back, "those long cushions from the sofa made a great bed—better than the one I've got at home. Turned on a little white noise, and I slept like a baby."

She poked her head back out of the bathroom door. "You guys

going to that prayer thang at seven? Don't wait for me. I'll meet you at breakfast."

SOMEHOW AVIS AND I BOTH GOT SHOWERED and dressed and down the elevator just as the lobby clocks ticked past seven. I had even managed to pour three Styrofoam cups of coffee made in the tiny coffeemaker perched on top of the in-room "mini-bar." Avis shook her head, which I translated as No-thanks-I-don't-drink-coffee, but Florida, seizing the moment, simply took a cup in each hand.

Strike one against spontaneous deep sharing with Avis. What did one do with a girlfriend if you couldn't go out and bare your heart over bottomless cups of coffee? Or celebrate with an occasional double mocha latte at Starbucks?

Nony Sisulu-Smith was the only other person from last night's group when we made our appearance in Meeting Room 7. She was on her knees already praying out loud, so we just sat down in nearby chairs and joined her. At least I closed my eyes and tried to concentrate on Nony's prayer. Her cultured voice rose and fell like a piece of classical music. But as I listened, her prayer sure did seem full of a lot of clichés.

" . . . You are the root and the offspring of David, the bright and morning star. The Spirit and the bride say, Come. And let him that heareth say, Come. Let him that is thirsty, come. Thank You,

Father! Thank You that You have said, Whosoever will, let him take the water of life freely . . ."

On and on she went, her voice growing stronger. "I will bless the Lord at all times. Your praise shall continually be in my mouth. My soul shall make her boast in the Lord; the humble shall hear and be glad. O magnify the Lord with me! Let us exalt his name together! . . ."

I opened my eyes and peeked. Nony's cheeks glistened with moisture. Avis was on her feet, murmuring, "Yes! Thank You, Father! . . . Thank You, Jesus! . . ." as Nony prayed. I closed my eyes again. Looked like Nony was going for the long haul.

"O God, we know that young lions do lack, and suffer hunger. But if we seek the Lord we shall not want any good thing . . ."

Speaking of hunger, wasn't breakfast at eight o'clock? I took a peek at my watch. Only 7:22. Just then I was aware of a presence behind me, and Avis whispered in my ear. "Psalm thirty-four."

Psalm thirty-four? Did she want me to look it up? I reached in my bag and pulled out my small travel Bible. Psalm thirty-three . . . thirty-four . . . My eyes skimmed over the verses. *Duh.* Of course! Nony was praying Psalm thirty-four. Had probably been "praying Scripture" all along. And Avis, no doubt, knew right where each Scripture verse came from. *Double duh.*

I squeezed my eyes shut. *Okay, God, I feel like a dork. I'm sorry for thinking Nony's prayer was just a bunch of clichés. You gotta help me here. Everything's just so . . . different. But I want to learn whatever You want me to learn this weekend . . . I think.*

5

The line for the breakfast buffet wound clear out of the hotel café when we arrived at eight, but Avis, Nony, and I managed to get a table for four by the time we got through the line about eight-thirty. The line had thinned, and a few minutes later Florida hustled over with a cup of coffee and a sweet roll. I waved her into the fourth chair beside Nony. "Someone offered us a hundred bucks for this seat, but . . . we saved it for you."

Florida chuckled. "You did right." She tore her sweet roll in half. "So . . . was the prayer group good?"

"You're looking at it," I said.

For a blink Florida stopped chewing. "Well, thank God! At least I wasn't the only delinquent." She waved her sweet roll at the rest of us. "Though I'm sure God was pleased that a few of you showed up to get your praise on."

I stifled a grin. Florida talked about "getting your praise on" like it was a blouse or a pair of shoes. Then her forehead wrinkled up. "It was optional, right? I mean, they'll probably have the prayer groups get together again during the conference, don't you think?"

"I'm sure they will." Nony slipped cream into her tea. "But I was just as glad there were only a few this morning. The prayer time was precious."

I studied the beautiful woman across from me. I'd never met anyone who seemed so totally unself-conscious when she was praying. Besides Avis, I mean. I thought maybe Avis had some special connection to God that was on "high" all the time. But Nony slipped Scripture in and out of her prayers so easily, it was like a second language.

With time slipping away and the first session of the day starting at nine o'clock, we mostly paid attention to our bagels, plastic cups of yogurt, and fruit juice amid small talk. I gave a quick glance around the room to see if I recognized anyone else from the night before. But mostly I saw women in a variety of "casual dress" with an occasional color-coordinated jogging suit. Guessed I was dressed okay in my beige slacks and off-white cotton sweater. Nony was wearing another African-print tunic over black pants, but she'd left off the headgear. Instead, a head full of tiny cornrows met at the top of her head and cascaded in a ponytail of coppery braids down to her shoulders. Gosh, it was gorgeous. I felt slightly cheated. My thin wash-and-wear hair would never do something like that.

"Hellooo, Jodi. I said, do you want to go back to the room with me?" With a start I realized Avis had stood up and was waiting for me. "I want to . . ." She pantomimed brushing her teeth. " . . . Before the session starts."

"If you get on up in there before me, save me a seat!" Florida called after us, still intent on her coffee.

Teeth brushed, a fresh application of lipstick, and Avis and I made our way to the ballroom. Once again the worship band and singers were up and running already by nine o'clock, even though women were still finding their seats. Once more we ended up in row five from the front with Avis next to an aisle. I piled my purse and Bible on the chair beside me to save a seat for Florida. *Unless Adele comes and dumps them back into my lap,* I thought ruefully. But that would mean she'd be choosing to sit beside me in a room with hundreds of chairs, and I was sure *that* wasn't going to happen.

Soon the lady in the red suit—except it was a creamy tan today that complemented her skin to a golden glow—was back on stage with the hand-held mike, song lyrics were up on the screen, and the place was rocking.

> We're blessed in the city! We're blessed in the field!
> We're blessed when we come and when we go!

After six or seven repeats of the same song—verses, chorus, *and* vamp ("Blessed! Blessed! Blessed! Blessed!")—the ballroom was filled with shouts of "Hallelujah!" and "Praise the Lord!" as the worship band quickly slid into another song. The ballroom doors stood open, and I saw some of the hotel staff peek in from time to time to see what all the ruckus was about. Even a house-maid or two. Later when I looked again, the doors were closed. Guess they didn't want us disturbing the other guests.

Avis was totally focused on worshiping. I tried. I really did. But my mind kept wandering, kept looking over the crowd to see if I recognized any of the other women in Group Twenty-Six. But we were pretty close to the front, so I couldn't really turn around and stare. I tried to clap and step to the music, but it was like patting my head and rubbing my stomach at the same time—I couldn't get coordinated. So I just sang along to the unfamiliar songs as best I could.

But after about an hour of chandelier-shaking music, I needed a break. I caught Avis's eye and mouthed that I was going to the bathroom. At least everyone was standing and moving and shout-ing, so it was pretty easy to slip out of the crowd unnoticed.

In the ladies restroom, I headed for the third stall. Funny. I always picked a stall in a public restroom and kept using that same one (unless it was already in use). Did other people do that? Or was I hopelessly in a rut even about bathroom stalls?

The noisy worship from the ballroom still throbbed in the background, but the peaceful ladies' room was like sitting by Walden Pond with a superhighway somewhere beyond the trees. However, my little oasis of quiet was broken by someone else coming in to use the facilities. While that woman was washing her hands—I heard water running—another person came in.

"Sister Monica!" gushed the newcomer. "I didn't know you were at the conference! How ya doin', girl?"

"All right. All right. I'm blessed. Highly favored by the Lord and coming into my prosperity. You?"

"Saved, sanctified, *and* satisfied. Can't complain."

The two women burbled on, but I closed my eyes and leaned against the industrial-size toilet paper dispenser. What was I *doing* here? These women talked a whole new language! I'd been a baptized Christian for thirty-plus years—forty-two, if I included my childhood years when "Jesus Loves Me" was my favorite goodnight song—but when someone asked how I was doing, I usually said, "Great," or "Fair" or "Not so good," depending on how I felt at the moment.

Either these women had cliché buttons that played on automatic, or they had an inside track on God's blessings.

I stayed in my stall until the other women left, then washed my hands with the perfumed hotel soap and hit the button on the hot-air dryer. *So, what is it, God? Am I blessed? Is that the same as being thankful for my blessings?*

I GOT BACK TO THE BALLROOM in time to hear another dynamo speaker who barely needed a microphone, then we were instructed to return to our prayer groups and pray for each other, that God would reveal the obstacles keeping us from living out our destiny.

Here we go again, I thought as the flood of estrogen energy flowed through the doors and into our respective meeting rooms.

My "destiny"? I didn't have a clue. And I wasn't sure I felt that comfortable with the jargon. I mean, we're supposed to do God's will as revealed in the Bible—obeying the commandments and stuff like that. And "bloom where we're planted," to borrow a worn-out cliché. As in, be faithful where God puts you. But living into our destiny? What did that mean?

Florida plopped down in a chair beside me in Group Twenty-Six. "Where were you?" I asked. "I saved you a seat."

"Oh, girl, I got there late and didn't want to walk all the way up to the fifth row." She leaned toward me with a conspiratorial whisper. "We gotta deprogram Avis, you know. The fifth row isn't any more spiritual than the fifteenth."

I chuckled. My sentiments exactly.

To my surprise, everyone from last night's circle showed up for this prayer time. Even Adele. Even Yo-Yo. Maybe Ruth dragged her since they came to the conference together. Again there was a bit of awkward looking at our shoes, wondering who would start this thing. *I* sure wasn't going to jump in again.

Finally Delores Enriques spoke up. "Why don't you get us started, Avis? You're the senior *señora* here, I think." She looked around the circle. "*Si?*"

There were murmurs of assent from several in the group. I was sure Avis felt put on the spot. But Delores was right. Avis was the natural spiritual leader in the group as far as I knew.

But the woman with all the earrings—Leslie Stuart—spoke up. "Why do we need a leader?" she said. "Let's just start, whoever wants to."

I wasn't the only one who glared at the woman with the long blonde hair who wanted to be called "Stu." She had a right to her viewpoint, but it felt like a put-down after Delores had suggested Avis.

Avis got off the hot seat. "Well, Stu is right. We can just go right to prayer. We don't need to know specifics in order to pray for each other. We can pray in the Spirit, mention each person by name. God knows better than we do what our destiny is, or the obstacles in our lives."

True, I thought, but I felt disappointed. I liked being able to pray specifically for a person—and sharing was a way to get to know each other.

But Stu wasn't finished. "I didn't mean that. I think whoever wants to should share what they'd like prayer for, and then we can pray for that person. I just don't see that that needs a 'leader.' "

Now I was really irritated—especially since I half-agreed with her about the sharing part and praying specifically. But I felt defensive for Avis.

Adele, on the other side of the circle, was sitting with her arms folded and foot tapping. "Leslie, is it?" she said in a voice that made me think of a teacher with a ruler. "I think I heard most of this group agreeing that we'd like to appoint a leader, and Avis is it. Let's not waste a lot of time here. I think you'll agree." The woman who operated Adele's Hair and Nails nodded at Avis. "Go ahead."

Zingo! Good for Adele, I thought. She had just redeemed herself in my eyes—for the moment anyway. But I sure wouldn't have wanted to be in Stu's shoes.

I felt a poke in my side. "Adele knows how to kick a little butt, don't she?" Florida whispered. Again I wanted to laugh.

"Well, I don't know that we really need a leader either," said Avis graciously. "But why don't we quiet ourselves and get in an attitude of prayer. Then if anyone has something to share that needs prayer, just speak out. No one has to share if they don't want to, but let's try to pray for each person during this time. Let the Holy Spirit be our guide."

She closed her eyes, lifted up her face, and began to murmur, "Thank You, Jesus. Thank You for who You are . . ."

Others around me began to pray in a similar way, all at the same time. Beside me, Florida rocked side to side, her eyes squeezed shut. "Thank ya, *Jesus!*" she said. No murmuring there. *"Thank* ya!"

My heart felt stretched. What had just happened here? I couldn't close my eyes. I just wanted to memorize the faces in this group. Even Stu seemed pacified. For a reason I couldn't fathom, I felt teary. I thought I had just seen spiritual leadership at work—though I'd be hard-pressed to explain it.

As I soaked in the murmured prayers and gazed around the group, I suddenly noticed something.

Nails. Lots of painted fingernails, no two shades of red alike. Not only that, but every dark hand, whether African or Caribbean or American, had painted nails. I glanced on either side of me. Even Avis and Florida. But most of the pale hands—Yo-Yo, for sure, but also Ruth and me and Hoshi—had bald nails, though

Hoshi's looked carefully manicured with very white moon-slivers at the tips.

Stu was the exception. Her nails were long, blue, and glittery.

Good grief, Jodi! Stop it! I squeezed my eyes shut. *Dear God, I'm sorry for getting distracted. Help me to stay focused . . . focused on You.*

6

By the time we stopped for lunch, we'd only prayed for half the group. Edesa asked us to pray for her family back in Honduras. (Honduras! Of course. No wonder she attended a Spanish-speaking church. I wondered what percentage of blacks lived in Honduras. That would be interesting for my third-graders to study.) Edesa's parents were believers, she said, but their town had been devastated by Hurricane Mitch in 1998. She felt guilty being away from home and experiencing so much plenty in the States, when her extended family was still struggling with grinding poverty.

Encouraged by Edesa, who mentioned families, Hoshi spoke up. Her parents were coming to Chicago to visit this summer and would be extremely displeased that she had forsaken the Shinto religion for Christianity. She wanted prayer to be strong to share her new faith.

"As long as we're praying for parents, y'all can pray for my mother. And me. I take care of her. And—you know—it's like having another kid." Adele spoke into the circle then retreated behind arms folded across her ample bosom.

Adele took care of her mother? I knew firsthand that was no picnic. Grandmother Jennings had lived with us for a time when I was a teenager. She had dementia (my brothers called it "demented"— but not in front of my parents, of course), and nothing my mom or dad did for her was right. As the only girl, I had to share my room with Grandma. One time I caught her going through my drawers and throwing out birthday cards and notes I'd saved under my sweaters and underwear. Boy, did I yell! When she died and I got my room back, I felt relieved and guilty at the same time.

I corralled my thoughts and tried to focus on Chanda, the Jamaican woman who said she cleaned houses on the North Shore. Had been doing it for ten years, had a good clientele. But the focus on "living into your destiny" had stirred up feelings of dissatisfaction. "I wan' to be doin' someting else, but I don' know what," she said. "Got tree kids, no mon. It's hard to jump the train."

Whew. I was glad people were opening up. Chanda was somebody you didn't really notice just sitting there. Average height, dowdy skirt and blouse, short black hair, cut but not styled, nothing that stood out. But the idea that God had created plain Chanda to be a "woman of destiny" tickled my fancy. Wished I had the gift of prophecy and could zap her with a "word." Well, not really. People who tried that at Uptown Community made me feel uncomfortable, even though I knew *some* people must have that gift because it was in the Bible.

Noting the time, Avis moved us into praying for Edesa, Hoshi, Adele, and Chanda, even though we hadn't gotten around the circle. Well, there was always the next time.

AT LUNCHTIME, the lines for the pay phones just off the lobby were three and four women deep. Lines probably would have been longer, but I saw a lot of women standing in the line for the lunch buffet holding one hand to their ear talking on their cell phones. I did a double take when one woman came marching through the lobby talking loudly to herself and making emphatic gestures— then I realized she had one of those handsfree cords hanging from her ear.

As I waited for a phone, bits of one-sided conversations merged in space above the pay phones, like little cartoon balloons.

"What color is it? . . . Orange? Sure it wasn't just a hairball? . . . Okay, okay, I know it's yucky . . . No, you *can't* leave it for me to clean up! . . . Just *do it*, Morris."

"I want to cancel my Saturday three o'clock . . . Do you have a two o'clock on Monday? . . . *Friday?* I'll look like my mother by Friday!"

"Of course I miss you, honey . . . You broke what? . . . No, no, Mommy's not mad . . . Why were you using my good— . . . Put Daddy on the phone. *Now.*"

Phones got hung up, and the lines inched forward. A new voice ahead of me sounded familiar, but I couldn't quite place it.

"Tomas? . . . Did ya check me lottery numbers on this morning? . . . On the refrigerator door, where they always put! . . . Gwan do it . . . Yes, I wait."

Dying of curiosity, I shifted my position, trying to identify the woman whose back was to me. Then the woman turned, caught my eye, and we both gave a slight nod of recognition. Chanda George.

Good grief! Chanda played the *lottery?* On a cleaning woman's pay? It might be legal, but surely it was unbiblical, or . . . or at least irresponsible. Didn't she have three kids? I strained my ears as she turned back to the phone. "Ya sure? . . . Ya double-check? . . . I was *sartin* I gwan be a winna . . . 'cause I been prayin' 'bout it all weekend."

Oh, brother. The prayers God had to sort through. I was afraid Chanda would speak to me when she hung up, and she'd *know* I was rolling my eyes. But just then one of the pay phones got free, so I dropped in thirty-five cents and punched in my home number.

The phone picked up. "Yeah?"

"Josh! Don't answer the phone like that!"

A pause on the other end. "Hi, Mom. Whassup?"

"Just calling to see how everybody's doing."

"Fine."

I leaned my forehead against the phone box. Why did talking with my seventeen-year-old always feel like Chinese water torture? "Where's Amanda and Dad?"

"Out somewhere." I ground my teeth, but Josh added, "I think they went out for brunch—you know, one of those dad-daughter things."

"Thank you, Josh," I said, my irritation somewhat pacified by this information. That was Denny, Mr. Spontaneous. A dad-daughter brunch—that was nice.

"Well, I'll be home tomorrow afternoon. Maybe we can go out for pizza tomorrow night. We'll do Gullivers—make it special."

"I think Dad said we're gonna order pizza tonight. Besides, the youth group is having a planning meeting for our summer trip tomorrow night."

"Oh." *Might as well stay another night,* I grumbled to myself. *Baxter household's not planning a big Mom homecoming.* "Well, tell Dad I called, okay? Love you."

"Sure, Mom." *Click.*

Right. I had as much confidence that Denny would get that message as I did that the phone was going to give me my money back. I checked the little slot. Nope.

I went through the lunch line by myself, but the buffet was good: a salad bar with lots of different pasta salads, spinach, and arugula greens (usually $4.99 for eight ounces at Whole Foods), lots of fresh fruit, and crusty bread. The hotel had a women's conference pegged right down to the menu.

"Darn," said a familiar voice behind me at the condiment bar. "Where's the mac 'n' cheese? I need me some greens."

I looked up and grinned. "Hi, Florida." (Well, maybe the hotel didn't have *this* women's conference pegged.) "You eaten already?"

She picked up a grape. "If you call this eating? Think they got a Popeye's nearby?"

"You're kidding, right?"

"Girl, no! I'm hungry. Wish I had some crispy fried chicken right about now. Anyway, gotta run. What time's the next session?"

"Uh . . . two o'clock, I think, followed by the prayer group. Then I think we break to get ready for the banquet tonight."

"Oh, yeah! The banquet." Florida perked up. "Maybe they'll have chicken. We gotta get sharp tonight, right?"

Right. I'd almost forgotten dressing up. Had seemed kind of silly to me at first, but maybe it would be fun after all.

I TURNED ON THE HOTEL SHOWER as hot as I could stand it and let the pulsing jetspray massage my head. Ahhhh. Now this was luxury. At home we barely got the "hot" water temperature in our old frame house past lukewarm. Not to mention that when the family on the second floor of our two-flat was doing laundry in the basement, the water pressure in our shower slowed to a trickle. But I'd paid for two nights in this hotel room, *all utilities included,* and I intended to get my money's worth.

I soaped up, lathered my hair with the hotel's silky shampoo, then just stood under the stinging hot water letting my mind and body relax. The afternoon main session had been again a boisterous burst of praise, but by now some of the songs had begun to feel familiar. After a verse or two of "Lift Him Up!" the cream-suited worship leader had stopped the musicians (except for the keyboardist, who kept up a running background) and talked about a verse in Hebrews 13, about offering a "sacrifice of praise" to God.

"Have you ever stopped to think what a *sacrifice* of praise is?" she'd asked, striding across the portable platform and back again. "If it comes easy, if it doesn't cost you anything . . . it's not a *sacrifice!* Now I know some of you would rather be upstairs on those king-size beds, taking a nap." General laughter. "Good for you. At least you're here. That's a *sacrifice.* Some of you other folks see women dancing and shouting and weeping, and you're thinking, *Uh-uh. No way am I going to make a fool of myself.*"

I squirmed a little. Now she was stepping on *my* toes.

The worship leader stopped at the podium, leaned across it, and lowered her voice—but it still carried loud and clear. "I want you to close your eyes and start thinking about *what Jesus has done for YOU.* Some of you were on drugs, your mind so muddled you had no idea what day it was, much less how many kids you had."

Shouts of "Glory!" and "Thank You, Jesus!" erupted from the crowd.

"Some of you have thought of suicide . . . maybe even tried it, but God stopped you. Some of you have been so broke you were digging through dumpsters, just to find something to eat."

The place was losing it now. But the worship leader just lifted the mike and raised her voice over it. "And *some* of you thought you were pretty good. You kept all the major commandments and managed to avoid the big mistakes. But let me tell you—you were *still* going to hell until Jesus saved you!"

I felt like she was talking right at me. But so must all five hundred other women, because all I could hear now were thunderous shouts of *"Thank* You! Thank You, *Jesus!"* On one side of me, Florida was jumping up and down and clapping her hands; on the other, Avis's eyes were closed and tears were flowing down her cheeks. I closed my own eyes and tried to focus on what I'd been saved from. It was hard, because by most anyone's standards, including my own, I'd had a good life. Intact family, not rich but not poor either, no major tragedies. Theologically, I knew I'd been "saved," but it wasn't something I *felt* very much.

The worship leader was hollering now. "Maybe you don't feel like praising today. Praise anyway. Give God a *sacrifice!* Maybe you don't feel like dancing. Dance anyway! Give God a *sacrifice!*"

That must have been a cue, because the worship band and singers lit into the perfect song: "When I think about Jesus, and what He's done for me . . . I could dance, dance, dance, dance, dance, dance, dance all night!" Women exploded into the aisles in every version of "sanctified dancing" one could imagine. I couldn't help but grin. Josh and Amanda would be horrified at all the middle-aged mamas, some seriously overweight, "gettin' their groove on." But why should they? Teenagers had Cornerstone; the "middle-aged mamas" had the Chicago Women's Conference.

Later, during the message, I looked up the passage in Hebrews 13 that the worship leader had mentioned. Sure enough, verse 15 talked about offering God a "sacrifice of praise." But the next verse went right on to say, "And do not forget to do good and to share with others, for with such sacrifices God is pleased." That was a version of Christianity I was more comfortable with—doing good and sharing with others. But the writer called both praise *and* doing good a sacrifice—

"Jodi?" A muffled voice on the other side of the bathroom door broke into my thoughts. "You going to be long?"

Oh, help. How long had I been hogging the bathroom? "Be right out, Avis!" I yelled back, shutting off the shower and grabbing a fresh towel so big and thick it felt like a bathrobe. Darn. I'd intended to shave my legs and pits, but . . . oh, well. Pantyhose and sleeves would cover the damage.

I came out toweled like a toga and grinned sheepishly at Avis, who had shed her clothes and thrown on her caftan. "Sorry I steamed it up in there," I said sheepishly. "I'm a sucker for a hot shower."

"Don't worry." She breezed past with mock unconcern. "I'll just get you later if I get a cold shower."

The hot water must have held out because the shower started up again. By the time Avis came out, I had dried my hair and was trying not to mess it up as I slid into my borrowed dress—a black slinky thing that would have made Denny's eyes bug out. "Mm, nice," she commented, moving into the sitting room to dress. "What did you think of the prayer meeting?" she called back.

"Great. I'm kind of surprised everyone has hung in there. Even Yo-Yo." I took a slim tube of mascara out my makeup kit and unscrewed the lid. "Can you believe she's taking care of her teenage stepbrothers all by herself?"

"Not that strange. Grandparents raise their grandkids, siblings raise siblings—happens all the time."

"Oh. Well, it kinda amazed me." I dabbed at my eyelashes with the mascara, trying to make them look thicker and longer.

"What's amazing," said Avis from the other room, "is that she asked us to pray for them. Kind of a breakthrough, don't you think? Considering what she said last night about not being into the 'Jesus thing.'"

"Uh-huh. Great." I started in on blush and lipstick. "Nony is kind of a mystery. She asked for prayer about whether to go back to South Africa, whether that's her destiny to help her people there. But it sounded like her husband—Mark, isn't it?—is American and wants to raise their kids here."

"Yes, well . . . that's a huge decision. Don't know that I'd want to raise my kids there."

"Mm-mm." I mashed my lips together to blot the lipstick. Kids? Probably grown though, since she had grandkids. "Let's see, who else shared . . . oh, Stu." I rolled my eyes at the closet door mirror. "She's a case."

Avis chuckled on the other side of the French doors. "Is that a pun?"

"Pun? . . . Oh." I laughed. "You mean 'cause she wants to quit real estate and get back into social work? Guess she was a case-worker for DCFS right out of college." The caseload for the Department of Child and Family Services was so huge, a lot of young idealistic social workers crashed and burned.

"Sounded like it from her prayer request—that newspaper story about the little girl who'd been left alone in her apartment for two days? Lord, have mercy!"

The French doors opened, and Avis came into the bedroom. "Wow!" I said. "You look stunning." She did, too. For someone her age—I guessed fifty-four, maybe fifty-five—the principal of Bethune Elementary always looked so elegant and smart. Tonight she was wearing black silky harem pants and a loose silky tunic with wide rag sleeves in a bright rose color, belted with a sequined belt.

She looked me up and down. "You look pretty good yourself, girl. Don't show up at church in that outfit, or Pastor Clark might preach a sermon on being a temptation and a snare."

I gawked at her, then giggled and checked myself in the mirror once more. I did look nice . . . even kind of sexy—which I considered a big waste at a women's convention. Still, it felt good to go toe to toe with the fancy dressers I'd seen. Hair tucked behind my ears, silver earrings, silver necklace, slinky black dress . . . mmm, I felt luscious.

"Mm-hm. You two all that an' a bag o' chips."

Neither Avis nor I had heard Florida come in.

"But, um . . . something has come up. The rest of the group thought it was a good plan, and I was sure you two would be willin' to make the sacrifice—"

I broke in. "Florida! What are you talking about?"

"Yo-Yo. She doesn't have a dress. Only those bib overall thangs she wears. She didn't realize there was a dress-up dinner—don't think she has a dress, even if she did. So she wasn't goin' to go tonight. But we thought—"

"We who, Florida?" Avis asked suspiciously.

"You know, Ruth and Stu and Delores and Edesa—the prayer group!"

"Thought what?"

"That we could *all* wear our jeans or slacks or sweats to the banquet tonight to support our sister. You know, all for one and one for all."

I could not believe my ears. I'd just spent an hour getting myself ready for the banquet. I might even be able to hold my head up among the "glitterati" I was sure would appear tonight. Now Florida was asking us—me—to wear my *jeans?*

I almost couldn't trust myself to speak. But I managed a weak "I need a little time to think about this."

"Sure. Banquet doesn't start for another half-hour. Besides, I gotta go check with a couple more folks in the group." And as quickly as she had come, Florida bopped back out the door, leaving Avis and me staring at each other.

7

*T*hink about it? I was mad! What I really needed was time to cool down before I said something I regretted. Excusing myself from Avis, I shut myself in the bathroom and plopped on the stool. The *nerve* of Florida . . . or whoever thought of this crazy idea. Committing the whole prayer group—still practically a group of strangers—to something so outrageous as showing up at a fancy banquet in our jeans and sweats. The very thought was ludicrous. Or embarrassing.

That's it, isn't it, Jodi? You don't want to look like a fool.

I wanted to hit something or scream. But given the fact that Avis was just outside the door somewhere, I stuck a washcloth in my mouth and shook it with clenched teeth, like Willie Wonka, our chocolate Lab, playing with one of Denny's socks. Then I caught sight of myself in the big bathroom vanity mirror. I looked so silly I didn't know whether to laugh or cry.

Taking the washcloth out of my mouth, I let out a big sigh. I felt trapped. Damned if I did, damned if I didn't. I could either go with Florida's bright idea and look like a fool in a context where I didn't feel on solid ground to begin with, or I could stay dressed up and be unsympathetic to Yo-Yo's plight.

Why didn't she just go in her overalls, and we'd all sit with her and show her we loved her anyway?

Would I do that if I were Yo-Yo?

No-o.

I sighed again. *You're a big hypocrite, Jodi Baxter. Not twenty-four hours ago you were thinking the idea of five hundred women dressing up like Oscar night was pretty silly. You were pining for the small, casual women's retreats up at Camp Timberlee. Now you have a chance to loosen up at this big women's conference—with a dozen other women willing to be just as casual—and you're having a fit.*

But I realized I didn't *want* to be casual tonight. I looked good. I looked as close to gorgeous as I've ever looked—recently, anyway.

Sacrifice.

The word popped into my head so strongly I looked around, thinking I'd heard a voice. *Sacrifice . . . a sacrifice of praise.* I frowned. What did that have to do with anything? *A sacrifice for Yo-Yo. She's not sure about "this Jesus thing," but she's here. She's in your prayer group. What a little thing to sacrifice to show you care about her.*

The tension slowly drained out of my body. But tears welled up in my eyes, and I swiped at them with the washcloth. The washcloth now had black streaks. *Oh, great, there goes my mascara.* But as I thought about what Florida wanted to do, I began to feel amazed . . . and humbled. Here was a black woman, a former drug addict by her own admission, a Christian only five years . . . willing to put aside people's expectations and do something humbling to show the love of Jesus to a white ex-con who landed in her prayer group.

Sacrifice. Sisterhood.

I felt like someone pulled a cord and opened the blinds on my eyes. Why should I care about impressing or fitting in with four hundred and eighty-some women I didn't even know . . . when I had a chance to be "one in spirit" with a group of twelve women who had been thrown into my life, even if just for this one weekend? We were a drawer of mismatched socks if there ever was one—I wasn't sure we even *liked* each other. But we were Prayer Group Twenty-Six. And we had the chance—I, Jodi Baxter, had the chance—to give God a sacrifice of praise and love a young woman who was fresh out of prison.

What was that scripture in Hebrews? "With such sacrifices God is pleased."

I stood up, glancing in the mirror at the black smudges under my eyes. So much for "all decked out."

I'd almost traded a chance to please God for a black silky dress.

AS IT TURNED OUT, not everyone in the prayer group had brought a pair of jeans, but I did, so I teamed it with my cream-colored cotton sweater and a pair of clogs. Sure enough, Yo-Yo showed up at the banquet in her bib overalls and worn athletic shoes. She would have kept right on going when she saw half the prayer group wearing jeans, too—even Adele—but Florida snagged her, and we pushed amoeba-like through the double doors into the ballroom. Avis, who had no jeans, just wore the harem pants outfit she already had on, and Nony topped off *her* jeans with the African print tunic she'd been wearing all day, but added a matching headscarf wound turban-like around her head.

But to tell the truth, it was fall-down funny. Before Florida came up with her bright idea, I don't think anyone had planned to go to the banquet "as a group." But there we were, all twelve of us squeezing into the ballroom-cum-conference room-cum-banquet hall, asking women to move so we could have one of the large tables. It was only set for ten, so we stole a couple of place settings from another table and crowded everybody in.

A chamber ensemble pouring their hearts into Mozart and Bach—hallelujah!—had replaced the worship band for the banquet. I'm not sure I could eat to the high decibels that had carried the worship sessions the last two days. Seemed like a long time before we actually got served, but at least there were carafes of hot coffee and baskets of rolls on the tables to help quell my rumbling stomach.

When the hotel waiters finally brought our plates of food, Florida caught my eye. "Chicken!" she exclaimed with a big grin. It wasn't deep-fried and crusty—smothered in some kind of creamy sauce, actually—but Florida seemed happy.

Tucked in between Nony and Avis and wondering what to do with my elbows, I picked up Ruth's voice on the other side of the table. "So I'm heading out the door, and Ben says, 'Where's my clean shirts?' And I said, 'Who do you think I am? A laundry service?'"

Florida's beads bobbed in agreement. "Uh huh. Housekeeper, fry cook, lover . . . and ATM machine."

Adele rolled her eyes. "Ain't that the truth."

Chanda snorted. "The mon only *say* they got no money. Last week? Took the kids to the library, who there but my baby's daddy. Cooin' and cuddlin' with his new girlfriend while they plannin' some cruise they takin'. 'Im who always say, 'I ain't got no money, honey.' So I'm 'fraid I lay down my religion for a minit and—"

Florida and Adele started hooting with laughter.

"They off on that cruise now," Chanda sighed. "I'm praying for a 'spirit of boredom' to follow them from stem to stern." She grinned at the rest of us. "Sorry. Guess that's not very sanctified."

By now our laughter was so loud we almost didn't hear someone at the microphone saying, "—an emergency telephone call. Is there a Delores Enriques in the house? You have an emergency telephone call."

"Quiet! Quiet!" I waved the others down. "Did you hear that?" I turned to Delores, who was sitting two seats away from me. "Delores, you have an emergency phone call."

Immediately eleven pairs of eyes turned to the Cook County nurse. Her dark eyes suddenly filled with fear.

"I'll go with you," Edesa said, scooting back her chair and helping Delores to her feet. The younger woman escorted her friend toward the ballroom doors.

The rest of us looked at each other, concern passing from face to face. Avis stood up. "I'll go see what's happening," she said quietly, leaving her napkin in her plate. "The rest of you—pray."

I watched her thread quickly toward the doors. What did Avis mean? Pray silently to ourselves? Obviously not, because at that instant Adele launched into a loud prayer for divine protection, "whatever this emergency is about."

Nony picked up the prayer. "O God, Your Word says that we who dwell in the secret place of the Most High will abide under the shadow of the Almighty. You are our refuge and our fortress. We trust in You. Spread Your wings over Delores; let her find refuge there."

The scripture was comforting. Maybe it wasn't a real emergency. Maybe just a kid with the flu or an injured dog. Didn't Delores say she had five kids? Could be anything.

Hoshi reached across Avis's empty seat and grasped my hand, and I reached out to Nony. The prayers passed around the table like a gift—Chanda . . . Florida . . . Ruth—each in turn. I noticed several women at other tables glancing at us from time to time. No wonder. One minute we were laughing uproariously, the next praying out loud.

I don't know how long our table had been praying—maybe only five minutes—when I felt a touch on my shoulder. I looked up at Avis. She was not smiling.

I cleared my throat. "Everybody? Avis is back."

All eyes opened. Avis leaned in to close out the hubbub all around us. "Delores's oldest son, José, was shot tonight. He's only fourteen. They don't know how bad—he's been taken to Cook County."

Amid a chorus of "Oh, no!" Yo-Yo asked, "Drive-by? Gang hit?"

Avis shook her head. "I don't know. But I'm going up to Delores's room to pray with her before she leaves, if anyone else wants to—"

The whole table stood.

AS IT TURNED OUT, someone wisely pointed out that all of us crowding into Delores's hotel room might be overwhelming. Nony went with Avis, and the rest of us piled into Meeting Room 7 to pray for the Enriques family. Somewhere far away we could still hear the general hubbub from the ballroom, sounding like someone had left the TV on in another room. How ironic. The banquet had shrunk from big deal to background noise.

Delores . . . I could only imagine the terror she must be feeling. José was fourteen? The same age as my Amanda. My heart squeezed as prayers poured out all around me. *O God! I've only known Delores for twenty-four hours, but . . . she's a mom, like me. Don't let her son die! Save him, Lord! Save him!*

About ten minutes later, Avis came back. "Sorry to barge in, sisters, but if Delores waits for her husband to pick her up, it might be another hour. A taxi would cost twenty-five, thirty dollars from here. She wouldn't take it from me. But if we all pitched in a few dollars—"

"Of course!" I said, joining the chorus as several of us fished for our wallets. Something we could *do.*

Stu stood up. "Never mind. I've got my car. I'll take her."

We all stopped with our purses hanging open.

"Are you sure, Stu?" said Avis. "You'll miss out on the last part of the conference."

Stu shrugged. "Doesn't matter. This is more important."

I should have been glad Stu volunteered to drive Delores to the hospital. But I felt cheated—like Miss-Fix-It-All had robbed the rest of us of a chance to help our friend. But . . . how petty was that? Getting Delores there was the important thing.

We all gathered in the hotel foyer to see Delores and Edesa off. Delores clung to each one of us. *"Gracias,"* she whispered, her dark eyes bright with tears. Beyond the revolving doors a sporty silver Celica pulled up with Stu in the driver's seat. Figured. Just the kind of car a real estate agent would drive. But she'd better think twice about driving that car into the 'hood if she got back into social work. We watched as Edesa squeezed into the tiny backseat of the two-door and Delores eased into the low-slung bucket seat in the front, while Stu stowed their luggage in the trunk. And then they were gone.

We looked at each other, unsure what to do. "Don't really feel like going back to the banquet, but . . ." Ruth shrugged. "Maybe we should eat." Several others nodded and moved halfheartedly toward the ballroom.

"I think I'll go back to the prayer room," Avis said. "Maybe some of the rest of you could come later. We could keep up a prayer chain for José tonight, then all meet in the morning at seven."

Florida jumped on the idea. "I'll take ten to eleven."

I opened my mouth to volunteer for eleven o'clock when Adele jumped in. "I'll cover eleven to midnight." I wanted to groan. The prayer chain was a good idea, but I sure didn't want to end up trying to keep awake in the wee hours of the night.

Seeing my mouth close, Ruth said helpfully, "We could always double up."

I hesitated. I didn't think I was quite ready to go one on one with Adele. Maybe I'd go with Avis now, or with Florida at ten. "Look," I said, digging in my tote bag for my notebook, delaying for time, "we can make a list." I quickly jotted down the hours from now till 7:00 A.M. and filled in the names of Avis, Florida, and Adele. Then I handed it to Ruth. "Just pass it around."

Florida snorted. "Girl, you are too funny."

I had no idea what she meant, but as it turned out, I got to sign up for 6:00 A.M. Not a bad time for me—especially if I could get six or seven hours of sleep first. Nony, Hoshi, Chanda, and Ruth volunteered for the other nighttime hours. But there were still a few gaps. Who hadn't signed up? I looked down the list, then up at Yo-Yo.

"Hey. Don't look at me," she protested. "I don't do chain prayers or whatever you guys call it."

8

*A*vis went to the prayer room while the rest of us returned to the banquet. But I think we'd all lost our momentum and couldn't get it back. The waiters had already cleared the tables—I couldn't even remember if I'd finished my food—and the program had started. They were giving out gift bags to the oldest woman present . . . the mom with the most kids (some brave soul had eleven) . . . the most outrageous outfit (the skinny leather skirt with leopard-print silk blouse and leopard-print shoes got it hands-down) . . . the first one to register . . . two somebodies who had birthdays today . . . and a few other things that brought squeals of giddy laughter.

I kept thinking about Delores's boy. Shot. Maybe dead and Delores didn't know yet. Was he in a gang? The Latin Kings or one of the other Hispanic gangs? Delores was such a nice lady— a Christian, too. How terrible if her son had ended up in a gang.

Whenever I'd read stories in the *Chicago Tribune* about another gang shooting, it always seemed so far away, like another universe. I'd look at my Josh, whooping it up with his dad watching the Bulls or the Bears, and feel relief that I didn't have to worry about gangs. And then I'd close the paper and forget.

But this time I'd met a mother, a mother like me . . . and I couldn't forget.

I sighed. To tell the truth, I wasn't enjoying the banquet anymore. Maybe I should go join Avis in the prayer room . . . or just go up to our suite. *That* appealed to me a lot. I needed some time alone.

Catching Florida's eye I mouthed, *I'm going up to the room,* got up, and threaded my jeans between tables of sprayed, gelled, braided, and sequined ladies till I reached the ballroom doors. Behind me, the bold notes of a brass trio—all women—playing "Shout to the Lord" brought the assembly to its feet, clapping and singing along. On the other side of the double doors I hesitated. Should I go pray with Avis? But instead I headed for the elevator.

I AWOKE WITH A START, struggling for breath, sweat soaking my sleep shirt.

The bedside digital said 3:30. The bathroom light I'd left on was off. A dream . . . thank God it was only a dream!

I'd been running, running through the streets of my neighborhood . . . calling for my boy, "Josh! Josh!" . . . but I couldn't find him! . . . It was night, dark . . . nothing looked the same . . . the shadowy buildings loomed cold, unfriendly . . . streetlights peered like dim eyes through the black, scrawny branches of trees on the parkway . . . parked cars fenced in the sidewalks . . . until I got to Sheridan Road, suddenly bright with winking neon signs and sodium vapor streetlights along the strip of video stores, corner groceries, art galleries, movie theaters . . . Sheridan, as bright as day. I'll look here, *I'd thought in my dream . . . but I still couldn't find him.*

Awake now, I forced my breathing to slow, to picture Josh . . . safe at home in bed, his clothes dumped in blessed piles on the floor, his radio on low just off the dial so that the music scratched like an old record player. Even at seventeen, he had a midnight curfew on weekends. Yes, Josh was safe. It was only a dream.

But José . . . José wasn't safe at home in bed. Neither was Delores Enriques. *Her* son had been shot. What was happening at Cook County Hospital right now, at three-thirty in the morning? Was Delores still there, sitting by the hospital bed of her son? Holding his hand? Praying that he would be all right? Weeping for her son?

I rolled out of the king-size bed and got down on my knees in the dark. I couldn't remember the last time I had prayed on my knees—maybe not since family devotions when I was a child. But prayer for a boy with a bullet in his body—a boy whose mother I knew by name—needed more from me than a quick prayer from beneath warm covers.

God, I'm sorry. I'm sorry I didn't take one of the nighttime hours to pray. I can't believe how selfish I am—worried about my sleep and signing up on the prayer chain only at a convenient time. Did You

wake me up to pray? I'm here now . . . but I don't know how to pray for
José! I don't know what happened, or how he is, or even if he's alive. Oh
God, help him . . . he's only fourteen . . . help Delores . . .

"Jodi? Are you okay?"

I looked up with a start. Avis was dimly silhouetted in the open
French doors between the bedroom and sitting room of the suite,
her voice a stage whisper.

"Yeah . . . yeah. I was just . . . you know, praying for José."

"Oh. I heard a moan and just wanted to be sure you're all right."

"Yeah, I'm okay. Just, you know, worried . . ."

Avis came over to my side of the bed and sat down. I was still
on my knees. "We don't have to worry," she said quietly. "God is in
control. He's bigger than this. He's bigger than the enemy. He's
already won this battle."

I frowned in the dark. How could she say that? What if José
died—or was already dead? I mean, sure, God was "in control"—
but bad things still happened.

I felt Avis's hand close on top of mine. "Jesus! Thank You for
what You're going to do in this situation. We know the battle is
already won, no matter what the enemy tries to throw at us. Don't
let us sink into worry and despair. Satan wants us to cower and
whimper. But we're thanking You, Lord. We don't know what
happened, or why. But we're thanking You!"

She was using "we," so I whispered, "Yes, please, God." But I
didn't know if my faith was that strong. My prayer had been more
of the begging variety: "Please, Lord, don't let him die. Please,
Lord, help . . ."

After praying awhile Avis left me, still on my knees, used the bathroom, and tiptoed back to bed. I could tell the other side of the king-size bed had not been slept in, though the pillows were gone. "Is Florida in there?" I whispered loudly into the other room.

"Yes," came the reply. "On the floor with the sofa cushions. Go figure."

MY TRAVEL ALARM WENT OFF under my pillow. 5:50 A.M. Parting the blackout curtains, I could tell the sun was already up. Trying to be as quiet as possible, I pulled on my jeans and sweater from last night, splashed water on my face—a shower would have to wait—and slipped out the door of our suite.

Meeting Room 7—an interior room created with expandable walls—was dark when I pulled open the door. I'd forgotten the list and couldn't remember if anyone had signed up for the five-to-six time slot. Guess not. I felt around until I found a light switch, but the light was so bright with only me in the room, I felt like a captured spy about to be interrogated. I turned it off and propped the door open.

Part of me wasn't sure I knew how to pray for a whole hour—especially without my morning cup of coffee. But maybe this was a chance to practice praying like some of the other women in the prayer group. For a while I walked around the circle of chairs in the dim room, silently praising God. Florida or Nony or Avis would've been saying, "Praise You, Jesus!" or "You are God Almighty from whom all blessings flow!" out loud, but I was chicken. Some hotel employee going past might hear me and think I was weird.

Remembering how Nony "prayed Scripture," though, gave me another idea—but I hadn't brought my Bible downstairs. I checked out the room by the light from the hallway and spied a Bible someone had left in one of the other prayer circles, a Contemporary English Version—I hadn't seen that one before. Dragging a chair near the open door—I still wasn't ready to "pray big" in a lighted room all by myself—I turned to the Psalms and began reading out loud. "The wicked try to trap and kill good people, but the Lord is on their side, and he will defend them when they are on trial." Oh, that was a good verse. Right on the money. I skimmed the psalm. "The Lord protects his people, and they can come to him in times of trouble."

What if I turned Psalm 37 into a prayer for Delores and her family? I tried it out loud. "Oh God, the wicked are trying to trap and kill Delores's son, but I know You are on their side, and You're going to defend them during this trial . . . You protect Your people, Lord, and Delores can come to You in this time of trouble." Goosebumps tickled the back of my neck. The words rang in my ear in a new way. Not third person but first person. *I* know *You are on their side . . . You protect Your people . . .* Did I *know* this—really? Could I declare it in faith?

I tried out several other psalms this way—and nearly jumped out of my skin when the lights suddenly flooded the room.

"Jodi! What are you doing in the dark?" Nony and Hoshi had come into the room. Both had sweats on.

"Uh, I was praying for Delores and her son . . . what time is it?"

"Seven. We came for the group prayer."

Seven already? I could hardly believe it. An hour ago I wasn't sure how I was going to fill up the time.

Within a few minutes, nearly the whole group showed up in various stages of morning dress—minus Delores, Edesa, and Stu, of course. Even Yo-Yo, though she sat off to the side, arms folded like a principal doing classroom observations. Yesterday morning, no one had shown up except Nony and Avis—plus me, tagging after Avis. But this morning, it was full house.

I'd always thought of "group prayer" as taking turns praying. But I was about to be introduced to no-holds-barred, every-woman-for-herself prayer. Avis, Adele, and Chanda moved around, praying out loud, all at the same time. Florida and Nony held forth on their knees. Ruth and Hoshi anchored their chairs, but I could tell they were praying.

I was the only one who saw Stu come into the room. I scanned her face. Bad news? Good news? "Stu! What's happened?"

The prayers abruptly stopped. Stu took a deep breath. "He's okay—shot in the back, but not fatal—"

"*Thank* ya, *Je*-sus!" Florida shouted. Chanda gripped her head and started jumping up and down. Several burst into tears and dropped to their knees. "Hallelujah!" . . . "You are a *mighty* God!" . . . "Ha! Satan, you're a liar!" filled the room for several moments.

I wanted to say, "Hush! Hush! Let's hear what happened." But obviously some of the other women had heard what they needed to hear. Delores Enriques still had her son! José was not dead! The "enemy" had been thwarted!

75

GRADUALLY THE STORY CAME OUT—what Stu knew of it, anyway. She and Edesa had not been allowed to see José, only family. They'd paced and prayed in the waiting room for a couple of hours while José had surgery to insert a tube in his chest cavity— she wasn't sure why. At one point several police came in, asking to speak to José Enriques. Stu and Edesa could only wait helplessly. Finally Delores came out, worry mixed with relief.

Evidently José had taken his siblings to the park near their house in the Little Village neighborhood. José's sister Emerald said a bunch of gangbangers—Spanish Cobras—were hanging in the park, "doin' business." José had told them to move somewhere else *(Unbelievable! Pretty brave for a fourteen-year-old,* I thought) so the kids could play. The Cobras started yelling, so José had corralled the little ones and was hustling them out of the park, when . . . here Emerald said she didn't know *what* happened. But she heard car tires screeching, then some gunshots—and suddenly her brother was down on the ground, groveling in pain.

Stu said Delores had broken down weeping at that point in the story. "It could have been Emerald—the twelve-year-old—or any of her 'babies.'" The police weren't making any statements at this point, Stu added, but witnesses in the park said José got hit by a bullet when a bunch of Latin Kings showed up and started a shouting match over Cobras doing business on King turf.

"King turf?" I blurted.

Yo-Yo spoke up. "Cobras makin' a *big* mistake if they mess with the Latin Kings. Kings are *everywhere,* and they don't take kindly to anybody messin' with their turf."

I stared at her. How did she *know* that? Prison education? But I'd heard enough. Kids getting hit by stray bullets just going to play in the park? I brushed aside the nagging thought that I'd been quick to assume José himself was in a gang, just because he got shot. I latched on to the most important thing: Delores still had her son; they'd get through this.

The big-faced clock in the room said nearly eight o'clock. Most of us still needed to get showered and dressed for the day—in a hustle if we didn't want to miss breakfast. Several others must have had the same idea, because we started drifting toward the door. Crisis was over.

But I heard Yo-Yo's voice again. "What are you guys going to do?"

I turned back, prepared to offer my short list: shower, clothes, breakfast.

"How do you mean, do?" Ruth asked in that funny, backward way of hers.

"About Delores. What are you going to do about Delores?"

There was an awkward silence, which Yo-Yo took as an invitation. "You guys been talkin' all night to the Big Guy upstairs about Delores's boy. Looks like He gave a pretty good answer . . . for starters. But everybody just goin' to go home? Like this prayer group never happened? Delores might still need you, you know."

9

Later, sitting with Avis and Florida in the Sunday morning worship service in the ballroom, I thought about what Yo-Yo had said. For somebody who wasn't into the "Jesus thing," Yo-Yo had sure seemed to nail the "Jesus thing" that time.

Avis had said it was a good question. "Let's meet one more time after the morning worship and talk about what we want to do."

Sunday worship was the fourth main session of the weekend—not counting the banquet—and to tell the truth, the pounding gospel music had begun to burrow its way into my soul . . . "The devil is defeated! We are blessed!"

That was true enough this morning. Last night I, for one, had thought Delores might be attending her son's funeral. Not Avis, though. She obviously wasn't about to accept defeat—hers or anyone else's—as long as she had breath to claim victory. That took faith—a lot more faith than I seemed to have. Funny. I'd always presumed I had a strong faith. *Let those Commies come and send me to Siberia unless I recant! Ha! Do your worst!* But on an everyday level, my mind tended to weigh in all the "realities." *Most people don't get healed from cancer . . . Denny got bumped from the high school coaching job he wanted . . . A lot of poor people pray, but they still go to bed hungry . . .*

The music was going over the top. "I'm coming back to the heart of worship . . . it's all about You, Jesus . . ."

I closed my eyes, for once oblivious to what Florida and Avis were doing. *I want to learn how to worship You, Jesus. I want a bigger faith. I want to learn how to pray. And, yes, I want to know what You created me for . . .*

When the morning speaker—Evangelist Olivia Mitchell again—asked, "Who wants God to show you who He created you to be? Who wants to step into your spiritual destiny? Come on down here to the front. We're going to pray for you," I planted my feet firmly. No way was I going up. I didn't want to cry or have hands put on me or get laid out. I could pray right here in my row, thank you.

But when both Florida and Avis went up—and I saw Nony and a couple of others from our prayer group up front—I reached down for some courage. *Jodi Baxter, didn't you just tell God you wanted to learn more about worship . . . about faith . . . about prayer . . . about yourself? Well, go get prayed for, girl!*

Fortunately for my shaking knees, there were so many women who came to the front for prayer that the speaker just touched each woman on the forehead with oil and kept praying as she passed down the line. But even that brought tears to my eyes, to feel that touch, to be included in the prayer. I had the strange sense I was being sent on an adventure into the unknown . . . without a map.

WHEN THE SERVICE WAS OVER, the ten of us in Prayer Group Twenty-Six—Edesa had stayed at the hospital with the Enriques family—gathered once more in Meeting Room 7. One of the other prayer groups was also meeting in the room, so we pulled our chairs closer together in order to hear.

"Well," Avis said, "Yo-Yo asked what we're going to do about Delores. What are you thinking, Yo-Yo?"

Yo-Yo slouched in her chair like a denim-clad log, shoulders and fanny barely touching the chair, her legs stretched out their full length, her hands jammed in the pockets of her bib overalls. "Yeah. The way I see it, something got started here, and you guys stood up with Delores in a big way with that chain prayer thing. But it ain't over yet."

We all glanced at each other, then a few suggestions trickled out.

"If we had her phone number, we could call her, let her know we're still praying for her."

"Or maybe some of us could visit José in the hospital—Cook County, wasn't it, Stu?"

I took a leap. "I've been thinking about what Yo-Yo said. There's no reason we couldn't continue this prayer group."

"Oh, really!" Adele snorted. "My guess is the folks in this room live all over the city. Lawndale . . . Little Village . . . Austin . . . and half a dozen other neighborhoods. Not an easy commute to get together at 7:00 A.M. for a prayer meeting."

I could feel my ears turning red. But I pressed on. "I realize that. But if we had each other's telephone numbers and e-mail addresses—"

"What? Like a phone chain?" Florida asked.

Stu groaned. "That could take forever to get around—or get stuck in somebody's voice mail."

"But how about e-mail?" I pressed. "If we had each other's e-mail addresses and each created a 'group list' in our address book, then if someone has a prayer request, they could send it to the whole group with one e-mail."

The idea sat out there for a moment or two, then Florida piped up. "I like that. That works for me."

Stu tucked a long blonde lock behind her ear. "But maybe not everyone has e-mail. Let's see hands of those who don't."

Yo-Yo and Chanda were the only ones who waggled their hands.

"Not to worry, Yo-Yo. My e-mail is your e-mail." Ruth patted Yo-Yo's knee. "I'll bring it to the café when I get my rugelach." We had no idea what rugelach was, but the rest of us couldn't help but laugh.

"But what about Delores and Edesa?" Stu pressed. "What if they don't have e-mail?"

"I'll call them and find out." I lobbed the ball right back into her corner. "Did you get Delores's phone number last night?" I dug around in my tote bag and pulled out my notebook. "Look, I'll send this around and everyone can put down their e-mail addy *and* their phone number. Snail-mail address, too. Then we can make a list—can't tell when it might come in handy."

"You are the queen of list-makers, girl!" Florida crowed.

"Um," said Hoshi. We all looked at her. The Japanese student had said so little in the group that even "um" got our attention. "I have e-mail, fine. But if we create a group list in our address book, we need a name. Not just 'Number Twenty-Six.'"

Chuckles rippled around the circle again.

"Just call it Prayer Group," said Stu. She sounded annoyed.

"Prayer Group, yada yada, whatever," said Yo-Yo.

Ruth twisted her motherly self to the side and looked at Yo-Yo like she'd just said something brilliant. "I like that. The Yada Yada Prayer Group. It means something, I think."

"Yeah. 'Whatever,'" echoed Adele. She shook her head as though she couldn't believe we were having this conversation.

I snatched back the initiative. "Yada Yada it is—whatever it means." I wrote it at the top of the page of my notebook, scratched my address, phone, and e-mail on it, and started it around the circle. "I kinda like it, too." *It kinda fits this motley crew,* I didn't say. *And we'll never agree on a name, so "whatever" is fine.*

Avis smiled. "Well, I don't know about Yada Yada as a name, but keeping in touch and sharing prayer requests by e-mail is a good idea. Jodi, will you send that list to all of us by e-mail? But we still have Yo-Yo's question to answer. What are we going to do about Delores? I think it would mean a lot if a few of us—wouldn't have to be everybody—could visit José in the hospital. And the rest of us could call Delores and share a promise from the Word or pray with her on the phone."

"Now you're talking," said Yo-Yo. "Sign me up to visit José."

I TENTATIVELY SIGNED UP to visit José Enriques with Avis on Monday night if he was still in the hospital—pending Denny's schedule, since he sometimes had to coach late afternoon sports at West Rogers High School. As we packed our luggage and said our good-byes to Flo, I felt really weird. We'd been thrown together for three days and two nights, right down to our toothbrushes and sleep shirts . . . and now I wasn't sure when—or if—I would see Florida again. Our lives were about as different as two people's could be, but I liked her. Really liked her. I could only imagine everything she'd been through, but she was so . . . so upbeat. So close to God. Where did that come from?

"Sorry about the snoring," I told her sheepishly as we folded up the sleeper sofa and returned the cushions to their rightful place. *"Next* time you take the bed, and I'll take the floor."

"Next time?" Flo wiggled her eyebrows. "Well, girl, you come visit me, and for sure I'll take the bed and give you the floor." She laughed. "Only got one bed, anyway. The kids are already sleeping on the floor."

I tried not to look flabbergasted. Kids sleeping on the floor? Oh, well. Not my business. But I did have something I was curious about. "Flo, when we were sharing stuff for prayer, you asked us to pray about getting your family back together again. What did you mean?"

Avis, coming out of the bathroom with her cosmetic bag and toilet kit, heard my question and gave me a look. Like maybe I was getting too personal.

"That's okay. You don't have to say," I added hastily.

Florida shrugged, her brow knit into a frown. "No, it's all right. Just hard to talk about. Truth is, I can't find my baby. DCFS took all three of 'em when I was strung out on drugs and put 'em in foster homes. Carl—their dad—wasn't in any shape to take care of 'em, either. Since I've been straight, I've got the boys back— Cedric, he's eleven, the one who's ADD, and Chris, he's thirteen. But my girl—she'd be eight now—the foster family who had her just . . . disappeared. Even DCFS can't find 'em." Florida's eyes puddled. "Scares me sometimes that maybe I won't find her."

"Oh, Florida!" I put my arms around her in a tight hug. I couldn't think of anything else to do.

"Not find her? Oh, no, we're not going to go there," Avis said firmly. "That's Satan telling you one of his rotten lies. Father"— and she started right in praying—"we rebuke Satan and all his lies. We reject discouragement. We claim victory right now for finding Florida's little girl . . ." The three of us stood in a little huddle for several minutes while Avis prayed. When she was done praying, I didn't want to let go of their hands, didn't want the moment to end. But we parted, finished packing quietly, and headed for the lobby to check out.

"You got a ride?" Avis asked Florida as we said our good-byes beside the hotel's revolving door.

"Yeah, Adele said she'd drop me off. We don't live too far."

"Are you in Rogers Park, too?" I asked, surprised. I hadn't had time to look at the list of addresses that had gone around.

Florida nodded. "Yeah. Almost to Edgewater. Only a couple of miles from you guys, though."

As Avis and I pulled out of the hotel parking lot, I saw Florida outside the revolving doors with her bag, a cigarette in one hand. At that moment, I didn't blame her. If I couldn't find my little girl, I'd probably be dragging on a cigarette, too.

10

vis dropped me off in front of the house. I couldn't believe it was already 3:30—but then our prayer group had gone past noon, so by the time we tried to get a "quick lunch" in the hotel café, the line had been pretty long. We'd made the deadline to check out by two o'clock—barely—but the traffic on I-90 going into the city crept along in typical freeway gridlock. We made better time once we got off on Touhy Avenue heading east toward Lake Michigan, even with stoplights.

"See you tomorrow," Avis said as I got out in front of our two-flat on Lunt Avenue in Rogers Park. "Back to real life. No more maid service."

I grinned weakly. I was glad to be home . . . but part of me hated for the weekend to end. I wasn't sure why—getting to know the women in the prayer group was part of it. But I wanted time to think about everything that had happened since Friday night, to sort it out. I couldn't wait to tell Denny—he'd be real interested to hear about it.

Picking up my suitcase, I walked up the steps to the porch and stood there. Should I ring the bell? Or use my key? I used my key, let myself into the foyer where carpeted stairs led up to the second-floor apartment, then unlocked our first-floor door on the right. Slipping off my shoes and hanging up my jacket in the hall closet, I could hear the television in the living room—a baseball game, no doubt. Then I heard male laughter—several adult voices.

Rats. Denny had company.

I could almost taste the resentment that surged upward from my gut. Didn't Denny know I'd be home about now? That we hadn't seen each other for two whole days and nights? That I'd want some time together to catch up with each other?

I swallowed, telling myself I was being childish. I didn't even know what the situation was yet. Pasting a smile on my face, I walked in my stocking feet toward the living room archway and stopped.

Three guys—four, counting Denny—lounged on the couch, the floor, and two overstuffed chairs, eyes glued to a Cubs game on the TV as they booed a call by an umpire. Willie Wonka, our almost-deaf chocolate Labrador, lay sprawled happily on Denny's feet. Nearly empty bowls of chips, popcorn, and salsa competed with a cardboard pizza box and cans of pop on the coffee table and lamp tables. And brown bottles. Bottles? The bottles didn't compute for a moment. And just then Denny looked up and saw me in the archway.

His face lit up. "Hey, babe! You're back!" He leaped up, bottle in hand, and gave me a big smooch.

Beer on his breath. The bottles were beer bottles.

He turned back to the other guys. "Larry . . . Greg . . . Bill . . . you remember my wife, Jodi."

I recognized the men now—coaches and assistants who worked with Denny at the high school. Larry could be Michael Jordan's brother, complete with shaved head. A chorus of "Hi, Jodi!" wafted my way, cut short by a whoop as the Cubs batter connected.

"Denny?" I said, giving the bottle in his hand a dark look.

He looked amused. "Don't worry about it, babe. One of the guys brought a six-pack. *One* six-pack. Not a big deal."

"But what if my parents walked in right now? . . ."

"Your parents, I assure you, are safely ensconced in Des Moines, Iowa, where they belong." I could tell he was teasing me, his gray eyes twinkling under dark eyebrows and the thick strand of dark hair falling over his forehead. "Say, did you have a good time at the conference?"

"Yeah, I—"

Loud groans from the living room. Denny stepped back where he could view the TV. "I want to hear all about it, hon. Only one more inning in the game." He still stood only three feet from me, but he was gone.

Turning on my stocking feet, I stalked down the hallway, past Amanda's bedroom on one side and the dining room on the other, past the one and only bathroom . . . I came back to the bathroom. The door was closed. I knocked tentatively.

"Busy!" came a female voice on the other side of the door.

"Amanda? It's Mom. I'm home."

"Oh, hi, Mom! Glad you're back," said the disembodied voice of my fourteen-year-old.

"Come see me when you're out—I'll be in my bedroom."

"Okay."

I continued on down the hall and peeked into Josh's room. No sign of life, except for the mold and unsightly creatures probably breeding in the piles of dirty clothes, CDs, schoolbooks, magazines, and snack dishes littering every inch of the floor. My mouth tightened. Didn't Denny tell the kids to clean their rooms on Saturday?

Probably not. Nagging was *my* job. Everybody was on vacation when Mom went away for the weekend.

I headed for our bedroom at the back of the house, tempted to slam the door with gale force, but I thought better of it with "company" in the house, so I left it open a crack. Throwing myself onto the bed, hot tears welled up and wet the comforter. I grabbed a tissue from the bedside stand and dabbed my eyes, then blew my nose.

Some homecoming.

"Mom?" My fourteen-year-old stood silhouetted in the doorway. "Ohmigosh. You've got big black smudges under your—" Amanda, her butterscotch hair twisted in a clump on the back of her head and gripped with a big white plastic claw, sat down on the edge of the bed and squinted at me. "You okay?"

I rolled my eyes and allowed a self-deprecating grin. "Yeah. Never learned the art of bawling without ruining my mascara. I'm fine. Just, you know"—I jerked my head in the direction of the living room—"disappointed."

She looked confused. "Why? Dad's just watching the game with some guys."

"I know. I just . . . never mind. How was your weekend?"

"Great! Dad took me out for brunch Saturday—we went to the Original Pancake House up in Wilmette. So cool, Mom! I had one of those Dutch babies—couldn't even finish it."

I smiled, trying to ignore the pang in my chest. It'd been a long time since we'd been to the Original Pancake House, a virtual North Shore museum of stained glass as well as to-die-for breakfast creations. "I'm glad, honey. That's neat."

"Oh. What time is it? Gotta go. The youth group is having a meeting at four-thirty about our service project trip to Mexico. Josh is already over there." She bounced off the bed then leaned over and pecked me on the cheek. "'Bye." And she was out the door.

Thirty seconds later she was back. "The game isn't over. Can you give me a ride to the church?"

I sighed. Welcome back to the real world.

WHEN I GOT BACK FROM TAKING AMANDA over to Uptown Community—it was only about a mile, but Denny and I didn't like her walking alone, even in the afternoon—the game was over, the guys were gone, and Denny was dutifully cleaning up the living room. "Hey," he said as I walked in. "Thanks for taking Amanda.

Hope you didn't mind. It was a great game—Cubs won by seven runs!" He had that hopelessly silly look of the sports addicted.

I shrugged. "Didn't mind. Got to steal a quick hug from Josh—who knows when I'll get to see him otherwise."

Denny balanced several bowls in each hand as he headed for the kitchen beyond the dining room. "Yeah. He's taking this 'youth leader' role for the Mexico trip pretty seriously. Hey! You sit down," he called back over his shoulder. "I'll finish this up, then I want to hear about your weekend! You want some coffee? Tea?"

"Tea." That would be nice. I settled in one of our secondhand overstuffed chairs in the living room—decorated in a charming hodgepodge that Denny called "early attic." I felt my spirit relax. I'd gotten myself worked up over nothing. The kids were gone . . . Denny and I could have some time to ourselves now . . . everything was okay.

Five minutes later Denny came back with the teapot, two mugs, the honey bear, and a couple of spoons on a tray. "Okay," he said, handing me one of the steaming mugs. "Tell me about your conference."

Now that I had his attention, I hardly knew how to tell him what had happened this weekend. So I just started at the beginning—our unexpected roommate . . . getting assigned to a prayer group for the weekend . . . wearing our jeans to the banquet ("You're pulling my leg!" he said, his eyes getting big; then he burst out laughing) . . . the news about José getting shot and the all-night prayer chain . . . and finally, our decision to keep the prayer group alive to pray for each other.

Denny set aside his mug and pulled me over to sit beside him on the couch. I nestled down into the crook of his arm, feeling warm and safe. "Sounds like an amazing weekend. How did it go rooming with Ms. Johnson?"

Ms. Johnson? I pulled back to look at him. He had a smirk on his face. Of course. That's what I always called Avis at school. She was the principal, my boss, after all. "Good. Good. We got along great." But suddenly I felt a bit schizophrenic. All weekend she had been "Avis"—a friend, a "sister." And yet, now that I thought about it, I didn't know a whole lot more about her than I did before the conference. Except that she could lose herself in worship—totally unlike her calm, reserved, everything's-under-control presence at school. I knew she had grandkids—their pictures were all over her office at school—but she'd never said anything about a husband. Was she married? Divorced? Never married?

How had we managed to get through the entire weekend—and all that sharing in the prayer group—and I still had no idea if there was a Mr. Avis?

I just sat in the crook of Denny's arm, thinking . . . when I spied a stray brown bottle on one of the lamp tables. "Denny?" I turned to look at him again. "What's with the beer? I mean, I thought we agreed, no beer in this house."

"Oh, is that what we did? I thought it was you saying *you* didn't want any beer in the house. Though you don't seem to mind the occasional bottle of good wine."

"Yeah, but . . . that's different." Denny knew my background; why was he being so cavalier about it all of a sudden? I was too little to remember much about my father's drinking—just the feeling of panic when the yelling started, my big brothers holding me in one of the back bedrooms, covering my ears to drown out the sounds of my father shouting at my mother and the crash of things getting thrown around. But then my father got saved at a little Bible church—saved and "delivered from the demon of alcohol," my mother often said. After that, drinking of any kind —along with smoking, gambling, and cussing—was right up there with the seven deadly sins. To my mother's delight, we became the church-goingest family in Des Moines, and everyone had marveled that Sid Jennings was a changed man.

Denny, on the other hand, came from a mainstream church background, where drinking wine and even beer was an accepted part of the social culture. By Denny's own admission, he'd been more of a church attender than a Christ follower till college, even got a little wild with the weekend parties. But then he'd had a real renewal of his faith with a Christian college group on the university campus—somewhat to the bewilderment of his parents, who were a little worried he might turn "fundy."

Denny's parents had graciously offered to buy the wine for our wedding reception, nearly giving my parents apoplexy. We managed to convince the senior Baxters that *not* serving wine at the reception dinner would be more "sensitive" to my family, who didn't drink— and besides, would save tons of money.

They gave us two nights in a luxury hotel instead.

"How different?" Denny's tone was not confrontive, but also not concerned.

"Just . . . different." I felt on the defensive. "People don't go out and get drunk on *wine*. But you hear about all these stupid beer parties at the universities, and . . . and, who do the cops pull over for DUIs? Beer drinkers!" Now I was finding my groove.

"Hey, hey, hey! Wait a minute." Denny's tone went up. "When did we jump from drinking a beer while watching a Cubs game to getting pulled over for drunk driving?"

"Well . . . it starts somewhere."

"Jodi Marie Baxter. You're being unfair. I'm totally on the same page with you about drunkenness! It's wrong. It's stupid. The Bible warns against it. But drinking a glass of wine with our meals—as you do from time to time—or drinking a beer with the guys in my own living room is not a sin. I didn't even buy it. Larry brought it, and I made the decision that to make a big deal about it would be to push him away, a 'holier than thou' thing. Especially when we drink wine from time to time. What kind of hypocrisy is that?" He paused. "Besides, remember that Bible study we did on Jewish festivals? Wine is a symbol of harvest, of God's blessings. You know that."

"Wine, not beer," I said stubbornly.

Denny stood up abruptly. "Oh, good grief, Jodi. Let's not fight about this. It's really *not* a big deal. Look, you just got home . . . I'm glad you had a good time . . . the kids and I managed fine . . . this is the first time the other coaching staff have been to my house, and they had a great time . . . Let's leave it at that." He picked up the tray and headed for the kitchen.

I sat motionless on the couch, wishing I still had his arm

around me, wishing I hadn't said anything. Tears threatened again, but I blinked them back stubbornly. Maybe Denny was right. Maybe I was inconsistent. Still . . . I didn't like him drinking beer in our house, not with the kids around, for sure, and I wished he wouldn't. For me, if nothing else.

The clock on the mantel of the gas fireplace struck six. I shook myself. I needed to go over my lesson plans for tomorrow—we were working on one-digit multipliers in math, and I'd wanted to develop some games to make it fun—and do the prayer group e-mail list.

A surge of energy got me up off the couch. The prayer group. If we were going to hang together as the Yada Yada Prayer Group, I needed to get on the computer and send out that list.

11

I settled down at the computer in the dining room—
might as well do the list first, I reasoned, before the kids
got home, suddenly remembering that they still had homework—and got out my notebook with the page the prayer group had
filled out. As I started to type in names, addresses, and e-mails,
I couldn't help but guffaw. I could practically guess whose e-mail
address belonged to whom, even without looking at who wrote it down.

AprinciPal@MMBE.org . . . Avis, of course.

Flowithflo@wahoo.com . . . guess who.

Yid-dish@online.net . . . oh, that *was* funny. Ruth, the Yiddish
Dish. Ha!

ShineBaby@wahoo.com . . . had to be Adele's shop.

Nony's was easy: BlessedRU@online.net.

Stu's was blatant advertising: GetRealStu@GetRealEstate.com.

I felt a little silly typing our family e-mail address on the list:
BaxterBears@wahoo.com. Denny's idea, of course, when the

Chicago Bears were hot. But now it sounded like a children's picture book. Oh well.

Hoshi had a Northwestern University address, and I didn't have anything for Delores or Edesa yet. Chanda and Yo-Yo did not have e-mail—hopefully Adele and Ruth would help us stay in touch with them somehow.

"Whatcha doin'?"

I turned to see Denny leaning in the doorway between the dining room and kitchen. His gray eyes were gentle, a little sad—that puppy dog look he got when he wanted everything to be okay.

"Making a list, checking it twice . . . to see who's been naughty or nice."

That got a laugh. So I told him about our conference prayer group wanting to stay in touch, even choosing a name for ourselves.

"The *Yada Yada* Prayer Group?" Now his eyes were crinkled up in silent laughter, the corners of his mouth twitching.

"Don't laugh," I ordered, but I was grinning myself. "If you met all these women, you'd see it fits this group perfectly."

"And it means . . .?"

"Don't have a clue. 'Whatever.'"

Denny moved behind me and massaged my neck. "Hungry? You want to go out for a bite somewhere? Kids aren't back yet . . ."

The last bit of tension between us seemed to evaporate. It was tempting . . . but. "Sounds great . . . but I want to get this done before Josh and Amanda get back and tell me they've got a ten-page paper due tomorrow morning, and will I *please* get off the computer?" I looked up hopefully. "But a toasted cheese sandwich sounds good. With horseradish. And a pickle. If you're offering."

"Coming up."

Denny went back into the kitchen, and I stared once more at the blinking cursor on the screen. Okay, I had the list done and ready to send, but I needed to make an address subgroup so I could send it with one click. And maybe I should summarize what different women had asked prayer for during the weekend and send that, so we could keep praying for those situations.

The foster family who has my little girl seems to have disappeared.

Flo's words popped into my head so strongly, I actually looked around, thinking she was standing right there telling me again. Ohmigosh. If we were going to be a real prayer group, we certainly should be praying for *that*. But . . . Flo had only told me because I'd blundered into her business. Would she mind if we prayed about it as a group? Why would she?

At least I could ask.

Working quickly, I created a subgroup in my address book called "Yada Yada," then copied the list into an e-mail message and hit "Send." Then I called up a new message:

To: Florida Hickman
From: Jodi Baxter
Subject: Prayer for your daughter

Flo! Hope you got home okay. How are the boys?

  I'm wondering . . . could Yada Yada pray about finding your daughter? Ever since you told me that the foster family has disappeared, I've been thinking THIS is the very reason we need to continue the prayer group. Please consider letting the group know how we can pray. In the meantime, I will pray . . . hard.

I stared at the message on the screen, realizing how little I knew this woman. Then a troubling thought crossed my mind: if Flo had e-mail, that meant she had a computer. A computer . . . but no beds for the kids?

Odd.

BEEP . . . BEEP . . . BEEP. I automatically flung out my arm and hit the snooze button on the alarm. For a moment, I was confused. Had the prayer group decided to pray before breakfast again? Had my snoring chased Florida out of the bed again?

Then I felt movement in the bed, and Denny's arm pulled me close under the comforter. I smiled sleepily as I pressed my back against his warm, bare chest. This was definitely better than sleeping by myself in the corner of a king-size hotel bed, even without maid service.

Five minutes later, the alarm went off again, and I flung off the comforter. Monday morning at the Baxter household had begun.

One hour and thirty minutes, four rounds of banging on the bathroom door, two slices of burnt toast, one shoe hunt, pooling pocket change for city bus fares, and three wails of "Where's my whatzit?" later, I headed out the front door for the fifteen-minute walk to Bethune Elementary. I felt like a bag lady in walking shoes, a bulging backpack (extra sweater and flat shoes to change into) slung over one shoulder, a huge canvas tote bag full of rectangle shapes (baking pan, old Christmas card boxes, box of cereal, and the like) for my students to measure the perimeter of rectangles in math, and my smaller canvas lunch-bag-with-water-bottle in the other.

"C'mon, hon! I'll give you a ride," Denny called, letting the engine of the minivan run while he cleaned bird poop off the windshield. My mistake. I'd left the car parked on the street last night after picking up the kids from church. Usually there weren't any parking places on the street—at least we had a garage off the alley—but yesterday, there it was, a parking place *right in front of the house*. An urban miracle! It would've seemed a shame to leave it empty.

But I forgot about the bird poop.

"No thanks! Need the exercise." I lifted the tote bag in a half-attempt at a wave and set off down the sidewalk at a good pace. Walking was my fifteen minutes of mental space between household chaos and school chaos every day.

I hummed as school kids passed me on the run, their book bags bumping on their backs like loose turtle shells. "Hi, Miz Baxter!" a few of them called. But for the most part, they seemed to function on the principle that school hadn't started yet and therefore they weren't obligated to acknowledge adults. That was all right with me. All too soon we'd all be on the conveyor belt that pulled us through the school day. Bells ringing . . . announcements on the loudspeaker . . . passing out worksheets . . . moving desks into modules for science projects . . . the constant hum of thirty eight-year-olds, like a classroom of crickets . . .

I'm coming back to the heart of worship . . .

It's all about You, Jesus . . .

I realized I'd been humming some of the worship songs from the conference. The words carried me along like inner breezes.

The playground was full of kids running—always running—backpacks and jackets dumped along the tall chain-link fence or against the deep red brick of the old school building. The May sunshine tempered a chill wind coming off Lake Michigan and prowling through any available open space.

I pulled open the double doors and stepped into the relative quiet of the before-school hallway. Glancing into the school office, I saw Avis talking with one of the secretaries. She caught my eye, and I gave her a smile, but I thought, *Good morning, Ms. Johnson. Back to the real world.*

But to my surprise, she held up her index finger in a wait-a-minute signal.

I lowered my tote bag to the floor. In less than a minute, she came out, dressed in a cranberry suit and chunky gold earrings. Were school principals supposed to look that smashing?

"Hi, Jodi." She smiled, but I wasn't sure if it was a "friendly principal" smile, or a warm now-we-know-each-other-a-little-better smile. "Recover from the weekend yet?"

"Not sure I want to. It was . . . great."

"Yes, it was. And you did the group list already! I was so surprised to get it this morning when I came into the office. That's great."

"Good." I nodded. "I'm glad."

"But I wanted to ask you . . . do you want to go see José Enriques tonight? And hopefully Delores, if she's there."

José! I had totally forgotten I'd signed the list to go with Avis tonight. I hadn't told Denny or checked to see if he needed the car or anything.

"Oh! Yes . . . I want to. Can I let you know for sure a little later?" I probably should offer to drive, since Avis had ferried me to the conference and back. But did I really want to drive around the Near West Side at night? Not really.

Avis agreed with a wave and turned toward her inner office while I picked up the tote bag once more and headed for my third grade classroom. It was pretty much as I had left it on Friday, except the floor had been swept, the trash emptied, and the desktops had been scrubbed free of dried paste and eraser marks. Bless the janitor. Through the bank of windows along one side of the classroom, I could see the blur of feet dancing in and out of a set of twirling jump ropes to the tune of a timeless childhood chant:

> Strawberry shortcake
> Huckleberry Finn
> When I call your birthday
> Jump right in . . .
> January, February, March, April . . .

Still a few minutes to get ready for the day. I unloaded my bags, changed my shoes, and stowed my lunch in the desk drawer . . .

noticing the paperback New Testament I kept there. Kept there, and it usually stayed there, too. This was a public school, for goodness' sake. But this morning I pulled it out. In my head I could hear Nony "praying Scripture," one verse after the other. I felt an inner longing to be that full of God's Word, so that it came pouring out like that.

Well, why not?

I opened the book and turned to the Psalms, included at the back. The pages fell open to Psalm 95. My eyes skimmed a few verses silently . . . *Come, let us sing for joy to the Lord; let us shout aloud to the Rock of salvation.*

I was struck by the irony. Reading "sing for joy" and "shout aloud" silently—that was me, all right. But if Florida or Nony were standing in my shoes right now, they'd take "Sing!" and "Shout!" pretty literally.

Well, why not?

"Come, let us *sing for joy* to the Lord!" I said in a loud voice, picking up a piece of chalk and proceeding to write down the day's new math problems on the board. "Let us *shout aloud* to the Rock of salvation!" I did a little dance step and moved down the board. "Hallelujah!"

Gosh, that felt good. So good it made me laugh, just as the bell rang.

I put down the chalk and stowed the New Testament back in the drawer. Time to hustle out to the playground, stand in front of the ragtag line known as "Ms. Baxter's third grade," and escort them back to the nest of learning. Another typical Monday . . .

Or was it?

12

That afternoon at the last bell, it took only ninety seconds for twenty-seven third graders—three were absent—to disappear from Room 3C, leaving behind the usual glut of forgotten items: two hooded sweatshirts, an overdue library book, several hair bands and barrettes, a red sock (a *sock?*), somebody's copy of the math homework page, even a blue-and-red backpack. I peeked inside the backpack. Johnny Butler's, of course. His backpack resided more hours in the classroom than it did at home. Unfortunately, his parents never seemed to notice.

Piling the left-behind items into my Darn-Lucky Box covered with gold foil—I charged the kids a quarter to redeem items, and they were "darn lucky" to get 'em back—I glanced at the clock: 3:05. I'd had no time to contact Denny at the high school during the day, and now he'd be busy with after-school baseball practice. I wracked my brain, trying to remember if anything was happening tonight in the Baxter family that would curtail my going to the hospital, but my mind was blank.

That was either a good sign or a bad sign.

Taking a chance, I made a quick trip to the office and told Avis (though I remembered to ask the school secretary, "Is Ms. Johnson available?") that I was pretty sure I could go tonight and would pick her up at six-thirty. *That* was a leap. *Okay, God, I'm counting on You to grab Denny by the scruff of the neck and haul him back home by six—and please don't let him bring half the team home for supper.* Well, it hadn't happened yet, but I wouldn't put it past him.

Back in my classroom, I consulted my lesson-plan book to see what I could do now to get a jump on the next day. Following my finger down the language arts column, I found "contractions." "Ha!" I announced to the empty room. These kids were pretty good at contractions already—*ain't . . . cain't . . . gonna . . . whassup*—though I doubted I'd find those in the third grade syllabus. I finally decided to make a puzzle out of strips of heavy paper so the kids could play with words like *do not* and *is not* that could be joined together, with "wild apostrophe" cards to cover the dropped letter. As for math, the kids had enjoyed measuring "real" rectangles, so I toyed with the idea of having a contest to see who could bring in the most interesting "rectangle" the next day—the class could vote and the winner would get a prize. Could be risky, though. No telling what the kids might come up with—and I didn't want to incur the wrath of a parent whose jewelry box went "missing."

For science, we were supposed to compare "consumable versus recyclable" household items. Jotted down another list of stuff to bring from home. Toothpaste . . . bath soap . . . shampoo . . . would do for consumables. The recyclables were easy too: newspaper . . . metal can . . . plastic grocery bag . . . glass bottle . . .

Glass bottle. Yesterday's upset with Denny dusted itself off and tightened my face. Sure hoped I could find an empty bottle besides the brown *beer* bottles I'd stashed under the newspapers in the recycling bin on the back porch.

I smacked the side of my head with the flat of my palm. *Nope. Don't go there, Jodi. Denny said it isn't a big deal, so don't make it a big deal.*

By four o'clock I was ready to change back into my walking shoes, gather up my bags, and head out of the school. The afternoon sun had warmed up to a comfy sixty-five degrees, and the walk home was pleasant—though if I had three wishes, I'd use two of them to be walking along a country road (one) and to be ten years old again (two).

On second thought, I didn't really want to be ten years old and have to go through puberty and pimples again.

"Hellooo," I called out as I let myself in the front door, mentally rehearsing what I could make for supper and keep hot if I had to leave. "Anybody home?"

Willie Wonka's nails scrabbled down the hall and slid to a stop around my dropped bags, snuffling and sniffing in each one.

"Hi, Mom." Amanda's voice floated from the dining room. "Just me. Josh and Dad are still at school . . . Hey, who's 'FlowithFlo'? We got a strange e-mail message from somebody, but *I've* never heard of her. Should I delete it?"

THAT'S IT, I DECIDED, as I slowed the minivan in front of Avis's apartment building. I've got to get my own e-mail address. Nearly gave Willie Wonka a heart attack by pounding down the hall screeching *"No!"* with—I hoped—the accuracy of a heat-seeking missile. Amanda had looked startled then rolled her eyes when I ordered her away from the computer. But, I'd reminded her, she wasn't even supposed to be *on* the computer unless Denny or I were home.

But it all worked out. The e-mail from Florida had simply said, "Okay to put my girl on the list. Her name is Carla." No signature; no context. (No wonder Amanda felt suspicious.) But I felt nonplussed; sounded like Florida was leaving it to *me* to write up the prayer request and send it to Yada Yada. But I didn't know diddly-squat about the situation! Why didn't she write it up and send it herself? She had the list now.

But as I stared at her daughter's name—*Carla*—on the screen, my attitude softened. What did it matter, really? I didn't have to say much. We just needed to pray that Florida could find her little girl, her Carla.

"Mom? Are you crying?" Amanda's voice behind me had sounded alarmed.

"No . . . no," I'd sniffed. "Well, maybe a little. Tell you later."

But I hadn't had time to tell her. I didn't want to write up the prayer request in a rush, so I told Amanda she could use the computer now and went into the kitchen to scare up supper. By the time Denny and Josh got home—by six o'clock, thank You, God—I had the makings for tacos on the counter assembly-line style, apologized for not giving Denny advance warning about going to the hospital this evening to see Delores's son, but did he mind if I took the minivan?

"No problem," he'd said. "But it's going to be dark by the time you get home. Want me to go with you?" I could tell he was a little worried about me driving in an unfamiliar neighborhood—with good reason. Even though we'd lived in the Chicago area for twenty years, even though we'd lived on Chicago's north side for nine months, I had never once been to Cook County Hospital.

But armed with a map Denny printed off from the computer, I kissed everybody good-bye—even Willie Wonka—and set out for Avis's address. But—as usual—I couldn't find a parking place, except a nice empty spot in front of a fire hydrant. Taking a gamble, I pulled in, left my hazards blinking, and dashed into the foyer. *D. Wilson . . . T. Coleman . . . A. Johnson . . .* that was it. I punched the white button beside her name.

The intercom crackled. "If that's you, Jodi, I'll be right down."

I grinned and ran back to the minivan so I could move it if a police car snuck up on me.

"Hi!" said Avis a few minutes later, opening the passenger-side door and climbing in. "Glad you found me okay." I noticed she was carrying her Bible, a big thick thing. It hadn't even occurred to me to bring mine—though if it had, I probably would have brought my pocket-size one. Avis clicked the seat belt. "Which way are we going?"

"Down Lakeshore Drive into the Loop"—the name of Chicago's downtown, circled by a loop of elevated trains—"then out the Eisenhower Expressway." I didn't know if that was the fastest way, but it kept me on major arteries. I glanced at Avis. "You been to Cook County Hospital before?"

She nodded. "Long time ago, though, in the old building. Haven't been there since they built the new one. I think it's called Stroger Hospital now—after the county commissioner."

That was news to me. I don't think I could have told anybody who the county commissioner was, and now they'd named a hospital after him.

The traffic was still pretty heavy as we headed into the heart of Chicago proper, but the lake was beautiful once we got on Lakeshore Drive heading south. Bikers and skaters filled the bike path that snaked for miles along the shore. On the other side of the drive was the Gold Coast, where classy old apartment buildings rubbed elbows with businesslike steel-and-glass condos. I reminded myself that I was driving and to keep my eyes on the road because I was tempted to gawk at the penthouses on top of the older buildings.

"I have this fantasy," I confessed to Avis, "of marching into one of those buildings someday and asking whoever lives in the penthouse if I could please just come up and look around. Ever want to do that?"

She bent her head and looked up as the buildings flashed by. "No. Never thought about it."

Okay. That one didn't fly. I didn't really want to talk about school—somehow I wanted Avis to be Avis tonight, not Ms. Johnson. So I told her about Florida's e-mail. That got her interest, and we talked about what to say to the group. Before I knew it, Avis was praying out loud for little Carla—her eyes open, talking just like Jesus was sitting in the backseat. "Jesus, we know *You* know where Carla is, and we pray for a hedge of protection around her right now. You know the foster family, too, and why they've gone missing. Thank You, Holy Spirit, for the work You're going to do in reuniting Florida's family. *Thank You!*"

I think we prayed right through the city, out the other side on the Eisenhower Expressway heading west, right off the exit ramp at Damen Avenue—just like Denny's computer map said—until we saw the huge hulk of the hospital loom just two blocks south of the expressway. The sign said, "John H. Stroger Hospital of Cook County."

THE ELEVATOR DOOR PINGED OPEN, and Avis and I got out on the sixth floor in the middle tower. It had taken a good while to find a parking spot in the parking structure, then we took an elevator to the ground floor and walked and walked—the length of a football field at *least*—past the outpatient pharmacy, past out-patient clinics for ophthalmology . . . oral surgery . . . pain control . . . clinic after clinic, each with its own waiting room with rows of connected black-and-tan steel benches, divided into "chairs" by steel armrests and individual vinyl pads on seats and backs. Finally, we came to the main reception area, stark and functional, and got our visitor passes. I'd seen signs for the ER pointing to the other end.

Did the hospital extend a similar length in that direction? It felt like a skyscraper lying on its side.

"This might be a new hospital," I murmured to Avis in the elevator, "but they sure didn't waste any money on carpets or wallpaper or green plants to soften all this glass and steel."

The young woman at the sixth-floor reception desk—still not a plant in sight—efficiently told us how to find our way to the patient rooms. After a few rights and lefts, we stopped at a nurses station and asked for José Enriques. A nurse in a blue-print tunic looked at the sign-in sheet. "He already has several visitors . . ." She let her voice trail off, as if hoping we'd offer to leave or wait. But we just let it hang there. "Guess it's all right if you don't stay long," she finished.

The door to José's room was slightly ajar. We heard a multitude of voices inside. I hung back and followed Avis into the room. In the first bed, a man in his late twenties or early thirties—dark-haired, nutmeg complexion—spoke rapid Spanish with two older women, one of whom kept fussing with his sheets and shaking her head. Probably his mother.

Beyond the curtain that hung between the two beds, I saw a man—short and solid—sitting mute and poker-faced in a chair in the corner, like a bullfrog on a log. But I picked out a familiar voice on the other side of the curtain: Delores. We pushed farther into the room, nodding apologetically to the man in the first bed.

"Avis! Jodi!" Delores Enriques, standing on the far side of the hospital bed, lit up with delight like we'd arrived with birthday cake. Beside her a girl about twelve with large dark eyes, her hair pulled back with a yellow headband, smiled shyly. "I'm so glad to see you!" Delores babbled. "Oh, my . . . and that girl, Yo-Yo, came last night. She really surprised me—oh!" Our friend put a hand to her mouth then gestured toward the bed. "Listen to me. And I haven't even introduced you to my son. José? This is . . . is . . ." Delores turned toward us in consternation and whispered, "I don't remember your last names."

Avis smiled at the teenage boy in the bed, who was looking at us through a mask of wariness and pain. "I'm Avis Johnson, José. And this is Jodi Baxter. We got to know your mother at the women's conference this weekend—before this happened. We've been praying for you."

The boy's eyes relaxed slightly. "*Señora* Johnson . . . *Señora* Baxter." He shifted slightly in the bed, wincing in discomfort. Suddenly I was aware of the tangle of tubes attached to various parts of his body, some clear and dripping various fluids, others gray and snaking to various machines behind the bed. One larger tube was strapped to his chest.

Delores turned toward the man filling the chair in the corner as though to introduce us—I'd already guessed he was José's father—when three knocks sounded on the door. "José Enriques?"

Avis and I stepped aside as a large black man in the uniform of a Chicago police officer entered the room and loomed at the end of the bed.

13

The police officer was followed by another, a woman with a short blonde ponytail, carrying a huge book like a photo album. "Mr. and Mrs. Enriques?" The first officer shook hands with Delores and extended a hand to the man in the chair but got only a short nod. "My name is Officer Clay, and this is Officer McCloud of the Victim Advocacy Unit. I was here Saturday night after your boy got out of surgery. We have a few more questions we need to ask José."

Avis and I had only just got there, but I suddenly felt like extra baggage above the limit at an airline security gate. "We can—" I jerked a thumb toward the door. "We'll find a waiting room."

"*Gracias,*" Delores nodded. "But please don't leave. *Esmerelda*"— she pushed the young girl forward—"show the *señoras* where to go."

Again the dark-eyed girl smiled shyly and—to my surprise— took my hand and led us toward the door.

"One moment," said Officer Gray. "Emerald, you were with your brother in the park when he was shot, is that right?"

The girl's smile faded. She nodded.

"If you don't mind, Mrs. Enriques, we would like to talk to the girl, too. We have some pictures—maybe she can identify someone."

The frog on the log stirred. "Leave the girl alone," Mr. Enriques muttered. "What can she know? She was scared. All our babies were scared."

But Delores mutely nodded at Officer Clay and shooed us out with her hand.

Outside the hospital room, I was sorry I'd suggested going to the waiting room. The policeman's presence had shut up the chatter around the other bed. They probably wanted to eavesdrop . . . just like me. If we hung around right outside the door, we might be able to hear the policeman's questions.

But Emerald, still holding my hand, led us around a corner to a room with large glass windows looking out into the hall. A sign said, "Waiting Room." Beneath it was the word, *"Espera."*

We waited. Emerald hummed a little tune, sitting on her hands. Avis had her eyes closed. Praying, no doubt.

"What grade are you in school, Emerald?" I asked.

"Seeex."

"What's your favorite subject in sixth grade?" That's what I said. But I wanted to say, *What did those gangbangers say when José asked them to leave the park? Were you afraid? What did you do when José got shot? Who called the police? Did anyone help you? What—?*

116

Emerald shrugged. "I don't know. Art maybe."

Art maybe? "I'm a teacher—did you know that? But I teach kids younger than you—third grade." I leaned over and lowered my voice to a stage whisper. "*Señora* Johnson is the boss of our school. *She's* the principal."

Avis arched an eyebrow and opened one eye. Emerald giggled. She clearly didn't believe me. "My sister Luisa is grade three. Rosa's the baby—she's in kindergarten."

I added up the names. "Aren't there five of you?"

The dark hair bounced up and down. "My other brother, R. J. He's ten."

"Were you all in the park—"

The door to the waiting room opened, and Delores and the two police officers came in. "Ladies, if you don't mind, we'd like to ask this young lady a few questions," said Officer Clay. We were clearly being dismissed.

"Go talk to José," Delores urged apologetically. "We'll come back in a few minutes."

Avis and I obediently found our way back to the hospital room. "Not sure I want to be alone with Mr. Stoneface without Delores," I murmured to Avis just before we went in.

The chatter had resumed around Bed One. We hustled past, nodded to Mr. Enriques, and came around to the other side of José's bed. My heart seemed to squeeze. Anchored by tubes to the hospital bed, José seemed younger than his fourteen years. A *child* with a bullet wound? It was crazy.

"It could have been the girl—or one of the others."

I jumped at Mr. Enriques's voice. It was as if Delores's husband had read my mind. Suddenly, I felt ashamed of my flippant attitude toward the man. He was obviously hurting, hurting badly, in his own way.

"We are terribly sorry this happened to your son, Mr. Enriques," Avis said gently. She turned to José. "But we are so grateful God spared your life, José. That's something to thank God for, isn't it?"

José nodded politely and winced.

Avis opened her Bible. I knew she was warming up now. "Your youth is a great gift, José—did you know that?" The pages of the huge Bible flipped. "Let me read you something." She turned a page or two more. "Here it is, First Timothy, chapter four . . . 'Don't let anyone look down on you because you are young—'"

"That's right," José muttered, his voice suddenly dark with anger. "Those Cobras just flipped me off 'cause they bigger. Makin' that park so nobody can use it but them. But they better watch out. One day they gonna be sorry they messed with me."

I caught Avis's eye. I didn't think this was where she'd been going with that verse.

"Let me finish the verse, José." Avis's tone held a bit of her "principal" authority. "'Don't let anyone look down on you because you are young, but *set an example* for the believers in speech, in life, in love, in faith, and in purity.'" She closed the Bible and laid a hand gently on José's hand, avoiding the IV line. "That was *you*, José—what you did in that park. Even though you are young, you were an *example* to your younger brother and sisters of doing the right thing—even an example to those Cobras, or whoever they were. That took a lot of courage. But you had that courage. Courage to do the right thing."

José frowned, as if considering what Avis was saying. Or ignoring it. It was hard to tell.

"Do you mind if we pray for you, José?" Avis said "we," but she didn't really wait for an *okay* from either the boy or me. She just began praising God for sparing José's life. A nurse came in to check José's tubes and machines; Avis just kept praying. When the nurse left, I began to pray, too, whispering, "Yes, God . . . Heal José's wounds, Jesus . . . Thank You for his courage, God"—an undercurrent to Avis's prayer, which was growing stronger and bolder.

"We're claiming *victory* for José's life, Father God! Right now, in the name of Jesus! Satan, you can't have him!—or his brother, or his sisters, or anyone in his family. Hands off, Satan! This is God's child!"

I couldn't help sneaking a peek through my eyelashes at the visitors for Bed One as Avis back-talked "the enemy." The two older ladies stared open-mouthed in our direction. I didn't look at Mr. Enriques to see how he was reacting to Avis's prayer. But I closed my eyes again, realizing it didn't really matter. Avis wasn't trying to offend anyone—but she believed in the importance of prayer so much that she just did it, even if it did.

Oh God, how many people have I not prayed for or with because I was too afraid of offending somebody?

"*Gracias, Dios.* Thank You, Jesus!"

119

I opened my eyes. Delores and Emerald had come back. I gave my new friend's plump body a squeeze as we clustered around the bed and pulled Emerald into the crook of my arm. But I felt a little hypocritical. I wasn't sure I could be so . . . so enthusiastic in *my* praise if that was *my* son lying in the hospital bed with a gunshot wound in his back.

IT WAS DARK by the time we got out of the hospital, and once we got on Lakeshore Drive heading north, the city was spectacular, dressing all the buildings in gossamer gowns of twinkling lights. To our right, the city lights lit up the foam atop the gentle waves of Lake Michigan, like so much liquid cotton rolling against the shore.

"Who's going to the hospital tomorrow?" Avis asked, as I pulled up in front of her apartment building.

"Nony, I think." I dug around in my tote bag, pulled out my notepad, and turned on the interior light of the minivan. "Right. Nony tomorrow, and Ruth on Wednesday. Stu is Thursday, and Adele on Friday if he's still in the hospital." The doctor had told Delores it would be anywhere from four to seven days until the hole in José's lung healed and they could take out the tube that was draining air and fluid from his chest cavity.

Avis was quiet a moment, thinking. "Maybe you should send those folks a reminder by e-mail. It'd be easy to forget."

"A *reminder?*" I rolled my eyes. My kids already accused me of nagging them to death. Would these grown women feel the same way? But I probably *would* remind the people on this list, because I couldn't help it.

Avis laid a hand on my shoulder. "Don't worry about it, Jodi. It's going to be hard to keep this group informed and praying together. Go for it. You're good at that."

I flushed gratefully. "Okay. I'll, um, send out Delores's and Edesa's e-mail addresses"—thank God I'd remembered to get them from Delores before we left the hospital—"and just add the visitation list so everyone has the same info."

She opened the car door. "Great. And don't forget the prayer request about Florida's daughter."

I laughed. "Now who's nagging!"

But as Avis got out of the car I felt a strange disconnect. I'd spent gobs of time with Avis the last few days and still knew nothing about *her* family, *her* background. On impulse I beeped the horn. She turned back and peered into the open passenger window, eyebrows raised as a question mark.

"Uh . . . would you like to have dinner with us sometime this week?"

"Dinner?" She glanced away, breaking eye contact. "I'm usually pretty beat after a day at school. But thanks for the invitation. Maybe another time."

With a wave she was gone. I'd been dismissed.

Five minutes later I pulled into our alley, clicked the garage door opener several times till our garage door finally rolled up, and parked the car inside. I hated the walk from the dark garage to our back porch at night, even though it was only twenty feet. I didn't feel truly safe till I got in the back door and locked it behind me. *A cell phone would be nice,* I thought, stabbing my key into the door lock. *Then I could call Denny when I drove in and he could come out to the garage and escort me in.*

"Woo woo woo," barked Willie Wonka, scrambling up from the mat just inside the back door where he always waited if anybody in the family was "out."

"That you, Jodi?" Denny's voice sailed from the front room, where I could hear the TV.

"Yeah, it's me! Be there in a minute!"

Noting gratefully that the kitchen had been cleaned up, I dumped my purse in the dining room and stopped by the kids' bedrooms before heading for the front room. Amanda had the cordless and gave me a wave, pointing to the phone. Josh was sprawled on his bed, working on homework in his lap, his boom box playing noisily at his elbow. I went in and stood by his bed, just looking at my son. Almost as tall as Denny now. Losing his adolescent gawkiness. Sandy-haired. Too short, though; almost a buzz cut. Not like Denny and me at that age, imitating the hairy hippies of the '70s. Ho ho! How Josh and Amanda laughed at our high school pictures, with those gaudy bell-bottoms and all that hair. That was ancient history now—the last century, Josh liked to remind us. Gosh, he was good-looking—especially when he laughed, which was often. Next year he'd be a senior, and then . . . off to college.

"What?" He looked at me funny. "You okay, Mom?"

"Yeah." I bent over and kissed him on the forehead. "Just glad you're alive."

TO HIS CREDIT, Denny turned off the TV when I brought in two mugs of tea and curled up on the couch beside him. He listened thoughtfully as I told him all about the visit to Cook County Hospital. "It's called Stroger Hospital now," I told him, feeling informed.

"Uh-huh." Denny was obviously not going to work too hard to change the name in his mind. I grinned. Me, either.

"Both José and Emerald picked out a mug shot of the guy José talked to in the park. José said he's a Spanish Cobra. That doesn't mean he's the shooter, though. Other witnesses say some Latin Kings drove up and started shooting. The police said they'd talk to the guy, though. It's a start." Suddenly I shivered, in spite of the hot tea. "Oh, Denny, I never worried about gangs before, because . . . I mean, it sounds terrible, but at least the gangs tend to leave the white kids alone and . . . what?"

Denny was giving me a funny look. "Jodi, there are white gangs, too."

"What do you mean?"

"Honey, at West Rogers High we've got Skinheads and Stoner groups . . . the Insane Popes here on the North Side are Greek, basically a white gang. And girls—don't forget girls. A lot of the gangs have female counterparts."

I just looked at him.

"Besides," Denny added, "that's not the point here. From what you say, Delores's son wasn't in a gang, just an innocent bystander. We've seen it in the newspaper before—some kid killed accidentally in a drive-by."

True, but it had always seemed . . . far away. Not up close and personal.

Denny reached out a finger and tipped up my chin. "Hey, don't get all morose. I wish I could meet these new friends of yours. I'm feeling left out. Sounds like an interesting bunch. An ex-con named Yo-Yo . . . an ex–drug addict . . . a Japanese university student . . ."

"You will . . . I hope." Suddenly I wanted to see the women in the prayer group—the Yada Yada Prayer Group—again. It had been great to see Delores tonight and meet part of her family and pray in person for José. How could we make that happen for the rest of the women?

"That reminds me," I said, pushing myself off the couch. "I've got to send out an e-mail. Won't take long."

"Promise?" Denny waggled his eyebrows suggestively then picked up the remote. "Okay. I'll catch the news for a few minutes, then come to bed."

Willie Wonka followed me into the dining room and plopped himself under the computer desk, leaving no room for my feet. The screensaver contorted on the computer screen, like a Slinky toy on amphetamines. I called up e-mail. Two or thee spam junk ads . . . a reminder from Uptown Community about the Mother's Day potluck after worship next Sunday, please bring a friend . . . and something to "Yada Yada Prayer Group" from "Yid-dish@online.net." Ruth.

Chuckling already, I clicked it open.

To: Yada Yada Prayer Group
From: Yid-dish@online.net
Subject: "Yada Yada"

So who's the brilliant person who came up with the name, Yada Yada? I knew it meant something. I looked it up in my Hebrew dictionary. "**Yada**: to perceive, understand, acquire knowledge, know, discern." And a whole lot more. Here's one I like: "To be known, make oneself known, to be familiar." And another: "To distinguish (yada) between right and wrong."

If we add an "h" it gets even better. "**Yadah**: to speak out, to confess; to praise; to sing; to give thanks." Later it says Yadah "essentially means to acknowledge . . . the nature and work of God."

How about those jewels, Yada Yada sisters?

Ruth

I sat staring at the computer screen, not quite understanding the tears that wet my cheeks.

14

When I got home from school the next day, Willie Wonka nearly bowled me over in his urgency to go outside. Normally we just let him pee and poop in the backyard in the morning and Josh walks him when he gets home from ball practice. But today I played on Amanda's sympathies and sent her around the block with Willie Wonka while I logged on to the computer.

There were several e-mails to Yada Yada, mostly in response to Florida's missing daughter. A couple of the responses said things like, "Oh, Florida, my heart aches for you. Of course I'll pray!" and "That's so awesome about what *Yada Yada* means."

Avis, of course, cut to the chase: "Cling to Romans 8, sister! 'If God is for us, who can be against us? He who did not spare his own Son, but gave him up for us all—how will he not also . . . graciously give us all things?' (v. 31–32)."

Nony's e-mail took it to the next level: "Satan, beware! You can't have this child, either! Florida, I'm praying Isaiah 10:1–2 for you and your precious Carla." Hmm. Would have to look that one up.

And then there was Stu's e-mail.

To: Yada Yada
From: GetRealStu@GetRealEstate.com
Subject: Missing foster family

Florida, I'd like to hear more about the situation. I worked at DCFS for several years after college and still have some contacts there. Maybe we can pull some strings and cut through some red tape to get your daughter back. E-mail me privately if you don't want to put out the details to the whole group.

Stu

I glared at the screen. Why did Stu's e-mail rub my fur the wrong way? She was only trying to help, right? Right. That was just it. Stu acted like she had all the answers. For half a second I hoped she wouldn't be able to find those "strings" she wanted to pull—and almost slapped myself. *Jodi Baxter, get a grip. Bottom line, you want Florida's daughter to be found, right? Who cares if God uses a real-estate-agent-wannabe-social-worker?* Okay, okay, I told myself. Still, it bugged me that she invited Florida to "e-mail me privately."

I clicked "next." A response from Adele: "Sure. Get the white folks to pull strings, and all will be well. Whatever. I'm praying, Florida."

Ouch. I didn't know whether to wince or giggle. Adele's sharp tongue sure could snap you like a rubber band. I kinda liked it when she set Stu straight. But what *exactly* did she mean by "get the white folks to pull strings, and all will be well"?

"Mom? Can I—?"

I jumped. "Amanda! Don't sneak up on me like that!"

"Sneak?! Willie Wonka and I got back five minutes ago! But I gotta use the computer—got a paper due tomorrow."

I sighed. Did *anybody* with teenagers have a life? Seemed like all I did was juggle around *their* schedules. They needed the computer . . . they needed a ride . . . they needed the car . . . could they eat early? or late? They had a practice, a game, a youth meeting . . .

I clicked the "close" box and headed for the kitchen. Oh, well. It was time to start supper anyway, and my plants could use a good soak. And lesson plans for tomorrow. Always lesson plans.

"Oh . . . Mom? You're supposed to sign this."

I turned in the dining room doorway. "Sign what?"

"This." Amanda held out a sheet of paper with all the enthusiasm of going to the dentist, making me walk back to take it. A Spanish test . . . with a big fat red F at the top.

"Amanda! What is this?" The school year was almost over! How could I not know she was doing so badly? "This isn't . . . this isn't . . ."

"No, it's not the final." She pulled a pout, a talent bestowed on fourteen-year-olds the day adolescence was invented. "Just a quiz . . . but my teacher said you had to sign it or I'll get an F for the semester. How fair is *that*?"

I grabbed a pen and scrawled "Jodi Baxter" across the bottom of the paper. "Fair? Fair? You're on rocky ground, young lady, talking about *fair.*" I threw the pen back onto the desk. "What's going to keep you from getting an F for the semester all by your own sweet self with grades like *that?*"

"But Spanish is *hard,* Mom." Amanda dragged out the word "hard" like she was pressing it into existence. "And the teacher doesn't teach good."

"*Well.*"

"What?"

"'The teacher doesn't teach *well.*' Forget it. But you can't blame the teacher, Amanda."

"I can't help it if I don't understand what he's saying." The pout deepened to personal injury. "Why'd you and Dad move us from Downers Grove anyway? *That* high school is rated one of the best in the state."

I winced. "Don't change the subject," I snapped. "What about homework? Have you turned everything in?"

"I guess. Yeah. Mostly."

I stood there, hands on my hips, feeling frustrated. Frustrated with Amanda for waiting this long—it was May, for goodness' sake!—to say she was struggling with Spanish. And only then because the teacher made her get a parent signature on a failing quiz. Frustrated with myself for not noticing. For not asking. What did her teacher say at the last parent-teacher conference? For the life of me, I couldn't remember. I'd never taken Spanish in high school; might as well be Greek to me. That was my excuse, anyway, for why I never asked to see her homework or how Spanish class was going.

Pretty lame excuse.

And then there was the sore point about Chicago schools. Amanda had been looking forward to entering high school with all her friends and had thrown a royal fit when we—mostly Denny—decided to move. Denny had been concerned too. Chicago schools in general seemed tougher, less endowed. We finally decided to send the kids to Lane Tech College Prep, one of the better high schools, even though it was farther away than West Rogers High where Denny got a coaching job. But . . . moving had been tough on both kids. A sacrifice.

I took my hands off my hips and rested them lightly on Amanda's shoulders. She did not pull away but slumped under my touch. "Honey, I'm sorry. Sorry I didn't know you were having a hard time. Maybe it's not too late to get some help. Can you stay after school? Ask your teacher—?"

"I don't want to ask him! He's . . . I don't know. I'd rather get help from somebody else. But I don't know who."

I opened my mouth to protest, then closed it again. Okay, so Amanda didn't click with this teacher. Maybe her own stubbornness; or maybe he "didn't teach good." We just needed to get her through this class, help her to pass, maybe get some help in summer school to prepare her for Spanish II. But who? That was a good question.

"Look. I'll talk with Daddy, see if he has any ideas. Just work on your paper." I hadn't even asked what paper she was writing. "What are you working on?"

"Oh, it's kinda cool. We had to read *To Kill a Mockingbird,* and now we're supposed to draw parallels—what's the same and what's different—between the social issues in that book and the social issues in our own neighborhood today. It has to be at least two pages long, double spaced."

I liked the way Amanda's eyes lit up talking about the paper. At least the funk she was in about Spanish hadn't spilled over to her English class. I was glad I'd asked.

DENNY WAS UPSET about Amanda's Spanish quiz, as I knew he would be. I didn't say anything till we were doing dishes after supper when I could speak to him privately. "I feel like it's partly my fault because—"

"Jodi! This is *not* your fault. Amanda has to take responsibility for her own grades. If she needs help, she should ask for it."

I glanced into the dining room to make sure Amanda wasn't parked in front of the computer. Empty. Competing CDs blared from both kids' bedrooms. "I know. It's just . . . I haven't checked on her homework or asked how the class is going for weeks." *Maybe months*, I thought.

"She could also *ask*. Haven't we drilled that into the kids? 'If you don't know, *ask!*' 'There are no dumb questions!' 'Learn how to learn!'"

He looked so comical, punctuating each axiom with a dirty plate before putting it into the dishwasher that I started to laugh.

"What?" He grinned. "Okay, you're right; we both should've

asked. Maybe I could help. I took three years of high school Spanish . . ." His voice trailed off, and he stared at me, another dirty plate in hand. His admission must have punched a rewind button in his mind, because he said, "Good grief, Jodi. That was over twenty-five years ago! Are we really that old?"

"Uh-huh. Twentieth anniversary coming up. Not that you'd forget or anything."

"Sheesh." Denny poured dishwasher soap into the little soap cups in the door and closed it with a *whump*. "Twentieth anniversary, huh?" He kissed the back of my neck as he headed out of the kitchen. "August . . . August, right? I didn't forget the month—just the year."

I watched his back as Denny went through the dining room and disappeared down the hall toward Amanda's bedroom. Nice bod. Stockier than when we got married twenty years ago, but still in good shape. Firm muscles, only a slight pot. I smiled, remembering those first couple of years before Josh was born. We'd moved to the Chicago area—but out in the 'burbs— because I wanted to teach and he wanted to coach. We thought there'd be a lot more opportunities in a large urban area. There were—but the head coaching job he'd wanted at a choice high school out in Downers Grove had never materialized. Too much competition. And the city schools—too many politics. Disappointing. But Denny wasn't the kind of guy to wallow in disappointment. He started volunteering at Uptown Community Church in their outreach program . . . and the rest, as they say, is history.

Almost twenty years married, though . . . that was some kind of milestone, all right. Some couples would take a cruise, or fly to Cancun for a weekend in the sun. Not likely for the Baxters. But we *would* celebrate, I vowed, drying the counter with the dishtowel and tossing it toward the towel rack. (Oops, missed.) Maybe a party, invite our friends . . . then sneak away to Starved Rock or some other resort out in what passed for "country" in Illinois. I wondered what I could get for cheap on Priceline.com?

The dining room was still empty—I could hear the muffled voices of my spouse and child, calm enough, from Amanda's bedroom—so I pulled one of the table chairs up to the computer and moved the mouse. The screensaver dance froze then disappeared into its little black hole or wherever screensavers hide when they're not needed.

I called up our e-mail server. Only one new message—from Nony.

To: Yada Yada
From: BlessedRU@online.net
Subject: José Enriques

Dear Sisters,

Picked up my two boys after school and took them to visit José today. I was so touched to see the answer to our prayers on the mend and in his right mind. Hallelujah! God is good . . . all the time!

Edesa was there when we arrived . . . then Delores came

after her shift ended. At first I thought it was just a nurse coming in to check José's tubes—took me a second to recognize Delores in her pink flowered pediatrics tunic and stethoscope. She looked so official. Got a laugh out of that.

Edesa left to pick up the other Enriques children at their after-school program. What a sweet sister she is to Delores.

José tried to be polite but seemed exhausted, so we went out to the waiting room to talk and pray. Delores says to tell EVERYBODY in Yada Yada that she appreciates our prayers and visits so much. Her other children are quite upset. We need to keep the whole family in our prayers.

My boys (Marcus, 11, and Michael, 9) were tongue-tied during our visit—but once we got in the car they had a zillion questions. A good teaching moment.

Love to all,
Nonyameko

P.S. I LOVE the meanings of Yada Yada/Yadah Yadah! Can we keep both meanings even though we spell it just one way?

Nonyameko. I'd forgotten that was her full name. How beautiful. And it was interesting to hear Nony talk . . . normal, like any other mom. Maybe it was the conference. Maybe it was those gorgeous African prints she wore. Maybe it was the way she "prayed Scripture" like it was her mother tongue. But I hadn't quite imagined her doing ordinary things like picking up her kids at school or laughing over Delores's nurse's uniform.

I called up "write message," typed in "Yada Yada," put "Prayer Request" in the subject line . . . then stopped. Any prayer request I had seemed so paltry and insignificant compared to Florida's missing daughter and José's recovery from a gunshot wound.

On the other hand, what was the point of a prayer group if we couldn't pray about everything? I went on.

To: Yada Yada
From: BaxterBears@wahoo.com
Subject: Prayer Request

Hi Sisters! Jodi again. This may not seem very important, but I just discovered my daughter Amanda is failing Spanish! I never took Spanish—for some reason I took French as my foreign language, which would make sense if we lived in Quebec or Europe. But Chicago? My husband took high school Spanish, but that was in the Dark Ages. (No comments needed.) Please pray that we find a tutor or someone who can help Amanda in the next few weeks to pass this class, and maybe get some help during the summer so she'll be ready for Spanish II next fall.

Thanks, Nony, for your report from José's hospital room. Anyone else who visits, please give our love to Delores and send us more praise or prayer reports. Delores is probably too overwhelmed right now to give us news and requests.

Everybody sleep tight! I'm so glad God put you—

The computer *pinged!* meaning I had a new message. I diminished the e-mail I was writing and called up the new message.

Another one from Stu.

To: Yada Yada
From: GetRealStu@GetRealEstate.com
Subject: Church on Sunday?

Hi, people—but specifically Avis and Jodi. What time does your church start on Sunday morning? I haven't really found a church home here in Oak Park. Thought maybe I'd visit some of the churches you all come from. Uptown sounds interesting. Could you tell me the address? I figure it'll take about 45 minutes from here to get to Rogers Park in Sunday morning traffic.

Or do they do a big sappy Mother's Day thing? Not sure I'm up for that.

Thanks! Stu

P.S. Florida, my offer still holds. Let's get your girl home!

I groaned. Oh, great. Just what I needed. Leslie Stuart the

Great coming to my church. Like we needed more white folks from the suburbs!

Resisting the urge to delete it, I closed her message and brought mine back onto the screen. I wished I'd sent my e-mail *before* Stu sent hers, so I could pretend I hadn't gotten it till some other day. Could I send mine now without answering her question about church?

Blowing out my frustration, I finished the last sentence: "I'm so glad God put you all in my life" . . . went back and deleted "all" . . . and hit "send."

15

Somewhere between breaking up a fight in the hall between two fifth graders and scraping fish sticks off the bottom of my shoe in the lunchroom the next day, I realized I missed Florida. She had plopped into my life—into my hotel room, to be exact—unexpected, unapologetic, and certainly a bit unusual. But she had accepted me at face value, talked openly about the challenges in her life, and seemed to have the determination of a locomotive on full throttle.

I wanted to be more like her.

Not the drugs. Oh God in heaven, thank You for sparing me from the dragons she's had to slay just to lead the semblance of a normal life!

But coming through the fire . . . whole, her faith intact, her will to overcome fueled by *knowing* what rock bottom is like. And thankful. I missed hearing her voice cry, *"Thank* ya, Jesus!" during worship. I missed the way she wrinkled her nose and said, "Girl, you are so funny" (which translated probably meant, "Jodi, I can't figure you out, but *whatever").* I missed her energy, popping in and out of rooms, looking out for other people. I even missed the matter-of-fact way she had to "step out for a cig," even though I hate the smelly things.

But that was Florida, the whole package. Take it or leave it.

We were together at the women's conference for less than forty-eight hours, yet I felt . . . changed, somehow, by knowing her. But unfinished, too, like taking a bite of chocolate and knowing I had set it down somewhere, because the expectation for the whole thing is still unsatisfied in my mouth.

I would call her tonight, I told myself as I herded my class back to our room after lunch. Within minutes I had to comfort a weeping LaKeisha, the child's small, bony shoulders shaking because Mean Old Kevin had poked a pencil through the watercolor picture she'd worked so hard on for Parents Day. Kevin, sitting in the corner as penance for his misdeed, rocked the chair legs back and forth and sent imaginary darts in my direction. Once LaKeisha had calmed down, we would practice "conflict resolution," which usually required some form of restitution from the perp—though for the life of me, I couldn't think what could restore LaKeisha's masterpiece to its original third-grade perfection. The pencil hole went right through the forehead of her portrait of our school namesake, Mary McLeod Bethune.

"It's still a beautiful painting," I pointed out, though that brought on even louder wails. LaKeisha was certain in her heart that wasn't so. "But," I went on, "Mrs. Bethune suffered a good many problems establishing a school for black girls a century ago. She might say that hole in your portrait is a good reminder of all the difficulties she faced."

Sniff, sniff. The wailing stopped, and I gave LaKeisha a tissue to blow her nose. "That—*hic*—really be so, Miz Baxter?"

"Yes, I think that's what she'd say."

Mollified, LaKeisha took her picture and pinned it proudly to the bulletin board. The crown of little beaded braids all around her head bounced—just like Florida's had at the conference.

Just like Florida's . . .

I walked over to the bulletin board. "LaKeisha, how old are you?"

She beamed up at me, tears forgotten. "Eight. But I'll be nine in June when I graduate to fourth grade." And she skipped away.

I don't know why I asked. I had a whole classroom of eight-year-olds, though at this time of year they were turning nine like popcorn. Eight years old. Just like Florida's Carla. If Carla went to this school, she could very likely be in my classroom.

The dismissal bell rang. The quiet work suddenly erupted into orderly chaos—but the faces of the children who filed past me froze in my mind, frame after frame, like pictures snapped with a digital camera. What if Carla *was* in my classroom, but her foster parents had given her a new name? No, no . . . that couldn't be so. That would be too weird. Too coincidental. There were scores of Chicago neighborhoods where Carla's foster parents might live —maybe they'd even skipped town altogether without telling DCFS.

But I was so rattled with the possibility that I forgot to ask Avis on my way out of school what to do about Stu's e-mail about visiting Uptown Community this Sunday.

AS IT TURNED OUT, I didn't call Florida that night or even the next. Josh had a soccer game against the Senn Bulldogs, Lane Tech College Prep's archrivals, so Denny, Amanda, and I sat on the sidelines yelling our heads off for the Indians—then had to cope with a disappointed Josh because Lane Tech lost by one point, which affected their standing in the playoffs. The following night—Thursday—was Bible study at Uptown, a rather mind-numbing affair with Pastor Clark trying to unpack the Book of Revelation and the meaning of endtimes prophecies. How can anybody really know what the leopard-like beast with ten horns and seven heads means, or who the "twenty-four elders" are? *Really* know, I mean.

Avis likes this study though. Denny, too. They like digging into prophecy verse by verse. Which is a good thing for me. If there's anything critical I need to know—like Jesus is coming back next week—I'm counting on them to tell me.

I caught Avis after Bible study. "Did you get Stu's e-mail, wanting to come to church here at Uptown on Sunday?" I paused, leaving her to fill in my meaning.

The outer corners of Avis's plum lipstick flickered upward a fraction. "Yes. Yes, I did. I answered it this morning—no, yesterday—when I came in to the office." She shrugged. "Gave her the address and told her it was a great Sunday to visit since we're having a potluck after worship, and no, Uptown didn't overdo the Mother's Day thing. 'Course I told her she didn't have to bring anything as a guest."

"Oh." *Knowing Stu, she would anyway. Probably flaming cherries jubilee or something equally exotic.* "I—uh—didn't know how you'd feel about that after she made such a fuss about *not* having a leader for the prayer group."

Avis wagged her head. "Jodi, if I got offended every time somebody said something insulting or silly or ignorant, I'd spend most of my life in a funk. Don't have time to be offended. Takes too much energy. I'd rather spend that energy on praising or praying."

I nodded like I understood. I didn't. How could she not be offended by that little episode? *I* was offended, and it wasn't even me Stu had dissed.

"Well . . . good. Just wanted to be sure one of us answered." *Lies, lies, all lies, Jodi.* "See you tomorrow." I did smile then. "Last week this time we were looking forward to the women's conference."

Avis chuckled. "Right. All we have to look forward to *this* Friday is staff meeting after school."

Oh joy. I had totally forgotten. "Right. See you then."

When Denny and I got home from Bible study, Josh was on the Internet—doing research for his American history paper, he said. "Huh," said Denny, peering over his shoulder at the long list of web sites about the Vietnam War. "Vietnam was 'current events' when I was in high school." He slouched into the kitchen, shaking his head.

"Midlife crisis," I murmured to Josh—then made him take a break to scoop Willie Wonka's poops in the backyard.

"But it's dark, Mom."

"I noticed," I said, handing him a flashlight.

I saved his research as the back door banged and called up e-mail for BaxterBears. Several new messages addressed to Yada Yada *pinged* onto the screen. Good. At least husband and off-spring had been quickly trained to not delete anything till I'd had a chance to read it, though Josh thought the name was a hoot. ("You starting a Star Wars fan club, Mom?" he'd teased.)

I opened the first message.

To: Yada Yada
From: Edesa55@CCC.edu
Subject: Spanish

Hola! I'm on the school computer and others are wanting to use it, so can't be long. God bless you all for the visits to José. It means so much to Delores and the whole family—even Ricardo, though he won't tell you so.

Jodi, about your daughter. I want to teach Spanish and could use the practice. Would you like me to tutor Amanda? Delores is taking two weeks off to stay with José when he comes home so won't need me for babysitting for a while. I could come to your house, if that works best for you.

Edesa

"Denny!" I screeched. "Amanda! Look at this!"

As they read the message over my shoulder, I told them what I knew about Edesa—that she was from Honduras and Spanish was her native language, that she was a student at Chicago Community College (I was guessing—but what else could <u>CCC.edu</u> mean?), and she babysat for Delores Enriques. "They met at Church of the Holy Spirit or something-or-other in Spanish."

"Cool," Amanda said.

"What does she charge?" Practical Denny.

"What's the party?" asked Josh, bungling in the back door with Willie Wonka and the pooper-scooper. When we told him he said, "Sweet. Can I have the computer back now, Mom?"

"Give me a few more minutes," I growled, shooing them all out of the dining room except for Willie Wonka, who leaned happily against my leg. I sent a quick reply back to Edesa, thanking her profusely for her offer and asking how much she charged, then opened the next message.

To: Yada Yada
From: <u>Yid-dish@online.net</u>
Subject: [blank]

To pray the foster family be located is good. To know the child is safe, smothered in love, and cared for like their own daughter—of course you want to know. But if all is well, is it the best interest of a child to be taken away and returned to a parent she may not even remember after so many years?

Ruth

I had to read Ruth Garfield's message three times before it sank in. Was she saying Florida's little girl *shouldn't* be returned to her? Then, horrified, I realized her message had gone out to the whole group. Including Florida.

I clicked "next," got something about Internet virus protection, clicked "next" . . .

A message from Florida. I was almost afraid to read it.

To:	Yada Yada
From:	FlowithFlo@wahoo.com
Subject:	Re: [blank]

Do I need advice? God is God all by Himself and knows what is best for me and my family. Do I need prayers? NOT IF YOU'RE PRAYING AGAINST ME!

16

I was so shaken by the exchange between Ruth and Florida that I tossed and turned all night. Why in the world would Ruth raise a question about whether Florida's daughter should be returned to her? And Florida . . . I was the one who'd urged her to share about Carla with the whole group. But I hadn't expected this!

All day long their e-mails haunted me. That, plus a rotten night's sleep, made me as snarly as the troll under the bridge in Three Billy Goats Gruff. I suspect the children had an extra reason to be glad when the dismissal bell rang *besides* the fact that it was Friday.

As I sat in the staff meeting after school trying to look alert—major agenda: Parents Day coming up the end of May, and Illinois testing—I wondered what Avis thought about the latest exchange between Ruth and Florida. But she was all business, and afterward several other teachers got to her first.

I thought about checking e-mail when I got home, but Amanda informed me that she'd been invited to a birthday party—tonight—which meant doing the usual parental inquisition: Why was I only hearing about this now? How well did she know the girls being invited? Would any boys be at this party? Any R-rated videos? Who was going to supervise? Which elicited the usual, "Mo-om. I don't know! Shelly just gave me the invitation today, and I'd like to go. It's just a birthday party, for cryin' out loud."

Why shouldn't she go to a birthday party? Jiminy Cricket from Disney World whistled cheerfully in one ear. *They'll gossip about all the boys at school, decide to color some poor girl's hair with a box of L'Oreal Ruby Fusion, squeal over birthday CDs, glitter eye shadow, and ankle bracelets, and gorge themselves on pizza and white bakery cake with "Happy Birthday Shelly" on top in gel frosting . . .*

Why should *she? Because her parents are probably out of town!* screamed Jiminy Cricket from the 'hood into my other ear. *Because you've never met this girl, because boys will crash the party with six-packs of beer—or worse, and next thing you know, you'll be getting a call from the police station!*

I tried to remain calm. "Let me call Shelly's mom and find out what's what." Which I did. Shelly's mom wasn't home yet, but I was informed by Shelly herself that her mom would be around all evening. Did I want her to call? "Yes," I said and left our number. But, I warned Amanda, if we didn't connect, she couldn't go.

As it turned out, Ms. Mom did call me back, sounding surprised I had any questions. But she assured me the party would be supervised, and no boys, beer, or bad movies would be allowed. "Is

PG-13 all right?" she asked sweetly. "We're going to the video store soon." *Depends on which movie!* I wanted to shout. But wasn't sure how far I should keep pushing. I let Amanda go to the party—at which point she asked if she could borrow ten dollars and could I drive her to Target on Howard Street to buy a birthday gift?

So much for my Friday evening.

Denny and Josh, who both had after-school games, only saw us in a blur as they came in the door and we absconded with the minivan. At Shelly's home—a condo half a block from Lake Michigan—I insisted on going up the elevator and delivering Amanda to the door, even though it meant leaving my car double-parked and risking a thirty-dollar fine. Amanda, of course, was *totally* embarrassed, but I said, "Just wanted to meet your mom!" to Shelly when she opened the door, giving her my sweetest smile. Amanda and Shelly disappeared somewhere into the labyrinth of hallways and rooms, but I stayed in the doorway till a woman dressed in a business suit with an extremely short skirt—never could figure out the rationale of that combination—came to the door. We exchanged a few pleasantries, then I excused myself with a cheery, "Well, gotta go. I'm double-parked, and if I get a ticket, Amanda's taxi bill is going to be thirty bucks!" I was just joking, but the lady gave me a very strange look.

No ticket. Just an irate car owner I'd been blocking, so I refrained from shouting, "Thank You, Jesus!" and beat a hasty retreat. By the time I nearly tripped over Willie Wonka inside the back door, I was ready to crash—but not before I shanghaied Denny to pick up Amanda from the party at ten-thirty. Not just because I wanted to go to bed early and fall asleep over a good book—I'd already decided *not* to check e-mail; whatever Yada Yada was up to could wait till I got a decent night's sleep—but mostly to let Shelly and her mom know that Amanda's dad was a Big Guy.

I WOKE TO A LUXURIOUS STILLNESS. The red numerals of the bedside digital said 5:47. Still early. I could go back to sleep, but— figuring I'd fallen asleep before ten last night—I'd already had almost eight hours. The prospect of some early morning quiet time all to myself lured me out of bed.

All bedrooms were quiet. Josh had been out playing pool at a friend's house; Denny must have retrieved Amanda with no problem. Good. Let 'em all sleep.

Willie Wonka followed me into the kitchen and whined at the back door. By the time he was ready to come back in, I had a big mug of fresh coffee and was looking for my Bible. With chagrin, I found it in the hallway, tucked inside the tote bag along with the journal I'd taken to the women's conference last weekend. Had the whole week really gone by and I hadn't once cracked it open?

Well, I wasn't going to beat myself up about it. Weekday mornings were hard, getting everybody off the school. But this morning I'd make up for it—just me, God, and Willie Wonka, I grinned, tucking myself into the La-Z-Boy near the bay windows facing the street.

For a while, I let the Bible just lie on my lap as I sipped my coffee, staring out the window at the waking world. A couple of dog-walkers, a car every now and then, a gradual brightening as the sun came up over the other side of the lake . . . but tucked in here among all the buildings, it would be quite a while before actual sunshine filtered in. I couldn't remember where I'd been reading the last time, so I just started to pray silently, thanking God for my family, our jobs, our health, our church—my usual litany of thanksgivings.

Whoa. I had a whole new list of people and things to pray for—all the requests people had mentioned in the prayer group last weekend, plus additions from the Yada Yada e-loop. My silent prayer became more specific as I remembered Edesa asking prayer for her family in Honduras . . . Yo-Yo taking care of her siblings . . . José Enriques coming home from the hospital, maybe today? . . . Hoshi's Shinto parents coming to the States from Japan this summer . . . finding Florida's daughter . . .

As I prayed, I closed my eyes and imagined the group of virtual strangers praying together at the women's conference. And all at once something felt wrong with my prayer. Something was missing . . .

Praise.

I must have said it aloud—loudly—because Willie Wonka's silky brown ears, hiding his growing deafness, perked up, and he looked at me with a doggy question in his eyes. "Praise," I repeated, rolling the word around in my mouth. "Willie, why do I always launch right into thanking God for this or that blessing in my life when I pray, and then whip out my list of things I want

God to do?" Willie Wonka must have decided this didn't really concern him, because he put his head back down and sighed.

I got out of the chair, dumping my Bible on the floor, and started pacing around the room. Why had it been so easy for the other women to praise God—just for who God is—at the women's conference? Not just in the main sessions, but in the prayer group, too. All our prayer times had started that way, with worship, just praising God, worshiping Him, being glad to know Him—no strings attached.

I never started my personal prayer times with worship, not really. Not like Avis and Nony did. Suddenly a great bubble of thankfulness welled up inside me for giving me a glimpse last weekend into a new spirituality—new for me, anyway—a spirituality my sisters of color seemed to possess in greater depth than I'd been exposed to.

I grabbed my Bible off the floor; I needed a prop. I flipped it open to Psalms and landed at Psalm 150. Okay, I was going to paraphrase like Nony did, and make it between God and me.

"God, I praise You in Your sanctuary! I praise You in Your mighty heavens! I praise You for Your acts of power, for Your surpassing greatness. I'd praise You with a trumpet if I had one—or a harp or tambourine! I praise You with dancing—"

Hey, I could do dancing. I twirled around the room, startling Willie Wonka and sending him scrambling for a safer spot. "Let everything that has breath praise You, Lord! Hey, hey, hey! Praise the Lord!" I tumbled onto the couch out of breath.

"Jodi?"

Denny's voice startled me right off the couch. How long had he been standing in the archway from the hall?

"Ohmigosh, Denny. I'm sorry. Did I wake you up?"

"Yeah. But it's okay." He scratched the back of his head. "What's going on?"

I started to laugh. "Just trying out what it would be like to 'get down' before the Lord—you know, like King David. Sorry if I woke you up . . . hey." I retrieved my coffee mug and pushed him onto the couch. "Don't go away. I'll get you some coffee, then I want to talk to you about something."

Returning with my refill and a fresh mug for Denny, I let the coffee do its job till my frumpy husband looked halfway awake behind his eyes. Then I told him about the two e-mails from Ruth and Florida.

"I know." He scratched his head again, as if waking up his brain cells. "I saw them last night after you went to bed."

"I don't know what to do! I'm the one who asked Florida if I could tell Yada Yada to pray about finding her daughter. Never dreamed it would turn controversial. Now maybe she's mad at me. Didn't Ruth know how her 'suggestion' would sound to Florida?"

Denny nodded thoughtfully. "That's one of the problems with e-mail. Too easy to shoot off a message without really thinking it through. And you don't have to look the other person in the eye when you say something."

The windup wall clock—a wedding present from my grand-parents—ticked loudly as we both sank into our thoughts. A tiny fear tickled the back of my mind. What if Yada Yada fell apart before it even got started? *Oh God, don't let that happen! I need this group. I need these sisters . . .*

"Denny!" I knew exactly what I needed to do. "I'd like to go see Florida today. Any reason that wouldn't work? What's happening today?" My mental calendar came up blank.

"The men's group at church is doing some repairs and painting at Uptown—told Josh he needed to put in a few hours with me. Guess you could have the car . . ."

"Don't need the car. I hate trying to find parking. I'll get her address and take the el or something."

Denny frowned. "What if you have to walk in an unfamiliar neighborhood?"

I smiled. I liked it when Denny worried about me. And I certainly wasn't above letting Mr. Big Guy part the waters or scare off the bad guys on my behalf. But I felt strong and confident today. "It's daytime. I won't take a purse. I'll keep to busy streets. Don't worry, I'll be fine—oh. What about Amanda? If you're gone and I'm gone . . ."

"Take her with you. I'd feel better if there were two of you anyway. She's a good screamer too."

"Whaddya mean, 'too'?" I threw a couch pillow at him—but it wasn't a bad idea. Amanda was a friendly kid; she'd probably hit it off with Florida's boys. I scrambled off the couch, eager to begin the day, but Denny grabbed my sleep shirt and pulled me back onto his lap. "On one condition—that we go out tonight. Both kids were out last night. They can just stay home tonight, and *we'll* go out. Promise?"

17

*D*enny decided to jog to the lake and back, but I opted to start the laundry that was crawling out of the bathroom hamper and inching its way across the floor. Ran down to the basement to throw in a load, then got in the shower, wondering how early I could call Florida. She had kids—she couldn't sleep in that late, could she?

Had my hair all soaped up when the water suddenly slowed to a trickle. Shoot! The washing machine was refilling. Wrapping myself in a towel, I ran down to the basement hoping I wouldn't bump into our upstairs neighbors, shut off the machine, and dashed back to the safety of the bathroom. Stupid water system.

Finally, squeaky clean and balancing two pieces of wheat toast on top of a glass of OJ, I turned on the computer and called up the address list I'd made for Yada Yada. There. Florida lived in the 5600 block of Magnolia . . . where was *that?* Digging out a Chicago map, I figured she lived pretty close to Broadway and

Bryn Mawr—not too far, maybe three miles. There was an el stop at Bryn Mawr too. Good.

Denny got back from his jog and jumped into the shower, bellowing "Buffalo Gals Gonna Come Out Tonight" slightly off-key—until the rinse cycle on the second load of laundry started in the basement, at which point he yelled bloody murder. I ran down to the basement and hit the stop button, making a mental note to turn it on again when he was out of the shower. Only eight-thirty . . . probably too early to call. Taking a deep breath, I checked our e-mail and skimmed through the forwards and ads and stuff addressed to Denny and the kids. Nothing from Ruth, nothing from Florida. Hmm. Was that good or bad after almost two days? There *was* a long e-mail from Stu citing case studies of foster children successfully being returned to their parents and giving web links to look up . . .

Oh, brother, I thought. I didn't even bother to read it.

And a new one, dated seven o'clock this morning, from Adele.

To:	Yada Yada
From:	ShineBaby@wahoo.com
Subject:	Prayer for our kids

Florida, don't let "friendly fire" shoot you down. Keep the faith, baby.

Saw José last night. Doctors are sending him home today. I think it's too soon—he's still in pain and has trouble breathing. "They" say he just needs time to heal. Delores says thanks for all the visits and prayers. Keep 'em up.

I winced. "Friendly fire"? That kind of language felt like throwing gasoline on live coals. I'd been worried about how Florida felt. But now I was worried about Ruth.

Was about to shut down when I realized I'd skipped over an e-mail from Edesa because it wasn't addressed to Yada Yada, but to BaxterBears: "You don't have to pay me—I need the experience! But when do you want me to come? I'm free this Saturday late afternoon." That was today!

I considered waking Amanda to ask if she had anything going on this afternoon and decided it didn't matter. She was failing Spanish, and this was her lifeline. She probably wouldn't appreciate me planning her *whole* day—but I could call going to see Florida a special mom-daughter time, like she had with Denny last weekend.

I picked up the phone and dialed Edesa's number.

BY THE TIME I TOLD EDESA HOW TO FIND US, called Florida and asked if I could "drop by" this morning, rousted Amanda and sweet-talked her into coming with me to visit one of my new friends ("instead of cleaning your room," was the way I put it), it was almost eleven when Amanda and I hiked the three blocks to the Morse el station. I bought a pass from the machine good for four rides, stuffed the card into the electronic turnstile, then handed it back to Amanda so she could put it through again.

We heard a train pull into the elevated platform above our heads and did a mad dash up the stairs, but it was northbound, heading for Howard Street—Chicago's northern city limit—where any remaining commuters would transfer to the Purple Line serving the North Shore communities.

"Did you tell your friend I was coming?" Amanda asked, stuffing her hands into her jeans and suspiciously eyeing two teenagers with low-slung jeans and zigzag designs shaved into their clipped heads. I suddenly saw Amanda as the male species must see her: butterscotch blonde hair pulled back into a ponytail at the nape of her neck, leaving wisps of stray hair curling around her face; a budding figure; rosy skin marred only by a few concealed zits on her forehead. *Humph!* I told myself. *I should have left her home.*

"Um, sure I did. And her name is Florida—Mrs. Hickman to you. She said she'd *love* to meet you."

I smiled, remembering Florida's barely disguised surprise when I called. *"Uh-huh. You and your daughter 'just happen' to be in my neighborhood and want to drop in?"*

"No, Florida," I'd said, realizing how easy it would've been to give that as a reason—but obviously, Florida was no fool. *"I've been missing you this week. So I said, 'Heck with the housework. I'm gonna go have coffee with Flo.' Or whatever you drink at your house."*

Flo had laughed out loud. *"Girl, you takin' your life in your hands with that one. Sure, come on. House won't look like Martha Stewart, but I'm cool. And I'd love to meet Amanda. I'll go kick my menfolk out of bed—time they was movin' they butts anyhow."*

The southbound Red Line pulled into the Morse Street Station with a metallic squeal, and the doors slid open. Only one person got out—Morse was the second stop after Howard Street and most people who got on at Howard were heading downtown. The boys who looked like they might trip over their pants held back and let Amanda and me get on first. Nice, I thought. I hadn't expected that. The car was about half-full, but Amanda and I got two aisle seats across from each other.

Denny and I always told out-of-town guests they had to ride the el if they wanted a genuine Chicago experience—though I suspect the riders who were privy to it for everyday transportation were unimpressed by people who rode the train "just for fun." As the train picked up speed, it snaked perilously close to apartment buildings whose second-floor windows looked out eye to eye with commuters on the elevated train. How could the people who lived in those apartments stand it? No wonder most of the windows had their blinds pulled. But how depressing was that?

"Look, Mom!" Amanda pointed out the window on her side of the train at a back porch loaded with hanging baskets and flower boxes, a profusion of bright colors spilling over the sides. "Cool," said Amanda. "Like 'bloom where you are planted.'"

Out of the mouth of babes . . . I shook my head. Could *I* bloom if God planted me with the back of my house butted up against the elevated train tracks with a deafening din clattering past every fifteen minutes? *Why not?* a voice argued from somewhere inside my head as another flower-bedecked rear porch flew by. *What does scenery have to do with it?*

"Morse" . . . "Loyola" . . . "Granville" . . . the el pulled up along each platform stop, exchanged passengers, then rolled out again. Shutting out the *clickety-clack, clickety-clack,* I listened harder to the voice in my head, remembering the speaker at the women's conference—Olivia Mitchell. Even when she got up to speak, the praise went on for several more minutes. *I don't need your permission to praise!* she'd told us. *You don't know where God has brought me from!*

"Mom? Mom! Isn't this where you wanted to get off?"

The train doors had slid open, revealing the word BRYN MAWR in block letters on the platform sign. "Yes!" I jumped up, grabbing Amanda's hand. "Let's go!"

We walked a few blocks on Bryn Mawr, crossed Broadway, and hit Magnolia just one street over. Florida's apartment building was just half a block south—a six-flat. In the foyer I punched the button that said "Hickman, 3rd Fl. N."

A tinny voice said, "Who is it?"

"Jodi and Amanda."

A loud buzzer echoed in the small foyer, and I jerked open the door.

"Mom," Amanda whispered as we climbed the worn, carpeted stairs, "I feel funny. I don't even know these people."

"I know, honey." I felt funny, too, and I *did* know these people—Florida, anyway. "But thanks for coming with me. Means a lot."

Two doors stood on either side of the landing at the top of the stairs. Before we could read the little paper names inserted in the door nameplates, the door on the right opened. Florida stood there in T-shirt and jeans, cigarette in hand, a big smile wrinkling her nose.

"Jodi! Give me a hug, girl."

I gave her a big hug, feeling like my own smile was wrapping itself around the back of my head. Gosh, I really had missed her.

"This your baby?" Florida stepped back and gave Amanda a head-to-toe once-over. I suddenly felt appalled. How stupid of me!—flaunting my daughter, when Florida's daughter was missing. But Florida seemed oblivious to my self-chastisement. "Why didn't you tell me she was such a beauty! Mmm-mm. You better get yourself a shotgun and keep it loaded." She held out her arms, the cigarette ash growing longer by the second. "C'mere, darlin'. Let Aunt Florida give you a hug."

This seemed to please Amanda tremendously, and she returned Florida's hug with a grin. Florida opened the door wider. "C'mon in. Don't mean to leave you out in the hall. Chris! Cedric!" she yelled somewhere over her shoulder. "Turn that thang down and come meet some friends of mine."

The living room to our left was dim, lit only by a video game bouncing on a TV screen. Two young boys reluctantly put down their controllers and came to the doorway to shake our hands. Chris, Florida told us, was thirteen; Cedric was eleven. Even though Amanda was only one year older, I noticed she towered over Chris by a good three inches. Both boys had Florida's warm hazelnut skin; embarrassed grins escaped as she bragged on how well they were doing in middle school.

"What game are ya playin'?" Amanda asked, moving into the living room. "I've never seen it before. Can you teach me how?"

"I guess," Chris shrugged.

"Sure!" beamed Cedric. "It's really fun."

161

I stared at Amanda's ponytail as the three kids settled down on the floor in front of the TV. Would wonders never cease? Two minutes ago Amanda didn't even want to be walking up the stairs.

"Come on back to the kitchen," Florida said, leading the way down a long narrow hall. "I've got coffee on."

I sneaked a peek into the two bedrooms to my left as we headed toward the kitchen—a double bed, unmade, in one; a double mattress on the floor in the other. The second room was so small the mattress practically touched both walls.

A man with tired eyes in an otherwise pleasant face sat at a round table in a room just off the kitchen that seemed to serve as all-purpose room. A computer monitor and keyboard sat atop a small desk in one corner, surrounded by schoolbooks and stacks of mail; a sewing machine sat on a recycled end table. The chairs around the table didn't match. The man must be—

"Carl, this is Jodi Baxter, one of the women I met at the conference last week."

Florida's husband reached out a hand and murmured a greeting, but he seemed puzzled as I shook his hand. "Not the same one who was here last night?"

Florida snickered and headed for the coffeepot. "You got eyes, Carl! Stu was taller, had long blonde hair."

I was startled. Stu was *here* last night? But Carl seemed embarrassed. "Sorry. Just took me a minute. You know, you both . . . you both . . ."

"White," Florida finished, returning from the small kitchen

with a big grin and handing me a cup of black coffee. "These white people all look alike, don't they?"

I couldn't help but laugh. "I'm really glad to meet you, Carl— your handsome boys, too," I said, trying to smooth the awkwardness. But what was there to say next? I couldn't ask about his job; Florida had said he was unemployed. I turned to Florida. "Stu was here last night?"

"Yeah." Florida sat down at the table and motioned me into a seat. Carl seemed to take the cue and excused himself. "She wanted to talk about Carla, get whatever information she could about the DCFS case. I . . . gave her the folder we had with letters, forms. She said she'd be sure to return it." Florida looked at me. "What? You think maybe that wasn't a good idea?"

She must have seen the strained look on my face. I certainly felt my mouth tighten, my forehead frown. But what *was* I thinking? That Stu had gotten here first. I had wanted to visit Florida in person, show her I really cared about her and her family . . . and Stu had beaten me to the draw.

I shook my head, trying to shake my petty thoughts loose. Florida seemed to be waiting for my answer. I made a stab at one. "Uh . . . I don't know. Maybe. Do you have copies of all those papers?"

"No. But Stu said she'd photocopy them and return my originals." Florida stubbed out her cigarette in an ashtray and muttered, "One of these days God and me gonna have a talk about *this* habit . . ." Her thoughts seemed to drift, then she sighed. "Guess I shoulda made copies first, but she seemed eager to get the process started. Though for the life of me, I don't know what she can do. She doesn't even work at DCFS. Not now, anyway."

I pushed past my own conflicted feelings to reassure her. "I'm sure Stu just wants to help if she can. But it would be good to get those originals back as soon as possible." I looked around the room. There was one framed poster on the wall—the poem "Footprints" done in fancy calligraphy. Christian pop art. But no framed photographs. "Do you have a picture of Carla? I'd love to see it."

"Those were hard times, Jodi. Didn't take many pictures." But Florida got up and rummaged in one of the desk drawers, then handed me a snapshot of a little girl about two years old, holding a ball. The quality was poor, but the grin on the little girl's face was bright, the eyes laughing—just like Florida's.

"She's adorable," I breathed.

Florida's shoulders slumped. "That's the last picture I have of her—two years old. She'd be eight now. I try, I really try, to imagine what she looks like, but I can't. And sometimes I'm afraid . . . afraid I won't find her again, or if we do, afraid she won't know me anymore, won't want to come back." Tears slid down her cheeks.

Tears were filling my own eyes. I clasped Florida's hands in both my own. "No, no. We're not goin' there." *Good grief,* I thought. *I sound like Avis.* "Look what God has done for you already! You're 'five years saved and five years sober'—isn't that what you said?"

"Yeah." Her smile was tentative, like a small break in the rain clouds. "Five years this June. After they took the kids from me."

"You've come so far, Florida! God has been putting your family back together again—look at your two beautiful boys! And your husband, too." I lowered my voice to a conspiratorial whisper. "Good-lookin' guy, you know, even if he doesn't have a job. Yet."

"Yep. You're right. God's been good . . . all the time. Hasn't brought me this far to leave me." The old fire rekindled in her eyes. "And I can't be around negative people who think otherwise."

"Ah. Ruth's comment." It couldn't be avoided. It had to get out on the table.

"You got that right!" she shot back. "What does she know about me, or . . . or Carla . . . or our situation, or . . . anything!"

AMANDA AND I STOPPED AT A LITTLE CAFÉ on Broadway for Chicago hot dogs and milkshakes before catching the Red Line back to Rogers Park. "That was fun, Mom," Amanda said, trying to keep the trimmings from falling off the bun as she took a big bite of her hot dog. "Chris and Cedric are nice. Thanks for bringing me along." These last words were muffled by the wad of food in her mouth.

I nodded. Aside from talking with her mouth full, I was proud of her. Amanda had really risen to the occasion. I wasn't so proud of myself. The visit to Florida had clearly shown me two things:

We had to patch up the rift caused by Ruth's comment before Yada Yada ripped apart at the seams.

And I really was jealous of Stu.

18

*M*y load of laundry was sitting on top of the dryer, sopping wet. Rats! I'd forgotten to turn the washing machine back on after Denny's shower. It looked like our upstairs neighbors—a working couple who never seemed to be home—had moved my unfinished load so they could do some laundry while we weren't home. With only two households using the washer and dryer, it usually wasn't a problem. But now I couldn't remember whether my load had been in the wash or rinse cycle.

I gave up and ran it through all over again.

When I came into the kitchen from the basement, I could hear Amanda and Edesa exchanging Spanish phrases in the dining room. *"Como te llamas?"* . . . *"Me llamo Amanda."* . . . *"Cuánta gente en su familia?"* . . . *"Hay cuatro personas en mi familia."* Caught that one. Something about "my family."

Edesa had arrived right at four o'clock. Amanda seemed to

take to her right away, probably because she was young and pretty and shook Amanda's hand with a delighted smile—unlike Mr. Ortez, Amanda's teacher, fiftyish, who seemed to have a perpetual frown engraved between his flabby jowls. Now that I thought about it, that frown would not make me want to ask for extra help, either. But Edesa hadn't wasted any time getting down to business. She'd asked for Amanda's last few quizzes to get an idea of what her weak areas were and they'd set right to work.

Denny and Josh came home from the men's workday at Uptown Community right in the middle of the Spanish lesson, and of course had to tromp into the kitchen for something to eat. I followed them, trying to get them to muffle the sounds of two hungry males pulling out chips and salsa and popping cans of Coke. "What's for supper, Mom?" Josh said in a failed attempt to keep it to a whisper.

"Your mom and I are going *out,*" Denny said. "Supper is whatever you and Amanda can find to eat."

Amanda's voice floated in from the dining room. "Can Edesa stay for supper?"

"No, no. That's all right. Thank you anyway," Edesa protested.

I looked at Denny. *Now* what?

As it turned out, Denny admitted later it was a delightful time getting to know Edesa over a quick supper of quesadillas—tortillas topped with melted cheese and piled high with shredded lettuce, chopped tomatoes, chopped green onions, and salsa—with a side of packaged red beans and rice. It was one of our "easy meals"—ready in thirty minutes—and I didn't think much about

168

it until Edesa held up one of the store-bought flour tortillas and said with a teasing grin, "My mama makes these from scratch . . ." *Pat-pat-pat-pat*—she flipped the tortilla from side to side between her palms. ". . . and bakes them in a brick oven. Mmmm. Now *that's* a tortilla."

I was horrified. Edesa must've thought we were trying to give her an "authentic" Honduran meal or something. But before I could get out a protest, she pointed at my face—I'm sure my mouth and eyes were round as Cheerios—and burst out laughing. Amanda, Josh, and Denny joined right in, though why they felt the joke was on *me,* I don't know.

But that sparked a lot of questions from Josh and Amanda about the town in Honduras where Edesa grew up. Most of the population, she said, was *mestizo*—mixed Amerindian and European—with blacks, whites, and indigenous Indians making up about 10 percent. Her people were descended from African slaves who rebelled in the Caribbean and were exiled to Honduras by the British. "Unfortunately, racism exists in Honduras, too," she said, her eyes liquid and dark, like looking into a deep well. "We are still considered 'outsiders.' When Hurricane Mitch hit the coast in 1998, no one sent us any aid, especially those of us who belong to Pentecostal churches—a small minority in a largely Catholic country."

By the time we finished talking, it was getting dark, and Denny was concerned about Edesa riding the el alone. So, for our "date" we gave her a ride home to the Near West Side—not too far from where Delores lived, she said. The night was clear, and the brightest stars could be seen in the darkening sky as we drove down Lake Shore Drive, in spite of the brilliant lights from Chicago's skyline. The Loop was alive with horse-drawn carriages, partygoers heading for restaurants or the theater, and families silhouetted against the colorful sprays of Buckingham Fountain enjoying the May evening. But when we had spit out of the other side of the Loop like a watermelon seed zipping west on the Eisenhower Expressway and finally turned off on the narrow one-way streets of the Near West Side neighborhood, the darkness seemed to close in around us.

"Sweet girl," Denny said, coming back to the car after walking Edesa into the dim pocket of her apartment building foyer and making sure she got inside okay. "Now what? Too late for a movie—unless you want to go for the late show."

"Uh-uh. Not with church tomorrow," I groaned. But I did have an ace up my sleeve. "Wanna try out the Bagel Bakery? I hear they got awesome Jewish pastries." I waggled my eyebrows knowingly and fished out a scrap of paper where I'd written the address from the yellow pages that afternoon. "On Devon somewhere."

Denny looked at me suspiciously. "Do I detect another Yada Yada conspiracy afoot? Jodi . . ."

"Only if you want to," I amended hastily.

"Hey," he said, turning the key in the ignition. "I'm only along for the ride." But his hangdog look was so exaggerated I punched him on the shoulder. "Okay, okay," he agreed. "Why not? I didn't have anything else to suggest anyway."

IT WAS ALMOST EIGHT-THIRTY by the time we pulled into the parking lot of the tiny strip mall on Devon, and the Bagel Bakery was hopping. Denny held the door for me. "Popular place."

Inside, a warm, homey smell pulled us into the waiting arms of the bakery. Loaves of bakery bread and freshly made bagels and bialies—rye, pumpernickel, onion, egg, wheat, cinnamon—and various sugary pastries filled the glass cases. An overhead menu—fast-food style—offered soup, bagel and bialy sandwiches, cheese blintzes, kugel, potato latkes, and kreplach, whatever that was.

Denny eyed the food as plates were handed to waiting customers, trying to figure out what was which, but my attention was drawn by a young woman with short, spikey hair behind the bakery counter. "Half a pound of ruggeleh?" she was saying to a customer. "Do you want the raisin-filled or raspberry . . . both? You got it." A moment later the customer walked toward the cashier with her white paper bag.

"Yo-Yo?" I ventured.

The young woman behind the counter stared at me for a moment, then broke into a huge smile. "Jodi? Hey, Jodi! Speak of the devil . . . and is that your man?"

I grinned. "Yeah. That's Denny." I pulled "my man" away from the food counter. "Denny, this is Yo-Yo, one of the women in my prayer group at the conference."

"Right. 'Yada Yada,'" he teased, as if giving the secret password. "I'm delighted to meet you, Yo-Yo, and everything looks so good I may stuff myself."

"Go right ahead! Get something to eat. I'll take a break in a few minutes and come join you." She turned to another customer. "What you want tonight, Mr. Berkenstein?"

Armed with a pumpernickel bagel piled with lox and cream cheese for Denny, and a spinach and cheese blintz for me, we looked around for a table. The place was full of men, women, and children—a gray-haired grandfather over there, tickling a dark-haired cutie who tried to protect her "tickle zones" amid peals of laughter . . . a mother scolding, "Eat! Eat! I paid good money for that kugel!" . . . teenagers huddling in a corner . . . and a table of four women, dyed heads all bent together like a cootie convention. I noticed that almost all the males—young and old—were wearing small, black, embroidered caps, anchored to their heads with clips or bobby pins.

"You need a yarmulke," I teased Denny, edging toward a booth that was being cleared by a young man in a white apron.

A few minutes later Yo-Yo came out from behind the counter, wiping her hands on her apron, revealing her signature denim overalls underneath. "Hey, Jodi," she said again, sliding in beside me on the yellow vinyl seat across from Denny. "What brings you here?"

"To see you," Denny offered. "We're supposed to be on a date, but . . ." He tried on his hangdog expression again.

"Don't pay any attention to him. He's fine. And he'll be fat, too, if he hangs out here much longer." I tipped my head toward the general hubbub around us. "This place always this busy?"

Yo-Yo shook her head. "Nah. But Saturday night after Shabbat ends, they flock in like bees around honey. Sunday morning, too."

"Shabbat?"

"You know . . . like Sunday for you, only Saturday. We close at sundown on Friday, open at sundown on Saturday." She shrugged. "Get Friday night and Saturday off, anyway."

"You Jewish, Yo-Yo?" Denny asked between bites of his bagel.

"Me?" She guffawed. "I ain't nothin'. But it's a good place to work. Ruth got me the job, you know. Speaking of Ruth . . ." Yo-Yo craned her neck, scanning the lively tables and the people who kept coming in. "Ruth and Ben usually come in Saturday night. Haven't seen 'em yet, though—oh. But you can meet Jerry." With hardly a break she raised her voice and yelled, "Jerry! *Jerry!* C'mere!"

A young boy about twelve or thirteen untangled himself from the knot of teenagers clustered around the corner table and came over to our booth. He wasn't wearing a yarmulke, though I thought he could've used one of those clips to keep the shock of lank, brown hair out of his eyes.

"Jerry, this is . . ." She looked blank for a moment. "Jodi!" she hissed. "What's your last name?"

"Baxter."

"Mr. and Mrs. Baxter, friends o' mine. And *this*"—she swatted the boy playfully on his rear—"is my kid brother. Say hi, Jerry."

"Hi Jerry." The boy snickered at his own joke, then gave a little wave. "Nice ta meetcha." He grinned and backed away toward the corner table.

"Kids," Yo-Yo snorted. "Ain't got the manners down yet. I'm still working on keeping 'em fed and a roof over their heads. Pete —that's the older one, he's sixteen—he's out with some friends tonight. Scares me to death to let him out of my sight."

The enormity of Yo-Yo's situation—working a full-time job, trying to raise two teenage brothers—left me speechless for several moments. Denny, too. I could tell he was watching the boy as he melded back into the group of young people.

"Yo-Yo," I said, "have you gotten any of the e-mails from Yada Yada this week? I know you don't have e-mail yourself, but Ruth said—"

"Yeah, yeah. Ruth has printed out stuff and brought it to me every couple of days." She lifted an eyebrow. "Hope it works . . . keeping that prayer thingy goin', I mean. People got some stuff, don't they?"

That was the truth. I desperately wanted to ask if Ruth had talked to her about that whole foster-care business, but Yo-Yo jumped in again. "Hey. Maybe Yada Yada needs to get together, rather than just computer talk, ya know? Got plenty of reasons. Why don'tcha throw Florida a party—a five-year sobriety party? Man, if *I'd* been on them drugs and stayed clean for five years? *I'd* want to party—not party party, but you know, with folks like you and the rest of them women I met at the conference. 'Cause that's major stuff—Hey! There's Ruth and Ben. Hey, Ruth! Ben!" she yelled across the crowd. "Look who's here!"

19

I saw Ruth Garfield's eyebrows lift as they came in the door, and she headed our way, her husband trailing behind. Yo-Yo hopped off the vinyl seat. "Look who's here—Jodi and . . ."

"Denny. Denny Baxter." Denny slid out of his seat, stood, and shook hands with both Ruth and Ben. Ben looked about sixty, with wavy silver hair and crinkly friendly eyes. "I'm really happy to meet you, Ruth." Denny clasped her hand in both of his. "This Yada Yada group seems to have taken over our house ever since Jodi got back from that conference." He motioned to the padded bench he'd just vacated and slid in beside me. "Sit down, please!"

Yo-Yo grinned at the Garfields. "The usual? I'll get it. You guys talk. I gotta get back to work anyway."

"Got any beer, Yo-Yo?" Ben gestured at Denny. "Want a beer, Denny?"

"Sure. Thanks."

"Make that two, Yo-Yo!"

I felt my face go hot. Denny was going to drink a *beer,* right here in public, in front of my new friends? One of which was a "Messianic Jew," or whatever a Christian Jewish person was called, and Yo-Yo wasn't a Christian at all! *What's wrong with this picture, Denny?* I wanted to yell.

I felt like the "picture" had flash-frozen, but it was probably only for a millisecond, because Ruth reached across the table and grabbed my hand. "Oh, Jodi, I *am* so glad to see you. You don't know . . ."

"Uh . . . me, too, Ruth. I know it's only been a week, but it seems like a year!"

"I know." She tossed a look at the two men, who were already jabbering away. "Looks like Ben and Denny hit it off."

I shifted nervously. What did she mean by that? Drinking buddies already?

"Tell me, how is everybody?" Ruth asked eagerly. "I mean, in Yada Yada. Have you seen anybody else since last weekend?"

My knotted muscles relaxed slightly. I'd been worried that Ruth had been blown out of the water by Florida's strong reaction to her "suggestion" about kids in foster care. But she seemed to genuinely want to know about the others.

"As a matter of fact, today especially! I saw Florida this morning"—I purposely dropped this in, but moved right on—"and Edesa, bless her heart, offered to tutor my daughter, Amanda, in Spanish, so she was at our house today. And let's see . . . oh, yes, Avis and I went to see José Enriques last Monday night, so we both got to see Delores—"

"Yes! I did too! On Wednesday. That poor boy—broke my heart, it did. But Delores . . . that's a strong woman! If my child had gotten shot . . ."

I leaned forward slightly. Denny and Ben were talking about the latest Cubs and White Sox scores. "Do you have children, Ruth?"

Ruth looked down at the Formica tabletop. But only for a second. She came up smiling. "No, no, never did." Lowering her voice to a stage whisper, she jerked her head slightly in Ben's direction. *"He's* number three. You'd think one of those times . . ." She brushed a lock of hair off her forehead, as though brushing off the subject. "Eat, you two! Don't wait on us. Ours is coming."

As though playing the prophet, Yo-Yo appeared with a large bialy—sliced and filled with something that looked like sautéed vegetables, pizza sauce, and melted mozzarella cheese—that she set down in front of Ben, and a bowl of matzo ball soup and an onion bagel that she set down in front of Ruth. "And these are for you," she said, whipping out two bottles of cold beer from the pockets of her tunic and setting them down in front of Ben and Denny. Last out of her pocket was a bottle opener. "Enjoy, folks. Gotta get back to work."

My mad came back. I couldn't believe it. Denny really was going to drink that beer, right here and now.

"How did you guys meet Yo-Yo and her brothers?" Denny asked, polishing off the last bite of his lox-and-cream-cheese bagel and washing it down with a swig from the bottle.

I wanted to snatch it out of his hand . . . but Ben said, "Ho ho, now that's a story." That got my attention; I'd been wondering the same thing all week.

"Story, schmory. Not such a big deal," Ruth protested, but I could tell she was warming up. "I work as a secretary, right? I type, I take dictation, I answer the phone, I smile, I make the coffee, I cheer everybody up. Always making the boss guys look good—but for what? So they can make money. *Pffffft."* Ruth thumbed her nose and rolled her eyes. I didn't dare look at Denny for fear we'd both burst out laughing. "So I tell God, I says, 'God? If I'm gonna smile myself to death, I want a better return on my efforts.' I'm thinking money, see? But I forgot to factor in God's sense of humor. God's got a cosmic sense of humor, you know. Remember Queen Esther? And Haman? Ho, ho, I nearly fall down laughing every time we celebrate Purim. To think—"

"Oh, no," Ben groaned. "Noodle, don't get started on Esther. Back to Yo-Yo."

Noodle? He called her Noodle! Oh, that's a stitch!

"What's the hurry? The place on fire?" Ruth gave an exaggerated sigh. "Okay, okay. You want a *short* story, you get a short story. A woman in my office—nice black lady—visits women down at the county jail. So I'm thinking, *That's nice.* Then I think, *If I have to make nice, I'd rather make nice on someone who can use it more than the fat cats I work for.* So I go with this lady to the jail one night. Turns out she does a Bible study—you know, a Christian thing—with whoever wants to come. But it didn't matter who—Christian, Muslim, Jew, whatever. These gals wanted to talk; I like to talk—"

"Got that right," muttered Ben, giving Denny the eye.

Ruth swatted him with her paper napkin. "You *said* tell the story!"

"Nah. I said, 'Now *that's* a story.'"

"Oh, please don't stop now," I interrupted. "I really do want to hear how you met Yo-Yo."

"See?" Ruth said, flicking her fingers at Ben like an annoying fly. "All right, where was I? . . ."

Ben hoisted his beer bottle with an indulgent smile of resignation.

IT WAS ALMOST MIDNIGHT by the time we got home. "Ben and Ruth . . . they're something else." Denny was grinning when we got back in the car.

I laughed. That was the truth. All the way home I thought about Ruth's story, how Yo-Yo had drifted into the Bible study at the county jail, always sitting in the back. When the "nice black lady" found out Ruth was Jewish, she asked her to tell some Old Testament stories to the women. That knocked my socks off! . . . Finding a common denominator even though Ruth wasn't a Christian. Apparently Ruth was a great storyteller. Yo-Yo kept asking, *"Why did God do this?" "How come God did that?"* Ruth said she didn't have a clue, but the Bible study lady started to explain how the Old Testament fit together with the New Testament.

"It got me thinking—" Ruth had said.

"Thinking, not talking, eh?" Ben winked at me.

Ruth had swatted him with the napkin again. *"So one day I went to this Jews for Jesus–type church—"*

"Yeah. Can you beat that? An oxymoron, if you ask me."

Ruth ignored him. *"So now on Saturday I go to synagogue with Ben—when he goes, that is—and on Sunday I go to church. With other Messianic Jews."*

"What's a guy to do?" Ben had shrugged. *"She's got a foot in both pots."*

In spite of all the banter, I suspected he adored her. "For that matter," I told Denny on the way home, "Ben seems more attached to Saturday night at the Bagel Bakery than Saturday morning at the synagogue. He wasn't wearing a yarmulke, for one thing."

Denny grunted. "Huh. You could be right."

Ruth had liked Yo-Yo from the start. *"A plain talker—when she talked,"* she had said with an eye on Yo-Yo, busy behind the bakery counter. Then one week Yo-Yo wasn't there. Or the next. Ruth found out she'd been given two years at Lincoln Correctional Center downstate. Eighteen months with good behavior. Ruth wrote a couple letters to Yo-Yo and got one back.

"That did it," Ben had butted in. *"She dragged me down to Lincoln to visit the girl. Not my idea of how to spend my day off—at a women's prison."* But a hint of a smile had softened his words.

That's when they discovered that Yo-Yo had two younger step-brothers she worried about plenty. Their mother had a "drug problem," and the boys were dropping through the cracks. *"Whatever she did to get arrested, I think she did it for those boys,"* Ruth had said.

"That's really something," I murmured as Denny turned the minivan into our alley and clicked the garage opener. "How Ruth and Ben hunted up Jerry and Pete and took 'em places and did things with them while Yo-Yo was in prison." Ben had said they'd only met the mother once, and she'd been so strung out when they came to the door that she hadn't asked any questions about who they were or where they were taking the boys. Just, *"Fine, go."*

All the lights were on, and both of our kids were still up when we got home—cat's away, the mice will play—but we chased them into their bedrooms and settled down on the living room couch with some chamomile tea, my stocking feet in Denny's lap. Willie Wonka flopped on the floor with a huge sigh.

"Whatsa matter, Willie?" Denny said, scratching the dog's silky ears. "Mad at us?" He put on a growly voice. "'Bout time you two got home. Don'tcha know I can't go to sleep till everybody's in?'"

I was only half-listening, still thinking about our evening at the Bagel Bakery. I had hoped to talk about Ruth's e-mail about "what's best for the child." In Ruth's shoes, I would probably be scared off from saying anything more to Yada Yada after Florida's hot reaction and Adele's sarcastic comment about "friendly fire." At one point, I thought I'd found the perfect opening to bring it up . . .

"It was Ruth's idea, really," Ben had acknowledged, *"to take those boys under our wing . . . kinda like foster parents, even though they didn't live with us. And she helped Yo-Yo get custody when she got out. She's got a knack for that."*

"Oh!" I'd said, little lights going on in my head. *"Have you worked with the foster care system, Ruth?"*

"Now that's another story," Ben had said. *"I'll need another beer if we go there. You, Denny?"*

I mentally glared at Denny, but to my relief he shook his head. Ruth, however, dodged the ball. *"Talk, talk, talk—that's all I've been doing. What am I, a monopoly? Jodi, how did you meet Denny? A good catch he is, I'd say! He could give my Ben a few pointers."*

And so we'd chatted and got acquainted right up till Yo-Yo kicked us out at closing time. My "good catch" had been thoroughly charmed by Ben and Ruth, and Yo-Yo, too—which was fine, but I was left still wondering if Yada Yada was going to hang together or not. At least Ruth had seemed eager to hear about the other women in the prayer group, even though we'd verbally danced around the "elephant" in the middle of the room as though it wasn't there. Maybe she was okay . . .

"Denny," I mused, nursing the last of the tea in my mug, "what do you think about throwing a five-year sobriety party for Florida, like Yo-Yo suggested? . . . Denny?"

Romeo was snoring softly at the other end of the couch. Well, let him. He was still going to get it for drinking that beer tonight.

20

I didn't feel like praising the Lord when I woke up. I overslept, the laundry was only half-done, I'd totally forgotten to plan something for the Mother's Day potluck—who came up with that dumb idea, anyway?—Denny seemed oblivious that I was mad about the beer, and Stu was coming to Uptown Community that morning.

Hallelujah.

For the next hour and a half we did the "Baxter Hurry Scurry," and at two minutes to ten we hustled up the stairs of the double storefront Uptown occupied to the large upstairs room that served as the sanctuary. Well, at least Josh and Amanda and I did. Denny was still driving around trying to find a parking space. I snuck into the kitchen with my Easy Chicken-and-Rice Casserole and hoped I'd remember to stick it in the oven at eleven o'clock.

I sniffed. Fresh paint. The work crew yesterday must have painted something.

The Reilly twins were passing out carnations to everybody as they came in—red if your mother was still alive, white if she had "passed on." In one corner of the large room the music group—two guitars and a keyboard—was warming up. Josh settled in at the soundboard—his new passion. Avis was talking with Pastor Clark at the front; she must be leading worship this morning.

And Stu had already arrived. She was wearing a smart lavender suit—overdressed for this crowd—her ash blonde hair coiled into a professional bun at the nape of her neck. She waved at us with the red carnation she was holding and pointed at the empty folding chairs next to her.

"Oh, Lord," I muttered, "she saved seats for us."

Stu was sitting in the third row near the front beside a young couple in jeans and T-shirts. Two street people dressed straight from the Salvation Army sat just behind her, a situation that was sometimes challenging to the nose. We often had more street people on potluck Sundays, I'd noticed. Otherwise our congregation was pretty much a casual mix of "wuppies"—white urban professionals—both married and single, who wanted something a bit different than traditional church, with a hopeful sprinkling of color here and there and a whole mess of kids. Kids . . . somewhere along the way I'd lost mine but spied Amanda sitting with some of the other young teens.

Get a grip, Jodi. I smiled back at Stu and headed—slowly—for the third row. *Just because Stu is a go-getter doesn't make her your rival or anything. Go on; she looks glad to see you.*

"Hey, Stu." I plopped down into a chair beside her. "You made it." The smell factor from the row behind us didn't seem too bad today.

"Yes! Found it with no problem." She grinned at me. "Guess you have to live a long way away to arrive early."

I opened my mouth and shut it again. Great. She just couldn't help commenting about me squeaking in at the last minute, could she?

Stu waggled her carnation. "This is nice. Everybody gets to celebrate Mother's Day."

Avis's voice filled the room from the microphone. "Praise the Lord, church! If you have your Bibles, please turn with me to Isaiah Fifty-Two." Hiding the flush that had crept into my face, I dug into my tote bag and got out my Bible. Avis's voice rang free and joyous, so different from her contained demeanor at school, like she'd just kicked off shoes that pinched after a long day at the office. "How beautiful on the mountains are the feet of those who bring good news, who proclaim peace, who bring good tidings, who proclaim salvation, who say to Zion, 'Your God reigns!'" she read. "Listen! Your watchmen lift up their voices; together they shout for joy. . . ."

Denny's familiar bulk sat down in the chair beside me. Parking place at last. Out of the corner of my eye I saw Stu turn slightly our way, waiting. "Oh," I whispered, trying not to interrupt Avis's Scripture reading. "Denny, this is Stu . . . Stu, my husband, Denny."

Denny reached a hand across my lap and shook Stu's warmly. "Yada Yada, right?" he whispered.

185

"Right," she murmured, giving him a bright smile. Too bright, if you asked me.

". . . The ends of the earth will see the salvation of our God," Avis finished, closing her Bible. "Let's stand and worship God this morning as men and women who have received good news! *Salvation* is ours because of Jesus Christ. *Peace* is ours because of Jesus. Like the watchmen on the walls, we can shout and sing a joyful song!"

The guitarists strummed an introduction as the words to a song based on Isaiah 52 appeared on the portable screen behind them. I found it hard to concentrate with Stu standing beside me but dutifully sang the words: " . . . How lovely on the mountains are the feet of him . . . who brings good news . . . good news . . ." We came to the end of the song, and immediately the music group launched into another. Uptown prided itself on providing "contemporary worship," but the quick way we hustled from song to song was certainly different from the worship at the women's conference last week, when one song seemed to last anywhere from ten to fifteen minutes. We had lingered over the words, singing them again and again till they worked themselves deep into the soul.

I watched Avis. As worship leader, she was mostly in charge of setting a theme, reading Scripture, maintaining the flow. As the music group galloped from song to song, she gradually seemed to tune them out, lost in her own worship of the Savior. Her eyes were closed—were those tears?—her hands raised, and I could see her lips moving—not to the song, but just saying, "Glory! Praise You, Jesus! I love You, Lord!"

How did she do that? It wasn't like anything profound had

happened today to kindle such deep worship. Last week, with five hundred other women worshiping over the top, sure, I could let go, too. Well, at least what passed for "letting go" for Jodi Baxter. But here at Uptown? Would I dare be the only one to shout out, "Thank You, Jesus!"

Probably not.

But with Avis . . . it didn't seem to matter. She worshiped the same here at Uptown as she did at the Chicago Women's Conference, regardless. How did she do that?

Because she is thankful. She loves the Lord with all her heart.

The words were so clear, it was like someone spoke inside my head. I squeezed my eyes shut. *Lord, I know I said I want to learn more about worship. But it's so hard. I get distracted . . . by people around me . . . by things I have to do . . . by my runaway thoughts.*

During the next song, I kept my eyes closed, shutting out everything around me. When the familiar words ran out, I just did what Avis did, filling in with "Glory!" and "Thank You, Jesus!" and "I love You, Lord!" More like a murmur than a shout, but my heart began to fill. God had been pretty good to me. I needed to be more thankful—and tell Him so.

THE SERVICE WAS OVER, and I was introducing Stu to the people around us when I saw several folks head for the kitchen. I stopped in midsentence: the potluck! And my casserole was still sitting on top of the stove, stone cold.

"Jodi? Are you okay?" Stu looked at me quizzically.

"No . . . yes! Yes, I'm fine. Denny?" I plucked on my husband's sleeve. "Could you introduce Stu to some folks? I've . . . I'll be back in a minute."

I didn't head for the kitchen. I headed for the women's bathroom, a two-stall affair with plastic flowers in a vase on the counter between the two sinks in an attempt to dress up the drab little room. Except it wasn't drab today. The small room had a fresh coat of sunny yellow paint. Well, good for the work crew.

The bathroom was usually pretty busy right after the morning service, and today was no exception. When a stall became free, I locked the door and sank down on the toilet seat. I wasn't sure whether to laugh or cry. Why did I forget today of all days? With Miss-Do-Everything-Right visiting. Why did I always end up feeling a day late and a dollar short when Stu was around?

On the other hand, Jodi, you forgot because your focus was on worshiping today. For a change.

I blinked back the tears that had started to pool. Okaaay. The bad news was that I'd blown it as far as the potluck went. How bad was that? There would probably still be plenty of food—or at least "enough." The good news was that I'd given God more of my attention than I usually did on a Sunday morning. I could live with that, couldn't I?

When I came back into the large room, Stu was talking to Pastor Clark, who had given a pretty good sermon that morning (I'd even taken notes). While she was busy, I slipped into the kitchen where half a dozen helpful people were putting out all the dishes on the counter that opened into the big room. Even my uncooked casserole sat among the others, still in its aluminum foil cover. Hoo boy, folks would get a surprise biting into that raw rice. With an apologetic smile, I whisked it away and stuck it in the refrigerator.

Denny and I sat with Avis and Stu at one of the many long tables that had been set up around the big room. To quell my guilty conscience, I didn't fill my plate very full, though I did make a point to take some of Stu's pasta salad. Okay, so I was wrong about the flaming cherries jubilee. "Where's your chicken-and-rice?" Denny asked, his mouth full of Avis's super cornbread. "I wanted some but didn't see it."

"Um, sorry. It met with a little accident. The pasta salad is good, Stu." Actually it was only so-so, but who was I to find fault? At least it was edible.

Denny stopped midbite and looked at me. "Accident? Ha. You forgot to put it in the oven, didn't you!" He thought that was very funny. "Oh, you should have seen us this morning, throwing that thing together. And then she forgets to put it in the oven! Ha ha ha ha ha!"

Thanks, Denny. Thanks a lot.

Stu grinned. "Well, at least we know what you're going to get for supper, Denny."

I decided to take it on the chin. "Yep. And Monday night, and Tuesday night . . ."

Everybody laughed.

"I enjoyed the service today." Stu pushed back her empty paper plate. "The teen mission trip sounds great. And the carnations were a nice touch—a nice way to include everybody on Mother's Day. I'd like to come back."

Oh, great, I thought. "Sure," I said.

"Watch out," Denny teased. "That commute from the 'burbs is why we ended up moving to Rogers Park."

"Actually," Stu continued, "I've been thinking about visiting all the different churches Yada Yada folks attend. If we really want to keep this prayer group going, I'd like to see each woman in her own context."

Hmm. Kinda liked that idea. Wished I'd thought of it.

"Even better—what if *all* the women in Yada Yada visited each other's churches? But we all came on the same Sunday?—say the last Sunday of the month till we've visited everybody. Shouldn't be too hard to organize through the e-loop . . ."

I figured *"I'll be glad to set it up"* would be her next words.

"I'll be glad to set it up," Stu finished.

Avis frowned thoughtfully. "But that could be five or six churches—a lot of Sundays to miss being at one's own church."

"Well, spread it out—maybe every two months."

Okay. So what if it was Stu's idea. I actually liked it, though spreading out those church visits over a year might be most realistic. But as long as we were talking about getting Yada Yada together, I decided this was a good time to float the idea about a five-year sobriety party for Florida.

"It's actually Yo-Yo's idea," I said modestly. "Last night Denny and I went to the Bagel Bakery where she works, got to see Ruth

Garfield and meet her husband, Ben, too." *Sorry, God, couldn't help dropping that in.* "It would primarily be a celebration for Florida, but we could also make time to share and pray for each other—like we did at the conference."

I would have checked with Denny, but he had disappeared across the room to talk to some of the street people. "We could host it at my house," I added.

Avis nodded thoughtfully. "Sounds good."

Stu nodded. "What about Memorial Day weekend? That'd give us two weeks to plan it."

"Can't be a Saturday," I said. "Yo-Yo works Saturday night—big night at the Bagel Bakery. And it was her idea."

"If we did it Sunday afternoon, we could invite the sisters to come to Uptown in the morning—the first 'church visit'—and then go over to your place." Avis seemed to be warming up to the idea.

"Do you want me to send out invitations, Jodi?"

"But speaking of Ruth . . ." said Avis, suddenly backing up.

Ah. The elephant in the middle of the room.

"Yes!" Stu immediately turned from invitations to indignant. "Why in the world did she send that e-mail? Implying that Florida wanting her daughter back might not be 'in the best interest of the child'! Sheesh."

"It was more generic than that," I defended. "Sometimes returning foster kids to the natural parent *isn't* in the best interest of a child."

"Yes, but why bring it up in Florida's case?" Stu shook her head. "What does she know?"

191

Good point. I'd wondered, too. "I wanted to ask Ruth about it when I saw her last night. But our husbands were with us and, you know . . ."

Avis's lips twitched in a small smile. "Right. Husbands. Women talk better when they're not around."

My ears pricked up. She said *husbands*. Was she talking about her own? Was she still married? Divorced? Avis was an extremely attractive woman, even in her mid-fifties—but as far as I knew she'd never mentioned a husband before. Why—

But the conversation had turned back to Ruth.

"Can't blame Florida for reacting the way she did," Stu was saying. "With friends like that, who needs enemies?"

Avis leveled a gaze at Stu that would stop most students at Bethune Elementary in their tracks. "I certainly hope you didn't say that to Florida. At worst, the comment was thoughtless. At best, Ruth may . . ." She didn't finish her sentence.

"May what?" I prompted.

Avis shook her head. "Never mind. We're all speculating anyway. We don't know. But . . . after the reactions she got, do you think Ruth will come to Florida's sobriety party?"

Good question. But at least we were finally talking about the elephant.

21

We had the *cooked* chicken-and-rice for supper, at which Denny and the kids had surprised me with a raspberry pie from Baker's Square and three flats of alyssum, petunias, and impatiens to plant in the backyard as my Mother's Day gift. I felt overwhelmed by the flowers, afraid they'd die in their little plastic pots before I had time to get them in the ground.

"So whaddya think?" I asked Denny, flopping down on the couch after finagling a promise from Josh and Amanda that they'd help me dig up the flowerbeds. "Should we make this party for Florida a surprise or tell her about it?"

"Huh?" Denny half-turned toward me, his eyes still glued to a documentary on public television about avalanches.

"Never mind." I got up.

"No, no, that's okay." He hit the mute on the remote. "What's up?"

I reminded Denny what Yo-Yo had said last night about a

five-year sobriety party for Florida and said both Avis and Stu liked the idea. "Should we make it a surprise or tell her about it?"

"Tell her. You want to make sure she'll come." He hit the sound back on.

"Uh, can we have it here?"

"What? Sure." On screen, the film crew was skiing for their lives, trying to outrace the avalanche. If I wanted a fur coat or a trip to Ireland, now would be the time to ask.

I called Florida. "Really?" she said. "Yo-Yo said that? That girl's all right."

She said Sunday on Memorial Day weekend would work for her. "Can I bring my kids? They're a huge part of what I got to celebrate."

Kids? I hadn't counted on *kids* when I offered to have it at my house. What would we do with kids? "Uh, sure. We'll think of something to keep them entertained." Something like Josh and Amanda. My name was going to be mud.

"You gonna invite the whole Yada Yada group?"

"Uh, sure. That's the idea. To celebrate with you."

A silence thick as wall putty seemed to clog up the line. Then, "Well okay. Can't nobody rob me of my joy, right?"

"Right," I said softly.

Everybody would be invited, but would "everybody" come?

I stood by the kitchen phone after we hung up. This whole thing didn't make sense. I liked Florida—really liked her. And I liked Ruth, too. What a stitch she was! I was sure they could be friends, if anybody could be in Yada Yada. What had happened?

"Hey, Josh," I said, stopping by the desk in the dining room, where he was pecking away at his history paper. "Let me know when you take a break. I gotta send out an invitation tonight."

BY THE TIME MEMORIAL DAY WEEKEND LOOMED on the calendar, I had gotten responses back from almost everybody saying, Great, let's do it, don't know about church but I'll see, what can we bring? Yo-Yo didn't have e-mail so I called her. Turned out she worked on Sunday, too, but was going to try to get off. Chanda didn't have e-mail, either, so I'd tried her number and left a message, but she hadn't called back. So that was everybody so far . . .

Everybody except Adele and Ruth.

Ruth . . . guess I wasn't surprised. She might need a little coaxing. Needed to call her, too. But what was Adele's excuse? It had been almost two weeks! How long did a simple yes or no take to send by e-mail?

Prayer requests from Yada Yada had been piling up, too. The most urgent was from Delores. On top of José's medical bills and slow recovery, her husband, Ricardo, had lost his job! "Without Ricardo's paycheck, I need to go back to work," she wrote. "Probably a good thing. Having both José and Ricardo underfoot all day is driving me *loco!*"

Hoshi had gotten a letter from her parents about their visit to Chicago this summer, but she still hadn't had the courage to tell them she'd become a Christian. "Pray for me I won't be afraid."

Nony wrote a long epistle detailing the growing famine in

Zimbabwe, Mozambique, Botswana, and other countries surrounding South Africa, and once again asked prayer about returning to Africa to work for the good of her people. "P.S. Mark and I would like to send Marcus and Michael to a Christian summer camp. Any suggestions?"

Hmm, I thought. *I could pass on the camp brochures we get every summer, since Josh and Amanda are going on the mission trip instead.*

And of course there was the ongoing prayer that Florida's little girl would be found. No word on whether Stu's efforts were turning up anything new.

I meant to pray every day for all these things; I really did. But school had been a zoo the last couple of weeks. End-of-year fever made nearly all the kids infected with can't-sit-still-itis until I was about ready to declare an epidemic and stay home. And Parents Day was coming up the week after Memorial Day, meaning that I'd probably spend most of the Monday holiday decorating my classroom. Bummer.

Chicago's lakefront officially opened on Memorial Day, and Chicagoans flocked to the parks and beaches like Ulysses clones drawn by the Sirens' song. Even a crowd-hater like me. For one thing, the mosquitoes and bees had not yet begun to recruit troops and draw up battle plans for Labor Day, pretty much leaving the parks bug-free. For another, people-watching was at its greatest as bikers, joggers, dog-walkers, and baby strollers were practically bumper to bumper, and everybody and his Uncle Jimmy hauled their Weber grills to the lakefront for a family reunion. It was as if Chicago itself shook off the winter doldrums to celebrate the beginning of summer.

Which made going back to school the next day—for three more weeks!—grounds for mutiny in the hearts of students and teachers alike.

But now that Saturday was here, I might as well suck it up and make the most of the three-day weekend. Like groceries. I hadn't done a serious shop since before the women's conference, just darting into the store to pick up milk or bread or hamburger on our way somewhere else. But, as Denny subtly pointed out, the vittles situation was starting to get serious when the only cans on the pantry shelf were dog food.

Besides, I had to shop for Florida's party. Which meant chicken. *Lots* of chicken. I hoped "Baxter grilled" instead of Kentucky Fried would be okay.

After reminding Amanda that Edesa was coming at four o'clock for tutoring and laying down the law to both kids that their rooms had to be clean—not just kicking stuff under the bed—before they could do anything with friends, I set out armed with my list of errands. I'd dropped off the dry cleaning and stood in line at the post office—both near each other on Devon—and was heading back up Clark Street toward the fruit market and new Dominick's grocery store when I saw the red-and-blue sign:

ADELE'S HAIR AND NAILS

I was so startled, I hit the brakes, meriting serious horn honking from the car behind me and getting a single digit salute as the driver swerved around me into the oncoming lane. I circled the block and drove slowly north on Clark once more, on the lookout for a place to stop and gawk. Adele's Hair and Nails—that was it, all right. I'd totally forgotten that Adele had said her shop was on Clark Street, a two-lane artery through Rogers Park boasting so many ethnic businesses that the shop signs looked like someone shook up the alphabet and scattered the letters like so many dice.

A car pulled out of a parking space, and I pulled in. Why not? I was here; Adele was in there, doing her thing. Why not just go in and ask if she could come to Florida's party? We were both Yada Yada. Why not?

Because you're a big chicken, Jodi. Adele hadn't exactly warmed up to me at the women's conference, and at least there I had the relative safety of the whole prayer group. But now . . .

I looked at the shop about two car lengths away. It looked innocent enough. Posters of women—mostly black women of different hues—with perfect skin and various hair styles ranging from waves to weaves stood behind an array of hair products in the window. Twinkle lights outlined the window—left over from Christmas?

Didn't look like a lion's den. But that's what it felt like as I locked the car, fed the meter, took a deep breath, and pulled open the door.

22

A bell tinkled over the door as I walked in, and I was greeted with a strong, not unpleasant smell reminding me of the Tonette home perms my mom used to give my grandmother. And music—a male vocalist singing gospel something. Three beauty-shop chairs were parked in front of the long mirror covering the wall to my left, but only one was occupied. On the right side, behind the counter, I could see a couple of hair dryers—those standard beehive contraptions that looked like hairdos on a *Simpsons* cartoon.

A young woman wearing a smock and tight-fitting latex gloves was sectioning the hair of a woman in the first chair and daubing on a white substance at the dark roots with a small, square paintbrush. She looked up. "Be with you in a minute."

I looked around the waiting area. Don't know what I'd expected, but not a comfy sofa and matching love seat making an L around a large coffee table. Another woman with light honey skin sat on the love seat paging through a copy of *Essence* and carrying on a conversation with the woman getting her hair done. "Her baby is just the sweetest thing," she was saying. "Sings like an angel."

"What? How old is he now?"

"Nine, maybe ten. He's good enough for the Chicago Children's Choir, I swear."

I edited my vision of an actual baby "baby" that could sing like an angel and sat down on the couch, giving the three woman what I hoped was a friendly smile. I picked up a copy of *O*—Oprah's magazine—from among the available reading materials: *Ebony, Jet,* and *Essence,* plus several issues of neighborhood newspapers. And a Bible.

"Whose CD is that she's got on? Kirk Franklin's new one?"

"Sounds like Fred Hammond to me."

I'm not sure which surprised me more: the Bible on the coffee table, the gospel music flooding the salon, or the coffeepot, half-full, plugged in on a little table beside the love seat. A cake server snuggled among the Styrofoam cups, powdered creamer, and packets of sugar revealed some kind of cake or pastry under its glass lid. Everything looked so . . . inviting. Sit down. Stay awhile.

Somehow, "inviting" and "Adele" were concepts that seemed like the north and south ends of a magnet.

"Can I help you?" the beautician asked, moving from the chair to the counter as she toweled white goo off her latex gloves.

I came to the counter, my mind scrambling. Should I just ask for Adele, or . . . maybe I should get something done. Nails! Why not get my nails done for Florida's party tomorrow? I was tempted to grin, remembering all the painted nails around the circle at the women's conference. Mine excluded. How much could it be? Might be fun.

"Um . . . do you take walk-ins for a manicure?"

Lifted eyebrow. "You don't have an appointment?"

"No, uh, you see . . . I was just driving by when I saw Adele's shop—Adele Skuggs, right?" I glanced past the young woman toward the back of the shop. "Is Adele here by any chance?"

The young woman arched both absolutely perfect eyebrows as if to say, *"You* know *Adele?"* but obediently called over her shoulder. "Adele? Lady here wants to see you."

"Give me a minute! I'm doing a comb-out!" That was Adele's voice all right. I smiled at the young woman, who returned to her client, and perused the shelves of beauty products that lined the wall just inside the door. Dudley's Oil-Sheen Spray & Moisturizer . . . Mizan Holding Spritz . . . KeraCare Detangling Shampoo . . . and several other brands of conditioners, moisturizers, and fixers, as well as small plastic packages labeled "Wave Caps."

"Well, look who's here. Jodi Baxter of the Baxter Bears."

I whirled. Adele had appeared behind the counter, big as life. Same short reddish 'fro. Same big gold earrings. Same little space between her front teeth. Same ability to tie up my tongue in a triple knot. The lion in the lion's den was looking at me with an amused smile.

"Hi, Adele. I . . . was just driving by and saw your shop! Decided to drop in and say hi . . . uh, *and* get my nails done, if you take walk-ins." I held out my fingers. "They're in pretty bad shape."

Adele did not look down at my hands.

"Or," I added hastily, "I could make an appointment for another time if you're too busy. Last-minute idea anyway. Just thought I'd get gussied up for Florida's party. Tomorrow, you know." I was starting to stumble over my own words, and I knew it.

Adele's eyebrows lifted a fraction. "Florida's party. Tomorrow."

"Right! I sent out an e-mail to Yada Yada about it, but maybe you didn't see it. A five-year sobriety party for Florida. It was Yo-Yo's—"

I stopped in midsentence. A little old lady with dark freckled skin and graying hair appeared in my line of vision, pushing a walker between hair dryers and beauty chairs and muttering loudly. "Cain't get nothin' ta eat in this rest'runt . . . lousiest service in th' South . . . jest gon' find mahself 'nother place ta eat . . . bunch o' pig-headed—"

"MaDear!" Adele grabbed but missed as the old woman shuffled past in her pink slippers—at a pretty fast clip, in my opinion—making a beeline for the front door. Adele caught her before she got to the handle and turned her around. "You want somethin' to eat, MaDear? Come on. I'll fix something for ya."

I stood transfixed, watching Adele usher the little woman in front of her, keeping a firm grip on "MaDear's" bony shoulders, which were encased in a faded blue housedress. Just as they were about to turn a corner beyond the hair dryers, Adele called out, "Come on back, Jodi. Think I can squeeze you in."

Startled, I glanced questioningly at the woman on the love seat. "Are you . . .?"

"Me? Nah. I'm waitin' on Takesha, here, to do my hair."

The young woman in the white smock—Takesha, presumably—nodded. "Go on. If Adele say she can squeeze you in, she can squeeze you in."

The woman in the chair, her hair standing stiffly at all angles, laughed. "Yeah. She the boss."

I walked toward the back and turned the corner into another leg of the shop. Two comfy-looking black vinyl chairs were poised on white porcelain pedestals that looked like mini-bathtubs. For soaking feet obviously, I told myself. Two more chairs were lined up in front of little white tables with all sorts of small gadgets and bottles of nail polish. Manicures.

Adele had parked her mother in a rocking chair and was tying her in with a padded Velcro belt. "Here you go." She handed her a sandwich that she took out of a small refrigerator.

The old lady patted Adele's hand. "Yo' sweet." She looked up quizzically. "What yo' say yo' name is?"

"Adele, MaDear." Adele blew out a breath, as though easing the level of pent-up frustration. "Since the day I was born."

She seemed to notice me then, standing in the middle of the narrow aisle. "Go on, have a seat. I've got a comb-out to finish. Be with you in five."

I sat down at one of the manicure tables, dizzy with the events of the past two minutes. Adele's mother was more "demented" than my grandmother ever was. Maybe it was Alzheimer's. Out of the corner of my eye I watched the old lady take her sandwich apart, laying each piece separately on her skinny lap: slice of bread, square of rubbery American cheese, slice of balogna, another slice of bread. Then she proceeded to lick the mayonnaise off each one.

"'Bye, Adele! See ya in a couple of weeks. 'Bye, MaDear." The comb-out waved in the general direction of Adele's mother and disappeared toward the front.

"Takesha!" Adele yelled after her. "Cash out Sister Lily, will ya?"

Then she was back. She eyed her mother. "Hmm. Oughta keep her busy for a while. Okay . . . you wanted a manicure?"

"Yes . . . I mean, if you're sure . . . I didn't have an appointment . . . how much do your charge?"

"Relax, Jodi." Adele was washing her hands in the hair-washing sink. "It's all right. I was kinda surprised to see you, I guess." She looked me up and down as she toweled her hands. "Sure you don't want a pedicure, too? Ten for the manicure, twenty for the pedicure . . . but I'll give you both for twenty-five. For coming in. Call it a first-time promotion."

I was tantalized. Why not? I'd cut it off the grocery bill—somewhere.

Sitting with my bare feet in the Jacuzzi footbath, I watched Adele lay out her clippers and scrubbers, oils and lotions. "Pick a color," she ordered, motioning toward the rows of nail polish. Oh, gosh. I didn't think I could go blood red. "That one," I said, pointing at a soft coral color.

"Ah. Living dangerously, eh?" Her shoulders shook in a silent chuckle.

But when Adele, big and black, pulled up a low footstool and took my left foot out of the bath, a sense of . . . of impropriety welled up inside me. I couldn't do this! Adele was practically kneeling at my feet, rubbing some kind of cuticle oil on each toe . . . it felt wrong! Like the old days, before Civil Rights, when white women like me sat up high and mighty on their thrones and black women scrubbed the floors.

"Jodi! Stop jerking your foot. I'm gonna gouge you good with this cuticle cutter if you don't hold still."

"Adele . . ." My voice came out in a squeak. "I feel . . . awkward having you work on my feet. I mean, you own this shop . . . don't you have a girl or somebody who does feet?"

Adele sat back and looked at me. Just looked at me. And for some reason, I started to cry. Big ol' tears just slid right down my face.

Finally she spoke. "Well, ain't you somethin' else. Know who you sound like, Jodi Baxter? Big ol' full-of-himself Peter. 'Oh, Master! You shall never wash my feet!' Just couldn't swallow it. And what did Jesus say?"

I just stared at her.

"He said, 'If I don't wash your feet, Big Boy, you ain't one of mine.' Well, something like that." She chuckled at herself. "Then ol' Peter says, Well if that's the case, give me the whole bath!"

Adele, still sitting on the footstool, put one hand on her ample hip and shook a finger at me. "Well, Jodi Baxter, I ain't gonna give you a whole bath, but feet are my business, and this *ain't* a big deal. And if we gonna do this . . . this Yada Yada thing, better get used to it. You wash feet sometimes; you get your feet washed sometimes. Ain't that the way it s'posed to be? Now hold still."

I PULLED INTO THE GARAGE an hour later than I thought I'd be, the back of the minivan full of groceries. Hitting the grocery store after getting all twenty digits oiled and lotioned and painted like a queen was a bit of a letdown. Here I was, still in my gym shoes covering up my now-gorgeous toes, when I *felt* like dancing barefoot in the grass wearing a gauzy gown, like those women who float through TV commercials for some kind of pain reliever.

But the temperature was creeping upward in the garage; it was going to be a warm Memorial Day weekend. Better get the cold stuff into the fridge right away—especially those packages of chicken for Florida's party tomorrow.

Sorry I'm late, I rehearsed telling Denny in my mind, *and I just spent twenty-five dollars we probably don't have—but it was worth it. Adele Skuggs is coming to Florida's party tomorrow, and she promised to bring Chanda—"minus Chanda's three kids if God has any mercy at all,"* was the way Adele put it.

Trying to be careful of my newly polished nails, I scuttled toward the back door, a gallon of milk in one hand and a bag of chicken in the other. "Sure hope Josh or Denny is around to help me haul in all these groceries," I mumbled. "And Josh and Amanda better have their rooms clean, too."

Willie Wonka was on hand to greet me, poking his nose into

the bag of chicken before I even got inside the door. I swatted his nose. "Anybody home?" I yelled. "I need help with the groceries!"

No answer. But I heard the shower running. Peeking into the dining room, I saw a couple of notes on the table, one in Amanda's pretty cursive, the other in Denny's scrawl.

"Finished my room. Dad said I could go to the mall with Trisha's family. They promised they'd get me back by 4:00."

"Jodi—Gone for a run. Josh playing ball at the park. Love you. D."

Humph. Denny must be back from his run and in the shower. So much for help lugging in groceries. But they got points for at least leaving a note.

I picked up the bag of chicken and opened the refrigerator door . . . and felt my own temperature rise. It had been almost empty when I'd left this morning. Plenty of room to store all that chicken until tomorrow. But now the lower shelf was full—with two six-packs of beer. Minus one bottle.

23

I hauled in the rest of the groceries like a queen bee with her stinger in backward. Now Denny was not only "having a beer with the guys" while watching a game, but stocking up the refrigerator! *(Stomp, stomp, stomp* across the back porch.) What was he stocking up *for?* Florida's party? Over my dead body. *(Slam* the car door.) How did he buy them anyway? *I had the car. (Slam* the back door.) And what's with the missing bottle? Drinking by himself? In the middle of the day? *(Slam* the refrigerator door)—

"Jodi? What in the world . . . ?"

I whirled around. Denny was standing in the kitchen doorway in his jeans, barefoot and shirtless, leaning on one arm against the doorpost. He looked pretty yummy—but I was *not* going to be distracted from my anger.

I flung open the refrigerator door and pointed. "That."

He didn't move from the doorway but folded his arms across

his chest. "That. Uh-huh. All this slamming of doors is because I bought some beer."

"*Some* beer? Looks to me like you laid in quite a supply . . . for what? Not Florida's party. She's a recovering *addict*, for goodness' sake, Denny." He wanted stubborn? He was going to get stubborn. I folded my arms across *my* chest.

A little grin tipped one corner of his mouth. "Hey. You got your nails painted." The grin widened. "Jodi Marie Baxter, Miss Simplicity herself, has gotten herself—"

"Don't change the subject." I tucked my nails under my folded arms . . . but I could feel tears gathering behind my eyes, like an anxious teenager who didn't get asked to the prom. I'd wanted Denny to notice my nails, to like it that I got dolled up—but not in the middle of an argument. I tilted my chin up. "When did you buy this stuff? *I* had the van. Why so much? You got a party planned I don't know about? And looks like the party's already started—"

"Good grief! Give me a break, Jodi!" The grin disappeared, and he half-turned to go—Denny's usual defense when I rode in with six-shooters blazing. But he pointed a finger at me. "You're right. You had the van and took your own sweet time getting home, too. Did you ever think I might have errands to do? But no problem, I decided to go for a run down at the lake. Beautiful day for a run— or hadn't you noticed?" Sarcasm dripped off his words as though sweating from the heat in his voice. "Worked up a real thirst on my run. Stopped in at the Osco on Morse on my way home to get something to drink. And you know what, Jodi? They had a special on cold beer. Buy one six-pack, get one free. And you know what else, Jodi? That cold beer looked mighty good and I drank one. One measly beer . . . and my wife wants to take it all the way to the Supreme Court. Sheesh." He threw up both arms in disgust and this time completed his exit.

I watched him disappear into the hallway beyond the dining room, trailed by Willie Wonka, who'd been standing between us, watching us with worried wrinkles above his doggie brows. My tears came out of hiding, pursued by silent sobs as I tackled the plastic grocery bags all around my feet.

Okay, so I probably didn't handle that the best way. I stuffed frozen orange juice, frozen vegetables, and hamburger into the freezer.

Should've waited till we could talk about it instead of jumping all over him. Canned goods, pasta, and cold cereal went into the cupboards.

Should've known that would backfire; always does. I dumped the bags of onions and potatoes into their little plastic bins under the sink.

Didn't say anything last weekend when he had a beer at the Bagel Bakery . . . huh! Look where that got me. Gave him an inch, and he took a yard. Paper towels, toilet paper, and napkins got squeezed into the tall cupboard by the back door.

What does this say to the kids? It's okay to have a beer? And he better not give me that "but even you drink wine sometimes" bit. Last time I read the papers, it was "beer parties" that got busted, not dinner parties. I pulled out the crisper and dumped in carrots, celery, and lettuce.

I paused with the refrigerator door open again, staring at the offending six-packs. It bugged me to have my refrigerator full of beer. I wanted them *out* before the kids got home. Not only that, but I didn't want them there with Yada Yada coming to my house tomorrow. People like Avis and Nony probably thought *any* alcohol was wrong. And it might be a stumbling block to someone like Hoshi, who was new in her faith . . . or Chanda, who seemed rather borderline when it came to Christian behavior.

I hauled out the six-packs and took them to the garage, setting them in a corner under an old bushel basket. I'd tell Denny before he "discovered" they were gone and . . . well, we'd deal with it later.

EDESA DECLINED OUR INVITATION to stay for supper after her tutoring session with Amanda at four o'clock—said she was going to babysit for Delores and Ricardo that night so they could get out of the house.

"Isn't José too big for a babysitter?" I teased.

"Absolutely!" she laughed. "But . . . he cannot take care of his younger brothers and sisters yet. Besides, he is bored. He likes me to play cards."

"What about tomorrow—can you and Delores come to Florida's party?"

She smiled. *"Si!* Wouldn't miss it. Can we bring Emerald?"

More kids. "Uh . . . sure." Emerald was sweet. She wouldn't be any trouble.

Josh, bless his heart, walked Edesa to the Morse Street el stop. While he was gone, I asked Denny if we could talk privately a minute. Amanda was on the phone talking to a girlfriend, so we went out on the back porch and sat down on the steps.

"Denny, I . . . I'm sorry I jumped all over you about the beer."

He pursed his lips and nodded, but didn't say anything.

"But I really don't want it in the house for Florida's party. The women in Yada Yada come from a lot of different churches and might . . . I just don't want to offend anybody."

He shrugged. "Sure. I'll put it down in the basement."

"Uh . . . I already took it out to the garage."

His smile tightened. "Fine. Garage."

The tension between us had deflated somewhat but still hung there, like a helium party balloon hovering two feet off the floor. "Do you want to talk about the beer?" I asked.

"Not really," he said. "Maybe some other time."

I felt relieved. I didn't really want to talk about it now, either. But I didn't like the distance between us. Any crack, no matter how small, always felt like a huge canyon. "But . . . do you forgive me for yelling at you?"

"Yeah."

We sat on the steps a few more minutes, listening to the *thump, thump* of kids playing basketball in the alley beyond our garage, punctuated with the *caws* of several large black crows flying around a big elm one street over.

"I ran into Adele this afternoon—you know, the lady that squashed me like a bug the first night of our prayer group." I made my tone light, chatty. Maybe Denny and I just needed a bit of time to close the gap. "She has a beauty shop right on Clark Street— I didn't realize it was so close."

"That where you got your nails done?"

213

"Yeah. Feet, too." I giggled and pulled off one shoe and sock. "Whaddya think?"

I was relieved to see Denny grin as I wiggled my coral-tipped toes. "You sat still long enough for someone to give you a pedicure? Your mom always said she couldn't even play 'This little piggy went to market' without you screeching bloody murder."

"It wasn't easy. In fact—"

The back screen door banged open. "Mom. Dad. I'm back. When's supper? Somebody from Habitat for Humanity is going to talk to us tonight about the Mexico trip. Do you realize we leave in exactly one month?"

I made a face at Denny. Oh well. I had a lot to do to get ready for the party tomorrow anyway. I'd find some other time to tell him how freaked I got about that pedicure—and not because I was ticklish, either.

"Edesa get on the train okay?" I asked, rising reluctantly and following Josh back into the kitchen.

"Yeah. I hung around by the ticket booth till a southbound train came. Didn't hear any screams, so I'm pretty sure she got on okay."

"Oh, get out of here," I said, snapping him with a dishtowel. "I take it back. Set the table."

I pulled some catfish fillets out of the freezer and popped them into the microwave to defrost. Through the screen door I could see Denny still sitting on the back porch steps. Probably wishing he had one of those beers I'd hidden in the garage . . .

Stop it, Jodi. Drop it till you have time to talk.

24

"Thank You, God," I murmured, pulling open the blind on the bedroom window the next morning and seeing blue sky above the garage roof. The prospect of having all twelve members of Yada Yada plus assorted husbands *and* children underfoot in the house if it rained today had filled me with anxiety, akin to the claustrophobia I'd felt the time I got stuck in an elevator with ten other sweaty people.

But blue sky and sunshine . . . that would help a lot. Our backyard wasn't very big—I could probably count the blades of grass —but at least Denny could grill the chicken out there and any husbands who came along could yak outside while Yada Yada had our prayer time together in the front room.

Kids, hmm. Maybe Josh and Amanda could haul them down to the lake and fly a kite or something. Didn't we have a kite somewhere?

Unfortunately, that was the extent of my prayer time that

morning. *I'll make it up to You, Jesus,* I promised, flitting from room to room like film footage that's been speeded up, munching a bagel while picking up magazines, shoes, schoolbooks, mail, and anything else that gave our house that "lived-in look." At least Avis would make sure we got prayer time at the party this afternoon . . . that would have to do.

I ended up making everybody wait in the car as I ran back to the house to set out a gallon glass jar filled with water and tea bags for "sun tea." When I climbed back into the car Denny said, "Relax, Jodi. It's going to be great. I'm looking forward to meeting the rest of Yada Yada. But . . ." He gravely fingered one of my earlobes. ". . . is this a new style? You're only wearing one earring."

BESIDES THE FACT THAT Denny saved me from looking foolish two Sundays in a row, his good-natured laughter as I ran back into the house for the missing earring had felt like a soothing ointment on the raw place between us. We walked up the stairs at Uptown hand in hand while Josh parked the minivan this time.

"Wonder if anybody from Yada Yada will come to church this morning?" I whispered, glancing about the upstairs sanctuary. I checked out the third row. "Whoa, you mean we got here before Stu this time?" My day was picking up.

"Mom, look! It's Edesa!" Amanda made a beeline for a couple of women whose backs were turned toward us, and sure enough,

Edesa turned around and gave her a big hug. I could see her introducing Delores and Emerald to my daughter.

I pulled Denny in their direction. "Delores!" I gave the shorter woman a hug and bestowed one on Emerald, too. "I didn't really think you'd be able to come to church as well as the party this afternoon."

Delores's round face dimpled. "Good excuse to have a girls day out." She rolled her eyes and tapped the side of her head with her finger. "My Ricardo *with* a job is a trial to live with. Unemployed? He is driving me—" She drew little circles at her temple with her finger.

We laughed but couldn't talk more because Avis was giving the call to worship. Some people moved over a couple of chairs so we could have seats together. I noticed Emerald, her jet black hair caught back from her face with a baby blue ribbon, jockeying for position between Edesa and Amanda. What a cutie.

We were singing the second song when I felt a poke in my ribs from the row behind me. "Hey, girl," came a loud whisper. "Why didn't you save me a seat?"

I'm sure I grinned from ear to ear. "Florida!" I whispered and gave her an awkward hug over the back of my chair. She was dressed in black slacks and a loose-belted tunic—rose on black—and her hair was different. The crown of little beaded braids had given way to a cascade of shiny finger curls slicked back from her forehead with tiny combs. Chris and Cedric, looking manly in their khaki slacks and open-necked dress shirts, both gave me a little wave. No Carl though. Denny might be odd man out at this party, after all.

That was all from Yada Yada who came to Uptown Community that morning, but it was a start on our "church visitation." I wasn't too surprised that others hadn't made it—after all, Adele had "MaDear" to worry about, and Chanda was a single mom with three kids. Probably getting a babysitter—or mother-sitter—for one afternoon was challenging enough. I was surprised about Stu, though. She had come again last week and talked like she'd be here this morning.

The service was nice, pretty typical for Uptown. From time to time I glanced sideways at Edesa and Delores, wondering how our medley of contemporary worship songs—sincere, but rather monotone in intensity, accompanied by a few hand clappers—compared to worship at their Church of the Holy Spirit. It would be fun to visit a Spanish-speaking church. I ought to go when Amanda could go with me.

During announcements, the teen group asked members of Uptown Community to sponsor work projects for the teens the first three Saturdays in June to earn the remaining money for the mission trip. It hadn't really hit me yet that both my kids were going off U.S. soil for ten days . . . without me. As people gathered around the teens to pray for them, I felt strangely warmed to hear Florida's familiar, "Thank ya, *Jesus!*" and "You are *so good,* Jesus!" join Avis's regular affirmations.

Our visitors had come by public transportation, so I got together with Avis right after service to work out rides to my house. Delores and Edesa wanted to run by Dominick's to pick up some potato salad; Avis said she'd take them so we Baxters could get home to get the grill going. That left Florida and her boys to ride with us.

I saw Pastor Clark talking to Florida and making a fuss over Chris and Cedric. *That's nice,* I thought. Pastor Clark carried a vision for more diversity in the congregation. Maybe he was trying to recruit them. But finally we all made it out the door and piled in the minivan that Josh had waiting—double-parked—in front of Uptown's storefront.

"Didn't know this was yours and Avis's church, Jodi," Florida said, followed by a stern, "Get that seatbelt fastened, Cedric; don't you be fussin' 'bout it."

"Yeah. Almost a year now—well, last summer. That's how I met Avis and found out about the job at Bethune Elementary."

"Ain't that somethin'," Florida murmured as we pulled away, which I thought was odd. She couldn't have been *that* impressed.

BY THE TIME AVIS ARRIVED with her carload and a pan of hot macaroni and cheese, it was almost one-thirty and Chanda and Adele had just arrived, bearing a couple of bags of chips and a big pot of greens respectively. "Get that mac 'n' cheese in the oven," Adele ordered, charging into the kitchen. She put her own pot of greens on top of the stove and turned the flame on low. "Nothin' worse than cold mac 'n' cheese."

For a flicker of a second my territorial instincts rose up: *You may be the boss of your salon, Adele Skuggs, but this is my kitchen . . .*

but instead I tried to make conversation. "Where's your mother today, Adele?" I *was* curious. What did one *do* with someone suffering from Alzheimer's like MaDear, who was always looking to "escape" with her walker?

"My sister takes her on Sundays. Gives me a day off." She seemed to notice the others who'd come in with Avis for the first time. "Hey, Edesa . . . Delores. Oh, my . . . this your baby? How ya doin', honey? How's José doin'?" Chatting all at once, the little group threaded itself through the back door.

"Amanda's out there somewhere, Emerald!" I called after them.

Chanda George had disappeared into the bathroom the moment she walked in the front door. Coming into the kitchen now, she caught sight of others in the backyard and made a beeline for the screen door, giving me a polite nod in passing. Then, as if on second thought, she stopped and enveloped a startled Avis in a big hug.

"That was interesting," Avis murmured a few minutes later as the two of us set things out on the dining room table, buffet style. "Maybe getting everybody in the prayer group together is as important for Chanda as for Florida."

"You think?" I hadn't thought much about Miss Lottery Ticket since the conference—Chanda didn't have e-mail, so we hadn't really communicated. I really had no idea what her life was like . . . single mom, three kids, cleaning houses for a living. Did we have *anything* in common? But I did appreciate that she had made an effort to come out on a Sunday afternoon—*sans* kids, thank goodness—to Florida's party.

Avis was staring at me, an amused smile on her face.

"What?"

She pointed. "Your nails. I thought there was something different about you today, but I didn't know what. You did your nails."

"Nope. Got them done. At Adele's salon." I waved my fingers under her nose, enjoying the "oh *really*" look on her face. I'd wondered if anyone would notice.

Josh and Amanda had Florida's boys and Emerald in the alley, shooting hoops against a neighbor's garage, while most of the women flirted with Denny, who was manning the grill. Okay, they weren't really flirting, but he was the only man present and was being his charming self, which meant giving each new arrival a big welcoming smile and talking like they were old friends. I knew I could count on Denny to help put people at ease.

The doorbell rang as Avis and I set out the last of the red-and-white paper plates and matching napkins and cold cups on a folding card table in the dining room. "I'll get it," I said, hustling down the hall and pulling open the front door.

"Nony!" I shrieked, and gave her a big hug—before realizing that an absolutely gorgeous hunk of a man stood just behind her, six feet three if he was an inch. His skin was nutmeg, a spicy complement to Nony's darker skin, with deep-set eyes, a perfectly trimmed moustache and goatee, and—good grief!—dimples.

"Hi, Jodi," Nony said, dressed as usual in a beautiful African thing—a royal blue dress with slits up the side, embroidered all around the neck and wide sleeves with a silvery design. "This is my husband, Mark, and . . ." She reached around behind her husband

and pulled out two shy boys, each one holding a couple of liters of soda pop. "Marcus," she said, tapping the slightly taller one, "and Michael." Spitting images of their father.

"Come in, come in!" I beamed, awed by this beautiful little family. "Everyone's out in the backyard. The guy in the apron manning the grill is my husband, Denny. He will be so glad you showed up, Mark—so far he's been the only male at this hen party. If you don't count kids, I mean."

Mark shook my hand warmly and gave a slight bow. "Delighted to meet you, Jodi Baxter." I felt like Anna in *The King and I*. Yes, I could imagine this man was a professor at Northwestern University.

"Is Hoshi coming?" I asked.

Nony shook her head. "Can't. Writing a history paper." She gave her husband a look. "*Some* professors expect way too much research."

"Oh, I'm sorry. Tell her we missed her . . . Oh. There's a chest of ice on the back porch for that pop," I said to Nony's boys . . . just as I noticed a bunch more heads bobbing up the porch steps behind the Sisulu-Smiths. I stepped aside as Nony ushered her family toward the back of the house then returned to the open front door to welcome the new arrivals.

Yo-Yo! Followed by Ruth and Ben, carrying a big paper bag that said "the Bagel Bakery." And lurking at the bottom of the steps, Yo-Yo's two teenage stepbrothers, whose slouch and averted eyes made it clear that they wished they were someplace else.

"Ohmigosh!" I said, dishing out hugs once more. "I didn't know if you guys were coming! Ben . . . Denny will be delighted.

Three husbands ought to be enough for this crowd, don't you think?"

"Yes, plenty," Ruth said. "They can do the dishes while we talk. No?"

Laughing, I gave her a big hug. "I am *so* glad you came, Ruth. You have no idea," I whispered in her ear.

She waved me away like a pesky mosquito. "What's not to come? You have food, we eat. We are women, we talk. The party is Yada Yada, we pray." But something in her voice made me think her bravado functioned more as an internal pep talk. Frankly, I suspected we had Yo-Yo to thank for getting them all here.

I hustled the latest arrivals out to the backyard—which seemed tinier by the minute—and for a few minutes hugs, squeals, greetings, and introductions degenerated into a general hubbub. I called Josh from the alley, who—if he was surprised at the growing number of kids, hid it well—managed to coax Yo-Yo's brothers, Jerry and Pete, to play three-on-three in the alley.

Well, that's everybody, I thought. Everybody except Hoshi . . . and Stu.

I snuck away, hunted up Stu's number on the Yada Yada list, and called. Three rings, then an answering machine picked up. I hung up without leaving a message.

Strange.

25

*F*lorida seemed to be having a great time. "That man of yours sure can barbecue some gooood chicken," she conceded to me, her plate piled high with blistered chicken, macaroni and cheese, greens, potato salad, and chips, before moving on to trade good-natured insults with Adele and Chanda, laughing and talking. I noticed she hadn't taken any of the potato kugel Yo-Yo and Ruth had brought from the Bagel Bakery. Shouldn't read anything into that, I told myself; she didn't go for the "yuppie" food at the hotel, either.

Watching the steady stream of nine kids—most of them hollow-leg boys—going in and out of the house with copious amounts of food, I began to worry about dessert. Stu was supposed to bring it . . . what did I have to substitute if she didn't show up? A quick inventory of the kitchen came up with two partially eaten half-gallons of ice cream and an unopened package of store-bought cookies. That would have to do.

On the way back out to the backyard, I snatched the camp brochure I'd put out on the counter to show to Nony. She was chatting with Avis but excused herself when I waved the brochure at her and pantomimed, *For you.*

"Didn't mean to interrupt," I apologized. "Just didn't want to forget to give this to you—you asked about a Christian camp on the e-loop, remember?"

"Oh, yes. Let me see."

Nony took the large brochure I handed to her and opened it up, disclosing a colorful display of photographs of kids zipping down a water slide, made up in clown faces, doing crafts, and riding horseback, sprinkled amid descriptions of the different age groups and specialty camps. "My kids have attended this camp for years," I put in. "They love it! It's got all sorts of great activities—parasailing, canoe trips, a ropes course, even a horsemanship camp—on top of the regular stuff. And they bring in lots of popular youth speakers. Amanda would probably be going this summer, except she's going on a teen mission trip to Mexico, and the dates conflict." I lowered my voice in that parent-to-parent confidential tone. "Good thing. No way we could afford both in one summer."

Nony studied the brochure for a moment or two longer, then folded it up and handed it back to me. "Thank you, Jodi."

"Oh, you can keep that."

Nony shook her head. "One look at that brochure and my kids would say, 'No way.'"

I felt like I'd been slapped. She must have seen me jerk because she added, "The pictures. Not a single black face in the whole brochure. Except one picture, and they're *all* black in that one."

I blinked. Really? I was sure I'd seen African-American kids at the camp when we took our kids or picked them up at the camp. At least one or two, anyway. "I'm sure they'd be wel—"

"It's not just that, Jodi," Nony said, not unkindly. "Look." She pointed to the one picture that showed several grinning dark faces just above a camp week described as "Urban Camp." "See that description? 'Underprivileged' . . . 'inner city' . . . 'scholarships.' That's the impression given by this brochure—that black kids are underprivileged, all live in the inner city, need scholarships, and come to this particular week of camp. Mark would have a fit."

A hot flash of embarrassment crept up my neck. What a dork I was! I should have noticed . . . but I had to admit, it hadn't even crossed my mind.

As if to soften the sting, Nony gave me a kiss on the cheek. "It's all right, Jodi. I appreciate you thinking of the boys." She retrieved her plate and moved off, as regal in our puny backyard as if it were a marble courtyard.

I retreated to the kitchen to stash the brochure . . . and started to feel defensive. I'd extended an invitation to share *my* world and been rebuffed. For that matter, how could this camp—an outstanding Christian camp in my opinion, at least up until the last five minutes—include any pictures of black middle-class kids having fun at camp . . . if they didn't *go?*

I wanted to go somewhere and stick a pillow over my head. *Suck it up, Jodi. You're the hostess of this party, remember?* I put the ice cream, a scooper, and the cookies on a tray then stood at the back door another moment or two, working up courage to go back outside and mingle, not knowing when I'd make a fool of myself again.

Standing at the back door, I had a sudden revelation. If all the kids in those pictures had been black, would Amanda or Josh think that camp was intended for them? Would *I* want them to be "token white kids," just to integrate the place?

No. I wasn't that noble. Sure, I'd welcome a healthy mix of kids, as I was sure Nony would, too. But, just like Nony, I'd mostly want my kids not to feel different, to feel like they *belonged.*

DENNY CLANGED HIS BARBECUE UTENSILS together. "Hey, everybody!" The general hubbub died down, and even the kids stopped slurping ice cream long enough to stare at my husband, who stood on the steps of the back porch in his silly apron.

"I've been forewarned," he said gravely, "that the Yada Yada Prayer Group plans to get together all by themselves right after we finish eating . . . leaving the gentlemen, by the way, to clean up—"

"What about these kids?" Ben Garfield glowered at Jerry and Pete, trying to look tough.

"No, no!" howled Yo-Yo's brothers. "We can't clean up. Josh is taking us to the lake to play volleyball!" The other kids lustily joined in the general protest.

Denny clanged his utensils together again. "All right, all right. Just put your own trash in that big trash can there, and it'll be half-done. But wait! Wait!" He held up the barbecue tongs as the kids made a mad rush for the trash can, intent on taking the promised hike down to the lakeshore. The hubbub settled once more.

Denny turned to Florida. "Before Yada Yada steals you away, we want to acknowledge our guest of honor, Florida Hickman, who is, I believe, 'five years saved and five years sober'! Let's give it up for Sister Florida!"

As cheers and clapping and laughter erupted, Denny hopped down and gallantly escorted Florida to the top step. "Speech! Speech!"

I grinned as Florida looked around the yard, tears sparkling in her deep brown eyes. This was perfect. Denny always did have a gift for the dramatic.

For a few moments, Florida didn't speak, her emotions doing a little dance between her big smile and the tears that threatened to flow. But as the happy clamor subsided, she lifted her chin. "There's only one guest of honor here—and that's Jesus. 'Cause if it weren't for Jesus—oh, Lord! If it weren't for Jesus—" She stopped and closed her eyes as the tears finally fell. She shook her head from side to side . . . but in a few moments opened her eyes again. "If it weren't for Jesus, I'd still be a mess for sure, still out on the street, still doing drugs, still stopping cars in the middle of the street, begging anyone and everyone for money for my next fix. But—praise Jesus!—He . . ."

My mouth slowly fell open. Florida went on talking, still giving God praise, but I no longer heard the words. My mind had stuck on the last thing she said: *stopping cars in the middle of the street, begging anyone and everyone for money . . .*

An old memory, a rainy day, way back when the kids were little, a wild woman stopping my car . . . could that have been *Florida?* Immediately, common sense told me that there must be thousands of drug addicts in Chicago. The odds that Florida and I had run into each other ten, maybe twelve years ago . . . impossible. We didn't even live in Chicago back then. Denny used to volunteer at Uptown sometimes, but Chicago was a big city—

". . . Uptown Community Church," Florida was saying. "Ain't God got a sense of humor, bringing me and the boys to that church today, the day y'all picked for my sobriety party? But it was one of the storefront churches I used to hit up for handouts. Didn't even remember the name, not until I walked in there this morning and saw the pastor—what's his name? Pastor Clark . . . right. He tried to get me straightened out a couple times, but I wasn't ready. Wasn't ready till they took my babies . . ."

Oh God. That was Florida.

"Jesus!" a piercing voice cried, yanking me back to the present. It was Chanda, shaking her head and waving one hand in the air. "Jesus!"

"Hallelujah! Glory!" Delores started clapping, and others joined in. A little way behind the others, Avis walked back and forth on the grass, head thrown back, lips moving in praise.

Still stunned at the revelation that our paths had crossed once before, I wanted to grab Florida, say something. But she stood on the back steps, one arm lifted heavenward, her voice rising over all the others: *"Thank* ya, Jesus! *Thank* ya!"

Looked like we were getting ready to have church right there in the Baxter backyard.

THE KIDS FINALLY ESCAPED under the supervision of Josh and Pete as the "oldest," volleyball in hand. Yada Yada moved into the living room, glasses of pop and iced tea in hand. (Though I'd been informed by Florida that adding sugar to cold iced tea just didn't do justice to the "real thing." "Girl, ya gotta add the sugar while the tea is *hot*. Ain't nobody ever told you how to make real 'sweet tea'—like they do down South?") The front windows were open and I'd put a fan in one, pulling a nice breeze from the open back door. Somehow, all ten of us found a perch, either on the couch or chairs or pillows on the floor.

"You got a real nice house, Sista Jodee," Chanda said. It was the first thing she'd said to me all afternoon.

"Nice nails, too," Adele quipped.

"Yeah. Look at you," said Yo-Yo, settling on the floor in front of Ruth.

At any other time, I would have enjoyed "joining the club" of nail-painted women. And it was the perfect time to give Adele and her salon the credit. But I didn't want to lose what had just happened in a flurry of small talk. "I gotta tell you guys . . . Florida and I met before. Twelve years ago."

The room was suddenly silent, and nine pairs of eyes looked at me.

"I . . . I didn't realize it until just now . . . out in the backyard! But, Florida, when you mentioned that you used to stop by Uptown Community to get a handout—"

Florida pulled back behind her stare. "Thought you and Denny have only been at Uptown since last summer."

"That's true! But before that, Denny had been volunteering there for half a zillion years, even when we were living in Downers Grove. The first time I drove into the city to pick him up . . . a woman jumped out in front of my car—Good Lord! Scared me half to death. It was raining, too. I could have hit her!—but all she wanted was some money. To feed her kids, she said. I didn't know what to do. At first, I told her to go to Uptown—they could help her. She said she'd been there, done that. But . . ." I tried to make eye contact with Florida, but she was leaning forward, hands clasped on her knees, her eyes focused on her hands. ". . . that's why I think it was you."

I couldn't tell what Florida was thinking. But a lump was growing in my throat. "Never in all my wildest dreams did I think God would put *that woman* in my hotel room at the women's conference . . . put her in my prayer group . . . in my home . . . in my life . . . as my friend."

"Glory," someone breathed. Probably Avis. But I kept my eyes on Florida.

She finally looked up. "So, what did you do—back then, I mean?"

"You don't remember?" I waited to see a slight shake of her head. "Well, I was going to take you to the grocery store to buy you some food and diapers—that's what you said you needed."

"Did you?"

"No." I dropped my eyes. "On the way we stopped at the church and . . . you were gone when I got back to the car."

"Stopped at the church to check me out?"

I swallowed. *Bingo.* I nodded.

Florida's face crumpled. "I don't remember it—stopped a lot of cars during that time." Her voice was hushed as though uncomfortable with the idea that one of the women in this room—the women who knew the Florida who was "saved, sober, and sanctified"—had met the "other" Florida.

"*I* think this is incredible." Delores broke the tension. "Don't you see? God had a plan all along to bring all of us together—and maybe it started that day when Florida and Jodi met by accident."

"Get out!" Yo-Yo arched back. "That was just coincidence, right?"

"There are no coincidences with God, Yo-Yo," said Avis.

"What's that mean?" Yo-Yo pressed. "God's got some big *reason* Florida hit up Jodi for money years ago? Some big *reason* this bunch of women got number twenty-six on their gold sticker at that conference?"

"Maybe." Avis smiled.

"'Fear not, for I have redeemed you; I have called you by name; you are mine,'" Nony quoted, flipping through her Bible. "Where's that passage, Avis?"

"Wait a minute," said Yo-Yo. "Don't go throwing Bible verses around. What's this name business? I mean, God calling us by name."

"Names have meaning," Edesa suggested.

"Yeah, right. Yo-Yo . . . a spinning toy going nowhere," Yo-Yo muttered.

"Here it is." Avis had her Bible open. "Isaiah forty-three: 'Thus says the Lord, who created you . . . "Fear not, for I have redeemed you; I have called you by your name; you are Mine. When you pass through the waters, I will be with you; and through the rivers, they shall not overflow you. When you walk through the fire, you shall not be burned, nor shall the flame scorch you. For I am the Lord your God, the Holy One of Israel, your Savior"' . . ." She looked up. "That's a good passage for this celebration."

"For Florida, yes. Praise God! But I was also thinking," Nony murmured, "about what Delores said about God calling us together as a group . . . and planning it a long time ago . . . and giving us a *name.*"

Delores got so excited she was practically bouncing on the couch beside Florida. *"Gloria a Dios!* Ruth, what did you say 'Yada Yada' meant—that Hebrew meaning?"

"Never heard what *that* was all about." Chanda pulled a face.

Ruth looked taken aback, as if she had not planned to speak. "What am I, a dictionary?" But she dug around in her purse, finally pulled out a square of paper, and unfolded it. "All right. Yada Yada like we've been spelling it—without an *h* on the end—means 'to perceive, to understand . . . to be known, to make oneself known.'" She frowned and read farther in the tiny text on the photocopied page. "'Often used to describe God's knowledge of man.'"

"And women," Adele sniffed.

"*Si, si,*" Delores said impatiently. "Don't you see? Jodi and Florida had absolutely nothing—nada—in common when that drug addict stopped that car. They didn't know each other, they didn't understand each other, they didn't think they'd ever see each other again—"

"You sayin' God knew?" Yo-Yo still looked doubtful.

"That's it," said Avis. "God knew them, He knew you, He knew each one of us back then—and wanted all of us to know Him . . . and maybe wanted us to know each other, too."

"For real?" Chanda's eyes were big. "You be sayin' that God planned all along for these here sistas to get together? And named us, too?"

I wasn't sure how all this fit together with the fact that I had "met" Florida for ten minutes twelve years ago . . . though it seemed terribly significant *somehow*. I still couldn't read Florida, though, what she thought about it. I wanted to get up and just give her a hug, let her know I was glad we'd met, glad God brought us back together again.

Nony was smiling and waving her Bible. "Don't know why God calling us by name shouldn't apply to a group as well as individuals. We *thought* we made up a name for this group just off the cuff—but look what it turned out to be. God's name for us."

"That's it. What's the other meaning of Yada Yada, Ruth?" Delores pressed.

"Yadah Yadah with an *h?* Hmm . . ." Ruth peered again at the tiny print, moving it to arm's length. "Yadah Yadah means—

among other things—to praise, to sing, to give thanks. It says here—"

The doorbell rang. Ruth stopped and looked up.

Rats, I thought. *Wish Denny would get it.* But Denny was in the backyard and probably didn't hear it. "Go on, Ruth, I'll get it." I stepped over Yo-Yo and Edesa, who were sitting on the floor and headed for the front door. Behind me I heard Ruth finish, "It says here, 'an expression of thanks to God by way of praising.'"

I pulled open the door. Stu was standing on the other side of the screen, her long hair tucked behind one ear, showing off the little row of earrings, and holding a nine-by-eleven pan of something. Dessert. *A little late,* I huffed to myself.

"Hi, Jodi. Everybody here?" Stu pulled open the screen door and practically charged past me into the living room.

"Hey, Stu. Get mugged on the way?" cracked Yo-Yo.

A few others started to call out greetings, but Stu held up her hand like a traffic cop. "Sorry I'm late. But I've got news." She paused, looking around the room, her eyes finally falling on Florida.

"I found Carla."

26

Stu's announcement surged from person to person like a slow-motion shock wave and pulled Florida off the couch. "You . . . found my baby?" Disbelief and hope, fear and longing tangled themselves around those words.

"Pretty sure. Everything seems to—"

Adele's big frame rose up from the La-Z-Boy like a protective mother bear. "Don't do this, Leslie Stuart, not unless you *know*—"

"Wait. Please. Listen to me." Stu shoved the pan of dessert into my hands and moved to Florida's side. She took the dark, trembling hands in her own and lowered Florida to the couch cushions, kneeling down beside her. "They don't know exactly how it happened, *how* Carla's foster family got lost in the system, but my contact at DCFS thinks the original social worker quit or got fired and Carla's files got lost, or misfiled, or something. That's why they couldn't find any record of her when you went back."

"Sounds like DCFS, all right," Adele muttered, and sat back down.

By now all of us were glued to Stu's words.

"But . . . there's a family with a foster child who recently applied to adopt the little girl, and DCFS can't find any of *her* records. That tipped off my friend, who had copies of your papers, Florida . . . and the facts fit: first name, date of birth, date taken into custody by DCFS, all that kind of stuff. He's pretty sure it's your Carla."

"You mean . . . the family didn't steal her? Or run off to some other state? Or . . . or hurt my baby?" The struggle to let go of her fears was written all over Florida's face.

Stu shook her head. "No. Don't think so. This family applied to adopt her, after all. They'd have to stand up to some scrutiny. And . . . probably means they love her. Enough to want to keep her."

The word "adopt" finally sank into Florida's awareness. "Keep her? But . . . no, no! I want my baby back. Now that she's found, I want my baby back!" She made an attempt to stand up, but Stu's firm grip on her hands kept her in her seat.

"Don't worry, Florida," Stu said patiently. "They've only applied for adoption. Nothing's final. Once DCFS matches up the paperwork, your own application to get your daughter back will certainly affect the adoption process. The fact that your husband and sons are back with you? Definitely a plus factor."

"*Si, si.*" Delores, who was sitting beside Florida on the couch, put an arm around her shoulder comfortingly. "*Muy bueno.* And we pray."

"Are the foster parents white? Or black?" Chanda's question interrupted the flow of encouragement like an open manhole that one had to dodge in the middle of the street.

Stu shrugged. "I don't know. Does it matter?"

"Matter!" Adele jumped in, screeching to a halt right in front of the yawning manhole. "White folks think they can raise black kids color-blind. But most of 'em don't know a whit about preparing a black child for life in this society. Huh." She folded her arms across the wide span of her bosom. "Takes more'n love or money or good intentions. Black kids need identity, the strength of they own kind. What else gonna—"

Stu stood up. "I disagree. There're too many kids wasting away in the foster care system—most of them children of color—to get all self-righteous about what color an adoptive family should be. We need more people wanting to adopt, period."

"Why don't you adopt, then?" Chanda asked.

I felt slightly smug that Stu was on the hot seat after riding in on her white horse to save the day. Adele had a point, of course, but to be honest, I agreed with Stu. I probably would've been rendered speechless by Chanda's challenge, though, but Stu lifted her chin. "I've thought about it. Seriously."

"Want a couple of teenage boys?" Yo-Yo snickered. "I need a break."

"Ah . . . this might make a good discussion at another time," Avis said. "But right now it's a moot point, since, as Stu says, we don't know. The important thing is . . . Carla was lost, but now she's found. What an answer to our prayers! We need to give some glory to God!" She stood up—I think it's against Avis's nature to praise God sitting down. "Glory to You, Jesus! Glory!"

Florida's tense body gradually melted against Delores's arm around her shoulder. "Yes . . . Yes! Thank ya, Jesus. Thank ya! *Thank* ya! You're a *good* God!"

Others began to join in the prayer and praise. I thought *hallelujah,* too—hallelujah that Avis had the wits to derail *that* discussion. I wanted to join in the praise and prayer, too—if Carla really had been found, that was worth shouting about!—but I was still standing in the doorway, holding Stu's nine-by-eleven pan. I slipped out to the kitchen and set it on the counter. Maybe it would keep the kids busy if they got back before Yada Yada was done.

The praise from the living room could be heard clear out in the kitchen—maybe even out in the backyard. I peeked in Stu's pan—yum, lemon bars—then glanced out the screen door. Denny, Mark Smith, and Ben Garfield had parked three lawn chairs in the shade of the garage. They looked relaxed, friendly. Sure were a funny trio. Denny, the all-american-guy high school coach . . . Mark, the svelte college professor, tall, dark, *and* handsome . . . and Ben, short, stocky, a shock of wavy silver hair, and features that could make him a stand-in for Itzhak Perlman if he played the violin. I could hear Ben's guttural guffaw as he raised a bottle to his lips.

Bottle? I squinted and peered intently through the screen door. Had Ben brought some beer to the party? Hadn't noticed any when they came in. Which meant—

I did a quick double-check of the other guys. Both Denny and

Mark held red plastic cups. I glared through the screen door. *That better be iced tea in that red cup, Denny Baxter—*

"Jodi?"

Startled, I turned to see Ruth standing behind me. Her face was red, her eyes bleary, and she was holding a tissue to her nose.

"Ruth! Are you all—"

"Need to get Ben . . . need to go." Ruth's voice wavered.

"Ruth . . . wait." I put my hands on her shoulders and could feel her trembling beneath my fingers. "Ruth, tell me what's wrong."

She began to cry in earnest then, stifling the sobs in an effort to be quiet. I pulled her into my arms, pulling past her resistance, pressing our heads together cheek to cheek, and just held her while she cried. A movement behind Ruth caught my eye, and I saw Avis hesitate in the doorway between the dining room and kitchen. I crooked a finger at her to come in.

After a minute or two, Ruth quieted and pulled back from my embrace, fumbling for a tissue and blowing her nose in a healthy snort. Avis came closer. "Ruth?"

Ruth turned her head. "I'm all right. Just need to leave . . . I'll get Ben—"

I was about to say, *You can't go! Then Yo-Yo will have to go, and her brothers aren't even back from the lake yet* . . . but Avis cut to the chase.

"Ruth, you've got a load as big as a dump truck on your shoulders. Let us help you carry it. Isn't that why God put this group together?"

Ruth just shook her head as fresh tears spilled down her cheeks.

"It has something to do with Florida and finding Carla . . . doesn't it." It was a statement, not a question. Avis put a firm arm around Ruth, who mopped her blotchy face and allowed herself to be walked back toward the living room. "Come on. Let's face into it. After all . . ." Avis gave Ruth's shoulder a tender shake. ". . . you're the one who told us Yada Yada means 'to be known, to make yourself known.'"

The group had gathered around Florida on the couch, their hands laid on her knees, her shoulders, her head as first one, then another, continued the prayers for Carla, for strength in the waiting, for a speedy reunion of Florida's family. Avis led Ruth back to her chair and waited quietly with her until there was a lull in the spoken prayers, even as various ones were murmuring, "Have mercy, Jesus" or, "Bless You, God."

I probably would have said a big "Amen!" at that point, bringing the prayer time to an end so Ruth could share whatever it was that was eating her up. I was afraid that if we didn't hurry, she would change her mind and leave. But Avis just turned the prayers.

"Father God, You have loved us so much . . . loved us in spite of all our imperfections. You sent Jesus and covered all our sins with His blood . . ." A general chorus of *thank Yous* and *hallelujahs* filled in the blanks. "Thank You for bringing Yada Yada together and allowing us to pray for one another. Thank You for answering those prayers, for sparing José's life, for finding Carla . . ."

The rest of the group pitched in. "Yes, You did!" "Thank ya!" "You're a good God!"

"Now give us that same kind of love for one another . . . give us ears to hear and hearts that are open to bear each other's burdens as we listen to our sister Ruth."

That took everyone by surprise. Eyes popped open as the women realized Avis meant it literally. I caught a few looks that said, *What's goin' on?* passing between folks as they took their seats.

"There's joy in this room because of the news Stu brought us," Avis said, "but there's also pain. One doesn't cancel the other out—we need to be able to bear both sorrow and joy at the same time." She lifted her eyebrows at the still-blotchy-faced woman beside her. "Ruth?"

For a moment, Ruth just shook her head and blew her nose, and I thought she couldn't do it. But then her voice croaked, "I . . . I wanted to leave, not spoil the celebration. But a mother hen, she is." Ruth jerked a shaky thumb at Avis. "Oh, Florida, of course you want your daughter back, and . . . and I want that for you. Yes, I do. But . . . but . . ." The tears started fresh.

"But what? What kind of 'but' you talkin' 'bout?" Florida's voice had an edge. Avis's prayer about "bearing each other's burdens" was going to be a hard sell if it had anything to do with not getting Carla back.

Ruth squeezed her eyes shut. Couldn't blame her. Maybe it would be easier to talk if she didn't have to look at the ring of skeptical faces.

"The family that's been raising Carla for . . . what? five . . . six years? I can't help thinking about *them.*" It was a good thing Ruth's eyes were closed, because Florida's eyes narrowed. Avis simply raised her hand to cut off any comments. "Because that's me," Ruth wailed. *"Me."*

More looks passed around the circle as Ruth took a big, shuddering breath. What in the world did she mean? When Ruth spoke again, her voice had lowered almost to a whisper and I had to lean forward to hear her. "A foster mother I was, years ago . . . three times I've been married and no kids. So my second husband and I, we decided enough of this moping! We'll adopt a kid through Jewish family services. Huh. But that process dragged on and on, so we went to DCFS and took a foster child, a beautiful little girl . . . mixed she was—Asian and black and maybe something else— and we had her for five years. Five years! And we loved her so much . . . and we wanted to adopt her. Nothing from her mother or father for five years—not a word! And all of a sudden, her daddy shows up and wants his 'baby girl' back. And they took her . . . they *took* her . . ."

The room was deathly silent except for Ruth's gut-wrenching wails. Yo-Yo was staring at her friend, open-mouthed. Avis simply held up her hand as if to say, *Just hold the comments and hear her out.* And, eyes still squeezed shut, Ruth's sobs finally quieted and she spoke again.

"Tore us apart, it did. My husband and I . . . we didn't make it. I . . . he . . ." Ruth seemed to sink into the memory, not crying this time, just revisiting the pain that drove them apart.

The room was hushed for a long time. Then Yo-Yo blurted, "But you and Ben—you practically took my brothers in while I was doin' time. And you smother-mother me, too, for that matter. Pretty good parents, if ya ask me."

Ruth opened her eyes and smiled at Yo-Yo in spite of her

dripping nose. "Yes, my Ben. Number Three. Helped me move on, Ben did. *And* meeting you and Jesus in the Cook County Jail. I thought I'd put it all behind me . . . until . . ." Ruth studied her lap, where she had shredded at least three soggy tissues. "Until Carla."

Florida leaned forward. "I'm gonna get Carla back, do you understand? Ain't gonna make no apologies for that. And I don't wanna feel sorry for the foster family that has to give her up. Does that make us enemies, Ruth?"

Ruth jerked her head up. "No! No . . . I'm sorry. So sorry. I shouldn't have—"

"Yes, you should," Avis said firmly. "Florida's story is her story . . . and Ruth's story is her story. A good reminder that *every* story has two sides, maybe more. And there's no way we can be a prayer group if we don't know each other's stories." She reached over and laid a hand on Ruth's knee. "Ruth, remember praying with Delores at the conference? All we knew was that José had been shot. Didn't know why . . . didn't know what. Some of us probably thought he was gangbanging, just didn't want to say it."

Ouch. Avis got me there.

"But did that stop us from praying? No, because Delores's pain became our pain. And we're praying with Florida, because she's our sister and God put us together in Yada Yada to stand with each other. If Yada Yada had existed when you were going through the fire, we would have prayed with you, too. It's not up to *us* to make the difficult decisions like King Solomon. What are we going to do, cut the baby in half?"

"Cut the baby in half? *What* are you talking about, Avis?" Yo-Yo sputtered.

The tension buckled and broke into laughter. Avis smiled. "Tell you later, Yo-Yo. All I want to say is, if the Yada Yada Prayer Group means anything at all, it means standing with each other *no matter what.*"

27

Denny and I stood on the front porch saying good-bye to our guests as Yada Yada, long-suffering spouses, empty dishes, and assorted offspring straggled out of the door. Emerald Enriques had a hard time letting go of Amanda and made Edesa *promise* she could come with her the next time she gave Amanda a Spanish lesson. Yo-Yo's stepbrothers kick-boxed with the other boys on the sidewalk until Ben Garfield pulled up in the car he'd had to park two blocks away—and even then he had to yell, "Get in the car *now* or you'll walk home!"

Florida turned down Denny's offer to walk her and her boys to the el. "We'll be fine—don'tcha worry none. Delores, Edesa, and Emerald have to catch the train, too." She patted him on the arm, like some granny thanking an overzealous Boy Scout. "But that's very sweet, Denny." Florida cast me an impish eye. "Better hold on to your man, Jodi Baxter. Ya don't want ta train 'im this well then lose 'im to some hungry hussy."

Everyone in earshot laughed as Denny turned red . . . but remembering the comment later, it seemed an odd thing to say, teasing another woman that she might lose her husband to some "hussy." I mean, *ouch*. After all, we didn't really know everybody's story in Yada Yada when it came to men. Who had fathered Chanda's three kids? Had Adele ever been married? Ruth was on number three! Even Avis's love life was still a mystery.

Not that I was worried about Denny.

Avis was the last to leave, cradling her empty pan. "You two need any more help cleaning up?"

"Nah. We'll just let Willie Wonka lick the rest of the dishes." Denny's smirk lasted only a brief second. "But seriously . . . what happened in there? Ben heard his wife wailing, and I practically had to tackle him to keep him from ripping in there."

Avis leaned back against the porch railing and nodded at me to go ahead. Briefly I tried to tell Denny how Florida's search for her missing daughter had stirred up a lot of painful memories for Ruth, who'd been a foster parent wanting to adopt, but the child had been taken away from her. "When Stu showed up and said that Carla had been found—"

"*Found!*" Denny's jaw dropped. "Florida's daughter has been found? Why didn't you say something?"

Avis shook her head. "Sorry. We couldn't. The kids came back, and Florida didn't want to get Chris and Cedric's hopes up before she could check it out. And since it's a holiday weekend, she's going to have to wait till Tuesday."

"Whew." Denny sank down onto the top step. "That's huge.

But what about Florida and Ruth? I can only imagine . . . *sheesh."*

I hadn't even had time to process for myself what had happened in my living room. Part of me wanted to just *think* about it for a while before trying to explain it. But Avis was studying a jet's contrail overhead, as though waiting for me to respond.

"Well, yeah. They both felt pretty raw . . . but Avis kept us from making it a 'foster care issue' and focused on what Ruth and Florida both needed in the painful situations they're in."

Avis shook her head. "Not me. That was God, no doubt about it. If I'd stopped to think about it, I would have hightailed it before putting myself between two she-bears with their fur up!"

Okay, so God deserved the credit. But I'd been awed by the simple truth Avis had spoken into the group, diffusing Florida's pointed challenge *("Does that make us enemies, Ruth?")* and enabling the rest of us to love both of them.

We had cried and prayed and hugged each of them and prayed some more. But the best moment for me was when Ruth reached out her hand to Florida and said, *"The wall I put between us . . . I am sorry. Can you forgive?"* And Florida, hesitating only a moment, had said, *"Guess I'd be poundin' new nails into the cross if I didn't forgive you, after all the forgivin' God's had to do for this sinner."* And she'd taken Ruth's hand and pulled her into an embrace.

We *really* had started having church then, but a few minutes later the kids arrived back from the lakefront, barging through the front door—all nine of them—and then standing in the doorway gawking at their mothers praising and crying and praying. Chanda had gotten so excited she'd started jumping up and down.

I'd reluctantly peeled myself away from the "party" and shooed the younger set toward the kitchen, where I let them dig into Stu's lemon bars and told them to hustle out to the backyard. When Avis closed out Yada Yada ten minutes later and we drifted toward the back of the house, the lemon bars were gone. Only crumbs.

Didn't matter though. We'd been having a feast.

EVEN AVIS WAS GONE NOW. We let Josh drive Amanda to youth group at church, and Denny bagged the last of the trash while I put away leftovers and filled the dishwasher.

"So, did I overhear Yada Yada deciding to get together regularly after this?" Denny asked, lugging a bulging plastic trash bag through the kitchen, followed by an ever-hopeful Willie Wonka, who so far had not gotten to lick any dishes.

"Uh-huh. Chanda complained that not everybody got to share stuff for prayer today, so couldn't we meet again real soon? Several folks work on Saturday, so we're going to try every two weeks on Sunday—like five to seven. Might visit each other's churches now and then, too." I noticed Denny's puckered lips. "What? Will the car be a problem?"

His lips unpuckered. "Nope. Gotta get the kids to youth group but . . . okay, I kinda hate to give you up Sunday evenings when the kids are gone. Especially now that summer's just around the corner. That's been our special time, walking to the lake, stopping for coffee . . . you know. But if it's just every other week . . ." He shrugged. "Guess I can deal with it."

I followed him out the screen door as he headed for the trash can in the alley. I probably should have talked it over with Denny first before agreeing to meet with Yada Yada on a regular basis. But I'd been so glad the others wanted to, I hadn't even thought about it. I think everybody realized we couldn't "yada yada" in *either* sense—"becoming known" or "giving thanks to God by praising"—unless we actually met face to face.

"Bring that recycling bin, will ya?" Denny called back over his shoulder.

I bent down to pick up the blue recycling bin on the back porch, overflowing with empty liters of pop and tin cans . . . and two brown bottles. Beer bottles. So my eyes hadn't been fooling me when I'd looked out the screen door. I looked after Denny, who had disappeared behind the garage. Should I—?

I felt torn. I didn't really want to get into a fuss with Denny after such an amazing afternoon. On the other hand, I couldn't just ignore it, could I? There they were, sitting right in the recycle bin. And I had specifically *told* Denny I didn't want any beer at this party.

I picked up the blue bin. We met on the sidewalk as he came back toward the house. I stood in the way.

"Denny? I thought we had an understanding—no beer at this party. *Especially* at this party." I held out the recycling bin.

Denny puckered his lips again and looked aside, as though studying our neighbors' fence. For a moment I thought he wasn't going to answer. But he turned back, his gray eyes flickering with ill-concealed impatience. "Jodi, I will tell you exactly what happened. But I'm getting tired of you questioning me like I'm a sneaky teenager." He took the recycling bin and walked it out through the back gate, then came back empty-handed.

"Ben Garfield came to this party. Remember Ben? Short Jewish guy who likes his beer."

I felt annoyed at his smart-aleck tone but kept my mouth shut.

"Mark and Ben and I are making small talk in the backyard while you and . . . and your Yada Yada thing"—he waved his hand in little circles toward the house—"go inside and do your stuff. And Ben asks, 'Say, Denny. Got any beer?' Just like that. And as it happens, I *do* have some beer. It's sitting out in the garage where my wife hid it. I didn't bring it up, I didn't put it out, but the guy asked for it. So what was I supposed to do, Jodi?"

This time I was the one who studied the neighbors' fence.

Denny shrugged. "So I told him, yeah, but it's not cold. Thought that might be the end of it, but Ben says, 'Stick a couple in the ice chest, will ya?' So I went to the garage, got a couple of beers, and stuck them in the ice chest. For Ben, Jodi."

Okay, so it wasn't Denny's idea. I should have dropped it right there. But I still felt betrayed. "What about Mark?"

"What about Mark?"

"What's Mark going to think? You didn't offer him one, did you?" My voice was rising and my temperature, too, imagining Mark telling Nony on the way home that Jodi's husband kept a stash of beer in the garage. "What about the kids? Did they see you drinking?"

Denny's eyes darkened, and he put his hands on his hips. "Last question, Jodi. *Ben* offered Mark one of the beers and Mark said, 'No thanks.' Simple as that. And yes, Ben was still drinking the second beer when all the kids came back. Nobody blinked an eye. Now . . . are we done here?"

No, I thought, *we're not done here. This wouldn't even be an issue if you hadn't bought those six-packs in the first place.* But Denny had already gone back into the house.

WHAT SHOULD HAVE BEEN a pleasant, peaceful Sunday evening after successfully pulling off Florida's sobriety party turned instead into Denny and me giving each other the silent treatment. I felt discouraged, like walking on a treadmill and getting nowhere. We had to talk about this sometime. What was with Denny, anyway? Why couldn't we talk about it without him getting all huffy? Or maybe I was the one who got huffy. But he *knew* this was a sore point for me. My parents would think we were on the road to perdition if they ever knew we had beer in the house with their grandchildren.

With Denny nursing his anger in front of the living room TV, I cast about for something to keep me busy. I supposed I *could* get a head start on those annoying construction-paper flowers to decorate my classroom for Parents Day . . . or make some baked beans for the picnic we'd been invited to tomorrow afternoon by some Uptown families who were barbecuing at Lighthouse Beach. But I didn't feel like it. Tomorrow was soon enough.

Ah. I spied the overflowing hamper in the bathroom. Hadn't touched the laundry all weekend. The perfect mindless task. Maybe I'd even do the kids' laundry—they deserved *something* for being such great party hosts for the Yada Yada kids all afternoon.

Dragging the laundry baskets from each bedroom into the dining room, I started sorting, wishing I was sorting wood and metal so I could drown out the canned TV laughter from some dumb "reality show" in the front room. I threw dark wash-and-wear into one pile *(bam! bam!* they'd go) . . . light-colored stuff into another *(crash!)* . . . bras, slips, and blouses into a cold-water pile *(bang!)*. . . jeans with sweats *(boom!)*—

Okay, I was angry. But the afternoon felt spoiled, like the yellowed underarms of my favorite white T-shirt. I tossed it in the pile of light stuff. There were other things I'd really wanted to tell Denny about what had happened that afternoon, like discovering that Florida and I had run into each other (almost literally!) twelve years ago. That still boggled my mind. *Couldn't* be just a coincidence . . . could it? I mean, not if I truly believed God was in charge of all our comings and goings. So what did it mean, that Florida had come back into my life, a totally changed person?

I tossed a pair of Josh's sweatpants onto the pile of jeans then picked them back up to remove a paper sticking out of one of the pockets. Why couldn't he remember to empty his pockets before he threw his clothes in the laundry? How many times had we had to tape dollar bills together or iron school papers—or worse, ruined a whole load with a renegade ballpoint pen?

I yanked the folded paper from the pocket and unfolded it.

Stylized yellow butterflies rode a swirl of brilliant colors from top to bottom, advertising something about a "Teen Rave." What in the world was a teen rave? Sitting down on the floor in the middle of the piles of laundry, I studied the copy separated by the lemon yellow butterflies. "Teen Club! . . . Dance! . . . Alcohol Free! . . . No One Over 17 Admitted! . . . Fun! . . . Teens Only! . . . Rockin'! . . ."

I looked at the sweatpants. Josh had been wearing those sweats when he and the other kids went to the lake this afternoon. Did he actually think we'd let him go to a teen dance club? "Alcohol free" sounded good, but "No one *over* 17 admitted"? What—no chaperones? Red flags went up all over the place with *that* little tidbit. Where did he pick this up, anyway?

Stomping feet on the back porch brought Willie Wonka's nails clicking down the hallway from the living room toward the back door. Couldn't have heard it—must have felt the floor shaking. The dog paused, confused by the piles of laundry between him and his goal, then he executed a few awkward leaps and met Josh and Amanda at the back door.

28

"onka!" Amanda draped herself all over the chocolate Lab, just like she'd been doing ever since she was a three-year-old.

"Hey, Mom." Josh paused at the doorway between kitchen and dining room. "Doing laundry? On Sunday?"

I waved the flyer at him. "What's this?" I pasted on a smile.

"Oh. That." Josh shrugged and started to pick his way through the piles of clothes on the floor. "Just something Pete gave me."

"Pete?"

He sighed patiently. "Pete Spencer—Yo-Yo's brother."

"Yeah," Amanda butted in, holding one end of Willie Wonka's old knotted play sock and pulling him into the dining room, his teeth clamped on the other end. "Pete asked Josh and me to go to this teen dance club thing next weekend. He said it's really fun . . . no alcohol allowed . . . a place high school kids can go to have fun."

My anxiety level pushed up into the orange zone. Amanda had been invited, too? She was only fourteen!

"Josh, hold it." My son was about to disappear down the hall toward his bedroom. "It says 'No one over seventeen allowed.' That means there's no adult supervision."

Josh actually rolled his eyes at me. "No, Mother. The club owners are adults—gotta be, right? They *say* that so the place won't be crashed by college kids and party types." He looked down on me from his five feet eleven. "I thought you'd want us to go."

"*Want* you to! Why?"

"Because it's Pete asking us to go."

"But you hardly know Pete! And he's had a very rough life—his mom's an addict, his sister was in jail. I mean, kids like that easily get caught up in smoking or drinking or doing drugs, and I don't want—"

"Mom." Josh's voice took on a weary tone, as though explaining something to a child. "This Yada Yada thing today? They were *your* friends. You acted like you wanted us to be friends with their kids, right? So . . . we're just trying to be friends." He threw up his hands, turned, and disappeared into his room. At that moment he looked just like his father.

"Yeah, Mom," Amanda echoed. "Besides, Florida smokes and she's *your* friend. She was smoking right here."

"What do you mean?" Of course I knew Florida smoked, but I hadn't noticed her "dipping out for a cig" today.

"Out front—you know, when we were all eating in the back. Yo-Yo too."

Oh, great. Just great. I wanted to be friends with these women in Yada Yada. I really did. But I hadn't counted on what kinds of things my kids might pick up from the lifestyles of such a diverse group.

"Well, you're right," I said. "But those are habits they picked up before—" But Amanda and Willie Wonka were already tussling their way down the hall toward the living room.

Grrr. Why did I keep ending up on the losing end of arguments in this house? But I still felt uneasy about that flyer. I needed to talk with Denny . . . when we were talking again, that is.

I tossed the flyer on the dining room table and took the first load down to the basement. At least the washing machine was free. In fact, I hadn't seen our upstairs neighbors all weekend. Maybe they'd gone out of town for the holiday. I kinda wished they'd seen our multicultural backyard party today . . . maybe they wouldn't be so standoffish.

Upstairs I heard the phone ringing, then Amanda's voice a moment later. "Mo-om! It's for you!" I hustled up the basement stairs and picked up the kitchen extension.

"This is Jodi."

"Sista Jodee?" The Jamaican accent on the other end could be only one person.

"Oh!" I tried not to sound surprised. "Hi, Chanda."

"Sista Jodee?" The voice on the other end hesitated.

What did she want? Did she leave something at my house this afternoon? "I'm here, Chanda. What is it?" I heard a snuffling noise, like she might be crying.

"Sista Jodee, I got somethin' for Yada Yada to pray about, but

. . . I don't have a computer. Could you send it to other people by e-mail? I can't wait till our next meeting."

Couldn't help feeling good that Chanda had called *me*. "Sure, Chanda. I'll get a pencil . . . okay, go ahead."

Again I waited through some snuffling. When she did speak her voice was so quiet I missed what she said. "Try again, Chanda. I can barely hear you," I said, plugging my other ear.

"I . . . found a lump in my breast," she whispered from the other end. "I'm so scared, Sista Jodee. My mother, she died from breast cancer. What if . . . what if I got it too?"

I FELT OVERWHELMED by Chanda's phone call. No wonder she'd acted like a scared rabbit when she first got here today . . . and no wonder she'd been so eager to have Yada Yada meet again. Without being able to get in on the e-mail loop, she was pretty isolated from the prayer group except for one-on-one phone calls. And who did she know well enough in the group to just call and talk? Adele? Maybe, maybe not.

The TV was still going in the living room. Sounded like the whole family was in there now, laughing at some show. I was tempted to join them, to just let everything be *okay*. I even took a few steps in that direction, and then stopped. I did promise Chanda I'd send her prayer request on the e-loop. And—I groaned—I still had all this laundry to do.

I was still sitting at the computer when I heard the TV go off and a noisy threesome tromping down the hall. "'Night, Amanda! 'Night, Josh!" I called.

"'Night, Mom," they called back, disappearing into their caves—though I knew good and well they'd stay up late listening to music or reading or talking on the phone, because they could sleep in tomorrow. The teenage version of Memorial Day.

I sensed Denny standing in the hallway behind me, watching my back. Half-turning my head I said, "Denny?"

"Yeah?"

I turned and faced him. He looked so boyish standing there in his jeans, hands in his pockets. I knew he hated the distance that came between us when we quarreled, hated it as much as I did. "I . . . wanted to say thanks for everything you did today to help pull off Florida's party. Grilling, cleaning up . . . but mostly just liking my friends and showing it."

Denny hunched his shoulders and propped himself against the open archway between dining room and hallway. "Don't know if Nony said anything when you guys were meeting today, but sounds like she's putting a lot of pressure on Mark to emigrate to South Africa. But from what Mark says, it just ain't gonna happen. No way does he want to raise his sons in Africa."

"No . . . she didn't say anything today. But I'm not surprised." This wasn't what I wanted to talk about.

"I'd still like to hear more about how Stu 'found' Carla. What in the heck does that mean?"

"Sure." I drew a breath. "Wanna talk now?"

He peered at me for a long moment. He knew good and well

what I really wanted to talk about. "Tell you what . . . we both got a day off tomorrow. We'll talk then, okay?"

I tried not to let my disappointment show. But he was probably right—tomorrow would be better. We were both tired now. "I've got to spend some time at school getting ready for Parents Day this week," I reminded him. "And we're meeting the Whittakers and the Browns at Lighthouse Beach around four for a picnic."

"We'll make time," he promised. "Coming to bed?"

"Yeah. Give me a minute."

I turned back to the computer and stared at the e-mail message on the screen I'd been writing . . .

To: Yada Yada
From: BaxterBears@wahoo.com
Subject: Prayer Request from Chanda

It was GREAT to see everybody this afternoon. (We missed you, Hoshi!) What a fantastic way to celebrate Florida's five years of sobriety!

Chanda called this evening with a prayer request: She discovered a lump in her breast (last week?) and is really scared. Her mother died of breast cancer. She really wants our prayers. Don't think she's seen a doctor yet. She could use lots of encouragement.

Florida and Stu, please keep us up to date on what happens next, now that Carla is found. (Like Avis said, what an answer to prayer! I'm still praising the Lord!) We still need to pray, right?

Just a reminder to mark your calendars for two weeks from today. Adele said we could meet at her house that Sunday, five o'clock.

I'd been kinda surprised when Adele volunteered to host the next get-together of Yada Yada. 'Course we weren't going to do a party—just prayer. Still, I hadn't expected Adele to be the first volunteer.

I moved my cursor to "send," then hesitated. ". . . *still praising the Lord"?* Hardly. I mean, yeah, *theoretically* I was still praising the Lord that Carla had been found. But I hadn't been doing any *actual* praising since Avis had said the last "Amen." And *"We still need to pray, right?"* Right. I seemed to recall promising God that morning that I'd "make it up to Him" when I hit the floor running with everything I had to do to get ready for church and Florida's party. But somehow it was easier to *talk* about praying for all these requests than actually *praying*.

I deleted the "still praising the Lord" phrase, hit "send," and shut down the computer.

I'd pray tomorrow. I really would.

29

*D*enny and I finally talked. Not exactly sure we came out at the same place, but at least we talked. I woke up early enough on Memorial Day to get some quiet time in the living room with my coffee, Willie Wonka, and Jesus. That was a good start. For a while I just soaked up the pleasure of not having to rush out of the house on a Monday morning and let myself fantasize about the day school would be out. Frankly, I could hardly wait. My first year teaching in a Chicago public school was hardly the high point of my teaching career—even with a good principal like Avis. Part of me longed for the third grade class I'd taught in Downers Grove, where everybody spoke standard English, and I only had to deal with thirty different personalities, not thirty different cultures.

I wasn't sure I was ever going to "get it." Frankly, I dreaded starting over again next fall with an entirely new class. A lot of the kids were sweet, but it only took one eight-year-old thug-in-the-making to ruin it for everyone, including me.

But I prayed. Prayed for Chanda and the fear she was dealing with, and that she'd suck up the courage to get to a doctor. Prayed for Ruth, for the loss of the little girl she'd hoped to adopt but instead lost forever. Prayed for Florida, that she could be reunited with Carla as soon as possible. Prayed for Carla, who hadn't seen her mommy in five years. *(Five years . . . I couldn't even imagine not seeing Amanda for five years.)* I even prayed for the foster family who would have to give her up.

And I prayed for Denny and me, that we could get over this little hump. *I mean, Jesus, we've been married almost twenty years— twenty good years—and we have learned to work out a lot of differences. How come we're suddenly tripping over this?*

I spent several hours at school, along with quite a few other teachers taking advantage of the holiday to decorate our classrooms, and felt pretty ready for the Parents Day coming up on Friday . . . providing Kevin kept his pencil to himself and didn't vandalize anybody's work, or we didn't have a bomb threat or something.

Denny and Josh were over at Touhy Park shooting baskets when I got home, and by the time they got home and showered, it was time to pack up the bratwurst, buns, charcoal, lighter fluid, and the hot beans I'd left baking in the oven and head for Lighthouse Beach.

So it was almost eight o'clock that evening before Denny and I had a chance to take a walk, leaving Amanda and Josh, over their protests about "homework," to clean up the picnic stuff. We walked hand in hand down Lunt Avenue toward Sheridan Road and ended up at Panini Panini sidewalk café, where we ordered iced coffee— decaf.

I told Denny everything Stu had told us about tracking down a foster child they thought was Carla. "That's gotta be tough," he said, twisting his iced coffee around and around on the round glass tabletop. "Tough for the family who's been taking care of her for five years, tough for Carla, tough for Florida who's been working so hard to put her life together again."

I pulled out the flyer Yo-Yo's brother had given to Josh and Amanda. "What do you think of this?" I asked, not wanting to wave all my red flags yet, since I didn't really have much ground to stick them in.

He gave it a good once over. "Hmm. I don't think so—not till we know a lot more about what goes on at these teen raves. So for this coming Saturday, anyway, it's out."

I gaped at him in happy relief. How did Denny do that? Yes or no—bam, that's it. Well, I'd let *him* tell Josh and Amanda.

We were silent for a while, slurping our iced coffees till we were sucking air at the bottom. After getting Denny's agreement on the teen rave thing, I hated bringing up a sore point. Maybe, like he said, I was making too big a deal over the whole thing. And I *could* take responsibility for jumping all over him.

I set down my plastic cup. "Denny? About yesterday . . . I really do see that you felt caught in the middle between Ben Garfield and me about the beer. And I'm sorry that I made it such a big issue . . ."

He tore his eyes away from the assorted species of humanity walking by the sidewalk café in everything from sloppy sandals to combat boots. "Okay, thanks. I appreciate your saying that."

"But I'm still confused about why you bought all that beer in the first place."

A finger tapped impatiently. "I thought we went over that."

"I know, but . . . " I'd thought of another point in my favor. "I mean, after your dad's heart attack last year, doesn't it make sense not to drink at all? I mean, that stuff tends to run in families."

He shrugged slightly. "Actually, there are a lot of studies that say a moderate amount of alcohol is good for your heart."

"But . . ." Frustration began to lick at the edges of our conversation. "It's not just that. We've got teenagers who are very impressionable. And what if we offend some of our new friends who got saved out of all sorts of addictions?"

He seemed to be studying my face. "That's really it, isn't it? It would embarrass you if your new friends saw a bottle of wine or some beer at our house."

"No! I . . ." I stopped. *Be honest, Jodi.* "Okay, yeah. I . . . I just don't want anybody to be offended, or think—"

"—or think your husband's a lush." Denny looked at me hard. Then, to my surprise, he leaned forward and took my hands. "Jodi. We've been married almost twenty years. Have I *ever* gotten drunk? Or abused alcohol in any way?"

I looked down at our entwined hands. "No, but . . ." Why couldn't he just not do it because I didn't want him to?

We sat in silence for a few moments as twilight settled over the city and the streetlights came on. The evening was warm and, if anything, the cars and foot traffic going up and down Sheridan Road grew thicker, like the ants that had found our picnic that afternoon.

Denny sighed. "Look, Jodi. It really bugs me the way you've been jumping all over me. Like you don't trust me. And I don't think I've given you any reason to do that. But let's call a truce. I won't stuff the refrigerator with beer, and I promise to be very circumspect when it comes to your friends. And *you* promise to give me the benefit of the doubt, okay? Romans fourteen, remember?"

I nodded grudgingly. Pastor Clark had given a good teaching last month from the fourteenth chapter of Romans on "Christian freedom" in what we eat and drink, while also being careful not to be a stumbling block for others or cause them to sin. But surely that wasn't the *only* Scripture passage that might apply here.

"Okay, come on." Denny pulled me to my feet. "That waiter is giving us the evil eye. 'Vacate that table, you miserable penny pinchers, or order some actual food!'"

I laughed as he pulled me toward the intersection to cross with the light. "Oh, gosh, Denny, I forgot to tell you the most amazing thing. Remember that time I picked up a panhandler—eons ago —and you got mad at me for being so naive?"

THE NEXT TWO WEEKS seemed to pile up on each other, like a rug runner that kept bunching up instead of lying flat. Parents Day was a success, more or less, though for the life of me I couldn't figure out why a third of my parents didn't even show. But now that June was here, the school day consisted mostly of corralling thirty young prisoners who had suddenly smelled freedom. "Get back in your seat!" "No, you went to the bathroom ten minutes ago." "Because I said so, that's why." "No punching!" The worst part was enduring the sullen looks of my young charges who acted like I had denied them parole.

If I had my way, it'd be against the law to have school after Memorial Day. But so far the Chicago School Board hadn't asked my opinion.

Josh and Amanda got several calls from church members for the Saturday teen workdays—washing windows, childcare, painting a stairwell—so they actually had an excuse when Pete called to ask if they were coming to the teen rave. I wondered if Yo-Yo had given permission for him to go. On the other hand, she worked at the deli Saturday nights. Maybe she didn't know.

Stu came to church on Sunday, but she said the earliest appointment Florida could get with DCFS was next week. Personally, I'd hate to be the social worker who told Florida she had to wait. Probably was walking around with a blistered ear.

I checked up on Yada Yada e-mail when I could. Lots more chatting since we'd met face to face at Florida's party. Even Ruth sent an e-mail telling Chanda to get her behind to the doctor right now or she'd come over and take her herself. I hit "reply" and reminded Ruth that Chanda didn't *have* e-mail, and she'd have to use the phone to threaten her.

Had to laugh, though. If we weren't careful, Ruth would smother-mother the lot of us. But I was so glad God had steered Yada Yada through *that* minefield.

Hoshi was still anxious about her parents' visit . . . Ricardo Enriques still hadn't found a job—or Florida's husband, either, for that matter . . . Nony wanted Yada Yada to visit her church in Evanston—the Worship Center, or something like that—but said we could decide on a date when we got together at Adele's . . .

By the time the second Sunday of June rolled around, I was eager to see everybody in Yada Yada again—not to mention I could use some prayer-and-praise encouragement to make it through the last week of school. How did Avis keep her poise through all the ruckus? Teachers were harried, parents were complaining about grades, a fifth grader even had to go to the hospital because a class-mate shot her in the eye with a rubber band and a paper clip!

Adele's apartment was practically close enough to walk to—only about ten blocks from our house—but Denny said, no, he wanted me to take the car and not be walking alone on the streets, especially coming home. Things were good with Denny and me since our talk—at least the "beer discussion" seemed to have dissipated.

I called up Avis and asked if she'd like a ride—one less parking place to have to find. As I packed my Bible and notebook into my tote bag, I noticed I still had the old flyer about the teen rave stuck in there. I was about to throw it out, then left it on the off chance I'd get a minute to ask Yo-Yo what she knew about these raves, since I could almost bet the subject would come up again.

It wasn't easy finding a parking place near Adele's apartment building on a Sunday afternoon. In fact, Avis and I circled the block at least two times hoping someone would pull out and leave us a space. Finally pulled into a lot that said, "For customers only! All others will be towed!" and crossed our fingers. Only had to walk two blocks to get to Adele's building.

We arrived at 5:10, afraid we were late. But Avis and I were actually the first ones. I sipped the glass of lemonade Adele pushed into my hand, and Avis admired Adele's collection of "All God's Children" figurines, while the others straggled in over the next thirty minutes. Couldn't really blame them—most had farther to come, and some, like Florida, didn't even have a car.

Adele's first-floor apartment seemed dark, and I realized all the blinds were pulled, even though it was still daylight. I had the urge to run from room to room, pulling up all the blinds and opening the windows, but I drowned the urge with more lemonade and joined Avis by the glass cabinet that held the cute collection of African-American figures. But finally everyone arrived who was coming, even Hoshi this time, who got a ride with Nony. Delores was on duty at the hospital, but Stu had picked up Edesa since she had to drive in on the Eisenhower Expressway from Oak Park anyway. I certainly hoped Stu's fancy silver Celica wouldn't be missing its hubcaps when we got done here today.

In my eagerness to give Florida a big hug, I knocked over the glass of lemonade I'd set on the floor, and it spilled all over my tote bag. "Better that than Adele's rug," Florida snickered under her breath, fishing out my Bible, notebook, keys, and wallet from the wet bag while I ran to find some paper towels in Adele's kitchen. When I came back to the living room, she was pulling out the now-soggy flyer.

"Hate to tell ya, Baxter," she teased, waving it around, "but you're over seventeen. If you're into Ecstasy, you'll have to get it at a forty-something rave."

I stopped, the wad of paper towels still in my hand. "What do you mean, Ecstasy?" Florida rolled her eyes. "Oh, girl, it's there right under your nose. Look." She shoved the flyer in front of my face. "See all those yellow butterflies? Yellow Butterfly—that's the street name for one kind of the Ecstasy drug. Red Camel . . . Boogie Nights . . . Cloud 9 . . . some others, too." She took the paper towels out of my hand and started to mop up the spilled lemonade. "You savin' that flyer for some reason?"

30

was so shaken by Florida's casual drop that street drugs were being advertised in the flyer Pete had given my kids that I sat in a stupor for the next ten minutes, only vaguely aware that Avis had gently prodded the group past yakking all at once to starting our prayer time with some Scripture. I couldn't believe I even *discussed* whether Josh and Amanda should go to that teen rave. *But how was I to know, God? Do I have to be a recovering junkie to be aware of what's going on out there?*

I glanced at Yo-Yo, who sat slouched in her usual position, feet straight out, hands stuffed in the pockets of her boxy overalls. Why did she keep coming to Yada Yada anyway? After all, she wasn't even a Christian . . . well, at least she wasn't sure about "this Jesus stuff." But did she approve of these teen rave things her brother was going to? She was his guardian, for heaven's sake!

"Jodi!" An elbow in my side and Florida's hiss got my attention. "You okay? You whiter than Whitey right now."

I glanced at her sidelong. "Yeah, I'm okay," I whispered back. Then I giggled. "Whiter than Whitey, huh?" and she started to laugh, too. "Could be my problem," I added.

Avis looked up from her Bible and peered at us over the top of her reading glasses. But we both put on straight faces so she continued reading. "Seek the Lord while he may be found; call on him while he is near. Let the wicked forsake his way and the evil man his thoughts. Let him turn to the Lord, and he will have mercy on him, and to our God, for he will freely pardon. 'For my thoughts are not your thoughts, neither are your ways my ways,' declares the Lord. 'As the heavens are higher than the earth, so are my ways higher than your ways and my thoughts than your thoughts.'" Avis closed her Bible. "From Isaiah, chapter fifty-five," she said.

"Can I see that?" Yo-Yo said, actually sitting up and peering at the Bible next to her in Ruth's lap. "You mean God might go away and not be able to be found?"

I carefully peeled apart some pages in my Bible still clinging together with lemonade. Isaiah 55 was one of my favorite passages: *"Come, all you who are thirsty, come to the waters; and you who have no money, come, buy and eat. . . ."*

"I think the main point of the chapter," I pitched in, "is that God *can* be found now. Look at all the invitations—'come' . . . 'come to me' . . . 'seek' . . . 'call on him' . . . 'turn to the Lord.'"

"And all the promises if we do," Nony added. "'Buy wine and milk without money' . . . 'eat what is good' . . . 'your soul will delight in the richest fare' . . . 'he has endowed you with splendor.'"

"Wait, wait." Yo-Yo leaned forward. "Talk plain English, will ya? I don't get all this water and wine and milk stuff."

"Those are just figures of speech," Avis explained, "meaning God wants to fill our lives with good things, like giving water to a thirsty person, or food to someone who's hungry."

"Oh, Lord. Ain't that the truth." Florida punched the air. "Thank ya, Jesus."

"So how do you get all that good stuff?" Yo-Yo wanted to know. "I mean, coming to God—is that like coming to this prayer group? Or going to church and listening to God-talk?"

I felt a twinge of conscience for my ricocheting thoughts just a few minutes ago, questioning why Yo-Yo was even coming to the prayer group. Her presence had been suddenly threatening to me because of her brothers, because they'd come to my home and brought their damnable flyer with them . . . but here she was, basically asking how to come to God!

"I talk; you don't listen." Ruth wagged her head. "I told you already, you must believe Jesus is the promised Messiah."

Edesa nodded. "And accept Him as your personal Savior."

"What's that song Donnie McClurkin sings?" Adele snapped her fingers and burst out Jamaican style, " 'Born, born, born again, yuh must be born again . . .' "

"Arrrgh!" Yo-Yo exploded. "There you go, using all those bozo buttons. You think people know what they mean, but *I don't get it.*"

I was intrigued. I'd grown up all my life with those "bozo buttons," as Yo-Yo called them. How did you break it down for someone like Yo-Yo who wasn't familiar with religious shorthand?

"It ain't that hard, girl," said Florida. "Remember Bob Dylan?—nah, you too young. But he had a song . . . 'Ya gotta serve somebody—might be the devil, might be the Lord, but ya gotta serve somebody'—or somethin' like that. Ya just gotta make a decision: Ya gonna sit on the fence? Or give your life to Jesus twenty-four seven—all day, every day. And if anybody asks ya what your religion is, you say, 'I'm a follower of Jesus Christ.'"

"Twenty-four seven?" Hoshi looked confused. "Is that what I should tell my parents when they come?"

"No, Hoshi." Avis tried to hide a smile. "Just tell them the last part—you're a follower of Jesus Christ."

"I get it." Yo-Yo sat back. "Okay. Let me think about that."

Avis nodded. "Do you have a Bible, Yo-Yo? I can give you some good scriptures to read."

"Nah. I tried reading the Bible. But it's too hard."

"Don't worry. We'll get you a modern translation—" She smiled at the face Yo-Yo made. "Sorry. A Bible in plain English."

"Okay."

"But Hoshi reminded us of one of the things we need to pray about—telling her parents that she has become 'a follower of Jesus Christ.' When are they coming, Hoshi?"

"First weeks August. Very short time."

"Any news about Carla . . . Florida? Stu?"

Both shook their heads. "Had me a meeting with DCFS last week," Florida said. "I think next time somebody needs to go with me so I don't lose my temper. Oh, girl, when they told me they were 'looking into it,' I let them have a piece of my mind. Ten, *twenty* pieces. Losing Carla's paperwork? Gimme a break! They better look into it *fast.*"

"I'm sorry, Florida," Stu said. "I'll try to go with you next time if I can."

"All right. We need to keep those prayers going." Avis glanced around the group. "Chanda, we've been praying for you since you put your prayer request on the e-loop. Any . . . news? Have you been to the doctor?"

Everybody looked at Chanda. As usual, she'd been sitting mute, her gray skirt and dark top blending into the dusky color of the room. Her hands started twisting the handkerchief she held in her lap. "Uh-huh, I did go, Friday . . . Ruth kept calling me up till I made an appointment at the St. Francis Clinic. But I don't got no insurance. Don't know how I'm going to pay for it—not 'less my numbers win."

Oh, brother. Not likely, I thought.

"The doctor, what did he say?" Ruth prodded.

"She. Doctor was a she, which helped some. She said it felt like a cyst thing. But she wants to stick a needle in it to make sure, and wants me to get one o' those mammogram things." Chanda's eyes filled, and her hands twisted the handkerchief tighter. "Oh God, I'm scared. Even if it's not . . . not . . . you know . . . I heard those mammogram machines flatten your breast like a pancake and it *hurts*. And I'm scared of needles. Even in my arm! But in my . . . in my . . .?"

"Oh, honey." Adele rolled her eyes. "You can do it. You a normal size. Now, me? They hardly know what to do with these things." She spread her arms and puffed out her large bosom. Thank goodness I wasn't the only one who laughed.

"The aspiration they do with the needle's not so bad." Avis chimed in gently. "Really. One of us will go with you to hold your hand."

"What do you mean, not so bad? How do you know, Sista Avis?" Chanda looked doubtful.

Avis was silent for a moment, as though she hadn't intended to go this far, and suddenly the group seemed to hold its collective breath. Then she said quietly, "Because I've been through the whole nine yards."

Chanda's eyes widened. "You had breast cancer? Did you . . . did they take . . . ?"

Involuntarily ten pairs of eyes strayed to Avis's chest. She always wore loose-fitting things—tunics, big stylish tops in bold prints. Did that mean—?

"Whoa! Slow down, everybody." Avis shook her head. "No, I did not have a mastectomy. I did have a lumpectomy, because I did have cancer—but they found it early. It hadn't spread anyplace else. But even that . . ." Avis's mouth twitched, almost smiled.

"What!" several people cried together. All of us had a morbid fascination with this conversation. Avis, of all people! She'd told us more about herself in the last sixty seconds than I'd figured out in the last ten months.

"It's nothing, just . . ." Avis's shoulders started to shake, and her smile grew bigger. Good grief, she was laughing.

"What?" a few more people begged.

"It's not funny," Chanda sniffed.

"No, no, it's not funny. I'm sorry, Chanda. It's just that . . ." Avis shook her head, still grinning at her private joke.

"You better tell us, Avis Johnson," Florida said, "or we all be thinkin' you crazy."

"Already thinkin' that," Adele muttered.

That was the truth. This wasn't like Avis at all.

"All right." Avis tried to control herself. "Like I said, I had a lumpectomy, and they only took about one-fourth of my breast. Which I'm grateful for, believe me. But . . . to be honest, when I looked in the mirror, I still felt deformed. And I was worried . . ." She blinked rapidly, as though fighting some lurking tears. " . . . worried my husband might think so, too. I didn't want him looking at me, afraid of what he was thinking about my body—even though he kept assuring me it made no difference to him."

So there is *a Mr. Avis! Or was.* I was dying of curiosity. Why hadn't she ever talked about him before?

"Of course I had to go for all these checkups, and the next time I had a mammogram, the technician put these two little black plastic dots on either side of the scar so it would show up in the x-ray picture. And when I looked down at my breast . . ." Avis's shoulders started to shake again as she tried to control her laughter. ". . . it seemed like this little old man with no teeth was looking back up at me—you know . . . the puckered scar, the two little black eyes, and this protruding dark nose . . ."

Florida laughed right out loud. "Oh, girl, I can just *see* it!" And by that time, all the rest of us were cracking up.

"What did you *do?*" Nony said, grinning as big as the rest of us.

"Well, I started laughing—laughing so hard I could hardly stop. And the technician, she looks at me like I'm crazy. So I told her—"

"You told her?" Adele sputtered. "You *was* crazy, girl."

"Yes, she did look at me funny—especially when I asked her if she would just leave the two little black dots so I could show my husband."

At this, we all howled.

"You didn't!" Chanda eyes popped.

Avis got out a tissue from her purse and wiped her eyes. "I did. When he got home from work, I made him sit down on the couch, and I unbuttoned my blouse—"

"You go, girl!" Adele shouted.

"—and showed him the little old man with no teeth . . ." She could hardly go on, she was laughing so hard. But finally she gasped, "And we had the best laugh we'd had in a *looong* time."

So did Yada Yada. It took us a good five minutes to pick ourselves up and resume some semblance of order. But when we did, Ruth bluntly asked the question that was burning in my mind and probably everyone else's.

"Your husband, where is he now?"

Avis took a long shuddering breath and was quiet for a moment or two. When she spoke her voice had dropped, and she spoke almost reverently. "That's the hard part. He died two years later . . . from cancer."

31

Whew. Finding out that Avis had had breast cancer and that her husband had died of cancer was *huge*. Who would have known, as serene as she always seemed and so ready to "give glory to God" in every situation? Her hilarious story about visualizing "the little man with no teeth" on her "deformed breast" seemed so out of character for Avis . . . and yet, maybe not.

"Laughing together was so healing for Conrad and me!" she told us. "In fact, it helped prepare us for what lay ahead when he was diagnosed with pancreatic cancer. They couldn't operate—the cancer was too far advanced by the time he was diagnosed. But God showed us that even in the midst of a crisis, we can look for His gifts of joy and peace." She shook her head, half-smiling at the memory. "He wouldn't let our daughters be all sad and gloomy around him, even at the end, when he was bedridden and in a lot of pain. He'd crack jokes and tease them . . . and I'm so grateful.

Their memories of their dad are happy ones right up to the end, even though they miss him terribly. I'm only sorry he never met his namesake . . . Conrad Johnson the third." She threw up a hand. "Don't get me started on the grandbabies! I think maybe it's time to pray for Chanda."

And pray we did, gathering around our sister who cleaned houses on the North Shore, praying with many voices for healing. As part of the prayer, both Avis and Nony read a whole litany of "healing scriptures," claiming God's promises for health and wholeness for Chanda. I certainly believed God could heal, but I wasn't always comfortable thanking God in advance, like we *knew* for sure that's what He was going to do. In fact, I felt a little confused; Avis's husband had died, hadn't he? It was a little easier for me to pray that Chanda would experience God's peace in the middle of the uncertainty and that she could trust that God loved her and was working out His purposes in her life.

While we were still praying, the door buzzer sounded. "Ain't time yet," I heard Adele mutter, but she padded silently in her slippers for the front door. Shrill voices from the stairway took shape as Adele opened the door.

"Don't know this place! Take me home!"

"MaDear, you *are* home. Here's Adele—see?"

"Adele who?"

We heard Adele's sharp voice. "Sassy, you wasn't s'posed to come till eight. I got company."

"I know, I know. But . . . had to bring her home. She . . . never mind. Talk later. But I gotta go now. 'Bye, MaDear. Don't be mad,

Adele. I'll call you." And footsteps retreated down the short flight leading out the front door of the apartment building.

The apartment door closed and Adele appeared back in her front room carrying a walker folded flat in one hand and dragging MaDear by the hand with her other. "Sit here," she commanded, lowering the elderly woman into the dining room chair she'd been sitting in earlier. "Shh, now. We're praying."

"Oh. Praying." Out of the corner of my eye I saw MaDear press her hands flat together in front of her sunken bosom and squeeze her eyes shut. "Yessuh, Jesus . . . thanks ya, Jesus . . . 'Alle-*lu*-jah . . . Yessuh, yessuh . . ."

Adele started to rejoin the group praying around Chanda, but Avis moved over to the little woman in the dining room chair and began to pray. The rest of the group followed her, several kneeling down in front of the chair, others taking MaDear's hands and holding them, and began to pray for Adele's mother as if she'd been there the whole time. MaDear's eyes opened and she looked from face to face, a smile beginning to soften the birdlike face.

"Adele? Adele? We having a party?" she said in her throaty voice.

"Sure we are, MaDear." Adele's own voice sounded husky.

Yada Yada prayed for MaDear for several minutes, then we drifted back to our places with the last few "Bless the Lords." Edesa opted for sitting on the floor with Yo-Yo so Adele could have her chair.

As the room quieted, Avis raised her eyebrows. "Anything else before we close out today?"

"What about you, Jodi?" Florida spoke up. "You always so busy keepin' everybody connected. What can we pray 'bout for you?"

Her question took me off guard. "Oh, well, I don't know . . . nothing really." That sounded lame, and I knew it.

"Maybe Jodi doesn't need our prayers." Adele's statement sounded more like a challenge.

"Of course I do," I tossed back. Where did she get off saying something like that? Every time I thought Adele and I were breaking ground, it felt like she broke the shovel over my head. "I *would* appreciate prayer for my kids . . . Josh and Amanda are going to Mexico on a mission trip the end of this month—a youth group thing. But I have to admit I'm anxious. All the terrorist threats . . . the turmoil in the Middle East . . . heightened security. It's not easy letting them go out of the country right now." *There*, I thought.

Avis nodded. "Of course. Anyone else?"

"Well, uh . . ." Yo-Yo scratched the back of her short, stand-up hair. "You all good at prayin', I know that. So maybe you can pray for me about this Jesus thing. You know, deciding to be a Jesus follower or however you said it, Florida."

Nony literally leaped out of her chair. "Halle*lu*jah!" she shouted. Adele's living room erupted with "Glory to God!" and "Praise Jesus!" Yo-Yo wanted to be a Christian! Now *that* was worth shouting about.

Yo-Yo stuck her hands in her pockets and hunched her shoulders till she could get a word in edgewise. "You guys finished? 'Cause it ain't like there's anything to shout about yet. I done some stuff . . . stuff I ain't proud of. What's God gonna say about that?"

I NEVER DID GET TO TALK TO YO-YO that evening about the teen rave flyer, but it seemed like a downer after the way we ended Yada Yada at Adele's apartment. I mentally made a note to call her sometime before we met again in two weeks, which Nony offered to host at her house in Evanston, just north of the city. "You're all invited to visit our church that Sunday, too, if you'd like," Nony had said. "Easy to find . . . the Worship Center on Dempster, just west of Dodge. Doesn't look like a church, though. We meet in a warehouse."

"Well, Jodi and Avis's church meets in a storefront," Edesa had joked. "Maybe you'll have to wait till Yada Yada comes to Iglesia del Espirito Santo to visit a *real* church."

Avis was ecstatic on the way home. "You know, it was really Yo-Yo who encouraged us to hang in there with each other after the conference—to keep praying for Delores and José, remember? And, thanks to you, you got us all connected by e-mail. Maybe she didn't know it, but it was God's plan all along for us to hang in there for Yo-Yo, too, don't you think?"

"Absolutely." I laughed. "Avis, I am so high, I don't even think the car tires are touching the ground."

"Here." She fished around in her big purse and pulled out a CD. "Stick that in your CD player." In a few moments the car was filled with a mixture of gospel and praise and worship music.

I pulled up in front of Avis's apartment building and spied a parking space not far away. It gave me an idea. "Avis, could I come up for a few minutes? I'd like to see a picture of your husband . . . if you don't mind. After the story you told tonight, I'd like to meet him because . . . that's part of you I didn't know about."

She hesitated just a millisecond. "Sure. Come on up."

I parked the car—thanking God for the mini-miracle of a parking space on the street at that time of evening—and followed Avis up to her second-floor apartment. It was . . . just like Avis. Elegant art prints on the walls, shiny wood floors—shoes off at the door, please—with bright-colored area rugs, beige-and-black furniture, bookcases filled with hardcover books, and silk flowers in curved opaque vases. Colorful translucent drapes were caught back from windows that boasted Venetian blinds, turned just so to let the light in and keep prying eyes from below out.

"It's beautiful, Avis," I breathed.

She walked over to a low bookcase, the top of which was covered with framed photographs, and picked up a five-by-seven silver frame. "This is Conrad."

The picture was actually Avis and Conrad, standing by the railing of a ship, his arm clutching her close. They were both wearing white slacks and marine blue shirts, setting off the rich deep color of their skin. Avis was laughing, holding on to a long headscarf that was blowing in the wind. Conrad was grinning at her, obviously thinking he was the luckiest man in the world.

"That was our twentieth anniversary," she said. "We took a cruise to the Caribbean. Our first and last." She pointed out the rest of the photographs. "Those are the three girls—Charette, Rochelle, and Natasha. Charette and Rochelle are married. This one is Charette's twins, Tabitha and Toby, last Christmas. And this . . ." She picked up a portrait of a toddler with loose black curls all over his head, grinning happily. ". . . is Conrad Johnson the third. Rochelle's baby. She gave the baby 'Johnson' as his middle name so he could carry his granddaddy's name."

"And Natasha?"

"She's in grad school at the University of Michigan. Comes home once in a blue moon."

I looked at the photo of Avis and Conrad on the cruise ship a long time, then finally set it down. "I wish I'd known him." I turned to her. "Why haven't you ever mentioned him before? He seems like a wonderful man."

Avis sat down on the love seat along the front windows, her gaze on the big elms lining the street. "Because . . . I miss him. It's not easy to talk about him. It's easier . . ." She hesitated. ". . . easier to just praise God for the good years we had, for giving him to me long enough to raise our girls." She turned away from the window. "But if you want to know the truth, Jodi, it's not easy to be around married couples. That's one reason I turned down your invitation to dinner, because I knew when I got home, I'd probably tear my hair out, I'd feel so lonely. I didn't mean to be rude, but . . ." She shrugged.

Avis . . . lonely? Tearing her hair out? I was trying to absorb this new picture of the calm, self-assured Avis Johnson, principal of Mary McLeod Bethune Elementary School, the praise and worship leader at Uptown Community Church, whose joy spilled over to the rest of us, helping us white folks worship, helping us be thankful.

"I'm so sorry, Avis. I didn't know." It was getting darker outside, and I really needed to get going. "How do you do it—keep going, I mean. You always seem so happy."

"I *am* happy. Really. As long as I keep my focus in the right place—right on Jesus and all the good things God has done for me. Or Satan rushes right in and makes me start feeling sorry for myself." She gave me a hug. "Thanks, Jodi . . . thanks for wanting to 'meet' Conrad. I think he'd like you, too."

THE DIGITAL CLOCK ON THE DASH glowed 8:13 as I turned on the ignition. Ohmigosh, I was supposed to pick up Josh and Amanda from youth group on my way home, and I totally forgot! I was sure they'd be home by now anyway, but just in case I drove down Morse Avenue past Uptown's storefront exterior . . . no lights.

Okay, so I blew it. We'd have to work out the Sunday night car thing on the nights Yada Yada wanted to meet. But I couldn't feel bad; the whole evening had been incredible. I reached over and turned up the volume on the CD player—and smiled. Avis had forgotten her CD.

I was halfway to the house from the garage before I noticed Denny sitting by himself on the back steps. "Hi! I'm home."

"Uh-huh. Heard you before I saw you."

"Heard me?—no, you didn't! The music wasn't that loud . . . was it?"

"Uh-huh. That loud." But he reached up and pulled me down on the step beside him. Twilight had settled over the neighborhood, smudging the row of garages along the alley into a gray base that sprouted a silhouette of treetops and power lines against the cobalt blue of the sky. Only then did I notice that he was balancing a bottle with one hand on his knee.

Well, what of it. We'd talked about it and called a truce. He'd asked me to trust him, and so I would.

"Um, sorry I'm late. Did the kids get home okay?"

"Yeah, they got a ride. But your name is mud."

"Oh dear." I sighed. "I better go apologize." I started to get up, but he pulled me back.

"Don't go. Not yet."

I waited, but he said nothing more. We sat in a circle of silence, hearing only the hum of traffic over on Sheridan Road and the muted squeal of an el train. I began to feel anxious; how long had Denny been sitting out here like this? I'd expected to find him in front of the TV watching baseball.

"Denny? Is something wrong?"

He took a big breath and let it out slowly. "The school board hasn't renewed my contract yet for next year."

"Hasn't . . . what does that mean?"

"Nothing yet. But they're talking budget cuts. And you know how it is: Last to come, first to go."

"Oh, Denny." I put my arm around his broad back and laid my head on his shoulder. "Oh, Denny . . . I'm so sorry." But for one brief second it tickled my fancy like good news. Maybe we'd move back to Downers Grove, pick up our life where'd we'd left off a year ago. Our old neighborhood, our old jobs, our old church . . .

But I knew that's not what Denny wanted. He'd had tenure at his job in Downers Grove, and he had taken the risk of moving into the city because he felt that's what God wanted him to do.

And Yada Yada . . . I suddenly realized I didn't want my old life. Not if it didn't include Yada Yada. Whatever my "destiny" was—as Evangelist Olivia Mitchell had put it—it had something to do with Yada Yada. We'd only been a prayer group for barely two months, and already it had been a roller coaster ride that left me breathless. Shaken up. Energized.

Wanting more.

32

But the idea of moving back to Downers Grove kept niggling at the edges of my thoughts, especially when I told Denny about the "yellow butterflies" on the flyer being a code for Ecstasy drugs at these teen raves. "I don't know, Denny," I said a couple of hours later as I turned back the handmade quilt covering our bed and crawled in. "This stuff scares me. Maybe we should have waited till the kids are out of high school and *then* moved to Rogers Park." My finger traced the circles of the "wedding ring" quilt my mother had made for us when we got married. Quilting . . . did anybody do that anymore? It seemed so quaint, so honorable, the stitches of a simpler life. Unfortunately, Amanda wouldn't get such a gift from my hands. Maybe I should give her this one . . .

Denny cut the bedside light and crawled in beside me, pulling me close, my head on his chest and our legs entwined. "Maybe. But we're fooling ourselves if we think our kids wouldn't face similar challenges out in the 'burbs. Drugs, sex, guns . . . they're everywhere. Remember Columbine? Safe town, safe school—or so everyone thought."

I shivered against the warmth of Denny's bare chest. I didn't want to think about Columbine. "What are we going to do, Denny?" I whispered into the dark. "About your job, I mean."

"Nothing yet. Pray, I guess. Hey—get Yada Yada praying. That ought to shake up the heavenlies."

FRANKLY, WE DIDN'T HAVE MUCH TIME to think *or* pray all that week, except on the run. Since it was the last week of school for all four of us, the kids had exams, Denny had to turn in phys ed grades and attend end-of-year award ceremonies for the different sports programs, and I had to give the bad news to three parents that their offspring would have to repeat third grade or get special tutoring this summer to bring their reading and math skills up to fourth-grade level. One parent did not take this well and accused me of everything from being a racist to committing "gross emotional abuse" for "letting" her child fail.

I wanted to go nose to nose with this outraged mother and tell her I would be more than happy to pass her child on to fourth grade because *I didn't want to have to suffer her kid in my class one more minute, much less another whole year!* But I didn't. She would, I said calmly, have to take up her complaints with Ms. Johnson.

On the last day of school, I used the money I'd collected from the Darn Lucky Box to buy Ho-Hos for my class, and gave back everybody's "lost" items who hadn't bothered—or been able—to redeem them with the requisite quarter.

When I got home, Amanda waved her report card under my nose. She'd passed Spanish! We celebrated by taking the kids out for pizza at Gullivers on Howard Street—Chicago pizza at its best, in our opinion. We might get an argument from friends who swore by Gino's or Giordano's or Carmen's . . . but let any visitor mention California pizza, or even New York pizza, and we united with one voice: *Any* Chicago pizzeria beat out the competition by a long shot.

Gullivers not only had great pizza, but it was practically a museum of Victorian chandeliers, antique wall mirrors, old paintings in ornamental frames, brass lamps in every shape and size, even marble busts and nymph-like maidens. The weather was nice enough that, we could have eaten in the inner courtyard, but we elected to sit in a booth, its thick wooden table polished dark and smooth by many arms and elbows. Denny slid in beside Amanda, and Josh beside me.

We had finished sharing the hot breadsticks and large Italian salad—"Ewww!" Amanda cried, throwing all the anchovies on Denny's plate—and had just started in on the large sausage pizza with mushrooms and black olives, when Denny brought up the yellow butterflies. "Did either of you know drugs would be available at that teen rave?"

Amanda's mouth fell open. "No! That's stupid! Why would they advertise it as 'alcohol free' and then sell drugs?"

"Good question," I muttered.

"Josh?"

Josh shook his head with a nonchalant shrug. "No . . . but I'm not really surprised."

"But you were actually thinking about going!" I protested.

"Hellooo. Mom, I see guys dealin' drugs all the time. If you want a guarantee that no drugs would show up *anywhere* I go, I'd have to join a monastery or somethin'."

I raised my eyebrows at Denny. *Say something!*

"Point taken," Denny said patiently. "But if kids get caught dealing drugs at school, they get busted. It's illegal. It's against the rules. The school works hard to keep drugs out. Even if it 'happens,' that *is* different from an event that blatantly sells drugs to teenagers. So, just to be clear: The answer is already 'no' to any party, social activity, or event that isn't supervised by responsible adults committed to a zero-tolerance policy when it comes to alcohol and drugs for underage kids."

"That wouldn't keep me from getting drugs if I wanted to." Josh tilted his chin defiantly.

I nearly choked on my pizza.

"*Chill*, Mom. I'm not going to pop some stupid Ecstasy pill or start doin' drugs. That's just my point. You guys sound like you don't trust us. It's my own *decision* that keeps me from messin' with drugs—not your rules."

I just stared at Josh, then at Denny, then at the pizza crust on my plate. I did trust my kids . . . didn't I? But I didn't trust the world "out there." They were still *kids*, after all!

"We do trust you, Josh." Denny's tone was gentle. "Amanda, too. We're proud of you both. But we're your parents, and we have a responsibility to put guidelines on what we feel is appropriate or not appropriate. At the same time, you're absolutely right. We can't protect you from everything—especially at your age, Josh. You're almost an adult, and bottom line? It is the decisions *you* make, the ones that come from within, that determine the way you will go."

Well, okay. That's a good speech from someone who was Mr. Party Animal in college. "Sometimes people make the wrong decisions." I kept my eyes on my plate, moving a piece of sausage around with my fork. "And some decisions have terrible consequences."

From the corner of my eye, I could tell Denny had leveled his gaze across the table at me. "Yes, people do make mistakes, Jodi. But sometimes that's part of the learning process."

Amanda sucked out the last of her soda. "Dad, can we get another pitcher of root beer? And about the party stuff . . . does that mean you don't want us to be friends with Pete and Jerry?"

"Yes, root beer . . . and yes, friends. But how about on your terms? Like inviting them to some of the youth activities at Uptown. Or a day at Great America or something."

Had to hand it to Denny. Frankly, I'd been thinking, *Friends? You gotta be kidding!* But that was a good idea, a Jesus idea, inviting Yo-Yo's brothers to stuff . . . maybe Chris Hickman, too, Florida's oldest. I didn't get the impression that Florida had found a regular church yet.

I just hoped my kids wouldn't get rebuffed like I had when I gave Nony that camp brochure.

JOSH AND AMANDA had another full day Saturday doing work projects to raise money for the mission trip. Hmm. We might have to pay our own kids to get the Baxter windows washed this year. But while they were gone, I decided to give Yo-Yo a call and just be straight up about the reen rave flyer—parent to parent. Besides, I'd been meaning to tell her she could borrow one of my modern English Bibles—or I'd give it to her, for that matter.

Yo-Yo picked up on the second ring. "Yeah?"

"Yo-Yo? It's me, Jodi."

"Oh, hey, Jodi. Whassup?"

I told her I had a "plain English" Bible she could have. "Okay. That's cool. Thanks, Jodi."

"Um . . . Yo-Yo?" Why was I such a big chicken about this? "Have you seen those flyers about teen raves—just for teenagers seventeen and under?"

"Yeah. I've seen 'em around."

"Did you know Pete gave one to Josh and Amanda and invited them to come?"

"*Pete* did?" The string of swear words that followed took me aback.

"I'm sure he was just trying to be friendly," I hastened to say. "But Florida clued us in on the yellow butterflies—"

"Jesus!"

I hesitated. I was pretty sure she wasn't calling on Jesus.

"Look, Yo-Yo, I'm not trying to get Pete in trouble or anything. We didn't let our kids go. Maybe Pete didn't go, either; I don't really know. Just wondered if you knew about it, and since both our kids—well, our kids and your brother—were talking about it, just wanted to compare notes, see what you think."

"He's busted; that's what I think." She expelled a long sigh. "But I gotta work evenings . . . it's hard keepin' an eye on what he's doin', 'specially Saturday night."

"Yeah, I know. We all gotta pray for our kids."

Yo-Yo laughed. "Guess I gotta get on the main line now, huh? Like all the rest o' you. Hey . . . you gonna visit Nony's church next week? Ruth and me was thinkin' of comin'—if I can get off Sunday. I'm tryin' to change my day off, but they ain't too happy about it."

As I hung up, I noticed my manicure was looking a little worse for wear. Rats. Guess there was no way it'd last long enough for the visit to Nony's church.

33

Only two weeks till the Uptown Community youth group left on their trip to Mexico, building houses with Habitat for Humanity. But now that school was out, we all slowed down in the Baxter household. Denny had been hired to coach some of the summer park leagues—not much money, but it helped, and he liked coaching the younger kids. Amanda had gotten hired as a "mother's helper" half-days for an Uptown mom who worked at home, so she was raking in the money big time. Josh wasn't so lucky. The ten-day mission trip made it difficult to pick up a summer job, so Denny put him to work painting the garage.

As for me, I had a list of "projects" as long as my arm that I wanted to do this summer. And for another thing, I'd promised God I'd be more faithful having a "quiet time" in the morning, to read my Bible and pray. But during my first "quiet time" of the summer, it occurred to me that that was an odd phrase. "Quiet time." That's what they called it at church camp when I was a kid, what every pastor or teen group leader or Bible study I'd ever been part of had called it—that, or "personal devotions."

No wonder I had never included out-loud praises to God in my devotions, or turned up the music and danced.

Denny and I had decided not to say anything to the kids about his job contract—not until we knew something for certain. So I hesitated to put that prayer request out on the e-loop, where Josh or Amanda might see it if any of the Yada Yada sisters commented on it by reply mail. We were meeting in less than a week anyway; I'd wait till then.

I checked e-mail from time to time but guessed the others in Yada Yada were like me. Now that we knew we were going to meet on a semiregular basis, fewer requests showed up on the e-list. But Chanda called me late in the week. She had an appointment for a mammogram the following Tuesday, and would I go with her? "Avis promised somebody would go with me," she pouted, "but everybody I've called so far got to work, and Avis doesn't return my calls. You done with school, though, right?"

I knew for a fact that Avis had gone to visit her grandkids this week, but she said she'd be back in time for Yada Yada on Sunday. But . . . this shouldn't have to fall on Avis's shoulders. "Sure, I could do that. Do you want me to pick you up?"

"That'd be great, Sista Jodee. That way I could take the babies. Didn't know where I was goin' to find a babysitter for them, anyway."

I smacked my forehead as I hung up. Taking care of Chanda's "babies" was the last thing I wanted to do after so recently shedding myself of my thirty third-graders. *Calm down, Jodi. It's only a couple of hours. Just pack a bag of goodies, and you'll be fine.*

But Chanda's call reminded me that I hadn't heard anything from either Stu or Florida about what was happening in Carla's case, so finally I just picked up the phone.

"Girl, them people got so much red tape, I could plaster my walls with it," Florida steamed. "I gotta fill out half a zillion forms, take a drop, get a home visit . . . don't seem like no end to it."

I murmured something sympathetic, but frankly, I felt at a loss.

"Jodi . . . I *am* gonna get my girl back, ain't I?"

She was looking for reassurance from me? I wished Avis wasn't out of town, or that I could get Nony in on a conference call. But it was just me—me and whatever faith I could muster. Reaching deep, past my gutless human skepticism, I reached for the promises I *said* I believed.

"We gotta believe it, Florida. What's that thing you're always saying? God didn't bring you this far to leave you, right? Jesus said it only takes two to agree on something and 'it will be done for them by My Father in heaven.' And we're *all* standing together with you on this one."

"Where's it say that, Jodi?"

Oh, Lord. I knew lots of Scripture verses, just couldn't remember where to find them on demand. "I'll look it up and e-mail you the reference, okay?"

"Thanks, Jodi. See ya Sunday at Nony's. You goin' to her church in the mornin'?"

DENNY AND THE KIDS decided not to go with me to the Worship Center because Nony warned us that it sometimes ran "late-ish," and they all had stuff they wanted to do in the afternoon. We argued about who was going to get the car, but three to one beat me out (even though they *could* have walked to Morse Avenue—barely a mile). "Okay," I said, "but I need to be at Yada Yada by five o'clock. Get the car back in time—promise?"

Denny shrugged. "No problem." So I gave in and called Avis. No answer. Maybe she wasn't coming back till this afternoon. Who else lived close to me . . . Adele?

Rats. I'd rather not have to call her. But it didn't look like I had any choice. I dialed.

Adele picked me up in her Ford Escort at nine-thirty Sunday morning. We found the Worship Center in Evanston easily enough, but like Nony had said, it didn't *look* like a church. A plain building hunkered down in a small industrial strip on Dempster Street.

Inside, a young African-American woman with a pretty smile gave us both a big hug and handed us bulletins. Adele wasn't the "huggy" type, but she allowed it and we both made our way into the main room, which was two or three times bigger than Uptown's worship space, though rather cavernous and "warehousy." The chairs were nice, though. *Padded.* Uptown should take a clue. Banners hung up and down the two aisles, and the platform was decorated with big green plants and flowers and a nice backdrop that looked like it might once have been a theater prop in a Victorian play.

I thought the service had already begun, even though we got there before ten, which is when Nony said the service started, because several men and women were walking back and forth at the front, praying rather loudly. Adele and I sat about halfway back in the middle section, and I twisted around to see if I could spot Nony but didn't see anyone I recognized. But as the praise team filed up onto the platform and the musicians took their places, Ruth plopped down on the padded chair next to me.

"Where's Yo-Yo?" I whispered.

Ruth shook her head. "She asks; her boss says, 'What do you think this is, the Pope John deli? We *work* on Sunday." She patted my hand. "But she's coming to Yada Yada later on."

"Huh," I grunted. Now that Yo-Yo had become a Christian, working at a Jewish deli might be problematic as far as going to Sunday services.

Over the next half-hour, the Worship Center praise team launched into several vigorous praise songs, which were shown by overhead projector on the wall. We had to jockey a few seats down the row in order to see around one of the steel pillars that held up the roof. As we were singing something about "My miracle is coming . . . my breakthrough is on the way," I saw Nony and Mark come in with their two boys—along with Hoshi and a whole string of young adults who looked like university students. The Smiths all gave us big smiles but sat closer to the front. Mark, in a dark suit, looked even more handsome than I'd remembered. Nony was wearing a black slinky dress with a gauzy black-and-gold shawl over it and big gold earrings. Gosh, that woman knew how to dress, I thought enviously—though I knew the same outfit would look like a Halloween costume on me.

We'd been on our feet worshiping about half an hour when Florida pushed Chris and Cedric into the row in front of us, followed by Stu, who must have picked them up. Not a bad representation from Yada Yada, I thought.

Nony had said the vision of her nondenominational church was to be "a church of all nations," but except for half a dozen white folks and a few Hispanic and Asian folks, everyone else was black. Guess it wasn't any easier for an African-American church to attract people of other races than for a well-intentioned white church. It crossed my mind that if we merged Uptown Community and the Worship Center, *nobody* would have to feel like a minority.

We finally got to sit down as the worship leader called up Pastor Lyle Foster, who'd been sitting on the front row—and everybody stood up again and clapped and cheered. That blew my mind! I couldn't imagine Uptown cheering when Pastor Clark got up to preach, even though most people liked his teaching.

This ought to be good.

But if I thought it was time for the message, I had another think coming. "Pastor Lyle," though not a tall man, seemed to fill the stage with his energy. The next thing I knew he had begun to sing a song that he seemed to be making up on the spot; the instruments—a full set of drums, bongos, two saxophones, keyboard, and a tall, lovely woman on electric bass—picked it up quickly, and the praise team was backing him up like they'd known it all along. Several times in the next half-hour he said, "You all can sit down now," so of course I sat down. But it was like he was teasing, because thirty seconds later he and the musicians were off and running on another song.

We finally did sit down, but the pastor came off the platform and began walking around, followed by his elders or ministers—both men and women—laying his hands on people and praying for them. He called one woman out of her chair and prayed for her in the aisle, and *bam!* She fell backward and was caught by two strong men who laid her down gently as a woman covered her legs modestly with a burgundy-colored cloth.

All this seemed to be right up Adele's alley, because she was thanking God and praying in tongues all along.

They finally took an offering, dismissed the kids to "Youth Ministry," and I thought it was finally time for the sermon. But the pastor came off the platform again and asked a woman who'd been part of the praise team to come to the front. She looked to be thirty-five or so, maybe a single mom because the pastor started talking about how she was struggling to keep her head above water and make a home for her kids. Then he said, "The Spirit of God is telling me that we need to encourage this mother. I want ten people who have a twenty-dollar bill in their pocket to come up and bless our sister."

For a split second I thought, *Oh, how embarrassing! What if ten people don't go up?* But within thirty seconds, not only ten people went up, but fifteen . . . maybe twenty, or twenty-five! One of the ushers stood by and held a bucket, and when everyone had gone back to their seats, the pastor took the bucket and turned it upside down, raining money down over this woman's head, who by now was weeping and jumping and praising God.

34

"ow. Quite a service," I told Nony as we stood at the back of the church afterward. I had hardly noticed the time, though now my stomach was grumbling and my watch said 1:10. People streaming by stopped to welcome us "visitors" with outstretched hands, smiles, and hugs. During the announcement time, Nony had made us all stand and told her congregation that we were part of her prayer group from the Chicago Women's Conference and that we were visiting each other's churches.

"Well, you can stop right here," the pastor had joked. "See you all next week at ten o'clock sharp."

But right now I was anxious to get home, since in another four hours we'd be meeting at Nony's house for Yada Yada. I wondered what Stu would do, since she lived all the way in Oak Park—an hour from here on stop-and-go streets—and felt guilty, because I didn't really want to invite anyone to hang out at our house. But finally I asked if she needed a place to stay till Yada Yada met this evening and felt relieved when she said, no, she and Florida were going to hang out at the lake with the boys for a while then take them home and come back up to Evanston.

Well, she and Florida are getting thick, aren't they! I thought, caught between wanting to go home and chill for a few hours and wishing they'd invite me, too. But they didn't, so I left as I'd come, in Adele's car.

It was almost two o'clock when Adele dropped me off. "Thanks a lot for the ride, Adele." I peeked back into the window of her Ford Escort. I really should return the favor. "Do you want a ride this evening?"

Adele shook her head, chunky earrings swinging. "Tell you the truth, don't know if I'm gonna make it tonight."

"Oh." Adele didn't offer any explanation and just pulled away. I wondered what that meant for Chanda. As far as I knew, Chanda didn't have a car; didn't she usually come with Adele?

I felt annoyed. Did that mean I should pick up Chanda? I wasn't even sure where she lived, though I could easily look up her address on the Yada Yada list. Then, still standing on the sidewalk, I scolded myself. *There you go again, Jodi, thinking you have to make everything work out. Nobody asked you to pick up Chanda. If Chanda calls, fine. But until then, just leave it alone.*

Feeling better, I ran up the steps to the front door and let myself in with my key.

"Anybody home?" I called, but was only greeted with the *thump, thump, thump* of Willie Wonka's tail. He had positioned himself in the hallway where he could keep an eye on both ends of the house. Notes on the dining room table said Denny was playing softball with some of the guys . . . Josh was out on his bike doing the bike path along Lake Michigan . . . and Amanda had gone over to a friend's house from church and would go straight to youth group from there.

I was half-disappointed, half-glad. Disappointed because I was eager to tell Denny about the worship service this morning, wishing he'd gone with me . . . glad because I relished nobody needing anything from me for the next couple of hours.

I made a tuna sandwich, poured myself a glass of iced tea, and stretched out on the living room couch with a novel I'd been wanting to read. Willie Wonka plunked down with a *whumph!* alongside the couch and closed his eyes. Ah, this was what Sunday afternoons were supposed to be like.

But the temperature was rising, and soon the hot, muggy air felt like a sweating gorilla sitting on my chest. Peeling myself off the couch, I turned the fan in the front window on high and glanced at the sky. Enormous thunderheads billowed like neon white mushrooms above the building tops along Lunt Avenue. A storm was brewing. Well, let it. Maybe it would cool things off . . . though it would probably bring Denny and Josh home sooner than they'd like.

A CRACK OF THUNDER so loud it nearly split the house in two sent me flying off the couch like an electric shock. Where was I? . . . Why was it so dark? . . . It took a few seconds to realize I'd dozed off over my book.

I looked at my watch in the greenish gloom. Four-thirty! I should be leaving if I wanted to get to Yada Yada on time. "Denny?" I called out. No answer. Why wasn't he home? He'd promised!

Well, I'd get myself completely ready so I could dash when he got here with the car. No call from Chanda . . . that was good. I wouldn't have to take extra time picking her up. Hoped that meant she had a ride.

At twenty minutes to five, I was standing on the front porch, eyeing each car that came by with its headlights on. No rain yet, but flashes of lightning periodically lit up the brooding sky followed by grumbles of thunder.

I kept glancing at my watch: 4:45 . . . 4:50 . . . Where *was* Denny? He couldn't still be playing ball—not with the skies about to open the floodgates.

I'm not sure what made me go out to the garage, except it was five minutes to five, there was no sign of my husband, and I was mad. Leaving my tote bag with my Bible and notebook on the front porch, I covered the distance between front porch and garage in determined strides. The garage, of course, was empty. And so was the corner where I'd stashed the six-packs under the bushel basket.

"Hellooo!" Denny's voice wafted out the back door. "Car's out front."

I stormed into the house. Denny, his sweats covered with grass stains and mud streaks, was washing his hands at the kitchen sink. "You're late," I snapped. "Now I'll be late."

"Whoa!" He shook the water off his hands and reached for a hand towel. "You told me to have the car back by five o'clock." He pointed to the kitchen clock. "At the tone, it is now . . . five o'clock."

"Very funny. I said I had to *be there* by five. I should've left twenty minutes ago." I could smell the beer on his breath. "You've been drinking," I said flatly. "How many did you have?"

Denny's eyes narrowed. "Jodi, give it a *rest*, will ya?"

"You took the beer from the garage."

"So? You don't want it around the house. Might as well enjoy it with the guys." He threw the hand towel on the counter and headed for the shower. "Oh!" he tossed over his shoulder. "It looked like rain, so I took Larry home first."

"Oh, *right.*" I followed Denny right on his heels. "You took Larry home first. You shouldn't even be driving, Denny Baxter."

Denny whirled at the bathroom door. "What is *that* supposed to mean?"

I crossed my arms and stared him down. "I can smell it on your breath. And if I can smell it, so could a cop! What if you'd had an accident? What if you got arrested on a DUI? What then, Denny? Your career as a coach would be over in a *blink*—not to mention any ministry with the guys at Uptown. Ever think of that, Denny? Huh?"

Denny was breathing hard, the muscles in his jaw pulsing.

The words kept coming. It was like I couldn't stop. I didn't even know whether I was mad or scared or worried or what. "And what about our reputation as a family? What about the kids? What about *me?* Don't you care?"

Denny snorted and leaned an arm on the doorpost. "Me? Nah. In fact, I did it on purpose. I said to myself, 'How can I make Jodi mad? I know, I'll give Larry a ride—that ought to waste ten minutes—and make Jodi late! And then, we'll get rip-roarin' drunk. That oughta be good for another ten.'" He rolled his eyes. "Sheesh!" Turning on his heel, he slammed the bathroom door behind him.

"Don't shut the door in my face!" I screamed. But the only sound on the other side of the door was the shower jets, turned on full force.

Shaking with anger, I glanced at my watch. Five-ten. Now I *really* was going to be late. I didn't even feel like going to Yada Yada . . . but no way did I want to just stand there being ignored, either. I stomped past Willie Wonka, who stood staring at me, tail hanging motionless, as I snatched up my tote bag on the front porch and headed for the minivan, which Denny had parked across the street.

Before I even got the door open, the clouds let loose.

By the time I got inside, slamming the door shut behind me, I was soaked.

"Oh, great," I seethed, turning on the ignition and flipping on the lights and windshield wipers. "This is just great. I'm going to look a mess."

I jerked the wheel and pulled the minivan out of the parking spot, slightly grazing the bumper of the car parked in front of me. Well, who cared. Not me. Denny shouldn't have parked so tight in that spot.

I clicked the wipers to their highest speed, but I still had a hard time seeing between the foggy windshield inside and the huge splats of rain coming fast and furious on the outside. But I navigated west toward Clark Street, the main drag that would take me north into Evanston.

Tears of frustration and anger rose to the surface. Why couldn't Denny just say, "I'm sorry" when he blew it instead of getting all defensive? I might still be late, but that certainly would've helped.

Not only that, but if I'd left *on time* I wouldn't have to drive in this deluge, either.

The windshield wipers chased the rain from side to side in a hopeless frenzy, but so far the downpour had showed no signs of slowing down. Had I even remembered to bring Nony's directions how to get to her house? They lived somewhere close to the university, in one of the north Evanston neighborhoods. It was going to be hard to see street signs and house numbers if the rain didn't break soon.

Clark Street was extra busy. A long row of headlights came toward me in the premature darkness; a long row of red taillights sparkled in the rain in front of me. Even as I gripped the steering wheel of the minivan, I tried to get a grip on my feelings. I didn't want to show up at Yada Yada mad as a wet hen and have to confess that Denny and I had just had a big fight about his drinking—what would that sound like? Besides, maybe it wasn't all Denny's fault. Had I just been mad at him for being late? Had I overreacted . . . again?

Up ahead, the next two lights turned green. Good. I'd make it through the first one for sure . . . could I make the next one at Howard Street, too? Howard was the east-west border between

Chicago and Evanston, at which point Clark Street became Chicago Avenue, a nice long stretch before another light. I pushed the accelerator slightly, keeping an eye on the speedometer to make sure it stayed near thirty miles per hour, even as the rain continued to hammer the roof.

The traffic moved steadily . . . I was going to make it . . . keep going, Jodi, don't slow down . . . just a couple more car lengths . . .

I was watching the light and didn't see the small hooded figure dash out into the street until I was almost upon it. "Oh God!" I yelled and stomped on the brake. I felt the car skid under me . . . in front of my headlights a face jerked my way—just a kid!

I jerked the wheel, but the car kept sliding sideways . . . I felt a sickening *thump* . . . "Noooooo!" I screamed, and only at the last second saw a pair of headlights heading straight for my driver's-side window—

35

*I'm swimming . . . upward toward the light . . . all is silent
around me, the silence of the ocean beneath the waves . . .
but my lungs are bursting . . . pain wracks my side . . . I
must break the surface and get a breath . . . but I can't move my arms
. . . why can't I move? . . . voices . . . there are voices, but I don't know
what they're saying . . . blurry faces above the water's surface . . . I must
break through . . . must struggle to the top . . . must get a breath—*

"She's coming around."

*I hear the voice . . . close, so close, but just out of reach . . . the light
behind my eyelids is bright . . . did I break the surface? . . . why does it
hurt to breathe? . . . if I reach out my hands, will I be saved? . . . but,
God, I can't move my arms!*

"Jodi? Jodi Baxter? Can you open your eyes?"

With great effort, I managed to crack open my right eye—then
closed it again against the bright light just inches from my face.
But try as I would, I could not open my left eye.

"Jodi, can you hear me?" The voice was male. Insistent. Kind.

Yes! Yes, I can hear you! I tried to nod . . . but the most I could manage was a twitch. Panic rose in my throat like bile. Why couldn't I move my head? Why couldn't I move *period?*

A hand touched my arm. "Easy, Jodi," said the voice, "don't struggle. We've got you in a cervical collar and strapped to a backboard to keep you immobile—just until we can assess your injuries."

Injuries? What injuries? "What . . . where am I?" Was that croaking my voice? My lips felt dry and cracked, the words dry and cracked, too. Once again, I tried to open my eyes and found myself staring with one eye at a bright light at the end of a long metal arm.

A masked face moved between me and the light and looked down. The masculine voice behind the mask said, "Jodi, I am Doctor Lewinski, St. Francis Hospital. You've been in a car accident. We've called your husband—he'll be here soon. But we're going to take you to get some x-rays, okay? Can you tell me what hurts?"

What hurts? I wanted to take a deep breath, but anything beyond tiny, rapid breaths sent fire shooting across my chest. "Chest . . . side," I croaked. I forced my mind to roam over my body, trying to pinpoint the pain. "And . . . my leg . . . thigh . . ."

"Okay, good girl. We're going to take care of that . . . just hang on. We'll get those x-rays so we know what we're dealing with."

"JODI? Jodi, it's Denny."

The familiar voice pulled me once more through the fog into

the light. I willed both eyes to open. Denny's face hovered close to mine. Seeing the crinkles at the corners of his eyes, feeling his breath on my skin, sent a tear sliding down my cheek. "Denny . . ."

"That's one heck of a shiner you got there, babe." I could hear both tenderness and terror in his voice.

"Denny . . . what—?"

"Shh, shh, don't talk. Just want you to know I'm here."

I closed my eyes. Everything was going to be all right. Denny was here.

"MR. AND MRS. BAXTER?" A tallish man with close-cropped brown hair and angular features parted the curtain and came into the narrow examining space. "I'm Doctor Lewinski, chief resident of the ER." Through my cracked lids I saw the doctor—*sans* mask—shake Denny's hand. "We've got some good news."

Good news . . . good news, he said . . .

Dr. Lewinski consulted the clipboard he held in one hand. "Jodi's CAT scan shows no epidural or subdural hematoma, in spite of the nasty knock she got on the left side of her head. X-ray of her spine is normal, which is why we took her off the board and got rid of the collar."

I felt Denny grope for my hand and squeeze.

"Also, no collapsed lung—which can easily happen if a broken rib punctures the lung."

"Broken rib . . ." Denny sounded dazed.

"Several. That's giving her the most pain right now. But the left femur x-ray shows a midshaft fracture. We've got it splinted and wrapped in cold packs to keep the swelling down, but we'll have to put a rod in there, as soon as we're sure she's stabilized. And . . ." The doctor paused.

"And?" Denny repeated. I could hear the fear creep back into his voice.

"The CAT scan of her abdomen shows a badly ruptured spleen. We may be able to treat it without surgery as long as she's stable."

"What about . . . the cut on her head, and all the swelling? You know, her eye . . ."

"Superficial. A few stitches, mostly in the hairline—you won't even be able to see the scar."

Through my half-opened eyes, I watched Dr. Lewinski walk around the end of the bed and come close to me. "Don't mean to talk about you in third person, Mrs. Baxter—may I call you Jodi? Once the swelling goes down, you'll have a beaut of a black eye, but that'll go away in a week or two . . . Oh, by the way. You have visitors." He nodded soberly and headed for the door. "I'll send them in—but only for a few minutes."

My fingers curled around Denny's hand. *Don't leave me . . . don't leave me.*

"Mom!" Amanda's voice bounced into the room just ahead of her distraught face. "Ohmigosh! Dad—what happened? Mom?"

I could see Josh, tall and grim-faced, right behind his sister.

"Mom? What happened?" Amanda asked again.

I searched for words. "I . . . don't know . . . don't remember."

"But there's cops—"

"Not now, Amanda." Denny's voice was suddenly sharp. "Just give your mom some love, and we can talk later. The doctor was just here . . . good news! Mostly."

Amanda opened her mouth, but a shake of Denny's head shut it again. She bent over the railing and kissed me gently on the right side of my face. "Oh, Mom, get better real quick, okay?"

Wordlessly, Josh bent over the bed and kissed me on the forehead. My mouth twitched in an attempt to smile. He smelled like Denny's aftershave. Josh straightened and jerked a thumb toward the door. "Avis is here. C'mon, Amanda." He and Amanda disappeared out of my vision.

I tried to turn my head, but the movement created a stabbing pain near my left eye. "Avis?" I croaked. *How did Avis—?*

A commotion somewhere outside the curtain stirred up like a pot coming to boil. Voices argued; grew louder. Denny bent close to my ear and started talking rapidly. "Avis called me, worried because you didn't show up at Nony's—only seconds after I got a call from the hospital. I called Pastor Clark and he brought me straight to the hospital. Avis picked up the kids at youth group."

Avis drifted into my view, clutching her big Bible. "Hey, sister." She went around the bed and took my fingers, avoiding the tubes taped to the back of my hand. Her touch was gentle, her face calm. "Why didn't you just tell us you wanted Yada Yada to meet at St. Francis?"

I stared at her face, confused. I had no idea what she was talking about.

Avis smiled gently. "Sorry. Lame joke. But Yada Yada is here, praying in the waiting room. Pastor Clark, too." She looked at Denny. "Denny, you okay?"

The churning voices outside formed words, invading our curtained space. "Where is he? Where's my baby? I want to see my baby!"

I searched for Denny's eyes. "Is . . . someone's baby sick?" I managed.

Denny just shook his head, avoiding my eyes. "You stay here, Avis. I'm going to go see the kids a moment." I felt his fingers leave my hand.

Avis paged through her Bible. "Satan gave you a good lick, sister, but we're not going to just stand by while he messes with you. Here, listen to Psalm 103 . . . 'Praise the Lord, O my soul, all my inmost being, praise his holy name. Praise the Lord, O my soul, and forget not all his benefits—who forgives all your sins and heals all your diseases, who redeems your life from the pit and crowns you with love and compassion—"

"What do you mean, *dead?*" One voice outside rose above the others to a shriek. *"Not my baby! Not my baby! Oh God, no-ooooo."*

My fingers groped for Avis's hand. "What's . . . happening out there?"

"No, you keep listening to me, Jodi. 'The Lord is compassionate and gracious, slow to anger, abounding in love. He will not always accuse, nor will he harbor his anger forever—'"

"Who killed him? *Who killed him!*" I turned my face toward the screams, ignoring the shooting pain in my head. "Tell me who! . . . He's going to jail for this! He's going to pay!"

Avis's voice clothed the naked screams, pulling me back into the sound of her voice. "'He does not treat us as our sins deserve or repay us according to our iniquities. For as high as the heavens are above the earth, so great is his love. . . .'"

I tried to concentrate on the words she was reading. But I felt strange . . . lightheaded. I heard a sound behind my head. *Beep* . . . *beep* . . . *beep* . . .

A nurse swept the curtain aside, checking the machines just out of my sight. "Ma'am, you need to leave," she said to Avis. "Now." She swept out again, calling, "Dr. Lewinski? Get Dr. Lewinski, stat, in Number Seven!"

"Hold on to Jesus, Jodi." Avis's dark eyes locked on to mine. "He who is for you is stronger than he who is against you." And then she was gone.

My breaths were coming fast and shallow. "Avis? *Avis!* . . . Denny! I want Denny!"

323

36

I was swimming again . . . swimming forward . . . but the water was loud, drumming on my head . . . something was holding me back, clutching my middle in a viselike grip . . . Oh God, it hurt . . .

Swipe, swipe . . . swipe, swipe . . . windshield wipers swept the water from before my eyes . . . follow the red lights . . . bright lights coming toward me . . .

A face! . . . a brown face in the water . . . lit up bright . . . lit up scared . . . lit up—

I forced my eyes open. I felt sick as a dog. Immediately Denny's face filled the space in front of my own. "You're awake." A smile crinkled his gray eyes. "Doc says surgery went smooth as glass—but you're going to have to stay a few days."

Pincers with jagged teeth seemed to grasp my whole left side, from my ribs down to my leg. I fought a wave of nausea. A tube hung out of my nose, taped to my face. "Hurts," I moaned.

"I know, babe. You're going to be okay, though. Just hang on."

I was vaguely aware when I got wheeled through the halls . . . an elevator . . . more halls . . . into a room. The bare walls were blue . . . no, gray . . . something. Tall ceilings, tall windows . . . like a reformatory or convent.

I dozed, fighting nausea every time I awoke. People came in and out . . . Dr. Lewinski . . . Pastor Clark . . . a male nurse . . . Nony and Mark . . . Piecing together different comments, I realized I was minus one mangled spleen and had a metal rod holding my left femur together.

"Where are . . . kids?" I asked Denny at one point.

"Avis took them home. Edesa is going to stay at the house with them. Josh is okay, but Amanda . . . well, she'll be all right with Edesa there." He brushed the hair from my forehead. "They love you, you know. They're worried . . . your folks, too. They'd be here in a millisecond, but your mom's had a bad chest cold and her doctor's worried about pneumonia. I told 'em to stay put; we'd take care of you."

I squirmed under his intense gaze. "I must look awful." I couldn't look good and feel this awful.

"You're alive. You look beautiful to me."

THAT FACE! . . . the arms flailing . . . lit up bright . . . lit up scared . . .

I opened my eyes. The pain had dulled. The nausea diminished.

Denny was asleep in a chair in the corner, one leg over the arm of the chair, his head slumped at an uncomfortable angle. A shadow of a beard covered his chin and jawline. I watched him, remembering . . .

We'd had a fight . . . I was late. Late and mad. It was raining—no, pouring. The kind of rain that flooded the sewers and left small lakes at every street corner. And dark too early. I was trying to make the green light, trying to hurry . . .

Denny stirred and stretched. "Hey, babe. How you feel?"

I took several slow breaths. It hurt, but I had to get some air. "I remember the accident."

Immediately Denny was at my side. "Don't think about it, Jodi. Right now you just gotta get—"

"A boy, he . . . he ran right in front of my car. It was raining. I could hardly see. I tried to stop . . . I jerked the wheel. That's . . . all I remember."

"That's okay, honey. We don't have to talk about this now." Denny fussed with my blankets and pointed to a basket of flowers on the windowsill. "Look. They're from Yada Yada—well, Stu sent them for everybody, I think."

I didn't see the flowers. I didn't see anything. *Only the face, the flailing arms . . .*

Another wave of nausea brought a vile taste into my mouth and I retched, but only spittle came dribbling out. Denny grabbed a tissue and dabbed at my mouth. "You okay?"

I focused on his eyes. "Denny . . . what about the boy? Is he . . . okay?"

Denny looked away.

"Tell me!"

Denny shook his head. "No. He . . . died last night."

I heard Denny's words, but they didn't compute at first. *Died? The boy died?* But as the words sank in, they flowed like ice water into my veins.

"I . . . hit him?"

Denny nodded, tears wetting his cheeks. "That's what they're saying. Nothing's for sure yet, not until they investigate—"

"They who?" My voice came out in a whisper.

"Uh . . . the police. When you're better they want to talk to you . . ."

I think Denny said more words, but it was like a dream and far away. *The boy . . . I hit him . . . I killed him . . . I killed a boy . . . somebody's child . . . killed him! Killed!*

I heard a scream, a scream piercing the blueness of the room, ripping it like fingernails on skin . . . I heard Denny's voice from far away . . . *"Don't, Jodi, don't!"* . . . footsteps came running . . . hands held me down . . .

The scream was my own.

WHEN I AWOKE, I couldn't remember where I was. What day was it? Why was I here? A blue room . . . bags of clear fluid hanging on a pole with long skinny tubes taped to my hands . . . my hands—tied by strips of cloth to the bedrails . . . why?

And then it all came back to me like getting smashed in the gut by a heavyweight boxer . . .

I screwed my eyes shut, trying to shut it out.

A car accident. I'd killed somebody. Killed . . . a boy.

The wail started in my aching gut and burst from my mouth. "Oh God, no-oo-ooo!"

"Jodi? I'm right here, girl." A cool hand touched my face, brushed the tears from my cheeks. I opened my eyes. Bright sunshine streaming in the tall window created a halo of light around Florida's dark face and tiny ringlets.

I groaned and turned my face away. *Oh God, does everybody know?* "Please! Pull the blinds."

"But the sun is shining! And look at all these flowers that keep coming in." She peered at the little cards. "Denny's folks . . . couple of families from Uptown Community—"

"I want it dark!" I snapped. I wanted to yell, *I don't want flowers, either! Don't people know I killed somebody? They oughta send the flowers to his funeral!*

"You gotta get a grip, girl, else they gonna leave you tied up so's you don't pull out all these tubes."

I refused to look at her. "Just . . . go away."

"Huh. You got some attitude there. Well, it won't work with me. I'm gone . . . all the way to this here chair." The room darkened, then I heard the plastic cushion on the corner chair *wheeze* as she plopped down.

I kept my eyes shut. Maybe she'd think I was asleep and leave. But I heard her humming and filing her nails.

Finally, I opened my eyes. "Where's Denny?" I whispered.

"Comin'. Avis, too. They gotta be here by ten o'clock. But

your man needed some sleep. He's been here nonstop since Sunday night."

I mulled on that for a moment. *Why ten o'clock?* Then it occurred to me that I didn't even know what day it was. "What's today?"

Florida got up out of the chair, came over to the side of the hospital bed, and looked me up and down. "Tuesday mornin'. When the sedation wears off, Doc says you can get up and walk a bit today—test out that walker over there."

She had to be kidding. "Don't feel like it," I mumbled. Tuesday . . . Tuesday . . . I was supposed to do something on Tuesday. But for the life of me, I couldn't remember what.

"Gotta. Doc says he'll take that tube outta your nose when you pass some gas."

I glared at her. "Why is the doctor telling *you* anything?"

Even in the now-shaded room, I could tell Florida was grinning ear to ear. "Told him I was family. The look on his face was priceless."

Oh, right. Like he believed her. I started to turn my head away again, then turned back. "Why ten o'clock?"

She shrugged. "Police want to talk to you, ask you about the accident. Denny said they had to wait till he could be here."

My lip trembled, and I started to cry. "I-I'm scared, Florida."

"Hey. Sure you scared. But it's gonna be all right. Police gotta do they job. They gotta talk to everybody when there's an accident—including you."

She thinks she knows what I did. Oh, God, if she really knew . . .

A middle-aged nurse I'd never seen before came in to take my vitals. "Good, you're awake, Mrs. Baxter. Can we take these off, now, hmm?" She looked at me over the tops of her glasses as if I were an erring child and proceeded to untie my wrists. I said nothing, just lay still and looked away.

Denny and Avis showed up shortly before ten. "My private taxi," he grinned, jerking a thumb at Avis, then leaned over the bed to give me a kiss.

I stared at the thin blanket making lumps and valleys over my body, gripping its edges in my fists. *Oh, right. I've also banged up the minivan, so now Denny has to bum rides from our friends.*

Avis touched my hand. "Yada Yada is praying around the clock for you, Jodi. Everybody sends their love."

Tears welled in my eyes, and I squeezed them shut. They could forget praying for me. They had *no idea* what they were praying about! Love me? Not if they knew. They should be mad—mad as hell! That would feel good. We could just yell at each other then. That's what I wanted to do . . . just yell! Yell bloody murder!

"Jodi?" Denny's voice broke into my stupor. "The, uh, police are here. They want to ask you some questions. Can you do that?"

"I don't know," I whispered, and started to cry.

"It's okay, honey. I'll help you."

I grasped the front of his sport shirt and pulled him close to me, "I don't want Avis and Florida here when the police . . ."

He turned and whispered something to Avis and Florida, who quietly left the room, passing two uniformed police officers who came in, holding their hats with the signature blue-checkered bands under their arms.

Déjà vu. Just a month ago, two Chicago policemen had come into José Enriques's room, and Avis and I had tiptoed out. I'd wanted to hang back and listen then . . . were Avis and Florida listening just outside my door? *Go away!* I screamed at them in my mind.

"Mrs. Baxter?" The first police officer was African American, a good six feet and two hundred pounds, with a bull neck as wide as his ears. The other police officer was also male, but younger, thinner, with straight black hair, olive skin. Maybe Puerto Rican. "I'm Sergeant Shipp, and this is Officer Carillo."

I gripped Denny's hand. *It's not fair, God! Why can't I have that . . . that female officer with the ponytail who came to see José?* I hoped they'd ask me questions I could just answer yes or no. But Sergeant Shipp went digging. "Can you tell us what you remember about the accident?"

I looked frantically at Denny's face. He nodded at me encouragingly. "Just tell them what you told me yesterday, what you remembered."

I closed my eyes to see it again, but *the face* rose up so quickly, I quickly opened them. Breathing as deeply as my tightly bound ribs would allow, I told them about the heavy rain and the darkness . . . about the green light at Howard and Clark Streets . . . about the hooded figure that ran into the intersection in front of the minivan . . . stomping on the brake and jerking the wheel . . . about the bright headlights coming straight at me. "That's all I remember," I said weakly.

"Mrs. Baxter," the sergeant said, "you know by now that this accident involved a fatality. The young pedestrian died of injuries sustained when he was struck by a vehicle, possibly yours. Do you remember striking the young man?"

Panic began to rise in my throat, but Denny broke in. "Sergeant Shipp, are you saying there's a question about *which* vehicle struck the boy? If so, then I don't believe my wife is required to answer that question."

Sergeant Shipp snapped his notebook shut. "All right. That'll be all for now, Mrs. Baxter." The two men made for the door, but Sergeant Shipp beckoned for Denny to follow them. In the doorway, the officer lowered his voice, but it still carried into the room. "Mr. Baxter, we have at least three witnesses who are saying it was your wife's vehicle that struck the boy, and there are conflicting reports about who had the green light. The state's attorney is prepared to press charges."

"What—what charges?"

"Vehicular manslaughter. With or without gross negligence."

"But . . . it was an *accident*. It was raining. The boy ran out into traffic—"

"That may well be, Mr. Baxter. But my advice to you? Get a lawyer."

37

enny!" I grabbed my husband's hand as he returned to my bedside. "What did he mean, vehicular manslaughter with—?"

Denny put a finger to my mouth. "Don't worry, babe. Don't worry. The family is naturally upset and wanting to blame somebody. This isn't going to go anywhere."

I stared at Denny's face, reading the twitch in his jaw, the reluctance to look me straight in the eye . . . *Oh God! Oh God! This can't be happening!*

I looked away. "What's his name?"

"Who? The officer?"

I swallowed with difficulty. "The boy."

"Jodi, don't—"

"What's his *name?*"

Denny sighed. "Jamal Wilkins."

Jamal Wilkins . . . somebody's child . . . no more.

"How old was he?"

"Jodi, don't torture yourself like this!"

"Tell me!"

Denny sighed again. "Thirteen." He wandered over to the window and pulled the cord opening the blind so he could look out. "His friends say they were trying to cross the street to get under the overpass to get out of the rain. Jamal had his sweatshirt hood up and didn't see . . ."

The overpass that took the commuter train tracks over Howard Street into Evanston. Just a few more yards to safety and shelter.

Denny turned. "Should I go tell Avis and Florida they can come back in now?"

I shook my head. "No, please . . . tell them I'm sorry, but I want to rest."

Rest. That was a good one. I wasn't sure I would ever be able to close my eyes again without seeing that face.

BUT I DID SLEEP—slept as much as I could so I didn't have to think or talk. And each morning when I woke up, somebody from Yada Yada was already in the hospital room—usually Avis or Nony, walking around the room praying over me, over the machines, over the doctors. Even Yo-Yo showed up one morning, slouching in the corner chair in her typical pose. Like everybody else, she had opened the louvered blinds to let in the sun, and like every other morning, I wearily asked her to close them.

The light seemed obscene somehow, given the circumstances.

The nurses made me get out of bed and walk a little farther each day, using a walker. I felt like a prisoner of war, dressed in a humiliating gown that wouldn't stay closed in the back, hobbling on one good leg and an old-lady walker, with a nurse-guard trailing me, pushing the ever-present pole of liquid goodies to make sure I didn't run for it.

Denny went back to work on Wednesday—he'd already missed two days of his new summer job—but I didn't lack for visitors. Besides Pastor Clark's daily visit, Delores, Edesa, Stu, and Ruth all popped in at various visiting hours. Somebody in Yada Yada had probably made a "Visit Jodi" list, and I didn't need three guesses to know who.

Adele had showed up at noon on Wednesday, bringing with her a huge tube of hand cream with aloe. "I had two cancellations in a row," she announced, as though needing a reason to be there in the middle of the day. She picked up one of my hands and examined it critically. "Hmm. Gotta do something about these chicken claws." She squirted a huge gob of cream into her palm and worked it into the chapped skin of my hands, around the tape and tubes connecting me to the IV pole. I felt awkward with her massaging my neglected hands, but it felt so good and comforting that I didn't want her to stop—ever. It was the first time in five days that I felt like a woman.

To my surprise, I'd liked Adele's visit. She didn't try to talk to me or cheer me up; just rubbed my hands, layer after layer of thick hand cream. "Thank you," I whispered as she stepped away from the bed to make room for a male nurse who came in with a large paper cup with a plastic lid and straw.

"Let's get that tube out of your nose." The young man grasped the nasogastric tube that had been pumping fluid from my stomach. "Now, when I pull on this, I want you to cough. Okay?" Round glasses perched on his rather thin nose were topped by a shock of limp brown hair, making him look like a grown-up Harry Potter. He pulled, and I coughed . . . again and again. Felt like kicks in my side as the tube slowly emerged.

"Heard you passed gas this morning, Mrs. Baxter." He acted as if he was making casual conversation.

I rolled my eyes. "Oh brother." I could hear Adele snickering in the background.

The nurse was unperturbed. "Now that we've passed that milestone, Doc says to try some ginger ale today." He handed me the paper cup with the straw. "But go easy . . . only little sips."

I took a sip, then another. It tasted so good. I hadn't realized how parched my mouth and throat were for real liquid. I took a bigger sip . . . and suddenly it all came back up and then some, splatting all over the bed and the nurse's clean white tunic.

He stared at me as if I'd done it on purpose. "The basin, Mrs. Baxter. You're supposed to use the basin." A big sigh. "Guess we're going to have to change this bed again." He snatched the paper cup and took it with him as he headed for the door.

"Sorry," I squeaked, lying back weakly on the upraised bed. Did he have any *idea* how much it hurt to throw up when you had a big incision in your belly and five broken ribs?

The moment he was gone, Adele appeared at the side of the bed with a warm wet washcloth for my face. "That boy needs a stronger stomach if he's gonna be any kind o' *nurse,*" she muttered, barely concealing a grin.

DENNY AND THE KIDS usually appeared about suppertime and stayed a couple of hours in the evening. I was glad to see Josh and Amanda, but I desperately wanted some time alone to talk with Denny about what the police officer had said. We didn't know a lawyer—and couldn't afford one even if we did! What were we going to do? But no one was telling me anything.

Not that I had the courage to ask. I clung to the veneer of normalcy, the stream of nurses and visitors popping in and out like pinballs, the annoying shots and medications in little plastic cups, trips to the bathroom to see if I could "go," even the hated walks down the corridor with the back of my gown flapping. I was even glad when the night staff woke me up at intervals to take my vitals—anything to keep the nightmare of *that face,* lit up in my headlights, from taking over my sanity.

When the kids arrived on Thursday evening, Amanda eyed the "supper" tray of Jell-O and clear liquids an aide brought in. "Can't you eat any real food yet? It's been four days!"

I sighed. "My abdomen is still bloated. Dr. Lewinski calls it 'post-op ileus'—doc-talk for saying that my intestines are in shock and can't handle solid food yet."

Amanda looked anxiously at her father then back to me. "But when are they going to let you come home?"

"I don't know—I was hoping by this weekend." I reached out a hand to my daughter. "Gotta see you off to Mexico on Sunday." I tried on a smile.

"Uh, Mom." Josh cleared his throat. "We've been talking to Dad and thinking maybe we shouldn't go—not with you banged up like this. I mean, Dad's gotta work, and you're gonna need somebody to take care of you when you get home."

I stared at my children. I wanted to hug them, bawl all over their shoulders, thank them over and over for thinking of me. Yes, yes, I needed them, wanted them, didn't want them to go away to Mexico with its dirt roads and crazy bus drivers and unsafe water and terrorists just waiting to sneak over the border—

"No. Absolutely not."

"No? Why not? Look at you, Mom!"

I had looked at me in the bathroom mirror, and it wasn't pretty. "Because you two have looked forward to this trip for six months, and you've worked hard to earn the money, and it'll be a great experience, and you're going. I'm not dead, and by all accounts I'm going to recover and be back nagging you to death about cleaning your rooms."

Denny couldn't repress a smile. "I knew your mother wouldn't go for it."

"But who's going to take care of you, Mom?"

I rolled my eyes. "I'm *supposed* to get up and get around. At least at home I can wear some decent clothes so I don't shock

Willie Wonka. See those crutches?" An aide had brought in a pair
of elbow crutches for me to use to avoid hurting my cracked ribs.
"By the time you get back from Mexico, I'm going to challenge
you to a three-legged footrace."

By this time my husband and kids were laughing. Amanda
leaned over and gave me a hug. "Thanks, Mom." She pulled back
and studied my face. "But . . . are you sure? Because we really
would be willing to stay."

"Absolutely sure."

The three of them left in high spirits. Mom was practically her
old self again. She wanted them to go. Everything was going to be
all right.

I watched the heavy door shut behind them, feeling heavy with
guilt. They thought I was being wonderful and selfless. They had
no idea how selfish I was being. I knew their offer to give up the
trip and stay home "to take care of Mom" was sincere . . . but they
would resent it. Resent *me*. Maybe even hate me for being so stupid and careless to have an accident, to ruin our car, and ruin their
Mexico trip on top of it.

I couldn't bear it. Somewhere out there was a family who
already hated me because I had taken away their son, their "baby."
"Taken away?"—huh. Killed him. *Bam!*—like that. They wanted
me in court, probably wanted me in jail . . . maybe wanted to ruin
my family.

Great silent sobs welled up inside me, each one painful as they
fought against my broken ribs and sore abdomen. Hot tears spilled
down my face, and my nose started to run. I couldn't reach a tissue,

so I just blew my nose on the bedsheet . . . but the tears wouldn't stop.

"Oh God! God!" I wailed out loud. "Where are You? Why did You let this happen? I don't care how banged up I am—but why did You let that boy die? Everything would be okay if he just wasn't *dead!* And Jesus isn't walking around Chicago these days raising dead boys back to life, is He! . . . *Is He!*"

The last two words were practically a scream, but the door stayed closed, and no visitors or nurses or aides came tripping in. I was alone . . . utterly abandoned and alone. Giving in to the fear and grief and confusion that were my life, I cried and cried and cried.

38

*D*r. Lewinski discharged me on Sunday. Guess I'd peed and pooped to the staff's satisfaction, because they started to give me real food the last two days and sent me home with a long list of instructions of what I could and couldn't (mostly couldn't) do for the next six weeks. "We'll need a follow-up x-ray on that leg and start you on some physical therapy," the doc said.

Denny picked me up in an old car that looked like something from Rent-a-Wreck. Somebody at Uptown was loaning it to us until the insurance paid up and we could get another car—but the insurance wasn't paying anything till they found out whether I was liable.

Guilty until proven innocent . . . now I knew what *that* felt like. But the loaner was okay if we didn't want to actually go anywhere—and it looked like I would be staying put for a while.

I got home in time to hug Amanda and Josh good-bye before they left in the church van for O'Hare Airport, where they would be boarding Mexicana Airlines for Mexico City. I hunched over my elbow crutches, looking at the two large duffel bags in the hallway, packed, zipped, locked, and ready. "I . . . wasn't here to help you get ready."

"Oh, Mom! Don't apologize! Edesa came over and helped us pack—except she made me and Josh wash our own clothes. Fold 'em, too." Amanda grinned, proud of herself. "But she knew just what to take for weather south of the border."

I wasn't apologizing, I thought mournfully. *I'm sad for me, that I missed it.*

And then it was another round of hugs and kisses and pats for Willie Wonka . . . and they were gone.

After waving good-bye from the front porch, Denny held the screen door for me. "Honey, let's get you in bed. You hungry? I could make you some tea and toast. And it's about time for your meds."

"Okay. Thanks." My whole midsection hurt, and I could hardly wait for the codeine-induced relief they'd sent home with me.

Denny turned back the wedding ring quilt on our bed, collected all the pillows from the kids' rooms to prop me up, and made sure I got in bed without falling over. Then he headed for the kitchen. I stared at the wedding ring quilt . . . and for the first time since the accident realized my long recovery was going to be hard on Denny, too. No sex, no cuddling, no fooling around.

Neither one of us had talked about the fight we'd had just before the accident. In a way it wasn't important, given the really big stuff we were dealing with now . . .

Or was it?

Willie Wonka pushed his nose over the side of the bed and tried to lick my hand, which was still bruised from the IV. I idly stroked his silky ears, but my thoughts were elsewhere, going backward, back to last Sunday night . . .

Denny had gotten home late. I'd said I had to be at Yada Yada "by five o'clock." He got the car home "by five o'clock" . . . so, okay, maybe that was a misunderstanding. I cringed, remembering how apoplectic I'd been that he made me late. I should probably apologize—

But wait a minute. Denny had been drinking; I had smelled it on his breath. Sure, I could apologize for the misunderstanding about the time—but what about *that?* Still . . . I couldn't very well say anything now, could I, since *I* was the one in deep doo-doo. He could throw it right back at me and get off clean as a whistle. After all, he wasn't the one who . . .

He wasn't the one who . . .

A horrible realization pushed itself into my consciousness. I'd accused Denny of being a danger behind the wheel—but *I* was the one who had been drunk on anger, driving hard, driving mad—

No! I couldn't think like that. It was an accident! It wasn't my fault! *It wasn't my fault!*

DENNY HAD BOUGHT A CELL PHONE and told me to call him immediately if I needed anything. He seemed really worried about going off to work and leaving me alone, but it was a relief. Small talk

345

was hard for me when my whole world seemed like it was spinning out of control. After a week of doctors and nurses, being poked, prodded, and paraded, good ol' Willie Wonka was about the right kind of company I needed: practically deaf, undemanding, just there.

But around noon I heard a voice holler, "Hello? Jodi?"

I was lying in my darkened bedroom, not reading, not thinking, just in a kind of numb stupor. But I roused myself on one elbow. "Who's there?"

Footsteps came down the hallway. "Avis! I brought supper." The footsteps diverted through the dining room to the kitchen. A few minutes later she pushed open the half-closed bedroom door. "You okay?"

I *had* been, thank you. "Yeah, I'm okay. How'd you get in?"

She came in all the way and sat on the end of the bed. She was dressed casually, in white summer slacks, a blousy pale green top, and white thong sandals that stood out against her rich brown skin, even in the dim light. "Denny didn't tell you? He gave me a key, asked me to check up on you while he was at work."

"Ah." I fiddled with the quilt over my legs, conscious of my still bruised face and limp nightshirt. "Thanks for bringing us supper."

She waved a hand. "It's just mac 'n' cheese. One of the few things I can cook—everything else I touch turns out raw or charred!" She chuckled. "Just don't tell Yo-Yo."

I tried to smile, but I wasn't very good at it.

Avis dug around in her big leather purse. "Look, I brought you some CDs to listen to. Especially when you're home alone, it'll be good to fill your days with praise." She looked at me closely. "You're going to need some Word you can draw on, Jodi, when the going gets tough . . . oh! And I brought you this." She pulled a piece of paper out of her Bible. "It's a list of healing scriptures. When you don't know what to pray—" She waved the piece of paper. "—pray these. Especially Psalm 103, the one I circled. That one's for you, Jodi."

She stood up. "Want me to put it with your Bible?"

"Uh, sure. It's in my tote bag somewhere . . ." My tote bag had been in the now-wrecked minivan. "I'll have to ask Denny. Maybe he knows where it is."

"Okay. Want me to put one of these on now?" She held up one of the CDs.

"Uh, no, that's okay. I . . . think I'm going to sleep now for a while."

She knew I was stalling. But we both let my lame excuse stand. She came over and put both the piece of paper and the CDs in my lap. "Jodi, I don't know why God is taking you through this valley, this 'valley of the shadow of death,' but He's got a reason. A big reason. Go *through*, sister . . . go through."

A few minutes later, I heard the front door close, and all was quiet.

Yea, though I walk through the valley of the shadow of death, I will fear no evil . . .

How many times in my life had I repeated Psalm 23, feeling safe and secure, like that little lamb in the Sunday school pictures being carried by the Good Shepherd? But I had never really thought about what it meant to "walk through the valley of the shadow of death," and I *was* afraid.

AVIS'S PAN OF MACARONI AND CHEESE was so huge, Denny and I figured it would probably feed us for the rest of the week. But after reheating some for lunch the next day, I decided to freeze the rest and bring it out when the kids got home from Mexico.

I sat at the dining room table, blinds darkened, my crutches propped on a nearby chair, picking at my lunch and thinking about what Denny had said last night. He'd been very quiet when he came home from work—not at all like Denny, who was usually full of funny stories about the kids he was coaching in the summer park program . . .

"I talked to a lawyer last week—"

"What lawyer? We don't have a lawyer."

"We have one now. Stu gave me a couple of names of lawyers who handle cases like this."

I'd pressed my lips into a thin line. That meant Stu knew why we needed a lawyer.

"He called me today on the cell, wants to talk to you before the arraignment—"

"Arraignment?" My heart seemed to skip a beat. *"What does that mean?"*

"Like a hearing where the charges are read and bail is set. William Farrell—our lawyer—says it's routine; you don't have to appear, especially not in your condition. The defense lawyer is given a copy of the charges by the state's attorney's office, then a preliminary hearing is set. Maybe even next week."

Next week? I could feel my heart beating rapidly. So they really were going to press charges; I really was going to have to go to court.

"Why didn't he call and tell me?" I hadn't meant for my tone to be so challenging, but that's the way it came out.

Denny hid his exasperation well. *"Because you've just been through a terrible ordeal, and I don't want the lawyer or anyone else calling out of the blue upsetting you about this!"*

"I'm upset already." Tears had brimmed in my eyes and splashed down into Avis's macaroni and cheese.

Denny had reached out his hand and closed it over my own. *"I know, honey. Let's just talk to the lawyer tonight and let him take it from there. Maybe you won't even have to go."*

Not have to go? I'd clutched at the hope. *"But . . . it's my life they'll be talking about. Don't I get to say anything? Tell my story?"*

"I don't know, Jodi. This is new for me too. We just need to pray about it and ask others to be praying."

"I don't want other people praying about it!" I'd wailed. *"I don't want everybody knowing I'm being charged with . . . with vehicular manslaughter, or whatever he called it."*

I don't know how long I'd been sitting there toying with my food, going over the talk with William J. Farrell, Esquire, in our living room last evening, when I heard the front door being opened and another "Hellooo! Sista Jodee?"

That didn't sound like Avis. A Jamaican accent, more like . . .

"Chanda!"

Chanda stood in the archway of the dining room, loaded to the gills with a bucket, a mop, rags, spray plastic bottles, and aerosol cans. "What in the world?"

She held up a key and grinned apologetically. "Don' mean to

scare you. Denny gave it to me. But you never mind. I be blessed quiet—'cept when I vacuum. You got a vacuum?"

"Oh, Chanda." What was Denny thinking? We had a zillion hospital bills we hadn't even seen yet! "Denny shouldn't have asked—"

"'E didn't ask. I just tol' the mon I was comin'.'"

Chanda . . . something about Chanda. Suddenly I remembered. *That* was what I was supposed to do last Tuesday—take Chanda to get her mammogram. And I hadn't once thought to ask anybody what the outcome was.

"Last Tuesday . . . I'm so sorry I couldn't take you to your doctor's appointment. Did you find another way?"

"Oh, sure. Avis took me."

"And—?"

"T'ot you'd never ask. Got a mammogram, got a biopsy of that ol' lump." A wide smile took over her face, making her almost . . . pretty. "No cancer! Hallelujah, Jesus! No cancer!" Chanda dropped the bucket and mop and did a little shuffle dance right there in the archway.

"That's wonderful, Chanda. I'm so glad."

Chanda wheezed and fanned her face. "Given me history, it's a *miracle*. Now if I could just win the Big Lotto to pay off those doctor bills . . ." She picked up the bucket and headed for the kitchen. "All right if I use this sink?"

Oh, help. She really is going to clean my house. If I didn't feel completely useless before, I certainly did now.

I turned in my chair so I could see her through the kitchen

door. "Chanda?" Did I dare say anything? "Chanda, why don't you quit playing the lottery and buy some medical insurance with that money? Just a suggestion—but I wish you'd think about it."

"Oh. That's what I plan to do. Soon as I get me some winnings, I'm goin' to buy life insurance, medical insurance, a car, and take the kids to Disney World!" Chanda poured some liquid in the bucket and turned on the water in the sink.

Well, at least she didn't get mad at me for asking. I watched her start in on the kitchen—the sink was full of breakfast dishes—then hobbled back to my bedroom. How embarrassing to have one of your friends cleaning your house. I cringed; the bathroom was the pits, though I couldn't blame Denny and the kids with the crazy week they'd had. We ought to pay her something—she did it for a living, for goodness' sake!—but she'd probably feel insulted if we did, since it was her idea.

Why was everyone being so darn nice to me? I didn't deserve it. It'd be easier if they all just left me alone.

I took another pain pill and lay on the bed in the darkened bedroom, listening to the faint sounds of Chanda singing "Winna Mon" in that patois accent of hers, water running, huffs and thumps and chairs scraping.

Jesus, You did a miracle for Chanda. Why can't You do a miracle for me?

But I knew there would be no miracle. Not for Jodi Baxter. A boy was dead because of me, and I would have to live with the consequences.

351

39

By the end of the week, I was weaning myself off the pain medication and getting around pretty well on the elbow crutches. My broken ribs and ten-inch abdominal incision only hurt when I took big breaths—or cried or laughed—so I generally put a lock on my feelings and moved through the days and nights in a sort of detached stupor.

The Fourth of July came and went without any help from us, though Denny had the day off and did the laundry, watered the lawn and wilting flowers, and grilled some salmon fillets.

I missed Josh and Amanda so much. Their absence felt like another huge hole in my gut, right next to where my spleen used to be. But I was glad they were gone, glad I didn't have to be cheerful for their sakes.

Denny was attentive, trying to anticipate what I needed before I even knew myself, but we didn't talk much about the upcoming preliminary hearing, which had been scheduled for the following

Monday. If I let myself think about it, I might just freak out. So we made small talk, watched TV in the evening, even held hands while Denny prayed for the kids, for the family that was grieving, and thanked God that I was healing . . . but things felt distant between us.

I knew what was wrong—everything was wrong!—but I didn't know how to fix it.

The doorbell rang late Friday afternoon. Grumbling, I pulled myself off the bed and hobbled down the hall in reasonably good time, considering, and hoped it wasn't someone who was going to mind me opening the door dressed only in one of Denny's extra-large T-shirts and a pair of slipper-mocs.

It was Florida, holding out a bag of sub sandwiches.

"So why don't you have a key?" I turned my crutches around and headed into the living room and the safety of the couch.

"Key? What you talkin' about, girl? I don't got no key to your house."

"Never mind. Just thought Denny handed out keys to everybody in Yada Yada." I lowered myself onto the couch, with my bum left leg stretched out and my right leg on the floor—which put my back to Florida coming behind me from the foyer. "Why aren't you at work?"

Florida moved to the overstuffed chair facing me on the other end of the couch. "Girl, don't mess with me. You know I work the early shift; I get off at three. Decided to come see you and bring you some supper. But I'm getting a little tired of the attitude."

I sighed. "I'm sorry, Florida. Really. I appreciate you and everybody else who's been checking up on me. But—"

"But what?"

Did I have to spell it out? I looked away, but my breathing got heavy, sending little jabs of pain shooting from my sore ribs. "You all act like I had a skiing accident or something. 'Oh, poor Jodi, let's bring her some flowers'. . . 'Hi, Jodi, here's some supper.' Chanda came and cleaned my house, for cryin' out loud."

"So? You got a problem with people doin' nice for you?"

I closed my eyes for a moment, trying to slow my breathing. When I felt in control again, I opened them. Florida was sitting on the chair, arms folded, eyeing me like some mama waiting to hear the big whopper her kid was about to tell her.

"Yeah," I blurted. "Because I don't deserve it! Everybody's acting like there isn't a dead kid who got hit by *my car,* whose parents are so angry at me that they want me in jail. I've even got a copy of the charges from the state's attorney's office: The State of Illinois versus Jodi Baxter. Vehicular manslaughter . . . or hadn't you heard? Oh. And nobody mentions the fact that the kid was African American and I'm *white*—but I wouldn't be surprised if his family tells the media that it was a . . . a hate crime, that I did it on purpose or something."

I shocked myself. Why was I saying all this? Why was I dumping on Florida, of all people? *Jodi, you're a real jerk. She just came by to see you, and you're blabbering like an idiot.*

Florida got up out of the chair. For a second I thought she was going to leave, and I couldn't blame her. I opened my mouth to apologize, to beg her forgiveness—but instead she stood over me, hand on one hip while she shook a finger in my face with the other.

"Suck it *up,* Jodi Baxter! What does *deserve* got to do with anything? You think the only reason you're my friend is because you *deserved* it?"

"No, no! That's not what I meant. It's just—"

"Oh, I get it. You think you done somethin' *so* bad God just can't forgive you. So you mopin' around, keepin' all you blinds dark, like life just came to a stop."

I squirmed, wishing she'd back off.

But she bent down closer to my face. "Well, what makes you think you deserved God's love *before* the accident? Huh?" She straightened and walked around the living room with its comfortable furniture, plants in the windows, and pictures on the wall. "Oh, you been blessed all right. Nice house, nice kids, good husband, good life . . . but don't take no credit for it. You was *born* middle-class. You was *born* white. You was *born* in a family that already knew God and raised you right. Them three right there gave you a leg up and a head start, while some of the rest of us are still strugglin' out of the starting gate."

I watched as she paused and shuffled through some of the CDs by the music cabinet. *Take credit for it? Sounds like she's blaming me for it.*

Florida turned. "Know what your problem is, Jodi Baxter? You don't want to accept that *you're just like me.* I didn't deserve God's love when I was strung out on drugs, now, did I? But the thing that turned me around? I discovered He loved me anyway. Jesus died on that bloody cross to save *me*—and look how far He's brought me! With all your blessings, all your middle-class-white-

American privileges, you don't deserve God's love, either. But *you* seem to forget that He loves you *anyway,* that He saved you, and ain't nothin' you can do gonna change that."

"I know all that." I pouted.

"In you head maybe. But deep down inside, you ain't figured out yet what it means to be just a sinner, saved by grace."

She looked at the CD she'd picked up and had been waving in the air like a punctuation mark. "Where'd you get this?" She held it out toward me. Somebody named Donnie McClurkin.

"Uh, Avis brought it, I think."

"You listened to it? . . . Or this?" She waved another CD at me. I squinted. Clint Brown. I shook my head.

"Girl, you a sad case. Well, you *listen* for a change. Maybe God let you have this accident to get your attention."

Florida put the first disc in the CD player, punched the "on" button, and handed me the remote. "I gotta go have me a cig—" She fished a pack of cigarettes out of her purse, then laughed. "Yeah, God's brought me this far, but I still got a ways to go." She headed for the front porch. "But you—just listen."

I couldn't very well turn off the CD player with Florida sitting just outside on the front porch, having her "cig." So I lay on the couch as the gospel music filled the room. How often did I take the time to really *listen* to music? Usually it was just background noise while I cooked supper or watered my plants or prepared a school lesson.

I listened . . . and by the third song, I had forgotten everything but the words filling the room, filling my head, pushing deep down into the emptiness of my soul. "Just for me-ee," Donnie McClurkin sang, "just for me . . . Jesus came and did it just for me."

Oh God, do I really believe that? Even if there had been no Hitler or Ku Klux Klan or gang murders or drug lords or 9/11 . . . would Jesus still have had to die on the cross to cover my sins?

A voice seemed to shake up the inside of my head. *"You're missing the point, Jodi! Not 'would Jesus have had to?' . . . Jesus* did *do it . . . just for* you. *Because God so loved you, Jodi . . ."*

I'm not sure I heard many of the next few songs until the end, when another grabbed my attention.

> We fall down, but we get up . . .
> For a saint is just a sinner who fell down . . . and got up.

If Florida came back in, I never heard her because I was weeping.

AMANDA CALLED LONG DISTANCE Saturday afternoon. She'd bought a calling card with her own money and breathlessly tried to tell us in three minutes how much work they'd gotten done on the cement block home they were building with Habitat for Humanity in the Mezquital Valley. "And I'm learning lots of Spanish, Mom! It's so different here! I want to take conversational Spanish next year. Edesa would help me, I know! Oh—are you getting better, Mom?"

"I'm fine. Just stay safe and boil your drinking water!"

The front doorbell rang, and Denny, who'd been on the kitchen extension, went to answer it while I got in a few words with Josh, then said good-bye.

Denny poked his head into the living room, where I was stretched out on the couch with the cordless. "Company." He sounded peculiarly pleased about something but ducked down the hall.

"Hey, girl." I heard Florida's voice before I saw her. After the way I'd treated her yesterday, I could hardly believe she was back already. Good. I wanted to—

"Got somebody I want you to meet." Florida sashayed into the living room, holding the hand of a young girl who followed reluctantly, sucking on two fingers.

I thought my heart was going to stop beating. "Oh! Is this . . . Carla?" I looked back and forth from Florida to the child, as though seeing Florida at eight years old. All across the front of her head, Carla's hair had been braided in tiny cornrows held with little butterfly clips, looking for all the world like a little tiara, behind which sprang a wonderful mane of bushy black curls. She stared shyly at the braided rug on the floor, clinging to Florida's hand.

Florida beamed in the dim coolness of the living room, "Praise God Almighty! Jesus! Yes it is." She tugged the girl closer. "Carla, this is Sister Jodi . . . she's been praying for you."

My chin quivered. I hadn't prayed for Carla even once since the accident.

Carla pulled Florida down till her ear was level with the girl's stage whisper. "Why is she crying? An' she's got a big yellow eye."

Florida glanced at the tears spilling down my still bruised face and smiled. "She's crying because she's so happy to see you." Florida sat down on the overstuffed chair and pulled Carla into her lap. "We get visits to start with. Carla's staying with me an' the boys for the weekend."

I found my voice. "Oh, yes, Carla. I am *so* happy to see you. Your . . . mommy is my very good friend, so—" I had intended to say, "*—so I know we'll be good friends, too.*" But I was having a hard time pushing words past the huge lump in my throat.

Just then Stu bustled through the open front door and into the living room. "Finding a parking place in this neighborhood is like going to the dentist," she announced. "No, a tax audit. Whatever. *Irritating* would be too mild a word." She stood in the middle of my living room, looking me over. "So, Jodi. You got dressed today. Good for you. What do you think of our girl?" She beamed at Carla.

I reached for a tissue and blew my nose, hiding the smile that threatened to put a crack in my crisis mentality, letting in a tiny ray of hope. If God could turn it around for Florida after all she'd been through, then maybe, just maybe, God would get me through this mess, too.

40

enny wanted me to go to church with him Sunday morning, but I couldn't face all the Uptown people yet—not to mention the flight of stairs up to the second-floor meeting room. I needed more time.

"You want me to stay home with you? You've been alone a lot this week." He truly seemed distressed about that.

"No, that's okay. Somebody ought to represent the Baxter family. And besides, then you can tell me about the service." This would be the third Sunday in a row I'd missed worship at Uptown, and I *would* like to go if I could be a fly on the wall and just take in the worship and singing and the sermon. But nobody was going to let me be invisible.

"Well, okay, if you're sure," Denny said reluctantly. "But how about if we get out and take a walk by the lake this afternoon. Maybe we'll drive up to Evanston's lakefront—they've got a lot of walking paths."

Evanston's lakefront. That sounded good. Not a chance in a million I'd run into anybody I knew up there.

But the moment I heard the garage door close and the old junker rattle down the alley, I had second thoughts about church. Maybe it was a bad idea not to go. At least I would have been distracted for a few hours. As it was, I couldn't avoid the terrifying reality that *tomorrow* was the preliminary hearing about the charges being brought against me.

I hobbled into the dining room on my crutches and looked at the computer. Hadn't checked e-mail since before the accident. Just couldn't deal with cute forwards, spam ads, or even what had been going on in cyberspace with Yada Yada. Now might be a good time, though. It was something to do.

But I felt overwhelmed at the long list of e-mails that loaded into the inbox after I'd logged on. Halfheartedly I scrolled down through the list. Just as I predicted: a lot of "Fwd Fwd Fwds" with "You gotta read this!" or "So true!" in the subject line. I didn't even have the energy to delete them. I scrolled past a scattering of messages from various members of Yada Yada . . . old friends in Downers Grove who'd heard about my accident . . . messages for Denny and Josh and Amanda . . .

But one subject line caught my attention: "Vehicular manslaughter." My mouth went dry. I checked the sender: William J. Farrell to Denny Baxter. As though pushed forward by an unseen force, I clicked on it twice to open it.

To: Denny Baxter

From: William J. Farrell, Attorney at Law
Subject: Vehicular manslaughter

Denny,

I'll try to answer your questions as briefly as possible:

< Why vehicular manslaughter?>
    This is not a killing with "malice aforethought," therefore not murder.

< What exactly are we facing here?>
    Vehicular manslaughter can be charged in two ways: with "gross negligence" or without it. The former is a felony. The latter is what we call a "wobbler," which means the prosecution has the choice whether to charge felony or misdemeanor.
    Your wife has no priors and wasn't drinking, so I am confident that *at most* she might face a misdemeanor charge. Depending on the evidence, a misdemeanor charge—if convicted—can carry with it the possibility of jail time up to a year, and/or a fine and probation.

< Does Jodi have to attend the preliminary hearing?>
    Usually, yes. But if she can't be there, I can get a continuance until she's more recovered. I haven't heard the state's attorney's actual evidence—that will happen

Monday. But I'm working on a number of fronts to counter whatever "evidence" they think they have. No matter what happens, we will, of course, plead Not Guilty.

< We won't have to post bail?>

No. The document Jodi signed releases her on her personal recognizance. Even the state's attorney doesn't think your wife is a flight risk.

I felt frozen to the chair, even though the temperature was already well into the eighties. How could words like "a killing" and "murder"—even "not murder"—be associated with *me*, Jodi Baxter? I'd only had one traffic ticket in my entire life, and that was years ago when I got stopped for having an expired registration tag.

I stared in disbelief at the message. Words like "if convicted" and "jail time" swam before my eyes. Suddenly, I felt desperate to get rid of it, make it go away. With shaking hand, I moved the cursor to "delete" then closed the window, shut down the computer . . . and as an added measure, squeezed my sore body around the side of the computer desk and pulled the plug.

Now I was sweating. I needed to lie down. I swung my crutches toward the living room and the comfort of the couch— but knew I had to fill my mind with something, or the words would taunt me, shout me down in the silence. I stopped by the music cabinet and picked up the other CD Avis had brought me. Clint Brown. Never heard of him. But I stuck the disc in the changer, took the remote and the CD insert with me, and collapsed on the couch.

I hit the "play" button.

The music filled the room, rolling around me, over me, through me. No cutesy songs. Every song was about Jesus, about resting in His presence, about finding "strength while I'm waiting," about Jesus being "my everything."

Florida had said, *"Listen!"* I listened. I wanted the lyrics to drown out the terrifying words still knocking around in my brain. *A killing . . . not murder . . . felony . . . misdemeanor . . . prison . . . fine . . . not guilty . . . guilty . . .*

I concentrated on the next song. "Where would I be? You only know . . ."

Did God know I would make such a mess of my life?

"I'm glad You see through eyes of love . . ."

Exactly what Florida had said.

The voice on the CD seemed to be singing from inside of me, capturing every thought, feeling, and dread of the past two horrible weeks.

"A hopeless case, an empty place . . ."

O yes, God! That's me, that's me!

". . . if not for grace."

My eyes, wet with tears of self-pity, flew open. I hit the "repeat" button and listened to the song again. There it was.

". . . if not for grace."

I played the song again . . . and again . . . and again.

". . . if not for grace."

SOMEONE FROM UPTOWN COMMUNITY sent home a wonderful Sunday dinner with Denny—chicken stew with dumplings along with homemade rolls, crunchy coleslaw, and peach cobbler for dessert. For the first time since the accident, I actually felt hungry.

Then, true to his word, Denny got me and my crutches in the candidate for Rent-a-Wreck and drove up to Evanston's lakefront, where we walked slowly along the jogging path for about half an hour then sat on a bench and gawked at all the bikers, in-line skaters, stroller pushers, and dog-walkers enjoying the lakefront park.

I told Denny I'd read the lawyer's e-mail. He looked pained. "I didn't mean for you to see that."

I took as deep a breath as my ribs would allow. "Can't hide my head in the sand forever, can I?"

The walk wore me out completely, and I practically collapsed into bed when we got back home around four o'clock and fell asleep. I had a dream that I was lying in a plain wooden coffin, but I wasn't dead, and the lid wasn't on. And stamped all around the outside of the wooden coffin was the same word again and again: Grace . . . Grace . . . Grace.

I woke with the dream still clear in my mind and lay there thinking about it. The funny thing was that in the dream I wasn't panicky, but I just lay in the coffin, peaceful-like.

As I lay on the bed in that twilight between sleep and being awake, I thought I heard voices . . . and laughter. Now I really was awake. Who on earth could be here?

I looked at the clock beside the bed. Five-thirty. Reluctantly, I swung my legs over the side of the bed and got my crutches. I didn't really want company. But I was curious. I hobbled down the hallway, but even before I got to the living room, I could pick out voices: Florida bragging on Carla while Delores kept exclaiming, "Oh! *Es* wonderful!" . . .

I stood in the archway leaning on my crutches, giving the living room a once-over. Practically everybody from Yada Yada was there . . . except Chanda and Edesa. And Stu. I cleared my throat. *"What* are you guys doing here?"

"Hey, Sleeping Beauty waketh!" Yo-Yo called out over the hubbub.

Yeah, right. Though I did look a little bit more like a normal human being today, after getting a shampoo from Denny last night. The bruising on my face was almost gone, too; I'd even put on a little makeup for our afternoon outing. And the denim skirt and sleeveless top I was wearing hid the scars on my leg and abdomen.

"Why aren't you home with Carla?" I growled at Florida.

"You think I'd be here messin' with Yada Yada if I still had Carla? Ha. I had to take her back by three this afternoon. If I was home, I'd just be blubberin' on my sleeve, so I might as well be here."

"It's the Sunday Yada Yada is scheduled to meet," Avis explained.

"Knew *you* wouldn't come out," Ruth butted in, "so . . . to you we brought the Yada Yada!"

Gosh, she looked smug. "Why didn't anyone tell me?" I asked, exuding patience.

"You? You would've said no; that's because why!"

"That's it" . . . "Got that right."

Florida snickered. "So we asked that soft-hearted husband of yours, who we got wound around our little fingers."

Figured. Wasn't Denny supposed to be protecting me from overstimulation? But I let slip a grin. I was glad to see everybody, in spite of myself. My sisters. All of them. Even Adele. A few weeks ago, I could never have imagined that this group of women—like so many pairs of crazy, colorful socks—would become the kick-off-your-shoes-and-let-it-all-hang out kind of girlfriends I desperately needed. Yet God put us together in time to help me through the most difficult days of my life.

Yo-Yo scrambled up. "Okay, everybody. Off the couch. Pegleg, here, needs a place to prop it up."

"No, no." I moved quickly toward a chair. "Just give me that footstool. I'll be fine."

"You sure?" But Yo-Yo dragged over the footstool, and I sat in one of the dining room chairs Helpful Denny must have carried in.

"We won't keep you long." Avis was sitting on one end of the couch with her big Bible in her lap. "But tonight seemed like a good night to keep you covered in prayer."

So. Everybody has probably heard about the preliminary hearing tomorrow. I sighed. Couldn't keep it under wraps forever. Well, they were here, and I certainly did need the prayer. I cast a glance at Adele filling the La-Z-Boy, remembering her comment: *"Maybe Jodi doesn't need our prayers."*

She'd been right. I hadn't felt any real *need* for Yada Yada's prayers, though I'd been willing to scratch out some prayer requests. But now . . . *Oh God, yes, yes, I desperately need their prayers big time—especially since I really don't have a clue how to pray right now.*

Avis opened her Bible. "Just wanted to share a short parable that Jesus told about how we should pray."

I didn't have my Bible, so I just listened as she read the familiar parable from Luke 18 about the two men who went to the temple to pray. The Pharisee—upright citizen, religious leader—stood tall and thanked God that he wasn't a sinner like other men. He didn't rob banks or commit adultery or plot evil. He wasn't even a lowlife like the tax collector standing nearby. And the things he *did* do! Why, he fasted (twice a week!) and was faithful to pay his tithes down to the penny.

But (Avis continued reading) the other man—a tax collector, generally assumed by everyone in that day and age to be padding his own pockets—bowed his head and beat on his chest in remorse, crying out, "God, have mercy on me, a sinner!"

Avis shut her Bible, but those last words rang in my ears: *"God, have mercy on me, a sinner!"*

Florida had said I didn't really know what it meant to be "just a sinner, saved by grace." Did she mean . . . I was like that self-inflated Pharisee? The realization was shocking. Everybody knew the Pharisees were self-righteous bad guys.

But it was true. I was proud. *Hey, God, it's me, Jodi the "good girl"! God, aren't You proud of me? I've been married almost twenty-years—unlike Ruth, who's on her third husband, or Chanda, who has kids by several daddies. And thank You for my kids, off on their mission trip to build houses for Mexico's poor—while Yo-Yo's brother is sneaking off to those teen raves and doing who knows what. You should be proud of me, God, because I know the Bible from cover to cover (even though I forget those pesky references). And don't forget, God, I've never done drugs like Florida or even smoked a lousy cigarette! Have never forged a check like Yo-Yo . . . or played the stupid lottery like Chanda. But I'm no fuddy-duddy, God—why I occasionally drink wine on special occasions, but of course I'd never get drunk . . .*

But Jesus had said that it was the *other* man, the one who *knew* he was "just a sinner," who went home forgiven.

That "other" Jodi, the one who's basically selfish and petty . . . who flies off the handle at her husband . . . who was "driving angry" a couple of weeks back . . . the one who was driving too fast for weather conditions . . . who hit a young kid . . . and killed him . . . killed him . . .

"Oh *God!* Have *mercy* on me! I'm just a sinner! Have *mercy!*"

I didn't even realize I'd cried those words aloud, except that everybody looked startled and stared at me. Both Avis and Florida moved quickly to my side and began to pray. I couldn't stop the tears, but they didn't stop the prayers. Someone stuck a tissue into my hand, and then I felt Yada Yada gathering around my chair, as first one hand and then another was laid on my stuck-out foot, my head, even a gentle hand touching my belly.

"*Thank* You, Father, for Your great mercy!"

"Thank ya, *Jesus!*"

"*Gracias*, Father God . . ."

Nony's voice rose above the rest, and I recognized the psalm

Avis had pushed me to read. "Thank You, Father, that You are compassionate and gracious, slow to anger, abounding in love! You will not always accuse, nor will You harbor anger against us forever! You do not treat us as our sins deserve . . . so great is Your love for those who fear You—"

I heard a strange sound out in the hall. Others heard it, too, and glanced at one another. It sounded like Denny . . . weeping.

I suddenly felt afraid. Why was he crying? I didn't think I'd ever heard my husband sob like that. I wanted to get up and go to him, but I saw Florida leave the huddle around my chair and head for the hallway. In a moment, she was back, her arm around Denny, pulling him into the middle of the circle.

Denny fell to his knees beside my chair, head bowed, hands on his knees, and continued to weep. I felt confused, but I reached out and laid my hand on his hair. Soft dark hair, flecked with gray. Beneath my fingers, I could feel the heaving of his body . . .

After several moments, his sobs quieted, and he pulled out his handkerchief, wiped his face, blew his nose, and looked at me. Around us Yada Yada seemed to hold its collective breath.

"I . . . heard you cry out . . . for mercy." Denny reached for my hand. "But I'm the one who needs to ask forgiveness—from God and from you. Because—" He swallowed. "Because I *did* have too many beers the Sunday of the accident. Four to be exact. It was . . . stupid. I was irritated that you'd gone off to visit Nony's church instead of coming to Uptown with the family, jealous that Yada Yada was taking up half of our Sunday evenings . . . and scared, too, scared that I was going to lose my job and that we'd made a big mistake moving into the city. So while I was out playing ball with the guys, I thought, *What the heck? What difference does it make? Live a little, Baxter.*"

"Uh-huh," Florida muttered. "Been there."

I couldn't believe Denny was spilling our business like this in front of other people—a bunch of women at that. But . . . maybe it felt safer than just talking to me.

"But I didn't mean to make you late, Jodi. I thought you said to have the car back by five o'clock—"

"I know, I know." I was shredding the tissue I'd been given into little pieces on my lap.

"But I did wait till the last minute. On purpose. I wanted to make you sweat—but still get the car back on time. But then you jumped all over me for making you late, and it made me mad. And it made me mad that you smelled beer on my breath and accused me of drinking too much . . . but—" His voice dropped to a whisper. "—you were right. I just couldn't admit it. Didn't want to admit it. Didn't want you to be right . . ."

The room was incredibly quiet. Denny seemed to have forgotten everyone else and just kept his eyes on me. "But when the hospital called and said you'd been in an accident, said there'd been a fatality, I was terrified, because . . . I knew it was my fault!"

"No, no, Denny!" I moaned. It wasn't fair, Denny taking all the blame. "I was angry. I was distracted. Too angry to be driving in that rainstorm." I could hardly believe what I was saying, admitting how wrong I'd been to be "driving angry." But for some reason it felt okay, even in front of Yada Yada. After all, I was "just a sinner"—just like everybody else. Except I was the last person to know it.

But it was like Denny hadn't even heard me. "Jodi, will you forgive me? I can hardly bear the suffering you're going through—not just the surgery and your leg. That's bad enough. But the *charges* they're bringing against you, the *hearing* tomorrow . . . I'm so sorry. So sorry."

Behind me I heard Florida mutter, "Oh God, if you ain't God all by Yourself. Glory!"

I couldn't say anything; the lump in my throat was too big. But Denny just wrapped his arms around me, and we cried together as Avis and Florida and Nony and the others started praising and shouting and crying and thanking God.

Don't know who put on the CD—probably Florida—but suddenly the song she'd made me listen to yesterday filled the room . . .

We fall down, but we get up . . .
For a saint is just a sinner who fell down . . . and got up.

41

I awoke Monday morning to sunshine trying to stick its fingers through the cracks in the miniblinds. The digital clock read only 5:32. But I knew I couldn't go back to sleep.

Today was the day of the preliminary hearing.

Denny was still asleep, rolled over on his side, just a sheet covering the foothills of his hip and shoulder. I reached out beneath the sheet to touch him, to rest my hand on the curve of his hip, then pulled back my hand. I didn't want to wake him—not just yet.

I lay quietly on my back, thinking about Yada Yada last night . . .

After Denny and I had quit crying on each other's shoulder, the group insisted that Denny stay. He'd settled down on the floor beside the footstool, his back leaning against my chair. Avis asked us straight out what was going to happen at the preliminary hearing the next day. Denny laid it all out, everything we knew.

"*You scared, Jodi?*" Yo-Yo never waited for niceties.

Nothing like ripping open my emotional walls. *"Terrified."* To my surprise, it felt so good to admit it. *"If I'm convicted even of a misdemeanor, it could still mean—"* I'd swallowed hard. *"—jail time."*

"Yeah?" said Yo-Yo. *"Well, you won't be the first person in this group who's spent time in jail, will ya? And . . . here I am."* She'd spread her arms out. *"Still in one piece. And wiser, too."*

"But . . . my kids." I was close to weeping again.

"Uh-uh." Avis had shaken her head emphatically. *"We are not going to go straight to the worst that could happen. What are we going to pray for, Hoshi?"*

Hoshi had been very quiet, as usual. But she'd perked up at Avis's question. *"A miracle."*

"Delores?"

"I pray that Jodi and Denny have God's peace, no matter what."

"Adele?"

Adele had shrugged. *"Might as well go for the gold . . . and pray that the charges would be dropped."*

Avis had seemed satisfied. *"All right. That's what we're going to pray for—a miracle, God's absolute peace, and that the charges will be dropped."*

"And that God will get all the glory," Nony had added.

And so they'd prayed, and toward the end it seemed like everybody was praying at the same time, just thanking God for His salvation, His mercy, His grace . . . and I realized after a while that it was no longer about *me.* Florida, Avis, Delores . . . each one was thanking God for His mercy and grace *toward herself . . .*

Willie Wonka's nails clicked on the floor as the dog came into the room and nuzzled Denny's hand hanging over the side of the bed. *Time to let me outside, people!* his eyes seemed to say.

Denny rolled over on his back then turned his head and looked at me. "You awake already, Jodi?"

"Um-hm."

"You okay?"

"Um-hm."

He rolled over onto his other side, facing me, and stroked my face, tracing the still tender scar under my bangs where my head had hit the side window. "What are you thinking?"

I was quiet a moment, relishing the gentle touch of his hand on my face. "I'm thinking I want to go to the hearing."

"What?" Denny sat up so fast he whipped the sheet off my prone body. "Jodi, you don't have to go—not till you've healed more. The lawyer said he could ask for a continuance."

"I know. But why wait? Maybe it's more important to face my demons."

"Your . . . demons."

"My demons . . . my fears. If I stay home, I'll just be hiding. Not wanting anyone to know it's Jodi Baxter who killed that boy. Not wanting to face the accusations against me."

Denny stared at me as if I were a stranger who'd crawled into bed with him. "But, Jodi. What if Jamal's family is there?"

I nodded slowly. "That, too. I . . . hope they are." The look on Denny's face was so odd, it was almost funny. But I didn't laugh. "Will you go with me?"

"Go with—?" Then he did laugh. "How else would you get there, you goose—hitchhike?"

THE HEARING WAS SCHEDULED for ten o'clock at the Second District Circuit Court of Cook County in Skokie. I'd been surprised it wasn't at the big county courthouse on the South Side, but Mr. Farrell had told us the Skokie court handled all the North Side Chicago cases.

Denny let me out as close as possible to the entry of the sprawling two-story red-brick building at nine-thirty then disappeared into the parking garage. The courthouse was surrounded by one of the local forest preserves, almost parklike . . . except for the police cars driving in and out. I wondered how I was going to get through the revolving door with my crutches, but a security guard on the inside waved me over to a regular glass door marked with the blue handicapped logo.

As soon as Denny came through the revolving door, we got in line to go through security, but I set off the metal detector when I hobbled through it, and a security guard made me pass through again. The third time he made me hand over the crutches and I hopped through. The alarm still went off.

Exasperated, Denny barely kept his cool. "Look, she broke her leg, and it's got a metal rod in it. Can't you just wand her and let her go?" Which they did, but they made Denny empty his pockets *and* pull off his belt. They kept his penknife and said he could pick it up on the way out.

We finally headed up the escalator to the second floor and found Courtroom 206 about ten minutes to ten.

I don't know what I expected, but the beige-colored room wasn't that large. The judge, a balding black man with grandfatherly jowls who amply filled out his black robe, was already hearing a case. Our lawyer, William Farrell, was sitting in the empty, cushioned, jury seats, waiting our turn, I supposed. His sunburned face, topped with a thick head of auburn hair, looked up, surprised, and he hustled our way as Denny and I slid into the first of three pewlike benches at the back of the room. "Denny. Jodi," he murmured, shaking our hands. "You didn't have to come, you know. I was going to ask for a continuance, citing recovery time for your injuries, Jodi."

"I know." How could I explain that I needed to do this—now?

Two cases were dispatched in fairly quick order as we waited— one involving a man in drab, Department of Corrections garb, flanked by two Chicago police officers, who pled guilty to abuse of a controlled substance. The judge gave him a one-year sentence on the spot, minus thirty-three days he'd already served.

I stared at the man's back as the police officers led him out, suddenly feeling claustrophobic, like I might never leave this room a free person. I grabbed Denny's hand and held on tight.

A door marked "Conference Room" opened along the right side of the room, and a middle-aged white man in a rumpled tan suit came in followed by an African-American woman with close-cropped hair, small glasses, and gold hoop earrings framing a thin, tense face. She was accompanied by two boys—one nine or ten, the other an older teen—wearing T-shirts, baggy jeans with crotches to their knees, and big gym shoes with floppy laces, who stared at me as they sat at the far end of the pews. Mr. Farrell murmured something to Denny, who turned to me. "That's the assistant state's attorney," he whispered.

Must be Jamal's mother with him, I thought, looking straight ahead. *Are those his brothers?* My hands felt clammy. *Why did I think I was brave enough to do this?*

Someone slipped into the row behind us. I turned slightly. Avis! What was she doing here?

She leaned forward. "Thought you weren't coming," she murmured.

"So why are *you* here?" I whispered back.

"*Somebody* needs to pray over this hearing."

I faced forward again, but at that moment, my heart ached with love for Avis, who came all by herself just to pray, not even knowing we were going to be there.

God, when I "grow up," I want to think like Avis . . . be obedient like Avis . . . pray like Avis.

I cringed when the clerk read, "In the matter of the State of Illinois versus Jodi Baxter . . ." Mr. Farrell motioned for me to join him at the defense attorney's desk, which I did, feeling like every eye in the room was boring a hole in my back as I awkwardly made my way around chairs and railings. I tried to listen as the indictment was read but was distracted by the assistant state's attorney whispering to an aide, who hustled quickly out of the room. But all I heard was, " . . . resulting in the death of Jamal Wilkins, male, age thirteen" and "vehicular manslaughter."

"Mr. Prendergast. Are you ready to present the state's evidence?" The judge peered over the top of his glasses at the prosecuting attorney. The man shuffled some papers then made his way to one of the two podiums facing the judge.

"Uh, my witness has not arrived yet."

The judge raised his eyebrows. "Your *witness* has not arrived yet? Witness . . . singular?"

"Yes sir."

The judge paged through the papers in front of him. "It was my understanding, Mr. Prendergast, that the court would hear three witnesses at this preliminary hearing—two young men who were with the victim at the time of the accident, and a bystander, with sufficient evidence to take this case to trial."

"That's true, Your Honor. But . . . ah . . . the bystander is now uncertain she can verify the information she first gave to the police, and one of the boys with Jamal that day has declined to testify. I did not have time to serve a subpoena before this morning."

I heard William Farrell snort beside me, scribbling something with his pen.

The judge made his fingers into a tent, tapping his lips with the tips. "And your other witness?"

"Uh, we're waiting for him to arrive, sir."

The judge shook his head. "Counsel, approach the bench."

William Farrell patted my shoulder and joined the assistant

state's attorney before the judge's bench. They bent their heads together, but I was close enough to hear the other attorney say something about "running a red light . . . exceeding the speed limit . . . talking on a cell phone."

I bit my lip to keep it from trembling. Running a red light? Exceeding the speed limit? I didn't . . . I hadn't . . . had I? But how could we ever prove it? It was going to be their word against mine. But the cell phone—that I *knew* wasn't true!

I glanced toward Denny. Behind him I could see Avis's eyes closed, her mouth moving . . . she was praying.

William Farrell was leaning on the front of the judge's bench, looking completely relaxed. He had told us that only the state's evidence would be presented at the "pre-lim"; the defense could cross-examine their witnesses, but any defense witnesses did not have to appear until trial. *What witnesses?* Just me?

The other attorney pointed toward Jamal Wilkins's family, obviously asking for more time for his witness to arrive. My heart was pounding in my ears. Would there be a continuance after all? We'd come today for nothing?

But the judged eyed the clock, leaned back in his chair, and shook his head. The two attorneys returned to their seats.

"Ms. Wilkins, I presume?" The judge addressed the woman sitting behind the prosecuting attorney. She gave a slight nod, her thin face a mask of controlled emotion. "I am deeply sorry for your loss, Ms. Wilkins. It is a terrible thing to lose a child in an accident such as this, and we do not want to discount the pain that you and your family are going through. But . . ." The tented fingers tapped his lips again. ". . . without witnesses, the state has failed to show any evidence that would sustain taking this case to trial. I have no option here but to drop the charges against Mrs. Baxter." He banged his gavel. "Case dismissed . . . Next case."

Denny was out of his seat in half a second. "Thank you!" I heard him say to Mr. Farrell, pumping his hand. "Thank you!" Then, "That's it? It's over?"

"Yes—though the state's attorney could subpoena the witnesses and ask for a grand jury indictment. But don't worry—even if it went to trial, Jodi would walk . . ."

Even as Mr. Farrell started bragging about the defense witnesses he'd lined up, I could see Jamal Wilkins's mother sitting perfectly still on the other side of the room, staring straight ahead. Mr. Farrell's voice sounded far away, as if I had water in my ears . . .

The driver of the car that slammed into your minivan is prepared to testify that you both had the green light . . . evidence technicians who examined the skid marks at the scene of the accident found nothing consistent with excessive speed . . . not to mention that no cell phone was found in the minivan at the time of the accident . . ."

Taking my crutches, I hobbled toward the other mother. Swallowing past the huge lump forming in my throat, I spoke.

"Ms. Wilkins? I'm Jodi Baxter. It was . . . my car that struck your son."

The woman's face turned slightly, her eyes cold. "I know."

"I just want to say how terribly sorry I am. I can only imagine the pain you must be going through. I would . . . give anything if it hadn't happened. Even exchange my life for Jamal's—if I could."

Jamal's mother just stared at me for what seemed like an eternity. Then she stood abruptly, gripping her purse with both hands. "But you can't . . . can you?" She pushed past me and strode out the door of the room, the two sullen boys trailing behind her.

I watched her go. I could hardly forgive myself. Did I really expect that she could forgive me?

Avis came over and gave me a long hug, saying nothing.

Denny and Mr. Farrell joined us. The lawyer held out his hand. "Well, Jodi Baxter, you can go home a free woman. What happened today took me by surprise, but even if we had gone to trial, we could easily have proven you were not guilty."

I shook his hand. "Not legally, anyway."

He looked at me strangely, but I just said, "Thank you, Mr. Farrell," and headed my crutches for the door of the courtroom.

DENNY WANTED TO TAKE AVIS AND ME OUT TO LUNCH to celebrate, but I shook my head, hoping Avis would understand. I just wanted to get home. I wanted to think . . . or pray . . . or something. But not talk.

Once we arrived home, Denny said he'd fix lunch while I got off my feet in the living room. The room was dim, air moving lazily through it from the window fan. I swung my crutches over to the front windows and, one after the other, opened the miniblinds, letting in the bright daylight.

Stopping by the music cabinet, I shuffled through the CDs

sitting in little stacks. I picked up one of the *Songs 4 Worship* albums and ran my finger down the list of songs till I found what I was looking for.

Putting the disc into the CD player, I punched the "forward" button until it came to the number of the song I wanted.

In Your presence, that's where I belong . . .

The music, slow and majestic, swelled until it seemed to take over my whole body.

Seeking Your face, touching Your grace . . .

In Your presence, O God . . .

Lifting my face and with awkward grace, on one leg and two crutches, I began to dance.

Yada Yada Prayer Group
Reading Group Guide

1. Which character in this novel do you identify with most? Why?

2. Why do you think it was important for the women in The Yada Yada Prayer Group to get off the Internet and into each other's homes?

3. What was the common denominator that kept the women in Yada Yada hanging in there with each other?

4. Jodi, a longtime Christian, experienced what it truly meant to be "just a sinner, saved by grace" for the first time. Does admitting you're *still* "just a sinner" like everyone else feel like blame . . . or freedom? How have you experienced "God's grace" up close and personal?

5. What "religious clichés" have basically lost their meaning for you? Brainstorm new ways to communicate old truths.

6. What particular barriers tend to divide people, even those who share the same faith, where *you* live? (Cultural or ethnic differences? Racial tensions? Doctrine or worship styles?) Brainstorm ways you could be intentional about "breaking down the walls."

7. What obstacles have you experienced in making friends—*real* friends—"across the color line"? (Be honest!)

8. Share instances when a cross-cultural relationship has been a gift for you. Or ask yourself: *How might an interracial or cross-cultural friendship enrich my life?* What would you be able to bring to such a relationship? What challenges might you face?

9. Do you have a group of friends that "yada" you—i.e., know you deeply, inspire you to praise ("yadah")? If you were to form a "Yada Yada Prayer Group," who would you invite? (Pick up the phone!)

10. What would you still like to know about the characters after reading this novel? What do you think is going to happen to The Yada Yada Prayer Group in Book Two?

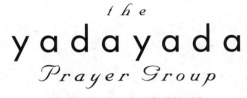

the

yadayada

Prayer Group

GETS DOWN

To Pat Hall

— the real "Bandana Woman" —

who is now my friend and sister in the faith

Prologue

CHICAGO'S LABOR DAY WEEKEND, 2002

The southbound elevated train squealed to a metallic stop on the trestles above Morse Avenue, and its doors slid open. On the street below, a slim figure slouching in the recessed doorway of the Wig Shop squinted intently through her wraparound shades at the train platform spanning the overpass. The commuter cars looked full, but only two women got off and started down the stairs to street level.

The woman in the doorway swore, sending expletives like a stream of spit toward the sidewalk. Three trains had come by already, and she hadn't seen an easy mark yet. Not with today being Sunday and tomorrow the Labor Day holiday. Mostly young folks heading downtown for the Jazz Fest in Grant Park—or coming back. The northbound would arrive soon, disgorging a handful of teenagers in baggy pants returning after a long day along Chicago's lakefront, noses burnt and ears plugged into their music. Maybe a few haggard parents who were smart enough to leave early with strollers, backpacks, and whiny preschoolers.

If only it was a workday! A bunch of skirts and suits would be coming home, tired, not so alert, twenties and fifties in their purses and wallets. Once they separated and headed onto the side streets of the Rogers Park neighborhood toward the brick apartment-buildings-turned-condos or the old two-story homes jammed between, hitting on a mark was usually just a matter of smooth timing.

But she couldn't wait till Tuesday. She needed some cash now. The ten blue Valium pills she'd washed down with a glass of vodka that morning hadn't suffocated the depression that was pulling her down, down into a bottomless black hole, threatening to swallow her, body and soul.

She had to get some smack. Soon.

The southbound pulled out overhead as the two ex-passengers spilled from the doors of the Morse Avenue station on street level. The figure in the doorway straightened, eyeing the pair. The first was a young woman, tall, nicely dressed in a white tailored pantsuit, straight black hair pulled back into a ponytail, a black handbag slung over her shoulder. And an older woman, her dark hair wound into a bun, wearing a navy skirt, red blazer, and sensible shoes with low heels. Their faces seemed long and flat, foreign. Asian. The watcher pulled back into the doorway as the pair crossed the street and passed right in front of her.

"Don't worry about your traveler's checks, *Mama-san*. See that drug store? It's got an ATM. I'll get some cash." The younger one took her companion's elbow as though to hurry her along, but the older woman shook off her hand, rattling off strange words that seemed to come out her nose, nasal and sharp.

A tight smile pulled at the corners of the mouth in the doorway, all that could be seen of a face masked with the wraparound shades and a red bandana tied tight around her head and knotted at the nape of her neck. She'd heard enough. *ATM.* She'd seen enough. *Two skirts at odds with each other, distracted.*

She waited a few seconds until the two women passed. Then, clutching the stiff paper bag with its long, hard object stuffed beneath her faded jean jacket, she stepped out onto the sidewalk behind them. *Watch ya feet, girl . . . don't bump inta no nickel feeders . . . be cool . . . don' call no 'tention to yo'sef.*

The two dark-haired women turned into the parking lot of the Osco Drug Store and disappeared inside. The woman in the jean jacket, skimpy tank top, and tight jeans leaned her backside against the corner of the store and fished out a nearly flat pack of cigarettes. She had to clutch the hidden paper bag with her elbow in order to light the cigarette with both hands. The long, flat object inside the bag made her feel confident. She wouldn't have to use it—just scare them. No problem.

The cigarette had burned only halfway when the pair came out of the store, but the woman flipped it into the street. So what if it was her last cigarette. She'd get some smack *and* a whole carton. Ha. Come right back here to this store and buy a carton straight up.

Or die. Didn't really matter.

She knew she couldn't keep this up—hooked on four habits. She'd tried to kick the heroin, signed up for that methadone program at the hospital. Yet all she'd done was pick up another habit. Most days she did all four—a handful of Valium washed down with vodka, a trip to the hospital for a slug of methadone, then back out in the 'hood to roll some sucker for money to pay for a bag of smack.

But none of it was keeping her from sliding deeper and deeper into that big black hole. It was going to come down on her one of these days. Maybe today.

She let the pair get several yards down the sidewalk before pushing off from the store wall to follow. She'd only taken a few steps when a loud voice behind her yelled, "Hoshi! Hoshi Takahashi! Wait up!" The mark—the young, tall one—turned and looked straight past her, a smile lighting up her long face.

The watcher swore under her breath. She couldn't stop now; she had to keep walking, right past the two women, who had now both turned back toward the running feet and yelling voice behind her. Why had she thrown the cigarette pack away? She needed something, some excuse to stop, to keep an eye on her mark. Desperation bubbled up in her throat. This had to work. Or it would go down—badly.

Her shoe. She'd retie the brand-new Nikes she'd lifted right under the nose of that stupid clerk at Foot Locker. She bent, untied one shoe, pulled it off, and shook out an imaginary piece of grit, rubbing the bottom of her bare foot and tipping her head slightly so she could keep the trio in her line of vision. Best thing about wraparound shades—you could watch people, and they didn't know you were looking.

A black woman, small boned, beaming, had joined the two Asian women, and the tall one was introducing the newcomer to the older woman. "You Hoshi's mama?" said the newcomer, pumping the woman's hand. The older woman smiled tightly, pulled her hand away, and nodded politely. Now they were walking again, right toward the woman bent over her shoe.

"Ain't this the bomb?" the newcomer crowed as the trio drew near, absently skirted the bent figure, and then passed on. "Yada Yada goin' to be blessed outta their socks to meet your mama. You just get off the southbound? I just rode up on the northbound, had to stand the whole way—on a Sunday evenin' too!" She laughed, a crown of tight coppery curls bouncing on top of her head. "Well, that's what happens on holiday weekends. So glad I ran into somebody from Yada Yada; don't have to walk by myself . . ."

The woman behind them straightened and swore again under her breath. Taking on three wasn't going to be so easy. The two foreigners—they'd give it up like melted butter. But this new one looked street-smart.

It was too late to wait for another mark. She knew they had money on them.

Two or three—didn't matter. It was do or die.

1

I bolted upright in the bed, soaked in sweat. *That face! Caught in my headlights, eyes round with fear. An eternal second . . .*

My thudding heart gradually slowed as the bedroom, bathed in early morning light, came into focus. I lay back down, begging the hands on the bedside clock to move because I did not want to close my eyes again.

Denny stirred on the wrinkled sheets beside me and cracked his eyes open mere inches from my face. "You okay, Jodi?" he murmured, slinging a heavy arm over my body and pulling me close. He kissed the back of my neck. "Happy anniversary, babe." Then he roused on one arm. "Gonna be a hot one, I guess. You're sweaty already."

I said nothing. The nightmare was still lurking beneath the surface, threatening to yank me back into its dark embrace. I forced myself to focus: our anniversary. Twenty years.

I'm so blessed. In spite of . . .

"I dreamed about the accident again." I wanted my husband to know how it haunted me, but could he ever know? How could anyone know what it felt like to have killed a child?

"Oh, Jodi." Denny pulled me closer against his bare chest. "I'm so sorry." He said nothing for a long while, just held me. And gradually his comfort eased my tense muscles like a long soak in the tub.

We slept again—maybe only ten, fifteen minutes—but this time when I awoke, Willie Wonka, our almost-deaf chocolate Lab, was licking my hand. His polite way of saying, "Don't you dolts get it? I gotta go outside—now!" Peeling Denny's arm off me, I limped out of our rear bedroom in my bare feet—boy, it felt good to walk without those annoying crutches!—circled through the dining room and kitchen, and let Willie Wonka out into the postage-stamp backyard of our two-flat. Sparrows darted and chirped in the trees along our back alley, but the usual crows were strangely silent. The West Nile virus stalking the Chicago area this summer, courtesy of ornery mosquitoes, had decimated the crow population.

Not that I missed them.

I waited at the back door for the dog to finish his business and grinned at the irony of this particular Wednesday. Getting married in *mid-August,* when the humidity in the Midwest can hover near tropic conditions, ranked as one of our stupider decisions—right up there with scheduling my two-month checkup after the car accident *today,* on our twentieth anniversary.

Though right now I didn't care. The nightmare had retreated into its dark hole and the day beckoned. I had a surprise for Denny he was going to love.

DENNY TOOK THE DAY OFF from his summer job coaching kiddy sports for the Chicago Park District to take me to my one o'clock doctor's appointment. At first I protested. "Josh can take me!" After all, what good is a seventeen-year-old with a driver's license if he can't chauffeur his parents around? Besides, a park district job doesn't have "personal days"; it's no-work-no-pay, and we were still waiting to hear if Denny's coaching contract at West Rogers High would be renewed for the 2002–2003 school year. Stupid politics.

But Denny just poured himself another cup of coffee and leered at me. "What? Work on my anniversary? Did I work on our wedding day? This family's not gonna starve if I take the day off— not till next week anyway. Besides, I want to hear what the doc says."

I took a long shower, letting the warm water run over my head long after the shampoo had rinsed out. *Thank You, Jesus, that I can wash my own hair again!* Frankly, I was doing pretty well, considering that I was minus one spleen and had a metal rod in my left leg. I didn't mind the scars on my leg so much—one about an inch long on my upper thigh and another down near my knee. Yet I was still self-conscious about the puckered pink line that ran from my sternum down to my pelvis, especially when Denny and I made love. It made me feel . . . damaged. And I still didn't know the consequences of walking around without a spleen. Didn't I need it? But so far I hadn't stopped breathing or anything, though Willie Wonka did look at me funny when I hobbled around the house with my stiff left leg.

And thank You, Jesus, that I didn't end up in prison! Did they have hot showers in prison? Green-apple shampoo? It had never occurred to me to wonder about that before I got charged with vehicular manslaughter. The prosecution tried for gross negligence, but the charges were dropped when no witnesses showed up at the hearing.

Grace. That's what it was. Only God's grace. It was an accident, yes. The boy had run out in front of my car in a pouring rain. Yet God knew I'd been driving angry. I was grateful—oh, so grateful!—that God had offered me mercy, forgiveness, and a legal acquittal, but . . . it was hard to forgive myself. After all, Jamal Wilkins was still dead; a mother was still grieving—

"Mom! Hurry up. I gotta baby-sit for the Fitzhughs today." I could hear fourteen-year-old Amanda rattling the bathroom door handle.

I turned off the shower, wrapped myself in a big towel, grabbed the hair dryer, and opened the door. "And happy anniversary to you, too, Mom," I said brightly in my best Amanda voice.

"Oh yeah. Happy anniversary, Mom." The tousled butterscotch hair disappeared behind the bathroom door, and I heard the lock click.

Teenagers. Amanda would be turning fifteen next week and starting her sophomore year at Lane Tech right after Labor Day. Josh would be eighteen next month, a senior. Where did the summer go?

I limped into the bedroom, toweled my wet hair, and pulled on some underwear. I knew where the summer had gone. My whole family—Denny, Josh, Amanda—had spent the last eight weeks getting Mom through surgery, through a court hearing, through recovery. My family . . . and my sisters in the Yada Yada Prayer Group.

I studied my reflection in the full-length mirror on the back of our bedroom door as I pulled on a jean skirt and white T-shirt. Who would've thought that motley prayer group from the Chicago Women's Conference last May would prop up Denny and me through the biggest crisis of our lives? *Florida Hickman* —"five years saved and five years sober!" *Avis Johnson*—the no-nonsense principal of Bethune Elementary School, where I taught third grade last year, and also the worship leader at Uptown Community Church, where Denny and I attended. *Yo-Yo Spencer*—ex-con and bagel chef, who was raising her two teenage half brothers. Plus several more "sisters" just as unlikely to end up in each other's living room.

I snorted and grinned as I flicked on the hair dryer. Only God could have put us together—and then kept us together. So far being part of the Yada Yada Prayer Group had been like riding a roller coaster without the lap bar. More than once I'd felt the group was on the verge of spinning off the planet—like when

Delores Enriques's son was shot by gangbangers while we were still at the women's conference. And when Ruth "Jewish Mama" Garfield had a falling-out with Florida Hickman over whether a foster child (Florida's daughter, to be exact) should be returned to her natural parents after such a long time. Not to mention Ms. Full-of-Herself Leslie "Stu" Stuart, a real-estate agent who had a talent for getting on my last nerve.

And then there was Adele Skuggs, big, black, and sassy, who could reduce my knees to Jell-O with one withering quip from her sharp tongue. But somehow God's hand always managed to bring us all back safely to the landing zone. So far.

I put down the hair dryer and held up a lock of limp, brown, shoulder-length hair in front of the mirror. Couldn't remember when I'd last had a haircut—before the accident anyway. Should've gotten a trim or something before my "anniversary surprise" for Denny this weekend. Oh well.

DR. LEWINSKI gave me a pretty good bill of health, but he scheduled me for physical therapy to build back the muscles in my left leg and gave me a lecture about the increased risk of infections now that my bodyguard spleen was pickled in a jar. "Bacteria that can cause pneumonia are normally filtered and killed by the body's defenses in the spleen," he said, peering over his reading glasses, which threatened to slide off the end of his long, thin nose any second. "We keep children under sixteen on prophylactic penicillin to protect them from severe life-threatening infections after a splenectomy, but"—he shrugged—"it's not routinely done for adults."

Hey, I thought. *I'm only forty-two. I'm not ready to go quietly with the "old people's friend,"* which is what my father called the pneumonia that took my grandmother. Dr. Lewinski simply cautioned me to drink lots of fluid and get plenty of rest during flu season, call my primary-care doctor if I suspected any chest congestion, and to "take care of yourself."

I'd given Denny a look. Primary-care doctor? We'd only moved to the Rogers Park neighborhood of Chicago a year ago, and finding new doctors hadn't been high on our priority list. Fact is, we hadn't seen the doctors we used to have out in the 'burbs for years. Who needs doctors when your kids are healthy teenagers and you're in your prime?

Me, I guess. Now, anyway.

Well, at least that was over. Now we could enjoy our anniversary. I glanced slyly at Denny, who was humming at the wheel of the borrowed car we were still driving while we waited for the insurance to settle on our wrecked minivan. I was sure he would take me out to dinner tonight, though he hadn't said anything about it yet. I hoped so, even though I knew our money was tight. I wasn't about to cook my own anniversary dinner—and besides, I needed a special atmosphere to spring my surprise on Denny.

I knew what he was going to say. "Jodi! We can't afford that right now." And I'd smirk and tell him I was doing sewing projects for some of the working moms at church to pay for it. But if he said, "You? Sew?" I'd throw a buttered roll at his forehead, like David bringing down Goliath.

I was so busy playing out that little scene in my head that I didn't notice we had kept going straight on Clark Street instead of turning off on Touhy Avenue. The street we lived on—Lunt Avenue—was one-way-going-the-wrong-way from Clark, which meant we always had to do this little square dance on one-way streets to get to our house. Instead, he had continued south on Clark Street, stopped, and was backing into a parking space.

I looked around at the plethora of small ethnic shops up and down Clark Street. "What's up?"

"Just be a good girl and don't ask questions." Denny came around to my side and opened the door of the old, rusted sedan.

"Okay," I grumbled, thinking this was way too early to be going out to eat—it was only two-thirty, for goodness' sake!—and besides, I didn't have my surprise along to give him.

He offered me his arm. "Close your eyes and trust me."

Oh, right. But I closed my eyes obediently and took Denny's arm, realized we were crossing the street—not at a crosswalk, because I heard horns blaring as he hustled me across—then walking down the other sidewalk at a good clip.

We stopped. I felt him pull open a door and heard a little bell ring. Where had I heard that little bell before? Yet it was the smell that gave it away—like the Tonette perms my mother used to give my grandmother back in Des Moines. What in the world?

I felt Denny's mouth brush close to my ear. "You can open your eyes."

I flicked open my eyes and jumped as several voices yelled, "Surprise!"

Adele Skuggs—owner and chief cosmetologist of Adele's Hair and Nails—stood smirking from behind the first chair of her shop, her hands encased in thin, plastic gloves. In the chair, Florida Hickman's hair—which for the past four months I'd only seen in perfect cornrows, braids, or tight ringlets all over her head—was sticking straight up like a bush of used Brillo pads, framing a big grin. Avis Johnson—my fifty-something boss—was sitting on Adele's vinyl couch under the front window, a copy of *Essence* on her lap and managing to look elegant even in her white slacks and embroidered denim shirt. And Leslie Stuart, otherwise known as "Stu"—the only other white woman I could see in the shop—sat in the corner chair next to the coffee cart, holding a mug of coffee and a slice of pound cake from the cake server.

All four of them were laughing at me. "Close your mouth, girl, before you trip over that bottom lip," Florida snickered.

Stu looked me up and down and shook her head. "You're right, Denny. She needs lots of help."

Oh, thanks a lot, Stu. Just what I need coming from Ms. Perfect herself. Stu wore her own straight hair long and blonde.

"Well, she's all yours, Adele." Grinning, Denny pushed me forward and backed toward the door. "Give her the works—hair, manicure, pedicure, whatever-cure. I'm taking her out on the town tonight!"

"You go, Denny!" crowed Florida as I heard the little bell over the door tinkle behind me.

405

2

I stood there, unsure what I was supposed to do, alternately feeling pleased at Denny's surprise and annoyed that he hadn't warned me. I should've scrubbed my feet while I was in the shower! The bottoms always got so tough and cracked in the summer from wearing sandals—

"You can sit down, Jodi," Avis said, patting the vinyl couch beside her and giving me her I'm-the-principal-but-I'm-not-going-to-bite-you look. "You're next."

Adele's big, gold earrings—like quotation marks around her short red 'fro—jangled as she resumed applying hair-straightening goo on Florida's head with a paintbrush.

"Yep." Stu washed down the last bite of her slice of pound cake with a swig of coffee. "Just relax. Don't worry about a thing." She smirked, which didn't comfort me at all. "We've already picked out your hairstyle and your nail colors."

"You're kidding, right? That's supposed to make me *not*

nervous?" I collapsed on the couch beside Avis, realizing my knees suddenly felt wobbly.

"Have some faith, girl!" Florida leaned forward in the beauty chair but was jerked back with a firm hand by Adele. "You ever see anybody walk outta here lookin' worse than when they walked in? My, my, my. You gotta trust your hairdresser."

Well, Adele wasn't exactly my hairdresser. I'd only been to her shop once before—to get my nails done on the spur of the moment. (Forty-two and I'd never had a manicure before!) Frankly, I didn't have a hairdresser. Amanda sometimes trimmed my hair, or I shelled out twelve dollars at Supercuts. Yet I had to admit that the women in Yada Yada who had started coming to Adele's Hair and Nails after we all met at the Chicago Women's Conference looked pretty spiffy after they got their hair done.

Adele peeled off her plastic gloves and said, "Leave that fifteen minutes—you watch the time." Florida grabbed a magazine and popped over to the other beauty chair in front of the long wall mirror. "In the chair, Jodi," Adele ordered.

I stood up, eyeing my friends suspiciously. Surely Avis wouldn't let Stu and Florida choose a really far-out hairdo for me—would she? "What about these guys?" I waved a hand at Stu and Avis. "Aren't they next?"

"In the chair, Jodi." Adele held the black plastic cape with all the patience of a mother counting to ten. I sat.

"I'm just here as a consultant." Stu grinned and tossed her long blonde hair over her shoulder, revealing the line of small pierced earrings running up the side of her ear.

Avis held up the back of her hand toward me, fingers spread out. "Nails. Soon as Corey gets done with her other nail appointment." Corey must be Adele's manicurist. I sucked in a tiny breath of relief. At least I didn't have to face Adele getting down and scrubbing my feet like she did the last time, which unnerved me no end.

Adele put on new plastic gloves and began wetting my hair with a spray bottle.

"Uh-huh," I said. "And how did you all *just happen* to be here all at the same time?"

"Denny thought you might need a little moral support, seeing as how we're doing a makeover here." Stu got in my face with a digital camera. "Smile! This is the 'before' picture."

When I stopped seeing stars from the flash, I glanced in the mirror. Adele was now running her fingers through my hair, holding up various lengths, and frowning, as though studying a serious scientific problem. "What happened to your other customers?"

"Huh. I can schedule whoever I want on today, 'cause I'm the boss." As though to prove her point, Boss Adele swung the chair I was sitting in away from the mirror.

"What? You're not even going to let me see what you're doing?" My protest was meant to be lighthearted, but I felt slightly panicked. Did Denny realize what he'd gotten me into? I mean, didn't Adele specialize in black folks' hair?

Adele allowed a big, rumbling chuckle. "Not to worry, Jodi. This hair can only get better. You've let this mess go too long."

Well, she had a point. Taking care of my looks hadn't exactly been high on my agenda the last two months. I closed my eyes, letting myself enjoy the cool spray wetting my head and Adele's firm fingers sectioning my hair and sticking clips here and there to hold it back while she started to cut.

"So has Denny told you where he's taking you tonight?"

I popped my eyes open at Stu's question. "No." I caught looks passing between Stu and Avis and Florida. "Don't tell me he told you guys."

"Uh-huh. Sure did," they chorused.

"So tell me! Yada Yada knows where I'm going on my anniversary before I do? How fair is that?"

"Uh-uh. Sorry. Promised Denny."

Adele's firm hand pushed me against the chair back. "Sit still, Jodi, or I'll cut something you'll wish I hadn't."

Stu grinned. "No problem. You could just give her a mohawk then. Or shave it. Women do bald now."

"Sheesh," I muttered. "Some moral support you guys are. You're making me a nervous wreck."

Adele left me in mid-cut to rinse Florida's head and condition it. When they came back, Florida was wearing a perky plastic cap, and Adele stuck her under a hair dryer, cap and all. Adele picked up her scissors once more.

"Avis Johnson?" A voice called out from behind me. "Corey says you're next."

A young teenager with glowing brown skin and braided extensions passed my chair on her way out, her nails not only painted but decorated with delicate flourishes, like so many tiny flowers.

"Thanks, Corey," she called toward the back. "Bye, MaDear!"

"Tell your mama hi," Adele said. "And remind her to bring me that mango salsa recipe she was tellin' me about."

"I will. Bye, Miz Adele." The bell over the door tinkled as the young girl went out. Avis got up from the couch, gave me an encouraging smile, and headed toward the manicure tables in the back.

"Speaking of MaDear, how's your mom, Adele?" I tried to make conversation as snips of dark brown hair kept falling to the floor.

"Mmph. Same. Same. She's all right. Doc gave her some new kind of medicine. Makes her sleep a lot—dozin' in the rocker in back. Kinda miss the ol' spitfire, but it's easier to manage the shop when she's not so hyper."

I could well imagine that. The last time I was here, MaDear had nearly escaped out the door with her walker, muttering something about the "lousy service in this here rest'runt." The spry little woman was quite muddled in her head, though Adele wasn't sure if it was Alzheimer's disease or plain ol' dementia.

Remembering the comical scene, I almost missed what Adele said next.

" . . . just as well. She's had a hard life. Needs to rest."

I didn't know whether I should ask what she meant by "a hard life," but just then Adele walked away, so I sneaked a peek at my haircut in the mirror. Still basically shoulder length, though the ends definitely looked fresher. So that was it? Just a trim?

Adele came back with a box full of pink plastic curlers. I couldn't remember the last time I'd had curlers in my hair. Who had time for curlers? Wash, blow-dry, bye-bye—that was my motto. But I was curious. What style had this conspiracy dreamed up? Would Denny like it? Would *I* like it?

"You goin' to let my head burn off?" Florida complained from under the dryer, scratching her head through the plastic cap.

"Yep." Adele calmly began rolling strands of my hair on the big pink rollers, anchoring them to my head with long clips. "Time I get Jodi here under the dryer be just about the right time to get back to you."

I had to admit it was fun getting fussed over, sitting under one of those serious hair dryers, looking no doubt like Marge Simpson with her beehive hairdo. Then—curlers still in my hair—the young woman Corey, who was maybe all of twenty, tall and slender with cocoa-rich skin, soaked and scrubbed my feet. Then she cut my toenails and painted them a daring rich burgundy.

"Whoo, some toes." Stu eyed me critically. "You'll have to wear open-toed shoes tonight. Do you have any open-toed heels?"

By this time, everybody was hanging out in the back part of the shop, and Adele was taking a break to spoon some yogurt into her mother's birdlike mouth. Open . . . spoon . . . swallow. Open . . . spoon . . . swallow.

"Um, no. Even if I did, not sure I could wear heels yet." I was only two weeks off my crutches. The very thought of teetering on high heels made me feel unsteady.

"Oh. Right. Of course." Stu backed off. She studied my hands as Corey patiently shaped the nails, put on a base coat, stuck them in the nail dryer, and then carefully began to brush on the wine-colored nail polish. "But seems like for your twentieth anniversary—I mean, good grief, that's a real milestone!—you ought to do something really special, not just go out to dinner. Take a cruise or something."

My turn to smirk. "We are."

That got even Adele's attention as the spoon she held paused in midair. Four voices chorused, "You are?"

"Well, not a *cruise*. Though I've been planning my own surprise for Denny."

"What? What?" Florida pulled a pout. "Girl, you shouldn't be keepin' anything from us."

"Oh, right. You should talk," I shot back, but I was grinning. Even Avis was still looking at me, waiting for the revelation.

"If any of you dare breathe a word of this to Denny . . ."

"Us? Breathe?" Florida looked offended. "Did we tell *you* about Denny's makeover surprise?"

Had to admit they'd kept me in the dark. In fact, I still didn't have a clue what my hair was going to look like or where Denny and I were going tonight.

"Well then." I took a triumphant breath, smiling at my own secret. "I have reservations at Starved Rock Lodge out near Utica for this weekend—two nights in one of their cozy log cabins, breakfast and dinner in the rustic lodge. Plus a swimming pool, hiking trails—it's gorgeous out there. We camped in Starved Rock campgrounds when the kids were younger, and I've always wanted to go back and stay in the lodge . . ."

I realized all four of my friends from Yada Yada were just staring at me. "What?"

Florida screwed up her face. "Girl, you tellin' me you takin' that hunk man of yours to a *log cabin* for your anniversary?" She turned to the others. "Now I know Jodi Baxter is outta her mind."

"What's wrong with that? Denny will love it!"

Stu rolled her eyes. Avis's mouth twitched. Adele just shook her head and slid another spoonful of yogurt into MaDear's mouth.

"Girl, now, you shoulda axed us for some advice." Florida, her head full of small, finger-size curlers, folded her arms across her small bosom. "For your anniversary, you go to one of them downtown hotels—"

"Like the Wyndham or the Drake," Stu cut in.

"Yeah, one of them fancy ones. You ask 'em for the honeymoon suite; you soak in the spa . . ."

"If you want 'back to nature,' you can take one of those horse-drawn carriage rides around the Magnificent Mile." That was Adele's contribution.

"All right, all right. I get it." But I was unmoved. "You wait and see. Denny will love my surprise and will promise to adore me for another twenty years."

For just a flicker of a second, a hint of pain clouded Avis's eyes, and I winced at my thoughtlessness. Avis and her Conrad had celebrated their twentieth anniversary with a cruise to the Caribbean, but he had died of cancer a few short years later. There would be no fortieth anniversary for the Johnsons. Yet the cloud passed and she jumped up, reaching for the almost-empty carton of yogurt. "Let me do that, Adele. Let's see what these beauties look like when you do the comb-outs."

With maddening casualness, Adele put Florida in the chair first, took out all the little curlers, and swept up a cascade of coppery ringlets on top of her head, anchoring them firmly with a crown of pins. Florida preened and strutted in front of the mirror then heaved an exaggerated sigh. "All dressed up and no place to go."

"Move, girl," said Stu. "Let's see what miracles Adele hath wrought with Jodi."

Once again, Adele swung the chair so my back was to the mirror. I could feel my hair spring and bounce as the curlers came out. Florida, Stu, and Avis stood front and sides, tilting their heads sideways, saying, "Mmm-hmm" or just nodding, making me as nervous as a turkey in November.

Then to my surprise, I could feel Adele twisting the sides and top of my hair, anchoring whatever-it-was with pins, then brushing and arranging and spraying the back. After thirty nerve-wracking minutes, she turned my chair around, facing the mirror.

I could hardly believe my reflection. Some other girl—yes, *girl*—from another lifetime looked back at me. Not the haggard Jodi Baxter who'd recently had major surgery, who woke several times a week from nightmares related to that awful accident, who'd worn the same basic hairstyle for the last ten years.

No, this Jodi was almost youthful . . . and pretty, even if I was only a month shy of my forty-third birthday. Little rows of

415

twists—not braids or cornrows—covered the sides and top of my head, then a small crown of sparkling pins announced the rest of my hair falling in soft waves down to my shoulders.

"Wow," I said.

Stu grinned. "You look great, Jodi. You really do." She fished out her camera. "Hold still for the 'after' picture."

"Wait!" Florida made a beeline for the front window. "Ain't that your wreck parking across the street, Jodi? Denny's coming!"

My heart actually started to pound like a sixteen-year-old about to meet her prom date.

"Get that cape off her," Stu ordered Adele, which was kind of cheeky, but Adele pulled off the plastic cape and let me stand up. "Come on, come on, Avis! Denny's coming."

"Don't let him in till I get there," Avis called from the back. "I'm bringing MaDear with me."

It was all too silly and funny and . . . wonderful. Would Denny like it? He had to! It was his idea. And to be honest, I hadn't looked this gorgeous in years.

Avis and MaDear joined the rest of us just as the bell tinkled over the door and Denny walked in, grinning foolishly, just like he had on our wedding day. "Oh my," he said. "Oh my, Jodi, you look absolutely—"

Denny never got to finish his sentence, because just then MaDear let out a horrible howl, like a cat with its tail slammed in a door. "You! You!" she screeched, raising her thin arm and pointing a shaking claw at Denny. "Git 'im outta this house!" With lightning speed, she grabbed a brush from Adele's supplies and hurled it through the air at Denny's head. The brush found its mark before Denny had time to react, cracking him on the forehead before it fell to the floor.

"MaDear!" Adele grabbed for her mother, but the old lady shook her off.

"Ain't you caused enough trouble, boy? How *dare* you come back here—an' with po' Larry hardly cold in his grave! Out! Out! Git out!" Adele's mother grabbed another missile—a hand mirror this time—and let it fly.

3

*T*his time Denny did duck, and the hand mirror shattered against the front door. The blood had drained out of his face, and his mouth hung open.

The rest of us stood glued to the floor, stunned. Adele finally got her big arms around her mother in a body lock, but MaDear was putting up a good fight. "Git 'im out! Git 'im out!" she continued to screech, flailing her bony arms—and then she started to cry. "No-o-o . . . nooooooooo. Not agin . . ."

Thoughts skittered like water bugs through my brain. *What's she talking about? What set her off? Why Denny? Who's Larry?*

"Everybody just leave," Adele ordered gruffly, wrestling the tiny woman toward the back room. "Go on. *Go.* 'Cept Avis. Avis, come on back and help me."

"But . . ." Denny reached for his wallet, his face stricken. "I haven't paid for . . . for—"

Florida stepped toward Denny and stopped him. "Don't worry

'bout that now, Denny. Come on, do what Adele says. Come on Jodi . . . Stu." Florida pulled open the door of the beauty salon and practically pushed Denny outside. Stu and I grabbed our purses and followed on their heels.

The four of us stood on the sidewalk, just out of sight of the salon's front window, and looked stupidly at one another. Denny gingerly touched the red mark on his forehead where the brush had clipped him. "What happened in there?"

Stu shook her head, mouth twisting in disgust. "It's just MaDear. She's nuts."

"Maybe." Florida's eyes narrowed. "But I think somethin' else was going on."

"Like what?" My initial shock was starting to thaw, and anger was bubbling up in its place. *Thanks, thanks a lot, MaDear, for ruining Denny's makeover surprise.* And, *That woman's dangerous! Adele should put her in an institution—under lock and key.*

Florida shook her head, setting her new crown of little ringlets dancing. "I dunno. She's confused, sure 'nough, but there's somethin' . . . somethin' real behind what just happened. Know what I'm sayin'?"

No, I didn't know what she was saying. MaDear's little tantrum had popped my bubble, and I was having a hard time getting back my enthusiasm for the day. Our day. Denny's and mine . . .

I looked at Denny. His shoulders were hunched, his hands shoved in the pockets of his Dockers, looking for all the world like one of Peter Pan's lost boys, in spite of the gray flecks in his dark hair. My anger softened. "You okay, Denny?"

He pinched his lips together and nodded, but he didn't look okay. He looked . . . distressed. Troubled.

"So, Denny." Stu shifted gears. "What do you think of our girl?" She took hold of my shoulders and turned me around. I almost shrugged off her hands, but it worked. Denny's face relaxed a bit into a smile.

"I like it. You . . ." The smile got bigger. "You look great, Jodi. Really great."

"All right!" Florida gave Stu a high-five. "Didn't I say you gotta trust your hairdresser? And your friends."

"Yeah," I admitted. Denny's sweet words soothed my ruffled spirit. "Yeah, thanks a lot, you guys."

"No problem, no problem." Florida laid it on thick. "Anything to help a friend. And you sure did need help, girl."

"Enough already, Florida! Stop while you're ahead!" I pulled a face, making her laugh.

"All right, all right." She grabbed Stu and started off down the sidewalk. "You two lovebirds have a good time tonight, ya hear?"

I watched them go, realizing that Stu had to go all the way back to Oak Park, west of the city, and Florida must have come straight after getting off her shift at the post office. They'd really put themselves out for me today. Avis too.

Denny checked his watch. "Hey, it's already past five. I got dinner reservations for seven. We better get home so I can make myself presentable. Don't want people thinking, 'What's that chick see in that old man?'"

I giggled like a teenager, flattered by the silly compliment—

421

and suddenly realized how patient Denny had been with my banged-up self the last few months. "So where are we going, Mr. Tambourine Man? You're full of surprises today."

The color had returned to his face—the dimples, too, creasing the sides of his face when he smiled. "Oh, thought we might go to the Bagel Bakery where Yo-Yo works, try out their kugel—ouch! I'm kidding!"

He deserved the punch on the shoulder. "I mean, where are we going *really?*"

Denny took my elbow and propelled me across the street, prompting another horn-blowing serenade. "Wouldn't you like to know? Guess you'll have to come with me to find out."

I WAS WORRIED that Denny might think he had to spend a hundred dollars on a five-star restaurant to make it a special date—especially since he didn't know yet that I'd already charged the Starved Rock Lodge on our credit card. The last time we'd tried out one of those super-fancy restaurants downtown (our tenth anniversary?—probably), we tried not to stare open-mouthed when the tuxedoed waiter put a huge plate in front of each of us with three long green beans artistically arranged on one side, a two-inch-thick "steak medallion" the size of a cookie cutter ("But wrapped in bacon!" Denny had pointed out), and half of a twice-baked potato, whipped up like a Dairy Queen. The food—what there was of it—had been melt-in-your-mouth tasty, but we decided the chef must be a former magazine editor who liked lots of "white space." Only the check came with generous portions.

So I was relieved when Denny ushered me into the Ethiopian Diamond Restaurant on Broadway Avenue. I should have guessed. Some of our friends had been recommending it for months. ("The food is to die for! And the portions are huge!" "So authentic! Lots of atmosphere.") The waiters were all Ethiopian, flashing bright-white smiles, and eager to explain the menu, which offered appetizers like *sambusas* (dough shells stuffed with vegetables or meat) and entrees like *gomen watt* (collard greens simmered in garlic and ginger sauce) and *kitfo* (seasoned steak tartare). There were no utensils on the white tablecloths, and I soon realized why by watching other diners, who were tearing off pieces of a pancakelike bread ("injera," our waiter informed us) and dipping it into the various bowls of stews and vegetables.

Denny and I held hands across the small table in the corner of the main room, where we had a good view of the five large paintings around the walls depicting scenes from different parts of Ethiopia. "This is great." I grinned. "Good choice." *Except for the eating-with-our-fingers part,* I thought, wondering if my newly painted fingernails would survive the meal. Denny looked delicious—open-necked black knit shirt, tan pants, and a wheat-colored sport coat setting off the even tan he got running around blowing whistles at peewee soccer players all summer. I wore the black slinky dress I'd borrowed for the Chicago Women's Conference last May but never got to wear. At least this time I got dressed up for my man, not for five hundred women I didn't even know. Even Josh had whistled at my new look. But Amanda said, "Mo-om! Didn't you borrow that dress from Sheila Fitzhugh? You better give it back *soon,* or she's gonna dock it from my babysitting money!"

I felt guilty for about one second. Yes, I would return it—tomorrow. Tonight I was going to enjoy feeling like a "babe."

Our waiter, whose name sounded like "Belay Wuhib," set down the steaming bowls of spicy lamb, strips of marinated steak, hummus, and vegetables we'd ordered, along with the ever-present injera flat bread and small dishes of cucumber and lentil salad in spicy vinegar, and we fell to. Between dripping bites, I prattled on about our wedding weekend twenty years ago when Denny's sophisticated Episcopalian parents from New York met my very conservative mom and dad in Des Moines, Iowa, for the first time, somewhat akin to a summit of East meets West. *Now* it was funny, but back then, it was hard to tell who was more shocked: the New York Baxters, trying without success to envision a wedding reception in the basement fellowship hall of the plain, nondenominational church my family attended, or the Midwestern Jennings, stuttering in dismay when Denny's folks offered to purchase the wine and beer for the reception "dinner." "Oh, uh, that won't be necessary," my mother had spluttered. "We're, um, well, there's not really a dinner, just simple refreshments with Red Zinger Tea punch—it's really good." I almost choked on a piece of injera bread, remembering how Denny and I had howled later.

Denny didn't smile, just nodded absently and said, "Uh-huh." In fact, I realized that for the past ten minutes I had been doing all the talking.

I picked up the cloth napkin and wiped my mouth. "Earth to Denny." At least that got his attention. "Are you okay?"

He leaned back in his chair and sighed. "Sorry, babe. It's just . . ."

I waited, but he'd already retreated behind his eyes.

"Denny, talk to me." I reached across the table and took one of his hands. "Is it what happened this afternoon at Adele's shop?"

He sighed. "I just can't get it out of my mind. She was so angry at me, and I don't have a clue about why."

"Well, it's obvious—I mean, she's got you mixed up with somebody else. It's not *you* she's mad at, Denny. I know it's upsetting— we were all upset—but you can't take it personally." *Or I'll get upset that a little old woman suffering from dementia is messing with our anniversary.*

"I know that—in my head, anyway. But *who* is she so angry at—and why? And why does she think whoever-it-is is me?"

I didn't want to think about MaDear and her problems—probably part of her "hard life" Adele referred to this afternoon. Whatever it was, it was past, nothing to be done about it—at least, nothing *we* could do about it.

I patted his hand, feeling more like Mother Hen reassuring Chicken Little than Denny's lover-friend-wife of twenty years. "Look, we'll call Adele tomorrow and ask if she's figured out what's going on with her mother, okay? Maybe that'll help you put it aside."

Denny nodded, though he didn't seem at all sure. I decided it was time to spring my surprise. Hopefully that would take his mind off MaDear's tantrum this afternoon.

I reached into my shoulder bag, pulled out an envelope, and slid it across the table. Denny looked at the envelope then looked up at me. "What's this?"

"Open it." I smiled, feeling impish and smug that I'd managed to pull off a surprise, too, in spite of crutches and being stuck in the house most of the summer. God bless Web sites that let you make reservations online.

Denny pulled out the paper and unfolded it. A good fifteen seconds went by as he read. I sucked in my breath. Maybe he didn't like the idea after all, like my Yada Yada "advisers" today had predicted. Then Denny looked up . . . and grinned.

"You rascal. When did you plan this?"

I let out my breath. "Several weeks ago—soon after the trial. I wanted to do something special to thank you for . . . for standing by me through, you know, everything."

His eyes registered pain. "Oh, Jodi, don't. Don't thank *me* for anything." He leaned forward and took both my hands, looking in my eyes so intensely I could almost feel their heat. "I've been to hell and back because of that stupid fight we had that day. But God has seen us through, *is* seeing us through, and you've forgiven me and . . ."

"Oh, Denny. You're not still blaming yourself, are you? It was *me* . . ."

We both just looked at each other, overwhelmed at the memories and feelings that were still healing. A stupid fight . . . me, late for a Yada Yada meeting, driving angry . . . a drenching thunderstorm . . . and now, a boy was dead. Charges had been filed against me: manslaughter with gross negligence. If the Yada Yada Prayer Group hadn't held both of us and showed us how much God loves us, even when—*especially* when—we don't deserve it, we might not have made it even this far.

"If you want to thank somebody, Jodi, thank God." Denny's voice was husky. "Where would we be without grace?"

I swallowed. The waiter cleared our dishes while we sat holding hands without speaking. "Coffee?" he asked. "Dessert?"

"Just coffee." Somehow the simple words dislodged the lump in my throat. We had to go forward, and forward at this moment meant Starved Rock this coming weekend—just Denny and me, no kids, no dog, no laundry, no cars gunning their engines at two in the morning, no apartment buildings crowding out the sun.

"Okay, my thanks go to God," I agreed, "but it's *you* I'm taking to Starved Rock Lodge. Deal?"

This time he laughed. "Deal."

4

*D*enny was up early and back to work on Thursday, leaving me with a second cup of coffee and a quiet house—momentarily at least, till the kids got up. I sat on the back porch steps, enjoying the relative coolness of early morning in the wake of a nighttime thunderstorm, mentally reviewing what I needed to do in the next two days in order to be gone for the weekend. I'd made the reservation for Friday and Saturday nights, but the earliest Denny could get off would be five o'clock on Friday. Day camps started early and ran late as zillions of Chicagoans parked their kids in summer programs—sports camps, arts camps, drama camps, sailing camps, a little-bit-of-everything camps—filling every moment of every day with activity.

Whatever happened to lazy summer days watching ants on the sidewalk, sucking "Popsicles" your mom made in little plastic freezer molds, or playing question-answer games with your best friend while swinging on the deserted school playground swings?

Probably a myth by now, created in simpler times when kids had daddies, and moms stayed home. Summer day camps were no doubt better than all those kids sitting in front of the television all summer.

Denny and I had always been grateful we both had school-year jobs that let at least one of us be home when the kids were out of school. Yet now that they were both teenagers, it drove me a little nuts that Josh and Amanda could easily sleep till noon if we let them. I wasn't a big fan of hanging out at the mall either. Denny solved that little problem by stopping their allowance in the summer. Any spending money they wanted they had to earn.

So far it was working pretty good with soon-to-be-fifteen Amanda. She kept up quite a cash flow with baby-sitting and "mother's helper" jobs—mostly families from Uptown Community Church. She enjoyed the independence of buying her own clothes and not having to beg us for money when she got invited to Six Flags Great America.

Josh was a different story. By the time he and Amanda got back from the youth-group mission trip to Mexico in July, most of the available summer jobs had been taken. Denny got him on as a sub at the park district, but so far that had only averaged one day a week of actual employment at pitiful wages. And the ancient garage behind our house had only so many sides that could be painted in one summer. I loved my tall, gangly son, but Willie Wonka was plenty when it came to inert bodies lying around the house.

One good thing: my recovery from the accident and lame leg

finally forced the kids to do their own laundry. We probably pushed up the water bill doing it that way instead of combining loads, but it was worth it. I'd been guilty of either nagging them to death about their laundry or finally giving up with an okay-I'll-do-it-myself martyr complex. But now? Couldn't do it; I couldn't do the basement stairs. If *they* didn't do their laundry, they had to wear it dirty. Ha!

Sometimes I wondered why it took a big crisis in my life to get some simple stuff straight, like not doing chores my kids should be doing.

On the other hand, they'd be happy doing some things for themselves I wasn't ready for yet—like staying home alone this weekend while Denny and I went away for our anniversary. I knew they'd both nix the idea of having somebody come to stay at the house. I could hear them now: "Mo-om! We're too big for a baby-sitter!"—though Amanda might acquiesce if I suggested Edesa Reyes, the black Honduran university student in the Yada Yada Prayer Group who tutored her in Spanish. Amanda and Edesa had hit it off big-time, but Josh was just old enough (seventeen) and Edesa just young enough (a very attractive twenty-one) that *that* didn't seem appropriate. Not for a whole weekend. I decided against it.

I heard the bathroom door bang back in the house. Shoot. I'd missed my chance for a leisurely shower. I better get off my duff and get on the phone. "Come on, Willie," I said to the dog, who was already into his morning nap on the back porch. "Let's put some rubber under these wheels."

TEN DISCOURAGING PHONE CALLS LATER—was everybody we knew out of town this weekend?—it was Amanda who came up with a solution that made everybody happy. Well, almost everybody. "Edesa said I could come spend a weekend with her sometime, Mom. I'd love to visit her church—it's in Spanish! And I'd get to see the Enriques kids too. Just ask her. I'm sure she'll say yes."

I couldn't help but smile. Amanda had quickly taken on the role of honorary "big sister" to several of the kids whose mothers were part of Yada Yada. Maybe this would work, though I felt a little nervous at Amanda spending a whole weekend on the Near West Side. José Enriques, Delores's teenage son, had been shot in a park in Little Village—only a mile from where Edesa lived—while we were at the Chicago Women's Conference, an event that solidified our ad-hoc conference prayer group into an ongoing prayer filibuster. Yet I knew Avis or Florida would say, "We can't live in fear!" So I dialed Edesa's number.

By the time Denny got home that evening, I'd walked over to the Fitzhughs' to return Sheila's dress, Edesa had agreed to keep Amanda for the weekend, and Josh had argued reasonably that he should stay home because "somebody's got to take care of Willie Wonka." Which was true.

Denny thought it was a good plan—until I told him Edesa offered to bring Amanda back on the El Sunday afternoon. "She and Delores are coming up anyway for Yada Yada—we're meeting at Nony's house." Denny frowned. "Uh, I offered to give Edesa and Delores a ride to Yada Yada after she brings Amanda back—

it's the least I can do." Nony Sisulu-Smith was hosting Yada Yada's bimonthly meeting this week at her home in north Evanston near Northwestern University, where her husband was a professor. I wanted to see where she lived. The only other time Yada Yada met at Nony's, I never made it.

Denny's frown deepened. "Did Dr. Lewinski say you could start driving yet?"

I shrugged. To tell the truth, I didn't want to get behind the wheel again ever, but I had to sometime. "Isn't the wreck we're driving an automatic? I should be okay. There's nothing wrong with my right leg."

"Going to Yada Yada just seems a bit much after a weekend away," he grumbled.

Ah. So that was it. I let it pass. Denny had apologized for getting jealous of our diminished Sunday evenings together, now that the Yada Yada Prayer Group had decided to meet every other week, but he still struggled.

After supper, Josh took off for Touhy Park to shoot some hoops, and Amanda had another baby-sitting job. I was feeling pretty accomplished lining up the weekend when Denny asked, "Did you call Adele today?"

I looked at him stupidly. I'd totally forgotten.

He winced. "This is important to me, Jodi. Maybe I should just call her myself."

I could tell he was frustrated—even more so when he had to go hunting for the phone, which he finally found in Amanda's room. I got him Adele's number and apologized for forgetting to call—

but to tell the truth, I felt relieved he was going to do it. What would I have said anyway? *"Say, Adele, got any explanation for why MaDear went off on Denny yesterday? Nice little fiasco."*

Denny dialed Adele's number, but I could tell from the tone of his voice that he just got her answering machine. "Uh, Adele? Denny Baxter here. Could you give me a call? I need some help understanding what happened yesterday with MaDear. I hope she's okay. Thanks." He hung up and stared at the phone.

"I'm sure she'll call you back," I encouraged, rubbing his shoulders. I certainly hoped so—tonight, while he was still home.

Yet Adele hadn't called by the time Denny left for work the next morning, taking Josh with him, who'd gotten a call at 6:30 a.m. to sub. So he asked if I'd please call the beauty salon and talk to Adele.

I thought of a half-dozen things I *had* to do before I could call Adele, but I eventually ran out of excuses. I picked up the phone.

"Adele's Hair and Nails," said a young voice. Sounded like Corey, the girl who did nails.

"Um . . . hi, Corey. Is Adele available? This is Jodi Baxter."

"Just a minute."

I could hear a CD playing in the background and indistinct voices. Then Corey came back on. "She's with a customer right now."

"She's with a customer right now." That was it? Not, *"Can she call you back?"*

I stumbled. "Uh, okay. I'll try again." *Dolt!* I scolded myself. *You should have left a message for her to call.* Well, I hadn't, so I'd just have to try again later. But how did I know when she'd be free?

I was packing the clothes Denny had washed last night when I heard the phone ring and Amanda pick up. "Mom! For you."

Whaddya know, I thought. Adele had called back after all. Yet when I said, "Hello? This is Jodi," it was Avis on the line.

"Hi," she said. "Just wanted to say good-bye before you and Denny take off for the wilderness this weekend. Will you be back in time for Yada Yada Sunday evening?"

"Yeah, planning to." I rattled off our weekend plans, including driving Edesa up to Nony's after she brought Amanda home. "You can pray for me! First time behind the wheel since—you know."

"You'll be fine." There was a slight pause. "You and Denny okay after what happened Wednesday?"

"Yeah." *Okay, Jodi, be honest.* "Well, maybe not. Denny is still pretty upset. He tried to call Adele last night to talk about it but only got her machine. He wants me to call today. I did once, but she was busy. Was going to try again in a while."

Another pause. "I'm not sure that's a good idea. You might want to give it a rest for a few days—at least till you get back from Starving Lodge or wherever you're going. Adele might be ready to talk about it then . . . but I'm not sure."

At any other time I would have guffawed at Avis's misstatement about Starved Rock, but something in her hesitation to have us talk to Adele set off alarm bells in my brain. I mean, I thought Adele would probably apologize for her mother's tantrum, assure Denny that he was just a victim of his mother's dementia, and say that MaDear didn't even remember it had happened. Surely that's what Denny needed to hear. So why . . .

"What do you mean?" My tone was sharper than I intended it to be. Then it suddenly occurred to me that Avis knew. She'd stayed behind to help Adele with MaDear; now she was urging us to "give it a rest" and not push Adele on it. "Avis, what's going on? Why did MaDear freak out when Denny showed up at the shop? Why doesn't Adele want to talk to us about it?"

"I think Adele should be the one—"

"You just said Adele doesn't want to talk about it," I was dangerously close to shouting, "but that leaves Denny and me hanging, filling in the blanks with . . . with . . . I don't know what!" I had no idea what she was talking about, but knowing my active imagination and Denny's despondency over what happened, I was pretty sure we could work up a pretty good stew over it.

"All right. I'll tell you what Adele told me, but promise me you won't try to talk to Adele about it just yet. Give her some time."

I tried to control my voice. "Okay. I promise."

As Avis filled me in on what happened after we left Adele's Hair and Nails last Wednesday, I slowly slid down the doorjamb of the kitchen doorway that I'd been leaning against until I was sitting on the floor, my elbow on my knee, my head in my hand.

When she finished I hardly knew what to say. Finally I whispered, "Okay. Thanks, Avis." I clicked the Off button and just sat in the doorway, hardly noticing Willie Wonka's wet nose in my face.

How was I ever going to tell Denny?

5

It took us almost an hour to get out of Chicago that evening—and that was *after* we dropped off Amanda at Edesa's apartment on the Near West Side.

Denny walked Amanda into the apartment building, carrying her sport bag of clothes for the weekend while she clutched her pillow and threadbare Snoopy dog she still slept with at fourteen. I watched from the car, double-parked in the street, as she waved and disappeared into the foyer. A few minutes later Denny was back. "Everything okay?" I asked.

"Uh-huh." He eased the clunker down the on-ramp into traffic on the Eisenhower Expressway as we headed back toward the Dan Ryan, where we would pick up I-55 heading south.

I bit my lip. Didn't he know when I ask if everything is "okay," what I really want to know is what Edesa said when they got to her door, and what he said, and did Amanda say good-bye or send any messages back to me? Did she seem nervous or anxious about us going away?

Probably not. What was one measly weekend when she'd weathered two weeks in Mexico without Mom and Dad just fine?

Friday night traffic was snarly as usual, with construction on I-55 backing things up for miles. I doled out turkey sandwiches and carrot sticks as we crept along behind a big truck, reading and rereading the stupid little sign on the back that said, "How's my driving?" and an 800 number.

"Did you bring your cell phone?" I asked.

"Uh . . . no. Why? We don't need it, do we?"

Denny had gotten the cell phone when I came home from the hospital so I could reach him anytime if I needed him during the long weeks of recovery. We hadn't used it much. I didn't think he even took it to work anymore.

"Oh, just thought I'd call that 800 number on the back of the truck. Do you think anyone ever does?"

Normally Denny would have laughed out loud at that. Even handed over the phone if he'd thought to bring it. But he just said, "Oh" and sank back into the silence that had hunkered in the car with us ever since we dropped off Amanda.

I rolled down the window, trying to catch what little breeze was created at fifteen miles per hour. My own mood that day had alternated between excited, worried, and ticked off. I'd really been looking forward to getting away with Denny, had been planning this Starved Rock getaway for weeks. But right now I felt like Pigpen in a *Charlie Brown* comic strip, walking around with a rain cloud over my head. A *big* rain cloud.

When Denny got home from work, I'd had stuff for the weekend all ready to go—two duffle bags, books to read, Bible and journal, swimsuits, Josh's portable CD player, sandwiches for the car, a cooler of lunch food so we didn't have to eat in the lodge dining room for every meal. I knew Denny still had to shower and change clothes before we could take off, but Amanda was raring to go, which helped. I dreaded the conversation about Adele and MaDear, arguing with myself all afternoon whether I should dump it all in his lap and get it over with, or put it off as long as possible. I knew I should feel bad for MaDear, but mostly I felt mad that we had to deal with this at all.

The first thing Denny did when he got home was ask if the mail had come. What he meant was, did he get anything from the Board of Education? School would be starting in a couple of weeks, and he still hadn't heard whether he'd been cut or retained. Didn't blame him for being frustrated. He'd started putting out résumés, but I could tell his heart wasn't in it. He was still hoping to go back to West Rogers High and pick up with the guys in the sports programs he'd been coaching all last year.

Yet Friday's mail had only contained the usual weekend ads, the gas bill, more medical bills from my surgery, and a note from my mother, saying she was feeling better now and maybe they'd come to visit for my birthday.

At least that was a good month away. I'd worry about that later.

As we had loaded the car, I'd decided to take the initiative. *"Oh. Tried to call Adele at the salon, but she never returned my call."* Denny frowned, but I'd just left it there. It wasn't a good time to tell him about Avis's call anyway, not with Amanda in the car.

439

Whatever was eating Denny obviously hadn't been left behind with the dirty pile of clothes he'd stripped off before his shower. He punched on the car radio, filling the moody silence with WBBM news discussing the latest tense negotiations with Iraq about UN weapons inspections. I waited till we finally made it onto I-80 heading west, where traffic opened up, the speedometer climbed, the air began to cool, and the sinking sun colored the high cirrus clouds like children with sidewalk chalk. When a string of commercials announced the top of the hour, I reached over and turned off the radio.

"Denny? Talk to me."

He glanced sideways, a rueful smile breaking his stony expression. "Sorry, babe." He jutted his chin toward the horizon. "Don't get to see a sunset like that too often. S'pose we could catch a sunrise over Lake Michigan, if we got up early enough, but—"

"Denny." I nailed him with a look. "I mean, talk to me about what you're thinking. This is supposed to be an anniversary getaway, but I feel like I'm riding with a robot, and you're"—I waved my hand in little circles—"off in la-la land."

He sighed. "Sorry, Jodi. Don't mean to be a wet blanket. It's just . . . I don't know. I feel like I should be home combing the want ads, searching the Net, sending out résumés, whatever. I'm kicking myself that I've waited so long to look for another job, but I kept hoping that no news was good news."

"I know." I turned my head away, watching golden cornfields zipping past. Half my mind wanted to scream, *It's just two measly days! If you wanted to sit home with the want ads, what about last weekend?!*" The other half of me realized I'd been ignoring the whole looming job disaster too. No way could we make it as a family on just my salary teaching third grade. Not with college on the horizon for Josh next year. Even without college! But, just like Denny, I'd kept hoping.

Behind the wheel, Denny cleared his throat. "And don't take this wrong, but . . . gotta admit I'm worried about the money—for this getaway, I mean. It's a great idea," he added hastily, "but I didn't know you were planning something, and with the 'salon surprise' and dinner at the Diamond and all . . ."

I put my smile on high beam. "Aha. That's one worry you can cross off your list. I'm paying for this weekend myself, with sewing projects I've been getting from some of the busy moms at Up-town—mending, table runners, curtains, stuff like that. Already got enough to pay for one night. One to go."

He turned to me, jaw dropping. "You? Sew?"

I grabbed a carrot stick and would have thrown it, but I didn't think braining him was worth sending the car across the median and piling into oncoming traffic.

"See?" I teased. "Twenty years married and there's still stuff about me you don't know."

He laughed then, and the last of the uncomfortable silence blew out somewhere on I-80. I scooted over as close as my seat belt and the console between the seats would allow and kissed the dimple on his cheek. Now maybe we could enjoy this weekend.

Yet one nagging thought tugged at me. I still hadn't told him about my talk with Avis about Adele and MaDear.

A CARVED SCULPTURE OF A BALD EAGLE greeted us as we drove into the lodge parking lot around eight-thirty, a half-hour before the dining room closed. Two dinners were included in our weekend package, so I convinced Denny we should take advantage of it before we even checked in. Didn't work. We had to have dinner vouchers from the front desk. So I left him to order salads and entrees in the rustic pine dining room while I hustled to the main desk and got us checked in.

When I came back with the vouchers, he was sitting at a small wooden table, lit only by a dimly burning candle lamp, sipping one of two glasses of red wine. I hesitated. Did I forget to tell him that drinks *weren't* included? And besides, this would be the first time alcohol had appeared on our table since the argument that led—

He cocked an eyebrow at me, reading my mind. "I know. Drinks not included. This is on me." He grinned and raised his glass. "To us. Twenty years."

I sat, wishing he hadn't, but he reached across the table and took my hand. "Thanks, Jodi, for . . ." He glanced around the lovely room, almost empty of diners now, with its big stone fireplace, wooden rafters, wilderness paintings, and stuffed game heads. "For this. We've needed to get away. Even with the job thing hanging over my head. This is good."

I relaxed. This was good. Even the wine was good. Our celebration. And no one had to drive anywhere.

Our waiter—a suntanned college-age kid, probably working at the state park for the summer—hovered over us, whisking away every dish the moment the last bite made it into our mouths. They wanted to close up. When we shook our heads at the dessert menu ("Dessert not included"), he seemed visibly relieved. We let him clear the table, and Denny paid for the wine, but still we lingered.

Suck it up, Jodi. You can't avoid telling Denny much longer.

"Denny?" I hated to break the mood, but carrying it alone was starting to eat at me. We needed to be able to talk about it. "I called Adele at her shop, like you wanted me to, but they said she was busy, and she didn't call back."

"I know. You told me."

I forced myself to keep looking at his face, even though I was twisting the starch out of the napkin in my lap.

"But I did learn something. Avis called. So I told her we'd been trying to call Adele but hadn't connected yet—remember Avis stayed behind to help Adele with MaDear after she freaked out? Avis got kinda funny, suggested we let it rest for a while."

Denny's eyes narrowed. "Why?"

"That's what I wanted to know, but you know Avis; she doesn't want to gossip. I told her that put us in a hard place—Adele doesn't want to talk to us, but we don't know why. Like it was our fault."

"And?"

I folded and unfolded my napkin. Anything to postpone saying what I had to say.

"Jodi. What did Avis say?"

"She said . . . she said that when MaDear was a little girl down in Mississippi, only her name wasn't MaDear, of course. Sally, I think. She was only ten or eleven, and her older brother . . ." *Oh God, help me.* It had been hard enough to hear the words, but saying them

443

. . . I could hardly push them out of my mouth. "A bunch of men—white men—came to their farm one night and dragged her big brother—his name was Larry—out of the house, yelling something about talking disrespectful or uppity or . . . or something. The family was terrified, and the next morning they went looking for him. And they found him, in the woods . . . strung up in a tree. Only fifteen. Lynched."

I dared to look at Denny's face. He didn't seem to be breathing.

After a few silent moments, he croaked, "And the other day, MaDear thought . . ."

I nodded, feeling miserable. "Thought you were one of the men who killed her brother, come back to get her—little Sally."

6

*D*enny spent the rest of the evening in a numb silence. I didn't blame him. What was there to say? I finally gave up the idea of cozy conversation and fell asleep over the novel I brought along.

When I woke up the next morning, sunlight and leafy shadows were dancing through the windows of the log cabin that was ours for the weekend. I stretched . . . and realized the other side of the bed was empty.

I sat up. "Denny?"

No answer. And the door to the tiny bathroom was wide open.

I raised my voice. "Denny!"

"Out here." His muffled voice came from the other side of the cabin's one and only door.

My left leg ached with its usual morning stiffness as I pulled on a pair of shorts under my sleep shirt and limped outside in my bare feet. Denny was sitting in a rustic Adirondack chair, cradling a large Styrofoam cup of coffee.

"Here." He reached down beside the chair and came up with a second Styrofoam cup. "Hope it's still hot."

Now this is nice. I lowered my body gingerly into a second wooden lounge chair and took a sip of the black coffee. The "Pioneer" cabins—as opposed to the "Deluxe" cabins—had no stone fireplace and no TV, and they were farther away from the lodge, but I figured, it's August! Too hot for a fireplace. And we had better things to do than park ourselves in front of a television. Besides, these were cheaper.

None of the cabins had kitchenettes, though. "Where'd you get the coffee?"

"Coffee shop."

We sat in silence for a while, with just the sound of the leaves whispering secrets and bird songs dipping and trilling.

"Did Avis say anything else?"

Denny's question shot out of the blue, like time had collapsed and we were still in the lodge dining room, still talking about Avis's phone call. It took me a minute to transition from peaceful-morning-with-coffee to the shadow that had obviously been lurking in Denny's soul all night.

"Anything else?" I repeated.

"Like why she thinks we shouldn't talk to Adele about it."

"Oh." I tried to remember. At the time, I'd been so shocked I couldn't say for sure if there'd been anything else . . . except— "Yeah. She said something about 'dealing with MaDear's memories was bringing up a lot of old demons for Adele.' And Adele couldn't deal with those and worry about our feelings too."

Denny's jaw tightened, and he just stared into the trees for several long minutes, his coffee forgotten. I battled my own feelings: sad for MaDear, who lived through such horror at a young age, worried about why this was so heavy for Denny, and irritated that it intruded so heavily on our weekend. *You gotta help me, Lord. What are we supposed to do with this? Can't You just make it go away for a couple of days?*

Pray. That was it. Why did it still take me so long to get to the first line of defense when upsetting things happened? Avis . . . or Nony . . . maybe even Florida . . . if they were here right now they'd be circling our chairs like warriors doing battle with fear, confusion, disappointment, anger. All those sneaky spiritual fiends out to trip us up. Hadn't I learned anything in the last several months, riding life with the Yada Yada Prayer Group? I could just hear Avis say, *"It's not your battle. It's the Lord's!"*

"Denny?" I reached out for his hand. "Let's pray about all this, okay?"

I HAD NEVER THOUGHT of prayer making me hungry, but Denny and I were both ravenous by the time we let go of each other's hands, wet with sweat and tears. Somehow we were able to "leave it there" in God's lap and enjoy our day.

After showering in the tiny shower stall and breakfast at the

Starved Rock Café, we hiked up to the actual "Starved Rock"—a huge flat-topped pinnacle at the edge of the Illinois River, where a historical marker told the grim story of a band of Illinois Indians who starved to death on top of the rock, surrounded by enemy warriors below. Hard to imagine all that fierce drama now as we made our way up a walkway with safety railings leading to the top.

Still, that little hike did me in, and I chose to soak my leg—okay, all of me—in the hot Jacuzzi next to the indoor pool while Denny hiked a longer trail. By the time he came back an hour later— muddy, sweaty, and grinning—I was sure this was the perfect treatment for what ailed me, not those physical therapy sessions Dr. Lewinski had ordered. I said so to Denny, but he merely showed off by swimming thirty laps in the pool.

We made love in the cabin in the afternoon, trying not to giggle as sightseers roaming the grounds walked past our cabin and tried to peer in the windows. "Wonder what these cabins look like inside?" called a woman's brassy voice. Fortunately, we'd drawn the muslin curtains. Still, it made me feel weird, like a couple of teenagers caught making out. *Really* making out.

The sightseers kept poking around, which put a damper on passion. "I could go to the door," Denny murmured, nuzzling my ear, "and ask, 'Can I help you?'" The thought of Denny confronting strangers at the cabin door, buck-naked, ended all restraint. I belly-laughed till I cried, and Denny laughed too. Loudly. The snoopers beat a hasty retreat.

Oh God, it feels good to laugh. Don't let the laughter die.

The yada yada Prayer Group Gets Down

WE DIDN'T TALK MUCH on the way home the next afternoon, but it was a different silence than the tension that had filled the car on the way out of the city Friday evening. We both knew the job thing was still unresolved and Denny would have to hit the ground running to find something at this late date. And MaDear's confusion . . . neither one of us knew how to compute that one, so we just kept praying all weekend. That felt good, just admitting, "We don't have a clue what to do, God," and "Heal her hurt, Jesus," and "Make a way out of no way about this job thing." It felt good praying together. Why didn't Denny and I do that more often?

As the Chicago skyline loomed out of the horizon, I smiled to myself, thinking about our personal "worship service" that morning in the cabin. Too bad the snoopers hadn't come back—they would've gotten an earful! We played some gospel and praise music on Josh's CD player and tried to sing along. Okay, it was a little hard to keep up with Kirk Franklin and the Family, but it was fun anyway. And our prayers changed when I said, "You know what, Denny? I always thank God *after* He's answered my prayers, but when we pray at Yada Yada, Avis and Nony and some of the others—they're always thanking God *before* He answers. Like, 'Thank You, Jesus, because we know it's already done,' or 'Thank You for what You're going to do.'"

So Denny and I tried it—just started thanking Jesus for what He was going to do—but it was hard to hang on to the richness of our weekend as our borrowed car joined the ever-increasing herd of semis, delivery trucks, cars, and minivans funneling back into the city. We'd left Starved Rock at noon on Sunday to give us plenty of time to get back home before Yada Yada, which started at five. But as I-55 slowed to a crawl, I wasn't so sure. Even weirder, I felt an odd relief. I might have a perfectly good excuse not to go tonight. . . . Why was that?

Deep down I knew. It would be awkward to face Adele at prayer group. Did she know Avis had told us about MaDear? How could it *not* come up? Not only Avis, but Stu and Florida had been at the shop that afternoon too.

Yet I'd promised Edesa I'd give her and Delores a ride—

My meandering thoughts were jolted by a thunderous roar overhead that felt like it was going to take the car roof right off. "Wow! Did you see that?" Denny shouted, poking his head out the driver side window and twisting his neck to look behind us.

"What?" I couldn't see a thing.

"A stealth bomber! I totally forgot—this is the weekend for the Air and Water Show."

Oh, great. Just great, I thought. *We'll never get home at this rate.* "Is it too late to take the Dan Ryan and stay west of the Loop?"

"No, no!" Denny's eyes practically glowed. "Let's take Lake Shore Drive. We still have time. Might get to see some of the air show!"

7

As it turned out, Denny and I got to see a lot of the air show as we crept up Lake Shore Drive. He tuned in WBBM radio, and a sportscaster's voice identified the low-flying planes screaming overhead—breaking eardrums if not the sound barrier—as an F-16 Falcon . . . an Apache helicopter . . . the Red Baron Squadron . . . and a finale by the Blue Angels. Guess we'd missed the aerobatics and parachute teams, much to Denny's disappointment. What did he expect? The show had been going on all day.

"I bet Josh is in that crowd somewhere," Denny moaned, scanning the thousands of bodies, shades, and sun hats populating the lakeshore. I was tempted to kick him out on the curb and drive home myself.

We finally pulled into our garage around four-thirty. *Sheesh.* Not early enough to freshen up before Yada Yada; not late enough to stay home. Oh well.

Amanda was already home, serving glasses of ice water for Edesa Reyes and Delores Enriques, who had come up on the El together. Left to themselves, Edesa and Delores often spoke rapid Spanish to each other, the younger woman obviously adoring her motherly mentor. It was easy to think of them as mother/daughter—except that Edesa had the rich, dark coffee-bean complexion of her Honduran heritage, while the Enriques family was "Mexican latte."

Willie Wonka was beside himself with joy that his family was back. He kept running from one to the other, leaving wet kisses on our knees and ankles. Denny was right; a note from Josh on the dining-room table said he'd gone to the air show. I hated to take off again without seeing him, but . . . *Hey,* I reminded myself. *At least he left a note.*

I splashed water on my face, dabbed on another layer of deodorant and a whisk of blush, and then came back out to the living room where Amanda was raving about worship at Iglesia del Espirito Santo that morning. "I understood a lot of the Spanish, Dad!" Our budding beauty then pounced on me. "Mom! Yada Yada *has* to go visit Edesa's and Delores's church! And when you do, I want to go with you."

Delores Enriques's round face beamed. "Why not next week? It's the last Sunday in August—time for Yada Yada to do another church visit. We can invite the others tonight." The older of the two women gave Amanda a warm hug. "Amanda, Amanda . . . she suits her name, *si?*"

Edesa laughed at Amanda's red face. "Amanda means 'lovable' in Spanish."

Amanda blushed. "Mom! Don't tell Josh. I'll never hear the end of it!"

Lovable. Well, my daughter could be at times. And to tell the truth, I'd rather stay home right now with my "lovable" daughter than get back in that clunker car again. Yet I held out my hand to Denny for the keys and turned to my Yada Yada sisters. "Ready?" I smiled, hoping I sounded more cheerful than I felt.

"Are you sure?" Denny mouthed at me as we trooped through the dining room on our way out to the garage. I gave him a half-hearted shrug and left him sorting through Saturday's mail.

I MADE IT FINE to Nony's house, even though my fingers tensed on the wheel as we approached the intersection at Clark and Howard streets, where I'd had the accident. Today was hot and sunny—nothing like the downpour that day, which had matched my ugly mood. For a brief moment, Jamal Wilkins's startled face rose up in my mind's eye, like a hologram—there but not there. The light was green, but I crept cautiously through the intersection, looking both ways, and then finally let out my breath. Edesa and Delores probably didn't even realize we'd just passed the site of the accident.

Evanston picked up where Chicago left off, and the Sisulu-Smiths lived on the north side near Northwestern University. We found Nony's home easily enough, a lovely two-story brick home on Lincoln Avenue with beds of impatiens hugging the house, and ivy clinging to the bricks and framing the windows. The house was modest by North Shore standards, but it was roomy enough for raising a family and "tastefully decorated," as Denny would say.

Nony met us at the door in a loose, caftan-type dress and gold-strap sandals, still managing to look like a *National Geographic* cover photo of African royalty even in her at-home attire. She led us past the polished wood stairs, through the spotless kitchen where Hoshi—who had been staying at the Sisulu-Smith home since NU dorms had closed last June—handed us glasses of iced tea on our way to the family room in the back, which looked out over a nice-sized yard with sturdy wooden play structures, big pots of flowers, and a tall hedge all around.

I sighed. Willie Wonka would *love* that backyard.

Most of the floors in Nony's house were polished wood, covered with patterned area rugs I presumed were African designs. On a trip to the bathroom I peeked into the dining and living rooms, both of which looked untouched by living human beings. I mean, did anyone dare sit on a white damask-covered couch?

Avis was already there, with Ruth Garfield and Yo-Yo Spencer. "Whoa," Yo-Yo sputtered. "Look at Jodi's new hairdo!"

After four days, I knew my hair didn't look quite as good as when I got out of Adele's beauty chair, but the little twists had held over the top and sides, and I'd actually rolled the back on some big curlers that morning to give it some bounce.

"Well, look at *you*," I tossed back. "Your overalls in the wash?" It was one of the few times I'd seen the twenty-something Yo-Yo in anything *but*. Tonight she had on khaki shorts and a rumpled

Bulls T-shirt. With her short, spiky hairdo, she looked like an ad for preworn Gap casuals. Yo-Yo just smirked.

"A picture she is! Denny had to beat off the competition, yes?" Ruth Garfield beamed at me from beneath her own frowzy bangs and planted a big kiss on my cheek that I was sure left red lipstick marks. "So!" she went on, giving me a big wink. "You and your *bubbala* had a—you know—great anniversary?"

The front doorbell ding-donged just then, and a moment later Florida Hickman and Chanda George tromped in. "Jodi! You back, girl?" Florida plopped down on a big floor cushion. "I thought maybe you lovebirds would still be at it." She grinned up at me.

"All right you guys, lay off. Denny and I had a great weekend, and that's all you're going to hear about it." I settled myself on the large, comfy couch beside Avis, knowing that everybody thought they knew what I meant. Truth was, I didn't want to admit that the incident with MaDear had threatened to derail our weekend big-time.

As it turned out, I didn't have to worry about prying questions, because Chanda had been practically dancing ever since she came in. "You gotta go to the bathroom, girl?" Yo-Yo butted in. "Go! You makin' me nervous."

"Nah, nah." Traces of Chanda's Jamaican accent spiced up her persona, which tended to be on the dumpy side, like the shapeless skirt and sweater hugging her extra pounds. A grin practically split her round face. "Nobody askin', so I'm a-tellin'." She paused for dramatic effect then squealed, "I won! I won!"

We all gaped. None of us took Chanda's weekly lottery tickets seriously, and the only time I'd worked up the courage to suggest she use her money more wisely met with unabashed optimism.

Ruth reacted first. "What are you now, a millionairess?"

"Nah," Chanda's smile was nonstop, "but I matched me t'ree numbers in the Pick T'ree game and got a hundred sixty dollars! Whoo-oo!" She did a little victory dance on Nony's African rug. "Me and the kids uppin' to Great America next weekend."

"That's *it?* A hundred sixty bucks?" Yo-Yo shook her head, probably thinking the same thing I was: *Bet you spent more than two hundred bucks winning that hundred-sixty.*

Chanda shrugged and sat down, still beaming. "My luck turnin' now."

Avis's eyebrows raised a hair—a twitch that usually meant, *Not going to go there. I have to pick my battles.*

Stu was the last to arrive, but she had the farthest to come, all the way from Oak Park. At least her silver Celica would be relatively safe in this neighborhood. "Aren't you tired of all that drivin' yet?" Florida wagged her head at Stu. "You goin' to church at Uptown, and you drivin' an hour each way to Yada Yada. You need a crib in the city, girl."

"Maybe when I change jobs." Stu took a seat next to Chanda, crossing her long, slender legs. "Right now most of my real-estate showings are in Oak Park—*what?*" she said to Chanda, who was grinning at her. "You win the lottery or something?"

Chanda's mouth fell open. "How'd you know?" Everybody cracked up.

Yet as I watched Chanda, something niggled at my mind—

besides the fact that she'd cleaned my house from top to bottom after my accident and wouldn't take any pay, even though cleaning houses is how she made her living. Then I realized what it was. Chanda had come in with Florida, which meant she'd ridden up on the el. Didn't she usually get a ride with Adele?

Adele wasn't here.

Avis must have had the same thought, because she said, "Guess we should get started. Adele's the only one missing. Anybody hear from Adele?"

"Yah." Chanda sighed. "I call her for a ride, but she say she not comin'. So I met up with Florida."

"She not coming" hung in the air for only a heartbeat, but I felt my mind pull two ways. Relief that Adele wasn't coming. But *why* wasn't she coming? Was she upset? At who?

I felt guilty—and resented the fact that I felt guilty.

Avis opened her Bible to the Gospel of Luke and read the passage in chapter 22 about the Pharisee who asked Jesus what was the greatest commandment of all. To which Jesus replied, "Love the Lord your God with all your heart and with all your soul and with all your strength and with all your mind, and love your neighbor as yourself."

"What?" Yo-Yo, who rarely brought the Bible I'd given her, grabbed Ruth's Bible off her lap. "Let me see that." She silently read the verse Ruth pointed out and then smacked her forehead. "You mean I gotta love my neighbors? But I *hate* my neighbors. I think they ate my cat for Thanksgiving!"

We couldn't help it. Every single one of us totally lost it. Nony's boys stuck their heads around the corner, no doubt wondering why all these women were laughing so hard. Even Avis's shoulders shook with helpless mirth. Florida kept howling, "I love it! I love it!" Yo-Yo was barely on the other side of her decision to "do the Jesus thing," and frankly, she didn't dress up her words any more than her clothes. When was the last time I was honest enough to admit I didn't like my neighbors? It wasn't the kind of thing a "good Christian girl" from Des Moines said out loud.

When we'd finally dried our eyes, Avis encouraged Yo-Yo to read the rest of the story when she got home, the story of the Good Samaritan who *did* love his rotten neighbor, but suggested that right now we move on to prayer.

I opened my mouth to ask for prayer about the messy situation with MaDear and Denny—after all, half the Yadas had been there when MaDear threw a fit; why shouldn't the others know about it?—then closed it again. *MaDear is Adele's mother, not mine. Maybe it isn't my story to tell.* On the other hand, Denny was my husband, the victim of mistaken identity—so wasn't it my story to tell too? I opened my mouth again, like a goldfish mouthing underwater O's. My hesitation cost me, because I heard Avis say, "Hoshi, have your parents arrived yet from Japan?" I closed my mouth and swallowed a sigh.

Hoshi was probably the quietest person in the Yada Yada Prayer Group, but her story had come out in bits and pieces. She had come to the U.S. a year ago to attend Northwestern University as a history major, ending up in a world history class taught by Dr. Mark Smith—Nony's husband. At a student reception for history majors, Nony invited the Japanese student to visit their home and also invited her to their "church of all nations" in Evanston, the Worship Center. Now Hoshi's decision to follow Jesus was about to be tested: her Shinto parents were coming from Japan to visit their daughter, and we'd been praying for Hoshi to have the courage to tell them about her newfound faith.

"No," Hoshi replied to Avis, "but soon." She was fairly tall, with silky black hair often pulled back into a simple ponytail at the base of her neck, and she had a tendency to nod a lot while she was speaking. "My parents—they will be coming in three days, for my birthday next week. Two weeks they will stay." A pink flush appeared on Hoshi's smooth cheeks. "I am scared so much to tell them that now I love Jesus. They will . . . feel very bad, very hurt. Maybe not speak to me again." Her eyes glittered with unshed tears.

"What are the names of your mother and father, Hoshi, so we can pray for them?" Delores's tender question broke Hoshi's reserve, and she started to cry.

"Takuya Takahashi, my father . . ." The tears slid down her cheeks. "And Asuka, my mother."

Nony moved quickly to the side of the student she had befriended and simply started to pray. "Thank You, Jesus, that You have said You will never leave us nor forsake us. We are bought with a price, therefore we glorify You in our bodies and in our spirits, which belong to You . . ."

I recognized the scripture Nony was paraphrasing, but as usual, I couldn't pinpoint the reference. I'd have to look it up in the concordance when I got home.

459

Several other sisters prayed for Hoshi, then Avis suggested we take turns calling Hoshi during the next two weeks to encourage her, to pray with her. Stu, of course, had a "better" idea. "Why don't you bring your mother to the next Yada Yada Prayer Group, Hoshi? To meet your new friends. If that seems like a good thing, of course."

"Oh, I don't know . . ." Hoshi was wide-eyed. "Please, I don't mean I am ashamed of you, but, I don't know. My mother . . ." She shook her head.

I wasn't sure it was a good idea either. The culture clash in our group could be pretty overwhelming, even for women who shared Christian faith in common. And somebody's mother, visiting from a foreign country, steeped in a foreign religion—it sounded like a recipe for disaster to me. But Avis said, "Well, you know she's welcome if you decide to bring her, Hoshi."

We moved on to the latest news in Florida's efforts to get her daughter, Carla, back from foster care. She'd been taken away before Florida got "saved and sober." Nothing could get Florida's eyes sparking like the subject of Carla. "I keep tellin' them that school is starting in two weeks, and it wouldn't do no good to Carla to start her in one school then transfer her to another, you see what I'm sayin'?" Her crown of copper ringlets bobbed as she jabbed a finger in the air. "Then they have the nerve to say, well, then, maybe Carla should stay with her foster parents another year. Almighty Jesus! Sometimes I am so tempted to lose my religion, just long enough to punch that social worker in the nose."

I didn't blame Florida one bit. I could hardly imagine all the red tape she was going through now that Carla had been located—so close, and yet still so far from "coming home." We prayed, stirring up a good storm in the heavenlies, binding Satan, rebuking red tape, and praying a hedge of protection around eight-year-old Carla.

As the prayers for Florida and Carla were winding down, I glanced at my watch. It was almost time to close, and nobody—not Avis or Florida or Stu—had brought up what happened at Adele's beauty shop last Wednesday. I wished *somebody* besides me would bring it up. Denny and I felt caught in the proverbial Catch-22 and certainly could use some prayer. Or would that be "telling tales" since Adele wasn't here? But all Avis said was, "Any other things that need prayer?"

"Yeah," I jumped in, but I chickened out about MaDear and offered up something safe. "Denny hasn't heard yet whether he still has a coaching job at West Rogers High. We're feeling pretty desperate."

"T'ree weeks till school be startin' and him still not know? Or it only be two? Well, no matter." Chanda shook her head. "Mm-mm-mm. Next t'ing they be tellin' us is the teachers on strike and our kids not goin' ta school."

The prayers of my sisters wrapped around my anxiety. Maybe this is what we needed to pray about anyway. First Ruth blurted, "Shake loose this constipated school system, God," which provoked a few chuckles. Then Nony prayed, "Oh God, the psalmist said he had never seen the righteous forsaken or their children begging for bread, so we ask You, Lord God, to be with Denny and Jodi right now, to provide for them beyond their expectations . . ."

I felt a hand on my shoulder. It was Nony's husband. Mark held up a cordless phone. "For you," he whispered.

I felt awkward leaving the group when the prayers were for Denny and me, but I slipped into the kitchen with the phone. "Hello?"

"Jodi." Denny's voice. "Sorry to bother you in the middle of your prayer time, but . . . we got some good news."

"Good news?" My heart leaped. *His job!*

"Yeah. The mail that came while we were gone? The insurance company sent us a check to cover the car. Won't cover a new one, but—"

"That's the good news?" I couldn't believe it. "You called me in the middle of our prayer time to tell me we got the insurance check?" I mean, of course I'd be glad to get rid of that borrowed clunker we'd been driving, but it could've waited.

"Partly, but thought you might also want to know I got my letter from the high school. Since Yada Yada was probably praying about my job tonight."

I sucked in my breath. *Uh-oh. Here it comes. The good-news/bad-news bit.*

"Somehow it got sent to the wrong address—can you believe that? Anyway, I was supposed to get it weeks ago." I could almost hear him break into a smile on the other end of the phone. "Good news, babe. They renewed my contract to coach another year."

8

*D*enny's news got a round of whooping and hollering when I came back into the family room grinning from ear to ear. "Thank ya, Jesus!" Florida cried. "Ain't that just like God—right on time." She punched the air in a victory salute.

More like right under the wire, I muttered to myself, remembering how much Denny had been sweating it out all summer. Yet I wasn't about to complain. At this point *any* job sounded like good news to me, and to be able to coach the same kids he'd had last year? Icing on Denny's cake.

We had a few more rounds of prayer and praise before Avis closed us out, and in the hubbub of everybody talking and leaving, we somehow also managed to agree that our next church visit would be at Iglesia del Espirito Santo this coming Sunday, and the next meeting of Yada Yada would be two weeks from today at my house.

I dug in my tote bag for my datebook to jot it down and realized with a jolt that two weeks from today was Labor Day weekend.

Chicago schools would begin right after Labor Day, and I hadn't even started to prepare.

Huh. I was gonna need prayer for *sure*.

THE NEXT WEEK rushed at me like a NASCAR video game—especially when it hit me on Monday that Amanda's birthday was only three days away, and I'd been so busy trying to pull off my Starved Rock surprise that I hadn't planned a thing. But while furiously sewing a set of curtains for a family at Uptown Community—I was going to pay off our Starved Rock getaway before school started or die trying—I got an idea: I'd make new curtains for Amanda's room for her birthday; maybe get her a new comforter too. The bedrooms in our two-flat were rather small and dark. Maybe she'd like to paint it a sunshiny yellow—though they probably called it "lemon chiffon" or "sunrise mist." Maybe I could talk Josh into helping me with painting.

Denny thought it was a great idea, though I'm not sure he really heard me. Every spare minute he wasn't at the high school getting ready for his new coaching year, he was looking in the *Tribune* for a good, used minivan. Besides, I knew he'd probably get Amanda a little something "just from Dad." He always did that. I'd be thinking our Christmas gifts to the kids were from both of us, and then little things we'd never discussed would show up under the tree "from Dad."

The yadayada Prayer Group Gets Down

Monday night was the first evening we'd sat down to supper as a family in four days. I made chicken fajitas—tasty and easy, twin requirements for a five-star rating at the Baxter household. "Oh, Mom," Amanda groaned, holding up a store-bought flour tortilla that I'd lightly seared over the gas flame on the kitchen stove. "This is truly pathetic."

"Pathetic? I thought you loved fajitas."

"I do. Did." She flopped the thing onto her plate. "But that was before I ate *real* tortillas in Mexico." She pronounced it "Meh-he-co," showing off her new aplomb at conversational Spanish.

"You don't want that?" Josh reached across the table with his fork and speared the lonely tortilla on his sister's plate, flopping it next to his own overflowing fajita.

"Give it back!" she screeched.

"Hey!" Denny yelled. "Josh, give the tortilla back to Amanda. Amanda, eat—and spare us the food critique."

Denny and I exchanged looks. These two were supposed to be young adults?

I passed Amanda the chicken fajita filling. "Speaking of food, what would you like for your birthday dinner?" For years that had been a safe question, since the answer was usually pizza or spaghetti. Last year, though, Josh had requested shrimp kabobs and twice-baked potatoes. I might have to ask for three choices and pick the one I could actually cook.

By now Amanda had stuffed half a fajita into her mouth. "Oh! Could I invite Edesa and Emerald to my birthday supper?" At least, that's what I think she said. It came out rather garbled. She swallowed. "And ask Edesa for her recipe for enchiladas. She made them for me this weekend, and they were *sooo* good."

That was different. Usually Amanda wanted a sleepover with some of her friends—but that had been back in Downers Grove, where she'd practically grown up with the same pack of girls from kindergarten through middle school. Last year at this time we had just moved to Rogers Park, and she'd settled for just one friend from our old church to come spend the weekend.

Now she was asking for her Spanish tutor and Delores Enriques's daughter, who was two or three years younger, to be her birthday guests. Was this the same teenager who'd been on the verge of failing first-year Spanish just a few months ago?

"Sure, but I'm not making any promises about the enchiladas." I caught Denny's eye again. *"Go ahead, tell them,"* I mouthed at him.

Denny cleared his throat. "Got good news," he said, refilling his own plate. "My contract at West Rogers High has been renewed."

"Great," Josh said. "Is there any more chicken?"

Denny opened his mouth then closed it again. Obviously the kids hadn't wasted any time worrying about it.

After supper, Josh took Willie Wonka for his evening walk, Denny and Amanda went out to look at used cars, and I tackled the final set of curtains for the Gage family. When would I be able to get to Vogue Fabrics up in Evanston to get some material for Amanda's curtains? Denny had preseason soccer practices at the high school, which meant no car during the day. Maybe tomorrow evening—if I could interrupt the car hunt—and then I'd have to find time to sew when Amanda wasn't around.

This might be more complicated than I thought.

I was almost done sewing the rod pockets when Denny and Amanda came in. "No luck on the car," he said and disappeared into the kitchen. A few minutes later he was back in the dining room, where I'd set up the sewing machine. "You about done?" He held up two sweating glasses. "Decaf. Iced." He headed for the back door with both coffees. "Come on out to the back porch when you can."

I sighed. I wasn't quite done, but Denny obviously wanted to talk. I turned off the sewing machine. Probably a good thing. My leg and midsection were starting to throb.

Denny was sitting on the back steps sipping his iced coffee. The cicadas were putting on a thunderous concert—if you call sawing away on one note a "concert"—but I liked it. Nature's refusal to take a backseat to urban noise.

He handed me my glass as I lowered my aching body to the steps. "Did, uh . . . did Adele or Avis say anything to you last night about MaDear?"

I shook my head. "Adele wasn't even there. Made me feel funny. Like she was staying away on purpose. I kinda hoped somebody would bring it up—after all, Florida and Stu were there too. But nobody said anything, so I didn't either."

Denny spit out an expletive under his breath. "Well, I'm gonna call Adele. It's driving me nuts. I feel bad for MaDear—but it's killing me, her thinking I'm some redneck racist who killed her brother. We gotta set this straight somehow." He stood up.

"Now? I mean, it's kinda late." I squinted at my watch. Nine-forty, to be exact. I wanted Denny to call—and didn't want him to call. Adele wasn't the easiest person to "get real" with.

Denny went inside to call Adele, and I prayed fervently into my iced coffee. *Jesus, we need some help here. Give Denny some peace about what happened—maybe erase MaDear's memory again. Wouldn't that work? Don't let Adele blame us for something that's not our fault—*

The back screen door banged. "No answer." Denny sat back down beside me. "I left a message." His shoulders hunched as he leaned his elbows on his knees. We both knew she wouldn't call back.

WITH AMANDA'S BIRTHDAY COMING UP, my sewing projects to finish, and school just around the corner—which meant shopping for school supplies and clothes for the kids, getting my classroom ready, updating my lesson plans, and attending the obligatory Professional Development days next week—temptation pulled me in two directions the next morning: roll over and go back to sleep, or hit the floor running.

Willie Wonka helped me decide by licking my hand and face—whatever skin he could reach with his doggy tongue—then clicking rapidly on the wooden floors toward the back door for his morning pee.

Okay, so I was up. As I waited for Willie Wonka to finish his business, I faced my next daily struggle: grab my to-do list or grab my Bible? Avis constantly reminded the Yada Yada sisters that the busier we got, the more we needed to "stay in the Word" and to pray. I knew for a fact that a morning devotional time would be hard to come by once school started, so as the dog came back into the house I muttered, "Okay, Willie. I'm gonna slow down these last two weeks long enough to get a half-hour for Bible reading and prayer before the rest of the family gets up. Hold me to it, okay?" Not that the deaf-as-a-doornail dog could hear my vow, but it felt good to tell *somebody*.

With a mug of fresh coffee in one hand and my Bible in the other, I draped myself in the recliner by the fan in the front window while Willie Wonka plopped down at my feet to start work on the first of his many daytime naps.

Prayer . . . It was still a challenge for me to get beyond my laundry list of "Dear God, bless so-and-so and please do such-and-such," a prayer routine perfected by family devotions as a kid, not to mention forty-plus years of Sunday school and church. Avis and Florida had given me several gospel and praise CDs when I was laid up after the accident, and that helped me focus on who God is and do some praising. But I couldn't exactly play loud praise music at six o'clock in the morning, or the neighbors upstairs would be knocking on the floor with a broom handle. And turning the volume low enough not to bother anybody didn't do justice to Donnie McClurkin or CeCe Winans.

My other challenge was a mind that skipped around like a pinball—and today was no different. *Two weeks till school starts—sheesh.*

I'm sure not ready for that emotional marathon. I tried to tell myself that I enjoyed teaching, that I loved third graders, but my first year at Mary McLeod Bethune Elementary hadn't exactly been a stellar experience. Half the kids in my room spoke something besides English at home, which made parent-teacher conferences like a debate at the UN—without the headphones and translators. *If* the parents bothered to show up. The no-show parents really made me mad. Out in the suburbs, I'd been used to a close partnership between school and home, but here, a good percentage of kids came to school without the supplies they needed. Or breakfast. A few of my students could barely read or write, but the school district seemed to push them along year after year, regardless of skill. And classroom management—don't even get me started.

My primary saving grace had been Avis—"Ms. Johnson" to the staff—who was the principal of Bethune Elementary. Yet she couldn't hold my hand all the time; she had eight grade levels and a large staff to oversee.

Trying to corral my thoughts, I opened my Bible to the Gospel of Mark, which I'd been reading in bits and pieces over the summer. Several of the women in the Yada Yada Prayer Group could quote reams of Scripture promises from the Old Testament—even from those pesky Minor Prophets—but my motto tended to be: "When in doubt, check out what Jesus said. And did." And right there alongside the little black ribbon that marked my place was the story of Jesus blessing the children: "'Let the children come to me!' . . . Then he took the children into his arms and placed his hands on their heads and blessed them."

Sudden tears filled my eyes. I'd read that story a zillion times at least. This week, though, it seemed like Jesus was giving it to me because I needed to carry it with me as I started my second year at Bethune Elementary.

The phone rang. So early? I could hear the shower running—Denny must be up—but someone answered, so I just shut my eyes, squeezing tears down my cheeks. *Okay, Jesus, You love the children. I guess that's why I'm at this school, so You can love them through me. But it was hard to love some of those kids last year, and now I'm going to have a whole new class. Everything from "sweeties" to "beasties." You're going to have to help me big-time—*

"Mom?"

I opened my eyes. Josh, pushing six feet, towered over my chair in a T-shirt, sweat shorts, and bare feet.

"Uh, Pastor Clark is asking if I'd take some kids to the beach today. He's helping their mom get signed up for Section 8 housing or something. I know I said I'd go with you to pick out paint for 'Manda, but . . ." He stared at me. "You okay?"

I gave him a bleary smile. "Yeah. God's just getting me ready for school."

9

*A*manda's birthday dinner was a great success. At least if you count that we laughed a lot. Edesa brought Emerald, who seemed delighted to be the only member of her large family invited.

My enchiladas, however, didn't measure up to Edesa's, even though she gave me her recipe—I could tell by the way Amanda politely said, "Good, Mom." Usually what I got from Amanda when I tried something new was either, "Eeewww, gross!" or "This is *so* to die for!" Guess company brought out her manners.

I'd taken the El up to Main Street Evanston to get material for Amanda's new curtains from Vogue Fabrics, and Denny and I got out to Home Depot in the evening to choose paint on the way to look at another used car. "Are you sure she'll like yellow?" Denny had asked—*after* the clerk had already mixed two cans of "summer sunflower."

I glared at him. "She better."

I had hoped to shop for a matching comforter, but Denny wanted to look at a promising Dodge Caravan he'd seen in the paper. The Caravan was only a couple of years old and in great shape, but the family who was selling it had decided they "only" needed two cars. "Understandable," Denny had said with a straight face. We bought it on the spot and drove it home—well, Denny drove it, and I followed in the clunker. By the time we returned our borrowed car to the Uptown family—bless 'em—who'd kindly loaned it to us after I totaled the Voyager, it was too late to shop for a comforter.

So I just made a coupon—"Good for a New Comforter!"—and stuck it in Amanda's birthday card. Josh paid for one of the cans of paint and promised to help paint her room—though I had a momentary heart palpitation when she said, "Can I exchange the paint? I was thinking of doing my room in red." But she gave it up when we said she'd have to pay for *that* herself.

My "fruit pizza" dessert with fifteen sparkle candles *did* go over big, as did Edesa's birthday gift: a Spanish-English New Testament. Emerald, looking like a Latina Alice in Wonderland with her thick mane of dark hair tied back with a baby blue ribbon, gave her a cloth bookmark that she'd stitched herself with Amanda's name. The way Amanda carefully put the bookmark in the Spanish Bible then hugged the book to her chest, I knew Amanda's fifteenth birthday would be held in her heart a long time.

And of course there was the "little something" from Denny: an ankle bracelet. How cool was that?

Denny and Amanda gave "The Two E's"—Josh's shorthand for

our guests—a ride home in our "new" minivan while I cleaned up the kitchen. Emerald gave me a hug before she left and whispered, "When *I'm* fifteen, my parents will give me a *quinceañera*—a big fiesta. You will come, *si?*"

"*Si,*" I replied, which used up my entire Spanish vocabulary, though I could only guess what a *quinceañera* was. "See you Sunday?" Emerald nodded happily before scurrying out the door after Amanda.

Visiting Edesa's and Delores's church on Sunday would be a treat. *Wonder who else from Yada Yada will show up? Does Adele even know about it?* I was usually the communicator to folks who missed a meeting, but I hadn't e-mailed Adele yet.

I gave the kitchen counter a last swipe with the dishrag, turned out the kitchen light, and limped into the dining room. My leg was *really* tired today. Maybe that physical therapy tomorrow would be good stuff. I lowered myself into the chair in front of the computer, turned it on, and called up our e-mail.

I scrolled past several birthday greetings for Amanda and the usual spam that made it past our blocker. Then I called up a note from Nony.

To: Yada Yada
From: BlessedRU@online.net
Subject: Hoshi's parents

Dear Sisters . . . By the grace of God Hoshi's parents arrived Wednesday. Mark and I and the boys (Hoshi, too, of course) picked them up at the airport. We offered our guest room to them during their stay, but Mr. Takahashi bowed quite formally and said they had instructed Hoshi to make reservations at the Orrington, so we just took them to the hotel.

Well, that made sense, since the Orrington in downtown Evanston was within walking distance to Northwestern's campus. On the other hand, so was the Smiths' house. Nony didn't sound offended, but it made me curious. Had Hoshi told her parents that her mentors were African-Americans? If this was their first visit to the United States, they were probably already in a state of culture shock.

The rest of Nony's e-mail was just a reminder to pray for Hoshi and to remember her birthday next week.

I called up a new message and typed in Adele's address:

To: Adele Skuggs
From: Jodi Baxter
Subject: YY church visit this Sunday

I stared at the blinking cursor for several minutes, wondering what to say. Just tell her about the church visit? Say nothing about MaDear? We'd left at least three phone messages for her, asking her to call. Surely she knew we wanted to talk about what happened last week. And why hadn't she come to Yada Yada last Sunday?

God, why does this feel like a minefield? I don't know what to say. I need some help here!

The y a d a y a d a Prayer Group Gets Down

It took me ten minutes of writing, deleting, and rewriting, but I finally ended up with:

Hi, Adele. Jodi here. You were missed Sunday evening! Delores and Edesa invited Yada Yada to visit Iglesia del Espirito Santo this coming Sunday (last Sunday of August). Can you make it?

Also, if you get a chance, Denny and I would like to talk about what happened last week at the shop. Avis told us a little bit about why MaDear was so upset. We are truly sorry your mom experienced such a tragedy in her past, but it feels bad to just leave it as is, given such a huge misunderstanding about who she thinks Denny is. Let us know when would be a good time to talk. Thanks.

I read it over at least twenty times . . . and finally hit Send.

SUNDAY MORNING wasn't too bad for Chicago in August: heading for the low eighties and humid. I had no idea what kind of church building Iglesia met in, but I tucked a couple of bottles of water in my tote bag along with my Bible and notebook just in case. Uptown Community wasn't air conditioned, just ceiling fans, and sometimes all those bodies in that second-floor room on a hot day could get stifling. *And* rather smelly if it was potluck Sunday, which always drew more street people with bathing issues.

I knew Amanda was eager to go with me this morning, even though she'd just been to Edesa's church last week. I was surprised, however, when both Denny and Josh said they'd like to come too. Denny hates to miss any Sundays at Uptown. But he'd spent all day Saturday there, coordinating the crew of volunteers who came from suburban churches to participate in Uptown's outreach to the homeless, so I guess he figured he could be absent with a clear conscience. He'd been one of those "commuting" volunteers for eons till last year, when the Baxter family had moved into the wildly diverse Rogers Park neighborhood near the church—a move I was still trying to reconcile with the girl who grew up with picket fences around our all-white neighborhoods in Iowa.

At least Denny remembered some of his high-school Spanish. Maybe he could help me decipher the worship service at Iglesia del Espirito Santo.

When we got to the address Delores had given to me in one of the west Chicago neighborhoods, all I saw was a large industrial-type building with no sign. I was about to wonder out loud if we were at the right place when Amanda said, "This is it." She practically skipped inside, where Delores and Emerald and a few of the younger Enriques children were standing in the foyer, waiting to meet us.

I wanted to ask why there wasn't any sign, but several good-looking young men in black suits and classy ties stepped up to greet us—Denny and Josh had come in slacks and silk sport shirts, considered "summer dressy" at Uptown—and directed us into a large room with tweedy, blue carpet and matching chairs.

"Whoa," murmured Denny. "Bet this room could hold about a thousand folks." Whatever its former life, the factory had been transformed into a bright and pleasant sanctuary. I poked Denny and waved my hand in front of my face. *Ahh. Air conditioning.*

Delores stayed in the foyer to wait for any other Yada Yada visitors, but Emerald took Amanda by the hand and led us to the left side of the building. "They have English translation here," the youngster chirped, leaving us for a moment then returning with four headsets. "But just during the message—oh! There's José!" She motioned to him vigorously.

Emerald's older brother sheepishly made his way toward where we were sitting. I could hardly believe he was the same boy I'd last seen lying in a hospital bed last May, shot in the back. His dark hair was nicely combed, he had on a white dress shirt and tie, and a healthy color warmed his cheeks.

"Buenos dias, José." Amanda took charge like we were visiting *her* church. "I think you met my mom already, but this is my dad and my brother, Josh."

"Hola." José stuck his hand out to Denny, then Josh. Josh towered over him by a good six inches. "Nice to meet you, but I gotta run." José flushed. "I'm on drums today."

I watched him head for the platform, where a truly amazing set of drums gleamed from behind a clear plastic soundboard. The instrumentalists were already warming up: a keyboard, electric guitar, and a small organ. The organist was obviously African-American, complete with cornrows that ended in tiny braids down to his shoulders—a fact that Florida didn't miss, as she scooted into the row beside me. "Look there. A brother. Now I know we gonna get some whoopin' and hollerin' today." She gave me a hug. "Hey, Jodi."

"Look. There's José," I whispered, tipping my chin toward the drums. I surely didn't want to thank God that José got shot, but I was suddenly overwhelmed with the realization that God had used that horrific event while we were at the Chicago Women's Conference to catapult our hodge-podge conference prayer group into the real thing.

"Uh-huh," murmured Florida. "And Amanda lookin' at him too."

I glared at her then dared to glance at my daughter—who was definitely watching the handsome teenager settling in behind the drums. I swallowed. *Oh God, I'm not ready for this!*

The seats all over the room were filling up. Delores and her brood ushered Avis and Stu into the comfy padded chairs in the English-translation section. Avis had picked up Florida but had gone to park the car; Stu came by herself. Edesa squeezed in beside Amanda and Emerald even though there were only two seats.

I thought that might be all from Yada Yada besides us Baxters, but just as the instruments brought everyone to their feet with the first worship song, accompanying a praise team of fifteen or so Latino men and women clapping enthusiastically, Ruth clambered over everybody in our row and dumped her things in the last free chair. She leaned across Florida. "Would Ben come?" she said loudly, barely audible over the pulsing music. "You'd think I'd asked him to eat pork. Suddenly he's Jewish." She rolled her eyes and leaned back. Florida and I tried to stuff it, but we couldn't help laughing.

Fortunately, the words to the songs were flashed on identical screens at both sides of the platform. Even though I didn't know Spanish, I tried to sing along.

> *El es el Rey de Reye*
> *El es Señor de Señores*
> *Su nombre es Christo . . .*

Josh leaned down to my ear. "Did ya catch it, Mom? 'He is the King of kings . . . Lord of lords . . . His name is Christ.'"

I nodded, wondering if I was too old to learn Spanish. My kids were showing me up and loving it.

The worship was similar to Nony's church—joyous, deeply felt, loud—but multiplied by five. The congregation was huge. By the time the pastor came onto the platform, the worship leader was glistening with sweat. The praise team sat down, but Pastor Rodriquez, a man with wiry black hair on the verge of gray, was still caught up in the spirit of worship. The musicians stayed right on his every word and gesture, providing background music as he spoke and launching immediately into this or that song—sometimes no more than a phrase or two—which he peppered throughout his message. His expressive face fascinated me. He smiled, grimaced, laughed, squeezed his eyes shut—and as far as I could tell, he hadn't even gotten to the sermon yet.

Was he speaking in Spanish? Or speaking in tongues? It was hard for me to tell until I noticed Amanda waving her headset at me from her seat on the other side of Denny. I put mine on; so did Florida and Ruth. Suddenly a woman's voice translating the pastor's words spoke clearly and passionately into my ears. "Brothers and sisters, yes it's a battle. But it's a battle that Jesus has already won. Hallelujah!"

Out of the corner of my eye, I saw Amanda looking up all the Scripture references in her new Spanish-English New Testament. *Okay, Lord, whatever it takes to get her into Your Word.*

The service went a good two-and-a-half hours, but the enthusiasm from both platform and congregation never abated. Several people gave testimonies: a man who was healed of cystic fibrosis after the church prayed for him; a woman who led her mother to the Lord; another who just babbled in tongues and cried and praised "Jesu" and I never did figure out what for. I wasn't sure how I felt about churches that majored in healing and tongues —but when the pastor gave an invitation to those who wanted salvation, the front was suddenly full. I squeezed my eyes shut. *Oh Lord, I'm so glad You're not limited by my own understanding. Whatever work You're doing here in the lives of these people, thank You.*

Finally we were back out in the foyer, getting introduced by Delores and Edesa to a steady stream of friendly faces that streamed past. I was curious. "Delores! Where's the sign for your church? If Amanda hadn't been with us, I'm not sure we would've found it."

Delores rolled her eyes. "*Si,* I know. Taggers. Spray-painted all over the sign. It's down for a face-lift." Then her smile tightened, and she leaned close to me. "Please pray for Ricardo. He hasn't found a job yet, and he's yelling a lot and drinking—when he's home." Her smile dissolved. "Just . . . pray."

I gave her a hug, kissed Emerald, said good-bye to the other Yada Yada sisters—and then realized Amanda wasn't with us. Denny went to look for her and came back with Amanda and a twinkle in his eye.

Good grief. She'd probably been hanging out with José. I glared at Denny, my message clear: *Don't encourage this!*

WE TALKED ABOUT OUR EXPERIENCE at Iglesia all the way home in the Dodge Caravan and through our lunch of BLTs and corn on the cob. Then Amanda and Josh headed for the beach, while Denny and I took advantage of their absence and snuck in a "nap." Willie Wonka, knowing good and well that we were in the bedroom, scratched and whined on the other side of the door till we finally let him in.

"Voyeur," Denny muttered.

Later, when the kids had gone to youth group at Uptown, Denny and I walked to the Heartland Café, the neighborhood's classic throwback to the hippie sixties, and ordered iced coffees while we sat in the screened-in area on the sidewalk behind the Morse El stop. Our walks to the lake would have to wait till my leg felt stronger. Neither one of us mentioned the obvious: Adele had not shown up at Iglesia that morning.

Not a big deal in itself—neither had Chanda or Yo-Yo or Nony or Hoshi. But I called up our e-mail before heading for bed, just in case . . .

No answer to the e-mail I'd sent her either—and it had been three days.

10

I stood in the middle of my third-grade classroom the next morning. What a mess—boxes, stacks of curriculum and old papers, and dust everywhere. Where to start? Eight days till school opened. If nothing else, last year's experience had taught me one thing: I had to think "outside the box." It wouldn't be enough to arrange the desks in friendly clusters or make sure I had all the materials I'd need to teach the first quarter's subjects or do my Welcome Bulletin Board. I'd also need to stock up on extra notebook paper and pencils for kids who came with not one thing on the supply list; juice boxes and granola bars for the ones who came to school hungry; even a stash of socks, underpants, shoelaces, mittens, and ear muffs to cover accidents and lost (or nonexistent) items. Most of this had to come out of my own pocket, though the Salvation Army store was a gold mine. Avis was sympathetic, but no way could the school budget fund these items for the entire school.

As I leaned against my desk, I realized I had a new resource this year: Yada Yada. Last September I'd felt totally alone and in way over my head. I knew Avis slightly from Uptown Community Church and knew her professionally at school. But it wasn't till she invited me to the Chicago Women's Conference last spring, where God plunged us both into a prayer group of twelve women from all over the city, that I began "to know and be known"—or *yada,* as we discovered the word meant in Hebrew. The Yada Yada Prayer Group had hung with me through the darkest days of this past summer, when I didn't believe anybody, not even God, could love a sinner like me.

Surely they'd hang with me through teaching third graders who came to school with no socks.

I stared at the bulletin board. What could I do with the tired old thing that would make my new class feel welcome? The story I'd read about Jesus blessing the children popped into my mind. *Hmm.* A bulletin board with Jesus Loves You! in big, colorful, construction paper letters? *Oh, right.* Even Avis wouldn't be able to stop the school board from firing me. Yet *something* that would let the children know, "I'm important. I belong here. Somebody loves me."

It wouldn't be easy. Sentimental notions aside, not all of them were lovable.

Lovable. That's what Amanda's name meant in Spanish. And suddenly I had an idea.

By the time I'd finished for the day, I'd done an inventory of classroom materials, filled out my purchase orders to turn in to the office, made a list of learning games to watch out for at garage sales, and begun work on my idea for the Welcome Bulletin Board.

It occurred to me that Yada Yada had been teaching me something else I could use to start off the school year: praise and prayer. Mostly because people like Avis and Florida and Nony—well, all the sisters of color—thanked God first then looked at the facts. Ruth Garfield, lugging her Hebrew/English dictionary, had also discovered that *yadah*-spelled-with-an-h meant "to praise, to sing, to give thanks . . . to acknowledge the nature and work of God." Whew. We'd had no idea when we pulled "yada yada" out of the air, almost as a joke, as the name for our prayer group.

I peeked into the hallway to see if I could do this uninterrupted for a few minutes, then I took the printout of my incoming students and stopped by the first short desk. "Lord God, bless Ramón. Help me to love this boy like You love him." I moved to the next desk. "Thank You for LeTisha." *Hoo boy.* I was going out on a limb thanking God in advance for this one. I'd had a LeTisha in my class last year, and that little girl knew more cuss words at age eight than I even knew existed. "Bless Chanté . . . thank You for Hakim . . . bless D'Angelo . . . thank You for Savannah . . . Britny . . . Sherrie . . . Darien . . ."

By the time I flipped off the light, I'd blessed that room from corner to corner and all the little warm bodies that would soon fill it. Juggling my bulging tote bag, purchase orders, and a stack of readers to mend, I gave the classroom door a firm bump with my hip. "Aaaa-men!"

MY GOAL OF GETTING MY SEWING PROJECTS completed before school opened was severely challenged by two Professional Development days and a Teachers' Institute. I was bored out of my mind listening to speeches by a rep from the teachers' union, another from the superintendent's office, and the president of the parents' group. I caught myself thinking, *Yeah, yada-yada-yada*— and had to guzzle from my water bottle to drown my giggles.

On the second day, Project JAM and the Howard Street Community Center, both of which offered after-school programs, perked my interest, but I'm afraid I faded out again during the PowerPoint presentation of "Curriculum Alignment with State Goals."

The Institute day got down to business for Bethune Elementary. Avis—*Ms. Johnson*, I reminded myself—introduced the new staff, several of whom were student teachers. Poor kids. Fresh from college, doing their student teaching, their notebooks full of ideas, idealism dripping from every pore. I hated to see their idealism dry up when reality smacked them upside the head with the first kid who spit or cursed in their face.

I felt sorry for one student teacher who hadn't been pre-assigned to a classroom. Avis asked for volunteers to add her to their classroom, but no one spoke up. She began calling names. Clara Hutchens, the owl-eyed matriarch of first grade, sniffed, "Can't. Already got a teacher aide." Tom Davis, who taught second grade, just shrugged. "Sorry."

The student—a tall, slender girl with dark, curly hair framing almost milk-white skin and wearing a wedding ring on her left hand—kept a smile pasted on her face, but I could imagine how awful she felt. I raised my hand. "I'll take her." Avis gave a silent nod, but her eyes were smiling.

The young woman scurried to my side as we broke into teams. "Thanks. I'm Christy James." She pumped my hand. "I thought I'd be aiding kindergarten or first grade, so you'll have to clue me in."

"Jodi Baxter." I smiled, hoping I'd done the right thing. A student teacher could be a godsend—or just another headstrong "kid" who thought she knew more than you did—but the wedding ring had convinced me. It said something about her. "You'll be fine."

I MISSED CALLING HOSHI on her birthday, but I sent her a "happy birthday" e-card a couple of days later. I wondered how the visit was going. Was no news good news? I'd been so busy that week I hadn't really been praying for her. Needed to change that.

I took the Labor Day holiday literally and "labored" all weekend at the sewing machine and doing school prep. My "bright idea" for the Welcome Bulletin Board took longer than I expected, but at least it gave me an excuse not to join the wall scrapers in Amanda's room, prepping for that coat of yellow paint. What a mess! I told Amanda it was fine to paint her room this weekend, but everything had to be back in her room by the time Yada Yada arrived at our house Sunday evening.

Stu was at worship Sunday morning, and Avis, of course. Seemed like Stu had pretty much adopted Uptown as her church, even though she had to drive all the way from the West Side. Wouldn't be surprised if she signed up for Pastor Clark's membership class in the fall. So far, Ms. Perfect hadn't "taken over" the church as I'd feared, but what if—as Florida kept prodding her— she moved into the neighborhood?

As much as I'd enjoyed Iglesia del Espirito Santo last week, I was glad to be back at Uptown, where I knew the words to the songs and could hear the sermon in my own language without earphones. Yet it had opened my eyes. No wonder the Hispanics and Pakistanis and Cambodians who populated Rogers Park didn't flock to our church. Diversity among blacks and whites was challenging enough, but at least we spoke English—though even then I wasn't sure we always spoke the same language.

Like Adele. Denny and I might as well have been speaking Chinese in the phone messages and e-mail we'd left for her, for all the silence we'd gotten back in return. So you could've knocked me over with a pinfeather when Adele showed up for Yada Yada at our house that evening at five minutes past five, marching past me with a crisp nod and taking up residence on one of the dining-room chairs I'd brought into the front room.

Other people arrived about the same time, or I might have given her a piece of my mind. *If you're gonna come to Yada Yada at my house, Adele Skuggs, couldn't you have come a half-hour early so we could talk about what happened when MaDear went off her rocker? You know Denny and I want to talk!* But she had already folded her arms across her wide bosom like an impregnable stone wall. She obviously wasn't here for talking.

490

Not that it would've done any good anyway. Denny and Josh had gotten the bright idea to invite Yo-Yo's teenage half brothers to go with them to the Jazz Fest down at Grant Park, and they'd left right after lunch to pick them up. It was part of our scheme to "invite them first" before we had another incident, like the time Pete Spencer invited Josh and Amanda to a teen rave, which— unknown to us babes-in-the-city—was practically advertising the drug Ecstasy on the flyer.

Bottom line: Denny wasn't even home.

Amanda had wanted to go with the guys, but she got her period in church this morning and had been in bed with cramps all afternoon. Poor kid. I ought to take her to a doctor to see why it hits her so hard. She was camping out in our bedroom, because hers was still a mess from prepping the walls and the first coat of paint.

Ruth Garfield bustled in alone, sniffing at the new-paint smell—Yo-Yo got called last minute to work at the Bagel Bakery, she grumbled. Chanda was home with sick kids. Edesa and Delores wouldn't be making it either; Delores had to work the evening shift at the county hospital and Ricardo had taken off who-knows-where, so Edesa was baby-sitting the Enriques kids.

So that was four who couldn't make it. Would Hoshi show up with her mother? *That* would be interesting.

I was especially sorry that Edesa and Delores couldn't come. I wanted to bounce my Welcome Bulletin Board idea off them and get their help with my Latino students' names. As I tried to figure out who else might be coming, Avis pulled me into the hallway.

"Just wanted you to know that I phoned Adele this afternoon and encouraged her to come tonight—to not let her mom's confusion isolate her from the group. But don't push her about what happened at the shop. She still needs time."

"Why can't we talk about it?" I knew I sounded exasperated, but I couldn't help it. "It would help clear the air. It's no fun that MaDear thinks Denny's some redneck racist who killed her brother."

"I know." Avis's voice was soft, almost swallowed up by the doorbell. "Let's talk later, all right?"

I hustled to the front door, which was standing wide open so people could walk right in. Hoshi and Florida stood on the other side of the screen door. "My mother insisted we ring the bell," Hoshi apologized. Even through the wire mesh, she looked stunning in a tailored white pantsuit, her long black hair caught back in the simple ponytail at her neck. Florida said nothing, but her amused grin said everything. "Mother" was standing a good five feet behind them, clutching her handbag.

"We are so glad you have come!" I said, a bit too loudly, pushing open the screen door. "Come in, come in!"

In contrast to her tall, svelte daughter, Mrs. Takahashi looked like a prim ladybug in a red blazer, navy skirt, and walking shoes, her own dark hair coiled neatly into a bun at the back of her head. Hoshi led her mother around the room and introduced her to Avis . . . Ruth . . . Stu . . . Adele . . . Florida she'd already met . . . and Nony, of course. Everyone greeted her and shook her hand, as warm and courteous as Wal-Mart greeters, but Mrs. Takahashi looked like she hadn't defrosted from the Ice Age.

"Any word about Carla?" I whispered to Florida as I headed for the kitchen to get cold drinks, but her smile died and she shook her head. *What does that mean?* I wondered as I returned with a pitcher of sweet tea for the sisters who grew up down South, and a pitcher of ice water for those not yet accustomed to drinking tea-syrup. *Will they start Carla in school near her soon-to-be ex-foster parents? How dumb could that be!*

The typical banter that usually characterized the first fifteen minutes of Yada Yada had been replaced by polite conversation directed at Mrs. Takahashi: "Did you have a good flight?" "How do you like Chicago?" "You must be very proud of your daughter." Except Florida couldn't resist bugging Hoshi: "Girl, why'd you bring your mama on the El? Ain't that hustlin' her cultural exposure a bit too fast?" She was grinning as big as a toothpaste ad and wanting to laugh, I could tell.

Avis suggested we start our prayer time, and Mrs. Takahashi perched on the edge of one of the dining-room chairs as if the back might be a pincushion in disguise. Her Royal Uptightness put me on edge, too, but I tried to focus on the psalm Avis was reading.

"Give thanks to the Lord," she read, sounding like she was giving a call to worship at Uptown, "for he is good! His faithful love endures forever. Has the Lord redeemed you? Then speak out! Tell others he has saved you from your enemies. For he has gathered the exiles from many lands, from east and west, from north and south."

She looked around the room. "Psalm 107 seems written just for Yada Yada, especially tonight, when Mrs. Takahashi has joined us all the way from Japan."

Those who had Bibles hurriedly flipped to Psalm 107 in our various translations as Avis continued. "We represent many lands: South Africa, Jamaica, USA, Israel, Asia—even Mexico and Honduras, though Delores and Edesa couldn't be with us tonight."

Ding-dong.

The doorbell? I set my Bible down and headed for the foyer. Who had come late? The door was still standing open to catch any evening breeze, but I didn't recognize the person on the other side of the screen. "Yes?"

"I gots yo' Avon order."

"Avon? I didn't order any Avon." I tried to speak quietly, so as not to disturb Avis's devotion going on in the front room. But as my eyes adjusted to the dim daylight on the front porch, I wanted to burst out laughing. I'd never seen an "Avon lady" wearing wrap-around shades and a tight red bandana around her head. This one looked like she'd been poured into her jeans too.

I suppressed a smile. "Sorry. Maybe it's for my upstairs neighbor. What's the name on the order? I could give it to her." I opened the screen door, ready to take the brown paper bag she held in her hand.

The woman in the bandana jerked the screen door right out of my hand. "It's for *you!*" The paper bag dropped, and in its place she held a butcher knife, waving it in my face. "Git inside!" she hissed. "Git inside *now.*"

494

11

I nearly wet my pants. *I can't let this crazy woman come in!* Then the woman shoved the knife just inches from my throat. Like stop-frame photography, I noticed the tip was broken off. Yet the blade itself was ten inches long—long enough to go through my neck and out the other side.

I backed up.

"Turn around an' walk inta that room." The hiss was low, like a talking snake. "Don't mess wid me, an' nobody'll git hurt."

My mind felt detached from my frozen body. Would my feet even obey me? But I turned around and started—slowly—for the living room. The stranger crowded behind me, something—her hand? the knife?—pressing into the small of my back. *Oh God! Oh God! What should I do?* Within seconds I'd be bringing danger into a roomful of unsuspecting women—my sisters, my friends. *Yell! Run!* But the words stuck in my throat, and my feet kept walking.

I could hear Florida's voice, then Ruth. Nobody paid the least attention as I mechanically crossed the hall into the living room, my shadow close on my heels. Suddenly the "Avon lady" shoved me aside. "Dis is a stickup!" she yelled. "Don't nobody move!"

The shove nearly sent me to my knees. I caught the back of a chair and managed to remain standing, though my legs felt like rubber bands. Someone screamed. I didn't recognize the voice till I saw Mrs. Takahashi's mouth stretched into a big O. Everyone else sat like ice sculptures. Ruth's hand hung in the air—she usually talked with her hands—and Avis's finger still touched the open page of her Bible, like she was about to make a point.

Mrs. Takahashi was babbling gibberish or Japanese. I didn't know which.

"Shut up! *Shut up, you—!*" The bandana woman pointed the knife straight at Hoshi's mother, spouting a string of obscenities.

Hoshi flinched and put a hand over her mother's mouth, like she was shushing a toddler. "Shh, shh, *mama-san*. Please don't." Tears puddled in Hoshi's eyes then ran down her face.

Oh God. She's terrified.

The intruder strutted into the middle of the circle, still waving her knife. "Jist do as I say. Ain't nobody gonna git hurt." She stopped in front of Nony, who was wearing a necklace of multiple chains and chunky gold earrings. "The jools. Take 'em off. Rings too." Nony's hands trembled as she obeyed.

The woman stuffed Nony's jewelry into the pocket of her denim jacket then held out her free hand to Stu. Stu had to fiddle a long time with the row of little earrings that ran from her lobe to the top of each ear, then she practically slapped them into the intruder's outstretched hand. The stranger pushed her wraparound shades right up into Stu's face. "Don't mess wid me, snow bunny."

My own legs wobbled so much I finally sank into the chair. The woman whirled at my movement. "Don't *you* go nowhere." She peered beyond me to the hallway. "Who else be here?"

Amanda! My heart thudded so hard in my chest, I thought sure it could be heard clear across the room. *Oh God, oh Jesus, keep Amanda out of this.* The last I'd seen Amanda she was reading a book in bed, earphones clamped over her head. And Willie Wonka. For the first time in my life I was grateful the old dog was almost stone-deaf.

I shook my head. "Nobody," I lied.

The intruder stopped in front of Avis. "Gimme dat." She pointed at a pin Avis was wearing that fastened the long, bright-colored scarf she was wearing around her neck. "An' dat." The woman pointed to Avis's wedding ring.

Avis looked up into the woman's face. She was calm, but a thin film of sweat glistened on her forehead and upper lip. "Please. Don't take my wedding ring. It's the only thing I have left to remember my husband."

"What? He dead?" The woman stared at Avis for a moment then motioned with her free hand. "Okay, okay. Just gimme da pin. Hurry it up."

Florida narrowed her eyes when the stranger stopped in front of her. "What? Do I look like I got jewelry?" Florida's voice dripped sarcasm. "I know where you're comin' from, scrub. You're pumped off your head. You snootin' snow? Shootin' H? What?"

"Shut up! Mind yo' own bidness." She moved on.

I noticed the wiry intruder avoided Adele, who sat with her arms crossed in front of her, big and foreboding. I got no such clemency. "Yo' rings, fool." She danced around, keeping an eye on the circle of women, waving her knife, as I tried to wiggle my wedding ring set over my big knuckles. I wanted to throw it, scream at her, do *something*—but I numbly put it into her hand and watched it disappear into her jacket pocket.

When she got around to Hoshi and Mrs. Takahashi, the older Japanese woman pinched her mouth like it was stitched together and pulled her handbag close to her chest. The thief pointed the broken tip of the knife. "You. Gimme da money."

Mrs. Takahashi shook her head.

The stranger grabbed for her purse. "I *saw* you git money outta dat ATM, slit eyes!"

Ohmigosh. She'd followed them here!

Fire smoldered behind the pressed lips and almond eyes. Hoshi's mother held on tight to the handbag and swatted at the knife waving in her face—and suddenly a wail filled the room. A line of bright red blood appeared across Mrs. Takahashi's palm down to her wrist.

"You *grabbed* it, you blasted fool!" the intruder shrieked. She whirled around and looked at me. "Git her somethin' quick. No! Don' leave da room—whatchu got?"

Blood was running down Mrs. Takahashi's arm. *"Mama-san! Mama-san!"* Hoshi cried. Her shoulders were shaking.

Ruth Garfield whipped out a large white handkerchief—Ben's,

no doubt—stalked over to Mrs. Takahashi's chair, and wrapped it tightly around her hand. "Press here," she commanded Hoshi, indicating a vein on her mother's wrist. "Hold her hand up—high." She turned and glared at the stranger. *"Vilda chaya!"* she spit out and stalked back to her chair.

"Whatchu call me? Din't I tell you nobody git hurt if ya do what I say?" The woman behind the shades was practically screaming.

Adele rose up out of her chair, like a bear coming out of hibernation. "That's *it.* You've gone too far. Get out." She pointed toward the front door. *"Get out.* You got what you wanted. Get out!"

I would've run, if it'd been me. But the bandana-headed woman eyed the big ruby ring on Adele's right hand, and her eyes seemed to glitter. With a sudden movement she grabbed Mrs. Takahashi out of her chair and held the frightened lady, still clutching her handbag, in front of her in a one-arm grip.

"I tol' you. I don't wanna hurt nobody—but I *will* if ya don't siddown *now,* Big Mama."

Adele didn't move. "She needs medical help!" The handkerchief around Mrs. Takahashi's hand was staining bright red.

The knife moved slowly to Mrs. Takahashi's neck. *"Siddown!"*

Adele slowly sat.

The intruder kept a grip on Hoshi's mother, who was too terrified to scream or cry, and caught my eye. "You! Tie up Big Mama there."

Tie up Adele? I couldn't have been more shocked if she'd asked me to walk on the ceiling. "With what?" *Think, Jodi! Say you've got rope in the basement then call the police . . .*

The woman gestured with the knife toward the box fan in the front window. "Use th' estenshion cord. An' hurry up, you—" She peppered me with all the cuss words in her gutter vocabulary.

I took a deep breath, hoping my rubbery legs would hold me up, and stumbled toward the fan. The rest of the room was deathly silent, except for Hoshi's stifled sobs and the intruder's raspy breathing. I unplugged the cord and turned to face our adversary. Surely she wouldn't make me—

"You! Big Mama. Put yo' hands behind yo' chair." Then she pointed at me. "Now tie her to the chair."

This was a nightmare! I couldn't tie up *Adele*—of all people! But the crazy woman was glaring at me from behind Mrs. Takahashi's terrified face, so I walked in a daze behind Adele's chair, knelt down, and began to wrap the extension cord around her hands. "I'm sorry, Adele—so sorry," I whispered behind her back, but Adele gave no sign that she heard me.

"She tied up?" the intruder's voice demanded. "Now take 'at ruby ring off her han', an' be quick 'bout it."

With dread practically dripping from my pores, I wiggled the ring from Adele's thick finger. *Oh God, Oh God . . . send somebody . . . do something!* Finally the ring popped off into my hand and I stood up—and nearly stopped breathing. The stranger's back was to the hallway, but over her shoulder I saw Amanda standing behind her in the doorway.

I wanted to yell at my daughter to run. Instead I said loudly,

"Here's the rotten ring" and stepped forward—but not all the way, making our captor push Mrs. Takahashi back into her chair before reaching out to snatch it. When I looked again, Amanda had disappeared. *Thank You, Jesus, thank You, thank You*—

"An' tie that one too!" The knife pointed toward Stu. "I don't like Cinderella's attitude."

Before I could obey—did we even have another extension cord in the living room?—I suddenly heard the click of Willie Wonka's nails in the hallway. "Woof! Woof!" The chocolate Lab skidded to a stop in the hallway just outside the living room. Willie hardly ever barked; he wasn't much of a watchdog. Yet he knew something wasn't right.

The dog's bark freaked the bandana woman. She whirled on the dog, slashing her knife through the air.

"He won't hurt you!" I yelled.

"Then git him to shut up, or I'll hurt *him,*" she snarled.

I knew Willie wouldn't leave voluntarily, so I grabbed his collar and dragged him over to the front window and made him lie down against the wall. Before I could straighten up, I heard a demanding male voice: "What's going on here?"

Denny! I looked up just in time to see the intruder whirl around to face my husband, pointing the knife at his throat. Where had he come from? Like actors in a tableau, Denny and the woman faced each other, motionless. My heart raced. But time seemed to stand still—half a second? half a minute? Then she lunged with the knife.

I screamed. *"Nooooooo!"*

12

It happened so fast, it was over in a blink. As the crazy woman lunged at Denny with the knife, he grabbed her wrist. The next moment she was on her back on the floor with Denny spread-eagle on top of her.

"Jodi!" he yelled. "Take the knife!"

My body parts suddenly came alive, and I scrambled toward the pair on the floor.

"Git off me, you—" The woman struggled beneath Denny's weight, letting loose a string of cuss words that made all the words she'd been throwing around for the last fifteen minutes sound like kindergarten babble.

"Take the knife!" he commanded again, trying to keep from getting kicked from behind by her flailing legs. The woman still held the handle of the butcher knife in her right hand—how in the world was I going to get it away from her? As Denny dug his nails into her wrist, she finally let go. I snatched it.

"Call the police!" he bellowed.

"I already did, Daddy." Amanda reappeared in the living-room doorway, barefoot, wearing only an oversized T-shirt, her brown eyes wide and her face chalk-white.

"An ambulance we need too." Ruth appeared at my side. "And take that horrid knife away, Jodi."

I stared at the ten-inch knife in my hand as though seeing it for the first time. A streak of Mrs. Takahashi's blood was smeared along the sharp edge. I had an overwhelming urge to throw it away from me, but instead I ran to the kitchen and dumped it into the sink. "Don't touch that!" I hissed at Amanda, who'd followed me. "And call 911 again for an ambulance." I ran back to the living room, just as I heard sirens screaming . . . coming closer . . . and screeching to a stop outside our house.

Stu was busy untying Adele. Nony, Ruth, and Avis huddled around Hoshi and Mrs. Takahashi, and Florida flung open the screen door for the police. The crazy woman was still cussing a blue streak on the floor.

Four big police officers—two black, two white—pounded into our living room. "Police! Don't anybody move!" One had his gun out of its holster. Taking in the scene at a glance, he pointed it straight at Denny's head. "Okay, buster, let 'er go. Put your hands behind your head."

"No!" I yelled. "Not him—*her!*"

Immediately the other women in the room started talking all at once, arguing with the police, pointing at the intruder on the floor, holding up Mrs. Takahashi's wounded hand.

"Quiet!" yelled the cop with the gun. He looked at me. "You. What's going on here?"

I couldn't believe this! "That . . . that woman on the floor came in here with a knife . . . and . . . and she robbed us . . . and cut Mrs. Takahashi's hand. And that's my husband—stop pointing that gun at him!"

"She's tellin' it," Florida declared. A murmur of assent rose from several others.

The intruder must have known it was all over, because she quit struggling.

"All right." A pause. The police officer holstered his gun. "We'll take her, sir. Get off easy, now. Fellas . . ."

The four police officers each took a wrist or ankle. Denny released his hold on the woman's wrists and scrambled to his feet. No sooner did the four men start to lift the bandana woman to her feet than she seemed to explode—kicking, scratching, cussing, and calling down all sorts of calamity upon their heads. The rest of us backed off, watching in disbelief. It took all four of them to finally get a pair of handcuffs on her, and still she kicked and screamed all the way to the paddy wagon, which was blinking its hazard lights in front of our house.

"Denny!" I ran to my husband, who was leaning over, hands on his knees. "Are you okay?"

He nodded mutely.

A few moments later, two of the officers came back in the house, brushing off their uniforms as if trying to regain their dignity. "Everybody sit down, please," said the one who seemed to be

505

in charge. His cheeks were ruddy, giving him a boyish look even though his paunch suggested he was older—forty, maybe fifty. "I'm Sergeant Curry. We're going to need a statement from each one of you."

"But my mother!" Hoshi cried. "She's hurt! She needs a doctor!"

Denny jerked his head toward the sound of another siren that suddenly choked off in midwail directly in front of our house. "We called an ambulance."

"And that thief just walked out of here with our jewelry in her pocket!" Stu stormed.

"Yes!" Nony wailed. "My wedding ring—please get it back." Even as she spoke, we heard the paddy wagon pull out to make room for the ambulance. Nony began to weep quietly.

The sergeant punched his walkie-talkie. "We need some ETs here. Lunt Avenue. On the double." He sighed. "I'm sorry, ladies. We're going to have to keep everything she had on her person as evidence. We'll"—he cleared his throat nervously—"be sure to return everything to you."

For the next few minutes, the house was full of medics who tended to Mrs. Takahashi's hand then trundled her out to the waiting ambulance. Nony insisted on accompanying Hoshi, so the second police officer also went along to get their statements at the hospital. No sooner had they left than two more police officers arrived. The evidence technicians, I presumed.

Sergeant Curry turned to me. "Ma'am, you mentioned a knife. Where is it?"

"I . . ." For a moment I couldn't think. "Uh, I put it in the kitchen sink." I led one of the ETs to the kitchen, where he pulled on a pair of rubber gloves, retrieved the knife, and put it in an evidence bag. Good grief. *My* fingerprints were all over that knife too!

When we returned to the front of the house, everyone else was sitting down again except Denny and Amanda, who was sobbing quietly under her daddy's arm as he leaned against the arched doorway. The officer in charge pulled out a small notebook. "Who encountered the woman first?"

I lifted my hand.

"Okay, let's start with you. Tell me what happened."

Tell him what happened? I just wanted them to leave! I wanted to hold Denny and Amanda. I wanted to hug my Yada Yada sisters. I wanted to go to the hospital to see if Hoshi's mother was going to be all right. I wanted to ask Adele if I hurt her when I tied her hands. I wanted to . . . to have a good bawl!

No. I was not going to cry in front of these police officers. I drew a breath. "Okay. We"—I indicated the other women—"were having, uh, a prayer meeting. My husband was out; my daughter was in her bedroom. The doorbell rang, but we weren't expecting anybody else. A strange woman stood at the door, said she had my Avon order . . ."

Sergeant Curry was busily taking notes. "Describe her, for the record."

"Well, she was black, wearing a red bandana and wraparound shades—"

Florida snorted. "That wasn't no black woman."

Stu frowned. "Sure she was. Light-skinned, maybe."

"That girl was *white*," muttered Adele.

I stared at Florida and Adele. From the moment I laid eyes on the "Avon lady," I thought she was black. The way she talked black or hip-hop or something. I looked at Avis for help.

Avis shrugged. "Hard to tell behind those shades, light-skinned as she was."

"Why'd you think she was *black?*" Adele was downright scornful. "Because she was whacked out on drugs? talked street jive? cussed you out?"

I looked helplessly at Denny. Could this get any worse?

The sergeant cleared his throat. "Ladies, it doesn't really matter. We've got the suspect in custody. Let's go on. What happened after she rang your doorbell?"

THE POLICE OFFICERS FINALLY LEFT after taking everybody's statements and making a list of the stolen jewelry. Adele started to follow the officers out the door, but Avis said, "Wait a minute, sisters. If ever we needed to spend time praying together, this is it. Ten minutes, tops. We've got some praising to do. Nobody got killed; everybody's going to be all right, even Hoshi's mother. We've also got some serious spiritual battle to do. That woman's drowning in darkness."

Reluctantly, Adele rejoined the group. Florida pulled Amanda and Denny into the circle, and we all held hands. I held on for dear life to Denny's hand on one side and Ruth's on the other. *Thank you, Avis! Yes, yes, let's pray. Otherwise I might just fall apart, right here and now.*

THE PRAYER WAS GOOD. It helped me calm down, let me focus on what we could thank God for in the midst of the trauma we'd just experienced. Nony called in the middle of the prayer, saying that Mrs. Takahashi had to have seventeen stitches in her hand but was going to be all right. Both Hoshi and her mother had been given a sedative by the emergency-room staff, and a police officer took them back to the Orrington Hotel. Now could someone come to St. Francis Hospital and pick her up? Nony's car was still at our house.

That's when I learned that Josh still had *our* car and was driving Pete and Jerry home. Which meant he'd dropped Denny off.

It had to be God.

So Stu went to pick up Nony at the hospital and brought her back to get her car. We hugged out on the sidewalk, and Nony shook her head, deeply concerned. "Pray without ceasing for Hoshi. Her parents are terribly upset."

Understandably. Stu's "great idea" for Hoshi to bring her mother to Yada Yada had turned out to be an utter disaster.

Can't go there, Jodi. It's not Stu's fault.

Finally everyone was gone. Josh came home and seemed rather

disappointed that he'd missed all the excitement. Amanda gave him a blow-by-blow account, puffing up her role a bit, I noticed, describing how she sneaked the cordless out of the house and dialed 911 from the backyard. Well, why not? She had behaved admirably under the circumstances.

At last Denny and I were alone in the living room—after I made sure our front and back doors were locked. "I'm starving," he announced. "Be back with a four-course dinner in two minutes." He turned at the doorway. "Turn on that fan, will you? It's hotter'n blazes in here."

I picked up the extension cord where it had dropped after someone—Stu, I think—had untied Adele's hands. I stared at the innocent-looking cord. Had I really tied up Adele Skuggs with this thing? Numbly, I connected the fan cord and the extension then plugged it into the socket. The cooling night air flowed into the room.

Denny returned with chips, salsa, leftover sweet tea, apple slices, and peanut butter. Not exactly the four-course meal he promised, but hey, he brought it out on a tray, and all I had to do was dig in. No complaint from me.

We sat on either end of the couch, our legs entwined, munching quietly for several minutes. Then Denny said, "God spoke to me."

I stopped eating. "What do you mean?"

"When that woman lunged at me with the knife. God told me, *'Grab her wrist. No one is going to get hurt.'* It was as if time slowed down, and everything happened in slow motion. She lunged. I grabbed. I pulled her across and tripped her. Not even sure how I did it, but I wasn't afraid. I knew God was helping me."

I shuddered. "I was afraid."

He leaned forward and began to massage my leg, the one with the steel rod in it. "You've had a pretty rough summer, babe."

Wasn't *that* the truth! I could get a good pity party going if given half a chance. Yet if Avis could look for things to thank God for only moments after being grilled by a police officer, maybe I could put the pity party on hold.

"Adele came to Yada Yada, as you saw," I mused. "Didn't get to talk to her, though. She seemed pretty distant—even before we got robbed. Avis told me to give her some space."

Denny heaved a big sigh. "Yeah. What happened tonight won't make it any easier, will it?"

We sat quietly for a few moments, munching on our snacks and washing them down with sweet iced tea. Then Denny started to chuckle.

"What?" I dug an apple slice into the peanut butter.

He tried to wipe the grin off his face. "It's really not funny, but . . . while I had that woman pinned, I thought, *'Does this crazy person have a name?'* I mean, it wasn't so bad tackling a cutthroat druggie, but what if she has a name like . . . like Susie or Denise or Tammy? I tell you, my superhero status starts to slip if I had 'Susie' spread-eagle on my living-room floor."

"No!" I started to laugh too, which wasn't easy with peanut butter in my mouth. "She couldn't have a name like Susie. It's gotta be some street moniker. Like Krazy Kate or Maniac Mama."

Denny's chuckles gave way to belly laughs. "Maniac Mama! That's it! I pinned Maniac Mama to the floor till the police came!"

All the tension of the evening erupted into hysterical laughter. I laughed so hard I almost lost all the snacks I'd just eaten. Even Denny was holding his side. Josh came out of his room, looked at us, and shook his head. "You guys are nuts."

Yet in the middle of the night, when I got up to go to the bathroom, my half-awake brain was jolted by the thought: *Florida was once a crazy drug addict.* My first memory of her flooded back: a tattered woman banging on the hood of my car, begging for money. Years ago. Just a panhandler then. Now she was Florida, my sister, my friend. Who but God could've done *that?*

I had a hard time going back to sleep. What happened to our intruder once that paddy wagon drove off? She wasn't just a thief; she was a woman—like me. Did they put her in a cell at Cook County Jail? Was she getting any sleep? Did she have a family? Did they know where she was?

Does she have a name?

13

*B*ecky Wallace. That was her name. We found out when Denny called the Twenty-Fourth District Police Station on Clark Street the next day and asked to speak to Sergeant Curry. It was Labor Day; we thought he might have the day off. But he called back a couple of hours later. I quietly picked up the kitchen extension but motioned madly at Denny to do the talking.

Sergeant Curry said "the suspect in question" was already in detox at Cook County Jail—a process that usually took about three weeks. After that, if she was found guilty, she was looking at some serious jail time. "Your wife and the other women she robbed willing to testify at her trial?"

Denny motioned at me to answer, but I shook my head and pointed back at him.

"Uh . . . probably," he said, rolling his eyes for my benefit. "Do we have to press charges or something?"

"No. We've got your statements. That will be enough for an arraignment. The state's attorney's office will decide what charges to file and will contact you if there's a trial."

I waggled my left hand across the room at Denny, indicating my bare ring finger.

"What about my wife's wedding ring and the other jewelry?"

A brief pause. "I'm sorry, Mr. Baxter. As I told you, it'll be awhile. Evidence."

"Right." Denny turned his back, as though he didn't want to get any more sign language from me. "What did you say the woman's name is?"

"Uh, just a sec. Got it here somewhere." We heard papers shuffling. "Wallace. She gave her name as Becky Wallace."

I just stared at Denny after we hung up. Surely the police sergeant was pulling our leg. The crazy woman who'd come charging into our house waving a ten-inch butcher knife and cussing like a gangbanger couldn't be a *Becky*.

Denny must have been thinking the same thing as he gave me a sheepish grin. "Sure glad I didn't know that before I threw her down. What would the guys say if they knew I'd manhandled a girl named Becky?"

I snickered. But knowing her name did feel weird. I kinda wished we hadn't asked. It was easier thinking of her as "that drugged-out crazy woman."

The last of the paint went on in Amanda's room—thanks to Josh and Denny—that morning, then Josh and Amanda took advantage of their last free day before school started to hang out at the lakefront, the last day the city lifeguards would be on duty. Well, let 'em. Tomorrow they'd stagger home with backpacks full of books and homework. And Josh had been getting college information in the mail all summer; soon he'd have to sit down and fill out applications and plan campus visits.

Let 'em have one more carefree summer fling.

As for me, I thanked God at least once every half-hour that today was a holiday. If I'd had to face the first day of school at Bethune Elementary after what happened last night, my emotions would probably be scrambled for life. I was sure Avis was grateful too. Everybody, in fact. We all needed a day to calm down and get our wits about us before facing real life.

Except Hoshi didn't have that luxury. What was happening with her? Her poor mother got the worst of it, and Hoshi was probably still picking up the pieces.

I dialed Nony. "Have you heard from Hoshi? How's her mother doing?"

A big sigh greeted my inquiry. "God in heaven, have mercy. The Word says the bruised reed will not be broken, nor the dimly burning wick extinguished . . ."

I waited. Sometimes it was hard to tell whether Nony was talking or praying. "What?"

She sighed again. "I went over to the hotel today. Mr. Takahashi insisted that they were leaving immediately. He was too polite to raise his voice in my presence, but he spoke sternly to Hoshi in Japanese, and when she shook her head, he stalked out of the room."

"What?"

"I'm getting there, Jodi! When her mother went to the bathroom, Hoshi told me her father said, 'This is what happens when a disobedient daughter turns her back on her parents and her religion.'"

"Oh no." I groaned. "He can't blame Hoshi! I mean, good grief! They've got crime in Japan, don't they?"

"They're upset, Jodi. Her father wanted her to go home with them. Today. Hoshi said no . . . she wants to finish her education."

"Are they paying her tuition? Could they—?"

"No. She has a full scholarship. But in Japanese culture, defying your parents' wishes is a very serious thing."

I felt heartsick for Hoshi—but part of me sympathized with her parents. How would I feel if Josh jettisoned his Christian upbringing for Shintoism? I'd freak out too. I managed to ask, "So where is Hoshi now?"

"She went to the airport with them by cab. I told her to come back to my house afterward. She really shouldn't be alone right now, poor thing."

I hardly knew what to think after I hung up the phone. What a mess.

DENNY DECIDED TO RUN OFF some of his pent-up emotions with a good jog by the lake. With everyone else gone, Willie Wonka followed me from room to room, standing in the way when I tried to move around the kitchen, lying on my feet if I sat down. He was getting on my nerves. Once I yelled at him to leave me alone—a lot of good that did, since he couldn't hear—but he looked at me reproachfully.

I relented. "Come here, guy," I said, plopping into a chair in the dining room and inviting him closer. Willie Wonka immediately stuck his face in my lap. *Humph.* Give a dog an inch, and he'll take a whole city block. I took his sweet doggy face in my hands. "You're still upset by what happened last night, aren't you? Well, so am I."

It was true. I felt so . . . violated. Like being strip-searched in a crowded room. A stranger had pushed her way into my home and threatened my family, my friends. I shuddered at what *could* have happened.

Willie looked hopefully into my eyes. So patient. As if waiting for me to say, *It's okay, don't worry, everything's going to be all right.* Why were dogs so trusting? Didn't they know we humans usually didn't have a clue? Unlike us, dogs seemed to love with no strings attached.

I stroked Willie's silky brown ears, my thoughts tumbling. Why was it so hard to trust God when things didn't go right? Surely *God* had a clue. I mean, He's God! That's His job description! I knew God loved me—and all of us in that room last night. So couldn't I stop stewing about it and trust God to work it out?

Okay. I was going to stop stewing and start sewing. "That's it, Willie." I got up abruptly, ending our little tête-à-tête. I had a sewing project to finish and research still to do on my Welcome

Bulletin Board idea. The computer was free; maybe I'd do that first while everybody else was out.

While I was waiting for the computer to boot up, my own thoughts came around again. *God loves all of us who were in that room last night. Even—*

Whoa. Even Becky Wallace?

I WORKED FOR A WHILE ON THE COMPUTER, using a search engine to chase down the meanings of the names of the students who would be in my class. D'Angelo was easy: "from the angels." So was Jade ("jewel") and Cornell ("hornblower"). But I was excited to not only find Ramón ("mighty protector") and Chanté ("to sing"), but also LeTisha ("joy") and Kaya ("wise child").

Hmm. So LeTisha meant "joy." This was going to be interesting. Last year's LeTisha had been anything *but*. I was starting to get excited. How would the children react to learning the meaning of their names?

What about Jodi? I'd never thought about it before. Did my name—

The phone rang. I thought I'd heard Denny come back and hoped he'd answer it, but it kept ringing, so finally I tried to make a dash to the kitchen phone. My leg had stiffened up sitting so long, and I almost fell. The answering machine started to pick up by the time I got there.

"Hello? We're here! Sorry it took so long."

"Jodi." I recognized Florida's voice, but there was something in her voice . . . Was she crying?

"Florida? Is something wrong?"

"No. It's good. I'm just . . . Jodi, DCFS just called. They're bringing Carla home. Today." Florida's voice faded; she must have put the phone down. Somewhere in the background I could hear her crying and praising. "Oh, thank ya, Jesus. *Thank ya!*"

"Florida? Florida!" I called into the phone. This was incredible! Wonderful news. She'd been trying to get her daughter back even before I met her last spring. Even after Stu—our wannabe social worker—had located Carla, the red tape had been like hacking through a jungle. I could hardly imagine how Florida got through each day, not knowing for sure when or if she'd get her daughter back.

Florida finally came back on the phone.

"Florida, that's wonderful," I said.

"Yeah, I know." Florida blew her nose. "But you gotta get the sisters to pray for us; that's why I called. Because they didn't *tell* me in time to get her registered for school"—Florida's tone got testy—"so I gotta take off work tomorrow, and—"

"Of course, Florida. I'll send an e-mail to everybody."

"That's not all." I could hear the tug between pain and joy in Florida's voice. "The social worker said Carla's upset. She doesn't want to start a new school. Wants to stay with her foster . . ." I could hear her crying again, softly. "Jodi? Am I doin' the right thing?"

14

had no idea how to answer Florida. The right thing? *The right thing, Florida, would've been not to get strung out on drugs and lose your kid in the first place!*

But I wasn't about to say that. After all, "the right thing" for *me* would've been not to have a stupid fight with my husband and end up driving angry behind the wheel of our car—which had had far worse consequences.

A spasm of regret made me feel sick to my stomach.

Florida was hurting and waiting for me to say something. I tried. "Flo, I don't know. Except . . . God's done some pretty big miracles in your life already, including DCFS returning Carla to you *today!* So she can start school! You're always saying God didn't bring you this far to leave you, and He's not going to leave you or Carla now either." I heard the words I was saying, desperately wanting to believe them.

We'd no sooner hung up than the phone rang again.

"Jodi!" It was Yo-Yo. "Heard I missed all the excitement last night! Had to work."

I was in no mood to joke about it. "Guess Ruth told you what happened."

"Yeah. Can't shut her up. She's beside herself about what that kook did to Hoshi's mama."

"Her name's Becky Wallace."

"Who?"

"The kook, as you called her." I was feeling testy, though I wasn't sure why exactly.

"Ha. She told you her *name?* Like, hey, my name's Becky Wallace. Pleased ta meetcha. Gimme all your jools." She laughed.

"No." My annoyance meter was rising. "Look, Yo-Yo. If you called for some reason . . ."

"Hey, sorry." Her tone sobered. "Must've been tough for you guys. *Really* sorry to hear what happened to Hoshi's mom. That perp musta been postal."

I was too tired to unscramble Yo-Yo's language. "Yeah."

"Uh, I really called to tell Josh and Denny thanks for taking my kid brothers to the Jazz Fest yesterday. They came home tanked— you know, all excited. Mostly 'cause somebody was payin' attention to 'em I think, though you'd never get either of 'em to admit it. Ben and Ruth used to do that kind of stuff with them—did it a *lot* when I was in the joint—but Ben's getting kinda cranky with them these days. Can't blame him; they drive *me* over the edge. They're, you know, mouthy teenagers. Anyway, tell your man thanks. Josh too."

"Okay. Sure." My insides relaxed a little. "Know something, Yo-Yo? If Denny had driven the boys home first instead of letting Josh drop him off here last night, no telling what might have happened."

"Yeah." A pause. "Guess the Big Guy upstairs was lookin' out for ya."

I smiled in spite of myself. Yo-Yo could never be accused of "churchy" language.

Neither one of us spoke for a moment. Then, doing a mental U-turn, I found myself saying, "Yo-Yo, remember when we were introducing ourselves at the women's conference last spring? I stuck my foot in it and asked where you learned to cook?"

The phone crackled with Yo-Yo's laugh. "Yeah. Wish you could've seen your face when I said prison."

"Yeah, I know." Even now I could feel my face getting red, but I pushed on. "You said, 'I had my reasons'—you know, for committing forgery. Uh, can I ask . . . what reasons?"

"Huh. Nosy chick, ain't ya." But she didn't sound mad. "School clothes. School supplies. Didn't know no other way to get what Pete and Jerry needed. My mom was in the ozone; she sure as heck wasn't getting them ready for school. It wasn't that hard to forge all those checks with my mom's ID. 'Course there wasn't no money in the bank . . ."

Did the crime, served my time. It's behind me now." That's what Yo-Yo had said last spring. Like it was nothing. I couldn't imagine even eighteen months shut away with people like . . . like Bandana Woman, who spewed filthy words five times in one sentence.

"What was it like?"

"What? Prison?"

"Yeah."

"Man!" That's all Yo-Yo said for a moment or two.

What were you thinking, Jodi? She obviously doesn't want to talk about it! I was just about to say, "Forget it," when Yo-Yo said, "It's tough, Jodi. Ya gotta *be* tough to survive in prison. Learned that the first day at Cook County. Was sittin' there in the common room, smokin' a cigarette an' mindin' my own business, when this big black girl comes over and says, 'Gimme a cigarette. *Now.*'"

I wondered why Yo-Yo mentioned the girl's race. It wasn't supposed to matter, was it? Yet it probably *did* matter in prison. "Like" allied with "like." I could just see Yo-Yo slouched in a chair, legs stuck out, one arm over the back—but probably without the overalls she always wore. Didn't prisoners at Cook County wear orange jumpsuits or something? Her skin was pale, and she rarely wore makeup; but her spiky hair with blonde tips called attention to itself. Yo-Yo wasn't a big person; she just seemed that way to me because of her blunt talk.

"Knew if I gave it to her," Yo-Yo went on, "it'd be over for me. I'd end up being some big mama's sissy. So I cussed her out good, told her to get out of my face. She backed off."

My knees literally got the shakes, and I had to sit down. I couldn't even bring myself to think beneath the surface of Yo-Yo's words. I wasn't tough. I was a wimp. I'd never have survived one day in prison.

I heard Yo-Yo sigh on the other end of the phone. "Didn't

especially like the person I had to be inside the joint, but that's the way it was. Ruth had to soften me up a bit once I got out."

Soften? "Soft" was not a word I would associate with Yo-Yo.

"Say, what's with all the questions?" she asked. "You got acquitted, remember? Don't go lookin' backwards."

"I know. Thanks, Yo-Yo. Sorry for getting so personal."

"It's okay, but gotta run. The Bagel Bakery is *not* closed on Labor Day."

We hung up, but for some reason I felt all confused. Uneasy. Yo-Yo forged checks to get school clothes—school clothes!—for her kid brothers and spent eighteen months in jail. I killed a kid in a car accident and *didn't* go to jail.

Then along comes Bandana Woman—yeah, that handle fit her a lot better than her so-called name—who terrorizes Yada Yada and cuts Mrs. Takahashi's hand and, frankly, I'm hoping she's going down for a long, long time. *She's a tough cookie,* I tell myself. *Nobody's going to mess with her.* Then an afterthought, *But if they do, it serves her right.*

MY PARENTS CALLED just as we were getting ready to eat supper.

I heard the phone ring, but it seemed like the phone had been ringing all afternoon—first Florida, then Yo-Yo, then Chanda, who was practically hysterical, even though she hadn't even been here last night. Somebody must have told her. Adele? They went to the same church—Paul and Silas Apostolic—but otherwise didn't seem to interact much. It annoyed me no end that I had to calm *her* down when she hadn't even been here to get robbed. "Oh, sista Jodee," she moaned. "Such a terrible t'ing." Her Jamaican accent got thicker, till I could hardly understand her. "So bad. So bad."

By the time Denny and the kids got home from their last fling with summer, the most I could manage for a Labor Day "picnic" was grilling some chicken in the backyard. Correction: Denny did the grilling. He knows I don't have the patience to sit there baby-sitting the grill, so the meat ends up BBB—"Blackened Beyond Belief."

Denny had just yelled, "Five minutes!" and I was putting some corn on the cob and fruit salad on the small back-porch table when the phone rang *again*. I was all for letting the machine pick it up, but Amanda can't resist a ringing telephone any more than Willie Wonka can resist scratching a flea. I heard her say, "Hi, Grandma! Yeah, it's Amanda."

My mother's timing is always exquisite. Just as we're sitting down to dinner, or just as we're rushing out the door to school, or even just as Denny and I are climbing into bed for a marital "roll in the hay." Which probably means I should call my parents more often when I do have a free minute—or ten, or thirty.

I heard Amanda say, "Yeah, we had a lot of excitement here last night—" I snatched the phone before my dramatic daughter could give her grandmother a blow-by-blow account of the robbery. "Hi, Mom!" I said breezily, shooing Amanda out the back door. *"Go ahead and eat,"* I mouthed at Denny.

"Hi, sweetie," my mom said. "Excitement? What excitement? You doing all right?"

My mom would probably never forgive herself for not rushing to my side when I'd had the accident earlier that summer. Yet she'd had a bad chest cold at the time, verging on pneumonia, and the doctor had advised her not to travel—praise be to heaven. I loved my folks, really I did. They were good parents, solid, full of faith, a bit too serious perhaps—but whew! They would've gone into shock when I got charged with vehicular manslaughter, even though it later got dropped. And what if they'd found out we'd been fighting that day over Denny drinking beer with the guys? Denny would never hear the end of it. Never mind that *I* was the one "driving mad."

No. God had created three hundred miles between Chicago and Des Moines, Iowa, which made it easier to keep things simple: *"It was raining. I had a car accident. A boy was killed—so tragic. I broke my leg and several ribs and lost my spleen, but I'm better now."*

"Sure, Mom. I'm fine. We all start school tomorrow, you know. The kids are excited."

"I know. That's why I called. Don't you think handling a classroom so soon after surgery will be too much? Maybe they could assign a substitute for a few weeks."

"No, Mom, really. I'll be okay. It'd be much harder to start late. How's Dad? You guys decide to get that motor home?"

"Oh, I don't know. It's secondhand, you know. Still in good condition, though . . ."

I closed my eyes as my mom fussed about spending the money, feeling relieved that she didn't pick up on the "excitement" we had around here last night—and guilty that I wasn't sharing things straight up with my parents. Yet I knew they'd be terribly upset and start fussing about why we were living in the city. Right now I could hardly handle my own raw feelings, much less theirs. There were some things you just didn't want to tell your parents—

Sheesh. Listen to me! Did Josh and Amanda think like that? What weren't they telling *us?*

Hmm. Maybe I should tell my parents. But later. I'd tell them later.

". . . come to see you for your birthday? Josh's birthday is the week after—maybe we could come the weekend between and celebrate both."

That got my attention. "Uh . . . sure, Mom. Let me check the calendar." *Oh God, give me strength.* Sure I wanted my parents to visit; the kids hadn't seen their grandparents all summer. At that moment, though, I felt overwhelmed. School was starting tomorrow. The upset at Adele's beauty shop was still unresolved. We'd just been robbed and terrorized right in our own home . . .

Well, at least that weekend looked free, between two Yada Yada meetings. And it was three weeks away. "Sure, Mom. That'd be great. Let's talk more about it later. Denny and the kids are eating without me, so I'll call you in a couple of days, okay?"

TRYING TO GET THE KIDS TO BED EARLIER because it was suddenly a school night was like trying to get a cat to heel. Finally I had a few minutes to send an e-mail to the Yada Yada list about praying for Carla and her reentry into the Hickman family. There were a few incoming messages—one from Stu, saying she had nightmares last night and for the first time in her life felt anxious about living alone, and she would have a hard time waiting another two weeks to pray together.

Hmm. That was a different side of Leslie "Stu" Stuart than I'd seen before. Nothing ever seemed to faze her. Guess she was human like the rest of us.

Nony had sent out a brief e-mail, bringing the group up to speed about the Takahashis leaving abruptly for Japan and urging us to pray for Hoshi, who was quite distraught. We all knew she'd been anxious about telling her parents she'd become a Christian, but this was far worse than anything she'd imagined.

Poor Hoshi. Maybe we could invite her to dinner soon and give her some emotional support. If I had any to give, that is. I moved that idea into a corner of my mind labeled "to think about later."

The last e-mail was from Ruth.

To: Yada Yada
From: Yid-dish@online.net
Subject: Rosh Hashanah

If Yada Yada wants to visit my Messianic Jewish congregation, the best time would be during our "high holy days" this month. I meant to invite you all last night, but with a robbery in progress, I can be forgiven, yes? But it can't wait till next time because Rosh Hashanah

(Jewish New Year) services are this weekend: 7:30 p.m. Friday and Saturday 10:30 a.m.

Or it could be Yom Kippur ten days later. Depends on whether you want to celebrate the New Year and EAT, or confess your sins and FAST.

Whichever, why doesn't Yada Yada meet at my house next time (right before Yom Kippur), and I could explain it all better then, though I'll probably have to throw Ben out.

Celebrating and eating sounds good to me, I thought. Something to get our minds off the trauma of yesterday's Yada Yada meeting, though this coming weekend might be a little soon for another church visit. Yet like Ruth said, the Jewish holy days weren't going to rearrange themselves for our schedule. I moved my cursor to Reply All and typed: "Great idea! Either holiday is fine by me. Jodi."

"Jodi?"

I turned from the computer screen. Denny was leaning against the doorway of the dining room, stripped down to a pair of boxer shorts. I thought he was going to say, "Coming to bed?" but he didn't.

"Could we"—he shrugged, as if embarrassed—"uh, pray together before we go to bed? I'm . . . I dunno. Just feeling un- settled. The business last night, but also Adele taking off without saying a word to me about MaDear and what happened. Still hasn't told me how much I owe her for your hair and nails either." He shrugged again. "Don't know why that bothers me so much, but it does. I've been trying to pray about it, to put it to rest, but seems like I go around in circles."

I just looked at my husband a moment, trying to read his face. Denny didn't often admit to "going around in circles." Or ask to pray together at bedtime. Unsettled? Yeah. I felt the same way. Like our private fears were lurking in the shadows, just out of reach, refusing to come into the light.

Standing there in his boxers asking us to pray, Denny looked about as vulnerable as I'd ever seen him.

15

The next morning the typical Baxter hurry-scurry kicked in, but we all managed to get out of the house roughly on time. Denny drove Josh and Amanda to Lane Tech in the "new" used minivan for their first day, then he headed for West Rogers High. I stuck the books I'd mended, the last pieces of my Welcome Bulletin Board, and a pair of loafers into my tote bag and headed out for the twenty-minute walk to Bethune Elementary.

I actually found myself looking forward to the first day of school. *Hoo boy!* Now if that wasn't a miracle!

Must have been the prayer with Denny last night. We'd just held each other in the dark in the living room, pouring out all the confusion and upset we'd both been feeling, telling Jesus it had been a rotten summer. We didn't know what to do about MaDear. Getting robbed in our own home had been terrifying. We also thanked God for a lot of stuff. Like Josh and Amanda and the rest of Uptown's youth getting home safely from Mexico and having a great time building houses with Habitat for Humanity. For the strength our Yada Yada sisters had poured into both of us with their prayers and their presence during those awful days following the accident. That the charges against me got dropped, and I was healing fast. That Denny still had a job at the high school.

Once we started, it seemed like there were so many things to pray about: Carla coming home to her family and starting a new school, Hoshi and her distraught parents, and even MaDear and the painful memories that haunted her.

"Good thing God is God all by Himself!" I'd muttered after our final amen. Florida's favorite phrase. "I'd sure hate to sort out all the stuff we just dumped in God's lap." That set us off laughing—but oh, my mutilated abdomen still hurt when I laughed.

I felt free this morning. Sort of like that old hymn, "Take your burden to the Cross and leave it there" . . . or something like that. Hadn't thought about that one for ages. We didn't sing hymns too often at Uptown Community, not like we did in the little Bible church I grew up in. I wondered if I had a hymnal somewhere; I could look it up.

Walking to school and carrying my heavy tote bag turned out to be a bit optimistic for the first day, because my left leg ached something fierce by the time I got there. But I was early enough to take a couple of pain relievers and told myself I'd make it through the day okay.

My student teacher was already in our classroom, looking as cute as Betty Boop with her short, dark, curly hair and a simple pale-blue jersey dress bringing out the blue in her eyes. "Blue is definitely your color, Christy," I said, giving her a hug.

She seemed a little flustered by the hug but gave me a big smile. "I'm really nervous, Ms. Baxter." She nodded toward the bank of windows that looked out on the playground. "All those children . . ."

"Feel free to call me Jodi when the children aren't around," I started unloading my tote bag, "but get used to being called 'Ms. James' when they are."

She giggled. "That will be so weird."

We set to work putting the finishing touches to the bulletin board. Christy had cut out each child's name in colorful bubble letters. Below each name I stapled a construction-paper cloud with the meaning of the child's name written in black letters.

"That is so cool, Ms. Bax— . . . um, Jodi." Christy studied the board.

The hands of the clock nudged toward 8:40. "Grab that class roster," I told Christy, heading for the door with a square of laminated paper that read "3-A." We made it to the playground just as the lineup bell rang. I held up the "3-A" sign, hoping parents had told their children which classroom they were in. A passel of energetic boys got in line pushing and shoving, their oversized backpacks bumping about on their skinny rumps. Most of the girls held back, out of the way of the pushers. I smiled at the first boy in line: a handsome child with hazelnut skin, brown eyes so dark they were almost black, and a nearly shaved head. Hmm. Without the hair I couldn't be sure about ethnicity—could be African-American or Middle Eastern. "What's your name, young man?" I asked.

"Xavier!" He shouted it out almost defiantly. The boy behind him giggled. *Still could be almost anything.*

The final bell rang. *Okay, Lord, this is it. See this line? They're mine for the year. Correction. They're Yours for the year. I'd appreciate a little help. Make that a lot of help.* I led them through the metal detectors that had been installed after 9-11 and down the hall to 3-A. Then I stood in the doorway as they jostled into the room.

As soon as each student—thirty-one of them!—found the desk with his or her name taped on it, I introduced "Ms. James" as my "team teacher" and wrote both our names on the chalkboard. We ran through the usual classroom rules—Respect People, Respect Property, Respect Yourself—and added my own clarifications: "When the teacher is talking, you're listening. Raise your hand if you have a question or need to use the washroom. No punching or spitting on other people."

Immediately there were a lot of spitting noises. I groaned to myself. *Shouldn't have given them the idea.*

I moved to the Welcome Bulletin Board while Christy sent the first child to join me. "Can you find your name?" I said to the little girl with three fat ponytail braids wrapped on each end with colorful rubber-band balls. She pointed to her name in bubble letters: Jade. "Can you read what your name means underneath?"

She squinted. "Jewel?" She looked up at me.

"Yes." I smiled. "Jade is a special kind of jewel, a very rich green color." I leaned toward her and spoke in a loud stage whisper.

"Green is one of my favorite colors."

I was rewarded with a smile, and Christy tapped the next student, a pug-nosed kid sporting an army-style buzz cut. "Cornell," he announced, pointing to his name. He studied the cloud underneath his name. "Horn blower?" he scoffed. "What's a horn blower?"

The other children laughed, but I held up my hand with a warning look. "Someone who can play a trumpet or a trombone or maybe one of those big baritone horns." I raised a quizzical eyebrow. "Did you ever think about joining the school band?"

"I don't got no horn!"

"You might want to think about it," I said, "with a name like that."

Now several hands shot up in the air, but Christy continued alternating a girl, then a boy, from different areas of the room. When Britny read, "From England," under her name, she scowled. "I ain't from no England." She certainly wasn't; she was as African-American as they come.

"But that's what your name means. Maybe . . ." I thought fast. "Maybe you could learn some things about England and tell the rest of the class. And maybe . . ." I whispered in her ear. "Maybe someday you will travel to England and see the queen!"

"Okay," she said and practically skipped back to her desk.

Now hands were flying everywhere. Everybody—well, almost everybody—wanted to know what their name meant. I tried to make a positive comment for each one, shamelessly bending some of them toward positive classroom behavior.

Ramón—"Mighty Protector." "Ah! Ramón must be our class

protector. He's going to protect anybody from getting bullied by somebody else."

"Yeah," agreed Ramón. "Any of you guys bully a little kid, I'm gonna smack you in the face." Laughter erupted once more, and I had to make sure Ramón knew that was *not* what I meant.

Xavier—*"Bright."* "Do you know what 'bright' means, Xavier?"

"Yeah." He spread his fingers on either side of his face, like sun rays. "I glow in the dark!"

Now the class was laughing nonstop. I was losing them. Just then the door opened quietly, and Avis slipped into the room. *Oh no.* I forgot that each classroom got a visit from the principal on the first day. She couldn't have come at a worse time!

I held up one hand like a traffic cop and waited till the children quieted. Then I turned back to Xavier. "Yes, that's one meaning of bright, like a dazzling light. It also means smart—very smart." I tapped the side of my head. "I think you are going to show us this year just how smart you are, don't you?"

Xavier strutted back to his desk, and I introduced "Ms. Johnson, our principal," who gave a little pep talk to the children about being good citizens of our school community and the importance of respect, rules, and teamwork. As she slipped back out the door, she caught my eye and tipped her head toward the bulletin board. "Clever."

The knot in my stomach untied. *Oh God, thank You for Avis!*

We went back to the meaning of our names, but when Christy tapped one boy on the shoulder, he scowled and scooted deeper in his seat. "Don't wanna. It's stupid."

I walked to where I could see his name on his desk. "Hakim?" I was surprised at his reluctance, but didn't want to force it. Instead I went back to the bulletin board and found his name. "Hakim . . . 'wise healer.'" *Oh dear.* I had no idea how to apply that to an eight-year-old. "Maybe," I tried, "you will be a doctor some-day."

"Don't wanna be a doctor." The boy's tone was fierce. "They ain't no good anyway."

Okay. Better just leave it alone. We moved on to the few remaining students.

THE TWO-THIRTY BELL RANG. The class started a stampede for the door, and we had to sit everyone down again and start over. "Line up! Everybody got your backpack and take-home folders? If you didn't bring the items on the supply list your parents got in the mail, there's a copy of that list in your folder."

As Christy led the line out the door, Britny suddenly stepped out of line and stood in front of me. "How come your name and hers"—she pointed at Christy's back—"ain't on the board? What do your names mean?"

We weren't supposed to use our first names with the children, but to tell the truth, I hadn't had time to look them up. *Jodi . . . Christy . . .* That would be interesting. I gave Britny a quick hug. "I don't know. Good question. I'll have to look them up."

I was so tired and achy when I got home, I just wanted to soak in the tub and crawl into bed. Amanda came home upset because she didn't get the teacher she wanted for Spanish II, and for a while there was a lot of door slamming between her room and the bathroom. Josh was his usual minimalist self, offering "Okay" and "Not really" to my questions about his first day as a senior.

Humph. So much for good communication with my teenagers. I took some iced tea out on the back porch, intending to sulk. Instead, the same hymn I'd been humming on the way to school popped back into my head. "Take your burden to the Cross and leave it there . . ." No, that wasn't quite right. What was it?

I dragged myself back into the house, found the red hymnal we used back at our church in Downers Grove, and turned to the index. There it was on page 353: "Leave It There." Except the actual phrase was, "Take your burden to the *Lord* and leave it there."

I squinted at the author: Charles A. Tindley. Wrote both the words and the music. Who in the world was he? I'd heard of Charles Wesley and Fanny Crosby, but Tindley? Curious, I looked in the author index to see if he wrote anything else. Yep. "Nothing between my soul and the Savior . . ." *Hmm.* I knew that one too.

I heard the back door bang. "Denny? Who's Charles Tindley?"

Denny appeared in the archway to the living room where I was sprawled in the recliner with the hymnal, his gym bag slung over his shoulder. "Hi to you too. Am I supposed to know this guy? I'm starving. What's for supper?"

He had to be kidding. He sounded like an Archie Bunker rerun. "Leftovers," I snarled. "Or PB&Js. Or we could go out to Siam Pasta. I'm beat." We didn't often take the kids out to eat—

not with their hollow legs—but, hey, we had all survived our first day of school. Cause for celebration. And Siam Pasta passed the test for a five-star rating from the Baxters: good food, lots of it, cheap.

Denny shrugged. "Why not? Beats PB&Js."

It actually turned out to be a good idea, because once we got the kids trapped in a restaurant booth—no phone, no distractions, no place to go—we actually got more lowdown about their first day of school. As for Denny, he said things went okay on the first day, though he had a lot of ideas that could improve communication among the coaching staff. "Though I don't think the athletic direc-tor wants to hear them from me," he grumbled. "Maybe he'll retire, and I can apply for his job."

I got a laugh out of Josh when I told them about our "mighty protector" threatening to smack anybody who bullied another kid. "Got the idea of looking up the meaning of their names from you, Amanda," I said. "Well, from Delores, really, when she said your name means 'lovable' in Spanish."

Amanda glared. *"Mom!* You weren't supposed to tell anybody!"

Oh. Right. Yet already I could see that trying to take it back would be like trying to retrieve dandelion fuzz after blowing it off its stem. I was sure the cogs in Josh's brain were clicking away, devising ways to hold this interesting fact over his sister's head. "Well, then, I'll just have to make the same rule for the family I made for the kids in my class: You can't use the meaning of some-body's name to tease them." *Oh, sure.*

Revived somewhat by supper "out," my curiosity got the best of me and I turned on the computer. No e-mail messages from Yada Yada—everybody was probably too busy recovering from the first day of school. I wondered how Carla Hickman's first day went. Did Florida get her registered? I decided not to call. The Hickman family needed space to adjust to this new wrinkle—a *miracle* wrinkle—in their lives.

Instead, I called up one of the name Web sites I'd been using to locate the kids' names and typed "Jodi" in the search box. I stared at the page that came up on-screen.

Jodi—a derivative of Joan.
Meaning: "God is gracious."

Maybe I was just tired. Maybe the long, difficult summer finally caught up with me. Maybe it was just a reminder of something God had been trying to tell me for weeks. But I put my head down on the computer keyboard . . . and wept.

16

God is gracious . . . God is gracious . . . I didn't tell anybody the meaning of my name right away. I wanted to tuck it into a private place in my mind and let it soak down deep. I'd looked up Christy's name too, just in case Britny asked again. All the variations of "Christine" meant "Christ follower." What would Christy think about that? Was she or wasn't she? We weren't supposed to talk about our personal religion in public school.

Not that we had much time for chitchat. The first week of school was like trying to stay one step ahead of a steamroller driven by thirty devious eight-year-olds. One misstep, and the kids would run right over me. In the back of my mind I worried about Hoshi and wondered how Florida's little girl was adjusting, but it was Thursday night before I got a chance to call either of them.

Wednesday night, I'd decided to go back to Bible study at Uptown with Denny—I hadn't been since I'd been in the hospital.

Pastor Clark was beginning a study of the book of James, which sounded promising. Good ol' James, a down-to-earth brother if there ever was one. Practical. Straight to the point. Unlike the apostle Paul, whose sentences rambled on and on like a sweater unraveling, with just as many knots to untangle.

I saw Avis at Bible study, but we didn't really get to talk except in passing, when she said she couldn't attend Rosh Hashanah at Ruth's church this Saturday, but she'd like to hear about it if I went. I told her Denny and I hadn't talked about it yet.

Thursday night things were quiet at the Baxter house. Josh was at Uptown, manning the soundboard for the praise-team practice; Amanda was baby-sitting the Reilly twins, nine-year-old sweeties whose mom sang on the praise team and dad played guitar. In the living room, Denny was watching videotapes of other soccer teams in the high-school league, trying to identify patterns and weak spots.

"Looks like it's just you and me, Willie," I said to the dog. "Whatcha wanna do?" Willie Wonka ignored me and waddled off to do some male bonding with Denny.

I took the cordless out to the back porch and called Nony. One of her boys answered. "Smith residence. To whom do you wish to speak?"

I nearly fell off the porch steps. He sounded like an English butler. Weren't Nony's boys only nine and eleven? "Um . . . this is Jodi Baxter. To whom am I speaking?" To *whom?* I hadn't been this correct since high-school English.

"This is Marcus. Hi, Mrs. Baxter. Do you want my mom?"

I wanted to hug him. He was going to be a heartbreaker some-day. He probably put his dirty clothes in the laundry too—unasked. "Actually, Marcus, I'm calling for Hoshi. Is she there?"

"I'll get her."

I waited for what seemed a long minute, then I heard Hoshi's quiet voice. "Yes? This is Hoshi."

"Hi, Hoshi. It's Jodi. I've been thinking about you all week. Nony told us your parents went home. Are you okay?"

"Yes, I'm okay." Her voice was only a few notches above a whisper.

"How is your mom?—her hand, I mean."

There was a moment's pause. "I don't know, Jodi. I haven't heard anything since they left last Monday. The Smiths let me call to Japan, but nobody answered." She started to cry.

"Oh, Hoshi." The poor girl was going through hell, and I just dragged it all up again. "I'm so sorry. I didn't mean to—"

"No, no, Jodi, it's all right. Wait . . ." I could hear her blowing her nose before she came back on. "I'm happy you called. Please pray for my parents. That's all I know what to do. Nony and Dr. Smith—they are very good to me."

"Do you . . . would you like to come to dinner sometime next week?" *Oh, you're rash, Jodi. You can barely scratch dinner together for your own family on weeknights.* "Or do your classes start next week?"

"No . . . I mean, yes, I would like to come. Classes don't start till the last week of September. It would be nice to share the table with your family."

We tentatively agreed on the following Tuesday, with Hoshi

545

coming by the El and then we'd take her home. After we hung up, I went inside to check it out with Denny, but he was taking intense notes while guys in blue-and-gold uniforms—probably the Sullivan Tigers—ran back and forth on the TV screen. I knew better than to interrupt that focused look.

I retreated to the back-porch steps again and dialed Florida. Another male voice, but this one was deep and brief. "Yeah?"

I took a stab. Had to be Florida's husband. "Uh, Carl?"

"Yeah."

"This is Jodi Baxter. Is Florida there?"

Carl Hickman didn't reply. He just yelled off to the side, "Flo! Phone for you."

This time it seemed like I waited two, maybe three minutes. Finally Florida picked up the phone. "Hey, Jodi. Whassup?"

"Whassup yourself. I called to see how it's going with Carla. You get her registered for school?"

We chatted for about five minutes. The social worker at Carla's new school had been very helpful, she said, even suggested some family sessions with a school counselor to help ease the transition at home as well as school. "'Course you know, Jodi, if Carl got hisself a *job*, that would be one big help. Then we could get a bigger apartment. Right now I got all three kids in that closet they call a second bedroom."

I remembered when Amanda and I had visited Florida's apartment—before the accident. All I'd seen in that little bedroom was a double mattress on the floor. Surely Carla and the boys weren't sleeping . . .

"Beds, Florida? You got beds for the kids?" I couldn't help it. Had to ask.

"Yes, thank ya, Jesus. Found a bunk bed at Salvation Army for the boys and an army-cot thing for Carla—actually, that's all we got space for till we get a bigger place. Sheets, though. We could use some twin bedsheets. And pillowcases."

"I'll see what I can rustle up." Amanda still had a birthday "coupon" for a new comforter for her bed. Maybe we should get new sheets, too, and pass on her old ones to—

I stopped myself. Why did I always think in terms of passing on the old ones? *Maybe you should get new sheets for Florida's kids, Jodi Baxter. Would you want someone else's old sheets for your kids?*

At least it sounded like things were coming along with Carla. Yet I still felt overwhelmed for her. What Florida said was true: they needed a bigger apartment, and Carl needed a job yesterday. Maybe I should ask Denny to talk to Pastor Clark about Carl.

The TV was still going in the living room when we hung up. Should I check up on anyone else? I'd talked this week to everybody who *hadn't* been at the robbery, and most everybody who had . . .

Except Adele.

Had anybody heard from her? Should I call? Just to see how she's doing after Sunday night? That would be reasonable, wouldn't it?

Instead, I headed back into the house, hung up the cordless, and pulled out my school bag. Really, I needed to review my lesson plans for Friday.

THE WEEKEND SLIPPED BY, and I never did call Adele.

When I got home from school on Friday, I was too bushed to even think about going to Rosh Hashanah services with Ruth that night. And when Denny got home, he'd immediately gone out to the garage to work on the car—"while I've still got some light"—so the car wasn't available anyway.

I did check e-mail to see if Ruth got any response to her invitation, but this weekend must have been too soon for most folks, because only Stu said she'd like to come, probably on Saturday. Why wasn't I surprised? Stu always seemed to be first up to the plate. Several other Yada Yadas said they'd try for Yom Kippur.

I had to admit I was curious about Ruth's Beth Yehudah Congregation. Did we have anything going Saturday? I'd never been to a Jewish service before, even though there were a lot of synagogues in Rogers Park. Of course, this would be a *Christian* celebration of the Jewish holiday. Would it be mostly like church? Or like going to synagogue?

Only one way to find out.

I printed out Ruth's invitation and went hunting for Denny. Found his legs sticking out from underneath the minivan. "Something wrong?" I asked.

"Nope," came a muffled voice. "Just changing the oil." He pulled himself out from under the car, oblivious to the little black smudges dotting his face. "What's up?" He stood up and leaned under the hood to change the oil filter.

"Um, wanna do something different tomorrow—you and me?"

"Sure. As long as it's cheap."

Can't get any cheaper, I thought, *unless they take an offering.* "Well, it's Rosh Hashanah, the Jewish New Year, and Ruth invited—"

"Ah. I get it. Another date sponsored by Yada Yada."

I couldn't see Denny's face under the hood. Was he having a problem with this?

"We don't have to go; it was just an idea. Or I could go alone." I knew that sounded whiny, but I *did* want to go, and I wanted Denny to go with me. "Unless you have a better idea."

"Not really." He appeared from under the hood and started wiping his hands on a rag. "Just feels like a lot. We visited Delores's church two weeks ago—which I enjoyed, don't get me wrong. Then Yada Yada meets at our house last week and turns into a three-ring circus. *Next* week it'll be Yada Yada again, and aren't your folks coming the weekend after that for your birthday?"

I didn't answer, just watched as he scrunched back under the car to cap the dripping oil. He was right; it did feel like a lot. On the other hand, if we didn't plan our Saturday, he'd end up in front of the TV watching a string of games—baseball, football—it didn't seem to matter who or where, as long as there were two teams fighting over a ball.

He reappeared, dragging out the container of old oil. "On the other hand—"

"Denny!" I shrieked. "That's the plastic pitcher I use to make iced tea!" I whacked him on the head with the rolled-up paper in my hand. "I can't believe you used that!"

"Oh." He grimaced. "Sorry. Couldn't find the old milk jug I usually use, and this was sitting on the back porch . . ."

I rolled my eyes. He looked really funny holding that iced-tea pitcher full of cruddy old oil, probably considering whether he could wash it out. I started to laugh.

He grinned—relieved, I'm sure. "Okay, let's go celebrate the Jewish New Year with dear ol' Ruth Garfield. On one condition: we go to the Bagel Bakery afterward and get some more of that lip-smacking lox and cream cheese. Just tell me what I'm supposed to wear. Unless"—he dipped a finger into the old oil and advanced toward me—"you'd like to go 'Goth': a black smudge here and there . . ."

"Don't you dare!" I flew out the door toward the house. Maybe Denny agreed to go because he felt guilty using the good plastic pitcher. Whatever. I gave him a chance to come up with a better idea, didn't I?

I'd better call Ruth. I had no idea where to go, what to wear, or what to expect.

17

Assured by Ruth Garfield that anything we wore would be fine ("Just not jeans or shorts—or halter tops, *oy vey!*"), Denny and I left a note the next morning for Josh and Amanda, who hadn't yet appeared in the land of the living, and set out in the Dodge Caravan for Beth Yehudah, Ruth's congregation.

"We're looking for what?" Denny said when I read him the directions. "Lincolnwood Presbyterian? I thought this was a Messianic congregation."

"It is. Beth Yehudah meets in a Presbyterian church on Saturday, so there's no conflict."

As we drove west from Rogers Park into Lincolnwood—indistinguishable from Chicago proper, as were all the other towns rimming the Windy City's borders—we saw numerous Jewish families walking to their local synagogue. Most of the men and boys wore yarmulkes; a few Orthodox could be identified by their traditional black-brimmed hats, prayer-shawl fringes dangling beneath their suit coats, and corkscrew curls in front of their ears. Children held their parents' hands or skipped ahead. Definitely a holiday feel.

I felt nervous, like I was intruding on their Sabbath. What did I know about Rosh Hashanah? These were Jewish holy days. Yet we'd been invited, I reminded myself as Denny pulled into the parking lot of Lincolnwood Presbyterian—a modern A-frame structure with lots of colored-glass windows in odd shapes. And these were fellow Christians, albeit Jewish ones. Maybe it wouldn't be so different.

We didn't see Ruth when we first came in, but a friendly greeter pointed us to the large "Fellowship Room," where most of the people coming in seemed to be headed. Folding chairs were set in rows facing a small oak table at the front, on which stood a tall wooden something—like a polished oak chest, up on end—with doors. Both table and chest had the same Hebrew inscription.

Another greeter handed us a booklet—the order of service, I supposed—and I nudged Denny into a row of chairs just shy of the middle, so we could watch what other people did but be close enough to see what happened up front.

I looked around, trying to spy Ruth. It all looked very ordinary—just a typical church building, a typical multipurpose room in the basement, and even the requisite keyboard, drums, and guitars off to one side at the front. As I scanned the people who were already sitting in the folding chairs, I noticed a familiar blonde head a couple of rows ahead of us. *Sheesh.* Stu had twice as far to drive as we did, and she still got here early.

Just then the blonde hair swung around, and Stu caught my eye. Getting up, she moved back to join us, booklet in hand, long hair falling over one shoulder of her neatly tailored navy pantsuit. Suddenly I felt underdressed in my khaki culottes, knit top, and sandals. "Hi, Jodi . . . Denny," she said, bestowing a bright smile on us as she settled into the seat next to Denny. "Seen Ruth yet?"

I shook my head. But just then we heard Ruth's voice over all the other murmured conversations going on. "*There* you are! Outside I'm standing, looking for you. How did you get past me?"

I smirked at Denny—*yeah right, she just got here and waited outside for thirty seconds*—then gave Ruth a hug as she plopped into the folding chair next to me, her hands clutching a roomy leather bag, her Bible, and the booklet, all of which she unceremoniously dumped on the empty chair next to her.

"Ben coming?" Denny craned his neck and looked around hopefully.

"Ben, Schmen." Ruth practically rolled her eyes. "Gave up attending temple years ago, he did—except for the occasional holiday—but set foot inside Beth Yehudah? He acts like God might strike him dead. But"—she leaned across me and winked at Denny—"he weakened when I told him *you* were coming today, Denny. He likes you."

"Maybe we could call him after the service and meet at the Bagel Bakery for lunch or something." Denny grinned at Ruth so wide his dimples showed. If it were anybody but frowzy Ruth, I'd swear he was flirting. But more likely he was thinking about that lox-and-cream-cheese bagel he had the last time we were there.

Now Ruth did roll her eyes. *"Goyim."* She lowered her voice. "It's *Shabbat,* Denny. It won't open till sundown."

I stifled a giggle, glad it was Denny who stuck his foot in his mouth, since I, too, had totally forgotten that the Bagel Bakery was closed on Saturday. Too bad. That would've been fun.

Several men and women were picking up instruments and testing microphones, and a middle-aged man wearing a gray suit with a white, fringed prayer shawl draped around his shoulders set up a portable lectern. Looked like things were about to get started. "What do the words on the table say?" I whispered to Ruth.

"'Holy to the Lord'—same as on the ark."

Ark? I peered closer at the upright chest thing. It didn't look like the ark of the covenant pictured in my Sunday-school pictures as a child, which always lay horizontal, like an old-fashioned hope chest.

A sudden long blast of a horn from the back of the room made me jump. I turned and stared. A tall young man with a dark beard was blowing a long, curved ram's horn—the "shofar" I'd heard about. Again and again he blew the horn, as if he were standing on a hillside, summoning all within the sound of the horn. Goose bumps popped out all along my arms.

As if on cue, the man at the front in a prayer shawl raised his arms and called out, "Wake up! Yeshua, our God and King, is coming soon! Wake up!" The sound of the horn died away, along with my goose bumps. "The Lord has given us these days for joy and thanksgiving—a new year! The blowing of the shofar also calls us to a season of repentance, a time to examine our hearts and confess our sins that we might be prepared for His return. Let us give thanks." The leader held up the booklet. "Please turn to page 53 and read responsively."

I fumbled for the booklet I'd been given and opened to the first page. Page 192? Then I heard Ruth hiss, "The back—it reads back to front."

Oh. I turned the book over. Sure enough, the back cover said, "Mahzor for High Holy Days." By the time I flipped to page 53, the leader had already started to read: "Give thanks to the Lord, for He is good."

Then the congregation chimed in: "His mercy endures forever."

"To Him alone who does great wonders."

"His mercy endures forever . . ."

After the responsive reading, an African-American woman, her head wrapped in an African-print cloth, stood up and began to sing—in Hebrew, I supposed, since the words were not English—accompanied by a tambourine, guitar, and piano. A Christian Jewish African-American? I had supposed that all Messianic Jews were probably Jewish first, but what did I know? I closed my eyes and let the unknown words sink in. The tune had a distinctly Israeli flavor, and I could almost imagine an Israeli folk dance. Then the Hebrew words flowed into English: "Blessed are those who know the sound of shofar, who walk in the light of Your presence, Oh Lord."

After the song, people stood and turned sideways, facing the wall. *What in the world?* "East, toward Jerusalem," came the whisper in my ear. The Hebrew words rolled easily off the tongues of people around us:

She-ma Yis-ra-el: A-do-nai e-lo-heinu, A-do-nai e-chad!
Ba-ruch shem ke-vod mal-chu-to le-o-lam va-ed!

And then the leader boomed out in English:

Hear, O Israel: The Lord our God, the Lord is One.
Blessed be his glorious name whose kingdom is forever and ever.

This declaration—the "Shema," Ruth informed me—was followed by a prayer from the leader, and then the instrumentalists started up again. The beat was decidedly bouncy. A young woman kept brisk time with the tambourine, and everyone began to sing: "Oh come, let us sing! Let us rejoice! Messiah has come! And He brought joy!"

I grinned at Denny. Celebrating that "Messiah has come!" was no doubt a Messianic addition to the traditional Rosh Hashanah service.

As the song continued, a few people at the front grabbed hands and began a line dance around the room. More people popped up and joined them—a mix of young and old, skipping feet, and bobbing yarmulkes of all different colors. When the line passed by the middle aisle, someone reached out to Stu, who was sitting on the aisle seat, and she joined them, her long hair flying as she quickly picked up the steps.

It looked like fun! I was tempted to join them, too, but dancing so soon after getting off my crutches was not a good idea. I'd probably fall down and make a fool of myself. And then it was over, and Stu collapsed, laughing, back in her seat. Lucky her.

The y a d a y a d a Prayer Group Gets Down

A few more songs, and then the congregation was invited to turn to the "Avinu Malkenu" in the *mahzor*. I noticed that on the right-hand pages, everything was printed in Hebrew script; the English translation was printed on the left. First the leader sang the Hebrew in a sing-song chant, and the congregation responded, also in Hebrew. I could hear even children's voices saying the Hebrew words and shook my head in amazement. Were they actually reading those exquisite squiggles and dots? I could imagine learning French or Spanish or any other language that had a similar alphabet to English—but Hebrew? Whew.

The Hebrew song-chant was followed by the English, simply spoken: "Our Father, our King, forgive and pardon our iniquities . . ."

After the Avinu Malkenu, two young men wearing prayer shawls strode toward the wooden chest sitting on the table. As if on signal, the congregation stood. They opened the box and reverently took out the Torah, dressed in a silk purple sheath with golden tassels, a brass plate hanging by a chain on the front—an "ephod," I guessed, like the priests used to wear in my old Sunday-school pictures—and topped with a crown. Everyone in the room seemed to hold their breath in a collective hush as the two young men removed the crown, then the ephod and the purple silken cloth, so the scroll could be unrolled.

"The Torah is read with great respect every Shabbat," Ruth murmured, almost causing me to miss the leader saying, *"Ba-ruch Adonai ham-vo-rach* . . . Blessed are You, Lord our God, King of the Universe, who has chosen us from all the peoples and has given us Your Torah."

One of the young men began to read in Hebrew from the huge scroll in a sing-song chant. Then the leader read the words in English from his Bible: "On the first day of the seventh month hold a sacred assembly and do no regular work. It is a day for you to sound the trumpets . . ." I noticed Ruth had her Bible open to Numbers 29. Other scriptures were read, then the Torah was re-dressed, and the two young men began to parade it slowly around the room and up the middle aisle. As they did so, people leaned out of their seats to touch it as it passed.

Ruth's breath brushed my ear. "The Jewish people hold the Torah in high reverence."

I couldn't imagine parading the Bible around Uptown Community. In fact, half the congregation didn't even *bring* their Bibles to church, much to Pastor Clark's dismay. Yet as I watched the Torah being carried about the room, I felt wrapped in awe. How little I really knew about the roots of my own Christian faith or my spiritual ancestors, even though I'd been raised on Old Testament stories along with the New.

When the Torah had been safely shut once more within the "ark," the leader began his sermon. I saw Denny hunch forward, elbows on his knees, chin on his hands, listening intently as the man in the prayer shawl began to explain the meaning of the various Jewish feasts and how each one prophetically pointed toward the coming of the Messiah.

Passover—the Lamb whose blood saved the people. Day of First Fruits—the resurrection. *Shavuoth,* or Pentecost (which traditionally celebrated the giving of the Ten Commandments)—the coming of the Holy Spirit, who now writes God's law on our hearts. Rosh Hashanah—yet to be fulfilled in Yeshua's second coming. And finally, Yom Kippur—when the Book of Life will be opened and read.

I was fascinated. I knew Jesus had broken the bread and passed the wine at Passover, saying, "This is My body. This is My blood." But I'd never really given any thought to the other Old Testament festivals as having anything to do with me.

"The days between now and Yom Kippur, the Day of Atonement," Beth Yehudah's leader continued, "represent the time we have been given to intercede for our people, that their names would be written in the Book of Life. Just as the prophets of old, we too must identify with the sins of our people—the sins of Israel and the sins of the church—and repent, calling on God for His mercy and forgiveness."

I felt Denny jerk upright beside me. I tried to catch his eye. Was something wrong? He seemed distracted, distant.

After the sermon, the instruments came out once more, thrumming a rhythmic song that reminded me of a slow dance in heavy boots: "Come back people . . . children of Abraham . . . open your eyes, your redemption is nigh." I closed my eyes, wondering what it meant to be part of a people by shared history and faith, rather than the American version of Christianity I grew up with: "just me and God." How presumptuous was *that?*

At the end of the service, the shofar blew again as we opened our *mahzors* and read the "Tekiah" (one long blast on the shofar) . . . the "Shevarim" (three short blasts) . . . and the "Teruah" (a string of staccato blasts that left the horn blower gasping).

After the service, people stood and chatted in little groups, while kids darted here and there. *"L'Shanah Tova,* Jodi," Ruth said, giving me a hug. "Happy New Year!" Stu squeezed past Denny's knees and claimed her hug from Ruth's plump arms. *"L'Shanah Tova,* Stu." Ruth beamed at us both. "Thank you so much for coming! You have no idea how much it means—"

Ruth stopped midsentence and peered behind me at Denny, who was still sitting in his chair like a brooding sculpture. The Thinker, with clothes on. "Denny? School's out—you can get up now." She frowned. "You okay?"

Denny looked up and blinked. "What? Oh. Sorry. Just thinking." He rose hastily and gave Ruth a hug. "Forgive my manners. Thanks for inviting us—well, for inviting Yada Yada." He jerked a thumb at Stu and me. "Hope you don't mind me tagging along."

I smirked at him. *That's okay, Denny. You don't have to admit I dragged you here.*

"Well, come on," Ruth ordered, heading toward a table in the back. "You can't leave till you've had some apples dipped in honey—traditional, you know."

APPLES DIPPED IN HONEY might be traditional, but it didn't make it as "lunch." Denny and I were famished. We splurged on huge burgers at a new Steak 'n Shake on Howard Street, so it was almost two o'clock by the time we got home. I tried asking Denny what he'd been thinking so hard about after the sermon, but all he said was, "Oh, all that stuff about 'repenting for the sins of the people.' Don't know what I think about it."

Didn't know what I thought of it either. Seemed one thing for Old Testament prophets to pray "on behalf of the people," but nobody else could repent of my sins, could they? Didn't I have to repent my own self? Wasn't that what "personal salvation" was all about?

Willie Wonka dashed past us as we came in the back screen door, as if he'd been waiting a long time for somebody to let him out. The back door was standing open—had the kids gone out and left the house unlocked?

Then I noticed the In Use button on the kitchen answering machine was blinking and the cradle was empty—somebody was talking on the phone somewhere. "Helloooo?" I called, dumping my tote bag on the dining-room table. "Amanda? Josh?" Then I saw a note in Josh's scrawl on the table. "Getting a haircut. Back by supper.—J"

A haircut? Denny usually cut Josh's hair with his old electric clippers. But if Josh wanted to use his own money to get his hair cut, more power to him. So it must be Amanda on the—

"Uh, hi Mom. Hey, Dad." Amanda appeared in the doorway between the hall and dining room with the cordless in her hand. "You guys went to church on *Saturday?*"

"Uh-huh." Denny waggled his eyebrows. "Yada Yada let me tag along."

"Oh, stop," I said. "It was interesting, Amanda. You would have enjoyed it." I tipped my head toward the phone in her hand. "Who's on the line?"

"Oh . . . nobody. Just talking to a friend. They hung up." She scuttled into the kitchen, replaced the phone in the wall cradle,

561

and then turned to me. "Can you take me shopping for a comforter today, Mom? It's been two weeks since my birthday and you promised."

Oh, yes. The birthday coupon. I sighed. "I guess. Just give me fifteen minutes before I have to get in the car again." Well, there went the rest of my Saturday. I'd been thinking about a good nap.

As I checked out the refrigerator, which looked pretty much like Mother Hubbard's cupboard, I felt slightly annoyed. Why didn't Amanda just say who she'd been talking to?

18

Amanda and I actually found something she liked for a decent price at Target—or "Tar-*zhay*" as the kids called it, bestowing a phony French accent on the name of the discount store. Of course, *I* would have preferred the comforter with big yellow sunflowers, but Amanda didn't give it a second glance and went for the yellow-and-black geometric shapes. I couldn't look at it too long or I started feeling dizzy.

While wandering the aisles of household items, I remembered Florida said Carla and the boys needed sheets. I stuck two sets of Spiderman twin sheets and one set with rainbows into our shopping cart.

"Uh . . . Mom?" Amanda curled her lip at the juvenile sheets. "No way!"

"Not for you. Florida's kids."

"Oh. Cool."

No complaint about needing new sheets herself. I wanted to

hug her. Amanda's soft spot for kids did indeed make her "lovable," but a hug right in the middle of Tar-*zhay* would *not* be cool.

After we got home I called Florida to see when I could deliver the sheets. "Don't go makin' no trip," she said. "I'll get them tomorrow."

"What do you mean? Yada Yada doesn't meet this week." Or did it? Wasn't the robbery just last Sunday?

"Nah. I mean I'm bringin' the kids to Uptown tomorrow. Gotta start goin' to church somewhere reg'lar as a family."

"Carl too?"

"Huh. Now wouldn't *that* be a miracle."

A door slammed, and I turned to see Josh coming in the back door. Florida's voice chattered on in my ear, but I didn't hear a word she said as I stared at my son's head.

"Hi, Mom," he said, avoiding my eyes while strutting past me, through the dining room, and disappearing down the hall toward his bedroom.

Josh's head had been shaved completely bald—except for a small ponytail high on the back of his head. A bright *orange* ponytail.

LORD, HAVE MERCY. *Why didn't somebody tell me raising teenagers was like trying to herd cats,* I muttered to myself as I struggled up the stairs to Uptown Community's second-floor meeting room the next morning, lugging the heavy bag of sheets in one hand and a chicken-and-rice casserole for Second Sunday Potluck in the other. I quickly ducked into the kitchen off to the left, both to deposit my casserole and to avoid people's dropped mouths when they first caught sight of my son's bald head.

"Why, Josh?" I'd wailed. *"You had such nice hair!"*

He'd shrugged. *"What's the big deal? Look at Michael Jordan."*

Humph. Michael Jordan, aging superstar, was one thing. Joshua James Baxter—my son—was another. Amanda, of course, said, "Cool!" I don't think Denny liked it, but he did pull me aside and suggested we basically ignore it. *Oh, right.* Ignore your son's head looking like a light bulb with an orange pull-chain on top.

I put on a smile and greeted Brenda Gage, who was sorting food by main dish, salad, or dessert. "I love the curtains you made for the baby's room, Jodi," she said warmly. "Main dish?"

"Uh-huh." Remembering the fiasco the last time I'd brought this dish—I forgot to *cook* it, much to the amusement of Stu, who was visiting Uptown for the first time—I stuck it in the big oven in the church kitchen and turned it on to 300 degrees. *There. Take that.*

As I came out of the kitchen, sure enough, Florida and her crew were coming up the stairs. She had eight-year-old Carla by the hand, followed rather glumly by Cedric and Chris, eleven and thirteen. "Got a ride from Stu," Florida huffed. "She's parkin' the car."

I handed the bag of sheets to Florida and lightly punched both boys on the shoulder. "Hey, guys. Good to see you." I got a mumble and a half-smile in return.

Then I knelt down on my good knee at Carla's eye level. "Hi, Carla. Remember me? You came to my house a couple of months ago . . . the first time you visited your mom."

Carla, her hair neatly combed into several fat ponytails tied top and bottom with colorful glass beads, looked questioningly up at her mother. Florida prompted, "The lady with the crutches—remember?"

Carla stared back at me. "Oh. You the same lady had the big ol' black eye?" She looked me up and down, like a kid expecting a magician to reveal how he'd done that latest trick.

I was saved by Avis's voice up front giving the call to worship, and we hustled to find seats. "Great Sunday to bring the kids," I whispered to Florida as we crowded into a row behind Denny and Amanda. "We're having a potluck after service." I craned my neck, looking for my son's bald head. Ah, good. He was manning the soundboard at the back of the room. At least I didn't have to look at it—or people's stares—all through service.

"Girl, I didn't bring no food for no potluck," Florida whispered back.

The praise team had launched into an enthusiastic version of "Shine, Jesus, shine! Fill this land with the Father's glory! . . ."

"Don't worry about it. There's always plenty."

She smirked at me. "Well, that ain't no pot*luck*, then. More like a pot *blessing*, I'd say."

Most everyone was standing in response to the stirring music. I closed my eyes, trying to get focused on worship. Pastor Clark often said we should come to the service "in an attitude of worship," but just getting everybody up, showered, fed, and out the door in time to make the 9:30 service rarely left me in an attitude of worship—*especially* not on potluck Sundays, when I had to throw together something edible to take with us.

At the end of the first song, Rick Reilly—the twins' father—gave up his guitar for a set of bongos as the praise team launched into "Hail, Jesus, You're my King! Your life frees me to sing! . . ." I noticed Chris and Cedric perk up and begin to clap along with the strong percussive beat.

I clapped too—it was almost impossible not to!—and sang, "Hail, Jesus, You're my Lord! . . ." That was one thing I liked about Uptown Community: we sang about Jesus a lot. No one who visited even one Sunday would go away thinking we preached a watered-down gospel about a generic God. Yet it occurred to me that at Beth Yehudah, "Jesus" was always translated as "Yeshua"—the Hebrew form of Jesus. And something else: in the *mahzor,* the names "God" and "Lord" were always printed as "G-d" and "L-rd." At first I thought it was a typo, but it happened again and again. I'd meant to ask Ruth about that but forgot.

We didn't have many traditions or liturgy at Uptown—a fact that appealed to people who were kind of burned out on church. Appealed to *me,* frankly. I'd grown up in a small, nondenominational Bible church, and liturgical worship felt kind of perfunctory whenever we went to church with Denny's family. But the Rosh Hashanah service had felt so . . . rich, somehow. It was easy to imagine Jewish people in hundreds of nations using a similar liturgy on this traditional feast day—though Beth Yehudah obviously expanded the meaning of the service to celebrate Yeshua as the Messiah.

After the last worship song, two of the men brought out a

small table covered with a white cloth that had figures representing children around the world embroidered along its edge. Communion today? It was usually the first Sunday. Must've been moved because of the Labor Day holiday last week when a lot of people were missing. Pastor Clark removed the cloth, revealing a round loaf of bread, a ceramic pitcher, and two ceramic goblets. I smiled to myself. I liked the way Uptown celebrated communion —literally "breaking the bread" and "passing the cup." Guess we had our own rituals, after all.

Pastor Clark, wearing a brown Mister Rogers cardigan and a truly awful green tie, read the familiar scriptures about Jesus saying, "This is My body" and "This is My blood." Then he added, "As we partake of these elements today, let us meditate on what the apostle Paul said about Christ's death: 'God demonstrates his own love for us in this: While we were still sinners, Christ died for us.'" Then he broke the loaf of bread in two and handed the pieces to the first two people who came forward. After they'd broken off a bit of bread, they each passed their hunks of bread to the next person, followed by the cup of wine.

I got up from my chair when the line wasn't very long. I could hear the murmured voices as I moved forward: "The body of Christ, broken for you . . . The blood of Christ, shed for you . . ." And then the hunk of homemade bread was put into my hands.

As I started to break off a small piece, Pastor Clark's admonition replayed itself in my ears: *While we were yet sinners, Christ died for us.* Oh . . . my. Suddenly I remembered the prayers yesterday at the Rosh Hashanah service, "repenting for the sins of the people." That had struck both Denny and me as a bit strange—to identify with the sins of others as if they were our own and ask God's forgiveness. Fact was, it felt challenging enough to identify my own sins and ask God to forgive *me*. I still struggled to feel forgiven for the accident that killed Jamal Wilkins.

But Jesus . . . whew! What Jesus did took that a *lot* further—identifying with the sins of others to the point of taking their punishment. That was the whole point of salvation, of course: Jesus died for *our* sins, not His own. But did the concept of "repenting for others" or "taking somebody else's punishment" have any application in our own day-to-day—

I felt a poke in my back. "Jodi!" Florida stage-whispered in my ear. "Ya gonna pass that bread on or what?"

Good grief. How long had I been standing there? Pushing my thoughts to the back of my mind, I put the bit of bread in my mouth, turned, and handed the larger piece to Florida. "The body of Christ, broken for you, Florida," I said—and wondered, *Would I be willing to take the responsibility for your sins, Flo?*

I couldn't imagine it.

19

What with Rosh Hashanah, Florida coming to Uptown on Sunday, and my son looking like a Hare Krishna, I almost forgot I'd invited Hoshi to dinner on Tuesday, except she called the night before to ask what time she should come. Minor panic threatened to consume my entire Monday evening. Should I cook Chinese? Bad idea. I didn't have a clue, beyond the sweet-and-sour pork roast my mom used to make, or stir-fry where we throw in whatever fresh veggies we happened to have on hand along with some beef or chicken.

Maybe Japanese people didn't eat Chinese anyway.

I polled my family. To a man—and girl—they told me not to make it a big deal. "Just cook one of your favorites, Mom," Josh said, banging the back screen door behind him as he took Willie Wonka out for his nightly constitutional.

It's annoying when your family is right so much of the time.

So I decided on pasta with a Gorgonzola cheese sauce, salad, and garlic bread. Simple, yummy—those two magic words—and I had all the ingredients, even a hunk of Gorgonzola in the freezer. I was good to go.

The second week of school was going pretty well so far, except some of the kids in my class were way below grade level. Kaya, my supposedly "wise child," didn't have a clue how to write a two- to three-sentence summary of a *Scholastic* article I'd assigned over the weekend, even though she'd raised her hand when I asked who had read it. I sent Christy to work with her awhile, but later she told me Kaya couldn't even read the title of the article, which was "Teamwork." *That* was discouraging. We'd talked about the article in class just that morning, even referring to the title several times. Christy persevered, covering up part of the word, showing how it was really made up of two words. Still no recognition from Kaya. Finally, when Christy broke it down even further, to just letters and sounds, Kaya laboriously sounded out the word.

My student teacher came to me in frustration. "Ms. Baxter, *what* is this child doing in third grade?" My thought exactly.

However, with a few exceptions, most of the children were getting into the rhythm of the school day, needing some reminders about the rules, but otherwise muddling along in good spirits.

Except Hakim. He wasn't rowdy or a troublemaker. But he didn't like to be called on and stubbornly refused to answer. I didn't want to force him and make a big scene; on the other hand, it would be all too easy to skip over him and pick on one of the madly waving hands, letting him slide into a black hole.

I was thinking about Kaya and Hakim while stirring the

Gorgonzola sauce Tuesday evening. *Okay, Jesus, You said let the children come . . . but what if they don't want to?* I didn't want to leave Kaya or Hakim behind, but I had to keep moving forward with the other children.

Grabbing a Post-it note from the counter beneath the wall telephone, I wrote, "HAKIM . . . KAYA . . . JESUS, HELP!" and stuck it to the hood above the stove just as the doorbell rang.

"Denny!" No answer. "Josh? Amanda?" Where *was* everybody? Somewhere in the back of the house I heard music coming from behind a closed bedroom door. Turning the flame to low, I ran for the front door—it'd be quicker to answer it myself.

Hoshi, dressed neatly in beige slacks and cotton sweater set, held out a bouquet of daisies as I opened the door. "Am I too much early?"

"No, no, right on time." I took the flowers and gave her a hug. "You didn't have to do this!"

She smiled—a bit sadly, I thought. "My mother would say, don't arrive at host's house with empty hand!"

"Well, come on—oh, help! My sauce!" I ran for the kitchen, hoping Hoshi would follow.

The Gorgonzola sauce had only begun to brown slightly on the bottom. *Major* save. I quickly poured it into another saucepan, dumped a box of linguini into the big pot of water boiling on the stove, and hunted for a vase for the flowers. As I cut off their stems and ran water into the vase, I craned my neck to look into the dining room but couldn't see Hoshi.

"Hoshi?" No answer. I retraced my steps and found her

standing in the archway of the living room, seemingly lost in thought. "Hoshi, are you all right?"

She turned quickly, as if I had startled her. "Oh. Yes, I am all right. Just . . . seeing this room makes me think about that terrible woman. How could she do that?—hurt my mother? We do not treat guests to our country that way."

I wanted to slap myself upside the head. It had never occurred to me how coming to our house—the scene of so much trauma the last time she was here—might make Hoshi feel.

"She hurt me too," Hoshi murmured. "More than if she had cut me with that awful knife. She cut me off from my family."

"Oh, Hoshi. I am so sorry." I felt so helpless. The cut on Mrs. Takahashi's hand would heal long before the cut in Hoshi's heart.

The corners of her mouth turned upward politely. "It is not your fault, Jodi. You are kind to invite me to dinner. Can I help?"

It was Amanda's turn to set the table, but I let Hoshi carry out the plates and utensils to give her something to do. I did drag Amanda out of her bedroom, though, and sent her out to the garage to fetch her father and brother, who were still tinkering with our "lightly used" minivan. Finally everyone was corralled in the dining room.

Hoshi, bless her, smiled like a saint at Josh, light bulb and all. We held hands around the table, and I marveled how long and smooth Hoshi's fingers were as Denny prayed. "Lord God, bless this food, bless the hands that prepared it, bless our sister Hoshi, and we also ask Your blessing on her family in Japan. Amen." Denny was not long-winded when it came to mealtime prayers.

Hoshi looked up. "Thank you, Mr. Baxter."

"Just Denny, please. Hey, this looks great, Jodi." Denny passed the pasta dish to Hoshi, followed by the salad bowl and garlic bread. I was glad to see Hoshi fill her plate. The kids had been right to keep it simple.

Amanda, of course, asked Hoshi what meals were like in Japan. Hoshi laughed. "Fish. Lots of fish. And rice. Japan is an island, you know. So fish is one of our main sources of food."

"Like sushi?" Amanda wrinkled up her nose.

"Well, yes, but we eat much fish, many kinds. Lots of shrimp, scallops, oysters. Also *ika-yaki*—grilled squid. And *hanpen,* a steamed fish cake. Also seaweed salad, called *kaisou.*"

I wanted to laugh. Josh and Denny were practically drooling, while Amanda looked like she'd just gagged on a fly. Yet I had to give her credit for not spewing the usual, *"Eewww. Gross."*

"Maybe you could fix us some Japanese food sometime." Josh was nothing if not direct.

Hoshi beamed. "Yes! I only wish I could cook like my mother. Now, she is good Japanese cook."

At the mention of Hoshi's mother, the table got quiet and the smile drained from Hoshi's face. I was tempted to cover up the silence with my usual blather, but instead I let it sit a moment. Then I said, "I wish we had gotten to know your mother, Hoshi— your father too. I am sure they are wonderful people."

She lowered her eyes and blinked rapidly. "Yes. Yes, I wish this too." Then to my surprise, she abruptly changed the subject. "Tell me, Jodi, about your school."

I was impressed. Hoshi obviously felt deeply about her parents, but she also seemed eager to move forward. So I launched into the saga of my first week of school, including Ramón's threat to "smack" anybody who bullied other kids, and Britny matter-of-factly accepting my suggestion to visit England someday, since that was the meaning of her name. That brought a smile to Hoshi's face. When I talked about Hakim and the shell he seemed to carry around him, her expression grew thoughtful.

"I wonder," she said, "if he is sad about something. Sad children do not volunteer to do things."

"Oh. Oh my." That was a thought. I laid down my fork. "Like what?"

"Maybe his mother and father just got separated or divorced," Amanda chimed in. "That would make *me* sad."

I caught Denny's eye. Did Amanda ever worry about that? We'd never given her cause—had we?

But Hakim, now. "That could be . . ." I murmured. Hakim had been the only one who didn't want to find his name on the Welcome Bulletin Board that first day. "I wanted to encourage him, so I told him his name meant 'wise healer.' Even suggested he might be a doctor someday. But he almost got angry. Said, 'Don't want to be a doctor. They ain't no good anyway.'"

"Hmm," said Denny. "Maybe his mom is sick or in the hospital."

"Or maybe his family lost someone they know in the 9-11 tragedy," Josh suggested. "It's the first anniversary this week, you know."

I nodded. What Hoshi said made so much sense. Whatever

was making Hakim sad, I hoped I could show him I cared and that our classroom was a safe place to come out of his shell.

HOSHI'S COMMENT stayed with me the rest of the week as I observed Hakim. He didn't react in any special way to the moment of silence our school observed the next morning in memory of the 9-11 victims. He didn't seem motivated at all, though when he did apply himself to his work—with constant nudging from me or Christy—he was bright enough. He balked when it was his turn to read in reading group, but he would read aloud if Christy sat with him one-on-one. "He knows most of the words," she reported. "Just doesn't seem to care what they say. If I ask him questions about meaning, he just shrugs."

I knew it. There was a smart kid underneath all that stubbornness. We were going to dig him out, I told Christy, inch by inch, like archaeologists carefully exposing rare bones with a toothbrush. And as the weekend finally arrived, I decided to ask Yada Yada to put Hakim on their regular prayer list.

I was glad Yada Yada was scheduled to meet this Sunday evening—the first time since Bandana Woman had terrorized us. We needed to get together (not at my house, though, thank goodness!) to catch up with each other and pray. Hoshi needed some healing, for sure. All of us did, for that matter.

Today was Saturday . . . what else was happening this weekend? I jolted my mind awake with a cup of hot coffee and checked the kitchen calendar. *Whoa.* It said, *"Jodi PT 11 a.m."* I had totally forgotten I had a physical-therapy appointment this morning—and Denny was out in the alley washing the car. I mentally rearranged my morning as I studied the calendar. Today was the fourteenth—almost two weeks since Bandana Woman had been arrested.

Was Saturday different than any other day at Cook County Jail? The sergeant had said B. W. was in detox, but had she been arraigned yet? My arraignment had been two weeks and one day after the accident—but then, I'd been in the hospital. How soon would her trial date be set? Soon, I hoped. I wanted my wedding ring back!

I refilled my coffee mug and wandered out to the alley, where Denny was hosing down the minivan behind our garage. "Hey, Denny. Forgot to tell you. I've got an eleven o'clock at the physical therapist. Will the car be done?"

"Guess so. I was gonna wax it, but I guess I'll do that next time."

I watched as he took a soapy brush to the front grill. "Um . . . would you be willing to call Sergeant Curry this morning and ask if a trial date has been set for Bandana Woman?"

He snorted. "Bandana Woman? Is that what you call her?"

Did I really say that out loud? "Well . . . yeah."

"Smarty. Same initials as her real name, huh?" he grunted, moving the bucket to the side and starting in on the wheels.

I frowned. Bandana Woman. Becky Wallace. B. W. *Sheesh.* It had never occurred to me. "Whatever. Will you call?"

"They said they'd call *us*, Jodi."

"I know, but . . . Yada Yada meets tomorrow night, and I'm sure people will want to know—especially if they're going to be called to testify." I picked up the hose and rinsed the still-soapy grill.

Denny sighed. "All right. I'll try."

"Great." I let the hose fall and headed toward the house.

"Or you could do it!" he called after me. I pretended I hadn't heard him.

THE THERAPIST put me through a bunch of range-of-motion exercises with my left leg, which I did pretty well except for a leg lift lying on my side, which nearly killed me. "That's the one you need to be working on," she said, jotting some notes for me. "One more session. Two weeks okay?"

I wanted an excuse to put it off. Only two weeks? I'd never be able to do that leg lift in such a short time. Yet I couldn't use my birthday and my folks coming as an excuse, since that was this coming week. I sighed and accepted the appointment card.

A thunderstorm rolled through our neighborhood that afternoon, watering our pathetic patch of straw-colored grass and leaving the air smelling like it'd just come out of the wash. Denny asked if I was up for a walk to the lake after supper. "We could stop at the Heartland Café on the way back," he tempted.

On the way to the lake, cars full of young Latinos passed us, honking and waving and flying huge Mexican flags from their windows—a sure sign Mexican Independence Day celebrations had started. I did okay on the walk to the lake, but I was glad to collapse at one of the Heartland's sidewalk tables on the way back. We ordered their homemade salsa and chips to split between us. The café was full, a buzz of conversation and laughter going on all around us. I sipped my ice water and watched people strolling by, enjoying the last weekend of summer with their babies or dogs or just their own selves before fall officially arrived next week.

"I called Sergeant Curry," Denny said.

"Huh?" I turned back to my husband. Our chips and salsa had arrived and I hadn't even noticed. "Oh . . . great! What did he say?"

To my surprise, Denny didn't answer right away.

"Denny? Did a trial date get set?"

He shook his head. "There isn't going to be a trial."

I couldn't have been more startled if he'd thrown his glass of ice water in my face. *"What?"*

20

I must have screeched, because several heads turned in our direction. I shrank down into my chair. Denny let out an exasperated sigh. "There's not going to be a trial, Jodi, because she pled guilty at the arraignment yesterday and she's gone. They took her to the women's prison in Lincoln today."

"Oh. I thought you meant they were going to let her go." I thought about what he'd said. "Doesn't everybody get a trial? You know, America and all that."

Denny shrugged. "Why waste time and money on a trial if a person pleads guilty? Guess the judge sentenced her right then and there."

"But we didn't even testify! How does the judge know what sentence to give if he hasn't heard the evidence?"

"The police took our statements, you know."

A big mad was building inside of me. Not good enough. I wanted a judge to hear firsthand how B. W. had barged into my home and terrorized all my friends. Hear Hoshi describe her frightened mother and that wicked knife, how the long-awaited visit had been cut short. Wanted Bandana Woman to have to listen too. Now she'd pled guilty and denied us the privilege.

All I knew was, she better get more than Yo-Yo's eighteen months.

I sucked in my breath. "So. Did Sergeant Curry say what her sentence was?"

"Yeah. Ten years for assault."

I took a sip of water to steady my nerves. "What does that mean? That she'll be out on parole in a measly five years?"

Denny shook his head. "Dunno. They've got 'truth in sentencing' now. Not sure when her parole could come up."

The waiter refilled our glasses of ice water, and we munched on the chips and salsa for a while in silence. So Bandana Woman got a short ride to prison. Wasn't that good news? Why did I feel so disturbed?

Denny and I held hands as we walked down Lunt Avenue toward our house, past the houses hunched between the newer apartment buildings. Had to admit he'd been pretty tolerant with my reaction to the news. I wondered what the sisters in Yada Yada would think. Should I e-mail them tonight or just tell them tomorrow? *Guess tomorrow is soon enough.*

As we reached our front walk, I stopped short. "Wait a minute. If Bandana Woman has gone to prison already, does that mean we can get our jewelry back?"

Denny shrugged. "Probably." He saw me open my mouth again

and beat me to the punch. "No, *you* can call Sergeant Curry and ask him."

AMANDA WAS WAITING FOR US when we came in, nervously bouncing in her socks. "Hi, Mom. Hi, Dad. Can I go to Iglesia tomorrow for church?"

I tried to catch Denny's eye, but he chose that moment to squat down and greet Willie Wonka, who assumed we were all standing in the hall for his benefit. Okay, if Denny wasn't going to deal with this, I would. "Honey, you were there two weeks in a row in August. A visit now and then is fine, but we need to be faithful at our own—"

"I've *been* at Uptown the last two Sundays!" she wailed. "Besides, the Mexican Independence Day parade is tomorrow— maybe Edesa would take me and Emerald after church." I'm sure she sensed that Denny and I were wavering, because she moved in to nail the deal. "We get extra points in Spanish for cultural activities, you know."

How Amanda talked us into letting her take the el to Iglesia del Espirito Santo by herself, I'm not sure—especially since she had to transfer. But she did the good-grief-I'm-not-a-baby-any- more bit and promised, "I'll take the cell and call you when I get there, okay?"

She must have gotten on the phone with Edesa because a short while later she popped her head into our bedroom and said, "All set!"

YADA YADA took Ruth up on her invitation and met at her house Sunday evening. I didn't want to leave before Amanda got home from the parade, but she called around four-thirty just as she was transferring to the Red Line, so Josh met her at the Morse Street station, and they walked from there to Uptown Community for youth group. Denny and I would have to hear all about the parade later.

Denny got the bright idea to drive me to the Garfields' and get Ben out of the house. *For a drink?* I wondered. Ben Garfield certainly liked his beer, and it wouldn't be the first time if he asked Denny to join him. But I needed to let Denny handle that. I'd gotten myself in enough trouble nagging Denny about it and jumping to conclusions.

The Lincolnwood area where Ruth lived wasn't easy to reach by public transportation, so everybody got a ride with somebody. Chanda called us at the last minute saying she needed a ride, so Denny and I swung by her apartment building in Juneway Terrace, a depressing concrete jungle that straddled south Evanston and Rogers Park.

"Ooo, that Ruth got herself a real cute house!" Chanda gushed as we parked in front of the Garfields' twenty minutes later. I glanced at the small brick bungalows lined up along the street like square Monopoly pieces. Frankly, they pretty much looked alike to me: Three concrete steps up to the front door, a tidy bay window on the right, one window on the left. The only variations were the curtains in the windows and what flowers or shrubs flanked the steps. Ruth obviously had a green thumb, because a profusion of

black-eyed Susans, decorative grasses, and fall mums brightened
up the front of her house.

Ruth's husband—number three—opened the door when we
rang the doorbell. Ben Garfield's silver hair was brushed back
from his broad forehead in a wave reminiscent of Itzhak Perlman.
"Where all of you women are going to sit in this shoebox is
beyond me," he grumbled, waving us into the small living room
behind the bay window, "but that's your problem. Denny, here, has
taken pity on an old man, and we leave you to your prayers."

"Oh, take yourself out of here, Ben Garfield," Ruth fussed.
"Thank you, Denny." She pecked Denny on the cheek. "Now
shoo, both of you." Ruth shut the door behind them and rolled her
eyes. "Men."

"Humph. Should be t'ankin' God you *got* a mon," Chanda
pouted, plopping down in a big easy chair.

We chattered for about ten minutes, emptying the bag of day-
old *rugelach* Yo-Yo had brought from the Bagel Bakery while waiting for the latecomers. Chanda downed at least six pieces of the
rich Jewish pastry as the others straggled in.

"Hey, Jodi. How ya feel?" Florida gave me a quick hug in passing as she and Avis shed their coats. We hadn't had much time to
talk that morning at worship—she'd brought the kids again—and
I wondered how her second week had gone with Carla at home.
Figured I'd find out soon enough.

Stu arrived last with her carload; they'd been delayed by
Mexican Independence Day traffic. Somehow we all found places
to sit in the small living room. It felt odd to be together again after

the robbery two weeks ago. We hadn't talked about it much online or even by phone. But it was comforting too. Hoshi got a lot of hugs and seemed a little overwhelmed by the attention. "I think everyone's here," Avis said finally.

"'Cept Adele," Chanda said with her mouth full. "She not comin'."

I'd pretty much guessed as much when Chanda called us for a ride. My feelings were mixed—again. With Adele not here, at least I could relax about that whole mess. On the other hand, wondering why she didn't come left me feeling annoyed. Like *we'd* done something to *her*.

"We should get started then," Avis said. "Does anyone have a song of praise to start us off?"

For some reason the hymn that had been bouncing around in my head the last two weeks popped out of my mouth. "Does anyone know, 'Take your burden to the Lord and leave it there'?"

"Oh, sure." Avis hummed a few bars. "One of Charles Tindley's hymns."

"Wait a minute. You know who Charles Tindley is?"

"Of course. Famous African-American preacher from Philadelphia. He wrote hundreds of hymns."

"My mama used to sing Tindley hymns when we was comin' up," Florida chimed in. "She was so proud of that man. She'd tell us the story—born a slave, taught himself to read, ended up the preacher of a huge church in Philly. My mama said they called him the Prince of Preachers. Ain't you never heard of him, girl?"

I shook my head.

"Huh. Well, I ain't surprised. White folks ain't been givin' black folks any credit if they can help it."

That stung. Yet I couldn't argue with her. We'd sung his songs, all right—at least the two in our red hymnal. Maybe more. But no one had ever bothered to mention that the songwriter was black or tell his story when they told stories about other famous hymn writers like Charles Wesley and Fanny Crosby.

"I'm sure Tindley wrote his hymns for everyone," Avis said, saving me from having to respond to Florida. "Whoever knows it, join in." Without further ado, she began to sing the words to the first verse, which I didn't know by heart, but I joined in with several others on the chorus:

Leave it there . . . leave it there . . .
Take your burden to the Lord and leave it there;
If you trust and never doubt, He will surely bring you out
Take your burden to the Lord and leave it there.

In gospel fashion, we ended up singing the chorus a couple more times before Avis led out with an impassioned prayer that we'd take the words of this hymn to heart "and bring our burdens to You, Jesus, and leave them there rather than dragging them around, letting Satan beat us down, all hangdog and discouraged." She could've been an old Baptist preacher herself, for she sailed right back into the last two phrases of the chorus: *"Mmmm-mmm . . . If you trust and never doubt, He will surely bring you out . . . Take your burden to the Lord and leave it there . . . mmmm-mmm."*

I stifled a grin. What would the teachers at Bethune Elementary think if they could see *this* side of their cool-headed principal? God must have prompted me to suggest that song because singing "Leave it there" with my sisters calmed the anxious spirit I brought to the meeting, though I wasn't exactly sure why I felt so unsettled. Too much unfinished business, I guess.

"These last two weeks been one thing after another, know what I'm sayin'?" Florida piped up after the prayer. "Ain't had no time to think about that robbery, though I get hot as pepper sauce when I do. But can't afford to be mad, 'cause I got a little girl who's mad enough at the world and especially me right now 'cause I took her away from her foster mama. Though it ain't all bad," she hastened to say. "We doin' all right. She out with her daddy and brothers tonight eating pizza."

Nony reached over and laid a hand on Florida's knee. "Please let us know what we can do."

"Probably what you doin' now—prayin'. Got sheets, thanks to Jodi. Now anybody who's got some sassy girl clothes to pass along, could use some of them. But you ain't no help in that department, Nony." A grin softened Florida's worry lines. "All you got is those two handsome boys."

"I've got girls," said Delores. "They wear out their clothes pretty bad, but I'll see what we can come up with."

Chanda's pout deepened. "Mi still hain't heard what happened at sista Jodee's house. Start at da' beginning."

Avis quickly discouraged simply rehashing the details. "We need to help each other move beyond the trauma to a place of faith."

"Uh-huh." Ruth considered that. "So spiritual, I'm not. Exactly how do you do that?"

Stu snickered. "You sound like Yo-Yo."

Yo-Yo, sitting cross-legged on the floor and cleaning her fingernails with a pocketknife, just grinned.

Avis took the question seriously. "By confessing the Word—"

"Avis! Plain English!" This time Yo-Yo did speak up.

"All right, plain English. But it's an important concept, so I'm going to break it down. *Confessing*—it literally means 'to tell, to make known.' *The Word*, of course, is what God says in the Bible. So we can either go around *confessing*, 'Oh, wasn't that awful' or, 'I'm so scared' or, 'I'm so angry about what happened.' Or we can *confess* the *Word*: 'I'm created in the image of God.' 'God knows and cares when even a sparrow falls to the ground; how much more He cares about me!' 'All things work together for good for those who love Him and are called according to His purpose'—to name just a few. That's what I call 'confessing the Word.'"

I knew I needed that kind of encouragement, to actually *speak* the Word. Say it out loud. Remind myself what *God* said about stuff that happens when my feelings are flying off in every direction. I certainly didn't do that last night when Denny told me that Bandana Woman had pled guilty and skipped a trial. On the other hand, that seemed like asking a lot of somebody who'd just suffered a trauma—especially Hoshi, who was suffering a lot more than the rest of us as a result of the robbery. Still, I was a little shocked when Stu put my thoughts into actual words.

"Avis, isn't that expecting people to deny their feelings?" Stu's voice got sarcastic. "I just got robbed at knifepoint—well, praise the Lord! Hoshi's family has disowned her—but all things work together for good!" Stu's chin went up. "I mean, maybe praise and thanksgiving are *your* first reactions when something bad happens, but I'll bet most of us would like somebody to say, 'Gee, that's tough,' or 'You have a right to be upset!'"

It suddenly felt like all the air had just been sucked out of the room. No one spoke. I didn't know where to look, so I stared at the curlicues in the carpet. Even Yo-Yo quit cleaning her fingernails. I felt defensive for Avis. Stu had just rejected everything she'd just said. At the same time, I'd been thinking pretty much the same thing—maybe others had too.

Finally Avis spoke. "Stu, I don't mean to deny anyone's feelings. We all have natural feelings—including me. Yes, I felt angry. Yes, I was upset. I don't think one day has gone by that I haven't cried about Hoshi's pain, and I don't know how God is going to work that together for her good. It looks pretty bad. But I do know that if I stay there in the natural, focusing on all my feelings, Satan gets a foothold in my heart. I begin to doubt God's love. My trust slips—is God really in control? All I'm saying is, what I need to do is confess the promises of God, and I need to do it right away. 'Satan, you're a liar!' 'God, Your ways are above my ways, so I trust You!'—even if I don't feel like it. Because that's the only way I can keep my feet on solid ground and my heart from giving in to fear."

Fear . . . had to admit that was usually my first reaction. Not just physical fear, but fear I'd look stupid or make the wrong decision. I glanced sideways at Stu. Avis had won that round in my book, but would Stu come out swinging?

It was Hoshi who spoke. "Thank you. It is what I needed, Avis. My heart is shaking. It is hard to trust God. I am new Christian and don't know all that God says. All I know is, I can't go back. God has been good to me, and what happened at Jodi's house— that was not God. Satan wants me to go back to my old religion, but I will not go back. Please, show me what God says to make me strong and not so afraid."

The carpet blurred beneath my wet eyes. I understood what Stu had been saying. To be honest, I felt that way too. But this— *this* was moving us toward faith.

21

*D*elores Enriques spoke up. "Fear dogs my footsteps every day, especially for José. He's a good boy, but . . . what if those gangbangers come after him, to make sure he won't talk? I have to keep telling myself, 'God hath not given us a spirit of fear but of power, and of love, and of a sound mind.'"

Good verse, I thought, *if you can get past ye ole King James English.* It still surprised me when Delores and some of the others in Yada Yada quoted the old KJV with all its "haths" and "cometh." Nobody at Uptown Community used King James. Well, maybe Avis. And Florida. None of the WASPs, anyway.

Soon Bible promises were popping like popcorn from others, not just for Hoshi, but for all of us struggling with anger and fear after the robbery. "Fear not, for I have redeemed you; I have called you by your name; you are Mine" . . . "I know the plans I have for you, declares the Lord, plans to prosper you and not to harm you, plans to give you hope and a future" . . .

I was scribbling references down as fast as I could so I could look them up later—and almost missed Florida's question.

"I wanna axe you all somethin'. What about this woman—the one who robbed us? She ain't that different from me five years ago, you know, 'cept I faint dead away at the sight of blood, so you know I ain't never gonna take up no knife."

The thought of Florida fainting dead away over blood stirred up some chuckles. "You didn't faint when Hoshi's mama was bleeding," I kidded.

"Too scared. *Couldn't* fall out."

Now we did laugh, and the atmosphere lightened up, like someone had opened a window. "Yes," Nony seconded, "I wonder about her too. How do we find out what's happening?" She held up her left hand with its bare ring finger. "And I want my wedding ring back."

I sucked in my breath. "Well, I've got an update. Denny called Sergeant Curry yesterday to ask if a trial date had been set"—I left out the part about me bugging him to death—"and guess what? The woman pled guilty at her arraignment on Friday and *bam!* She's already down at Lincoln serving a ten-year sentence."

Everybody looked at me like I was making it up. "Honest. That's what he said."

"Humph. Don't blame her," Yo-Yo muttered.

I frowned. "What do you mean?"

Yo-Yo hugged one denim knee to her chest. "Prison ain't no picnic, but it's a heck of a lot better than bein' stuck for months at

Cook County Jail. What's-her-name—Becky, right?—probably got put right off in the wing with other violent offenders. If I was her, caught in the act and knew I was goin' down for sure? I'd plead guilty, too, just to get outta Cook County, 'stead of waitin' months for a trial date."

Now everybody stared at Yo-Yo.

"How do you know her name?" Hoshi said, her voice barely above a whisper.

Yo-Yo looked up at me. "Didn't you tell me her name was Becky Something?"

Was Yo-Yo really the only person I told? And she hadn't even been there that night. I nodded, feeling guilty that I'd sat on it. "Yeah. Becky Wallace. That's what Sergeant Curry said her name was." *Bandana Woman . . . B. W. . . . whatever.*

Stu made a face. "Feels funny to know what her name is."

"Humph." Ruth folded her arms across her bosom. "A disgrace to such a pretty name, she is."

Yo-Yo snorted. "In case you guys never thought about it, everybody in prison has a name. Maybe you guys—" She checked herself. "Maybe *we* are s'posed to, you know, pray for her. Or visit her. You know, like Ruth did for me."

"Oh, who's sounding 'spiritual' now?" I snapped. "Ruth wasn't your *victim*. And all you did was forge a couple of checks." I shut my mouth, afraid of the sudden anger that heated my words.

Yo-Yo just shrugged, unperturbed. "All I'm sayin' is, this *is* the Yada Yada *Prayer* Group, ain't it? So . . . pray."

Where did she get off getting so holy all of a sudden? Yo-Yo hadn't been a Christian more than a few months, didn't even go to church yet. What did *she* know?

She knows what it's like on the other side.

The thought was so loud in my head I looked around the room to see if somebody had spoken it aloud. But no one was looking my direction.

"Well, now, the way I see it is . . ." Florida jabbed her finger at no one in particular. "I don't like this woman. Wouldn't mind if I never saw her again all my born days. Same time, I didn't like myself five, ten years ago either. And God still saw fit to give me another chance. So I say, maybe some of us *should* go visit this woman, this Becky whoever. And 'cause I been where she is—not in prison, thank ya, Jesus!—but drugged out and desperate, I might go visit her if some of you all would come with me."

No one else spoke for a long moment. Then Yo-Yo said, "Well, I been where she is, too—not drugged out, 'thank ya, Jesus!'"—she smirked at Florida—"but stuck in prison for long enough. Some people don't have nobody to visit 'em."

"*Mmm.* Lord have mercy," Avis murmured. Her lips continued to move, like she was praying in tongues or something.

Hoshi put her face in her hands and started to cry. "No, no. I couldn't . . . couldn't."

Nony put an arm around her. "Shh, shh. No one's asking you to, Hoshi. It's all right."

"Besides," Yo-Yo went on, "you can't just show up at Lincoln to visit somebody. They gotta put you on their visitors' list."

My ears perked up. "What do you mean?"

"Somebody has to write and tell what's-her-face that we want to come visit her, and she'd have to put our names on a list."

Oh! Relief surged through me. *No way would Bandana Woman put any of our names on her visitors' list!* That would be bizarre beyond belief. I felt let off the hook.

But my relief was short-lived.

"Maybe Jodi could write and axe her to put our names on the list—she's good at that sort of thing." Florida talked like I wasn't even there, but when I glared at her she just grinned back at me.

"I don't know," I mumbled. "I don't think . . ."

"Won't hurt to ask. All she can do is say no." Yo-Yo's logic was maddening.

Avis broke in. "I don't think we ought to decide anything for sure right this moment. This might be the right thing to do—or not. Let's pray about it and see what God says. If she's already been sent to Lincoln, she's not going anywhere soon. We have time to pray."

I flashed Avis a grateful look then bowed my head, all ready to tell God privately that this wasn't such a hot idea, didn't He agree? But Ruth said, "Um, before we pray . . . could I say something? Jodi and Denny and Stu came to the Rosh Hashanah service at Beth Yehudah last weekend, which I appreciated, can't begin to tell you. Tomorrow is Yom Kippur—some of you are coming, yes?" A few heads nodded around the room. "I want to explain about the Ten Days of Awe—the period between Rosh Hashanah and Yom Kippur. Because, to tell the truth, I think it applies to what we've been talking about here."

There was an awkward pause. This certainly sent the flow of the meeting on a detour, but Nony graciously said, "Of course. I would like to hear. Mark and I and the boys are coming tomorrow."

I felt impatient to get on with our prayer time but settled back reluctantly, hoping Ruth wouldn't go into a long description of everything we'd already heard at the Rosh Hashanah service.

"Rosh Hashanah, the New Year, begins a time of introspection, looking back at the mistakes of the past year and planning the changes to make in the coming year—a spiritual inventory, as it were." Ruth's face took on a flush of excitement, like a babushka showing her grandchildren around the ancestral farm. "Although it's not spelled out in the Torah, most Jews consider the blowing of the shofar during Rosh Hashanah to be a call to repentance."

"Yes, I remember that from the sermon that your rabbi gave at Rosh Hashanah," Stu put in.

Ruth gave her a look, just like the one my mother used to give me and my brothers that meant, *I'm doing the talking here. Zip your lip.* "Pastor," she said impatiently. "Beth Yehudah's got a pastor like everybody else. He's not a Jewish rabbi."

I wanted to snicker. *Sorry, God.* But I did love it when Stu got put in her place.

"Messianic Jews," Ruth went on, "believe *all* the Jewish festivals and holy days are not only a remembrance, but a foreshadowing of Messiah Yeshua. During the Ten Days of Awe, we are preparing our hearts for His return."

"This is so interesting." Avis leaned forward. "All the years I was coming up in the African-American church, we identified strongly with the Old Testament stories and the history of the Jewish people. Now that I think about it, a lot got focused on God's deliverance of His people from Egypt and the meaning of Passover—not the meaning of the others feasts and festivals."

"Uh-huh. 'Go down, Moses!' and 'Let My people go!'" Chanda rolled her eyes. "Rev'rend Miles at Paul and Silas Apostolic? He preachin' on that two, maybe t'ree times a month!"

Nony tossed her head, setting her newest 'do of curls dancing behind a bright-colored head wrap. "A lot of white Christians presume we're stuck there too. Mark and I were invited to a gospel concert at a big North Shore church, and the choir mostly sang spirituals from slavery times, as if that was the sum total of black contribution to gospel music. Why is that?"

Florida snorted. "'Cause ya sing spirituals slow, and white church folks can't sing fast and step and clap at the same time."

That got a laugh, even from us "white folks." Except Ruth. She was giving Avis "the look" for getting us offtrack again.

"Sorry," Avis said, trying to hide her smile. "Go on, Ruth."

"Where was I?" Ruth frowned, hands on her knees.

"The Ten Days of Awe."

"So I was. During the Ten Days of Awe, we not only confess our own sins, but we intercede on behalf of our people. Not just asking God to bless us, but asking God to forgive the sins of our people. For Messianic Jews, that means the sins of our fellow Christians as well. All of which culminates in a time of fasting and prayer at Yom Kippur."

Ruth sat back in her chair. The room was silent till Yo-Yo said, "That's it?"

"Well, no, there's lots more, but that's mainly what I wanted to say."

"So . . . how does that relate to what we were talking about?" I didn't mean to make that sound so challenging—or maybe I did.

"I think I know," Stu offered. "We can 'intercede' for our thief—uh, Becky, did you say?—because she's probably not at a place she can do that herself. Like European-Americans needing to take responsibility for how our ancestors treated the Native-American people—or ask forgiveness from African-Americans for the terrors of slavery."

Oh, thanks, Stu. I didn't ask you. Sounded like a lot of "politically correct" stuff from the current crop of social activists.

Florida muttered, "That would be the day." Ruth just nodded.

We finally got to our prayer time, though it seemed shorter than usual. I heard the front door open while Delores was praying for "the Becky woman" in prison and whether we ought to visit her. Then I heard Ben's voice mutter, "They're still at it," and the door closed again. Finally we ended with some good old-fashioned praise, did a lot more hugging, and got ready to go.

Just as I was trying to catch Chanda's eye to say Denny was waiting for us outside, Delores pulled me aside. She hadn't said anything about Ricardo tonight—I wondered if things had gotten worse. I looked at her expectantly.

"You know Amanda came to Iglesia this morning, *si?*"

"Well . . . sure. She said she wanted to go to the parade with

Edesa and Emerald afterward." *Oh dear. Guess I should have called Delores and checked it out with her, since it involved Emerald. Is she upset?*

Delores seemed embarrassed. "I wondered about that . . . but thought you should know. Amanda called the house last night and asked José to take her to the parade."

22

It drove me nuts that we had to give Chanda a ride home, so I couldn't talk to Denny about Delores's revelation the whole way. The moment Chanda got safely inside the front door of her apartment building, I exploded. "I'm going to strangle that girl!"

Denny looked at me as if I was crazy. "Who? Chanda? *What* are you talking about, Jodi?"

I told him what Delores had said. "Amanda never called Edesa about going to the parade! She lied to us, Denny!"

"Hmm." Denny frowned as he turned off Clark Street at the Rogers Park Fruit Market to do the "square dance" around the one-way streets to get to our house. "Sure sounds like it."

"*Sounds* like it! She said she was going to call Edesa, but Delores said she called *their* house and asked *José* to take her! If that's not a lie, I don't know what is."

"I know. Just . . . let's not go off half-cocked till we hear what Amanda has to say."

Half-cocked, my foot. I was ready to go into the house with both barrels blazing. What was Amanda thinking, anyway? Why didn't she just say she wanted to go to the parade with José? *Oh, right, Jodi—like you would have said yes. She's no fool.*

I was, though. I should've obeyed my instincts and said no to the whole crazy scheme in the first place.

Denny drove the Caravan into the garage and turned off the motor. "You ready to go in the house, or do you want to calm down first?"

"Don't patronize me, Denny," I snapped. "Why shouldn't I be upset? Why shouldn't Amanda *know* we're upset?"

He didn't answer, just made no move to get out of the car. I sighed. He was probably right. I needed to calm down before we confronted Amanda. But what was with that? Seemed like parents used to tell their kids what's what and didn't stress so much about their kids' feelings.

After a minute, Denny spoke. "What are you most upset about, Jodi? That Amanda told us a lie? Or that she went to the parade with José? What if she had asked us if she could go with José—would we have let her?"

I opened my mouth to say, *"That she lied, of course!"* but I shut it again. Yes, I was upset by the lie, but if I was really honest, I was more upset about her going with José.

Denny waited. Finally I worked up courage to voice my thoughts. "Okay, both. I mean, I like José—he seems like a nice boy, what little we know about him. But I like him mostly because I care about Delores, and I know she tries her best with those kids.

They all seem sweet. Yet . . . cultures are different. Expectations are different. I don't know."

"We've got to think about this, Jodi. If there's a problem, we've got to address the real problem, not a bunch of vague fears and prejudices."

Oh, thanks, Denny. Play the prejudice card.

"There *are* real concerns, Denny. For one thing, José's only fifteen—too young to be responsible for Amanda in a rowdy crowd like that parade. I thought she was with Edesa, an adult. You *know* forty or fifty people usually get arrested for disorderly conduct whenever there's a big parade in one of the Chicago neighborhoods. Edesa would be wise enough to take the girls out of harm's way. But José—he's just a kid himself! And Delores said she worries some gangbangers will go after him someday to keep him from testifying against the guys who shot him." I hit my forehead. "Sheesh! A big Latino parade like that? Probably crawling with Latin Kings and Spanish Cobras. Didn't even *think* about that when we said she could go."

Denny gave me a hard look. "Did anybody ever get arrested for shooting José that day in the park?"

I shook my head. "Don't think so—not that I've heard. José didn't see who did the shooting, though I suppose he could identify the Spanish Cobras he talked to just before it happened."

"José had asked them to leave so the little kids could play, right?"

"That's the story."

Denny blew out a sharp breath. "Does sound dangerous. Guess

it's a good thing we found out. But Jodi, *not* because of José. He's not to blame here. It wasn't a wise situation, and Amanda was wrong to deceive us. *That's* what's wrong here. We agreed on that?"

My eyes felt hot, like I wanted to cry, and it was hard to swallow past the lump in my throat. *Oh God, I don't want to have to deal with this. It's too big, too complicated. I just want to raise my kids someplace safe . . . and normal . . . and . . .*

I finally nodded. "Agreed."

AMANDA gave us a deer-in-the-headlights look when we appeared in her bedroom doorway. I could practically see her thoughts: *"Busted!"* She had to know we'd find out, since I'd just spent the last couple of hours with Edesa and Delores. Amanda protested that she *had* gone to church at Iglesia and thought maybe everybody—Edesa and the whole Enriques family—would go to the parade afterward, and she'd just go along with them.

"Amanda, *stop.*" Denny nipped that bit of nonsense in the bud. "You let us think you called Edesa and that it was 'All set,' when in reality you called José and planned all along to go with him. That's deception. That's a lie."

Amanda hung her head and wiped her nose with the sleeve of her sweatshirt.

"And *did* you go to the parade with 'everybody'? Or just José?"

She started to cry. "Just José," she whimpered. "We didn't do anything wrong, Dad, honest! I just . . . " She wiped her nose on her sleeve again. "José was telling me about the parade and it sounded like fun, but I *knew* you guys wouldn't let me go if I said José asked me."

"And why is that?" Denny put it right back in her lap.

Amanda pulled a pout. "'Cause you guys get all weird if a boy asks me to do *anything*. And"—she lifted her chin defiantly—"'cause the parade was in Little Village. Not exactly your comfort zone, Mom."

A few choice words would have put Miss Sassy in her place, but I pinched my lips together. I didn't like it, but what she said was true.

"Don't forget," Denny said, "we *did* let you go when we thought you'd be with Edesa, an adult we trust—or even if the rest of the Enriques family had been with you too. But big crowds can be dangerous for a young girl in an unfamiliar place, even with José."

Humph. *Especially* with José, I wanted to say, if some Spanish Cobras out there wanted to silence him for good, but again I held my tongue. Maybe Denny didn't go there for a reason.

Amanda was grounded to the house for the rest of September —a little over two weeks—no phone, no TV, no new baby-sitting jobs, no outside activities except school and church. Frankly, I wished we could've come up with some other consequence, like doing the dishes for the rest of her natural life or something. I hated grounding, because we ended up with a glum teenager kicking around the house 24-7. But what else can you do when they're fifteen?

I said as much to Delores when I called later to let her know the story from our end. "*Si*, I know what you mean," she said. "Too big to spank; too young to kick out of the house."

Denny got on the phone to make it clear that as far as we knew, the fault was Amanda's alone. José might have asked Amanda to go to the parade, but it was Amanda who chose to deceive us. "Please make it clear we are not angry with him, Delores—only that Amanda lied to us."

We heard Delores sigh on the other end of the phone. "*Si. Gracias.* But I don't know . . . you think they are sweet on each other?"

DELORES'S QUESTION was still dogging my heels when I walked into my third-grade classroom on Monday morning. Was it *that* obvious that Amanda and José were "sweet" on each other? What was going on that I hadn't noticed? Lots of phone calls, obviously. But why did Delores sound so concerned? I thought she liked Amanda! Did *she* worry about the cultural and racial differences?

That gave me pause. It never occurred to me that anybody would have concerns if their child wanted to date one of *my* kids. I mean, Delores should feel darn lucky if José was sweet on Amanda—

Just listen to yourself, Jodi Baxter! You're about as two-faced as a smiling thief.

Ouch. *Okay, God, You really gotta help me out. I admit it—I'm*

uncomfortable with this cross-racial dating, especially when it's my kid.
. . . Aren't there some real concerns here?

I had to shelve my thoughts and get on with the day before my students realized I wasn't paying attention. While I was taking attendance, I noticed Hakim turning around in his seat and snatching things off the desk behind him. Something inside me cautioned, *Don't single him out; don't give him attention for misbehavior.* So as I asked for volunteers to go to the board and solve the math problems I had written there, I casually walked around that side of the room and laid a firm hand on his shoulder for one full second without even looking down, then walked on. Out of the corner of my eye I saw Hakim glare at me. Then he turned back to his own desk and put his head down on his arms.

I sighed. Didn't know which was worse: Hakim acting up or Hakim slumped inside his shell. *Darn. Forgot to ask Yada Yada to put Hakim on their prayer list.* Well, I'd send it around by e-mail tonight. Hakim and I needed prayer *now*—we couldn't wait two weeks.

When I got home from school, the house was empty except for Willie Wonka, who needed to go outside. Amanda was supposed to come "straight home" from school—but what did that mean when she had to catch a city bus from Lane Tech? Traffic . . . a missed bus . . . a full bus went by the stop—there were plenty of realities she could use as excuses for being late. We better pin that one down.

I sat down at the computer to send out the prayer request about Hakim—then remembered that I promised to let the group know how we could get our stolen jewelry back. So I reached for the phone book, looked up the number for the Twenty-Fourth District Police Station, and dialed.

Sergeant Curry wasn't in, so I asked if someone else could help me retrieve my stolen property. I gave our case number to the officer who came on the phone then had to wait for several minutes while he looked up the file. I walked around the kitchen with the cordless cradled in the crook of my neck, pulled some chicken pieces out of the freezer, popped them into the microwave to thaw, then started loading the breakfast dishes into the dishwasher—

"Mrs. Baxter?" The man's gravelly voice came back on so suddenly I nearly dropped a glass. "That property will be released later this week. Call back Wednesday or Thursday. You can probably pick it up this weekend."

"Where? At the police station?"

"Normally, all recovered stolen property is sent to Twenty-Sixth and California for trial." My heart started to sink. Twenty-sixth and California was the address for the Cook County Courthouse, way on the south side. But the officer continued. "However, in this case the perp pled guilty before we had time to send it down there. So you can pick up your property here. Do you know where we are? Clark and Schreiber."

"That's great. Thank you! But, sir? . . . Sir?" I thought he was going to hang up. "I have another question. Can I pick up *all* the stolen property? It was all taken from my house, but it doesn't all belong to me. We were robbed while I had guests at my—"

"Sorry, ma'am. Can't do that." The officer's voice sounded

extremely impatient, like I'd gone over my limit of questions. "The statements taken the night of the incident described what was stolen from each victim, so each of those individuals will have to come down to the station and claim their own property."

"Oh. All right. Thanks." I hung up. *Bummer.* Seemed like a lot of unnecessary trips. But at least we could all get our jewelry back. I tried to think who'd had stuff stolen: Nony's ring and necklace . . . Avis's pin, though not her wedding ring—that was *so weird* that Bandana Woman didn't take it . . . my wedding ring set . . . Stu's earrings. Nothing from Florida 'cause she didn't have anything, and not even Mrs. Takahashi's money. I had to smile, remembering the grip Hoshi's mom had kept on her purse. Anybody else?

Adele. Bandana Woman had made me take off Adele's big ring myself.

I stood in the middle of the dining room, looking back and forth between the computer and the telephone. Adele needed to know that the thief had been sentenced already, and we could get our jewelry back. Should I just send out that information to everybody in an e-mail, including Adele . . . or should I tell her myself by phone?

It made a darn good excuse to speak to Adele person to person, and I was tired of this little game we were playing.

I picked up the phone.

23

*A*s the phone rang, I chastised myself. This was dumb, calling the shop. Adele was certain to be busy, and a message from me would just make her wary. I was about to do a quick hang-up when someone answered the phone. "Adele's Hair and Nails."

Adele's voice.

"Oh. Hi, Adele. It's Jodi. Sorry to bother you at work. If this isn't—"

"It's all right. What's up?"

What's up?! Like we haven't left a zillion messages in the last four weeks. "I wanted to let you know about your stolen ring." *That'll keep her on the line.*

"What about it?"

"Well, Sergeant Curry, the officer who took our statements that night—"

"I *know* who Sergeant Curry is."

Easy, Jodi, that's just Adele's way. Don't get jelly-knees over it.

"Well, Sergeant Curry told us that . . . that . . ." *Becky Wallace? Bandana Woman?* ". . . uh, the woman who robbed us pled guilty, and she's already been sentenced to ten years at Lincoln Correctional Center."

"What about my ring?"

"That's just it. Since there isn't going to be a trial, they're releasing our stolen jewelry. No evidence needed. You can pick it up at the Twenty-Fourth District Police Station on Clark—not too far from your shop."

"So I gotta go pick it up?"

"That's what they said."

"All right. Thanks, Jodi—"

"Wait. Adele, do you have another minute? I really need to talk to you about what happened the day you gave me the makeover for my anniversary."

For a moment only silence answered me from the other end.

"Adele?"

I heard a sigh. I could well imagine Adele's large chest heaving in exasperation, and I was glad we weren't actually face to face. "Just a minute" was all she said, then her voice moved away from the phone yelling, "Corey! Can you keep an eye on the desk? An' answer the phone if it rings—line two. My four-thirty's late. If she comes in, tell her to wait."

I couldn't hear what Corey said in reply, but it must have been in the affirmative, because I could hear Adele walking—a soft *shush, shush, shush*—then a door closed.

"All right. You wanna talk."

Ohmigosh. My mind was suddenly blank. Where should I start? "Yes. Uh . . . first of all, how is MaDear?"

Another big Adele sigh. "She's hangin'. Has some good days an' some bad days. Nights are worst. Nightmares, screaming . . ."

"Oh, Adele." My heart sank. "I'm so sorry." I paused, but Adele didn't offer any more. "Avis told us why MaDear screamed at Denny that day—I mean, who she thought he was . . . and what happened when she was a girl."

Silence.

"Adele, Denny and I had no idea she had suffered such a terrible tragedy. I wish there was a way we could communicate to her how sorry we are."

"Wouldn't help. Would just set her off. Just . . . leave it be."

I tried to gather my courage. "That's hard, Adele. It really hurts Denny to think your mother thinks *he's* the guy who . . . who murdered her brother. That's like . . . like a false accusation!"

"Look." I heard Adele suck in her breath, and her tone got hard. "Don't go telling *me* MaDear's making a 'false accusation.' She's got dementia or Alzheimer's—whatever. Don't take it personal, but as long as she thinks that way, do me a favor and just stay out of her life, okay?"

I winced. Adele's words were hard, unsympathetic. But I pushed on. "Okay, but why are you staying out of our life?"

"Whaddya mean?"

"You know. Not returning our phone calls, staying away from Yada Yada. I feel like you're blaming us for something we didn't do." There. It was out. I held my breath.

The silence was long and heavy on the other end. Finally Adele spoke, her words measured and tight. "Look. Right now, I can't really be worried about how you and Denny are feeling. What happened that day . . . *get over it*. It's not a big deal for you; just a misunderstanding by a senile old lady. But it is a big deal for me. It is a big deal for my mother, who wakes up at night terrified, and it's two, sometimes three hours before I can get her back to sleep."

I heard the front door slam. Usually Amanda called out, *"I'm home!"* but all I heard was something being dumped on the floor—backpack, probably—and footsteps stalking down the hall. I caught a glimpse of my daughter as she stomped past the dining room doorway and into the bathroom. Another slammed door.

I stifled a groan. It was going to be a long two weeks.

"And to be honest?" Adele continued in my ear. "It's brought up a lot of old feelings I thought I'd dealt with. My uncle was murdered—*murdered*, Jodi—by a bunch of white racists for who-knows-what stupid offense. Acting like a human being, no doubt. That was before my time, and my sister and me, we always rolled our eyes at the old stories. We pretended everything was different now, even when we got chased out of stores just for lookin' and when Daddy got stopped by the cops just for 'drivin' black.' But seeing how that lynchin' still terrifies my mother . . . yeah. I got some feelings. And I'm sorry if that's steppin' on your toes."

I had no idea what to say, so I didn't say anything, just sat slumped over the table with the phone at my ear. I half-expected Adele to slam down the phone, but Adele was on a roll.

"As for what happened at your house a couple of weeks ago?

That was just the last straw. I talked myself into coming to Yada Yada that night. *Big* mistake. I know, it was traumatic for everybody. Wasn't your fault—wasn't nobody's fault. But with MaDear half off her rocker 'cause of what white folks did when she was a kid—not to mention everything my family has put up with from ignorant bigots all the years I was comin' up—the last thing I needed was some doped-up white floozy messin' with *me*. Tie me up? Steal my grandmother's ring? If I think on it too long, I'll get crazy myself, probably do something I regret." She blew out a breath. "So. You asked. That's my answer. I'm takin' a break from Yada Yada, and from white folks in general if I can help it. And don't come crying to me about how bad you feel. What you feel ain't *nothin'* compared to what I'm dealing with right now, and I don't have time to worry about your hurt feelings. Get over it, Jodi—that's all I can say."

A dozen backlashes sprang to my tongue, but I knew I wouldn't say them. I wanted to yell, I wanted to cry—but mostly I wanted to get off the phone before I did either. "All right, Adele." My voice came out in a croak. "You made yourself plain. I'm sorry. That's all I know to say." And I hung up.

I was so mad and so hurt, I wanted to throw pots and pans or break a window or something—anything. Instead I just clenched my fists and sputtered, *"Arrrrrgggghhhh!"* at the top of my lungs. I paced back and forth between the kitchen and dining room, holding a hundred angry dialogues with Adele in my head, telling her *she's* the one who needs to "get over it" instead of taking it out on friends who never did anything to her—not just me and Denny, but all the Yada Yada sisters.

I got out a pot, dumped it into the sink, and filled it with water for chicken noodle soup. I banged it onto the stove, slopping some of the water and putting out the gas flame. By the time Denny and Josh walked in the door, the soup was almost done, the kitchen was a mess, Amanda was holed up in her room, and I was in no mood to be social. "Dish up some soup when you get hungry," I grumbled. "I'm taking Willie Wonka for a walk."

WILLIE WONKA lasted about twenty minutes—long enough for us to make it to Touhy Park, which normally took five minutes— but I hadn't figured on Willie stopping to sniff every tree, leaving his "mark" to let the next dog know who'd passed by. By the time we got to the park, he was huffing. I found a bench and sat down so Willie could rest up for the walk home.

The conversation with Adele kept replaying in my mind. *"Don't come crying to me about how bad you feel . . . ain't nothin' compared to what I'm dealing with . . . get over it, Jodi . . . don't have time to worry about your hurt feelings . . . I'm taking a break from Yada Yada and white folks in general . . ."*

But rehashing it only fed my festering anger. I sighed. *Okay, God. What am I supposed to do now? You tell me—'cause I don't have a clue.*

It was starting to get dark by the time I dragged Willie into the front door forty-five minutes later. Denny and Josh were in the living room flipping channels and watching sports news, empty soup bowls cluttering up the coffee table. Amanda, no doubt, was still sulking in her room.

Denny glanced up. "Good. You're back." His tone was reproachful, like, *"Okay, you're mad, but don't make me worry about you."* I stood in the doorway a minute, wishing he'd jump up and say, *"You upset about something, honey? Wanna talk?"* But I knew it wouldn't happen. When Denny's feelers pick up that I'm working on a mad, he usually backs off and leaves me alone till I cool off.

Grow up, Jodi. He probably thinks you're mad at him *for who-knows-what.* I unsnapped Willie Wonka's leash and straightened. "Yeah. Sorry I went off like that. I had an upsetting phone call with Adele. Had to blow off steam before I was ready to talk about it."

That got Denny's attention. He even got up off the couch and followed me to the kitchen, leaning against the doorway while I dished up a bowl of chicken noodle soup. "Wanna tell me about it?"

I nodded, and we sat at the dining-room table while I recounted the conversation as best I could between spoonfuls of soup. The hot, salty liquid felt good going down, like a hot water bottle soothing my ruffled feelings. Denny was hearing the conversation for the first time, and by the end he was pacing around the room, rubbing the back of his head.

Finally he threw up his hands. "Well, that's it. I don't know what else to do. Maybe Adele's right. Just get over it." He practically threw himself down on a chair.

"Yeah. Except . . . it's hard to 'just get over it' when she's dropping out of Yada Yada too. All the sisters are gonna feel hurt."

I pushed away my empty soup bowl, and we both sat silently at the table, hugging our own thoughts. It suddenly occurred to me I was still thinking mostly about me. In the quiet of the dining room, with only the TV providing distant background noise, I rehearsed our conversation once more, but this time paying more attention to what Adele was feeling . . .

"It is a big deal for me . . . my uncle was murdered, Jodi—by a bunch of white racists . . . my mother wakes up at night terrified, and it's two, sometimes three hours before I can get her back to sleep again . . . my sister and me got chased out of stores just for lookin' . . . Daddy got stopped by the cops for 'drivin' black' . . . everything my family has put up with from ignorant bigots . . ."

I looked up at Denny, who was still slumped in one of the dining-room chairs. "I know what we can do."

"What?"

"Pray for Adele and MaDear."

He cocked an eyebrow at me. "O-kaaay. Sounds, uh, virtuous."

I giggled. "I know. But I'm serious. How many times do I actually pray for my so-called enemies—or even someone who makes me upset? I stew . . . I fret . . . I try to work it out. But Adele's right about one thing—I wanted to talk to her to make *me* feel better."

Denny sighed. "Yeah. Me too. Okay, let's pray for Adele and MaDear. But there's something else I gotta do."

"What?"

He got up and grabbed the checkbook we kept in the computer desk. "Pay Adele something for your anniversary makeover. Don't want that to come back to bite me."

24

I called Avis the next evening to get her best "guess-timate" at what my hair and nails would cost at Adele's Hair and Nails, and I ended up telling her about the phone call. I felt slightly guilty blurting it all out—was I gossiping about Adele? But I decided that at least Avis should know what was going on. We'd asked her to be the leader of our prayer group, and Adele's decision to drop out definitely affected everybody. I needed to be careful, though. It would be tempting to "let others know" in subtle ways that made Adele the Bad Guy and us the Poor Innocent Bystanders.

"Uh . . . Avis. Maybe I'll let you figure out what to say to Yada Yada about Adele's absence. Florida and Stu may figure out it has something to do with what happened at the shop, but nobody else knows what happened that day. Are you okay with handling this?" There. That made me accountable to Avis. As well as let me off the hook.

"All right. Guess that's best. The Lord is going to have to give me the right things to say . . . but I don't think we should say too much. Nothing is written in stone—not since the Ten Commandments anyway. Let's give the Holy Spirit some room to work."

Room to work? Please! Take all the room You need, God! Then—I swear—a voice in the back of my head said, *Then you need to get out of the way, Jodi.*

I was so startled that I almost missed Avis's next words. ". . . any thoughts since Sunday about writing a letter to Becky Wallace?"

It took me a moment to reorient my brain. "Letter?"

"Right. Yo-Yo's suggestion that some of us go visit her at the prison."

"Uh . . ." My thoughts scrambled. I had put the whole idea out of my head the moment I walked out of Ruth's front door. "I thought you said we weren't going to make a decision about that yet—that we were going to pray about it."

"True. I was just wondering if you'd been praying about it and what God had been saying to you."

Whoa. Why was this all coming back on me? I decided to be honest. "Sorry, Avis. Haven't thought about it. Haven't prayed about it. What has God been saying to *you?*"

"Mmm. Not sure I have any wisdom about what's best, but in my prayer time, I was impressed that a couple of the sisters—Florida and Yo-Yo, at least—are willing to visit her. So the Holy Spirit seemed to say, 'If Becky Wallace is willing to have visitors, then God has opened a door.' We won't know unless we write, will we?"

"Um . . . okay, I'll think about it."

"Pray about it, Jodi."

"Right."

Denny poked his head around the door as I hung up. "Did she say how much?"

I must have looked at him blankly, because he waved the checkbook.

"Oh. She suggested sixty for hair and nails."

He considered. "I'm gonna add ten more. I'd rather err on the plus side at this point. Okay with you?"

I waved him away. *Whatever.* I didn't want to think about Adele . . . or Becky Wallace . . . or any of that mess right now. Didn't want to pray about it either. I just wanted to go to bed.

I WOKE UP THE NEXT MORNING before the alarm, fighting off a familiar anxiety dream: I was back in college, facing my final biology exam—but I hadn't been to class all semester! *Humph.* Wasn't hard to put my finger on the causes of my anxiety . . .

Adele.

Letter to Bandana Woman—or not.

And my parents were arriving tomorrow. For my birthday.

At least it wasn't the nightmare again. I pushed that thought up to "thankful" category and padded to the back door to let Willie Wonka out. I glanced at the kitchen clock—fifteen minutes before I normally got up on a school day. Good. I could—

You could pray, Jodi.

I sighed. *Right. Said I was going to pray for Adele and MaDear. And I practically promised Avis I'd pray about writing that letter to Bandana Woman. Guess I can pray about my parents' visit while I'm at it.*

I left Willie Wonka out in the backyard, realizing the sun hadn't even come up yet. Did I dare put on some music? Something quiet . . . meditative. I picked up the new Clint Brown CD Denny had picked up for me while I was laid up after surgery and scanned the back. There. The song, "You Are" was quiet and meditative.

I turned on the light long enough to stick the CD into the player, punched in the number of the selection, then flopped on the couch and soaked in the words.

You are . . . the hope that I cling to . . . You are my everything . . .

Willie Wonka barked at the back door, and the alarm was going off in our bedroom, but the words to the song kept me rooted to the couch.

. . . couldn't take one step without You . . . don't have the strength to make it on my own . . .

Didn't exactly get much praying done, but maybe this was like "pre-op"—necessary preparation for the kind of "surgical prayers" I needed to do. Surgery on my attitude, frankly.

I DON'T REMEMBER PRAYING ACTUAL PRAYERS that morning, but by the time I got home from school on Wednesday, I felt like God and I had been "doing business" on the side all day, and we'd struck a deal: why *not* write that letter to Bandana Woman? She wasn't likely to want any of us to visit her—how weird was that?—but if she did, wasn't God big enough to handle it?

Yet how in the world would I get a letter to her? Didn't I need her prison ID number or something?

Amanda came in the door in what passed for "straight home" from school, and for some strange reason, I told her what Yada Yada was thinking about doing and my problem about how to get a letter to a prisoner. To my surprise, her face perked up.

"Google it, Mom. They've got everything on the Web."

"What do you mean?"

Dumping her backpack on the floor, Amanda booted up the computer and then called up the Internet. She typed "Lincoln Correctional Center" into the Google search engine and began following the various prompts: "Visitation Rules" . . . "Inmate Search" . . .

"What's her last name, Mom?"

"Um . . . Wallace. Becky Wallace."

A list of Wallaces in the Illinois Department of Corrections came up, and there she was: name, prison ID, everything. *Sheesh. Hanging out on the Web for all the world to see. So much for privacy.* Amanda clicked on the name in the list, and a new page appeared.

Somebody named Becky Wallace stared back at us from the screen, a front and side view. All her vitals were listed—weight, height, race . . . I squinted at the tiny print: "Race: White." *Huh.* Guess I was wrong about *that.* Under sentencing information, it read: "Armed robbery. Sentence: ten years. Projected parole date: 2006."

Amanda let out a breath. "Wow. That's her? She looks different."

She did look different without the wraparound sunglasses and bandana. An actual face looked back at me—short dark hair, dark eyes—but it was the same woman, all right. Her mouth was hard, and I could almost hear the obscenities she'd spewed around our house that night, like a sewer that had backed up and overflowed.

I grabbed a notepad and wrote down her ID number and the address to send inmate mail. "Thanks, Amanda." I glanced at the clock. Denny and Josh would be home soon—better get supper going. It was Bible study night at Uptown, but I was going to make a case for staying home, since we had to get the house ready for my parents' arrival the next day. I'd write the letter later.

DENNY DISAPPEARED AFTER SUPPER, saying he had to run an errand. I washed towels and sheets so I'd be sure to have clean linens for my parents, hid the two bottles of wine—one half-empty—that we had sitting on top of the refrigerator, and gave Amanda and Josh a choice: run the vacuum, sweep the hallway and dining room, or clean the bathroom.

They chose vacuuming and sweeping, so I ended up scrubbing the tub. Rats.

Lathering hand cream on my water-wrinkled fingers after finishing the bathroom, I sat down at the computer and started drafting a letter to the woman who had robbed us—and immediately ran into problems. How did I address her? "Dear Ms. Wallace? Dear Becky?" One sounded too respectful for the likes of B. W., and the other sounded too friendly. So I finally settled on "Dear Becky Wallace."

No sooner had I stated the purpose of my letter and wrote the names of the two women who wanted to visit her than I realized we had another big problem. Neither Florida nor Yo-Yo had a car. How in the world were they supposed to get to Lincoln, which was at least two to three hours away by car?

The back screen door banged, and in a second or two I smelled Denny's aftershave and felt his lips on the back of my neck. "Whatcha doing?" He leaned over my shoulder. "What's this? A letter to *Becky Wallace?*" He pulled over a dining-room chair.

I told him what Yada Yada had talked about at Ruth's house— a little detail that had gotten lost in the revelation that Amanda had lied to us and gone to the Mexican parade with José—and how Avis suggested testing the waters to see if she would respond. "But if—big *if*—she says okay, how in the world would they get down there?"

Denny was quiet a long time. He leaned forward, elbows on his knees, chin resting on his clasped hands—like he did after the Rosh Hashanah service. Finally he leaned back. "I'll drive them."

"Really?" His offer surprised me. I had to be careful about Yada Yada making decisions that implicated him. He was already borderline resentful of our twice-monthly meetings, the extra phone calls, the church visits. "You don't have to make this your problem, Denny."

He snorted. "Becky Wallace robbed *my* house, frightened *my* family, terrorized *our* guests, and pointed her butcher knife at *me*. I'd say it's already my problem."

I swatted him on the shoulder. "You know what I mean."

The smile vanished. "If anybody's going to go, maybe it should be you and me, Jodi. After all, she did barge into our house, and I was the one who wrestled her to the floor. We've got a lot of feelings too. Maybe it would be good to face her. Maybe it would be good for her to face *us.*"

I rolled my eyes. "She's *not* going to put us on her visitors' list."

But in the end, I typed all four names into the letter: Florida Hickman . . . Yolanda Spencer . . . Denny and Jodi Baxter.

25

EEEEEEEEEEEEEEEEEEEE! I bolted upright in the bed. What was that? . . . The fire alarm! Throwing off the quilt, I vaulted out of bed as quickly as my morning-stiff leg would allow and grabbed for my robe in the dark. Just as I stuck my arm in the sleeve, the obnoxious racket stopped as abruptly as it had started, and two seconds later Denny poked his head into the bedroom door.

"Sorry. It backfired on me."

By this time I was totally awake and robed. "What backfired on you?" I followed him out into the hall, where a bleary-eyed, bald-headed Josh was standing in the doorway of his bedroom, looking totally confused. A plaintive wail rose from Amanda's bedroom: "Da-ad! Is there a fire? Or can I go back to sleep?"

"Sleep!" Denny called. "For fifteen more minutes!"

Josh sighed and disappeared behind his own door.

I stopped at the archway to the dining room where shadows

and glowing lights danced all over the walls. Whichever way I looked, candles in all shapes and sizes flickered warmly in the dining room . . . kitchen . . . living room . . . even the bathroom.

Denny stood in the middle of the dining room in his T-shirt and sweat shorts, holding the dismantled fire alarm. A sheep couldn't have looked more sheepish. "Uh, sorry, babe. I wanted to start off your birthday special—didn't know all these candles would set off the alarm."

I started to laugh. "Oh, this is *special*, all right. I'll never forget it—and I'm never going to let *you* forget it either!" I headed for the candlelit living room. "You can make it up to me by bringing me a *big* mug of coffee, because I am going to sit in the recliner and reign like a queen for at least fifteen minutes."

"Yeah, well," he called after me, "if you're going to be queen, you better check your royal robe—you've got it on inside out!"

BIRTHDAY OR NO BIRTHDAY, we all had to be at school at our regular time. With just minutes to catch the city bus to Lane Tech, Amanda was fishing in the desk drawer in the dining room. "Mom! Don't we have any more stamps? I need a stamp!"

I couldn't remember the last time Amanda actually wrote a letter. "I think so—somewhere in there. Do you need it now?"

"Yes, I need it *now!* . . . Never mind. I found one." Her tone by now was decidedly cranky, and she slammed the front door behind her.

Who was Amanda writing to? We'd said no phone calls; we didn't think about letters. Couldn't be any of her friends at school—she saw them during the day.

I sighed. *Probably José.*

I tried not to let Amanda's surly mood and my parents' impending arrival distract me from my lesson plans for that day, but I wished I felt better prepared emotionally. How would Dad react to Josh's light-bulb head? Mom would silently disapprove, but Dad would definitely say something. *I should have warned them,* I scolded myself, as I set up a balance scale for today's lesson on "Find the missing addend." *Given them some time to get used to the idea.* After all, it had taken me awhile to get used to it—no, take that back. I *wasn't* used to it, didn't like it, and would be very glad when he let it grow back in again. Or at least shaved off that orange topknot!

My students had fun with the balance scale. I wrote "2 + ? = 5" on the chalkboard and let "helpers" place two counters on one side of the scale and five on the other. I explained that they had to place the correct number of missing counters on the "addend" side of the scale in order to make it balance with the "sum."

Kaya carefully added one at a time to the two already on the scale—one . . . two . . . three—and beamed happily as the scale balanced with the sum of five. I wrote a second problem on the board: "5 + ? = 7." Cornell dumped a whole handful of counters on the addend side and took some off one by one till it balanced with the other side—but then he didn't know how many he had "added." Well, try again. "Who'd like to be next?"

Hakim's hand shot up. "Me! Let me do it, Miz B."

I was so surprised, I ignored his calling me 'Miz B.' Hakim's math papers so far had been pathetic. Trying to act matter-of-fact, I wrote another problem on the board: "3 + ? = 10," and put the known number of counters on both sides of the scale. Frowning, Hakim studied the scales a moment, then picked up seven counters and piled them next to the three already on the scale. When the scale balanced with the ten, a wide smile broke his face.

"Hakim, how did you know how many counters to put on the scale?"

He looked at me scornfully. "See those three there? An' ten there? Just counted backwards three times—ten, nine, eight. Seven to go. Didn't you know that?"

Christy and I both rewarded him with big grins. "I did indeed, Hakim. But you are smart to figure out that you have to *subtract* to find the missing addend. Why don't you show the rest of the class how it's done?" I put two more problems on the board then wrote them again as subtraction problems to get the same answer after Hakim figured out the missing addends in his head and balanced the scale both times. Now more hands shot up wanting to find the missing addend "in my head."

I was so elated by Hakim's participation and success that I was still grinning inside when the dismissal bell rang. Gathering up my stuff quickly, I determined to get home before my parents arrived who-knew-when. But as I made a beeline for the front doors of the school, the school secretary stepped into the hall and waved me down. "Ms. Baxter? Ms. Johnson wants to see you for a minute."

The yada yada Prayer Group Gets Down

For a second I felt like a kid being called to the principal's office. What had I done now? *Don't be stupid, Jodi. This is Avis, remember?*

As I peeked into her inner office, Avis Johnson was on the phone, but she waved me in, motioning for me to shut the door. Shut the door? Maybe it was something serious.

Avis hung up the phone and smiled. "Hi, Jodi. How was your day?"

I relaxed. Couldn't be too serious if we were doing first names. "Good. Real good." *Should I tell her about Hakim's little break-through?* I decided not—at least until I found out what this meeting was about.

"Wonderful." Avis opened one of her desk drawers, pulled out a glittery gold gift bag with tissue paper and an envelope sticking out of the top, and handed it to me with a smile. "Happy birthday."

"Oh, Avis!" I was so startled I just stood there like a carved duck. "You didn't need to—"

"Jodi." Avis leveled her eyes at me. "Just take it. And enjoy!"

I dropped my tote bags on the floor. "Thanks, Avis. Can I open it now?" This was too much—a birthday gift from my principal! I opened the card first. A Mahogany card about "A friend who is like a sister to me . . ." I could hardly speak. I took out a small square box from the bag and opened it: a scented candle. Green apple.

That made me laugh. "Oh, Avis, if you only knew! I gotta tell you how my day started this morning!"

BEFORE I LEFT THE SCHOOL OFFICE, I remembered to ask Avis if she got the copy of the "Becky Wallace letter" I'd sent to her by e-mail attachment last night. I'd also sent copies to Ruth (for Yo-Yo) and Florida. "Any feedback?"

She arched an eyebrow. "I noticed you added yours and Denny's names to the visitors' list. That's good. I stand in agreement with you. Now . . . we pray."

Well, yes, I thought a few minutes later, walking fast to make up for lost time. *But am I praying that B. W. will* or *won't put us on her visitors' list?* After one block at a good clip, I realized I better slow down to a steady pace so I'd make it still in one piece. Didn't want to have a relapse the minute my parents walked in.

A familiar light-blue Buick sedan was double-parked in front of our house, the trunk lid up. *Help! How long had they been waiting?* "Mom! Dad! Here I am!" I hustled the last half-block as my father, still wearing the old tweedy English driving cap he'd had for years, threaded his way between two parked cars and set suitcases on the sidewalk.

Sidney Jennings was not a large man—maybe five-ten, thin, almost wiry, a testament to his farm heritage. He straightened, a wide smile creasing his face as I dropped my tote bags on the walk by the suitcases.

"Here's the birthday girl!" My father held his arms wide and enveloped me in a bear hug. Old Spice aftershave tickled my nose. "How's that for timing?" he said, letting me go. "We just drove up. Couldn't find a parking place, though. Clara? Clara! Come on, get out of the car. Jodi's here now."

The y a d a y a d a Prayer Group Gets Down

I hustled up the porch steps to unlock the front door as my dad helped my mother out of the car. My left leg and abdomen were aching from my effort to get home quickly, but their backs were turned so they probably didn't notice as I pulled myself up the steps by the railing. By the time I got the door open and had dumped my bags on the floor of the entryway, my mom—hair graying, no makeup, but cheeks pink and eyes twinkling—was coming in the door. *Oh Jesus, I am glad to see her,* I thought, giving her a big squeeze. I looked over her shoulder and yelled, "Dad! Drive around to the alley. I'll open the garage so you can park there!"

By the time I got my parents and their bags settled in our bedroom—no way would it work to put them on the foldout in the living room since they usually went to bed at nine—Amanda had come in from school, forgetting her poor-me pout long enough to give her grandparents a big squeal of welcome. Both kids had had to downsize to small bedrooms and single beds when we moved from Downers Grove, but at least they didn't have to give up their rooms now when the grandparents came. That fell to Denny and me—a fact that Denny grumbled about last night, but he finally agreed it was the only thing we could do under the circumstances.

Amanda gave my parents a quick tour of our first-floor apartment in the two-flat, including a peek at our postage-stamp backyard and a trip to the basement, while I filled the teakettle and hunted for cookies. I could hear their voices in Amanda's room. "Painted it myself," Amanda bragged.

Oh, right. With a little help. I finally found the package of lemon crèmes, my dad's favorites.

"That yellow paint sure brightens up this small room." My mom's voice had that find-something-nice-to-comment-on quality that irritated me, because it barely masked a veiled comment. *Small room.*

The tour over, they came back to the dining room. "Now don't go fixing your own birthday supper," my dad chided as I poured hot tea and passed the plate of cookies. "We're taking you out." He chucked Amanda under the chin. "Oh, all right; I guess we'll take you, too, princess."

My father may be the only person alive who could treat Amanda like a little girl and get away with it. But going out was fine with me. I'd be thrilled not to cook my own birthday supper.

I knew Josh had a soccer game and wouldn't drag in till close to seven. As we chatted over our tea at the dining-room table, my mother suddenly peered at me closely as if she had x-ray vision. "Are you all right, Jodi? After the accident, I mean."

"Of course she's all right!" My dad waved a lemon crème in my direction. "She looks great!"

Thanks, Dad. I really can talk for myself.

He leaned toward me and talked behind his hand, pretending my mom couldn't hear. "Your mother simply can't forgive herself for not being here for you, Jodi. I told her you'd mend better without us."

What did he mean? Because Mom had been sick herself? Or did he suspect I hadn't wanted them around? "Oh, Mom. I know you wanted to come, but you just couldn't." *Much to my relief at the time,* but I didn't say it. "Please don't worry about it. In fact, I could ask you the same thing: how are *you* doing since that terrible bronchitis?"

My dad butted in with a rundown of my mother's illness that had kept them in Des Moines last June. I only half-listened, annoyed at his habit of answering for others. I was concerned about my mom. She looked . . . older. More frail than I remembered. What was she: seventy-one? seventy-two? Not very old. It occurred to me that my parents would not be around forever.

I suddenly felt incredibly selfish. We needed to make sure we saw them more regularly. Des Moines wasn't *that* far. Maybe we could go visit them for Thanksgiving or during the Christmas break.

I glanced at the clock: 6:45. Denny and Josh ought to straggle in any minute. Amanda was in the middle of telling her grandparents about the Uptown youth group's mission trip to Mexico, when I saw my mom glance at something behind me, eyes widening; her hand went to her mouth. I turned to see Josh in the kitchen doorway, school backpack slung over one shoulder, his sport bag over the other.

Rats. I totally forgot to warn my parents about Josh's bald head.

26

Frankly, I told Denny later, it went better than I expected. "Hi, Gramps!" Josh had said with a wave. "Hi, Gram."

He went to his grandmother and gave her an awkward hug from his six-feet-on-the-hoof down to her five-four perched on one of the dining-room chairs.

"Your . . . head!" my mother said, blinking rapidly. Couldn't blame her; I'd had exactly the same reaction.

"Oh, that." Josh casually ran his hand over his smooth dome. "Just trying to imitate Gramps here." He leaned over and patted my dad's rapidly receding hairline.

My dad frowned, eyeing the orange tuft on the back of Josh's head. "At least the hair I've got is a natural color," he growled.

"Hey. Had to be sure people could tell us apart." Josh grinned.

Oh, Josh, you're good, I thought.

My son looked around at the tea things and lack of supper activity in the kitchen. "Isn't it Mom's birthday tonight? What's happening?"

At least he remembered. I told him Gramps was taking us out and we better get ready so we could leave when Dad got home with the minivan. With only one bathroom, it took a bit of shuffling for everybody to "use the facilities," as my mother insisted on calling it, but we were more or less ready when Denny came in the front door. "There's a monster in the garage with Iowa plates!" he said in mock horror. "Flee! Flee!"

"Oh, Daddy." Amanda rolled her eyes. My father guffawed. He liked Denny's sense of humor, even if he was slightly suspicious of his son-in-law's New York, mainline-church upbringing. I caught my husband's eye as he hugged my parents, hoping he could read my mind: *Garage okay?* We hadn't talked about it, but I didn't want to risk parking my parents' car out on the street, even if it had been bought several years ago—"in the last century," Josh liked to point out.

Denny went back out to retrieve the Dodge Caravan, which he'd had to park in the next block, and we all piled in for the short trip to Bakers Square, Rogers Park's best bet for decent Americana food, really good pie, and a tab that would be easy on my dad's wallet. Over thick burgers dripping with avocado, bacon, and sprouts (Josh, Amanda, and me), honey-mustard chicken with rice pilaf (Denny and Dad), and a grilled chicken salad (Mom), our conversation bounced from the Chicago Bears' poor start— *again*—to Hakim popping out of his shell long enough to show the third-grade class how to "subtract in your head," to Josh's soccer game tomorrow night. "Wanna come, Gramps?"

My dad seemed pleased. He turned to Amanda. "What about

you, princess? You want to keep Gramps company at your brother's game?"

Uh-oh. We hadn't talked about how to handle Amanda's grounding while her grandparents were visiting. "Sure!" Amanda smiled sweetly at her grandfather, ignoring the warning look I sent her. I kicked Denny under the corner booth that accommodated the six of us, but he just gave a short nod that meant, *"Later."*

We were all too full to eat dessert right away, so we bought a triple-berry pie to take home. As we climbed into the minivan, I noticed that my dad had cornered Josh out of earshot in the parking lot. *Hmm. What's that about?*

Back home, Denny made decaf coffee and warmed up the pie while I opened presents: large wind chimes from my parents that looked like organ pipes, a pair of silver drop earrings from Josh and Amanda, and a slinky black dress from Denny.

"Try it on, Mom," Josh urged. Denny just grinned.

I hustled into the bedroom and slid on the dress. *Mmm, yummy.* I gave a quick brush through my hair, which was back to its old basic style, stuck my bare feet into a pair of low heels— I could stand it for a minute—and sashayed out into the dining room.

Denny whistled. My dad clapped. Mom smiled sweetly. Who knew what she *really* thought? But I didn't care. Even the kids nodded approval. "Next time we go somewhere fancy," Denny said, "you won't have to borrow a dress."

"So there's going to be a next time?" I fluttered my eyelashes shamelessly.

"Well, yeah. Our fiftieth anniversary is coming up in another thirty years."

My father thought that was knee-slapping funny. Then he stood up abruptly. "Well, it's off to bed for us. Happy birthday, sweetheart." He gave me a peck on the cheek. "Come along, Clara."

My mother obediently got up and trailed Dad toward our bedroom. I dashed ahead of them to grab the clothes I'd just taken off and a few other necessities we'd forgotten. The door shut behind me.

Well, one day down; three to go.

I made up the foldout in the living room while Denny cleaned the dessert dishes. On my way to the bathroom, I knocked quietly on Josh's bedroom door. "Yeah?" came the muffled reply. I poked my head in. Josh was sprawled on his bed doing homework, earphones to his CD player cradling his ears.

I shut the door behind me. "Just curious. What were you and Grandpa talking about in the parking lot at Bakers Square—or dare I ask?"

Josh slid off the earphones. "He wanted to know why I left the little tuft of hair when I shaved my head. Said it made me look like somebody into Eastern religion."

Humph. I'd wanted to say that very thing to Josh myself.

"Told him I *wasn't* into Eastern religion, and Jesus said people shouldn't judge other people based on how they look, and that oughta include hair."

Okay. Josh had a good point. Brave of him to challenge my dad. "What'd he say to that?"

"He agreed, sorta, but he said how people dress is often a statement of who they identify with. Asked me to think about it."

"What'd you say?"

Josh shrugged again. "Said I'd think about it." He put the earphones on again. Conversation over.

ON FRIDAY, my parents decided to visit the Museum of Science and Industry since the rest of us would be at school all day. If they got back by three o'clock, I hinted, they could stop at Bethune Elementary to see my classroom. "You'll miss rush-hour traffic that way," I added.

Sure enough, I saw my dad peeking in the window of my classroom door just as the dismissal bell rang. Hoping they wouldn't get run down by the herd of eight-year-olds stampeding for their hard-earned weekend, I called them in, introduced them to my student teacher, and showed them around the now-empty classroom.

My dad stopped by the stove-size, foil-covered box I used as a lost-and-found. "What's a 'Darn Lucky Box'?" I explained that if kids left their things lying around, into the box they went, and the kids were "darn lucky" to get them back—*if* they paid a twenty-five-cents fine.

My mother frowned. "But did you have to say 'darn'?"

I decided to let that one go and hustled them out of the classroom. "Someone I want you to meet." I hoped Avis was still in her office.

She was. I ushered my parents in and closed the door. "Ms. Johnson, these are my parents, Sid and Clara Jennings. Mom and Dad, this is the principal of our school—Avis Johnson."

Avis, as usual, made a good first impression: professional and attractive. She shook my parents' hands warmly. "Jodi is a great addition to our staff," she said graciously. My parents beamed.

"Avis is also the worship leader at our church, and we're in the same prayer group."

My parents hardly knew what to say to that. I'm sure it wasn't what they expected of a public-school principal. Or maybe they were surprised that an African-American was the worship leader at their daughter's church. Or was it that she was a *woman* leading worship? I couldn't tell.

My dad recovered first. "Well. I am so glad to see that God is still allowed in the public school. Praise the Lord!"

Yikes. Had my dad's voice carried to the outer office?

A smile tickled the corners of Avis's mouth. "Praise the Lord, indeed," she said, lowering her voice to a conspiratorial whisper. "Though we aren't supposed to shout about it in a public school."

"Nice lady," my dad commented as we walked toward their Buick in the school parking lot. At least I got a ride home.

Amanda was grumpy that she had to come all the way home from school if we were just going back to watch the Lane Tech soccer team play Wheaton North at five o'clock. Pulling her out of earshot of my parents, I told her she was welcome to stay home with her grandmother, who was tired out from walking around the museum and electing to stay home and rest. Or she could quit grumbling and count her blessings that we were letting her out of the house to go to Josh's game. She heaved a persecuted sigh and followed my father and me to the garage.

Once at the game, however, she forgot she was sulking and yelled, screamed, jumped up and down, and otherwise cheered the Lane Tech Indians, even though they trailed behind all the way and lost to Wheaton North's Falcons. She also managed to talk to a lot of school friends who came by, I noticed. *Oh well.* At least she stayed in our general vicinity.

After the game, Josh clomped over to us in his soccer cleats and muddy green-and-gold uniform. "You *don't* want to hug me!" he warned, but he seemed pleased that the three of us had come to the game in spite of the loss. By the time we waited around for Josh to change, I knew supper was going to be very late. At least I'd remembered to bring the cell.

I got Denny on the third ring. "Just got home myself," he said. "Don't worry about it, Jodi. I'll order a couple of pizzas."

After polishing off two medium pan pizzas from Gulliver's, we played table games—well, not Josh. He excused himself to go play pool at a friend's house. Amanda went head to head with her grandmother for the highest Scrabble score. My mom won by two points—a feat that put pink splotches of pleasure into her cheeks.

Later, after my parents had gone to bed, Denny and I lay on the foldout watching the news. "Kinda nice that Amanda's grounded," I murmured during a commercial. "She's hanging around her grandparents more than she would normally."

"Shh. I wanna hear this." Denny turned up the volume as the news came back on.

I pulled the blanket over my head. Two days down; two to go.

Even though it was Saturday morning and I could sleep a little longer, I woke up at the usual time. *Ah, a few moments to myself.* I let Willie Wonka out into the backyard, started a pot of coffee, and booted up the computer. Hadn't checked e-mail for a couple of days. Hadn't thought much about the Becky Wallace letter either. Still time to chicken out.

But there were e-mails from both Florida and Ruth with "Re: Letter to Becky Wallace" in the subject lines.

"You write a good letter, girl!" wrote Florida. "See? I knew you were the one. Glad you and Denny deciding to come too."

Ruth's was even shorter. "Yo-Yo says fine. Send it."

Then I saw one from Nony, dated late last night. I clicked it open.

To: Yada Yada
From: BlessedRU@online.net
Subject: Urgent prayer

Dear sisters,
I just got word from my brother in Pietermaritzburg, SA. My mother had a stroke. My brother says not to

come; she will recover most faculties in time. But it is terribly difficult to be so far away from my family at such a time. I want to take the boys to see their grandmother while she still knows who they are. Mark does not think I should take them out of school. Please pray that we will have wisdom—and agree on what to do.

Love, Nony

Oh wow, that's tough. I clicked on Reply and sent back a quick message: "Praying for you big-time." *Huh. Easy to say, Jodi. Better do it.*

By the time I printed out the Becky Wallace letter, hunted up an envelope and a stamp, and spent some time praying for Nony and her family, I could hear Denny folding up the couch in the living room and my father's footsteps shuffling toward the bathroom. Better start breakfast. It wasn't too warm for oatmeal, was it?

"Ah! My favorite breakfast!" my father said, coming into the kitchen ten minutes later. "What's on the docket today, princess?"

Grr. When was my dad going to figure out I wasn't his "little princess" anymore? But I put on a smile. *"Somebody's* got to hang that monster mobile you gave me for my birthday."

"Watch out!" He rubbed his hands together gleefully. "Once I get my hands on a hammer and nails, no telling what's going to get nailed down."

Amanda wandered into the dining room as the four of us— Denny and me, Mom and Dad—were starting in on our oatmeal. "Got enough for me?" She plopped down in an empty chair.

My mother leaned over and patted me on the hand. "Glad to see that the kids eat a good breakfast, at least."

It was all I could do to keep from yelling. *Okay, Mom. So they've had burgers and pizza the last two nights. It hasn't exactly been a normal two days. Sheesh.*

I started to pull my hand away, but my mother suddenly held on, staring at it. Then she looked up at me accusingly. "Where is your wedding ring, Jodi?"

27

My wedding ring! I mentally raced through possibilities. *"It's getting cleaned"* . . . *"It got too tight"* . . . "What? Didn't Mom tell you?" Amanda piled brown sugar and raisins on her oatmeal. "Her ring got stolen when that crazy robber—"

"Stolen!" Both my mom and dad yelped like Willie Wonka with his tail caught in a door.

"Wait! Wait! Calm down." I waved them back into their chairs. "I'm getting it back. In fact, I'm picking it up today."

"Picking it up?" my mother croaked. "Where?"

"Uh, the police station. It's not far."

"You mean to say," my father said slowly, "they caught the burglar, and he still had your ring? How . . . ?"

"Wasn't like that," Amanda piped up. *"Dad* caught the—"

"Amanda!" Denny's gruff voice stopped her midsentence. "We'll do the telling." He turned to my parents. "The thief was caught in the process. We called the police, the thief pled guilty and is now in prison, and they said we can pick up our jewelry." He shrugged. "That's pretty much it."

Amanda rolled her eyes. "'Scuse *me.*" She headed for the bathroom, locking the door behind her.

"She gets a little dramatic." I put on a lame smile.

My father was still frowning. "Why didn't you tell us?"

"I'm sorry, Dad. We didn't want you to worry." That was certainly the truth. "The thief was caught right away, and I'm getting my ring back—it didn't seem necessary."

The four of us sat in awkward silence for a long half-minute. I didn't think I was fooling my father; he still looked troubled. But my mother patted my hand again. "Well. At least it's not, you know, you and Denny—"

I jerked my hand away. *"Mom!* Is that what you thought? That Denny and I are having marital problems, and I took off my *ring?"* I must have looked so horrified that Denny started to laugh. My mother smiled tentatively; even my father chuckled. I gave up and laughed too.

MY FATHER hung the wind chimes on the back porch, practically giving *me* a heart attack as he climbed up on a rickety stepladder from the garage. Asking him to do this was a bad idea, but he whistled as he worked, came down the ladder in one piece, and gazed proudly at the result. A small breeze cooperated by moving the chimes, which gave off a melodic *ding-a-ling-dong.*

Nice in the daytime, I thought. Not sure how I was going to feel about those chimes on a windy night with my bedroom window mere feet away.

We needed groceries, and I'd planned to sneak in a trip to the police station to pick up my ring while I was out. Now that my stolen wedding ring was common knowledge, I asked my parents if they wanted to run errands with me "and see the neighborhood."

"Oh, you go on." My mother settled in the recliner with her bag of knitting. "I had enough walking yesterday."

My dad, though, pulled on his windbreaker and tweedy driving cap, ready to go. We took my folks' sedan so Denny could have our minivan. A group of suburban volunteers were coming to Uptown today for orientation to the church's outreach ministry, and Denny was going to give them a tour of the Rogers Park area.

Dad and I hit the new Dominick's on Howard first, and he patiently wheeled my cart up and down the aisles. Then we pulled into the Rogers Park Fruit Market on Clark Street, where ten bucks went a long way. As usual, the Greek owner was omnipresent, greeting customers by name, helping to bag groceries, talking to delivery drivers. "Hey, Nick!" a dark-haired man yelled in the owner's direction. "You got any African yams?"

As we pulled out of our parking space ten minutes later, I told Dad to go around the block and get back on Clark. "I think I can find the police station—it's on Clark Street, not too far from here." I wasn't sure how far, but I remembered the modern two-story brick building, looking out of place on this long strip of storefronts, laundries, and ethnic eateries. Sure enough, a couple of blocks south of Pratt I saw the dusky brown bricks spelling out the word POLICE in a huge half-moon, standing out in stark relief along the front side.

Dad drove around to the parking lot in the back. As we got out of the Buick, I saw a policeman assisting a teenage girl—jeans, sweatshirt, athletic shoes, long brown hair—into the back seat of a squad car. *Giving her a lift home or something?* Then I noticed that the girl's hands were handcuffed in front of her. My heart felt like it lurched upward into my throat. *Oh God. She's just a kid!*

My knees suddenly felt rubbery. I didn't want to go inside. I'd had more involvement with the police in the past few months— interrogating José Enriques in the hospital after he got caught in gang crossfire, getting charged with reckless homicide after the terrible car accident that killed Jamal Wilkins, and having my house full of police and evidence technicians after the robbery— than I'd had in my entire life. None of which I'd told my parents about.

Trust your parents more, Jodi.

"Jodi? You all right?"

I didn't realize I'd stopped right in the middle of the parking lot till my dad spoke. "Uh, sure, Dad."

The police station bent like an L around a small plaza on the corner of Clark Street and Schreiber, which boasted a couple of benches and a modern sculpture of who-knows-what rusty beams. We headed for the revolving door set into a long bank of floor-to-ceiling windows, hesitating long enough for the person pushing through from the inside to come out before we made our move.

As the woman exited, charging out in a steamy huff, my eyes

bugged. Close-cropped reddish 'fro, chunky gold earrings, substantial bulk inside her long coat—

"Adele!"

Adele Skuggs stopped short and looked at me, then at my father, then back at me as if she needed to process who I was. "Jodi."

"Uh, Dad, this is Adele Skuggs—another woman in my prayer group." *Or was.* I blundered on. "Adele, this is my father, Sid Jennings."

Adele gave a distracted nod in my father's direction. "If you're here to pick up your jewelry, don't bother. Man told me I had to go down to Twenty-Sixth and California to pick it up. Like I got *time.*"

"What? The man I talked to—"

Adele snorted. "Maybe so. But just now, the man's telling me I gotta take off from work, go all the way down to the south side, just to get my own property back. Humph." She started to leave.

"Adele, wait! I'm *sure* the officer on the phone told me we could pick up our stolen property here. Let me see what I can find out." I headed into the revolving door, not even waiting to see if my dad was following.

Two white officers sat behind the long desk that cut kitty-corner across the airy foyer. Signs that said, "Do not enter beyond this point" stood at either end of the long slab, prohibiting access to the rest of the building without authorization. One officer was talking to a young couple filing an accident report. The other one looked up. "You being helped?"

"Not yet." I stepped up to the counter, gave my name, and stated my business. I was aware that my father had come in and was standing beside me.

The man nodded sympathetically. "I'm sorry, ma'am. You'll have to pick up your stolen property at Twenty-Sixth and California. That's where they keep evidence till after a trial—"

"I know." Stubbornness gave me courage to plunge ahead. "But there was no trial. The perpetrator pled guilty and was sentenced inside of two weeks. I was told the stolen property hadn't left this station, and we could pick it up here."

The officer frowned. "Do you have the case number?"

I dug in my purse and pulled out a scrap of paper. "Here."

The man scribbled the case number on a piece of paper and left the room. I turned to see if Adele was still waiting and realized she had come back into the station and was standing a few feet away, watching. I gave her what I hoped was an encouraging smile.

A month ago, I probably would have gone over to chat with Adele while we waited. Though after what she said when I called earlier this week, I didn't think she felt like "chatting" with me. I kept my eyes forward and waited for the officer to return.

The man eventually came back with a metal box. "You are?"

"Jodi Baxter."

"ID?"

I dug out my wallet.

The officer consulted a list, opened the box, and handed me a stiff plastic Ziploc bag. "Here you go."

I smiled. My wedding ring. Safe and sound.

Then I remembered Adele. "Sir? My . . . friend had her property stolen at the same time." I motioned to Adele. "Adele Skuggs. She's on that list."

"ID?"

Wordlessly, Adele handed over her driver's license, her eyes smoldering.

The man fished through the plastic bags in the box and handed one to Adele. "Will you both sign this release that you have picked up your property?" He handed a form to each of us.

Adele scrawled her name with one of the cheap pens lying on the desk and threw it back down. Then she jabbed a forefinger at the officer behind the desk. "You wouldn't listen to *me*, would you? How come I couldn't get my property till these white folks show up? Huh?"

Adele did not wait for an answer. She whirled around and made for the revolving door, pausing only long enough to nod at my father and say, "Nice to meet you, Mr. Jennings." And then she was gone.

I was so startled I barely remember walking back to our parked car. Once inside, however, my father did not turn on the ignition. Instead he looked at me. "Jodi? I think there's a lot more to this than you've let on. What's going on?"

The voice in the back of my head nudged me again. *Trust your parents more, Jodi.* I hesitated. Where in the world would I begin? It was all so . . . so complicated, with the Yada Yada Prayer Group getting robbed at my house, including Adele, and how frightening it was, and feeling so violated. But even before that, the day at the beauty shop when MaDear accused Denny—on top of all the trauma surrounding the accident that had killed Jamal Wilkins, the haunting nightmare that still plagued my sleep . . .

I took a deep breath and opened my mouth, but instead of words, an involuntary sob escaped from my throat. And then tears. Suddenly I was sobbing in my father's arms. Weeks of pain and loss, fear and frustration, guilt and remorse came spewing out like the discharge hose of my washing machine, spraying water everywhere through the wire mesh lint trap left too long, full of crud.

28

I watched my parents' Buick head up our one-way street, hoping they'd find their way out of the city without any traffic tie-ups. Never could tell, even on a Sunday. They'd decided to leave right after church, not even taking time for lunch, so they could get to Des Moines before dark. "Call us when you get home. Promise?" I'd said, sounding—good grief!—just like my mother.

Denny and the kids headed back inside, but I stood out on the sidewalk until their car disappeared. *This is good. We have the rest of the day for some downtime, to get ready for next week.* I lingered on the porch steps. All in all, it had been a good visit. I was glad they had come. I'd wondered how they'd react to worship at Uptown Community, which was pretty tame compared to the churches I'd visited with Yada Yada but probably still a stretch for my parents, who'd been in the same church, singing the same hymns, accompanied by the same upright piano for the past forty years.

My dad seemed to hit it off with Pastor Clark—they were about the same age—and my mom kept making a fuss over Florida's kids. Too much fuss, if you asked me. Like she was trying too hard. "I just love how they do little black girls' hair, don't you, Jodi?" she'd said while I mentally willed the ground to open and swallow me. Or her. Momentarily, anyway.

But lots of Uptown people greeted them after the service, giving me a chance to grab Florida for half a minute. "Flo! How's Carla doing?"

Florida shrugged. "We hangin'. She visited her foster parents yesterday—part of the deal set up by DCFS. When they brought her back—oh, Lord. What a scene! Was afraid the neighbors would think we were beatin' the life outta her, she screamed so." She pressed her lips into a tight line. "Just keep prayin' for us. We gonna make it, though."

Now I sank down on the front porch steps, remembering my own crying jag in my dad's car outside the police station yesterday. To my surprise, he had pretty much just listened as I dumped everything into his lap. "Guess you can tell Mom too," I'd snuffled, finally blowing my nose, knowing my face was probably red and blotchy. I knew I couldn't do it again. As it was, I felt like I'd just turned my insides out inside that car.

I'd expected my dad to give me some fatherly advice or tell me we'd bitten off more than we could chew by moving into Chicago, but to my surprise he said no more about our "talk" till they were ready to leave. Mom was already in the car when he pulled me aside. *Uh-oh*, I thought. *Here it comes.*

"Jodi, your mom and I worry about you—and what you told me yesterday tells me we have good reason to worry! But this morning I was reading in Philippians." He pulled out his little pocket New Testament, which had print so tiny I was surprised he could still read it. "Chapter four, verse six. 'Be anxious for nothing, but in everything by prayer and supplication, with thanksgiving, let your requests be made known to God . . .'"

My father stopped midsentence, and he got a funny look on his face. I was familiar with these verses and could probably have finished quoting them myself, but I waited. And when he started reading again, his voice was husky. ". . . and the peace of God, which surpasses all understanding, will guard your hearts and minds through Christ Jesus.'" He stuck the Testament back in his pocket and pulled on his driving cap. The funny look had settled into a rueful grin. "Hmm. I was reading that for your benefit, but maybe that verse is supposed to be for your mother and me."

And then they were gone.

I got up from the front steps and made my way back into the house. Josh was sitting on a stool in the kitchen, and Denny was in the process of shaving off the little lock of orange hair with the hair clippers.

"Josh!" I couldn't believe this. "Why didn't you cut it off while your grandparents were still here? They'd have been delighted!"

My son just gave me a knowing smile beneath the purr of the clippers.

Kids. Honestly!

JOSH, NOW LOOKING LIKE A HIP-HOP Mr. Clean instead of a light bulb, drove Amanda to youth group—hallelujah! The caged animal was out of the house, so Denny and I took a walk to the Heartland Café, where I finally got a chance to tell him what happened when we ran into Adele at the police station. Denny shook his head. "Didn't she even say thank you for helping her out?"

"No. I think she was too upset about getting the runaround until we 'white folks' showed up."

"Man." He threw up his hands. "Can't win with Adele. Damned if we do; damned if we don't."

"Maybe." I shrugged. After getting all the frustration off my chest with that good cry in my dad's car, it was easier to see what happened from Adele's point of view. If I'd been in her shoes, it would've been embarrassing for me too. Like getting treated like a child. Not worth the bother for them to go check.

And as I headed for Bethune Elementary the next day, I determined not to let all the unfinished business with Adele get me down. After all, we'd survived one week of Amanda's grounding; only one week to go. (Frankly, I wasn't sure who got punished more by a grounding—the kid or the parents who had to put up with her! Still, I was pretty sure Amanda would think twice before lying to us again.) After Hakim's unexpected participation last week, I felt hopeful as I walked into my third-grade classroom. Maybe we had turned a corner with one kid, at least.

My high hopes were short-lived. I gave the same math problems we'd done with the balance scale on a quiz, and Hakim missed every one. What was *that* about? And twice that week I had to break up schoolyard fights between Hakim and D'Angelo. Neither boy would tell me what the first fight was about, but when it happened again, Britny tattled that D'Angelo had been bragging, saying *his* big brother could lick anybody else's brother.

That's a twist, I thought wryly. *Didn't it used to be, "My dad can lick your dad"?*

Yet we had to nip this little rivalry in the bud. I told both boys that if it happened again—and I didn't care who started it—they'd both get sent to the principal's office and face suspension. Fighting would not be tolerated in this school. We had parent open house coming up on Friday evening. It would be good to meet Hakim's parents, maybe get some clues how best to get through to him.

Josh's birthday snuck up on me again—ours were just a week apart. Eighteen! "Be nice to me," he said at breakfast that Thursday, reaching for the milk to pour on his heaping bowl of corn flakes. "I'm old enough to drop out of school and join the military."

I snatched the milk out of his reach. "Josh! That's not funny." Since 9-11, more and more U.S. soldiers were getting deployed to the Middle East, and now it looked like we were headed for another war with Iraq. This was no time to drop out of high school. *"Promise* me."

"Okay."

I handed him the milk.

"How about dropping my curfew instead?"

"Nice try," Denny said. "When you've got a diploma."

Josh *was* pleased by the extra set of car keys Denny gave him when he opened his gifts after supper. "Hey, could I drive the car to Great America on Saturday, take a couple of friends? Maybe Yo-Yo's brother would like to go too."

It happened every fall. Chicagoland's huge amusement park beckoned on weekends, one last day of thrills before shutting down for the winter. I checked the calendar. *Jodi PT 10 a.m.* it said. "I've got physical therapy at ten, but I oughta be back by eleven or so. My last appointment. Yea!"

"So you wanna come with us, do a few roller coasters?" Josh knew he was safe with *that* invitation.

"Oh, right. I'd have to start physical therapy all over again. You go. Have fun. Happy birthday."

"Everybody's having fun except *meee!*" Amanda wailed.

Josh knuckled the top of Amanda's head. "Wasn't going to take you even if you *weren't* grounded, shrimp."

THE PARENT OPEN HOUSE on Friday evening was a bit nerve-wracking—like getting inspected by the Big Brass at army basic training. We left the Welcome Bulletin Board up so that parents could enjoy the meaning of their kids' names and gave a demonstration of the balance-scale activity. That's when I realized neither Hakim nor his parents had shown up. Disappointment mingled with my irritation.

Figured.

When I got back from my doctor's appointment on Saturday,

clutching a list of exercises I was supposed to do and one bag of groceries I'd picked up at the fruit market, Josh was waiting impatiently for me. I started to hand him my keys, but with a gleeful grin he dangled his own set in my face and took off in the Dodge Caravan to pick up Pete Spencer and two other friends. I vaguely wondered how Pete could afford the pricey one-day pass but figured Josh—or Denny—was handling it.

I brought in the mail, sat down with a sandwich, and rifled through today's offerings: vitamin catalog, two pizza ads, coupon booklet, gas bill, and a long envelope addressed in unfamiliar handwriting. Pencil. I squinted at the return address—and nearly dropped the envelope.

Becky Wallace, LCC, Lincoln, Illinois.

I hardly knew what to think. Avis had encouraged us to "test the waters" by going ahead with the letter, and we'd know what God wanted us to do if Bandana Woman wrote back. Now that her letter was staring at us in the face . . . well, Yada Yada was meeting at Avis's apartment Sunday night, and we could decide what to do then.

JOSH DROPPED ME OFF at Avis's apartment on Pratt Avenue— good thing; it didn't look like there were any empty parking spaces in the whole block—then he and Amanda went on to youth group at Uptown. I was supposed to hitch a ride home with somebody.

By the time five-thirty rolled around, Avis had a full apartment.

Everybody had shown up, puffing and complaining about the climb to the third floor, then *oohing* and *ahhing* over the polished hardwood floors, shelves of books and pictures, and plants hanging in the windows. Everybody except . . .

"Where's Adele at?" Florida asked. "She ain't been to Yada Yada since the robbery. What's goin' on?"

"Longer than that," Stu said. "She came the night of the robbery, but she hasn't come to anything else since MaDear went off on Denny back in August. Taking it a bit too far, if you ask me."

"Whaddya mean, MaDear went off on Denny?" Yo-Yo looked around the group. "Did I miss somethin'?"

Avis came to the rescue. "Let's get started, have some prayer, and then we can fill you in on why Adele isn't here. We've got some major prayer concerns this week—and decisions too. Oh, Father!" Avis moved right into her prayer. "We need Your presence now more than ever in our lives . . ."

We spent the next five minutes, not praying for any requests, just praising God and remembering promises. Finally Avis said, "Amen."

All eyes fixed on Avis. *Oh God, I'm so glad she agreed to do this!* I was feeling pretty tongue-tied even *thinking* about talking about Adele.

Avis gave a brief rundown of what had happened at Adele's Hair and Nails back in August when Denny had brought me for an anniversary makeover. "Since then," Avis continued, "MaDear has been going through a difficult time with painful memories, and Adele is stressed. At my urging she tried coming to Yada

Yada on Labor Day weekend, but . . . well, we all know what happened at *that* meeting. Right or wrong, it was 'the last straw' for Adele. She's trying to simplify what she's dealing with, and unfortunately, that means pulling back from Yada Yada."

"Just for now, right?" Delores's eyebrows rose hopefully.

Avis shook her head. "Honestly? I don't know. She needs space, which we need to respect. But maybe down the road . . ."

Chanda pulled a pout, looking for all the world like a ten-year-old. "You mean ta say that Jodi, Avis, Florida, and Stu all knew 'bout dis ting what happened a whole month ago, but you jus' now tellin' us?"

Well, I would have liked to tell Yada Yada weeks ago—but I didn't say it.

Edesa spoke. "Jodi. How's Denny?"

Bless you, Edesa! Somebody around here realizes it's been tough being the target of MaDear's misplaced anger. I opened my mouth, but just then Stu snickered. "MaDear didn't throw the hairbrush *that* hard, Edesa! He's fine—right, Jodi?"

I stifled an urge to smack her. "No, he's not fine. Physically, sure, but emotionally, it's been really hard knowing MaDear thinks he's some kind of racist murderer." I blinked rapidly, hoping I wouldn't start blubbering. "Especially since Adele won't talk to us about it."

There. It was out.

"Well, stuff like that sure did happen back then," Florida muttered. "Don't really blame Adele. Hard to deal with if it happened in *your* family."

Avis cut in. "The point is, we need to be praying for Adele and MaDear—*and* Jodi and Denny. Sometimes we need to learn how to wait. And this seems to be one of those times."

The group prayed then, and the prayers were comforting. Once again, Avis had reminded us that we need to stand with each sister in Yada Yada, even when it seemed that our life experiences put us on opposite sides of the problem.

At the end of that prayer, Avis said, "Nony? You have something to share."

I tried to catch Avis's eye, pulling a corner of the letter from Lincoln Correctional Center out of my tote bag. She glanced my way and nodded, but she turned her attention to Nony.

Nony sighed. "You know my mother had a stroke last week. I want to take the boys to see their grandmother before it is too late, but Mark . . ." Tears puddled in Nony's large eyes. "He doesn't want the boys to go. Not till Christmas, when school is out. Then, he says, we can all go to South Africa together."

"But your Mama is sick now!" Florida pointed out.

"Humph." Chanda fanned a paper in front of her face. "No mon be tellin' *me* I canna go see my mama if she sick, even if it be on da' *moon.*"

Nony waved her hand. "No, no, don't misunderstand. Mark says of course *I* can go now to see my mother, but about the boys . . . we do not see eye to eye."

Avis looked thoughtful. "How do you want us to pray, Nony?"

The large eyes flashed. "To change Mark's mind! I *must* take the boys."

Several heads nodded around the circle. "Keep your own bank account, I always say," Ruth muttered.

Avis gently pressed. "I think we should ask God to show you *and* Mark what is best for all of you and to give you one mind and heart. And for you, Nony, to trust God for the outcome."

Nony nodded slowly, and Yada Yada prayed once more, clustering around our sister, so far from her family, her country. We prayed for Nony's "mother heart" that yearned for her sons to know their heritage; her "daughter heart" that yearned for her mother to know her grandsons. We prayed that God would knit the hearts of this family together and that Nony and Mark would trust God in each other.

But I missed Nony's own prayers, the way she "prayed Scripture" into whatever we were praying about. Tonight she was quiet, her eyes closed and lashes wet, letting the prayers rain down on her head.

We finally resumed our seats and Avis raised an eyebrow in my direction. Finally! I pulled out the letter and read the return address.

"You've *got* to be kidding!" Stu's mouth dropped and her eyes bugged, making her look like one of those thin, pale fish that stare at you through the glass at the Shedd Aquarium. "That woman had the nerve to write back?"

"Apparently." Ruth tapped her knee. "Jodi. Read."

I unfolded the single sheet of notebook paper. "She doesn't say much. No salutation . . ."

Chanda snickered. "You mean, she don't say, 'Dear sistahs' . . . ?"

Ruth glared at Chanda. "Just read the letter, Jodi."

"She just says, 'I put your names on the list. Sincerely, Becky Wallace.'"

Silence reigned in the room for at least five seconds. I noticed that Hoshi was staring at the floor.

"That's it? 'I put your names on the list'?" Stu was still incredulous.

"Rather a miracle, don't you think?" Avis said.

"*Sí!*" Delores shook her head. "I can hardly believe it."

"So now what?" Yo-Yo hunched her shoulders inside her overalls. "Florida said she'd go, and me. And Jodi and Denny's names are on that list too. So . . . when we gonna go?"

29

We agreed to go the following Saturday, the first week-end in October, depending on whether we could get Yo-Yo back in time to work Saturday evening and if Denny's coaching schedule was clear. Personally, I wasn't sure why it had to be so soon. Sometime in January would've been soon enough for me. Good grief, let Bandana Woman get oriented to prison life first, clean up her mouth, have some time to think about her sins, finish detox. Whatever.

Nony and Hoshi dropped me off after Yada Yada, and Denny met me at the front door. "Was that Nony?" Something in his voice . . .

"Uh-huh. Anything wrong?"

He shrugged and followed me back toward the kitchen, where I put on the teakettle. "Mark called while you were at Yada Yada."

"Nony's husband?" Now *I* was curious.

"Yeah." Denny leaned against the refrigerator. "He was pretty sure Nony would ask Yada Yada to pray about taking the boys to visit her mother in South Africa." Denny lifted an eyebrow at me, waiting for confirmation.

"Well, yeah, she did."

Denny sighed. "He's scared, Jodi. Scared she won't bring them back."

"What?" I nearly dropped the mug I was getting out of the cupboard. "Why wouldn't she bring the boys back?"

Another shrug from Denny. "He thinks . . . to pressure him. To move the family to South Africa. She knows he's not going to lose his family."

Well, of course not! True, Nony often talked about her desire to move back to South Africa—her heart's longing, for sure—but from everything I could tell, she and Mark had a stable, loving marriage. No way would they split over this.

The teakettle whistled frantically. I turned off the burner. "Whew." This was huge. Hard to believe, though. "What did you say to Mark?"

"Mostly listened. He . . . asked me to pray for him." Denny's mouth twisted in a half-grin. "Not sure I've ever prayed with another guy on the phone before—though I know you Yada Yada sisters do it all the time. Uh, could I have a mug of whatever you're making there?"

"Oh. Sure." I'd totally forgotten about the tea water. I grabbed some herbal tea bags and another mug.

"And," Denny added, "I told him to trust his wife—and the Spirit of God within her."

The y a d a y a d a Prayer Group Gets Down

I smiled as I poured the hot water. Now that was a good answer.

THE FOLLOWING SATURDAY found all four of us—Denny, me, Florida, and Yo-Yo—sailing south on route I-55 toward Lincoln, Illinois, but it took a lot of juggling. Yo-Yo had spent the night at our house, along with Pete and Jerry—Yo-Yo on the foldout; the boys camping out in Josh's room—so we could get an early start. It wasn't easy dragging Amanda out of bed at 6:00 a.m. so we could drop her off at Edesa's for the day, leaving Willie Wonka in charge of the three boys. On the way to Edesa's, we picked up Florida in the Edgewater neighborhood, dropped off Amanda on the Near West Side—never mind my uneasy realization she would be spending the day only a mile or two from José Enriques—and finally made it out onto the interstate.

I'd brought two thermoses of hot coffee, four travel mugs, some sticky pecan buns I picked up at Dominick's in-store bakery, and a bunch of bananas to pass around for breakfast on the road. "Now this is nice," Florida said, pouring a refill into her travel mug. "No kids all day, fancy breakfast food. Almost like a vacation."

I twisted around in the front passenger seat. "I can think of a *lot* of places I'd rather spend a vacation day than going to a prison, Florida."

"Yeah. Me too," Yo-Yo said glumly. "Didn't think I'd be going back voluntarily."

Denny chuckled from behind the wheel. "Better voluntarily than *not.*"

Yo-Yo guffawed. "Ha! Ya got that right."

"What are Carla and the boys doing today, Flo?" I asked.

Florida sighed. "Carla goin' to her foster family again today—s'posed to be the first and third Saturdays every month for a while. I know they care about her, but don't see how these visits help *us* none." She was silent a moment. "Still, it'd be harder to make this trip if she was home. So maybe just as well . . . say! I usually have a cig with my morning coffee—mind if I light up? Just *kidding,* Jodi! But we'll be stoppin' along the way, right?"

Denny glanced in his rearview mirror. "Just say the word, Flo."

"Hey, those trees are real pretty," Yo-Yo said. A cold snap the preceding week had turned the usually boring countryside along the interstate into a kaleidoscope of color. Golden elms and maples, rusty brown oaks, crimson sumac bushes, and the occasional brilliant red maple flashed by, resembling a colorful afghan tossed on a large, flat bed. "Wish Pete and Jerry coulda come. Don't think they ever been out in the country."

"My babies neither," said Florida.

I twisted in my seat again. "You mean . . . they've never been outside Chicago?"

Florida and Yo-Yo answered like a chorus. "Nope."

I was flabbergasted into silence. We'd always taken *some* kind of vacation when I was a kid, even if it was just visiting my grandparents on the farm. And then there was that memorable car trip West one summer, to see the Grand Canyon splitting the earth like a gigantic gash to the bone, then heading north to gawk at Old Faithful and the bears at Yellowstone National Park. I could still remember the rotten-egg smell of the sulfur hot springs and the amazing mud pots going *blop, blop, blop*—marred only by my brothers' incessant teasing that they were going to push me in.

I couldn't imagine never setting foot outside Chicago in my whole life. *Oh Jesus. If you ever plop a million dollars into my lap, I'm gonna buy a huge bus, hire a driver, and take Florida and Yo-Yo and Chanda and all their kids and whoever else wants to come and see the whole country . . .*

The other half of my brain put on the brakes. *Oh, right, Jodi. All those kids? Sounds like a recipe for disaster.* Well, it wasn't like I was going to actually *get* a million dollars—though for half a second I felt tempted for the first time in my life to play the lottery.

We stopped twice at roadside rest stops to stretch our legs and get some cold drinks. It took a little longer than usual, because Florida and Yo-Yo sat out on a picnic table for a cigarette break both times. So it was almost eleven o'clock by the time we drove up to the gate of the Lincoln Correctional Center. We had to state our business, open the back of the minivan, and get out while a security guard did a cursory check of the car. Then we were permitted to drive into the parking lot.

Chain-link fences and rolls of razor wire stretched out on all sides of us as far as I could see. Beyond the wire, off in the distance, lay a typical Midwest town nestled among the colorful trees, church steeples sticking into the blue October sky. So close, yet so far. I swallowed. Is this where I'd be if the charge against me

673

of vehicular manslaughter had stuck? My knees felt rubbery as the four of us walked toward the main entrance.

A lot of visitors were checking in at the main desk, but finally it was our turn. We immediately ran into trouble. Each of us was asked, among other things, if we had ever been convicted of a crime or incarcerated. Now it was Yo-Yo's turn to gulp as the truth came out.

"We can't let you visit an inmate without special permission of the chief administrative officer," the freckle-faced security officer at the desk said flatly.

We all looked at each other.

"Sir, we've driven all the way from Chicago." Denny was exceedingly polite. "Would it be possible to get that permission, uh, today?" He turned to Yo-Yo. "Ms. Spencer was a former inmate here at Lincoln—her records must be available. Given the nonviolent charges against her and her clean prison history, I'm sure you will see that she does not present a risk."

Florida kept her mouth shut, but *You tell him, Denny!* was plastered all over her face. I wasn't so sure Denny's charm was going to work with this buster, though. The man gave us an impassive stare, excused himself, and left us waiting.

It took another hour to get clearance for Yo-Yo, but somehow it happened. "Thank ya, Jesus!" Florida crowed, which earned her a funny look from the freckle-faced guy. We were then ushered into security areas—this way for women, that way for men—to be searched. Florida, Yo-Yo, and I had to take off our shoes, which were shaken and examined before we were allowed to put them back on. We were each assigned a locker for our purses, jackets, and personal items. Then we were patted down by a female guard and made to walk through a metal detector. *Sure glad I wore a pair of jeans,* I thought. I could hardly bear to think about being patted down under a skirt.

We met Denny outside the visitors' room and walked in together. The room was devoid of any color or decoration—just gray walls, beige floor tile, gray plastic tables, and gray plastic chairs. At most of the tables, a female inmate wearing street clothes—mostly jeans, sweatpants, and T-shirts—was surrounded by mothers or sisters and kids of all ages. At two of the tables, a man—boyfriend or husband—held hands with a woman across the gray plastic tabletop. Not a DOC uniform in sight.

The four of us sat at an empty table, pulling over another chair so we'd have five. And waited.

I hardly recognized Becky Wallace when a guard let her in the room. In fact, I didn't realize who she was until I saw the guard point toward us. A wiry woman wearing a shapeless T-shirt and baggy sweats walked slowly in our direction. Instinctively, all four of us stood up.

Florida thrust out her hand. "You Becky Wallace?"

The woman nodded, her dark eyes darting from one person to the next. Her dull brown hair was cut short; her skin was sallow, devoid of makeup or natural color. She looked tired, like an old woman who wasn't getting enough sleep.

Except she was young—not more than twenty-five. Her birth date must've been on that file I'd pulled up on the computer, but somehow her age hadn't registered.

"Well, I'm Flo Hickman. This here's Yo-Yo Spencer. And them two is Jodi and Denny Baxter."

We each shook her hand, which she extended reluctantly, and we all sat down. For a moment no one spoke. *Oh God*, I moaned inwardly, *this is so awkward.*

Finally Becky spoke. "You all at that house the night I got busted?"

Denny nodded. "Except Yo-Yo. She had to work that night."

The woman's eyes narrowed in Yo-Yo's direction. "Why you here then?"

Yo-Yo stuck her hands behind the bib of her overalls and slid down the chair into her customary pose—feet straight out, fanny and back resting at two points on the chair. "Wasn't there that night," she said, "but I been *here* and came out better'n I went in. I'm thinkin' the same about you."

The woman's lip curled. "Why should you care?"

Yo-Yo didn't blink. "'Cause somebody cared about me. Made a difference."

I was still tongue-tied. My emotions bounced around like little pinballs. Why *did* we come anyway? Wasn't she going to apologize for terrorizing us that evening?

Becky looked Denny up and down. "You the guy that pinned me down?"

Denny nodded. I could see a little twitch at the corner of his eye. Ha! Denny was nervous too. "I . . . hope I didn't hurt you."

"Nah. Ya did whatcha had to do."

The silence stretched out long again. It didn't seem the right time for small talk. Finally Florida spoke. "You finish detox?"

Becky's eyes dropped. "Huh! Got out of Cook County 'fore my three weeks' detox was up. Hit withdrawal big-time when I got here." She cussed under her breath. "Worse pain ever had in my life." She eyed Florida. "You?"

"Uh-huh. Writhin' all over the floor, screamin' for somethin', anything. Sure been there."

"You clean now?"

Florida grinned. "Yes, thank ya, *Jesus!* Five years saved and five years sober!"

The woman's lip curled again. "You all religious types?"

"Yep! That's what we was doin' when you came in the door— havin' a prayer meetin'." Florida nodded at Denny and me. "At their house."

Becky Wallace squirmed in her chair. "Guess I gave y'all somethin' to pray about, huh."

That's it? That's all she's going to say about what happened that night? I swallowed the sharp retort that rode the tip of my tongue. "Yes. We did too. Pray for you that night, I mean. And ever since."

Becky's mouth twitched. "Don't bother," she muttered. "Ain't worth it. Save your prayers for that lady what got her hand cut."

I noticed she didn't say, ". . . *for that lady whose hand I cut.*"

"Oh, we prayin' for her too," said Florida. "And her daughter. They was all shook up."

Becky shot us a wary glance. I could practically read her thoughts: *Knew it! Knew you guys are just itchin' to tell me how what I done made you feel.*

But nobody said anything more. Finally she seemed to slump

inside her ill-fitting clothes. "Didn't mean ta cut that lady," she mumbled, staring at the table. "Didn't want ta hurt nobody. Jus' . . . jus' needed money for a fix."

"I know," Florida said. "We all know that."

We asked if she had family. She shrugged. "Somewhere. Ain't heard from 'em in a long time." We asked if she had kids. Her eyes twitched. She gave a short nod. "Lil' boy. Don't know where he be, though. His daddy took 'im away from me. Said I wasn't fit." Did she need anything? She shook her head. "Nah. What's ta need? I ain't goin' nowhere."

The clock on the wall inched its way toward 1:00. My stomach was rumbling. Maybe Becky Wallace had missed lunch too. But if Avis were here, no way would she miss an opportunity to pray. Why not? I had absolutely no other idea how to end this awkward visit. "Could we . . . uh, pray for you before we go?"

That seemed to unnerve her. She stood up. "Ya can pray all ya want after ya get on outta here. I gotta go." She started to leave, then she turned back. "Don't know why y'all come on down here, but I . . . I 'preciate it." Without waiting for a reply, she strode quickly across the room, motioning to the guard to let her out the locked door.

And then she was gone.

30

None of us said much as we left the prison and climbed back into the car. I felt irritated that my mental image of Bandana Woman didn't stand up to the dull-eyed, pathetic creature we'd just left. But I didn't want to feel sorry for her. *Isn't some anger appropriate, God? After all, Hoshi's relationship with her parents is a wreck now, thanks to B. W. If we're going to actually relate to this woman, she needs to face that somehow.* With a twinge of satisfaction, I felt my level of anger—righteous anger, of course—nudge back up a notch.

She was so young, though . . .

"How old do you think she is?" I said to no one in particular.

"Dunno," Yo-Yo said. "Maybe 'bout my age."

"Which is?"

"Uh . . ." She paused, like she had to think about it. "Gonna be twenty-three in a week or so. Say, we gonna eat? I'm hungry."

We found a McDonald's in the town of Lincoln and got milkshakes to go with the sandwiches and apples I'd brought along. Got the coffee thermoses filled up again too.

Florida eyed the wheat bread suspiciously as she took a sandwich. "You got somethin' against white bread, Jodi?"

I stifled a snort. She probably meant that cheap spongy stuff in long "family-size" loaves that passed for bread in the grocery store. Might be good for *something*—like maybe caulking leaky windows in an emergency. I smiled apologetically. "Sorry, Flo. Just used what I had on hand."

We munched in silence for a while before I noticed that Denny had not gotten back on the interstate. "Taking the back roads home?"

He shrugged. "Thought we might find a roadside stand that sold pumpkins."

"They sell 'em at the *store*, Denny," Florida said, her mouth full of sandwich.

Denny grinned. "I know, but it's kinda fun to buy them right off the farm."

"Josh and Amanda still carve pumpkins? Them big kids?"

"Sure," I piped up. "We do it every year." Or was it Denny and me who carved the pumpkins now?

Sure enough, we saw a hand-painted sign boasting "Pumpkins, Apples, Squash." Denny pulled into the farm driveway. "Pick out a pumpkin for Carla and the boys, Flo. My treat." He eyed Yo-Yo. "You want a pumpkin? Take your pick."

Yo-Yo got out of the car, taking in the rows and rows of pumpkins lined up on the ground like so many Munchkins from the

Land of Oz with big orange heads and little green hat-handles, sorted by size behind signs that said, "Large $5, Medium $4, Small $3." She jammed her hands in the low pockets of her overalls. "Never had an honest-to-God *real* pumpkin before."

I stared at her. "Never?"

Yo-Yo shrugged. "My mom wasn't big on holidays. Maybe Christmas now and then—if she was sober."

"What about birthdays? She made a cake, that kind of thing, right?"

Yo-Yo shook her head. "Nah, but it's okay, ya know. I try to do somethin' for Pete and Jerry when it's their birthday. But we never had a pumpkin." She moved over to the rows of "Small" pumpkins. "If I get one, would one of ya tell me how ta, y'know, make it glow?"

I laughed, but I felt like crying. *"My mom wasn't big on holidays . . ."* How much I took for granted! Never thought that some families—families I rubbed shoulders with—didn't even do *birthdays*. "Sure. Maybe we should have a pumpkin-carving party. You wanna, Florida?"

"Cool. I'll bring Carla. Chris and Cedric gonna think they too big. Can I have this big 'un here, Denny?"

"Yeah. They gotta be big for carving. You guys pick out three big ones. I'll go pay." Denny headed for the outdoor counter.

"Pay for four, Denny!" I yelled after him. "I'm gonna get one for Chanda's kids too."

As we pulled back on the road, Yo-Yo stared at the field next to the roadside stand, where pumpkins dotted the ground, still clinging to their sprawling wilted vines. "Huh. So that's how they grow." It was a statement of wonder, like the way I felt watching Neil Armstrong set foot on the moon on my TV screen.

We finally got back on I-55. Denny didn't ask me to drive, and I didn't offer. One of these days I needed to muster up the courage to drive at highway speeds again. But not today. Nobody talked much about our visit to Becky Wallace on the way home. Maybe we all needed to digest the experience for a while.

I stuck in a *Songs4Worship Gospel* CD and glanced back into the second seat as the Colorado Mass Choir filled the car with "Let everything that has breath praise Him!" I turned the volume down a notch. Florida was sleeping in spite of all that coffee; Yo-Yo just stared out the side window of the minivan, nursing her own thoughts.

An idea began to percolate in my head . . .

AS FAR AS I COULD TELL, our kids had handled the day pretty well. Amanda volunteered that she and Edesa had gone over to the Enriqueses' house to make "real" tortillas with Delores and Emerald. *And to see José,* I guessed. Yet did it really matter, if the whole family was together? What harm was there in that? Josh and Yo-Yo's brothers played video games, ate the two frozen pizzas I had in the freezer, cleaned us out of ice cream, and left all their dishes in the sink. So what else did I expect? Though I was a little rattled by the cigarette butts I found out by the garage. Who'd been smoking—Pete? Well, so did his sister-guardian. Not much I could do about that.

At Uptown Community the next morning, Florida got up during the testimony time and shared briefly about our visit to Lincoln Correctional, mentioning the robbery that had preceded it "at the Baxters' house." I saw heads swivel as people looked at us, no doubt surprised that they were just now hearing about this. "That girl needs some serious prayer," Florida said. "So I'm askin' the church to keep her covered. God saved me, so I know He can save her too. Pastor?" She handed the mic to Pastor Clark and started to sit down, but Pastor Clark motioned her to stay up front and asked Avis and Stu and the Baxter family to join her and be included in his prayer.

Funny. I hadn't really thought about asking Uptown to pray about stuff related to Yada Yada. For one thing, Yada Yada was women from a bunch of different churches—not really an Uptown thing. And prayer requests shared in the group were confidential. Yet maybe Florida was right. This was bigger than any of us, bigger than Yada Yada. My eyes misted as Pastor Clark prayed for protection, for healing of the experience, for Becky Wallace's salvation.

Well sure, let's pray for her salvation. *Just don't turn her back out on the street, God,* I added as we sat down again.

Once back into the school week, though, I didn't have time to think much about Becky Wallace. On Monday I congratulated myself that my third-grade class was starting to gel. On Tuesday, Terrell tripped Darian as they came into the classroom, and the day seemed to unravel from there. Chanel was absent for three days, and we had to send a note home to all the parents that said, "A case of lice has been reported in your child's class, so please take the following precautions . . ." When Chanel returned with her head wrapped in a blue scarf, all the kids knew who the "case of lice" was, and I had to keep her in the classroom during lunch to prevent the inevitable meanness, in spite of the lecture I'd given the class on respecting others' feelings.

The week wasn't a total loss, though. I turned Christy James loose to plan our reading segment for the next couple of weeks, since that seemed to be of special interest to my student teacher. She started reading the story of Johnny Appleseed to the class, then she encouraged the students to write a poem using the letters of his name as an acrostic. The results weren't terribly creative, but some were pretty cute. Most of the kids seemed proud of their "poems," decorating their papers with round red blobs that were supposed to be apples.

Hakim, however, just sat and looked at his paper, as if he didn't have a clue. My heart constricted. Why was written work so hard for him? He was obviously very bright—the balance-scale episode proved that. I motioned him to a table at the back of the room. He came reluctantly, like he might get yelled at. "It's okay," I said. "Look, let's do it this way." I covered up all the letters of the acrostic except for the J and asked him to make up a sentence beginning with that letter. "You tell me what you want to say, and I'll write it down," I said. That seemed to make a difference. Working this way he finished the acrostic poem.

The y a d a y a d a Prayer Group Gets Down

J—Just the other day
O—On my way to the store, I
H—Hollered to the old man
N—Next-door . . .

Not bad. It actually rhymed. "It's the written work that trips him up," I murmured to Christy as we tacked the papers up on the bulletin board after school. "I wonder if he's ever been tested?"

On Friday, Christy brought a couple of bags of apples to class, a big plastic bowl, and a roll of paper towels and let the kids "bob for apples" as the last activity of the day. I should have advised against it, but I didn't want to squelch her ideas. The kids were already squirrelly, given that it was late in the school day just before the weekend, but it might have gone all right if Cornell hadn't started acting smart by rocking the bowl. Before we could stop him, the bowl tipped over, and we had water all over the floor—which meant a trip to the janitor's closet for a mop and bucket and a dozen disappointed kids who hadn't gotten to bob for apples yet. Ramón yelled at Cornell for ruining their turn, Cornell slugged Ramón, and we ended up having to send both boys to the office.

"Sorry, Ms. Baxter," Christy said sheepishly as she gathered up the remaining apples and the bowl. (The paper towels had paid the ultimate sacrifice mopping up the floor instead of kids' faces.)

"Don't be sorry, Christy. It was a great idea. Next time we'll just nail down the bowl." For a second there, I think she thought I was joking.

ON MY WAY OUT OF SCHOOL that Friday, I caught Avis on the fly and told her Yo-Yo would be twenty-three "in a week or so" but had never had a birthday party. "What do you think of celebrating her birthday Sunday night at Yada Yada? She'd really be surprised."

"*This* Sunday?" Avis frowned. "Well, okay . . . but Natasha's coming home from college this weekend—her high-school homecoming, I think—and Charette is coming up from Cincinnati with the twins. We're all going to the South Side to see Rochelle and the baby. I won't have time to plan anything. Not even sure I'll be at Uptown on Sunday. Might go to church with Rochelle."

"That's okay. I'll—"

"Where would we meet?"

"Meet? I thought we agreed on Nony's at the last meeting. Haven't been there since August."

"Yes, but Nony called me last night and said she and the boys are leaving for South Africa on Sunday. Not sure how long she'll be gone—several weeks anyway."

Nony *and* the boys? I hadn't said anything to Avis about Mark's phone call to Denny. "Well, good for Mark." Avis looked at me funny. *Oops! Did I say that out loud?* "I mean, good that our prayers were answered—you know, that they came to an agreement," I amended hastily. I made a mental note to give Nony a call before she left.

But where to meet? Only about half the group was able to host a Yada Yada meeting. Stu lived too far away; Delores had too many kids . . . I shrugged. "Guess I'm next on the list, if it's not too soon after the . . . you know."

The y a d a y a d a Prayer Group Gets Down

Avis raised an eyebrow. "We're not going to let Satan rob us of anything, Jodi—not our joy, not where we meet for Yada Yada." She looked at her watch. "Look, I've got to run. Let me know if you want me to bring something. I'll be there."

"Just a card for Yo-Yo!" I called after her as she flew out the door. By the time I crossed the parking lot to head home, her car was gone. Must be anxious to see her grandkids.

SURE ENOUGH, Nony had plane tickets for Sunday afternoon for herself, Marcus, and Michael. "I'm so sorry, Jodi, not to tell you sooner," she said when I called, "but it's been so hectic, getting passports for the boys, getting their schoolwork so I can home-school while we're gone. I don't know why Mark changed his mind, but God's name be praised! Will you let the rest of the sisters know? And give them my love."

Indeed. Just don't stay too long, Nony.

I sent out an e-mail Friday night to Yada Yada, telling them about the change in location for Sunday's meeting and Nony's news. And since I knew Yo-Yo didn't have e-mail, I broadcast my idea for a birthday surprise. "Just bring cards," I suggested. "I'll make a cake."

When I went to the store on Saturday to get a card for Yo-Yo, I couldn't find anything that seemed appropriate. What could I say to encourage a young woman who'd once said about her name, *"Oh, right. Yo-Yo—a spinning toy going nowhere."*

687

That actually gave me an idea. Back home I got on the computer, called up the Web site where I'd found the meanings of names for my Welcome Bulletin Board at the school, and typed "Yolanda" into the search. I blinked when the meaning came up on the screen.

"Yolanda. From the Greek: 'Violet Flower.'"

Wow. If I were going to hang a flower on Yo-Yo's name, I'd choose something hardy, sturdy enough to weather all sorts of conditions. Like marigolds or mums. But in the Bible, names had significant meaning. Maybe there was a meaning for Yo-Yo here that wasn't that obvious.

I was just about to shut down the name site, when a curious thought popped into my head. *What did Becky Wallace's name mean?* Immediately followed by: *Why should I care?* But I was curious enough to type "Becky" into the search bar and waited while that name page came up.

I stared. Was this possible?

"Becky. A familiar form of Rebecca. From the Hebrew: 'Bound, tied.'"

Oh God.

31

I was so focused on trying to pull off Yo-Yo's birthday surprise that Amanda's request after church on Sunday almost didn't register. "Invite who to youth group tonight?" I said absently, studying my recipe for red-velvet cake, wondering if I'd have to run out to Dominick's for two bottles of red food coloring.

"*José.* Mo-om! Aren't you listening?"

Well, she had my attention *now.* I leaned back against the kitchen counter and looked at my daughter. Okay. Should've seen it coming. After all, her two-week grounding had been for lying to us, not for being friends with José Enriques per se. However, I'd been hoping that the budding romance would wither on the vine for lack of attention—ignoring, of course, that "absence makes the heart grow fonder."

I sighed. "Don't they have a youth program at Iglesia?" *Oh brother. That was lame.*

She shrugged. "Sure. Some weeknight—Thursday, I think. What's your point?"

Watch it, young lady. I took a breath. What *was* my point? "I . . . is something special happening at Uptown tonight?"

"Kinda. The Reillys are gonna be talking about the music teens listen to—I thought José might be interested. They told us to bring friends. And our CDs."

"That's a long way to come—"

"Mom! Mrs. Enriques is coming to Yada Yada tonight, right? Here at our house? José could come with his mom, and we'll take him to youth group." She zeroed in for the kill. "Besides, isn't that what you and the other Yada Yada women do? Visit each other's churches?"

I hated it when my kids pointed the finger back at me to get what they wanted. The next item in her bag of tricks would be to remind me we'd told her that if she wanted to see José, to invite him up here.

I tried to back out gracefully. "Sure. Good idea." Amanda disappeared with the phone before I even got the mixer out.

As it turned out, the idea spread, and Josh called Ruth Garfield to ask if she'd bring Yo-Yo's brothers, ". . . since you and Yo-Yo are coming anyway." Chris Hickman came with Florida too. We didn't have that many high schoolers at Uptown, so the "youth group" started at eighth grade. It was a bit hectic at first, with Yada Yada arriving and teenagers leaving, but eventually we got everybody sorted out. Denny decided to go with the kids and "learn something about teen music." Poor guy.

I was glad to see Hoshi made it, since Nony was probably somewhere over the Atlantic by now. I made a mental note to take Hoshi back to campus after Yada Yada so she wouldn't have to ride the el alone after dark.

By mutual agreement, nobody said anything about Yo-Yo's birthday when we first started. Right after our beginning prayer and praise time, Avis asked for a report of the visit to Becky Wallace. *Oh, help.* I didn't know what to say. Admit I was still hanging on to my mental mad, even after meeting B. W. face to face and seeing her as a real person?

Florida saved the day. "I know what happened here that night was bad news. But that girl—why she's only a day or two older'n Yo-Yo here. Just a baby. Why, she—"

Yo-Yo loudly cleared her throat. "Just a baby, huh?" We all laughed.

"Oh, girl, ya know what I mean. She's got her whole life in front of her, and if somebody don't do somethin', it's gonna be messed up big-time."

"Messy, schmessy," Ruth huffed. "Seems like she's already done a good job of that. What are we, the local rehab?"

Exactly what I was thinking.

Stu frowned. "Why would you say that, Ruth? You befriended Yo-Yo in prison, looked after her brothers, got her a job . . ."

Chanda wagged her head. "If dat what you tinkin', don't look at *me.* I canna give no reference to mi ladies on de North Shore. You wants ta go in dey houses, you gots ta be squeaky clean. No drugs, no rap sheet, no nothin'."

I noticed Hoshi sat stiffly on her chair, twisting and untwisting a handkerchief with lacy edging.

Avis steered us back to center. "It's rather a miracle that Becky Wallace agreed to let some of us come visit. One step at a time. Right now, the most important thing to do is keep praying, but before we do that . . . Yo-Yo? Or Jodi? Anything you want to share from the visit to Lincoln?"

Yo-Yo shook her head. "Glad I went, though. Reminded me I don't wanna go back. Inside, I mean."

My turn. "To be honest? Don't know if I'm glad I went or not. I mean, it was probably the right thing to do, but . . . it's kinda hard to give up my feelings about what she did, barging in here and terrorizing everybody and hurting Hoshi's mother." Out of the corner of my eye, I saw Hoshi stop twisting the handkerchief and just stare at the floor. "Yet she didn't seem like a monster when we visited her in prison. Just someone sad and pathetic and lonely. Which is hard for me to accept, because I don't want to feel sorry for her. She really hurt us—all of us."

Hoshi spoke, her voice low and intense. "Yes. I don't want to feel sorry for her. Maybe that is not good, but that is how I feel."

I was glad Hoshi had the courage to say that. It wouldn't be fair to her if we were more concerned for the perp than for the victim. But even as I entertained those thoughts, I realized an unsettling truth: Visiting B. W. *had* taken away the sting of that night. I no longer felt the same fear when I thought of her. And maybe that was a good thing?

Tentatively I voiced this new realization.

Avis nodded. "When we hold on to our anger, we allow the person who hurt us to keep hurting us again and again, every time we think about what happened. That gives Satan way too much power! That's why the 'Jesus way' points us to reconciliation and forgiveness. But"—she held up her hand like a stop sign—"maybe that's something for us to think and pray about. God understands we need time. Why don't we pray for Hoshi and her mom and all of us still struggling with the after-effects of the robbery? And pray for Becky Wallace too."

Everyone seemed willing to get into the prayer time, also remembering to pray for Nony and her boys making their way to South Africa that very moment . . . for Mark Smith, home alone without his wife and children for several weeks . . . for all our teenagers at Uptown this evening. Edesa, bless her, prayed for Delores's husband, still without a job, still drinking too much to drown his discouragement.

During a short lull, I said, "And, Jesus, I want to pray for Adele . . ." Yet I had no idea what to pray *for,* so I just left it hanging there. Others filled in the gap with "Yes, Jesus!" and "You said You'd never leave her or forsake her!"

When it seemed like Avis was wrapping up the prayer time, I slipped out to the kitchen to light the candles on Yo-Yo's cake, smothered in whipped-cream frosting. I was realizing that twenty-three was a *lot* of candles when Stu slipped into the kitchen too. "Here, you need help with that." She struck a match and started in on the other side. *Humph.* Not *"Can I help you with that?"* Just *"You need help with that."* Which was true, but still.

We got all the candles lit, and Stu picked up the cake plate. "You go first and start them singing 'Happy Birthday.' I'll follow with the cake." She stood aside for me to go ahead of her.

Now I really was annoyed. Good grief! *I* made the cake, and *I* wanted to carry it in.

"Is that for Yo-Yo?" Stu nodded at the gift sitting on the counter, loosely tied up in lavender tissue paper and white ribbon. Darn if she wasn't right. I couldn't carry both the gift and the cake, even if I wanted to. I picked up the gift and started for the living room. *Okay, God, I know this is no time to get all hot and bothered by Stu's bossiness. Just keep me from smashing that cake in her face.*

We made it to the doorway just as Avis pronounced the final, "In the name of Jesus!" Perfect! As people's eyes popped open, I started singing, "Happy Birthday," and everyone joined in—even Yo-Yo, looking around as if trying to figure out who we were celebrating. When we all sang, " . . . dear Yo-Yo," Stu carried the flaming cake across the room and stood in front of her. "Happy birthday to you."

Yo-Yo's mouth dropped open, then her eyes darted this way and that. "Me?" she finally said. Man! Why didn't I remember my camera? The look on her face was priceless.

By now everyone was clapping and hollering. "Hey! Happy birthday, Yo-Yo!" "Blow out the candles! They're gonna drip all over the cake!" and "Make a wish first!"

"But it's not my birthday."

"When is it?" Ruth demanded.

"Uh . . . Tuesday."

"So? What's two days? Blow!"

Firelight from the shrinking candles danced on the blonde tips of Yo-Yo's short, spiky hair. "Okay, okay," she said and blew—spraying wax all over the frosting. But who cared. We all cheered.

Stu started to hand off the cake platter to me, but I held up the gift in my hands. "Oh. Could you cut the cake, Stu?" I asked sweetly. "But don't go yet. Got another presentation here."

"Hey, hey! Quiet, everybody," Ruth ordered.

I sat down on the floor in front of Yo-Yo's chair. She hunched forward, elbows on her denim knees, chin in her hands, staring at the toes of her sneakers. "Do you remember," I started, "when we were talking about what 'Yada Yada' means, and Avis or Nony—somebody!—said God calls us by our name? Well, I looked up the meaning of Yo-Yo's name—Yolanda, actually—and here it is." I held out the tissue-wrapped gift.

Yo-Yo stared cautiously at the lumpy gift. "Bite you, it won't," Ruth grumbled, waving her hand at her. "Open it!"

Yo-Yo let me place the gift in her hands. Hesitantly, she untied the white ribbon and the tissue paper fell away, revealing a large African violet with small clusters of bright purple flowers. Yo-Yo looked up. "I don't get it."

I smiled. "That's what your name means: 'Violet flower.'"

"Now dat nice," Chanda murmured.

Yo-Yo nodded. "Oh. Thanks. It's nice. Though . . . don't think that describes *me* very well." Leaving the plant on her lap, she held her arms wide, as though reminding us of her shapeless, same-old denim overalls.

I gave her a hug. "Oh, I don't know about that. My mom raised African violets all the time. And they'd just sit there growing leaves for months, then we'd get up one morning, and those gorgeous flowers seemed to have burst out overnight. Personally? I think there's a lot of beauty inside you that *you* might not see, but the rest of us do."

"You got that right," Florida crowed. And the clapping and cheering started all over again.

"Me tinks it be time to *party!*" Chanda jumped up, waving a CD she'd brought with her. "Go! Go! Cut dat cake," she said to Stu, who was still holding the cake platter, waving her away toward the dining room. "Jodi! How dis player work?"

In moments, Chanda had popped in the CD, turned up the volume, and was pushing furniture out of the way. The words to "Shout Hallelujah!" filled the house, while a tidal wave of drums, keyboards, and electric bass rumbled from the speakers.

> Come on and shout! hallelujah
> It's the highest praise!
> Dance! the devil is defeated
> He's under my feet! . . .

It was impossible *not* to dance to that music. Chanda pulled Yo-Yo to her feet, and pretty soon the two of them were doing a step-shuffle-and-shake number in sync. Avis and Florida were each "gettin' down" too. Ruth, Delores, and Edesa joined in, with results that looked a cross between a Jewish line dance and the

Macarena. Me—I didn't really know how to dance, but I tried to copy Chanda and Yo-Yo's steps. The results were pretty sloppy, but nobody seemed to care. Even Hoshi clapped along from the sidelines, a smile cheering up her face.

Shout! . . . Dance! . . . Clap! . . .

The CD was full of good "dance" songs, but it didn't take long for my left leg to start aching. Feeling guilty that Stu was off cutting the cake, I slipped down the hall to the dining room and took the cake knife from her. "Go on, I'll finish up. Go dance." I smiled at her and actually meant it.

We ate cake, gave Yo-Yo our cards, laughed, played music, and danced till the kids and Denny came back. They stood in a ragged line in the living-room doorway—Chris, Jerry, Pete, Josh, Amanda, and José—staring at their mothers and friends like a freak show. "C'mon, c'mon," Chanda waved at them. "Show us!" She put on the "Shout Hallelujah!" song again.

With a sly grin, José took up her challenge, and Pete followed—though how he could dance in those baggy crotch-around-his-knees pants, I'll never know. Feet flying, shoulders shrugging, the two young men did a hip-hop something to the pulsing praise music, while Chanda and Yo-Yo copied their moves. Everyone clapped and whooped. Encouraged, the rest of the kids joined them—even Josh and Amanda. *Hmm.* Where did they learn to move like that?

The living room was definitely crowded now, so most of Yada Yada faded back and let the young folks dance, while we cheered them on.

Not sure how I heard the doorbell, but I saw Denny go to answer it. *Good,* I thought. *If it's another Bandana Woman selling Avon,* he *can handle it.* But he came back and motioned to me.

"Upstairs neighbor," he said in my ear. "Complaining about the noise."

Oh, brother. It wasn't like we had a party every weekend—or even *once* since we'd moved here! I glanced at the clock. Good grief. It was only nine o'clock! And tomorrow was Columbus Day—a school holiday, anyway. But I turned down the volume on the CD player.

DENNY, BLESS HIS HEART, took Chanda and Hoshi home, and Stu somehow squeezed Delores, José, Edesa, Florida, and Chris into her two-door silver Celica. *Hope she doesn't get stopped by a cop,* I worried. As Ruth and Yo-Yo's brothers headed out to Ruth's car, Yo-Yo gave me a hug. "Thanks for the party, Jodi. And the African violet. Never had a birthday party before, you know."

I hugged her back. "I know."

Even after everyone was gone, the house seemed to ring with music and dance. *("Shout! . . . Dance! . . . Clap! . . .")* I sat down at the dining-room table with my school bag and pulled out my lesson-plan book, just to get an idea how much I needed to do tomorrow. A Post-it note stared at me from the cover. *"Send a note to Hakim's parents, suggest he be tested."*

Hmm. Should have asked Avis about that. Well, I'd write the note and check with her on Tuesday before sending it.

32

I managed to talk to Avis about three minutes on Tuesday, but she thought the testing could be arranged if Hakim's parents agreed. Satisfied, I sat down at my desk while Christy was reading *Ramona the Pest* to the class and pulled out the envelope with the note I'd written to his parents. I'd written the note in a friendly tone, even signed it "Ms. B" in quotes, which Hakim insisted on calling me. Only one problem: since neither his father nor his mother had come to the parent open house in September, I had no idea whether I should address it to "Mr. and Mrs. Porter," or just "Ms. Porter."

"To whom it may concern" didn't seem like an option.

I finally addressed it to "Ms. Porter" as the safest bet and asked Hakim to take it home to his mom. He eyed it suspiciously. "You gettin' me in trouble? I didn't fight nobody."

I smiled encouragingly. "Nothing like that. You've been fine. I just want to talk to your mom about how to make school better for you."

He frowned, like I'd just spoken gobbledegook, but he took the note and stuck it in the pocket of his sweatshirt. "Don't forget to give it to her," I called after him as he disappeared out the classroom door.

To my surprise, he brought the note back the next morning, with "Ms. Porter" on the envelope crossed out and "Ms. B" written in a strong, bold hand beneath it. Well, good for him. At least he remembered to give it to his mom. I didn't have time to read it at the moment, so I stuck it into the pocket of my corduroy skirt, intending to wait till lunchtime. Then I got so busy setting up our science experiment about ecosystems and the greenhouse effect that my student teacher was lining up the kids to come back in from the gym before I remembered the note.

Pulling the envelope out of my pocket, I opened the same sheet of paper I'd sent home with Hakim. The word *testing* had been circled in red ink, and at the bottom of the page was a note scrawled in the same bold handwriting: "Ms. B—Hakim is a smart kid. He does not need to be 'tested.' Testing is a cover-up for poor teaching. Just do your job." It was signed, "Geraldine Porter."

My whole face stung, like I'd just been slapped. *Poor teaching?!* The nerve of that woman!

I was so upset, I asked Christy to take over the class while I went to the teachers' restroom to pull myself together. I couldn't get rid of the accusing words ringing in my head: *"poor teaching . . . just do your job."* After ten minutes of pacing back and forth between the electric hand dryer and the overflowing trash can by the door, scorching my brain cells as I indulged in a one-side mental tirade at the lady, I decided to go see Avis.

A quick peek through the window in the classroom door satisfied me that Christy would survive another five or ten minutes without me, and I headed for Avis's office. She was on the telephone, but she motioned me inside. I shut the door.

She finally put down the handset. "Are you all right, Jodi?"

"No!" I handed her the note and pinched my lips while she read it.

"I see." Avis was quiet a moment. "Tell you what. I will do an informal evaluation of Hakim, just to assess the situation for myself. We better not do more than that, especially since we've asked and the mother has said no. Then, possibly I can contact the mother if we feel we need to pursue this further."

The principal contacting the mother sounded good to me. *Real* good. My steam level began to dissipate. "Hakim is bright, I agree. He shines when we do hands-on stuff. But put a sheet of paper in front of him, and he seems to freeze. Plus, he does have some troubling behavior problems. Either sulking and keeping to himself—or lashing out."

"Well, let's pursue it quietly for a while longer." Avis eyed me critically over the top of her reading glasses. "Don't let it get you down, Jodi. Leave it to God." Then she smiled, almost a tease. "And just do your job—like you've been doing."

LEAVE IT TO GOD . . . *Leave it to God . . .*

Avis's admonition followed me the rest of the week. Actually, it helped. I knew I was doing a good job—not perfect, but pretty darn good—teaching those third graders, and if I wasn't, I'd hear about it during staff evaluations. Like Avis said, I just needed to keep doing my job. And, I tried to tell myself, if Hakim's mother didn't want him to get tested, that was her problem.

No! I couldn't accept that. Because even though Hakim was bright, he *was* falling behind. And that wasn't fair to him.

Yet I had a whole classroom of kids to worry about. I couldn't tutor Hakim all day—unfortunately. Still, I determined to look for ways to give him more individual attention, especially with written work and reading. And parent-teacher conferences were coming up in a few weeks along with report-card pickup. Maybe that would provide a natural time to talk to Hakim's mom. If she showed up.

The weekend arrived before I noticed that the pumpkins we'd bought on the way back from Lincoln Correctional were still sitting in the garage. Yo-Yo and Florida had elected to leave theirs at our house since we'd talked about having a pumpkin-carving party with their kids. And I'd totally forgotten to say anything to Chanda.

But, hey, why not? It could be fun. I hadn't met Chanda's kids yet—this might be a good time. So I got on the phone with Florida, Yo-Yo, and Chanda, and we lined it up for the next Saturday. That gave a few days to enjoy the jack-o'-lanterns before Halloween, but not enough time for them to rot.

Since the Bagel Bakery was closed Saturday for the Sabbath, Yo-Yo didn't have to be at work till they opened at sundown. She didn't think she could drag either of her brothers, though. I laughed. "That's okay. You gotta hit twenty before you realize how much fun it is being a kid. Just bring yourself."

Fortunately, the weather cooperated—one of those treasure days of late October, when summer made one last attempt to return. Josh and Denny had soccer games on Saturday, but they both got rides, so I offered to go pick up Chanda and her kids.

"Why didn't you invite Emerald Enriques?" Amanda demanded, following me around as I hunted for my car keys. *Right. And José would have to come along to escort his sister on the el, I suppose.* I spied my keys on the stove—the stove?—and snatched them up before Amanda made a comment about me having a "senior moment."

"Next time." I smiled sweetly and pecked my daughter on the cheek. "Tell you what. You can either clean your room as usual or make some sugar cookies for our little party—pumpkins, with orange frosting or something."

I backed the minivan out of the garage, feeling smug about my little deal with Amanda. Of course, she might get huffy and not do either—you never could tell with fifteen-year-olds.

There was no quick way to Juneway Terrace on a Saturday afternoon, even though it wasn't that far. I mentally tossed a coin and headed for Sheridan Road. "So, God," I muttered as I waited at a red light on the busy north-south street. "What should we do about Amanda and José? Let them date? Figure it's puppy love and it will go away? What?"

The light changed to green and the line of cars crept forward, but the light turned red again just as I got to the intersection. Why didn't they widen this road? It was only two lanes, with parked cars crowding both sides. Drumming my fingers on the door rest, a man with dreadlocks and walnut-colored skin crossing the intersection in front of the minivan caught my eye. I half-expected him to be wearing an embroidered tunic over wide cotton pants, but the dreadlocks were pulled back into a ponytail, and he was wearing a tan sport coat, open-necked shirt, jeans, and carrying a briefcase. Then, for some strange reason, he turned beside my right front headlight and made his way between the Caravan's passenger door and the car parked along the curb.

Instinctively, I glanced at my door locks. *Not locked.* I pushed the button at my fingertips. The locks snapped into place with a loud *click.*

The man paused, slowly bent down, and caught my eye through the passenger side window. "That's right," he said loudly through the glass. "Lock your doors! But you really should keep them locked all the time, lady."

Ohmigosh. He heard me lock the doors! To my chagrin, the man pulled out a set of keys, unlocked the door of the four-door sedan parked along the curb, and got in.

Sheesh, Jodi. He was only getting into his parked car. I was so embarrassed that I didn't even notice the light had turned green until horns started to honk behind me. *Oh, God, he probably thinks I locked the doors because he's black and male and wearing dreads.* I pulled forward, but I wanted to go back. I wanted to say, *"I'm so sorry, sir. You're right. I should keep my doors locked all the time. I didn't mean to offend you.*" But a glance in my rearview mirror showed the sedan pulling around the corner and disappearing down the cross street.

For some reason, the incident rattled me. *Look,* I told myself as I double-parked in front of Chanda's apartment building and honked the horn. *You locked the doors because a man was coming close to your car door and you didn't know why. Not because he was black.* Or . . . did I?

Chanda and her three children trooped out of the apartment building door dressed like they were going to a party. The boy even had a bow tie! The kids piled into the backseats while Chanda climbed into the front. I tried to push the incident out of my mind.

"Dat big one in the back, he Thomas," Chanda announced. She pronounced it To-*mas*. "He eleven. Then Cheree. She seven. And Dia. She five. Say hello to Miz Baxter," she ordered over her shoulder.

A chorus of hellos echoed from behind us.

"Hi, kids." None of the kids looked alike. Made me wonder. "This car is kinda funny: it won't move until all seat belts have been fastened."

Chanda's eyes widened. "That true?" She wagged her head. "Cars too smart for dey britches now." She pulled her seat belt across her chest and clicked it.

Yo-Yo, Florida, and Carla were already in the backyard spreading newspapers on a couple of card tables when we pulled into the garage. Carla hid behind her mama while Chanda introduced her kids, but by the time I brought out black markers to draw faces on the pumpkins and serrated steak knives to cut them out, Carla, Cheree, and Dia were already giggling behind their hands.

"So glad Carla could come," I whispered to Florida. "This isn't the weekend she visits . . .?"

A shake of her head. No coppery ringlets or beaded braids today. Just pinned back with a few bobby pins. "Uh-uh. Just first and third weekends. But I tell you one thing—it ain't gonna be that way for long." Florida pinched her lips into a determined line.

Cleaning out those big pumpkins of their seeds and stringy matter proved to be a big job. Yet Thomas played the man, rolled up his sleeves, and dug out the gooey mess from two of the pumpkins, and Yo-Yo and I did the other two. The faces that got carved into the orange shells were rather lopsided. "But they'll look great with a candle inside when it's dark," I promised.

Amanda—will wonders never cease?—brought cutout sugar cookies, still warm from the oven, and a bowl of orange frosting. This was a big hit, as the girls dug in with table knives and blobbed frosting on the cookies. Thomas was content just to eat them, which he did in rather alarming numbers. But Chanda didn't stop him, so I didn't either.

That girl is really good with kids, I mused, watching Amanda hugging Carla and teasing Chanda's kids. Even Thomas warmed up to her. She made a game of stuffing the dirty newspapers and pumpkin innards into a trash bag, and the only fight the kids had was who was going to take it out to the trash can.

Yo-Yo left her pumpkin at our house and asked me to bring it when I came to Yada Yada tomorrow night at Ruth's house. Yet by the time I dropped off Florida and Carla at the Morse El station and took Chanda and her kids home, I was bushed. Not even sure I wanted to go to Yada Yada the next night.

Did I dare tell Yada Yada what happened today with that man? Made me look like a dork, for sure. Or revealed my prejudices beneath my smug exterior. Part of me wanted to tell them—or tell Avis, or somebody. Somebody African-American, who would affirm my motives. *"Of course you should've locked your doors! I would've! The man's just got a problem."*

On one level it didn't matter what my real motives were. The *man* obviously experienced it as just one more white woman protecting herself from a black man. And there was no way I could go back and fix it.

33

Denny let us out in front of Uptown's storefront the next morning as usual then drove off to find a parking place. A stiff, cold wind chased bits of trash down Morse Avenue. Yesterday must have been summer's last gasp.

Funny, I thought. *No lights on.* I pulled on the door handle. Locked.

"Hurry up, Mom!" Amanda whined. "I'm cold."

I shrugged. "It's not open." I checked my watch—almost nine-thirty. Should be open. Unless the Rapture had taken all the Christians during the night and the entire Baxter family had been "left behind." Or maybe Pastor Clark changed the time of service and we weren't paying attention. Or—

"Uh-oh." Realization dawned. "It's the last weekend of October. Daylight Savings Time ended last night. It's only"—my kids were going to kill me!—"eight-thirty."

Amanda's jaw dropped like I'd just announced the end of civilization as we know it. "Mo-om! We could've slept in another hour, and you got us up at the old time?" Josh gave me a dark look that said, *"Bad, bad mother"* and hunched his shoulders against the wind.

Denny came trotting up the sidewalk, trying not to be late, but he looked confused when he saw us still standing at the front door. When I told him we'd *all* forgotten to turn the clocks back—no way were they going to pin this on just me—he immediately moved into his okay-let's-fix-it mode. "So we've got an extra fifty minutes? Let's go eat! I'm still hungry."

We nixed going for the car—it would take too much time to drive anywhere—and opted for a neighborhood grill that advertised, "One egg, grits, bacon or sausage, toast, and coffee" for $2.99. The regulars—an assortment of men who all needed a shave and looked like they lived in a single-room-only hotel—stared at us kinda funny as we walked in and dropped into the chairs by a window table.

"Hey! There's Florida!" Amanda jumped out of her seat, pulled open the door, and waved them in. Florida looked confused, but she came in, followed by Carla, Cedric, and Chris, looking like chilly penguins. Her kids had the same reaction when they found out she'd dragged them out of the house an hour early, but now it was getting funny. At least we weren't the only ones who forgot the time change.

By the time we got to church—ten minutes earlier than our usual mad dash up the stairs to the worship space—Carla was hanging onto Amanda, Cedric was saying, "Hey, Ma. Let's forget to set our clocks next year and have breakfast again!" and Chris and Josh were still arguing about who was the best R&B singer on WCRX radio.

Stu waved at us from the second row. "Thought about calling

you guys and reminding you about the time change, but I see you remembered." She smiled approvingly.

I didn't dare look at Florida, or I'd bust out laughing. I felt her deliberately step on my toes, and I got the message: *"I won't tell if you won't."*

FLORIDA AND HER KIDS came home with us and spent the afternoon till it was time for Yada Yada. The kids seemed content with tomato soup out of the can and toasted cheese sandwiches, followed by popcorn and a heated game of Monopoly. Carla lost interest in the game, so I set her up on the floor with paper, markers, scissors, and tape. She immediately dumped out the markers and began to draw, saying something I didn't quite catch.

"What's that, Carla?"

Her head remained bent over the paper. "My other mommy gave me stuff like this too."

"My other mommy . . ." I looked up quickly to see if Florida had heard, but her spot on the couch, where she'd been watching the Monopoly game, was empty.

I found her out on the front porch "having a cig." I grabbed my coat from the front hall and joined her outside. She acknowledged me but returned to staring at the trees lining our street. "You okay, Flo?"

She didn't answer for a long minute, dragging on the cigarette and blowing smoke into the nippy air. Finally she stubbed it out and leaned against the porch pillar, hands in her pockets. "Don't know if me and Carl gonna make it, Jodi."

Oh God, not this. "What's wrong, Flo? Did something happen?"

She shrugged. "Nothin' in particular 'happened.' It's just . . . things ain't fallin' together for us." She was quiet for a few moments, and I just waited. "It's hard on a man when he don't have no job, know what I mean? He gets ugly—takes it out on me and the kids."

"Not . . .?" I couldn't say it.

"Hit us? Not me or Carla, anyway. But he whup those boys sometimes. Not that I don't think they need a good whack from time to time, but he yells—a lot. Makes the kids cry. Chris—he's just getting mad."

My heart was sinking. "Oh, Florida. You guys just got Carla back!" *Oh God. What would a bust-up in that family do to that little girl?*

Florida nodded. "I know. And if anything good in Carl's life, it's getting his baby back. She's his angel, but . . ." She didn't finish, just leaned on the post and shook her head.

I couldn't help it. I pulled Florida's hands out of her pockets and started to pray—out loud. Her usual *"Thank ya!"* was absent—just a muted "Oh Jesus" now and then. At the end of the prayer she squeezed my hands and said, "Thanks, Jodi. Just keep prayin'. That's all I know to do right now. Pray."

WELL, DENNY'S NOT HERE *to rescue Ben Garfield tonight,* I thought as we piled out of Avis's car in front of Ruth's house a couple of hours later. Denny had offered to drive Florida's kids home if we could get a ride with somebody. Yo-Yo showed up with another bag of day-old Jewish pastries from the Bagel Bakery, which we demolished in record time—some of us still had our mouths full when Avis called us to prayer. The prayer-and-praise time was a little muted till everyone had swallowed and got their voices back, then it was "praise as usual"—at least as usual for Yada Yada. Everyone talking to God at once, some clapping, some phrases sung from favorite praise songs, punctuated with "Glory!" and "You're a good God!" And we hadn't even shared our prayer needs yet.

Yet something was missing. Then I realized what it was: I missed Nony's rich voice praying Scripture verses, translating them in midprayer to make them personal. Where was Nony right now? How was her mother? Did she say when she was coming back?

"Did anyone hear from Nony?" I asked when the praise time was over and we had scrunched together on Ruth's small flowered couch, a couple of overstuffed chairs, and a bunch of folding chairs. "How about you, Hoshi?"

Hoshi, her willowy body almost swallowed up in Ruth's fat easy chair with the little lace doilies pinned to the back and arms, shook her head. "Nony has not contacted me. I did speak to Dr. Smith after class on Thursday, but he just said it would be awhile." She shrugged her shoulders, encased in a soft, baby-blue sweater set that set off her silky black hair. Her dark eyes shone with moisture. "I miss her," she added.

I could've kicked myself. Had I called Hoshi? Checked up on her since Nony left? *How hard would that be, Jodi?* Nony and the

Smiths were the closest thing to family Hoshi had in the States—but she couldn't very well go over to the Smiths' home with Nony and the kids out of the country and Mark home alone.

I made a mental note to call Hoshi at least once a week, maybe twice—but knowing me, a mental note wouldn't do it. I fished in my tote bag for a pen and some paper to make a to-do list, almost missing Hoshi's quiet voice as she continued.

" . . . have been thinking about what Jodi said about talking to the woman in jail, face to face . . ."

My head jerked up. Said? What had I said?

" . . . that the fear was gone after talking to the woman as a person—a person with a name." Hoshi tilted her chin up. "I'm thinking it would be good for me to go to the prison with you next time—if there is a next time."

"Alabanza Jesús!" Delores breathed. "Oh, Hoshi, that is . . . is . . ." She seemed to be searching for the right word. ". . . *valiente. Si, muy valiente.*"

"Very brave," Edesa translated, smiling at Hoshi.

Ruth shook her head. "Brave, maybe. But necessary? Why must she go? Three Yada Yadas already visited that Becky person in prison—like the Bible says we should do. Represent us, they did. *Everybody* doesn't need to go."

"That's right, Ruth," Avis said gently. "Everybody *doesn't* need to go, but if the Holy Spirit is prompting Hoshi to go, it may be an important step in the healing God wants to do. As she said, facing her fear. Because fear is not of God. Also"—she began thumbing through her big Bible—"it might prepare the ground for forgiveness." Avis found what she was looking for. "From the Lord's Prayer, the model Jesus gave us to pray: 'Forgive us our sins, *as we forgive those who sin against us.*'"

The living room was quiet, except for the sound of a TV from somewhere in the back of the house. *As we forgive* . . . Yeah. That was one of those sticky little things Jesus said which we piously recited as part of the Lord's Prayer, but when you came right down to it was hard to swallow. Almost sounded like a contract: "God will treat our sins in the same way we treat other people's sins." Ouch.

The silence was broken by a little laugh from Hoshi. "Do not talk me out of it—I will accept any and all excuses not to go!" But she leaned in my direction. "Jodi, will you write another letter to . . . to the woman, and ask if she will put my name on her visitors' list?"

Well, yeah, but that means you need a ride down there, so either Denny and I need to go again, or somebody else with a car needs their name on the list. I tried the back-door approach. "Sure, I'll write the letter. Anybody else want their name on the visitors' list?" I was hoping someone with a car would speak up, like Stu or Avis, or even Ruth—not likely—but no one volunteered. *Great. Just great.*

Avis moved on, collecting other prayer concerns. Florida didn't say much, just, "Pray for the Hickmans. Lot goin' on, not all of it good." We put Nony on the prayer list, and Avis volunteered to call Mark Smith to find out when she was coming back.

Chanda piped up. "Mi not get even t'ree words out of Adele at church dis mornin', but someone say it be her birthday week from tomorrow—four November. Yada Yada didn't visit nobody's

715

church all month. Why don't ever'body come to Paul and Silas Apostolic next Sunday? Be a *big* surprise for Adele's birthday."

"Ahh . . . maybe too big a surprise, Chanda," Stu said diplomatically. "I think it would be very awkward. Avis said to give her space, remember?"

Heads nodded around the room, including Avis.

Yo-Yo spoke up from the floor, squeezed between Ruth's chair and a corner of the flowered couch. "But showing Adele we haven't forgotten her—that'd be good. Maybe we could all send her birthday cards."

"A good idea, that is!" Ruth beamed. "Kill her with kindness."

Stu groaned. "We're not trying to kill her, Ruth."

Humph, I thought. *It'd take a lot more than kindness to kill Adele anyway.*

34

Avis dropped me off after Yada Yada, and I let myself in the front door, dumping my tote bag and hanging up my jacket. *Hope Denny has changed all the clocks by now.* I kicked off my shoes and headed toward the light in the dining room. *No way do I want to show up at school tomorrow an hour early.*

Josh was at the computer, surfing the Net for college info. So much for writing that letter to Becky Wallace—not that I minded putting it off. With a hint of glee I noticed that Josh's head sported a brown shadow, like a thin mat of Astroturf. He was probably getting tired of having to shave it every two to three days. "Where's your dad?"

Josh grunted. "Living room, I think." He resumed clicking the mouse, intent on the computer screen.

The living room? It was dark when I came in. I headed to the front of the house. "Denny?"

"Yeah. In here." His voice came from the recliner near the bay windows.

"What are you doing sitting in the dark?" I shuffled in my sock feet toward the recliner, illumined only by the pale streetlights outside, and almost tripped over Willie Wonka, who was snoring right in my path.

Denny held out a hand and pulled me down onto the arm of the chair. "Just thinking."

Yuck. He smelled like cigarette smoke. I almost said something but caught myself, hoping he'd let me in on whatever he was pondering. Besides, we might argue over his occasional beer, but I *knew* he wasn't lighting up on the side. Not the way he jumped all over his student athletes if he caught them smoking.

"Florida get home okay?" he asked.

My perch on the arm of the chair was a little precarious, but I snuggled closer, in spite of how he smelled. "Yeah. She got a ride with Stu, who was taking Edesa and Delores home. Not really on the way, but you know Stu. Have car, will travel." *Listen to yourself, Jodi!* Even though Stu got on my nerves with her "instant solution" to everything, I had to admit she was generous to a fault, picking people up, taking people home, giving of her time to make Yada Yada happen.

"I met Carl."

"You met—oh! When you took Florida's kids home?"

"Yeah. Carla fell asleep in the backseat, so I carried her inside. Carl buzzed us in, but I'm sure he was expecting the kids to come up by themselves—at least he just stared at me when he opened the door and saw me standing there with Carla over my shoulder. I said, 'Hi, I'm Denny Baxter. Where should I put her?' And once inside . . . I dunno. Figured this was my chance to meet Florida's husband beyond just hi and good-bye."

"Ah. That explains why you smell like an ashtray." I sniffed pointedly.

"That bad, huh." He chuckled. "Well, yeah, he seemed pretty nervous. Must've smoked half a pack while I was there."

"Half a pack! How long did you stay? Did you guys actually, you know, talk?" *Oh, wow, God.* And I hadn't said anything yet to Denny about what Florida told me out on the porch.

"Yeah. Well . . . as much as guys talk who are sizing each other up like tomcats in an alley. Mostly we talked about his kids—I figured that was safe territory. Told him how much I enjoyed getting to know them; thanked him for sharing them with us. He seemed kinda surprised by that. We talked about Carla too—that opened him up a little. His face lit up talking about Carla."

"Did he say anything about needing a job?"

"Nope. I think that's kinda touchy. But I did invite him to church. Told him to come with Florida and the kids, that I'd be really glad to see him."

"And?"

Denny shrugged. "He said, oh yeah, yeah, he would. But who knows. Still, now that we've talked a bit, maybe I'll invite him to our next men's breakfast at Uptown."

Now I was sure this meeting was God-inspired. I told Denny what Florida had said on the porch that afternoon. "Maybe knowing some guys who care will make a difference."

"Maybe."

I rolled off the arm of the recliner and pulled up the frayed ottoman. *Ahh, much better.* Somehow I wasn't as flexible with a steel rod in my leg. "So why are you sitting here in the dark? I thought something was wrong." By now my eyes had gotten used to the dim light of the streetlights, and I could see Denny's face, puckered in a frown.

He sighed. "I don't know. Just started thinking on the way home. Thinking about a lot of things, stuff that's happened. I've been involved in Uptown's outreach for the last ten years, but that's nothing compared to the stuff we've confronted since Yada Yada walked in our door. You'd think I'd know something by now, but you know what?" He smacked the arm of the chair so hard, even Willie Wonka jumped. "I feel pretty darn helpless to make a difference! Carl Hickman? It's tempting to tell him to shape up and support his family, but what do *I* know about what he's had to face in his life? And Becky Wallace . . . what does God expect of us in that situation? I still get mad when I think about all the danger my wife and daughter and our friends were in that night."

He fell silent again. I laid a hand on his knee, but he didn't seem to notice. "Know what, Jodi? Want to know what bothers me the most?" His voice broke a little. "Adele. Adele and MaDear. Why did God let that happen? I'm not the man MaDear thinks I am—but it still rips me up that she thinks I am."

He pulled out a handkerchief and blew his nose. When he spoke again, I knew it'd been a cover for the tears he was fighting back. "Heck. I don't have a clue why we moved into Chicago. Thought I could make a difference. Ha."

I DIDN'T THINK OUR CONVERSATION in the dark was the best time to bring up the fact that Hoshi wanted—maybe needed—to visit Becky Wallace and face her fears, which obviously implicated Denny, since he and I were the only people with a car on B. W.'s visitors' list so far. Unless I drove.

Not sure I'm ready for that.

I put off writing to Becky Wallace for a few days, caught up in a school week that included Halloween, TV specials about ghosts and ghouls, and an entire classroom that would be high on sugar the next day. Not the best week to see what Hakim could do with some one-on-one attention, but between Christy and me, we managed to spend at least twenty minutes a day working with him verbally or hands-on in different subjects. Working that way, he seemed to catch on quickly, came up with clever answers, and beamed when he solved problems. Once, to test him a little, I waited half an hour then gave him the same comprehension questions we'd just discussed written out on paper. He got angry, drew a big X over the paper, and refused to cooperate the rest of the day.

"I think he has a learning disability," I told my student teacher. "Makes me so mad his mom won't get him tested."

"Maybe we can talk to her at parent-teacher conferences in a couple of weeks."

"We?" I pulled a face. "I was going to let *you* do that conference."

Christy's eyes widened under her cap of dark curls. "Ms. Baxter! You wouldn't!"

Wouldn't I? "Just kidding. Don't worry. Got any ideas for something fun we can do on Halloween—*besides* bobbing for apples?"

She grinned sheepishly. "We could let them 'wrap the mummy.' All we'd need is five or six rolls of toilet paper."

So on Thursday, Christy and I used the last half-hour of class time to divide into teams and let the kids "wrap a mummy." It was loud and chaotic, but most of the noise was laughter and squeals of excitement—except for the moment when Ramón pushed over his team's "mummy" because she wouldn't stand still. We sent the winning team out the door with red apples and gave yellow apples to all the runners-up. My feeble antidote to the usual candy frenzy.

Uptown Community sponsored a "Hallelujah Fest" at the church as a Halloween alternative—ghoulish costumes strongly discouraged—and Denny, Josh, and Amanda were shanghaied along with the rest of the youth group to help with games, eats, and a costume parade. I stayed home to answer the door for neighborhood trick-or-treaters, though I'd been told by Uptowners that "kids don't trick-or-treat in Rogers Park—it's too dangerous." Last year—our first in Chicago city limits—we'd gotten a few in our neighborhood, which still boasted a lot of houses, so I decided to have treats on hand "just in case."

At the last minute I remembered to light the jack-o'-lantern in the front window as daylight faded. Ugh, it was starting to rot. "Hang in there for a few more hours, buddy," I told the pumpkin, propping it up on the windowsill. "Then you can rot to your heart's content out in the garbage can."

The doorbell rang a few times, but the bowl of Tootsie Roll

Pops and bubble gum pretty much stayed untouched. So I figured this was as good a time as any to write Becky Wallace. Redeeming the time, so to speak. As I called up our e-mail, my heart did a leap as a new message joined the clutter in our Inbox: a note from Nony! I could hardly click it open fast enough.

To: Yada Yada
From: BlessedRU@online.net
Re: Hello from Kwazulu-Natal!

Dear Yada sisters,

Please forgive me for not writing sooner. Mark says, "Please e-mail Yada Yada! They keep calling to ask if I have any news about you!" I feel glad for your concern. My brother finally helped me access my e-mail online at his office, so now I can let you know how things are with us in South Africa.

What a joy to see my mother! She is still in hospital, but she improves a little bit each day. However, visits tire her, so we are limited to only one hour. I am not sure when she will be able to come home. I would like to stay until she is released from hospital, to help make arrangements for her care and see that she is settled.

Hmm, I thought. *Wonder how Mark feels about that? Her return date sounds rather vague.*

In the meantime, I am getting reacquainted with my country. Kwazulu-Natal is called "The Garden Province" with good reason! The summer season has just begun, so everything is in bloom. Lilies everywhere! African lilies, bugle lilies, lion's tail . . . the flowers must enjoy the humidity (though I confess, I don't). My mother is in hospital in Pietermaritzburg, but I am hoping to take the boys to visit their cousins who live along the coast and maybe even take a "safari" into the savannah—like real American tourists!

But, dear sisters, my heart is also heavy. It is one thing to read statistics about the AIDS pandemic in Africa. It is quite another to learn that my old school chum's teenage daughter was raped by her uncle, because he thought he could be cured of the disease by having sex with a virgin. Now she is HIV. Myths and ignorance abound! Proverbs 13:16 is so true: "Every prudent man acts with knowledge, but a fool exposes his folly." My brother, Nyack Sisulu, who does social research for the KZN Department of Health, told me that half of all fifteen-year-olds in South Africa and Zimbabwe will eventually die of AIDS. It is so hard to see the suffering and do nothing!

The doorbell rang again—*Okay, this is it,* I decided—and I dispensed candy to a Harry Potter look-alike and a ghost in a pillowcase with eyeholes. "Cute!" I said, waving to an adult standing out on the sidewalk. The ghost stood on my porch, pawing through his—her?—sack of goodies, trying to see what I put in there. "Go on, honey," I urged, casting an anxious eye down the block. I wanted to get the porch light turned off and the pumpkin blown out before any late trick-or-treaters took it personally.

After darkening the front of the house, I hustled back to the computer wondering just what Nony planned to "do" about the AIDS crisis. I scanned the page on my screen trying to find my place. Ah.

As elsewhere, the poorest people pay more for less. Food prices are soaring in the Eastern Cape—a direct result of the political chaos in Zimbabwe, which used to provide one of our food staples: maize. Without their export, the price of maize has skyrocketed. And for South Africa's poor, maize is the primary food that they buy. Can you imagine spending over 50 percent of your income just on food?

No, I couldn't. Yet right now I was more concerned about Nony. Was Mark right to be worried that Nony's heart would find reason to stay in South Africa? I read on.

But as always there is hope. This week the Sunday *Times* told a story about schoolchildren right here in Pietermaritzburg who collected 240 rand, or about thirty-three dollars, to help feed the Eastern Cape's starving children. One boy gave his taxi money, which meant he had to walk forty-five minutes to get home. Another gave his birthday money. Many come from indigent families themselves. The children saw a need, set themselves a goal, and made personal sacrifices. These children are my heroes! And they give me reason to hope.

Love to all. I do so miss the Yada Yada prayer meetings.

Nonyameko

P.S. Marcus and Michael have their own new hero—Makhaya Ntini, a star player on South Africa's cricket team! SA is playing a series of tests against Bangladesh here in Kwasulu-Natal, and everyone is as excited as if the Chicago Cubs were playing in the World Series. Not sure the boys are going to want to come home.

Ha! Denny and Josh would get a kick out of that. The Chicago Cubs in the World Series. *Don't we wish.*

And then I read her last sentence again.

35

J called up New Message, wrote "Got Nony's e-mail. How do we pray???" and sent it to Avis. Nony had sent her e-mail to the entire prayer group, so it wasn't like telling tales. But it was a whole week till the next Yada Yada meeting, and I felt an urgency to be praying for Nony and Mark and their boys. I also felt perplexed. Maybe taking Marcus and Michael to South Africa was a mistake. I mean, a visit was great, but the boys couldn't help picking up on their mother's strong desire to return to South Africa to live.

I was still at the computer working on the letter to B. W. when Denny and the kids got back from the Hallelujah Fest. I handed Denny a printout of Nony's e-mail. "Maybe you should call Mark; see how he's doing."

He read the note, nodded, then leaned close to my ear. "Guess who showed up to play keyboard for the Hallelujah Fest?"

Keyboard? Who played keyboard? One of Yo-Yo's brothers? Florida's Chris? Or . . . *Duh. Of course.* "José." I sighed.

Denny waggled his eyebrows.

"Denny! You think this little romance is cute!"

He grinned. "Well, yeah, kinda. José is a neat kid."

"But, it's"—how did I say this without sounding narrow-minded?—"complicated."

He shrugged. "Love is always complicated."

I sucked back a sharp answer. *Huh.* This wasn't love. This was a teenage crush. I mentally rehearsed all the good reasons we should discourage this infatuation, wanting Denny to stand with me in a united front, but I knew that just before heading for bed was no time for an argument. Maybe I'd have to enlist Delores's support.

I FINALLY GOT THE LETTER to Becky Wallace in Saturday's mail, along with a birthday card for Adele I'd found at Osco Drugs. I'd vaguely wondered if I could do something with the meaning of her name, like I'd done for Yo-Yo, but the name Web site came up with: "Adele—a familiar form of Adelaide. Meaning: 'noble, kind.'" Noble? Kind? Not the first words that came to mind when I thought of Adele. So much for name meanings.

So I'd stood in the card aisle at the drugstore for the better part of thirty minutes, wondering what kind of card you sent a person who'd basically shut you out of her life. I passed over "To a Special Friend" and "Funny, You Don't *Look* Over the Hill," and finally settled on a card with a Maya Angelou quote: "Women should be tough and tender, laugh as much as possible, and live long lives."

"Yada Yada should've sent a card 'From the Whole Gang' and been done with it," I muttered as I stood at the mailbox. Even signing it had been a problem. *"Love, Jodi"*? Didn't think so. *"Your friend"*? Assumed too much. *"Praying for you"*? Too pompous. I'd finally settled for *"Wishing you God's best on your birthday—Jodi."*

Okay, God, You do the rest. I pulled open the yawning mailbox mouth, which gobbled both envelopes and practically smacked its lips.

It was the first Saturday of November, and hopefully parents were signing up for the midmonth parent-teacher conferences and report-card pickup at Bethune Elementary—first come, first served. Teachers didn't have to be at signups; too often, parents wanted to start talking right then. Call-ins had to take whatever slots were left. I was tempted to phone all thirty of my kids' parents and give them a lecture on the importance of parent-teacher conferences. After all, barely half of them had shown up for parents' night in September. Made me so mad! How could the school do its job without support on the home front?

When I got to school on Monday and checked the sign-up lists, I was pleased to see twenty-plus time slots filled. I ran my finger down the list, sometimes having to check the "Student's Name" column to figure out who was who, because last names didn't always match. *Ramón's father—good. Ebony . . . Kaya . . . Hakim . . .* Hey! Hakim's mother signed up. There it was: Geraldine Porter. Hallelujah! But on second glance the signature looked kind of funny. I squinted closer. The cursive was obviously juvenile—not the bold signature Geraldine Porter had scrawled on her note.

I paused by Hakim's desk while the class was doing silent reading. The third-grade reader sat closed on his desk, and he slouched in his seat. Like he was waiting.

"I see your mother signed up for the parent-teacher conferences, Hakim." I smiled encouragingly. "Did your mother come in, or did someone else sign up for her?"

The dark eyes got wary. "She works Saturday. Sent my cousin."

"Your cousin? How old is your cousin?"

Hakim squirmed. "She's fourteen. They said it was okay."

"It is! I'm just glad your mother is coming. I'm looking forward to meeting her." *Oh, right, Jodi. Like a toothache.* I touched the reader. "Would you like me to read with you awhile?"

He shrugged, his eyes still wary. "You gonna tell my mama I'm doing bad?"

I wanted to hug him. "On the contrary, Hakim. I'm going to tell her how smart you are when Ms. James and I let you work the way you do best." I tapped my head . . . and nearly fell over.

Because Hakim smiled at me.

HAKIM'S SMILE lifted me off my feet all day. Maybe I did like teaching at Mary McLeod Bethune Elementary. Maybe I could make a difference with some of these kids. Not to mention that Hakim's shuttered features—which usually kept you at a distance, like a barbed-wire fence around his soul—had been transformed by that smile. Today . . . the child radiated beauty.

I felt so upbeat that I made chicken cacciatore over fettuccini for supper, even dug out the half-full bottle of Chablis we'd hidden under the sink when my parents came to visit and added some to the sauce. Still some left—unchilled, but too bad—so I got out two wine glasses for Denny and me then gathered a bunch of candles, all different sizes, and lit them as a flaming centerpiece.

"We got company?" Josh asked when I called for supper, lifting the lid of the serving dish. "Yum."

Denny arched a questioning eyebrow. I could see him sorting through the possibilities in his mind. *"Not our anniversary—we did that. Birthday? Did that too."* "Okay, I give. What are we celebrating?"

I laughed, ready to say *"Monday,"* when out of the blue I remembered. "It's Adele Skuggs's birthday!" I laughed even harder at the look on his face.

"Oh. Adele's birthday. Balloons. Good cheer and all that." He sounded very much like a two-legged Eyeore.

By now even the kids thought it was a hoot. We joined hands for the dinner blessing, which Amanda offered. "Thanks for the food, God, and whatever got into Mom to make her celebrate a birthday for somebody who's not even here. Amen."

When all our plates had been served, Denny lifted his wine glass to make a toast. "To Adele. May she . . ." He paused, searching for words. "May she 'be anxious for nothing,' 'give thanks in all things,' and experience a 'peace that passes all understanding.' And . . . I do mean that."

We clinked glasses. Then I raised my glass again. "To Adele—noble and kind."

Denny's glass paused in midair. "Noble. And kind." His expression begged for an explanation.

"That's what the name Adele means: noble and kind."

He grunted. "I think she missed her calling."

"Or maybe that's how God thinks of her," Amanda said. Denny and I stared at our daughter as she nonchalantly shoveled in another mouthful of cacciatore.

Out of the mouths of teenagers, Lord . . .

I checked e-mail after supper while Denny and Josh did the dishes, which, I pointed out, shouldn't be a big deal since I'd already washed the cooking pots. (Big brownie points for Mom.) I scrolled through the pileup in our Inbox. Squeezed in among a bunch of spam and a dozen messages for Josh or Amanda were two messages to Yada Yada. "Denny!" I called into the kitchen. "We really do need to set up individual e-mail addresses for the kids!"

"Yeah, Dad," Josh echoed. "Ever heard about privacy?" Denny's only response was a noncommittal grunt.

The first message was from Stu: "Did everybody remember to send birthday cards to Adele?" I rolled my eyes at the screen before hitting Delete. *Yeah, yeah, we're all grownups, Leslie Stuart.*

The second was from Avis with "Re: Prayer for Nony" in the subject line: "Sisters, remember: we're not God. We may think we know 'what is best' for Nony and her family, but let's not get in the way of the Holy Spirit. We can certainly pray for unity of heart and mind for Nony and Mark, for safety for Nony and the boys, and that God will use this trip to further His purpose in the Smith and Sisulu families." Then: "P. S. Next Yada Yada is at my apartment, right? Just checking—don't want to clean house for nothing. Smiles."

I snorted. Frankly, I doubted if a speck of dust would have the courage to settle on one of Avis's spotless surfaces. As for the prayer focus, guess I needed to scrap the one I'd been praying: *"God, get Nony home quick!"*

I LOVED MEETING at Avis's apartment. Just being there seemed to gather up all the loose ends flying around in my rather scattered spirit, knitting them for the moment into a warm, comforting shawl for the soul. Why Avis had that effect on me, I wasn't sure, because at the same time the striking art prints on her walls, brimming bookshelves, stacks of Bibles and devotionals, and framed photos of her deceased husband and beaming grandbabies also seemed like a crossroads where past and present, the exotic and the familiar, work and worship, her world and my world met. And it was all good.

Not everybody made it to our first November meeting that second Sunday. Chanda's kids were sick, and Delores had to work at the hospital. *Rats. I wanted to talk to her about Amanda and José.* But I was able to tell Yada Yada that I had written to Becky Wallace about adding Hoshi to her visitors' list, and Avis once again prayed that Becky's answer would be our answer. Carl had not come to Uptown with Florida the last two Sundays, even though Denny had invited him, and Florida didn't even want to pray about it. "We pray about it, I go getting my expectations up," she groused. "If God wants to get Carl to church, He can just surprise me."

I wondered out loud whether anyone had heard from Adele. Did she receive our cards? "Yes," Stu said, looking perfectly positioned for *House Beautiful* on Avis's beige-and-black furniture. "I called her last Monday on her birthday. She said she'd received several cards from Yada Yada and to tell you all she appreciates it."

I waited, but Stu was done. I'd been hoping that all of us remembering Adele's birthday would break down the wall she had built around herself, and she'd say she was coming back to Yada Yada. But . . . Guess it was still good that we sent the cards.

We spent a lot of our prayer time praying for Nony, with Avis praying a long time "in the Spirit." Frankly, it seemed appropriate to pray in an unknown tongue and let God figure it out, since we didn't really know how to pray for Nony right now. We also gathered up other concerns, so I threw the upcoming parent-teacher conferences in the pot, being careful not to make Avis-the-Principal think Jodi-the-Teacher was too stressed out about them.

Yet I was. Last year's fall parent-teacher conferences—my first at Bethune Elementary—had been grueling. For one thing, I'd felt very self-conscious, like a glaring white crayon among a sea of hues in a box of sixty-four Crayolas. Admittedly, most of the parents who showed seemed genuinely concerned about their children and expressed appreciation for anything that smacked of improvement.

But I'd had three doozies: one father who showed up an hour late reeking of alcohol and got angry that I wouldn't see him *now;* a Pakistani mother who couldn't speak a word of English, so we ended up just nodding and smiling at each other and saying, "Good, good"; and another mother who kept complaining about "the neighborhood," as if I was personally responsible.

I determined not to approach these parent-teacher conferences like the "old Jodi." After all, my name meant "God is gracious," and I had a new weapon: praise. So for the next few days, I kept the gospel and praise CDs going before and after school, focused on praying for each of my students by name as I walked to and from school, and as Wednesday dawned, even thanked God for whatever He brought my way that day.

Conferences started at noon, since we went till eight that evening. This was Christy James's first experience as a student teacher with parent-teacher conferences, and she was a trooper. She even ducked out a couple of times to bring back fresh coffee and Krispy Kremes from the convenience store a block away, leaving the carrot sticks and apples I'd brought from home languishing in my tote bag.

No one had signed up for the 6:45 slot, which was strange since that was "prime time" for working parents, but I still had four more parents to go: LeTisha's . . . Hakim's . . . Chanté's . . . and D'Angelo's. Well, okay. All four had positive reports, as well as "areas that need improvement." Since I had a breather, I ducked out into the hall to see if I could catch Avis. It might be helpful if she sat in on my conference with Hakim's mother so I wouldn't be the only one encouraging some testing. But Avis wasn't in the office or in the hallways—she must be meeting with another teacher and student.

Shoot. I should have arranged this ahead of time. *Okay, Jesus, guess it's just You and me.*

Both of LeTisha's parents came to the conference, *with* LeTisha, which sent their approval rating on the Jodi Baxter Parent Scale right up to the top. I even told them LeTisha was living up to her name in the classroom: "joy." The mother teared up at that and told me they'd almost lost LeTisha to a heart defect when she was a baby. "Baby, look at you now," the father teased, chucking the embarrassed eight-year-old under the chin.

I was still smiling as they left. "You can send the next parent in!" I called after them.

Christy took LeTisha's folder from me and handed me the next folder: Hakim Porter. I barely had time to glance at my notes when I heard a boyish voice: "Hi, Miz B. Me an' my mama came."

I looked up to give Hakim a welcoming smile—and froze.

Standing before me was a woman I'd seen once before. In a courtroom at the Second District Courthouse. A woman who'd wanted to see me in jail.

Every inch of my body wanted to scream: *How can this be?* Because standing in my classroom was the mother of Jamal Wilkins, the boy I'd struck and killed with the Baxter car.

Recognition dawned on the other woman's face at the same time. Her dark eyes narrowed. Her mouth drew tight, leaving room to spit out only one word: *"You!"*

36

I groped for the desk behind me, trying to steady myself.
Oh Jesus . . . Jesus! Help me! Hakim and Jamal—*brothers?*
But the names! Porter . . . Wilkins . . .

"You!" The woman spat again, slicing into my jumbled
thoughts with her sharp, piercing eyes. Hakim's eyes pooled into
confusion, swimming back and forth between us. His mother suddenly seemed to realize he was standing there and spun him
around. "Go back into the hallway, Hakim!"

"But, Ma—"

"Now!" The woman thrust her finger toward the classroom
door.

Out of the corner of my eye, I noticed Christy quietly lead
Hakim out into the hallway, easing the door shut behind her. *Oh
please, Christy, go get Avis Johnson! Hurry!*

As the door closed with a soft wheeze, Geraldine Porter swung
her accusing finger into my face. "What kind of diabolical joke is

this?" Her fury slashed at me, like barbed wire whipping in the wind. "You . . . you kill my son! You walk away scot-free! Now here you are, acting like nothing happened, messing in my family's life, hiding behind a clever smokescreen—'Miz B' or whatever you call yourself." The barbs melded into a sneer.

I gulped for air. "No, no! Ms. . . . Ms. Porter, believe me! I had no idea Hakim was—"

"Well, I won't have it, do you understand me?" Geraldine Porter trampled my protest. "I . . . will . . . not . . . let . . . you . . . teach . . . my . . . son!" Each word hit me like a shotgun pellet.

Suddenly she whirled, her eyes sweeping the room. "Where's Hakim's desk?" She marched up and down the rows, glaring at the names taped carefully to each one. "Don't just stand there—show me where my son sits!"

Barely trusting my legs to hold me up, I made it to Hakim's desk then watched helplessly as she pulled out dog-eared pocket folders, pencils, a knit cap. "Ms. Porter, *please,* can we talk? Hakim is so bright, but he needs some special help. And I want to help him." My words tumbled out, almost falling over each other in my urgency to salvage something from this disaster. "If he could be tested—"

"Tested!" She slammed the top of the desk down. "Oh, yes, I know about this *testing*. It starts now, doesn't it—tracking kids into dumb and dumber, prettying it up under fancy titles like 'special needs.'" She was shouting at me. "Well, get this straight, Ms. Baxter. You don't have to worry about testing Hakim, because I am going to transfer him out of this classroom! Out of this school! Jesus!" Suddenly her features crumpled and her words descended into a moan. "Jesus! How much can one person bear?"

Instinctively, I reached out to her, but she jerked back, pulling her moment of vulnerability behind her flashing eyes. She straightened, and once again I saw the woman, hardened in her grief, who had faced me down in the courtroom after the charges against me had been dropped "for lack of evidence."

"Goodbye, Ms. Baxter. You won't—"

The door of the classroom opened. We both jumped. I caught a glimpse of royal blue as Avis Johnson came into the room and made her way quickly to where we were standing by Hakim's desk.

"Ms. Porter," she said, her composed, authoritative voice spreading calm like foam over a wildfire. She extended her hand to Hakim's mother. "I am Avis Johnson, principal here at Bethune Elementary. I don't believe I've had the pleasure."

The woman seemed taken off guard. "Wilkins-Porter," she corrected. "Geraldine Wilkins-Porter." She lifted a determined chin. "I would like to have my son transferred out of this classroom immediately."

Oh God! My spirit sank. *She really is going to take Hakim out.* I didn't know whether to try to explain to Avis, but by now I was fighting back tears. Did she recognize the woman? Avis had come to the hearing and sat in the back of the courtroom—to pray, she'd said. This woman had been there too. But if Avis knew what this was about, all she said now was, "Why don't we go to my office, and we can discuss it."

Hakim's mother tossed her head. "There is nothing to discuss.

Hakim will not be back in school until the necessary arrangements have been made. I will call you." She pressed the collection of items from Hakim's desk against the front buttons of her trim, navy-blue suit and strode resolutely toward the classroom door.

Out in the hall I heard Hakim wail, "Why we goin' home, Mama?" and a sharp, "Because—that's why!" before the door closed again.

Avis and I just stared at each other. Finally, Avis broke the fragile silence. "That was . . . Jamal Wilkins's mother?"

I nodded, not trusting myself to speak. The tears I'd been fighting back slid over the edges and ran down my cheeks.

"Lord, have mercy!" Avis sucked in her breath as though gathering her wits about her. "How many more parent conferences do you have, Jodi?"

I held up two shaky fingers.

"Christy can do them—I'll sit in with her. You go to the teachers' lounge and pull yourself together. But don't leave until we talk, all right?"

I was so grateful, I wanted to throw my arms around Avis or fall down and kiss her feet. Nodding mutely, I found the box of tissues on my desk, blew my nose, and moved numbly toward the door.

HOW I MADE IT THROUGH the teeming hallway without running into a distracted parent or an open door, I'll never know.

Mercifully, the teachers' lounge was empty, and I collapsed on the lone, saggy couch just as the dam of frustration and humiliation burst in a flood of tears. *Oh God, Oh God, Oh God, Oh God . . .* For some reason my desperate prayer got no further, and I let the silent sobs take over till they shook my whole body.

Finally I mopped my face, blew my nose, and tried to corral my wildly bucking thoughts. *What did she mean, 'hiding behind a smokescreen'? I'd only signed that note 'Ms. B' because that's what Hakim called me. My full name had been on room assignments mailed to each student's family, hadn't it? Surely she remembered my name from the hearing—probably kept it pinned to her wall and threw darts at it. Hadn't I tried to reach out to her that day, tell her how terribly sorry I was?* The helpless feeling washed over me once more. *Oh God, what more can I do?* I'd give anything if I could change what happened that dreadful day! But—

"But you can't, can you?" That's what Jamal Wilkins's mother had said to me after the hearing.

I felt cornered. What good was God's forgiveness if the person most affected by the accident that snuffed the life from her son wouldn't—couldn't—forgive me?

The door to the lounge opened and shut. I barely looked up but saw Avis's blue suit move toward me. I knew my eyes were puffy, my mascara probably smudged, my skin red and blotchy. I didn't care. Avis had seen me worse in the hospital.

Bethune Elementary's principal sat down beside me on the couch; I caught a whiff of silky perfume. Avis's presence, her smell, her voice usually filled me with a quiet joy, as though the Spirit of

God within her filled the space wherever she went. Today, the sweet scent seemed dissonant, like rose petals wafting through a garbage-strewn alley. *Ha!* Even Avis couldn't fix *this* mess. How many other parents and teachers had heard Hakim's mother yelling at me? What were they thinking right now? Would this cause a scandal for Bethune Elementary?

Geraldine Wilkins-Porter was right about one thing: it was some kind of sick joke.

I started to laugh—harsh, unhappy laughter. My shoulders shook again, and I threw my head back against the couch and howled.

"Jodi, stop."

I couldn't. *Jamal Wilkins . . . Hakim Porter—who could've known? I killed one. I was teaching the other.* It was hysterical when you thought about it. I shrieked. I let it all come out. I didn't care who heard me.

"Stop."

I stopped. It was the slap that did it. Avis Johnson slapped me.

"AVIS . . . SLAPPED YOU?" Denny drew back and stared at me as I told him the whole sordid story an hour later.

I nodded sheepishly. "I know what you're thinking. *Very* un-professional. Except we weren't 'Ms. Johnson' and 'Ms. Baxter' at that moment—just Avis and Jodi. I deserved it, I'm afraid. I was getting out of control."

The yada yada Prayer Group Gets Down

When I'd finally gotten home from school about nine o'clock, I pulled Denny away from *Law and Order* on TV—high-school conferences had been the previous week—and said I really, really needed to talk. Now we were sitting on our bed, backs propped against as many pillows as I could find, door shut against all intruders—except Willie Wonka, that is, who scratched and whined at the door till we let him in. Now the chocolate Lab sat with his white-whiskered chin resting on the side of the bed, brow wrinkled like tire treads, knowing in that peculiar way of dogs that something was wrong.

"Frankly, I'm mad, Denny—*really* mad at God, because I *prayed* about these conferences, prayed for all my students, and . . . and I feel *tricked.* How could God let this happen?" Avis had just listened to me rant and cry for a while, and so did Denny. I finally blew my nose. "Then she hugged me and said we'd talk later and sort it out somehow. And she promised to call Hakim's mother"—*Jamal's mother!* a voice in my head accused—"to talk about the situation."

Denny nodded. "You've got to let Avis handle it, Jodi. It's out of your hands. There's nothing you can do."

He reached out and pulled me against him, and I tried to relax in the curve of his arm, but my emotions still bounced around like ping-pong balls. Was that true? It was out of my hands? There was nothing I could do?

Denny's just trying to comfort you, Jodi, trying to help you let go.

But, my mind argued, hadn't I started something with Hakim? Something good? Why wouldn't God let me finish what I'd started?

743

Hadn't I been learning about His grace? Even my name: *God is gracious.* Yet maybe grace wasn't enough—

"—not if she won't forgive me!" My loud voice in the dark quiet startled me. *Good grief, I said that aloud.*

Then I heard Denny's whisper muffled against my hair: "Yeah. Goes for me too."

37

I had the nightmare again during the night, except the face lit up in my headlights kept shifting: *Jamal's eyes, wide with sudden terror . . . Geraldine Wilkins's face, an ice sculpture of fierce anger . . . then Hakim, looking straight at me, betrayed, accusing.* I made myself wake up and go to the bathroom, even chugged a whole glass of water. Yet the moment I laid down again, the three faces recycled behind my closed eyelids like a PowerPoint loop.

I was exhausted when the alarm went off. Still, I put my body on autopilot, let Willie Wonka outside, started the coffee . . . and suddenly realized what Denny had meant last night when he said, *"Yeah. Goes for me too."* He meant MaDear and Adele. The three of them, trapped in a tragic dance. Forgiveness would be so freeing, but . . . whom to forgive?

When I got to school, the halls were empty. Good. I'd deliberately left home twenty minutes early so I wouldn't run into any of

745

the other teachers and have to explain what happened last night. I collapsed at my desk and tried to pray, but all I could do was mumble over and over, "Oh God, help. Please help me—"

"Jodi?"

Startled, I looked up at Avis's voice. I hadn't heard the door open. The royal-blue suit had given way to a casual pair of black slacks and mocha sweater set. She pulled up a chair beside my desk. "Good. I'm glad you came early. I wanted to talk to you a minute before the school day started."

I just looked at her, too worn-out to use up extra words.

"You said last night that you're mad at God," she began. I didn't need reminding. I was still mad. "But can you handle the truth, Jodi? God has promised that He is working *all* things together for the good of those who love Him, who are called according to His purpose. *His* purpose, Jodi. His purpose for *you*."

I recognized the scripture she was quoting: Romans 8:28. *Oh sure.* One of the bedrock verses I'd memorized as a kid, convenient to haul out whenever anything went south. But I wasn't sure I really believed it at that moment.

Avis rested a hand on mine, which were clenched together in front of me on the desk. "Be encouraged, Jodi. I know it's hard to see right now, but if you have a minute before the kids come in, read Isaiah 55." She stood to go then turned back at the door and smiled. "Frankly, I think God is doing something big—very big."

She was gone, although I could still feel the touch of her hand on mine. I didn't move for a few moments, thinking about what she'd said. Then I glanced at the clock—five minutes till the bell rang.

Christy would be here any moment. Curious, I dug into my tote bag and pulled out the small Bible I'd started to carry around, even at school, and flipped pages until I found Isaiah 55.

I skimmed the passage and landed on verse eight. *"'For my thoughts are not your thoughts, neither are your ways my ways,' declares the Lord . . ."* I almost snorted. *Guess not! Wouldn't mind if God checked with me before putting me through a meat grinder, though.* I kept reading. *"So is my word that goes out from my mouth: It will not return to me empty, but will accomplish what I desire and achieve the purpose for which I sent it.'"*

Hmm. That's what Avis just said—that God was going to accomplish *His* purpose. It'd sure be nice if He gave me a clue now and then what that was.

I heard voices in the hallway and was just about to shut the Bible when my eyes caught the next verse: *"You will go out in joy and be led forth in peace . . ."*

The door opened, and Christy rushed in. "Sorry I'm late, Jodi. I'll go out and bring the kids in." My young student teacher, cheeks pink from the nippy air outside, looked at me kindly. "Are you okay after—you know, last night?"

I nodded. Even smiled. Yes, I was going to be okay . . . *I think.*

HAKIM WAS NOT IN SCHOOL that day or the next, and then it was the weekend. I tried to put him out of my mind and focus on the other children in my classroom, but they were all safe, just being their same squirrelly selves. But Hakim . . . what had his mother told him? Did he think I was some kind of monster? That I didn't care about him anymore? What was he doing today? Did she really put him in another school? Or was he just sitting at home, watching TV, pulling back into his shell?

My heart ached. Was this how the shepherd in Jesus's parable felt about the one lost sheep when He left the ninety-nine others safely corralled in the sheepfold and went looking for it?

I also read and reread the scriptures Avis had given to me that morning in my classroom until I thought the pages might fall out. On Saturday, after Denny left early to pick up Carl Hickman for the men's breakfast at Uptown Community—we were both surprised he had agreed to go—I turned the verses into my version of a "Nony prayer" and wrote it in my prayer journal:

"Okay, God. I'm going to trust that You are working all this mess together for something good, according to Your purpose—which, I admit, looks pretty foggy to me. Yet You made one thing clear: Your ways are not my ways. So I'm choosing to believe that 'Your Word' will accomplish Your desire and achieve Your purpose. Not just for my good, Jesus, but Hakim's too." I reread my prayer, then wrote: *"And for Hakim's mother too."*

By the time Denny got back around eleven, I wouldn't say I'd gotten all the way to "joy," but I was starting to feel some of that peace Isaiah talked about—not because I had any answers, but because I decided to start trusting God to figure it all out.

"Kids up yet?" Denny asked, opening the refrigerator door.

I shook my head. "Still zonked. Haven't heard a peep." A weird thought crossed my mind. Both kids could've snuck out in the wee hours, and I'd probably never know it, because I never checked on them once they were in for the night.

Stop it, Jodi! They're teenagers—they're just sleeping till high noon. I left Denny still rummaging in the refrigerator and did a quick room check. Two familiar lumps of covers in the dim bedrooms. *See, Jodi? Don't borrow trouble.* I headed back for the kitchen. "Didn't you guys just eat breakfast?"

Denny was forking cold leftover spaghetti straight from the Tupperware. "Two hours ago." His fork paused in midair. "Guess what? Mark Smith came too."

"Carl Hickman *and* Mark Smith?" Now there you had polar opposites. But if their wives—Florida Never-Been-Out-of-Chicago Hickman and Nonyameko World-Traveler Sisulu-Smith—could be sisters in the same prayer group, why not their husbands? I stared at my own husband with interest.

Denny set down the empty plastic container and belched. "Asked Mark Smith to come for Thanksgiving—hope that's okay."

"Thanksgiving! Don't you think Nony will be home by then?" Thanksgiving was less than two weeks away, and she'd been gone five weeks already. Still, if she wasn't . . .

Denny shrugged. "I don't think Mark knows yet. Said he would, unless his family comes home."

Thanksgiving. I hadn't given it a smidgeon of thought—except that we wouldn't be going to Iowa, since my folks had decided to drive to Denver to spend Thanksgiving with my oldest brother, Jim, and his family. Jim and Jeff . . . hadn't seen either one of my brothers for a while. I felt a small pang. It was so easy for families to drift apart.

Or fall apart. "Maybe we ought to invite Hoshi too," I said suddenly. "If Nony's not back, she won't have any place to go either." I sat down to make a list. Who else in Yada Yada might be alone? Not Avis—she'd be with her daughters and grandbabies on the South Side. Most of the others probably had family in the Chicago area. Anybody else? Stu?

I suddenly realized I knew nothing about Stu's family. She was single, she lived alone in Oak Park, she worked as a real-estate agent, and she'd latched onto Yada Yada and adopted Uptown Community as her church—that was all I knew. She had never offered information about any family, and I had never asked. Well, okay, I'd ask. Yada Yada was supposed to meet at my house the last Sunday of the month, just before Thanksgiving. If Mark and Hoshi were coming, I might as well invite a few more.

AVIS CALLED ME AT HOME that Saturday afternoon while Amanda was running the vacuum cleaner. "I had a meeting with Hakim's mother after school Friday."

"Just a minute—I can hardly hear you." I headed for my bedroom and shut the door, then took several deep breaths till my insides calmed down. "Okay."

"I met with Hakim's mother yesterday afternoon. She is adamant about removing Hakim from Bethune Elementary. However, school transfers are not that automatic, and I made it quite clear to her that further absence would be truancy. So we came to a compromise."

"What compromise?"

"Hakim will return to school on Monday but will be placed in the other third-grade classroom while she pursues a transfer. And, Jodi . . ."

"*What?*" That came out more snappish than I intended, but there it was.

"I agreed that you would not try to talk to Hakim, interact with him on the playground, or create any activities that would bring Hakim under your supervision."

"Avis!" How could she betray me like that? "He's going to think I don't care about him anymore! That *hurts,* Avis. Really hurts."

"Mmm. I'm sure it does. But I want you to know that I didn't promise that *I* wouldn't talk to Hakim. Actually, it didn't come up"—I could almost hear her stretching into a smile—"and I fully intend to talk to Hakim on Monday, maybe even check in with him daily. We don't know yet how he is reacting to all of this, but I will let Hakim know that you *do* care about him."

I let out a long sigh, paying out the head of steam I'd been building. "Thanks, Avis. Really. Don't know if this is good news or bad news. It'll be hard to see him in the school and not say anything."

"I know. Smile and wave—from a distance."

My thoughts scrambled. "Did you figure out why she had no clue that I was Hakim's teacher? I mean, my name should've rung a bell. And"—this question had been bugging me for days—"the two boys with her in the courtroom . . . does Hakim have more brothers?" I'd guessed their ages at the time as about ten and maybe sixteen. If so, why wasn't the ten-year-old a fifth grader at Bethune Elementary?

"Mmm, not sure. She didn't mention any other sons. Might've been cousins. From what I gathered, Geraldine had been living with her sister looking for a place to live in this area when the, uh, accident happened last June. Finally found a place in September— probably explains why she didn't pay too much attention to school notices. Also, she works as a night-duty LPN, so Hakim spends a lot of time at his aunt's house."

"Okay. It's just . . . so weird." *"A diabolical joke,"* the woman had said. I quickly shook off the thought. Couldn't go there. If I chose to believe that, I might as well give it all up right now. After I got off the phone, I dug out my journal and reread the prayer I'd written that morning. Then read it aloud to drown out the accusing laughter in my head.

I DECIDED NOT TO HIDE THIS MESS from Yada Yada—not like the incident with MaDear, where I kept waiting for someone else who'd been at the beauty shop to bring it up. I didn't even check with Avis, just wrote a long e-mail spelling out what had happened at the parent-teacher conferences, the scriptures I was hanging on to, and the focus I was trying to keep—that God would work this out not only for my good, but for Hakim and his mother too. ". . . even though," I admitted, "nothing can bring Jamal back. I know that. It's a reality I live with every day. So please, help me pray."

The y a d a y a d a Prayer Group Gets Down

The responses I got from different Yada Yada sisters reinforced the impression I had when "Prayer Group 26" first met at the women's conference last spring—that drawer full of crazy-colored, mismatched socks. It didn't matter; just knowing my sisters cared kept me going that whole awkward week, catching glimpses of Hakim, trying to send him a smile and wave from a distance but only getting a head down in return. For solace, I kept the Scripture reading and prayers going and checked my e-mails each evening.

"*Si!* Of course I will pray!" Delores wrote. "I consider it a privilege to pray for you, my sister—a small payment on the debt I owe for all the prayers Yada Yada has spent on the Enriques family."

Ruth's note made me laugh out loud: "Go shopping. Forget about your troubles for two hours and buy a new hat." Hadn't she noticed yet that I never wore hats? Still, it was actually tempting. A wild, crazy hat. What would Denny think of *that?*

Hoshi's note was brief: "Praying for you as you requested. Did you get an answer yet from the woman who cut my mother?" *Sheesh.* Hoshi had her own demons to fight. I hit Reply and typed, "Not yet. Will let you know." Then I hit Send.

Even Stu responded. "I am so sorry, Jodi. I wonder if Hakim's mother has gotten any counseling to help her deal with the loss of Jamal. It sounds like she's a ticking time bomb." *Okay, Stu, I'll let you suggest it.*

Florida didn't bother with e-mail but called me up. "Girl! You attract sticky situations like that nasty ol' flypaper! But don't you worry none. God's got your back. Say, that man of yours around? Wanna thank him for taking Carl to that guy breakfast last Saturday. He say much to you about it?"

"Who? Denny? Not really. Mark Smith came too." Had to admit I'd been kind of distracted and hadn't really pressed Denny for details. "What did Carl say?"

"Not much—Carl ain't a big talker. But he did say Pastor Clark got the guys shootin' off their mouths about what they think a 'real man' is. Guess it was some list." She laughed. "I think Pastor gave each man a Bible verse to look up, maybe to compare God's design with their own bright ideas, 'cause my Bible went missin' for a day or two then showed up again."

"That's great, Florida. Are things any better—at home, I mean?"

She snorted. "Ain't seen any miracles yet, but maybe it's a chink in the wall. Say . . . Yada Yada is meetin' at your house next Sunday, right?"

Which was true. And Chanda—who didn't have e-mail, so she didn't get my long version of what happened when Hakim's mother showed up—fussed at me up and down when Sunday evening rolled around and she discovered she was the only one at Yada Yada who didn't know what happened.

"I'm sorry, Chanda. I should have called," I said, even though I knew I couldn't have gone over the whole thing again on the phone. Now that Adele—who used to share e-mails with Chanda—was off the loop, Chanda did seem to get left out a lot from the online "chatter" between Yada Yada meetings.

We spent a long time that night praying for "the Hakim situation" and also for Nony and her boys. As far as we knew, there was still no word about when she planned to bring the boys home. I felt surrounded by the prayers of my sisters, like a wall of protection, and I wondered . . . did Nony sense our prayers halfway around the world? Feel that protection?

I did have one "answer" to prayer: a second letter from Lincoln Correctional Center. "Just arrived yesterday," I said, waving it in the air.

That got everyone's attention, especially Hoshi's. "Read it please, Jodi," she said, sitting straight, hands folded in her lap. Her eyes flickered, like Christmas lights ambivalent about whether they were going to burn bright or go out.

I unfolded the single sheet of paper. "Dear Mrs. Baxter," I read. "Don't know why Miss Takahashi want to be on my visitors' list, but can't feel any worse about what happened than I already do. Guess any visitors are better than no visitors. Sincerely, Becky Wallace. P. S. Last time you all was here you asked if I need anything. Could sure use some hand cream or the like. I'm working in the kitchen and my hands red all the time. But you can't bring it. Has to come straight from the store."

No one spoke for several moments while I refolded the letter. Hoshi looked down at her own hands, long and smooth. "Yes, I will go."

Guess that means Denny and I are driving to Lincoln one of these Saturdays.

"What dat she need?" Chanda piped up. "Maybe we chip in and buy her two or t'ree t'ings—hand cream or fancy bath stuff. You know, be a Christmas present."

Edesa nodded. "*Sí.* I will contribute, but it would be easiest to send it with Hoshi and whoever goes to visit her, wouldn't it?"

Yo-Yo leaned back in her chair and stuck a leg out. "Can't. Security reasons. Any gifts gotta come straight from the store or get ordered on the Internet or something. An' forget the fancy bath stuff. Gang showers ain't conducive to beauty baths."

Ruth groaned. "Now *that's* a reason not to get yourself arrested."

"Well, I'll be glad to order something and get it sent," Stu jumped in, "but I'll need her address. Just give me that envelope, Jodi." She held out her hand for the letter but shook her head when several people reached for their purses. "Later, okay? I'll buy something then figure out how much everybody owes. If we all chip in, should only be a few dollars each."

I handed over the envelope and remembered: I was going to ask Stu if she'd like to come for Thanksgiving. *Humph!* Maybe she'd like to organize the whole meal?

38

Stu arrived at one o'clock sharp on Thanksgiving Day, her silver Celica loaded with a veggie tray, a big bag of chips, two kinds of dip, homemade cranberry bread, small paper plates with a Thanksgiving motif, and a tin of mixed nuts. "Hey. Real food," Josh salivated, helping her carry the goodies into the living room. He had the bag of chips opened and a handful into his mouth before I even got the front door closed.

"You didn't have to do that, Stu," I said, watching her dump the chips into a basket she'd brought along and arrange the snacks artfully on our beat-up coffee table. "Didn't I tell you to just bring yourself?"

"I know, but you can always use munchies on Thanksgiving Day—right, Josh?" She beamed at my eighteen-year-old Hollow Leg, who was now sampling the tin of mixed nuts.

Not if you want your kids to actually eat dinner at two, I grumbled to myself. Yet I had to admit the cranberry bread looked tempting.

I got a cutting board and bread knife from the kitchen and cut a thin slice. *Oh my, to die for.* "Thanks, Stu. Yummy. I've got mulled cider. Want some?"

By the time Amanda and I got back with mugs of steaming cider—Amanda had insisted on garnishing each mug with a cinnamon stick, which of course didn't want to be found—Stu had curled up in the recliner by the front windows with a paper plate of veggies and dip. "Mark and Hoshi not here yet?" she asked, taking a mug from Amanda.

"Not yet. I told them one o'clock, so they should be here any minute."

As it turned out, Denny had finished grilling the turkey outside, stuck it into the oven to keep warm, and the hands on the clock were nudging up toward two o'clock before the doorbell finally rang.

"Sorry we're late, Jodi," Mark Smith said, ushering Hoshi inside then thrusting a large bouquet of mixed mums into my arms—eye-popping yellows and oranges and rust against a bed of leather leaf and delicate baby's breath. "Hope we didn't hold anything up." He helped Hoshi take off her long coat, adding it to the pile on the coat tree in our entryway.

"Mark! They're beautiful!" I said, taking the flowers. "You aren't that late . . . though we were starting to worry that maybe something had happened." I headed for the kitchen to hunt up a vase, passing Amanda in the hall carrying a tray with two mugs of cider on it. I gave her a thumbs-up. "Help yourselves to some snacks in the living room," I called back over my shoulder. "Denny! Mark's here!"

It took me a good five minutes to cut all the stems and get the mums arranged into a vase, but it certainly dressed up our dining-room table. I needed to remember that little nicety: bring a hostess gift when invited to dinner. At Uptown Community, we tended to pooh-pooh that mentality, opting for just-come-on-over-and-bring-yourselves simplicity. But the flowers were nice. Thoughtful. Gallant.

When I got back to the living room, Hoshi was saying, " . . . stopped by a policeman and made to get out of the car. I was worried for Dr. Smith."

"What's this?" Denny sat forward on the couch.

Mark quickly shook his head. "Nothing. Just one of those things." He smiled at me—a little forced, I thought. "Are you call-ing us to dinner, Jodi?"

"Well, yes. Everything's ready. Might as well eat." But I defi-nitely wanted to hear more about what happened. *Sheesh.* That's all Hoshi needed was another scare.

Stu, Denny, and Amanda helped me put the food on the table: grilled turkey (Denny's big idea, of course), candied yams, stuffing that hadn't been "stuffed" in the turkey, fresh green beans with almonds, store-bought dinner rolls, mashed potatoes, and gravy. I had to cheat on the gravy, though, because I didn't have any turkey drippings this year. After everyone had found a seat, I lit the candles, and we joined hands around the table to sing the Doxology: "Praise God from whom all blessings flow . . ." I grinned to myself as Hoshi's sweet soprano, Stu's alto, and Mark Smith's deep baritone added to the Baxter bash of voices. We actually sounded decent.

After the "Amen," I opened my mouth to give passing instructions, when Mark said, "Would you all like to sing the African-American version of the Doxology? Same words."

"Cool." Amanda grinned.

And so we sang it again, but this time Mark started low and slow: "Praise . . . God . . . from . . . whom . . . a-all . . . ble-essings . . . flow . . ." The rest of us chimed in as we caught on until the last phrase swelled to a stately crescendo. We all sat there after the "Amen," still holding hands, awed at the fresh power of the old words. The same way I felt when I heard Mahalia Jackson slow down "Amazing Grace," savoring each word, each truth.

"Sweet," Josh said. "Let's eat." Everybody laughed and started passing platters and bowls.

"What? No macaroni and cheese?" Mark said, filling his plate and winking at Amanda.

"Macaroni and cheese? At Thanksgiving?" Amanda asked.

"Hey. Thanksgiving wasn't Thanksgiving without mac 'n' cheese as I was coming up." He grinned, spreading his thin moustache, which dipped down on either side of his mouth and outlined his chin in a faint goatee. "Turkey and ham and mac 'n' cheese and two kinds of sweet potatoes, and greens—not to mention sweet-potato pie at the end of the food chain. Add two dozen relatives dropping in all day long to graze at my grandma's table, bringing all kinds of baked things and mysterious things dripping in sauce."

My mouth was probably hanging open. I had imagined Mark Smith growing up in a wealthy upper-class home, sort of like *The Cosby Show.*

"Sounds scrumptious," Stu said. "Did you grow up in the South?"

Mark turned out to be a wonderful storyteller about growing up in small-town Georgia. Amanda and Josh hung on every word as he described the "go-carts" he and his friends built out of baby carriage wheels and orange boxes, racing them down red-dirt hills and smashing them—and themselves—into trees that got in the way. "Shouldn't even be alive today," he laughed.

From what I gathered, he and a younger brother were mostly raised by his grandmother and a great aunt. He didn't offer what happened to his mother, and we didn't ask.

"You've come a long way, Mark—small-town Georgia to a major university," Stu said.

Mark grinned wryly. "You could say that. First person in my family to go to college, much less get a Ph.D. Grandma and Auntie Bell told me once a day, if not twice, that God put a gift in me, and it'd be a sin not to be the 'somebody' I was created to be. I'll probably never know what they sacrificed to get me there, but you should've seen those two when I got my doctorate. Jumping up and down, weeping and carrying on—though Grandma made it very clear I still had to wipe my feet at the front door and say 'Yes, ma'am' at *her* house."

That got a chuckle from the rest of us. But even as we laughed, I noticed a small frown gather on Mark's face, and he pushed his potatoes around absently. "Then there are days I realize we haven't come very far, after all," he said softly.

The table got very quiet. What did he mean? Civil rights?

Progress for blacks? Of course we'd come a long way . . . hadn't we?

"I think," Hoshi said in her quiet voice, "Dr. Smith refers to what happened today with the police."

"Tell us what happened, Mark," Denny said. "It's important for us to know."

Nony's husband laid down his fork and sighed. "Just one of those things, really." He half-laughed and shook his head. "Shouldn't be surprised, but I was. Since our dinner date wasn't until one o'clock, I decided to run up to Highland Park Hospital to see a colleague of mine who is recovering from surgery. Hoshi asked if she could ride along instead of picking her up later, since this man is one of her professors too. I was glad for the company and decided to drive up Sheridan Road—you know, to gawk at all the big mansions along the North Shore, show Hoshi how the upper crust *really* lives. I actually forgot about 'driving black' in an all-white area—stupid me. Next thing I knew lights were pulling me over. Cops made me get out, patted me down, ran my license plate . . . and got very vague when I asked why I'd been stopped."

Tiny beads of sweat gathered on Mark Smith's face, and his jaw muscles tensed. "They even asked Hoshi if she was 'all right.' Bless her—she got indignant and said, 'Of course I am all right. We are going to the hospital to visit a sick friend!'" He quoted her in that "correct English" way of hers with a brief smile. "But I admit to a moment of panic. If they'd kept asking questions and discovered she was a student and I was her teacher . . ." He threw his hands open. "Well, there you have it. They let us go with a warning to 'drive careful, now.'"

Denny was incredulous. "What did they think—that you'd stolen the car or something?"

"Dr. Smith," Amanda said, her brow creased with confusion, "why didn't you just tell them you're a professor at Northwestern? They probably got you confused with somebody else."

He grimaced. "Unfortunately, you're right about that, Amanda. Once I step away from Northwestern's campus, I'm just another black man. Whatever those particular cops think about blacks in general, well, that's what they see." He clapped his hands. "Enough about that! I think I need some more of those sweet potatoes. Almost as good as my grandma's, Jodi. Not quite, but almost." His teasing grin was back.

I swallowed my mouthful of candied yams with difficulty. *Just another black man . . .* That was what the man who'd heard me lock my car doors had probably been thinking: *"All she sees is just another black man."*

AFTER DINNER, Amanda snared Stu, Hoshi, and Josh into a game of King's Cribbage that she'd gotten from the grandparents last Christmas. To my surprise, Mark joined Denny and me in the kitchen, rolling up his sleeves and scrubbing pots while I put away food and Denny loaded the dishwasher. I don't know why, but suddenly I blurted out my whole awkward encounter with the man getting into his parked car.

"To be honest, Mark," I said, standing in the middle of our

not-too-big kitchen with a box of plastic wrap in one hand and the remains of the green beans in the other, "I waver between feeling badly about how I made him feel . . . and feeling like he was judging me too. I go over it again and again in my mind, imagining that the man is white or Asian or Italian or from Mars, and I *still* think I would have locked my car doors."

I don't know what I expected Mark to say, but he was quiet for a minute—a *long* minute—while he gave particular attention to a sticky baking dish in the sudsy water. He seemed about to say something when the phone rang. "Josh? Amanda?" I yelled into the living room. "Get that, will you? . . . Sorry, Mark."

He finally turned around, leaning back against the sink. "Unfortunately, Jodi, both blacks and whites in this country, no matter how well-meaning—and I do believe you didn't mean to humiliate him—end up living with the sins of the past. That means some racist cop will assume I'm up to no good if I show up in the wrong community until I prove otherwise, and it means that brother will assume you're just like all the bigoted white folks he's had to deal with in one way or another all his life until you prove different. We're all involved in an anxious dance, like the Jets and the Sharks in *West Side Story*, trying to survive on the same streets, in the same society, but not sure what's going to happen if we step over the line."

"Dad? Mom?" Amanda stuck her head in the doorway. "Um . . . José wants to know if he can come up to see us. You know, hang out. Play games or something."

"See us" my foot. I glanced at Denny. He gave a brief nod.

"Okay," I said impatiently. "Next time excuse yourself. We were talking." But Amanda had already disappeared.

I turned back to Mark, frowning, mulling over his "anxious dance" comment. "So, how do we tango instead of . . . you know, tap-dancing on eggs like boxers waiting for the knockout?"

Denny laughed out loud; even Mark grinned. I hadn't meant to be funny, but even I had to laugh when I realized I was still standing in the middle of the room waving around the plastic wrap and leftover green beans.

39

José Enriques showed up about five o'clock, handing me a tin with some kind of sugary cookies. *"Pan de polvo,"* he said, nodding politely. "Mama made it for you, *Senora* Baxter." He flashed a grin in the direction of my shoulder, and I wondered briefly if the boy had trouble looking adults in the eye—then realized the dazzling smile was directed at Amanda, who stood slightly behind me. I tried not to roll my eyes. *Oh Lord, give me strength.*

King's Cribbage gave way to a two-pack card game of Slap Jack that José taught us that soon had my head spinning. Mark Smith seemed to hit it off with José and caught on fast to the game. The rest of us lost all our cards one by one, and a fierce competition developed between Stu, Mark, and José. Amanda parked herself close to José, murmuring encouragement. In the spirit of fairness, Josh—his hair grown out to an astonishing half-inch—blatantly cheered every time Mark Smith won a hand.

Finally out of cards, Stu threw up her hands. "Can't keep up with those two. Just as well. Time to get home. I've got three real-estate showings tomorrow. I'm in the wrong business when it comes to holidays—but *that's* going to change." Hoshi and I walked her to the front door after she said her good-byes to the crew in the living room. Stu gave me a buss on the cheek. "Thanks for the invite, Jodi. Best Thanksgiving I've had in years."

I wanted to ask about her family—didn't she ever see them at holidays?—but she abruptly changed the subject, looking at Hoshi curiously. "Did you guys settle on a date for your prison visit?"

Both of us shook our heads. But before Hoshi left that evening, we decided this coming Saturday, before Hoshi's semester exams, was maybe the best time to make the trip to Lincoln Correctional Center. Denny agreed. "December weekends get awful busy with Christmas stuff."

"Holiday stuff," Mark teased, helping Hoshi into her coat. "You teach in a public school, remember?" Then a cloud crossed his face, like a remembered pain. "Thanks for getting me through *this* holiday. It's . . . tough without Nony and the boys. Pray for us, okay?"

Denny frowned. "Still no return date?"

Mark shook his head. "Guess this is something she needs to do." Then he laughed, but it was hollow. "Last thing she said? Oprah Winfrey is coming to South Africa next week to film a Christmas special highlighting the plight of AIDS orphans, and they need local volunteers at each of her stops. Nony thinks it would be an awesome experience for Marcus and Michael." He shrugged, but the pain had not left his eyes. "It would . . . if it didn't keep us on opposite sides of the world."

JOSÉ STAYED until nine o'clock then shrugged off an offer for Josh to run him home. "I can get home by El—*no problema*. See you Saturday."

I shut the door behind him and turned to Amanda. "Saturday? What's this about Saturday? Aren't you supposed to *ask* before you—"

"Mo-om! It wasn't even me. Ask Josh! Good grief!" She flounced off to her room.

I stared at Josh. "What?"

"Parental unit on overload. Begin cool-down cycle." Josh headed for the living room, where his father had turned on the TV to catch highlights of Thanksgiving Day football. "Youth group, Mom," he said over his shoulder—a tad too smug, in my opinion. "Service project, remember? We're going down to Jesus People USA on Saturday night to help serve dinner to the homeless. José heard us talk about it and said he'd like to come. I might ask Yo-Yo's brothers too. They'd fit right in at JPUSA." He grinned. "Can I have the car? I volunteered to drive."

I followed Josh into the living room, somewhat mollified that it was a youth-group activity. "No, I don't remember—and the car's a problem. Dad and I are taking Hoshi to visit Becky Wallace on Saturday. Downstate."

"But Mom! I said I could drive! And if Yo-Yo's brothers go, I have to pick them up."

So what's wrong with public transportation? I groused to myself—even though I knew when it came to my own kids, I'd much rather they get a ride. "Talk to your dad," I said, heading for the kitchen to clean up the remains of the apple crisp I'd made for dessert. *Let Denny figure it out.*

AS IT TURNED OUT, Denny didn't think it'd be a problem. "We'll leave early, be back by four. Then Josh can have the car." Amanda had dance practice at Uptown Saturday morning for this Sunday's Advent candle lighting—could the Christmas season be upon us already?—so we ended up leaving both kids at home. Had to admit it was a lot easier than the juggling act we pulled off the last time to get Amanda to Edesa's for the day. I took the cell and told her to call us if she made any other plans.

At the last minute Florida got wind that we were going to the prison this weekend and called to see if she could go along. "Carla's foster parents got her this weekend, and I'm about to go crazy if I stay here. I'm still on the visitors' list, right? Do you mind picking me up?"

So once again we hit Route I-55 heading for Lincoln, Illinois, on an early Saturday morning with our thermoses of coffee, some fruit and sweet rolls, and what was left of Delores's *pan de polvo*. The sky was overcast, like it was thinking about snow. "Sure hope that weather holds off till we get home," Denny muttered to no one in particular.

Right away Florida piped up from the second seat of the van. "All right now, Jesus. You heard the man's prayer. We're askin' for good weather all the way to the prison and back again, and we thank ya in advance for whatcha gonna do."

Denny and I exchanged grins. *Yes, God, make my prayers as natural as breathing . . . or talking.* I turned back to the passing landscape, stripped of the brilliant colors we'd enjoyed on our last trip. Now bony tree-fingers jabbed the sky and blankets of tired, yellowed grass lay crumpled everywhere, waiting . . . waiting for winter.

Hoshi didn't have much to say on the trip downstate. She was probably apprehensive. At least the three of us were along to help her sort it out if she wanted. Pawing through the CDs that were starting to collect in the van, I picked up one of Integrity Music's *iWorship* albums and stuck it in the player. The first track nearly blasted the car off the road till I frantically turned down the volume. "Sorry about that," I muttered. "Josh must've driven the van last."

Now that we could hear the words, the song seemed to speak to the raw feelings we all had after that awful night when Becky Wallace broke into our Yada Yada meeting: "I'm trading my sorrows . . . I'm laying them down for the joy of the Lord . . ."

"I like that," Hoshi said. "Can you play it again?"

I hit the Repeat button, and the last line was still going through my mind when we pulled up to the security gate at Lincoln Correctional Center at eleven o'clock. *"Though the sorrow may last for the night, His joy comes with the morning."* I took Hoshi's arm as we entered the door of the stark, gray building and headed for the visitors' desk. Had to admit it was as much for my own comfort as to comfort Hoshi. Even though this was my second visit, I was nervous. Again. I mean, how weird was it to visit the thief who'd terrorized us all with a knife? *We could all use some of that morning joy, Jesus.*

Hoshi's lip trembled when a female guard patted her down and made her leave her belongings in the locker. Didn't blame her. Getting searched made *me* feel like a criminal. But without Yo-Yo's prison history to delay us this time, we were soon shown into the visiting room and found an empty table.

And then we waited. Ten minutes . . . fifteen. "Maybe she changed her mind and does not want to see us," Hoshi said. She didn't seem to know what to do with her hands and kept fidgeting with an opal ring on her right hand.

Denny got up and spoke to a guard stationed at the door that let prisoners in and out, and the guard mumbled something into his walkie-talkie. Finally Becky Wallace stepped into the room. Not the same Becky Wallace. Healthier, fresher. She also looked incredibly young in a tank top, tight jeans, and jean jacket. She seemed to take a big breath then headed for our table.

"Hi." Her dark eyes were wary, but she sat down and greeted us each in turn. "Mr. Baxter . . . Miz Baxter . . . an' Miz Hickman, right?" Then she looked at Hoshi. "An' you must be Miss Tak—" She stumbled. "Takahashi."

Hoshi nodded but said nothing, like she had stage fright.

"First names are all right," Denny said. "May we call you Becky?"

"You lookin' better, girl," Florida blurted. She did too. The dull brown hair had grown an inch or two, even had a little wave and some shine. The dark circles around her eyes were gone, her face fuller. I noticed she even had on a hint of blush and mascara.

Good grief. She's almost pretty. I hardly knew what to do with the revelation.

Becky's lips twitched . . . not quite a smile. "Yeah. Been clean for two months. I'm sleepin' better. Food ain't so hot, but at least it's three squares a day."

Stillness settled around us like an invisible cocoon, muffling the hum of conversation at the other gray plastic tables. We just looked at each other or down at our hands, wondering what to say next.

Florida broke the silence. "What 'bout your kid? Heard anything?"

Becky nodded, but she swallowed several times before speaking. "Got word that DCFS put 'im in foster care." She shrugged and looked away, blinking rapidly. "Prob'ly best. Jus' . . . dunno if I'm ever gonna see my boy agin."

Florida reached out and gripped Becky's wrist. "Girl, I been there. But God gave me my baby back. Tell you what. We gonna track down your kid and make sure they send you word regular. We got just the friend to sic on DCFS!" Florida grinned at Denny and me and actually laughed.

Oh, Stu is going to love this, I thought.

"Really? You'd do that? After what I done ta . . ." Becky stopped and glanced at Hoshi. "Told these guys last time, but I . . . I didn't mean ta hurt yo' mama. Hope she's okay."

It wasn't exactly an apology, but the words seemed to electrify Hoshi. She sat up in her chair, looking lovely even in those drab surroundings. She quit fingering her ring and looked into Becky's face across the table. "Yes. She will be all right. I . . ." She stopped. We waited. The unspoken sentence hung in the air. Becky had no way of knowing that the cut that hurt the deepest was not her mother's hand. Would Hoshi say something?

To my surprise, Hoshi held out her hand, her long, tapered fingers with the perfect white moons reaching for the nail-bitten hand of Becky Wallace. "It is not easy to say, but . . . I forgive you. God forgives you too."

Their hands touched. Then Becky pulled back. "Nah. God ain't about ta forgive *me*. Y'all don't know the stuff I done."

"God forgave me—why not you?" I was startled to hear my own voice.

Becky looked me up and down with nothing short of a leer. "You? What do *you* know 'bout needin' forgiveness? You had a bad thought? Snitched cookies when yo' mama said not to? Huh!"

"No. I . . . killed somebody. A boy."

Becky's eyes widened, and we just stared at each other. For some reason, the meaning of her name resonated in my head: *"Bound."* And in the next breath, the meaning of my own: *"God is gracious."* And for a jumbled moment, the two names and the two meanings merged in my understanding. *I was bound . . . but God is gracious and set me free.*

Becky's eyes darted at Denny. "For real? She kill somebody?" She clearly did not believe me.

"Yes." Denny's eyes begged my permission before he continued. I nodded, then closed my eyes while he told the short, sad story of our stupid fight, me driving angry in a storm, a boy trying to get out of the rain, the terrible crash, a life snuffed out.

"But it be an accident, right?"

I opened my eyes. She was looking straight at me. "I didn't hit him on purpose, if that's what you mean. And the charges against me were dropped, but his mother can't forgive me, just the same. Yet God has forgiven me. That's what gives me courage to go on." *Say it, Jodi, say it! It's true—even though you don't always believe it. Becky Wallace needs to hear it!* "You already have Hoshi's forgiveness, Becky, and God will forgive you too. Just . . . ask Him."

Becky looked from Denny to me, then to Florida and Hoshi, testing the story with her eyes. "Man! You guys are a trip!" She slowly stood and looked toward the "inmate" door then, like she'd forgotten something, turned back and shook each of our hands. "Thanks for comin' ta see me. You guys all right."

She walked across the room and was gone.

The four of us just looked at each other. Finally Denny scratched his head. "Well, it wasn't exactly the Four Spiritual Laws, but"—he smiled big, making his dimples cave in—"I think something important just happened for our 'Bandana Woman.'"

40

We left the prison parking lot in silence, a little afraid to break the spell. At least, I was wondering what Becky Wallace was thinking right about now. What had Hoshi's words, "I forgive you," meant to her? Especially since B. W. hadn't actually come out and said, "I'm sorry."

Huh. Not that you've ever fuzzed the edges of an apology, Jodi Baxter. Well, okay, so it was a lot easier to say, *"I didn't mean to"* or, *"Guess I messed up."* Saying "I'm sorry" was downright admitting that a wrong had been done, a wrong that needed forgiving. And to be honest, I wasn't very quick on the forgiving end either. Didn't want to let the person who wronged me off the hook *that* easy.

But I told Jamal's mother I was really sorry—hadn't I? Or had I? Sorry about what? That the accident had happened? That she'd lost her son? Or sorry that I'd been driving angry, distracted from my driving, responsible for—

"I am glad I came." Hoshi's quiet voice from the backseat broke into my tumbling thoughts. "My only memory of that woman since that night was her screaming at us, waving that knife around, looking like a wild woman. Every time I thought about her, I felt afraid all over again."

I turned my head so I could see Hoshi, staring out the window behind Denny. "Yeah, know what you mean. Except whenever I thought about her, I just felt angry. Kinda resented finding out she was a real person."

Hoshi kept her head turned toward the window, as if talking to her own reflection. "I could not imagine saying, 'I forgive you,' but when I saw her today . . . it wasn't so hard. Not after she said, 'I'm sorry.'"

I started to say, *But she didn't, really*—then realized that Hoshi had given Becky the benefit of the doubt; she had listened beyond her words to her heart.

"Uh-huh," Florida muttered. "It's when they *don't* say 'sorry' that forgivin' gets hard. Still, sometimes ya gotta do it for your own sanity. Maybe that's why Jesus told us to forgive our enemies—more for our sake than theirs."

I twisted further in my seatbelt so I could see Florida behind me. "What do you mean, Flo?"

"Girl, it's just like Avis said a couple of weeks ago. If Hoshi didn't forgive Becky Wallace, she be lettin' that woman hurt her all over again every time she thinks 'bout what happened. But you watch. A little forgiveness goes a long way. Gonna take the sting out."

As I straightened around in my seat, I saw Hoshi turn from the window and take Florida's hand, a teary smile on her face. *Huh,* I thought, watching the bleak landscape slide past my own passenger side window. *Never thought about it like that.* I'd always thought "love your enemies" and "do good to those who persecute you" was kind of a be-holy-like-I-am-holy test. Never sounded fair—or even possible!—though of course a good Christian girl from Des Moines, Iowa, would never actually say so. Maybe Florida was right, though: maybe God wanted us to forgive people for our own good too. Even people who didn't say "sorry."

"For my own good," I whispered, watching my warm breath spread a misty cloud on the cold window.

THE SNOW HELD OFF till late that night, and then it was mostly lake-effect snow, whipped up by a chilly wind, laying down an inch or two, but not serious enough to even get out the snow shovel.

"Lucky you," I told Josh as he drove us to Uptown Community Church the next morning. "This was only a teaser. Wait till January. You'll have to set your alarm two hours earlier to shovel us out before school."

"That's why we need a snow blower," Josh countered. "Then Amanda can do it."

"Ha!" Amanda swatted the back of his head with a glove. "Just drive, muscle man. I need to get to church early, remember?"

Denny, riding shotgun in the front seat, didn't bother to tell

Josh that our short sidewalks—front and back—could practically be measured in inches, so forget a snow blower. In fact, Denny had been unusually quiet on the way home from the prison yesterday. Didn't even ask many questions about the youth group's service project at Jesus People USA last night, though both Josh and Amanda had said it was "cool." Whether they meant serving a couple hundred meals to homeless men and women and scrubbing pots and pans afterward, or just hanging out with a bunch of "Jesus people" who all looked like they'd just been roped in off the streets, I wasn't sure. By the time they got home from taking Pete and Jerry back to Yo-Yo's house after dropping José off in Little Village, Denny and I were heading for bed.

Not exactly the kind of youth-group activities I was weaned on, I thought as we headed up the stairs at Uptown Community, leaving Josh to go park the minivan. *Bible sword drills . . . Youth for Christ rallies . . . an occasional roller-skating party—the "sanctified" substitute for dancing.* I felt a pang. Nostalgia for a simpler time? Or realizing just how unprepared I'd been for how complicated and untidy the Christian life felt at the moment. Ever since the Yada Yada Prayer Group dropped into my life, frankly.

Amanda disappeared to get ready for the Advent candle dance, and Denny and I had our choice of seats for a change. Even beat Stu getting to church—now *that* was a first. She came in a few minutes later, sat down behind us, and leaned forward. "How did the visit to the prison go yesterday?"

"Good," I said. "Tell you more later, okay?"

I wanted to be quiet for a moment, to focus on the upcoming

worship service. An Advent wreath was suspended from the ceiling by purpoe ribbons; four fat candles representing each Advent Sunday nestled among the fake greenery. Advent . . . the beginning of the Christmas season. Communion Sunday, too, by the looks of the small table off to the side, covered with the cloth embroidered with "children of the world" figures.

The upstairs room filled. The lights dimmed. Three recorders began the familiar Advent hymn, and we all joined in on the words: "O come, O come, Emanuel . . . And ransom captive Israel . . ." Josh slipped into the seat beside Denny. *Sheesh. He must've had to park six blocks away.* And then someone else sat down. I leaned forward.

José Enriques. *Oh Lord, he must've come to see Amanda dance!* This was getting serious.

I was so distracted for a moment I almost missed Amanda and two other teenage girls coming down the aisle like bridesmaids at a wedding, bearing lighted candles—though the black skirts, white socks, and white tops kind of spoiled the "bridesmaid" image. As the music swelled—"That mourns in lonely exile here . . . Until the Son of God appears"—the three girls fanned out gracefully across the front, causing their tiny lights to flicker and dance in the darkened sanctuary.

"Rejoice! Rejoice!" we sang. My eyes were glued to Amanda's face as she lifted her candle heavenward. Her own eyes glowed in the candlelight as she lifted her face, following the light. And then, "Emmanuel . . . Shall come to thee, O Israel." Amanda and the other two girls turned and dipped their tapers toward the wick of the first candle in the Advent wreath. The room seemed to hold its collective breath until the fat candle glowed, the dancers blew out their tapers, and the candle wreath shone with the first promise of Advent.

Beautiful. I glanced at Denny. His eyes were swimming.

The lights came on, and I expected Avis to get up and launch us into some spirited praise and worship. Instead Pastor Clark came to the front—*Somebody's got to tell him to lose that awful green tie*—and said we were going to do things a bit different today. I swept my eyes around the room. Where was Avis, anyway? And then I saw her, sitting toward the back. And there was someone with her—a man. An older man, maybe late fifties, with graying hair at his temples. An African-American man at that.

I faced forward once again, my spine tingling. Avis with a man? *Calm down, Jodi. Maybe it's her brother or cousin or uncle, here for Thanksgiving.* I grinned to myself. *Yeah, right.*

" . . . not only the first Sunday of Advent," Pastor Clark was saying, "but the first Sunday of the month, when we celebrate the Lord's Supper." And the two celebrations, he said, have a great deal to do with each other. "During Advent, we celebrate God's promise to send the Messiah and 'ransom captive Israel.' Because not only Israel, but all of us are stuck—stuck in our sins. But in breaking the bread and sharing the cup of the Lord's Supper, we celebrate the purpose for which the Messiah came: to sacrifice His own life, taking on Himself the penalty for *our* sin. He suffered whips, humiliation, crucifixion, and finally death—none of which He deserved. That was *our* punishment. For our sins, our mistakes, our oversights, our weaknesses, our failings."

He paused for a long moment, lost in his own thoughts, almost as if he'd forgotten about the rest of us. And then he said simply, "So that we might live. Forever."

I forgot about Avis and the mystery man. I forgot about José. I almost forgot to stand when it was my turn to go up to receive the bread and wine. For some reason Pastor Clark's powerful words echoed something Mark Smith had said at Thanksgiving: *"Both blacks and whites in this country end up living with the sins of the past."*

Stuck. That's exactly how I'd felt when Mark said that. Stuck with the legacy of sin hanging over our heads. If Jesus was our example, though, the way out was *repentance . . . forgiveness . . . ransom . . . sacrifice.* I felt on the verge of something incredibly important—but for the life of me, I wasn't sure what it was.

I put the piece of bread in my mouth. *Christ's body, broken for me.* I took a sip of wine from the ceramic goblet. *Christ's blood, shed for me.* I turned, and passed both bread and wine to Denny. "Christ's body, broken for you," I whispered.

I'll never forget the look in his eyes.

WHEN WE GOT HOME AFTER CHURCH, the answering machine light on the kitchen phone was blinking. I pressed the Play button while I unwound my long neck scarf and unbuttoned my coat, still thinking about meeting Avis's "old friend" from Philadelphia. "Jodi, this is Peter Douglass," she'd said. "An old friend of Conrad's." I had tried to give her a meaningful look, which she totally ignored. But she wasn't going to get away that easy.

"Denny or Jodi. It's Mark." The answering machine sprang to life. "Nony's mother has taken a turn for the worse. Nony called last night, asking me to come . . ."

"Denny!" I yelled. "It's Mark! Come listen!"

" . . . bit of a mess, with term papers and exams coming up," Mark's message continued as Denny appeared in the doorway between the dining room and kitchen, "but I think I need to go. So, as soon as I can make arrangements with my department, I'm leaving. Jodi, will you ask Yada Yada to pray? For Nony and"—I almost didn't catch his next words—"for me."

The machine clicked off. "Wow. Wonder what that means? It's good, I think. Don't you, Denny?"

Denny nodded. "Uh-huh." He seemed deep in thought— thoughts he'd been carrying for days, it seemed, like Frodo Baggins, intent on getting that ring to Mount Doom in spite of all the obstacles . . . slowly, but surely. I gathered up my coat and scarf. *Guess he'll tell me when he's ready.*

I started for the front hall to hang them up, but Denny stopped me. "Jodi, how long does Adele's Hair and Nails stay open on weeknights like tomorrow?"

41

onday. Back to school after the Thanksgiving holiday. Christy James's last week as my student teacher. Back to kids already revved up for Christmas . . . and Hanukkah, and Kwanzaa, and the TV-commercial glut otherwise known as "the holidays." Back to seeing Hakim from a distance, lining up with the other third-grade teacher, hardly daring to wonder what he must think of me now. The lady who'd killed his brother.

"Okay, God, I know it's not just about me," I muttered out loud as I hustled to school with my tote bags, trying to keep warm. The rod attached to my left femur ached in the cold. "So please give Hakim what he needs in the other classroom. Finish what You started in him, okay?"

Denny hadn't told me what he had in mind for tonight, just asked if I would go with him if he went to see Adele and MaDear at the shop. *"But why?"* I'd argued. *"Adele made it clear we would only upset MaDear."*

He had stood hunched in the middle of the dining room, one hand in his pants pocket, the other rubbing the back of his head. *"I just know it's time. And today during Communion, God gave me peace that it's going to be all right."*

I pulled open the double door of Bethune Elementary and headed into the welcome warmth of the hallway. *Problem is, "our time" and "Adele's time" might be light-years apart.* I peeked into the office to see if Avis was there. I was dying to know more about the "old friend" from Philadelphia—he didn't look so old to *me*—but the inner office was empty. Oh well. I'd get her later.

I realized how much I was going to miss Christy when I sent her out to bring in the kids from the playground while I set up the day's lessons. The kids trooped in noisily, shedding coats, mittens, and scarves to a cacophony of, "Hi, Miz Baxter!" "That's *my* hook." "Stop steppin' on my scarf!" "See my new mittens?" Thank heavens the snow had fizzled. At least we didn't have to deal with a pile of boots as well.

I was helping Kaya and Chanel stick their mittens in their coat sleeves when I heard Avis's voice behind me. "Mrs. Baxter? Could I see you a moment? Hi, Britny. Yes, I see your new mittens. So sparkly!"

I motioned to Christy to take over the mitten situation and hastened to the door, which Avis was holding slightly ajar. Sounded like "business"—guess I'd have to ask her about Mr. Philadelphia later. She motioned me out into the hall.

A child, still bundled in a brown-and-black padded winter jacket, its hood up and tied with a long, red knit scarf, was sitting

in the chair that stood outside the classroom door, swinging boyish athletic shoes against the chair legs. *Thump. Thump. Thump.*
I peered around the hood to see who Avis had brought. A new
student?

Familiar dark eyes peered out at me. "Hakim!" Startled, I
looked at Avis.

Avis smiled pleasantly, as if this was really not a big deal.
"Hakim is coming back to your classroom. Is his desk still available?"

My heart was thumping so hard I could hardly get my breath.
"Uh . . . yes! Absolutely!" I beamed at Hakim. "It's been waiting
for you."

Hakim jumped off the chair and took my hand. "Tol' Miz
Johnson no other kid better be sittin' in my desk."

My head was spinning. What had brought about this miracle?
I let Hakim lead me back into the classroom, but not before I
jabbed a finger at Avis and mouthed, *You wait right here! I'll be
back in a sec!*

I handed Hakim over to Christy to deal with the jacket-scarf-
mittens routine, ignoring her dropped jaw, then poked my head
back out into the hallway. "What in the world?" I asked.

Avis was leaning against the wall, perfectly calm in her two-
piece gold-and-black dress. "It was Hakim. He kept telling his
mother he wanted to go back to 'Miz B's class.' Made such a
fuss—'raised holy hell' was the way she put it—she finally let him
come back. Plus, he was acting out big-time in Ms. Towers's
class. Ms. Towers came to me last week looking a bit frazzled and

highly recommended he be placed back 'in his own classroom.'"
Avis was grinning big-time now.

"But you didn't say anything to me!"

She shrugged. "Didn't know anything for sure, but Hakim showed up this morning with the aunt and a note from his mother. I don't think she's happy about it, but at least she's considering what's best for Hakim." Avis pushed off from the wall and headed down the hall with a wave. "Have a great day, Jodi."

WOULD WONDERS NEVER CEASE? I was so happy to have Hakim back in my class that the whole day felt like a Christmas gift from God, wrapped in gold ribbon. Hakim seemed happy too. Even asked for me to read with him one on one while Christy led group-reading time.

Couldn't wait to tell Denny, but only Willie Wonka was there to greet me when I got home. "Guess what, Wonka?" I said, taking the dog's face in my hands and kissing his soft brown forehead. "God is gracious! God is soooooo gracious!" Willie Wonka had natural urges on his mind and wiggled free, heading for the back door. I let him out into the backyard but felt like I wanted to dance, so I hunted around till I found the *iWorship* CD we'd been listening to lately and put on the first track by Darrell Evans.

> I'm trading my sorrows
> I'm trading my shame

The y a d a y a d a Prayer Group Gets Down

> I'm laying them down
> For the joy of the Lord

I was right in the middle of hopping around the living room to the spunky vamp—"Yes, Lord, yes, Lord, yes, yes, Lord!"—for about the umpteenth time when the Baxter crew all showed up, raiding the kitchen and giving me looks that said, *"Mom's gone off again."* I just laughed at them, turned down the music, and told them about my miracle.

"That's great, Mom." Amanda actually gave me a hug. "When's supper?"

Denny wrapped his arms around me and held me for a few moments. "I'm glad, Jodi. Really glad," he murmured into my hair. Then he pulled back, but I could see he was frowning slightly. "Uh . . . what time did you say Adele's shop closed?"

Good grief. I'd completely forgotten about promising to go with Denny to Adele's Hair and Nails. "Seven," I said. "Can't we do this another evening? I don't want to spoil this great—"

"I gotta do this today, Jodi. Before I lose my nerve. Please?"

Every nerve in my body wanted to protest, but something told me that if I didn't go, Denny would go by himself. I sighed. "I'll go. As soon as we eat supper, okay?"

He shook his head. "Don't think I can eat. Maybe when we get back."

So I pulled out Sunday's leftovers for Josh and Amanda, tanked up Denny and myself with some fresh coffee to take along, and headed for Clark Street.

We pulled into a parking space across the street from Adele's shop about six-forty. The white twinkle lights around the shop's window had been replaced with multicolored ones and wound with silver tinsel, giving a festive holiday air to the shop. Through the window, we could see a customer still in the chair getting a comb-out. And so we sat, motor running so the car didn't get too cold.

I had no idea what we were going to say when we got inside. But maybe MaDear wouldn't remember a thing about the previous incident, wouldn't even recognize Denny. After all, sometimes MaDear even forgot who Adele was! That would be the best scenario of all, as far as I was concerned. We could all just start over, clean slate.

The customer left about ten minutes later, calling back cheery good-byes. Denny turned off the engine and we got out, walking across the street hand in hand at a break in the traffic. We both hesitated at the door, then Denny pulled it open.

42

The air was warm with the pungent smell of hair perm— and cinnamon. A wreath of cinnamon pinecones hung on the inside of the door, underneath the bell tinkling our arrival. A gospel version of "O Come, All Ye Faithful" pumped out of the small speakers above the wall of mirrors.

Adele's other hairstylist—Takeisha, if I remembered her name right—looked up from the counter where she was writing in the log book. She looked slightly puzzled. "We're closed in ten minutes, but I'd be glad to give you an appointment."

"No, that's all right," Denny said. He cleared his throat. "We actually just came to see Adele Skuggs for a moment."

The young woman turned to give the familiar yell—*"Adele! Someone to see you!"*—but at that moment Adele herself appeared. Her short "natural" was no longer red but black tipped with gray, which looked like a mat of tiny silver springs. I tensed, not sure what she would do. Yell at us? Throw us out?

She did neither. Just looked at us, surprised. Finally she spoke. "Jodi and Denny Baxter. What can I do for you?" Her tone was calm but guarded.

"Adele, could I please see MaDear?" Denny spoke quickly, as though afraid he'd lose his nerve. Adele started to shake her head, jingling the big gold loops in her ears, but Denny rushed ahead. "Adele, this is so important. Tell her . . ." His grip on my hand tightened. "Tell her it is the man who killed her brother, come to ask forgiveness."

I whipped my head around to stare at my husband. I opened my mouth to cry, *"No, Denny!"* but the words stuck in my throat. My brain was scrambling. We should have talked about this! Why feed into the old woman's delusions? How would that help? Didn't MaDear need to see that Denny was *not* the evil man who killed her brother? Wouldn't that lay this whole mess to rest?

Almost as if I'd said my thoughts aloud, Denny said, "That's what MaDear thinks. We have to start there." He was speaking to Adele, who was staring at him, lips parted, revealing the small space between her front teeth.

To my utter astonishment, Adele suddenly said, "Well, hang up your coats" and motioned for us to follow her. At the doorway to the back room she held up her hand for us to stop. Then she went inside, and we heard her say, "MaDear, the man who killed Uncle Larry is here. He has something he wants to say to you."

I sucked in my breath, but the salon did not erupt into mayhem. In fact, all I heard was mumbling, something like, "Huh. What he want?" A moment later, Adele motioned us into the back room.

MaDear was sitting in a wheelchair, hunched birdlike over a lapful of curlers and rollers, picking them over, like she was sorting green beans. She looked up sharply as we came in, eyes flashing.

She stared at us angrily for a moment, then her lip began to tremble, and I thought she was going to cry. It may have been only a few seconds, but it was like time slowed to slow-frame . . . and suddenly I saw Jamal and Hakim's mother sitting there, confronting the person who had killed a loved one. *This isn't just about Denny.* I, Jodi Baxter, was "MaDear's white man" to that other mother. We could talk till we were blue in the face—Denny really wasn't that guy; it really was an accident that killed Jamal—but generations of racial division, injustice, pain, and distrust made subtleties hard to distinguish, facts almost irrelevant.

Suddenly I realized what Denny wanted to do and why. *Jesus gave us the way to break the legacy of sin . . .*

Denny let go of my hand and knelt down beside MaDear's wheelchair. I knelt down with him, kneeling low so that she was looking down on us. "Mrs. . . ." Denny looked up at Adele, searching for MaDear's real name.

"Skuggs," said Adele. "Sally Skuggs."

"Mrs. Skuggs," Denny continued, his voice husky, "what I did was wrong and evil. You have every right to be angry. But I have come to ask if you could forgive me. I . . . I can't bring your brother back, but I ask you to forgive me for how we white folks wronged your people, and your family in particular."

The room was hushed. No one spoke. Somewhere I could hear the melodic words to "What Child Is This?" softening the electricity in the air. And then MaDear reached out and patted Denny on the head, tears streaming down her face.

My own eyes blurred, and I groped for a tissue in my skirt pocket.

"I knew yo' mama," MaDear said, stroking Denny's hair. "My mama took care o' you when you was no bigger'n a sucklin' pig, she did. But after Larry was dragged off, found hangin' the nex' day, yo' mama couldn't look my mama or me in th' eye. She done *knew* it was you and yo' daddy and yo' uncle. But ta look us in th' eye an' admit it . . . she couldn't do that. Couldn't do that." MaDear shook her head sorrowfully. "Went to her grave, she did, not knowing we woulda forgiven her for what her menfolk did if she'd asked us to."

Denny's shoulders were shaking, and I handed him a wrinkled tissue. MaDear just kept stroking his head. "Now the son comes," she mused, almost to herself. "Yes, sonny, I forgive you. Big load off my mind."

Suddenly I felt her thin, bony hand reach for mine. "This yo' woman, sonny?" She took my hand in her own and peered closely at it. "What? These hands like chicken claws! Nails a mess, all dry . . . Adele!" She looked up at Adele, who was standing speechless, leaning against the refrigerator as if she needed something to hold her up. "Adele!" MaDear screeched again. "Take this child and do somethin' with these hands. You be ashamed to let her walk outta here with hands like that."

She let go of my "claw" and flapped her hands at me. "Go on—shoo! Soak those nails. Get some paint on 'em." MaDear wagged a maternal finger at Adele. "An' don't you go chargin' this child nothin' either." She mumbled, "All the years I put food on yo' table an' clothes on yo' back, yo' can do one lil' favor for me. Huh." And MaDear started picking through the curlers and rollers in her lap.

Denny blew his nose, and we stood up. Adele and Denny and I just stared at each other. None of us knew what to say, but I had a lightness in my spirit I had never felt before and thought I might just float away.

Adele broke the silence. "Well, come on. If MaDear says you need your nails done, Jodi Baxter, we better do 'em. She's the boss—right, MaDear?"

"You got that right!" MaDear yelled then fell back to studying her lap.

Adele started moving things around at one of the nail chairs in the back room. "Adele, it's really all right," I whispered. "I know you close at seven and weren't expecting us."

"Sit." Adele lowered her bulk onto the stool in front of the little table and poured liquid into a bowl. "Soak."

So I sat, lowering my fingers into the soothing liquid. Denny blew his nose again and took a seat in the corner, resting his elbows on the chair arms and making a tent with his fingers. Watching.

"Takeisha!" Adele yelled toward the front, finally taking my hand from the liquid and starting in on my cuticles. "Turn that music up!—stop jerking, Jodi, or I'm gonna jab you."

I closed my eyes and smiled as "Go Tell It on the Mountain!" in rich gospel beat suddenly took over any need to talk. In my mind I began composing an e-mail to a bunch of crazy, praying sisters. They were never going to believe what God had done today!

On the other hand . . . sure they would.

Yada Yada Prayer Group Gets Down
Reading Group Guide

1. The theme of *The Yada Yada Prayer Group* (Yada Yada #1) was *grace*—discovering what it means to be "just a sinner . . . saved by grace." What do you think is the main theme of *The Yada Yada Prayer Group Gets Down*? Why?

2. With whom did you empathize more in the incident at Adele's beauty shop: MaDear or Denny? Why?

3. The Yada Yada prayer group was traumatized by a crime. Have you or someone close to you ever been the victim of a crime? If so, how do you feel toward the perpetrator? If you had a chance for a face-to-face meeting, what do you think would happen? What would you want to happen?

4. How did Yada Yada's decision to visit Becky Wallace in prison affect the different sisters in the prayer group? How did it impact Becky Wallace?

5. If you were the mother of Jamal Wilkins—the boy who Jodi Baxter killed in her car accident in Yada Yada #1—how would you feel to discover her relationship to your other child? How does this discovery affect (1) Jodi? (2) the mother? (3) the child?

6. Jamal's mother can't forgive Jodi, even though Jodi asked for forgiveness at the end of Yada Yada #1. How does this affect Jodi? If the person she has wronged won't forgive, how can she ever be free of the guilt? However, if Jamal's mother does choose to forgive Jodi, what would that forgiveness look like?

7. What prompted Denny's response to MaDear in the final chapter? Why do you think his response was so healing? What questions does his encounter with MaDear raise for you about "repenting for the sins of others"?

8. Examine your own attitudes that may hinder fellowship with other groups of Christians. What is the most difficult or challenging area for you? What would it mean to repent of this attitude?

9. How might we "repent of" or "take responsibility for" past sins of our nation or people group? No matter what your race or ethnicity, what could *you* do to help bring about racial healing among God's people? How can we help each other?

10. Are there relationships in your own life—of any nature— that need healing through repentance or forgiveness? Whether you have "sinned" or "been sinned against," do you have the courage to take the first step?

Get Real

party edition
Now with Recipes & Celebrations

the
yadayada
Prayer Group
GETS REAL

a Novel

NEW
PARTY EDITION
INCLUDES
RECIPES &
CELEBRATION
IDEAS

neta jackson

The Yadas thought they had a handle on
forgiveness, but it seems God has them
on a crash-course to an even deeper level
in this third novel of the series.

Get Tough

party edition
Now with Recipes & Celebrations

the
yadayada
Prayer Group
GETS TOUGH
a Novel

NEW
PARTY EDITION
INCLUDES
RECIPES &
CELEBRATION
IDEAS

neta jackson

The Yadas have grown close in the past year,
but they're about to learn the real meaning of
togetherness in this fourth novel of the series.

Get Caught

party edition
Now with Recipes & Celebrations

the
yada yada
Prayer Group
GETS CAUGHT

a Novel

NEW
PARTY EDITION
INCLUDES
RECIPES &
CELEBRATION
IDEAS

neta jackson

For the Yadas, gettin' caught up in troubles
isn't the problem; it's how to get free
in this fifth novel of the series.